Richard Laymon wrote over thirt... May 2001 *The Travelling Vampire S...* ... ... the Bram Stoker Award for Best Horror Novel, a prize for which Laymon had previously been shortlisted with *Flesh*, *Funland*, *A Good, Secret Place* (Best Anthology) and *A Writer's Tale* (Best Non-fiction). Laymon's works include the books of the Beast House Chronicles: *The Cellar*, *The Beast House* and *The Midnight Tour*. Some of his recent novels have been *Night in the Lonesome October*, *No Sanctuary* and *Amara*.

A native of Chicago, Laymon attended Willamette University in Salem, Oregon, and took an MA in English Literature from Loyola University, Los Angeles. In 2000, he was elected President of the Horror Writers Association. He died in February 2001.

Laymon's fiction is published in the United Kingdom by Headline, and in the United States by Leisure Books and Cemetery Dance Publications. To learn more, visit the Laymon website at: http://rlk.cjb.net

'In Laymon's books, blood doesn't so much as drip as explode, splatter and coagulate' *Independent*

'A gut-crunching writer' *Time Out*

'Incapable of writing a disappointing book' *New York Review of Science Fiction*

'No one writes like Laymon and you're going to have a good time with anything he writes' Dean Koontz

'One of the best, and most underrated, writers working in the genre today' *Cemetery Dance*

'This author knows how to sock it to the reader' *The Times*

'This is an author that does not pull his punches . . . A gripping, and at times genuinely shocking, read' *SFX Magazine*

Flesh

and

Resurrection Dreams

headline

FLESH first published in Great Britain in 1987
by New English Library

RESURRECTION DREAMS first published in Great Britain in 1988
by New English Library

First published in this omnibus edition in 2006
by HEADLINE BOOK PUBLISHING

A HEADLINE paperback

1

ISBN 0 7553 3172 9

Typeset in Janson by Avon DataSet Ltd, Bidford on Avon, Warwickshire

Printed and bound in Great Britain by
Mackays of Chatham plc, Chatham, Kent

Headline's policy is to use papers that are natural, renewable and recyclable
products and made from wood grown in sustainable forests. The logging and
manufacturing processes are expected to conform to the environmental
regulations of the country of origin.

HEADLINE BOOK PUBLISHING
A division of Hodder Headline
338 Euston Road
London NW1 3BH

www.headline.co.uk
www.hodderheadline.com

Flesh

THIS BOOK IS DEDICATED TO
DEAN AND GERDA KOONTZ
WHO CONSISTENTLY TOP
THE LAYMON TIMES
'BEST-PEOPLE LIST'

Chapter One

Eddie, in his van, had the road to himself.

Except for the bicycle.

When he first saw the bike from the crest of the hill, it was below him and far ahead. At such a distance, he couldn't tell much about the rider.

He knew it wasn't a kid.

The bike was one of those high, streamlined jobs, not like you see kids pedalling around on. And the rider looked big enough to fit the bike.

Could be a teenager, Eddie thought.

Could be a gal.

Squinting, he leaned towards the windscreen. The bottom of the steering wheel sank into his belly, filling the crease between his rolls of fat.

Could be a gal, he thought.

With the back of his hand, Eddie wiped his mouth.

He was halfway down the hill by now, picking up speed and closing the gap between his van and the bike.

The rider's brown hair was somewhat long. That didn't prove much. A lot of men wore their hair that long and longer.

But you don't see a lot of guys in red shorts.

Eddie sped closer.

Close enough to see how the rider's hips flared out from a small waist.

A gal, all right.

On both sides of the road were fields with trees here and there. No buildings. No people. The road ahead to where it curved and vanished was deserted. Eddie checked his side mirrors. Behind him, the road was clear.

'Her it is,' he said.

He pressed the gas pedal to the floor.

1

Though the rider didn't look back, she must have heard the rising engine sound. Her bike moved to the right, gliding away from the middle of the lane and taking up a new position a yard from the road's edge.

Eddie bore down on her.

She was hunched over her handlebars. She kept pedalling.

Her T-shirt was so tight that Eddie could see the bumps of her spine. Bare skin showed between the bottom edge of her shirt and the elastic band of her shorts.

Her left arm swung out. She waved Eddie by.

At the last instant, she looked back. Eddie was near enough to see that her eyes were blue.

She was very pretty.

He turned his van towards her.

I like the pretty ones.

Her front wheel jerked right.

Pretty and young and tender.

He waited for her to meet the windscreen.

But she was being hurled the wrong way – forward and to the right. She was no longer on her bike. She was above it, legs kicking overhead, as Eddie's van smashed through it.

No problem, Eddie thought.

She won't go far.

I'll get her. Oh, yes.

His right-side tyres bounced over the gravel shoulder of the road and he was about to steer back onto the pavement when he came upon a bridge.

He hadn't even noticed it before.

He glimpsed the sign as he sped past it.

Weber Creek.

Not much of a creek.

Not much of a bridge – but it had a concrete guard wall four feet high.

Chapter Two

'Are you all right?'

'Do I *look* all right?'

She was sitting on the ground with her back to the road, her head turned to look up at him. Above her right eyebrow, the skin was scraped off to her hairline. The raw place was striped with beaded threads of blood. It was dirty, and a few bits of straw-coloured weeds clung to the stickiness.

Jake sat down beside her on the edge of the ditch.

Both her knees and the front of her right thigh were in about the same condition as her forehead. Her right arm hung between her legs, knuckles against the ground. She held the arm with her other hand while it shook. She didn't appear to be trying to hold it still. The other hand seemed meant to soothe it the way someone might lay a hand on an injured pet.

'Do you think it's broken?' Jake asked.

'I wouldn't know.'

Jake took out a notepad. 'Could I have your name?'

'Jamerson,' she said. The corner of her mouth twitched.

Jake wrote. 'And your first name?'

'Celia.'

'Thanks.'

She turned her head to look at him again. 'Shouldn't you be doing something about *that*?' Her eyes shifted towards the blazing van fifty or sixty feet to her left.

'The fire truck's on the way. My partner's keeping an eye on things.'

'What about the . . . driver?'

'We can't do much for him.'

'Is he dead?'

A shish kebab, Chuck had remarked when he saw the driver's remains hanging out of the windscreen.

'Yes,' Jake said.

'He tried to hit me. I mean it. He had the whole road to

3

himself, I'm over by the shoulder and I signal him to go around and I look back and he's actually swerving right at me. He's grinning and he swerves right at me. Must've been going sixty.' Her face had a puzzled expression as if she were listening to a bizarre joke and waiting for Jake to feed her the punchline. 'The guy meant to kill me,' she said. 'He creamed my bike for me.'

She nodded towards it. The bike with its twisted wheels lay in the weeds on the far side of the ditch.

'What happened, I turned quick to get out of his way and the bike flipped on me. Just before he hit it, I guess. The van never touched me. Next thing I knew, I was landing in the ditch and there was this crash. Bastard. That's what he gets, going around trying to . . . what'd I ever do to *him*?'

'Did you know him?' Jake asked.

'I've heard of these guys, they'll run down dogs just for laughs. Hey, maybe he thought I was a dog.' She tried to laugh and came out with a harsh sobbing noise.

'Had you ever seen the man before?'

'No.'

'Did you do anything that might've angered him?'

'Sure, I flipped him a finger. What is this? Is it suddenly my fault?'

'*Did* you?'

'No, damn it. I didn't even see him till he was about a foot off my tail.'

'As far as you're concerned, then, his action was totally unprovoked?'

'That's right.'

'You say that you heard the crash just after you landed in the ditch?'

'Maybe I hadn't hit yet. I really don't know.'

'What happened next?'

'I think I conked out. Yeah, I'm pretty sure I did. Then what happened, I heard your siren. That's when I got up and—'

'Hey, Jake!'

Jake looked over his shoulder. Chuck, fire-extinguisher in one hand, was standing by the open rear door of the flaming van and waving him over. 'I'd better see what he wants. Sit tight, there should be an ambulance on the way.'

Celia nodded.

Jake stood up, brushed off his seat, and walked over to meet his partner.

'Take a look-see here,' Chuck said, pointing to the ground.

The pale dirt of the road's shoulder was speckled with a few dark blotches. Jake crouched for a closer look.

'Looks like blood to me,' Chuck said.

'Yeah.'

'Was the girl over here?'

'Not according to what she told me.'

'We better find out for sure. 'Cause if she wasn't . . . know what I mean?'

Jake heard a distant siren. He saw a smear of blood on the grey asphalt of the road. The fire truck or ambulance wasn't in sight yet, so he rushed across both lanes. Chuck trotted along beside him, still hanging onto the fire-extinguisher.

'How'd someone survive a crash like that?' Chuck said.

Jake shook his head. 'Just lucky.'

'Yeah, I guess it can happen. You hear about folks making it through airline crashes. *There*.'

'I see it.'

A slick of blood on a blade of crabgrass.

Jake stepped into the weeds. He scanned the ditch and the field beyond it. Both were overgrown with weeds that had flourished and bloomed under the recent spring rains. The uneven terrain of the field was dotted with clumps of bushes. There were a few trees scattered around.

He saw no one.

Chuck cupped his hands to the sides of his mouth and yelled, 'Hello! Hey, out there!'

Jake, though standing beside him, could barely hear his voice over the noise of the siren.

Then the siren died. Chuck called out again. Jake heard the groan of air brakes, the tinny crackle and voice of a radio. He looked back and saw the town's bright yellow pump truck.

'How come you suppose he wandered off?' Chuck asked. 'It was me got banged up, I'd stick around and wait for help.'

'Maybe he's in shock and doesn't know what he's doing. More likely, though, he wanted to haul ass out of here. The girl says she was riding her bike along minding her own business and the van tried to run her down on purpose. Which would mean the guy's not a model citizen. You take care of matters here, I'll see if I can dig him up.'

'Don't take all day, huh? I'm getting the hungries and my stockpile's dry.'

The stockpile was the cache of fruitgums, chips and candy bars that Chuck kept in the patrol car.

'You'll live,' Jake said. He slapped Chuck's paunch, then climbed down into the ditch.

After looking for traces of blood, he climbed out of the ditch on its far side.

Back on the road, the firemen were blasting at the flames with chemical extinguishers. Chuck was walking over to Celia, who was standing now – bent over a bit and still holding her right arm.

Jake wondered if she was from the university. She was the right age, and he probably would've known her if she was a local. Also, there was her wiseguy attitude. *Do I look all right?*

Don't hold it against her, he told himself. She was hurting.

A good-looking woman, even with her face scraped up.

Came damn close to getting her ticket cancelled.

He turned away and continued searching.

Two in the van, one was killed and the other got away. The dead guy was obviously the driver. The survivor must've been in the back of the van, or he would've gone out of the windscreen, same as the driver. And Celia didn't mention seeing anyone in the passenger seat.

If he was in the back, maybe he wasn't part of it.

No, he was part of it or he would've stuck close to the van after the crash.

Wandering back and forth, Jake spotted a dandelion with a broken stem, a smear of blood on its blossoms. It was a few yards north of where he'd come out of the ditch. In his mind, Jake connected the two points and extended the line across the field. It led to a low rise a couple of hundred yards to the northwest. The high ground was shaded by a stand of eucalyptus trees. He headed that way.

From behind him came the blare of another siren. That would be the ambulance.

Nice response time, he thought.

He checked his wristwatch. 3:20 p.m. He and Chuck had spotted the smoke at 3:08. They'd reached the accident site two minutes later and called in. So the ambulance took ten minutes.

Good thing nobody's life was depending on it.

Jake waded into Weber Creek, peering up and down the narrow band of water. On the other side, he stopped long enough to check the area for signs. The weeds were nearly knee-high. He couldn't find any traces of blood or trampled foliage. Maybe the guy had changed course. Looking back, though, Jake could only make out the faintest sign of his own passage.

I'm hardly the world's greatest tracker, he thought.

And if the guy had made any effort to be careful, he could've skirted the places with high weeds and stuck to areas where the ground cover was sparse. Or maybe followed the creek.

Maybe I already passed him. If he stretched out flat . . .

Sneaking up on me . . .

Jake whirled around.

Nobody there.

His gaze swept over the field. Then he looked towards the road. The van was still smoking, but he couldn't see any flames. Chuck was standing close to Celia. An ambulance attendant was heading their way.

Jake continued towards the rise, but he began to feel that he'd lost the suspect. He didn't like that. In spite of the blood, it was apparent that the man hadn't been severely injured. Hurt, sure, but not incapacitated.

A potential killer.

Jake didn't want to lose him.

What kind of man pulls a stunt like that – tries to run down a bike rider, a total stranger, in broad daylight? He wasn't driving, of course, but he was an accomplice, Jake was sure of that.

Maybe they never intended to kill her, just run her off the road, rack her up enough to take the fight out of her, and snatch her. That Jake could understand. A good-looking young woman, get her into the van, have their fun with her, dump her later on, maybe dead.

If Celia's account was accurate, though, they actually tried to smash her with the van. It would've killed her for sure. And messed her up pretty good. Hardly your typical MO for a pair of travelling rapists.

They wanted her dead first?

Sick.

Outlandish, too. There just aren't that many necrophiles running around; the odds against two of them linking up must be staggering.

It could happen.

More likely, though, they would have just left her.

Thrill killers.

Combing the roads in a van, looking for suitable victims.

If I lose this guy . . .

Jake turned slowly, scanning the entire expanse of the field. Then he trudged to the top of the rise. He made a quick circuit around the trees. Nobody there. On the other side, the ground sloped down to a narrow road. Beyond the road, the field continued. The foliage and trees were heavier on that side. Plenty of places for a man to conceal himself.

Jake spent a long time watching the area. Turning around, he gazed at the field he had crossed.

You lost him, all right.

Get up a search party, go over the area inch by inch. The logical step, but not very practical. How do you get together enough men on short notice to do the job properly?

He leaned against a tree. He kicked a small rock and sent it flying down the slope. It landed in a clump of bushes, and he imagined his suspect crying out, 'Ouch!' and making a run for it.

Dream on, Corey.

Shit.

He looked up the side road. It led only to the Oakwood Inn. The old restaurant had been closed for years, but a couple from Los Angeles were planning to reopen it. He saw a station wagon parked in front. The folks must be there, fixing the place up.

I'd better warn them.

The damned restaurant only looked as if it was a quarter of a mile away. Weary and discouraged – and gnawed by guilt for losing the creep – Jake shoved himself away from the tree and made his way down the slope. He waded through the weeds. Once he reached the road, the walking was easier.

He kept a lookout, though he no longer expected to find the suspect.

Suspect, my ass, he thought.

This guy's into wasting random victims.

And I lost him.

Maybe the accident, losing his partner, took some of the starch out of him.

Right.

Goddamn it.

I lost him and it'll be my fault if he . . .

The distant sound of a car engine broke into Jake's thoughts.

Chuck coming to fetch him?

He turned and realized that the sound came from the direction of the Oakwood Inn. He remembered the station wagon.

Snapped his head forward.

He was standing in a dip.

He saw only the road.

From the noise, the car was speeding.

And he knew.

He'd been slow – he should've guessed it the instant he saw the car sitting there, vulnerable, in front of the restaurant.

Your van is totalled, you're on foot and hurt, you spot an unattended vehicle . . .

Heart racing, mouth gone dry, Jake Corey snatched out his .38, planted his feet on each side of the faded yellow centre line of the road, lowered himself into a shooting crouch, and waited.

He aimed at the road's crest fifty yards away.

'Come on, you mother.'

Jake wished he had a .357 like the one Chuck carried. With that, he'd be able to kill a car.

Jake would have to go for the driver.

He had never shot anyone.

But he knew this was it. He couldn't let the bastard get away.

Six slugs through the windscreen.

That'll do it.

The car burst into view, bounced on loose shocks as it hit the downslope, and sped towards him.

Wait till he's almost on you, blow him away, dive for safety.

9

Jake's finger tightened on the trigger.

Brakes shrieked. The car skidded, fishtailed, and stopped thirty feet in front of him.

Jake couldn't believe it.

'Let me see your hands!' he yelled.

The driver, a thin and frightened-looking man of about thirty, stared at Jake through the windscreen.

'I want to see your hands *right now*! Grab the steering wheel *right now*!'

The hands appeared. They gripped the top of the wheel.

'Keep 'em there!'

Jake held his revolver pointed at the man's face while he approached the car. The head turned, eyes following him as he walked to the driver's door.

No one else in the car.

Jake pulled the door open and stepped back. Crouching slightly, he had a full view of the man.

Who wore a blue knit shirt.

And Bermuda shorts.

Who didn't appear to be injured in any way.

'What's going on, officer?'

'Place your hands on top of your head and interlace your fingers.'

'Hey, really . . .'

'Do it!'

Why are you keeping this up? Jake wondered. It's a charade. Because you don't know. Not yet. Not for sure.

The man put his hands on top of his head.

'Okay. Now climb out.'

As he followed orders, Jake got a look at his back. No blood or sign of injury there, either.

'Turn around slowly.' Jake made circular motions with his left forefinger. The man turned. Jake looked for bulges. The knit shirt was skintight. The only bulge was at the rear pocket of his shorts – a wallet. Good. Jake didn't want to frisk him.

'Will you tell me what's going on?'

Jake holstered his weapon.

'Could I see your driver's licence, please?'

The man took out his wallet. He knew enough to remove the

10

licence from its plastic holder. Probably been stopped for traffic violations.

Jake took the card. His hand was trembling. It reminded him of Celia's shaking arm. He looked at the licence. Ronald Smeltzer. The photo matched the face of the man in front of him. The home address was Euclid Street in Santa Monica, California.

'Thank you, Mr Smeltzer,' he said, and returned the licence. 'I'm sorry about stopping you that way.'

'A wave would've sufficed.'

'I was expecting trouble. I assume you're the new owner of the Oakwood.'

'That's right. Could you tell me what's going on? I realize I was taking the road a bit fast, but . . .' He shrugged. He was obviously upset, but showing no belligerence. Jake appreciated his attitude.

'I was on my way to speak with you – to warn you, actually. We just had an incident over on Latham Road.'

'We were wondering. We heard the sirens.'

'On your way to investigate?'

'No. As a matter of fact, we haven't got ice. My wife and I. We've been working all day, trying to get the place in shape. No refrigerator, yet. It's supposed to be delivered tomorrow. We thought we'd relax over cocktails for a while, but . . .' He shrugged. He looked as if he felt a little foolish. 'No ice. What can I say?'

'Your wife is back at the restaurant?' Jake asked.

The man nodded. 'You mentioned something about warning us? About what?'

'I don't think you want to leave her alone just now. We've got a situation. Give me a lift to your restaurant and I'll explain.'

They both climbed into the car. Smeltzer turned it around and headed back up the road at a moderate speed.

'Pick it up,' Jake told him. 'I know you can do better than this.'

Smeltzer stepped on the gas.

As the car raced towards the restaurant, Jake explained about the attempt to run down Celia Jamerson, the blood behind the van, his search for the injured passenger. Smeltzer listened, asking no questions but shaking his head a couple of times and frequently muttering, 'Oh, man.'

The car lurched to a stop at the foot of the restaurant's stairs.

Smeltzer flung open his door. At the same moment, a door at the top of the stairs swung wide.

A woman stood in the shadows. She stepped out onto the porch as Smeltzer and Jake climbed from the car. Her perplexed expression altered into a frown of concern – probably as she realized that Jake was a cop.

She had nice legs. She wore red shorts. This is my day for beautiful women in red shorts, Jake thought. The front of her loose grey jersey jiggled nicely as she trotted down the stairs. The jersey had been cut off, halfway up. Any higher, Jake thought, and he'd be seeing what made the jiggles.

'Ron?' she asked, stopping in front of the car.

'Honey, this is Officer . . .' He looked at Jake.

'Jake Corey.'

'I ran into him on my way out. Almost literally.' He gave Jake a sheepish glance.

'Some kind of trouble?'

Jake let Smeltzer explain. His wife nodded. She didn't say, 'Oh, man,' after each of his sentences. She didn't say anything. She just frowned and nodded and kept glancing over at Jake as if expecting him to interrupt. 'Is this true?' she finally asked him.

'He covered it pretty well.'

'You think there might be a *killer* hanging around here?'

'He didn't kill anyone today, but it wasn't for lack of trying. Have either of you seen anyone?'

She shook her head.

'But we've been working inside,' Smeltzer said.

'You folks have a home in town, don't you?' Jake asked. He seemed to remember hearing that they'd bought the Anderson house.

'I was on my way there,' Smeltzer said, 'for the ice.'

'It's certainly your decision, but if I were you, I'd close up here for today and go on back to your house. There's no point in taking unnecessary risks.'

Husband and wife exchanged a look.

'I don't know,' Smeltzer said to her. 'What do you think?'

'We've got to get this place in shape before they bring in the equipment.'

'I guess we could come in early tomorrow.'

12

'It's up to you,' the wife said.

'This guy does sound like he might be dangerous.'

'Whatever you say, Ron. It's your decision.'

'You'd rather stay,' Ron said.

'Did I say that?'

'I think we'd be smart to leave.'

'Okay. It's settled, then.' She smiled at Jake. It was a false smile. *See? You got your way.*

Hey, lady, he wanted to tell her, sorry. Just thought you might want to know there's an asshole in the neighbourhood and maybe you're his type. Forgive me.

Smeltzer turned to Jake. 'Could we give you a lift?'

'Yeah, thanks. I could use a ride back to the road.'

'Fine. We'll just be a minute. We need to lock up.'

He and his wife headed up the porch stairs.

Jake glanced at the woman's rear end. He didn't find it especially interesting. She was a fine-looking package, beautifully wrapped, but Jake had the idea that he wouldn't like what he found inside.

So much for lust.

They were inside the restaurant for longer than Jake expected. At first he assumed they were probably delayed by a heated discussion about leaving ahead of schedule. Then he began to worry.

The guy from the van was in there and got them?

Not very likely.

But the possibility stayed with Jake. He counted to thirty, slowly, in his mind.

They still weren't out.

He went for the stairs, took them three at a time, and reached for the door handle.

The door swung away from him.

'Sorry it took so long,' Smeltzer said. 'Had to use the john.'

'No problem.' Jake turned away, not even trying for a glimpse of the wife, and trotted down the stairs.

From behind him came her voice. 'This really *is* the pits.'

'Better safe than sorry,' Smeltzer said.

'Of course.'

Chapter Three

A few classes were still in session and Bennet Hall had terrible acoustics that seemed to magnify every sound – especially on the stairways – so Alison climbed to the third floor with excessive caution, holding onto the old wooden banister to keep herself steady.

Alison knew she was early.

She couldn't help it, though.

She'd tried to stay away until four, but Chaucer let out at two and she had no classes after that on Tuesdays and Thursdays and it just isn't easy, killing two hours. The walk home only used up ten minutes. Neither of her roommates were there. Too bad. A conversation with Celia or Helen would've been good for making the time pass.

She'd tried to study, but couldn't concentrate. Not on the book, anyway. Just on the clock, the minute hand of which seemed to move one space every ten minutes. If she could just take a nap and wake up at a quarter to four . . . So she set her alarm clock and stretched out on the bed. Sure, sleep. She shut her eyes, folded her hands on her belly, and tried very hard. It was no use, of course. She couldn't even lie still, much less sleep. Finally, she gave up the idea, put the waitress uniform into her flight bag, added a paperback, and left.

She had reached Bennet Hall at 3:20. That was early, even for her – a whole fifteen minutes earlier than her arrival time on Tuesday. So she took her usual seat on a concrete bench that encircled the broad trunk of an oak tree, and tried to read. And watched a squirrel eat a nut. And watched a couple of yelling lower classmen, probably freshmen, toss a Frisbee around. Watched Ethel Something stroll towards the library holding hands with Brad Bailey. Tried to read. At last it was ten to four. She couldn't wait any longer. Besides, she told herself, the class might let out early.

So she entered Bennet Hall and made her way as quietly as

possible to the third floor. The hallway was deserted. She heard the slow tapping of a typewriter from a faculty office, and a few faint voices drifting into the hall from open classroom doors.

She stopped near the open door of the last classroom on the left. The students were out of sight, but her position gave Alison a clear view of Evan.

She'd been with him only last night, but she felt as if far too much time had gone by since then. Too much time with a hollow ache in her chest. The ache didn't go away now. It seemed to get worse.

Come on, Alison thought. Dismiss the class.

Apparently Evan hadn't noticed her arrival. He was looking forward, probably at the student who was asking about a minimum length requirement for the term papers.

'It should,' he replied, 'be like a young lady's skirt – short enough to keep one's interest but long enough to cover the essentials.'

A few of the students chuckled.

'But how long does it have to *be*?' the voice persisted.

Evan arched an eyebrow. Alison smiled. He was so cute, acting the pedant. 'Fifteen pages minimum.'

'Is that typed?' enquired a different voice.

'Typed. Black ink. White paper of the eight and a half by eleven variety. Double spaced. One-inch margins all around. If possible, refrain from using erasable paper – it makes my fingers sticky.'

They were freshmen. Probably taking notes on his every utterance.

Evan folded his arms. He was standing in front of his desk, its edge pressing into his rump. Taking off his wire-rimmed glasses, he asked, 'Any more questions?' While he waited, he wiped the lenses on a lapel of his corduroy jacket. Without the glasses, his face looked bare and somehow childlike. He put them back on and became the scholar again. 'No? Your assignment is to read pages 496 through 506 in Untermeyer and come to class on Tuesday prepared to astonish me with your knowledge of Mr Thomas's craft and sullen art. You are dismissed.'

Alison stepped away from the door. There was no stampede to leave the classroom. The students took their time departing, some coming out alone, others in groups of two or three. The bell rang. More students wandered out. Alison waited impatiently, then peeked around the doorframe.

A girl in the fourth row was still in the process of stacking her books on top of her desk. Finally she stood, lifted the precarious pile to her chest, and strolled towards the front. 'Have a nice weekend, Mr Forbes.'

He grinned. 'I shall spend the weekend continuing my quest for naked women in wet Macintoshes.'

'Huh?'

'Have a nice weekend, Dana, and Friday, too.'

Alison entered the room. The girl stepped around her, and was gone.

'Naked women in wet Macintoshes?' Alison asked.

Evan grinned. He slipped a book into his briefcase. 'A line borrowed from Mr Thomas.'

'Your friend Dana will think you're daffy.'

'Daffiness is expected from English instructors.'

Alison shut the door and went to him. He latched his briefcase, turned to her, and stared into her eyes.

'How you been?' she whispered. Her throat felt tight.

'Lonely.'

'Me, too.' She eased herself against him, arms moving beneath his jacket, head tilting back, lips waiting for his mouth.

He kissed her. He pressed her body closer and she snuggled against him. This was what she wanted, what she had longed for since last night – being with him again. If it could only go on and on. If they could only go from here to his apartment and be together, make love, eat supper, spend the evening and the night . . . But it couldn't be that way, and the knowledge was a whisper of regret that tainted the moments in his embrace.

Alison ended the kiss.

She pressed her mouth to the side of his neck, squeezed herself hard against him, then lowered her arms and slipped her hands into the rear pockets of his corduroy pants. 'It feels so good,' she said.

'My ass?'

'Just holding you.'

'The clothes get in the way.'

'It's still nice.'

'Nicer still would be naked on the floor.'

'Undeniable.'

'How about it?' His hands went to her rump. They cupped her buttocks through her skirt, squeezed.

'Not a chance.'

'Give me one good reason.'

'The door doesn't have a lock.'

'Aside from that.'

She smiled up at him. 'Isn't that enough?'

'A minor detail.'

'You think so, do you?'

'It would be well worth the risk.'

'No way, pal.'

'A coward dies many times . . .'

'And discretion is the better part of valour.'

'Methinks the lady doth not want to screw.'

With a laugh, Alison pushed herself away from him. 'Walk me to work?'

'Well, I don't know. One good turn deserves another, and . . .' He shrugged.

'You're kidding, right?'

'Nobody's going to come in here.'

'How do you know?'

Evan reached out and opened the top button of her blouse. He started for the next button. Alison took him by the wrists and pushed his hands away. 'I said no. I meant it. This isn't the time or the place.'

He pressed his lips into a tight line and breath hissed from his nostrils. 'If you say so,' he muttered.

Alison looked into his eyes. His gaze, which before had seemed so deep and searching, now had a blankness to it as if something inside him had shut down and he no longer saw her at all.

He turned away. He opened his briefcase and took out a fat manilla folder.

'Evan . . .'

'I guess I'll stay here for a while. I've got some papers to grade. Besides, I want to see if anyone comes in during the next half-hour or so. Call it curiosity.'

Alison stared at him a moment longer, not wanting to believe he was doing this to her. Then she walked to the door.

'Come on, Alison, what's the big deal?'

She didn't answer. She left.

In the corridor, then on the stairs, she expected Evan to hurry after her. He would apologize. *I'm sorry, it was a stupid idea. I shouldn't have brought it up.*

By the time Alison pushed her way through the main door, she knew he wasn't going to run after her. He'd meant it. He was staying. Still, she kept glancing back as she crossed the lawn.

How could he do something like this?

Evan had walked her to work almost every day during the past two weeks. A couple of times he couldn't do it because of meetings or something. But this – this was just spite.

A punishment.

Because she wouldn't put out.

Put out. What an ugly term.

Put out or get out.

All day she had been looking forward to seeing him. A hug and kiss in the classroom, holding hands as he walked her to the restaurant. Talking, joking, just *being* with him. And both of them knowing that he would meet her after work, that they would walk to the park or back to his apartment and he would be inside her.

Not today, folks.

The sidewalk was blurry. She wiped her eyes, but they filled again.

If it was that important to him, maybe . . . it *shouldn't* be that important. What's the big deal? Well, it was obviously a very big deal to him.

I'm suddenly the bad guy 'cause I won't let him screw me on the classroom floor.

And you thought he loved you.

Well, think again.

He loved you all right – he loved putting it to you, that's what he loved.

Goddamn him.

Alison rubbed her eyes again. She sniffed and wiped her nose, and stopped at the kerb. Gabby's was only a block away. She didn't want to walk in there crying.

She didn't want to walk in there at all.

Not today.

She wanted to shut herself inside her bedroom and stay there. And sleep, and forget.

But when the traffic signal changed, she stepped off the kerb and continued towards the restaurant.

Maybe he'll show up later on, meet me at closing time just as if nothing had happened.

What then?

She walked past the windows of Gabby's. Only a few of the booths were occupied. Still too early for the supper crowd. She hoped it would be a busy night, busy enough to keep her from having time to think.

The entrance was on the corner. She pulled open one of the glass doors. It seemed heavier than usual. Inside, she managed a smile for Jean, who was heading her way with a tray of empty beer steins.

'Early today,' Jean said.

All she could do was nod.

'You all right?'

'I'll be okay.'

Jean stepped up close to her. 'You need to talk, you give me a holler. I raised three girls, and it weren't always rosy, let me tell you. But you just name me a problem, you can just bet your tush I've run into it one time or another.'

'Thanks.'

'Get on along, now.' Jean moved her head a fraction to the left. Taking the cue, Alison looked over Jean's left shoulder. 'Careful Prince Charming don't follow you into the john.'

Prince Charming sat alone at the last booth.

'Trying to cheer me up, are you?' Alison asked.

Jean winked and stepped around her.

Alison tried not to look at Prince Charming, but couldn't help glancing his way as she hurried towards the restroom. He was hunched over the table, pulling and twisting a long greasy hank of black hair in front of his face. Pasty skin showed through a hole in the shoulder of his grey sweatshirt. The sweatshirt looked as if he'd been wearing it for months.

A bowl of vegetable soup was on the table under his face.

Lucky Jean, getting to serve him.

Was he trying to wring something out of his hair and into the soup?

Alison averted her eyes. She caught a whiff of him as she rushed by.

Thank God he didn't look up at her.

She entered the restroom and locked the door.

Prince Charming, at least, had succeeded in taking her mind off Evan.

Evan.

The hurting started again.

If I want to feel bad, she thought, I should trade problems with Prince Charming out there.

She hoped he would be gone by the time she finished.

She put on her make-up slowly. Then she draped her skirt and blouse over the door of the toilet stall and opened her flight bag.

Most of the other waitresses wore their costumes to work. Alison didn't like to wear hers in the street, and especially not on campus. The yellow taffeta skirt was several inches too short and had a dainty frilly-edged apron sewn to the front. The short-sleeved matching blouse had her name stitched in red over the left breast. The fabric of both, thin enough to see through, had obviously been selected by someone who wanted to give the male customers an extra treat.

Alison put on a short slip, then the costume.

She folded her street clothes. Spreading open her flight bag to put them away, she saw her toothbrush and black negligee.

For later.

For Evan's place.

She might as well have left them at home.

Squeezing her lower lip between her teeth, she stuffed her clothing into the flight bag and zipped it shut.

She stepped out of the restroom.

Prince Charming was gone.

My lucky day, she thought.

Chapter Four

'In a way, it's a relief,' Ron said.

'You'll be singing out of the other side of your face, my dear, when we have to get up at five o'clock in the morning.' Peggy sipped her vodka gimlet, being careful not to spill. She was at a bad angle for drinking, but it felt good to be leaning back against the sofa cushion, her legs stretched out and feet propped on the coffee table.

'I don't think we'll need to get up quite *that* early,' Ron said.

'Think again. They're coming in at ten with the appliances, and the kitchen floor has to be stripped and waxed before they arrive.'

'That won't take five hours, will it?'

'You don't think so?'

'I'm sure you know best.'

Peggy nodded. An icy drop fell from the bottom of her glass onto her bare belly below the cut-off edge of her jersey. She flinched a bit, then rubbed the glass against her shorts. It made a dark smear on the red fabric. She took another drink.

'We should've done the kitchen after lunch,' Ron said.

'My dear, we'd planned to do it after supper – having no idea, of course, that the long arm of the law, so to speak, would reach out and fuck us over.'

'He was just trying to help.'

'I can live without that kind of help, thank you very much.'

'We didn't have to leave.'

'You couldn't wait to get out of there and you know it.'

'I still think it was the wise thing to do. Why should we put ourselves in a possibly hazardous situation when it can be avoided?'

'Why, indeed?' she muttered.

'I really don't appreciate your attitude,' Ron said.

'Too bad.' She started to take drink.

'*Damn it, Peggy!*'

Her hand jumped. The chilly liquid sloshed, spilling down her chin. 'Shit!' She sat up. It trickled down her neck. With her left hand she lifted her jersey and blotted herself dry. 'You didn't have to yell.' Her throat felt thick and her eyes burned. 'Now I'm all sticky. Jeez, Ron.'

'I'm sorry.'

She tugged the cut-off jersey down to cover her breasts, took a drink, then set her glass on a coaster. 'Excuse me.'

In the bathroom, she wiped her chin and neck with a damp washcloth. Ron appeared in the medicine-cabinet mirror. His hands caressed her belly. 'I am sorry,' he said again.

'Me, too,' Peggy said in a small voice. 'I've been such a bitch. It's just that I wanted to get it over with tonight.'

He lifted the jersey. His hands covered her breasts.

'I was worried about you,' he said. 'That's all.'

'I know.'

'If you want to stay here, I'll go back tonight and get a start on the floor.'

'By yourself?'

'I could take the gun,' Ron told her.

'I've got a better idea. Take the gun, and we'll both go.'

Jake Corey, sitting with his back to the trunk of a eucalyptus tree, scanned the fields with the binoculars he'd brought from home.

It was dusk. A breeze had come up and it felt good, a real improvement over the afternoon heat that had punished him during the long trek after he'd left his patrol car.

He must've hiked two miles or more, searching, criss-crossing his way through the weeds before coming to the high ground to settle down and watch.

'Don't waste your time,' Chuck had said at the shift's end.

'I haven't got anything better to do.'

'Bullsquat. You oughta go out and get yourself some action, it'd do you good.'

Jake was in no mood for the kind of action Chuck meant. If he didn't do this, he would spend the night alone in his small rented house, reading, maybe catching some TV, hitting the sack early. There would also be guilt for letting the crash survivor slip away from him.

This way, at least, he was doing something about it.

The guy could be miles gone by now.

On the other hand, he might be nearby. The fields were far from flat. He could've found himself a depression and stayed low, resting and waiting. Biding his time until he felt it was safe to start moving.

That was the scenario Jake counted on.

That was why he waited, well concealed among the high weeds with the tree to his back, scanning the area through the binoculars.

Especially the area near the deserted restaurant.

That's where you would head, he thought.

You're hurt. You've been lying low in the weeds for hours. You're hungry and parched. You're starting to want a glass of water more than just about anything in the world.

Well, there's the creek. You could get your drink there.

You'd still head for the restaurant.

You're not just thirsty, you're hungry, too. And this is, after all, a restaurant. You're not from around here, you've got no idea it's been closed for years. You only know that it isn't open tonight. So it's closed on Thursdays. You're in luck. Get inside, you can have a feast. Take enough when you leave so you'll be fixed up for days.

Jake's position on the high ground gave him a good view of the restaurant. At least of its front and south walls. The other side and rear could be approached by an army, and he'd never know. Not from here.

Maybe the guy's already inside.

Jake wished he had checked the place out before settling down for his vigil. At this point, he was reluctant to leave his cover.

Wait for dark.

That wouldn't be long now. Colour was already fading from the landscape, the bright greens and yellows dimming, turning shades of grey.

Dark in a few more minutes.

Like waiting at a drive-in for the movie to start.

Jake was in his Mustang. With Barbara. His window was rolled down, the speaker hooked over its edge. Almost dark. Almost time for the movie. Kids were on the swings and roundabout of the play area under the screen.

Barbara. In a white knit shirt, white shorts, socks and

tennis shoes. Fresh and beautiful. Her skin dusky next to all that white.

A walk to the refreshment stand. It was always popcorn and Pepsi during the first feature, then back at intermission for an ice-cream sandwich or liquorice shoelaces. Usually liquorice.

A lot of fooling around went on with the liquorice shoelaces. You could whip with them. Or tickle. Or tease. You could each take one end of the same piece of liquorice in your mouth and chew your way towards the middle.

Until you met Barbara's mouth. Her cherry-flavoured mouth.

The sound of a car engine snapped Jake back into the present, and he felt as if he'd awakened from a sweet dream.

Headlights appeared on the road to the restaurant.

The car approached. As it passed below him, Jake saw that it was a station wagon.

Terrific.

So much for his warning.

And so much for his plan to check the place out.

He watched the red taillights rise and fall with the dips in the road. When the brake lights came on, he raised the binoculars. A door opened. The car's interior light came on.

Smeltzer and Smeltzer. The dynamic duo.

Ron opened the rear door. He pulled out a double-barrelled shotgun.

The door shut. Jake lowered his binoculars and watched the couple climb the stairs. They spent a few moments on the porch, Ron at the door. Then they both went in. Seconds later, light appeared in the bay windows.

So what gives? Jake wondered. Why'd they come back?

Forgot something? If that's the case, they'll be out in a minute. Unless they get jumped.

Jake realized he was holding his breath, listening for a shotgun blast. Or a scream.

He got to his feet. He started down the slope to the road. Still listening. He heard his own heartbeat, the foliage crunching under his boots, the normal constant sounds of crickets and birds.

Maybe the guy doesn't jump them, Jake thought. Maybe he hides. He would've heard the approach of the car. An old restuarant like that, it must have plenty of good hiding places.

If he's in there at all.

He might just as easily be in the trees beyond the restaurant. Or two or three miles away. He could be anywhere. Hell, he could be lying in the weeds, dead from his injuries.

Or he might be crouched in a dark corner of the Oakwood Inn, watching for a good chance to pounce.

From a high spot on the road, Jake could see the station wagon and restaurant. But not the Smeltzers.

They didn't forget a damn thing, those idiots. They came back to work.

Not a big surprise.

Jake picked up his pace.

The woman, that afternoon, had obviously been reluctant to leave. Ron was the sensible one. But weak. The little wife must've persuaded him that they shouldn't let a minor detail like a possible killer in the vicinity stand between them and their chores. Scared? Take the shotgun. You stand guard while I sweep up the dust bunnies.

'Smart move, folks,' Jake muttered.

He hoped they were smart enough, at least, to check the doors and windows carefully. Assuming they had locked up before leaving (and they'd certainly taken long enough, Jake remembered), then the guy probably couldn't have entered without breaking something.

Unless he was already inside before they secured the place. Hiding.

What if they know?

The thought astonished Jake. He stopped walking and stared at the restaurant. And toyed with the idea.

They weren't hostages – that didn't fit at all. But what if they were cooperating with the guy for some reason?

What reason?

Money? Maybe the guy's loaded and bribed them to help out. Ron's story about going for ice always did sound fishy.

And they spent an awfully long time inside when they were supposed to be locking up. Maybe discussing the situation with their new friend.

They leave with me. Come back after dark. With a shotgun.

A shotgun for their pal.

Jake started walking again, frowning as he gazed at the restaurant.

What do I know about the Smeltzers? he asked himself. Next to nothing.

Hell, the van might've been on its way *here* when somebody got the bright idea of running down Celia Jamerson.

You're stretching it, aren't you?

Just covering the bases. Taking a good look at every angle. That's how you avoid surprises.

Do you really believe they've thrown in with the guy?

The wife, maybe. Yeah, I could believe that. But Ron?

Maybe Ron's a terrific actor.

Jake doubted it.

They had to both be in on it, or neither of them. So it was neither. Probably.

As Jake neared the restaurant, he decided that, in all likelihood, the two had simply decided to ignore the risk, bring a gun along for protection, and spend a while finishing up their chores. But he couldn't dismiss the other possibilities, remote as they might be.

Better safe than dead.

He chose not to knock on the door.

Instead, he silently climbed the porch stairs and peeked through one of the bay windows to the right of the entrance. He saw no one. The area beyond the window would be the cocktail lounge. A long darkwood bar with a brass footrail ran the length of the room. It had no stools, but there were a couple of folding chairs and a card table in front of it, about halfway down. The card table held a small collection of bottles and cocktail glasses.

There's some evidence for you, Jake thought. They *had* been planning to drink here. Ron must've been telling the truth about going for ice.

Jake crept to the other side of the door. Through the window there, he had a full view of the main dining-room. Without any tables or chairs, it looked huge. The dark panelled wall to the left had half a dozen windows. Sconces were hung in the spaces between the windows, between the windows at the rear, and along the wall to the right. The wrought-iron sconces each held three imitation candles – white stalks with glowing bulbs at the top.

Apparently they didn't provide enough illumination for the Smeltzers. One table lamp rested on the floor, casting a pool of light across the glossy hardwood.

Next to the lamp stood a vacuum cleaner. A broom was propped against a step ladder. There was an open toolbox on the floor, and an assortment of rags and cans and bottles of substances to be used for cleaning and polishing.

Jake figured that the wall on the right must close off the kitchen area. About halfway down it, light spilled out from the batwing doors.

Jake climbed down from the porch. He made his way around to the right side of the building and approached one of the glowing windows towards the rear.

Quiet music came from inside, so he realized that the window was probably open. He crept towards it cautiously.

The window was open, all right.

It was high off the ground, its sill level with Jake's shoulders. Bracing himself with a hand against the rough wood wall, he peered in at a corner. He smelled a faint odour of ammonia.

Ron, in a far corner of the kitchen, was bent over a bucket, levering dirty water out of a sponge mop with a long handle. He wore jeans and no shirt. His shirt was draped over the counter close to the radio.

Jake spotted the shotgun. It stood upright, barrels propped against the wall in a nook probably intended for a stove or refrigerator.

He couldn't see the wife.

Ducking low, he made his way along the side of the building. He stepped around the corner, and peered through a rear window.

The wife was at the other end of the kitchen, down on her knees, scrubbing the floor. She still wore her red shorts. But nothing else. Her back was arched. She held herself up with one hand and scrubbed with the other. Her breasts shook as she worked.

Jake suddenly felt like a voyeur.

He stepped away from the window, leaned back against the wall, and stared out at the dark field and nearby woods.

So much, he thought, for checking out the Smeltzers.

It was pretty obvious they weren't harbouring his fugitive.

Whether or not they were safe – that was anyone's guess. But they had chosen to assume the risk, and they'd at least taken the precaution of bringing a firearm. Jake had done his duty; he'd warned them, even sneaked around here to check on them. He couldn't see himself knocking on the door to warn them again – especially not after spying the half-naked woman.

He had an urge to look again.

Don't be a jerk, Corey.

He headed away.

'Did you hear that?' Peggy asked.

'Hear what?'

'Turn off the damn radio.'

Ron dragged the sponge mop behind him to the counter and silenced the radio.

Peggy let go of her scrubbing brush. She straightened up, wiped her wet hands on her shorts, and stared at him.

'I don't hear anything,' he whispered. He looked frightened. His eyes were wide and his mouth hung open a bit.

A drop of sweat trickled down from Peggy's armpit. She brought her arm against her side and rubbed it away.

'Maybe you just imagined it,' Ron said.

'I didn't imagine anything.'

Ron's head swivelled, eyes darting from window to window.

'Not out there,' Peggy told him. Raising her arm, she pointed at the closed door to the cellar.

The colour went out of Ron's face. 'You're kidding,' he muttered.

In a harsh whisper she said, 'I heard something, damn it, and it came from there.'

'Oh, shit.'

'Don't just stand there, get the gun.'

He looked over at it, then back at Peggy. 'What *kind* of dose up noise was it?'

'A thud, a thump, I don't know. For godsake, Ron . . .'

'Okay okay.' He tiptoed across the kitchen, lifted the shotgun, and held it at his side, barrels pointing at the cellar door.

Peggy glanced sideways. Her folded jersey was on top of the counter, just out of reach. Bare to the waist, she felt very vulnerable. She watched the cellar door, and inched her way towards the counter on her knees. She realized that she was afraid to make any quick movements. She couldn't take her eyes off the door. Reaching up, she patted the counter until she touched the jersey. She pulled it down. Holding it at her belly, she gazed at the door and fingered the jersey until she found its opening. She slipped her hands through the armholes, raised her arms high, and let the jersey drift down. For a moment, it blinded her. She tugged it quickly down off her face.

Gripping the counter top with one hand, she stood up. 'Let's get out of here.'

'You mean leave?' Ron asked.

'*Yes.*'

'You must be kidding.' The tone of his voice pried Peggy's gaze off the cellar door. She looked at him. His face was still pale, but a corner of his mouth twitched as if he was working on a grin. 'We haven't finished the floor,' he mocked her.

'Ron.'

'I really do think we owe it to ourselves to finish the floor, don't you? Otherwise, we'll have to get up at the crack of dawn and . . .'

'*There is someone in the cellar!*' she hissed.

'Look who's the chicken now.'

'I never called you a chicken.'

'Didn't you? Seems like you did. Or maybe I just imagined it.'

'This is no time to be . . . let's just get out of here, okay?'

'You're going to let a little noise scare you off? After you dragged me back here?'

'You want to stay, stay. Give me the car keys.'

'And what am I supposed to do, walk home? Spend the night? No thank you. I've got a better idea. I'll go down and search the cellar, and when I come up you'll apologize. You'll repeat after me, "Ron is not a wimp or a coward." '

'You're not a wimp, you're not a coward. Now let's go. Please!'

He smirked at her. Then he stepped boldly towards the cellar door, lowered the shotgun, and wrapped his left hand around the knob.

'You idiot!' Peggy rushed forward, ready to grab him and stop the craziness, but her bare foot hit a wet patch and her leg flew up. She landed hard on her rump.

The mockery left Ron's face. 'Did you hurt yourself?'

'I'll live.'

'Here.' He searched a pocket of his jeans, pulled out his key case, and tossed it to her. It thumped and jangled, striking the floor between her knees. 'Go ahead and wait in the car.' He pulled open the cellar door. 'I'll come and get you after I've checked it out.'

'Don't go down there. I know you think I'm nuts. You think it was just a mouse or a rat or some damn thing, but . . .'

'Right.'

He flicked a light switch, and started down the cellar stairs.

Peggy snatched up the key case. She clutched it tightly as she listened to Ron's feet on the wooden stairs. Slowly, quietly, she gathered in her legs and pushed herself to her knees.

The sounds of Ron's descent stopped.

'Ron?' she called. He didn't answer.

Peggy got up. She crept to the doorway and looked down. The cellar was lit, but she could only see a small area at the foot of the stairway. Ron wasn't there. 'Are you all right?'

'Yeah, fine.'

She leaned against the doorframe. 'Why don't you come up now?'

'Just a minute. Haven't been down here before. This is kind of . . . *SHIT*!'

The jolt of outcry jerked Peggy rigid and knocked her breath out. Stiff in the doorway, she gazed down. The thought flashed through her mind that if she had to run, she wouldn't be able to.

She tried to call down to him. Her voice seemed frozen.

God, oh God, what had happened to him!

'Damn thing,' Ron said.

She felt relief, but not enough. She still couldn't speak. She gasped for air.

Ron stepped into view at the bottom of the stairway. He smiled up at her, looking rather pleased. 'You should've seen it. Scampered out of nowhere, right in front of me.' He started to climb the stairs. 'Biggest damn rat I ever saw. Of course, I must admit, I've never *seen* a rat before.'

Peggy staggered backwards. Away from the door. A hand pressed to her chest.

She stopped when her rump pushed against a counter. She cupped her hands over the counter's edge to brace herself up.

Ron reached the top of the stairs. He frowned. 'Are you okay?'

She took a few deep breaths. 'You . . . scared the hell out of me . . . yelling like that.'

'Sorry. The thing gave me quite a start.'

'A rat.'

'A rat. Didn't I tell you there was nothing to worry about?' Ron smiled and raised the shotgun.

'Hey, don't fool around with . . .'

Jake Corey, hiking up the middle of the road, having called it a night and decided to take the easy way back to his car instead of trudging through the dark fields, heard a gunshot.

He whirled around and ran.

Aw Jesus.

I knew it.

Aw Jesus I shouldn't have let them stay. I knew it I knew it was wrong I knew he was there I knew it I should've forced them to leave. Those goddamn idiots I warned them so what more could I do plenty that's what I could've made them leave. They knew what they were doing like hell they did. Thought it couldn't happen to them it's always somebody else well maybe Ronnie boy blasted the bastard and not the other way around fat chance I'll just bet one of them's deader than cold shit maybe both of them by the time I get there can't you goddamn it run any faster!

The restaurant was ahead of him, jarring in his vision as he sprinted for it.

Past the car.

Up the stairs three at a time, snapping open the holster and drawing his .38, still at full speed when his shoulder hit the door.

Wood splintered and burst and the door flew open.

Nobody.

He ran for the batwing doors.

He dived through the doors, tumbled into the kitchen, came up in a squat and took aim.

He didn't fire.

He didn't know what he was seeing.

The woman in the red shorts was sprawled on the floor, face up. Face up? She didn't have a face. A chin, maybe.

Ron was hunched over her, his face to her belly.

No one else in the kitchen.

The cellar door stood open.

'Ron? Ron, which way did he go?'

Ron lifted his head. A bleeding patch of his wife's flesh came with it, clamped in his teeth, stretching and tearing off. He sat up straight. He stared back at Jake. His eyes were calm. He calmly chewed. Then he reached back for the shotgun.

Jake Corey's bullets slammed him down.

Chapter Five

Alison filled two pitchers with draught beer and carried them to a booth crowded with Sigs. Two of the guys were seniors: Bing Talbot and Rusty Sims. She'd dated Bing a few times in her freshman year. She'd been in classes with him and with Rusty, and knew they were with the Sigma Chi house. The other four packed into the booth were undoubtedly also frat brothers – they had that look about them.

They'd already killed two pitchers and six Gabby-burgers. They were still working on the chilli fries.

Alison set the two full pitchers down on the table.

One of the younger Sigs waved at her. 'Hey, hey!' He pointed at the name stitched on her blouse above her left breast. 'Wha's 'at say?'

'Alison,' she told him.

'Wha'd'ya call the other one?'

'Herbie,' she answered.

He fell apart, giggling and slapping the table.

Alison started to turn away, but Bing caught her by the skirt. Stopping, she smiled down at him. 'You want it? It'd look good on you.'

'Wait, wait,' he said as if he hadn't heard her.

The others had definitely heard her. They were having fits, hooting and whistling over the remark.

'Wait,' Bing said again. He let go of her skirt. 'What'd the waitress say when she was sitting on Pinocchio's face?'

'Lie! Lie!'

Bing slumped. 'You heard it b'fore.'

'How 'bout joining us?' suggested a skinny guy who was squeezed between two of the huskier frat brothers.

'Not enough room.'

'You can sit on my lap.'

'No, mine!'

'Mine!'

'We'll draw straws.'

'I'm not allowed to fraternize with the customers,' Alison said.

'Awwww.'

'Frat-ernize,' Rusty said.

'I geddit, I geddit!'

She backstepped quickly as Bing made another grab for her skirt. 'Enjoy, fellows,' she said, and turned away.

'Ah, what a lovely derrière.' The voice was wistful.

Yes indeed, Alison thought. And it's about time to haul the derrière out of this joint. She checked the wall clock behind the counter. Two minutes to ten.

Eileen, behind the cash register, looked up as Alison approached. 'You taking off?'

'Yep.'

Eileen, who was wearing red beneath her tight uniform, glanced over at the Sigs then back at Alison. She grinned. 'At last, my chance at table six.'

'Enjoy,' Alison told her. She went into the kitchen, said goodnight to Gabby and Thelma, and picked up her flight bag. When she came out, Eileen was already on her way to table six.

She went to the restroom, intending to change into her street clothes, but the door was locked. With a shrug, she left. She didn't mind walking home in the costume. At night, it didn't seem to matter so much.

She started down the sidewalk, coins from tips jangling in her apron pocket. After a few steps she crouched, opened her flight bag, and took out her purse. She transferred handfuls of change from her apron to a side pocket of the purse. She was still doing it when someone approached.

And stopped in front of her.

She recognized the beat-up ankle-high boots.

Her heart quickened.

She looked up at Evan.

'So,' she said, 'you came after all.'

'I never said I wouldn't.'

'I guess not.' She finished emptying her apron, buckled down the purse flap, shut the purse inside her flight bag, and stood up.

'Can I carry that for you?'

'If you like.'

She handed it to him. Evan pretended it was too heavy, gasped with surprise and staggered sideways. 'Whoa! *Mucho* tips, huh?'

Alison found that she couldn't smile.

'Hard night?' he asked.

'Hard afternoon.'

'Oh.' He took her hand and they started walking. 'Nobody came into the room, by the way. I stayed until after five.'

'So it would've been perfectly all right, is that it?'

'Yeah. I knew it would be.'

'Good for you.'

'Hey, come on. We didn't do it, okay? You won. So what's the big deal?'

'No big deal,' Alison muttered.

They waited at a street corner for the light to change, then started across.

'Am I some kind of creep because I wanted to make love with you?'

'Not exactly.'

'Hell, we've done it in the park. Not just at night, either. What about Sunday afternoon?'

She remembered the bushes, the sunlight, the feel of the blanket, the feel of Evan. It seemed a long time ago.

'I don't happen to see the big difference,' he said. 'A park, a classroom.'

They stepped onto the kerb and started down the next block. They passed closed shops, a bar with the sounds of clacking pool balls and jukebox music drifting from the open door, more deserted shops.

'So what is the big difference?' Evan asked.

'There's not that much,' Alison told him. 'It doesn't have to do with that.'

'You lost me.'

'It doesn't have to do with the difference between the park and your classroom.'

'I still don't get it.'

She looked at him. He was frowning. 'The thing is, you dumped on me.'

'I see.'

'It didn't bother me that you wanted to have sex. It was your reaction when I said no.'

'Just because I wouldn't walk you to Gabby's?' He sounded as if he considered that a silly reason to be upset.

'Sort of,' Alison said.

They reached the corner of Summer Street's intersection with Central Avenue. Evan's apartment was four blocks to the right, just off Summer. The house where Alison lived was straight ahead, two blocks past the end of the campus, on a road off Central. As she expected, Evan led her to the right.

She didn't resist.

Her heart pounded harder.

Earlier, she had made up her mind against going to his apartment tonight. She had doubted that he would meet her after work anyway, but if he did come she would simply have to tell him no.

That kind of decision was easy, she realized, with Evan gone and the confrontation somewhere in the vague future.

Not so easy to stick by when the time came to act on it.

And it would get more difficult with every step. Before long, they would be at his apartment.

'Wait,' she said. Stopping, she pulled her hand free.

Evan looked at her.

'I don't think so,' she said.

'You don't think what?'

'Not tonight.'

In the dim glow from the streetlamp, she saw his brow crease. 'You don't mean it.'

'I mean it.'

A side of his lip went up. He looked surprised, annoyed, disgusted – as if he had stepped on a mound of dog waste. 'What is it with you?'

'I don't like what happened, that's all.'

'Christ,' he muttered.

'It changed things. It made me think. It made me wonder if all you really care about is the sex.'

'That's crazy.'

'I don't know, is it?'

'Of course.'

'Then you won't mind too much if we . . . abstain.'

'You don't want to make love tonight,' he said quietly as if explaining the situation to himself.

'It's not that I don't want to.'

'But.'

'But I won't.'

'I didn't walk you to work, so now you're going to punish me by holding out.'

'That isn't why.'

'No? That's how it sounds.'

'I'm "holding out", if you have to call it that, because I need to find out what's there – what's there without the sex. I mean . . .' Her throat tightened. 'Do you drop me, or what?'

'Alison.'

'Do you?'

Evan looked confused and hurt. Raising a hand to the side of her head, he gently stroked her hair. 'You know better than that.'

'I wish I did.'

'I love you.'

'Even without sex?'

'Of course. Come on now, let's go to my apartment and you'll see that I'm marvel of restraint.' He took her hand.

'No, not to your apartment. We both know what would happen.'

'We'll just sit down and talk. On my honour.' He smiled. 'Unless, of course, you should happen to change your mind, in which case . . .'

'I'm going back to my place,' Alison told him. 'Are you coming along?'

'You've got *roomies*.'

She reached her empty hand towards her flight bag.

'Never mind, I'll come along. Can't have you wandering the streets alone – not with all these tips.'

They returned to the corner and crossed Summer Street.

'Another thing,' Alison said.

'You mean there's more?'

'It's not just for tonight.'

'This celibacy kick?'

'It wouldn't mean anything, just one night.'

'Hey, it means a lot to *me*.'

'Obviously.'

'Come on, I'm just joking around.'

They walked in silence for a while. Finally, Evan asked, 'About how long do you have in mind?'

'I don't know.'

'A week, a month, sixty years?'

'It'll depend on how things go.'

'What, exactly, do you hope to accomplish by this little manoeuvre?'

'I thought I already explained that.'

'You mean to see what sort of relationship we have without the sex?'

'That's about it.'

Evan shook his head. 'Can't we vote on this?'

Encouraged by his light tone, Alison said, 'It doesn't have to be so bad. We'll still see each other. Won't we? You said . . .'

'We'll still see each other.'

'We'll find other things to do when we're together.'

'No more idiot box – no pun intended.'

'What do you mean?'

'One time in high school, my folks got the bright idea I was spending too much time in front of the idiot box – the television. They said there's more to life than watching TV. So they cut me off. I was supposed to broaden my horizons and forget the tube.'

'And did you?'

'Sort of. I read a lot of books. I played cards – solitaire. I spent more time on my homework. My grades improved. I did all kinds of stuff.'

Alison smiled. 'We can read to each other, play cards, study . . .'

'Strip poker?' He squeezed her hand. 'There's a side effect that I haven't yet mentioned. I became obsessed with television. Whenever I could, I finagled my way over to friends' houses to watch theirs. And sometimes I even snuck downstairs after my folks were asleep. I'd turn on the TV in the family room and sit in the dark about a foot in front of the screen with the volume so low I could hardly hear the voices over that humming noise you get. It was pretty neat, actually. I was like a starving man at a feast.'

'Stolen sweets.'

'Precisely.'

'And you think being deprived of sex will have a similar effect?'

'It's bound to.'

'What are you going to do about it?'

'You don't leave me much alternative. I guess I'll just have to jack off with your yearbook pictures.'

'Evan!' Laughing, she shoved her elbow into his ribs. He stumbled off the sidewalk.

'You got a better idea?' he asked.

'How about cold showers?'

'I hate cold showers.' He took her hand again. 'It is all right, I take it, to hold your hand?'

'Don't be silly.'

'What about kissing?'

'We'll see.'

'Ah, the prices we pay for our tactical errors.'

At the south end of campus, they waited while a car approached on Spring Street. After it turned onto Central, they crossed. They walked past the A&W root-beer stand where Alison had first met Evan.

She remembered that rainy evening, standing at the counter while she waited for her order and hearing a voice behind her intone, 'She walks in beauty like the night.'

A glance back.

Evan Forbes gave her a smile.

'Talking to oneself is a sign of madness,' she informed him.

'Ah, but I was talking to you. Is that also a sign of madness?'

'Could be.'

She had seen Evan around campus, knew that he was one of the small cadre of graduate students in English, and had noticed the way he watched her the previous night when she served him at Gabby's.

She picked up her hamburger, fries and root beer.

'Do you mind if I join you?'

'No, fine.'

Evan followed her to a table.

'Aren't you going to order something?' she asked.

Shaking his head, he sat across from her and took one of her French fries. 'I'll eat yours.'

'Oh.'

He chewed it up. 'As a matter of fact, I've already eaten. I spied you leaving the library, and tailed you here.'

She felt a blush warm her face. 'That's a lot of trouble to mooch a French fry.'

Remembering, Alison found herself smiling. 'You ate *all* my fries,' she said.

'Nerves. The fries kept me from biting my fingernails.'

'Probably tasted better, too.'

They crossed the railroad tracks, walked past the laundromat where Alison took her dirty clothes once a week, and turned down Apple Lane. Professor Teal's house was third from the corner. Its porch light glowed, but the ground-floor windows were dark. The front windows upstairs were bright, however, so Alison assumed that at least one of her roommates was in. Helen, probably. Celia would still be at Wally's, more than likely, raising hell and soaking up beer.

A wooden stairway angled up the side of the house to the upstairs door. The light above the door was off.

Evan stayed beside her on the walkway across the yard and

remained at her side, though it meant walking on the dewy grass as she followed the flagstones past the front of the house. They climbed the stairs together. At the top, he set down her flight bag.

'Are you going to ask me in?'

'I don't think so.'

The quiet, mellow sound of a Lionel Richie song came from inside.

'One of your roomies is here to protect your virtue.'

Alison squeezed his hand. 'I'm tired. I just want to go to bed.'

'Sans Evan.'

'Will I see you tomorrow?'

He nodded. 'What now? Am I permitted to kiss you goodnight?'

'I think that's allowed.'

In the moonlight, she saw him smile. He lifted her hand to his mouth and kissed the back of it. 'Until tomorrow, then.' He released her hand and turned away.

'Evan.'

He glanced around. 'Yes?'

'Don't be this way,' she murmured.

'Fare thee well, chaste maiden.'

Alison leaned against the doorframe and watched him descend the stairs. The planking creaked under his weight. At the bottom he didn't turn to follow the flagstones, but headed straight across the lawn towards the sidewalk.

Alison yelled, 'You snot!'

Then he was gone.

She unlocked the door. As she entered, Helen peeked out of her bedroom. 'It's okay,' Alison told her. 'The coast is clear.'

'What *happened*?' Obviously, she had heard the parting shot.

'A little disagreement.'

'Little?' With a glass of cola in her hand and a bag of potato chips between her arm and side, Helen went over to the recliner and sat down. She was wearing her bathrobe and sagging purple socks. 'I heard you come up the stairs, so I made myself scarce. I thought you might bring him in.'

'Nope.' Alison set her flight bag on the coffee table. She sat on the sofa, kicked her shoes off, and swung her legs onto the cushions. Sitting down felt great. She sighed.

'Want a Coke or something?'

'No thanks.'

'Chips?' Helen lifted the bag. 'They're sour cream and onion.'

'I'm too upset to eat.'

'That's when food is best. Fills up that empty feeling.'

'If I ate every time I got upset . . .'

'You'd be a tub like me,' Helen said, and poked a potato chip into her mouth.

Alison shook her head. 'You're not so fat.'

'I ain't skin and bones.'

Helen might have been described as 'pleasingly plump', Alison thought, if she had a cute face. She didn't even have that going for her. Far from it. She had a pasty complexion, a broad forehead, buggy eyes behind her huge round glasses, an upturned nose that presented a straight-on view into her nostrils, heavy lips and a neck so thick that it enveloped whatever sunken chin she might have.

'So you want to tell me about it?' Helen asked as she chewed.

'Evan's annoyed with me because I wouldn't put out.'

'Figures. He's a man. A man's an ambulating cock looking for a tight hole.'

'Real nice, Helen.'

'Real true. Take it from me.'

'You've had some bad experiences.'

'So you think I'm wrong?'

'I'd be hard pressed to argue it,' Alison said, 'the way I'm feeling right now.'

'I've never in my life been out with a guy who cared about anything but getting into my pants. Never. And that's saying something. I mean, take a look at me. You'd think they wouldn't want to touch me with a ten-foot pole. A six-inch pole, that's another story.' She gasped a short laugh, blowing out a few crumbs of potato chips.

Alison had heard all this, and more, on numerous occasions during the time she had been rooming with Helen. The young woman was bitter, and with good reason. She had been sexually used and abused by many men, including her stepfather.

Before meeting her, Alison had assumed that men would tend to stay clear of someone with Helen's looks. Not so.

If Helen understood why she was frequently targeted by men, she never let on. But she rarely dated any more, so maybe she had reached the same conclusion as Alison: that the men saw her as easy prey – that anybody with a face and body like Helen had to be hard up – that she would gladly spread her legs and be grateful for the attention.

'I take it back,' Helen said, after washing down a mouthful of potato chips with cola. 'I did go out with a guy once who didn't try to make me. He turned out to be a homo.'

'I want a man who will be my friend,' Alison told her.

'Gotta find yourself a homo, then.'

'But I like sex, too.'

'Then what's your beef with Evan?'

'It's turned into too big a deal. I don't want sex to be the only thing. Maybe not even the *main* thing.'

'Yeah, you and me both. I used to think, if I could just find some guy who looks like he got beat over the head with an ugly stick. But that hasn't worked out, either. The ugly ones are just as messed up as the handsome ones – maybe even worse.'

'The pits,' Alison muttered.

'So did you and Evan break up, or what?'

'Not exactly. I just told him we need to abstain for a while and see how it goes.'

'Oh boy.'

'Oh boy?'

'I bet he wasn't too crazy about that idea.'

'He didn't take it very well.'

'Surprise surprise.'

'If he dumps me over something like this, I'm better off without him.'

'Don't worry, he won't dump you.'

'I don't know. He was acting . . . pretty spiteful.'

'Sure. He was looking forward to some whoopy. Major disappointment, sob sob. By tomorrow, though, he'll be telling himself you just had a bad night, and he'll be expecting you to come to your senses by the next time he sees you. He'll probably treat you extra nice, just to be on the safe side.'

'He'll be in for another disappointment.'

'How long are you planning to hold out?'

'Just long enough to see what happens.'

'Know what I think?' Helen asked, brushing some crumbs off the front of her robe.

'What?'

'I think you've just had a bad night, and tomorrow you'll come to your senses and put out for the guy.'

'You on his side?'

'I know you. You're angry at him right now, but anger has a way of softening pretty fast and you're an easy mark. First thing you know, you'll be feeling sorry for him – and feeling guilty because you're the reason he's so miserable. Then you'll do what's necessary to cheer him up. This time tomorrow night, you'll be in the sack with him.'

'No way.'

'You'll see.'

Alison heard the faint scuffing sound of footsteps. Someone was climbing the outside stairway. Very slowly. Helen stopped chewing and raised her thick eyebrows.

Alison's heart pounded hard. 'Maybe it's Celia,' she whispered.

Helen shook her head. 'Try again. Wally's doesn't close till two.'

'Oh, God. I don't need this.'

'Want me to tell him you're in the shower, or something?'

The footsteps came to a stop on the landing just outside the door. 'No, I'd better . . .'

A key snicked into the lock. Alison's stiff body relaxed, sinking back into the sofa. Mixed with her relief was a hint of disappointment.

Then Celia came in, and Alison jerked upright.

Celia's right arm was held across her chest by a sling. A bandage covered the right side of her forehead from her eyebrow to her hairline.

'Whoa,' said Helen.

'What *happened*?' Alison asked.

'I got creamed, that's what.' With her left hand, Celia swept the jacket off her shoulders. She dropped it, along with her purse, onto the floor beside the door. 'Some bastard tried to turn me into a road pizza.'

She limped towards the sofa, wobbling a bit, apparently not

43

only injured but somewhat drunk. After easing herself down beside Alison, she carefully raised her legs onto the coffee table, stretched them out, and moaned.

'You and that stupid bike,' Helen said. 'I *told* you you'd get nailed.'

'Take a leap.'

'You were on your bike and a car hit you. Tell me that I'm wrong.'

'How about getting me a drink?'

'Don't you think you've had enough?'

'It helps the pain.'

'I'll get you something,' Alison offered. 'What do you want?'

'Anything but beer. I couldn't look another beer in the face. Bushnells. Bring me the bottle, okay?'

Alison hurried into the kitchen. She grabbed the bottle of Irish whisky from the cupboard, got a glass, and returned to the living-room. She filled the glass halfway and handed it to Celia. 'You're a bud,' Celia said.

'How'd it happen?' Alison asked, sitting down again.

'Some bastard tried to run me down. I was over on Latham Road, you know? On my way back from Four Corners. And this van came down on me. The guy had all kinds of room to go around, but he steered right *at* me. He *intended* to hit me. Some kind of a nut. Anyhow, I tried to get out of his way and the bike flipped. That's how I got busted up.' She sat up slightly, wincing, and took a drink. Then she settled back. She rested the glass on the lap of her sweatpants.

'He *intended* to hit you?' Helen sounded sceptical.

'You bet your buns.'

'Why would someone . . . ?' Alison began.

' 'Cause he was a fuckhead, that's why. And no, I didn't flip him a finger. I didn't do *anything*.'

'I'll just bet,' Helen said.

Celia glared at her. 'What's your problem, your vibrator go on the fritz?'

'Matter of fact . . .'

'Come on, Helen,' Alison said. 'Lay off. She's hurt, for godsake.'

'I'm pulverized.' Celia took another drink.

'Anything broken?' Alison asked.

'No bones. What I've got are sprains, strains, contusions, abrasions and general fucking mayhem from head to foot. I was in the emergency room about two hours. On the bright side, my doctor was a hunk. A guy that really enjoyed his job. He checked me out where I wasn't even hurt.'

'Every cloud has its silver lining,' Helen said.

'Yeah. I'll probably be hearing from him.' She lifted her glass, held it in front of her eyes, and stared at the amber liquid. 'You wanta hear the good part?' she asked. From the tone of her voice, she didn't sound overjoyed by the 'good part'. Helen frowned. Celia kept her eyes on the whisky. Her jaw moved slightly from side to side, rubbing her lower lip across the edges of her teeth. 'The guy that did this to me . . . he bought the farm.'

'What?' Alison asked. 'You mean he . . . ?'

'Crumped, croaked, bit the big one. His van went onto the shoulder of the road after he tried to kill me, and ploughed into the guard wall of a bridge. Killed him dead. Then he got his ass cooked.'

'Holy Jesus,' Helen muttered.

'Served the bastard right,' Celia said, and drank her glass empty. 'I didn't even know the guy. So what's he doing, trying to kill me? Huh? Can't even go riding my bike without some nut trying to murder me. Served him right. What'd he wanta do that for? He didn't even know me. But he sure paid. He paid. Wish I coulda seen the look on his face when he hit the wall. Boy, I bet he was surprised.' She smiled and her chin trembled and she began to weep. She lowered the glass to her lap. It fell over. A few drops of whisky trickled onto her sweatpants. Squeezing her eyes shut, she pressed her head back against the sofa cushion and sobbed.

Alison put a hand on Celia's thigh. 'It's all right,' she whispered. 'It's all right.'

'Christ.' Celia sniffed. 'The guy got cooked.'

Chapter Six

The buzz of the alarm clock startled Jake out of his sleep. He killed the noise and pushed himself up on one elbow. Ten o'clock. That made seven hours of sleep. So how come he felt like death warmed over?

'Cause of yesterday.

Groaning, he swung his legs off the bed, sat up, and rubbed his face.

Yesterday. One charbroiled man hanging out of the windscreen. One woman with pieces of her brain and skull clinging to the wall and spread around in clumps on the kitchen counter. One man munching on her flesh.

Jake felt sick, remembering.

Then his sickness changed to fear as his mind did a slow-motion replay of Smeltzer going for the shotgun. The patch of skin in Smeltzer's teeth flapped lazily, sprinkling blood as he turned and reached. Jake thought, *He's going for it!* He thought, *This is it*! He fired, feeling the revolver jump, feeling the blasts slap his ears, smelling the pungent smoke, watching Smeltzer jerk each time a bullet kicked into him. He saw again how one slug opened his throat and how he drifted backwards hosing Jake with blood, the skin still clamped in his teeth, then his spastic twitching after he hit the floor, the blood raining down on him.

Jake took a deep, shaky breath, and got to his feet.

I had to do it, he told himself. I'd be dead if I hadn't dropped him.

It wasn't an excuse, it was the truth. And he had reminded himself of that truth so many times since last night that he was tired of it.

He went into the bathroom and turned on the shower.

Last night, the water going down the drain had been pink from Smeltzer's blood. He'd showered until the hot water ran out. Then he had waited half an hour, and taken a second shower. This would be number three.

He stepped under the hot spray and began to soap himself and saw Smeltzer look up at him, ripping a patch of flesh from the woman's belly. The flesh tore away and he started to turn. *He's going for it!*

'Turn it off!' he snapped. 'We've seen it, we've seen it a hundred times, thank you very much. What is this, the goddamn network?'

Just what it's like, he thought. How many times had they shown the footage of Hinkley blasting away at Reagan, or the Challenger rising beautifully into the sky and blowing up? And each time they start to show it you hope it'll be different this time, you hope they rewrote the script and Hinkley waves instead of shoots and the Challenger makes it into orbit, and you go charging into the kitchen and Smeltzer and his wife are busy mopping the floor and they look at you as if you're nuts. But the script never changes. Each replay is identical to the last one, no matter how hard you wish it different.

They aren't mopping. She's on the floor with just her chin on the end of her neck, and Smeltzer is down on her. *My God, what is he doing!*

Oh, I do not need this, not one little bit. It's my day off, how about my memory taking the day off, too? Pick up Kimmy in about an hour. That should help. A lot. Call Applegate first, though, find out when he'll be winding up the autopsy on Smeltzer – guy must've been drugged out, probably Angel Dust, which is about the only logical explanation for what he did. Eating her. Jesus! Had to be Angel Dust.

But how does Angel Dust connect with the van? The two incidents must be related, somehow. Mustn't they?

When he finished showering, Jake got dressed and made a cup of instant coffee. Then he dialled the morgue. 'Betty? It's Jake.'

'How you doing, fella?'

'Hanging in.'

'I heard about last night. Pretty rough, I guess.'

'I've had better times.'

'I'm free tonight, just in case you could use a little loving.'

'Thanks for the offer,' he said. Betty's idea of a little loving was a lot of hard work. She was a twenty-two-year-old blonde beauty. She had been a champion gymnast in high school, and now her performances were confined to the bedroom. She was truly awesome. Jake's several encounters with her had been real adventures, but exhausting, and afterwards he had always somehow regretted the time spent with her.

He was glad, now, that he had an honest excuse for avoiding Betty. 'Afraid I can't, tonight. This is my weekend with Kimmy.'

'Just let me know.'

'I'll be sure to. Is Steve around?'

'He's out for the day.'

'You're kidding.'

'I wouldn't kid you, fella. He got a call first thing this morning from Dr Willis – the coroner over in Marlowe? Willis wanted him to take a look at some stiff they turned up.'

'We've got stiffs of our own.'

'Willis and Steve are old pals. And Willis has a country club in his back yard. I think there was more to it than just a professional consultation. Steve took his golf clubs.'

'Great. And tomorrow's Saturday.'

'He told me you'd be calling. He said to tell you he'll be in tomorrow, for sure, and do his number on your guy first thing.'

'Okay.'

'You sure about tonight? What time does your kid hit the sack?'

'I wouldn't be much fun, anyway.'

'Sure you would. But hey, it's up to you.'

'I'll be in touch,' he said. 'Take it easy now.'

'You too, Jake.'

He hung up.

Fifteen minutes later he swung his car onto the circular driveway and stopped it behind a red Porsche with the cutesy licence plate, BB'S TOY.

BB's toy would look best, Jake thought, wrapped around a tree. Then he felt guilty. After all, she was Kimmy's mother. Kimmy loved her. Poor taste on the kid's part, but you love the mother you get, even if she is a slut.

His chest felt tight, his mouth dry, as he stepped onto the front porch and pressed the doorbell. From inside came the faint sound of chimes playing the opening bars of Beethoven's Fifth.

Harold Standish opened the door, stepped back, raised his hands high and said, 'Don't shoot.'

Jake stared at him. The man's routine hadn't been amusing the first time he pulled it, over a year ago. It had become less amusing with each repetition. This morning it gave Jake an urge to tear off Harold's trim little moustache.

'Just pulling your leg, Jako. Come on in. The little woman's getting the Kimmer ready for her big day.'

Jake stepped onto the marble foyer.

Harold headed for the living-room, walking sideways and smiling, keeping his eyes on Jake – apparently afraid to turn his back. Jake had never spoken a sharp word to the man, had certainly never threatened or assaulted him. But Harold knew what he had done. And, quite obviously, he knew what he deserved.

What Harold did not know was that Jake never blamed him for the situation. It might have been different if he'd seduced Barbara with good looks and charm, but Harold was a skinny guy with a receding hairline, a nose like a turkey's beak and all the charm of a fieldmouse. He was a wimp. A wimp who made big bucks filling teeth. And Barbara, not Harold, had been the seducer.

She hadn't dumped Jake for a man. She'd dumped him for a handsome bank balance and plastic cards with dreamy credit lines. Harold was a piece of excess baggage that came along with the good stuff.

If it hadn't been Harold, it would've been someone else.

Barbara was the one who deserved . . .

'Could I get you some coffee, a sweetroll?' Harold asked.

'No thanks.'

Harold sat on a recliner, but didn't settle back. He stayed on the edge of the seat as if ready to rush off, and cupped his hands over his knees. 'So,' he said.

Jake sat on the sofa.

'So, how are things in the law-enforcement business? Keeping the criminals in line?'

'We try.' Apparently Harold hadn't heard about last night. That was fine with Jake.

Harold nodded as if pondering the response. He gazed at the floor. He seemed nervous about the silence. Afraid Jake might take the opportunity to bring up an unpleasant topic, such as adultery? Ah, he must've thought of something. His eyebrows lifted and he looked at Jake. 'How do you feel about the hand-gun initiative?'

'I'm against it.'

'One would think that a man in your line of work, who sees the tragedies caused by private ownership of guns . . .'

'We had a seventy-two-year-old widow, last month, who woke up to find a stranger in her bedroom with a knife in one hand and a hard-on in the other. She shot him four times with a pistol she kept on her nightstand. Me, I'm glad she had the gun.'

'But statistics show . . .'

'Save it, Harold. You want the bad guys to win, that's *your* business.'

Harold dared a condescending smile. With a shake of his head, he stood up. 'I'll see what's keeping the ladies,' he said, and backed his way out of the living-room.

He was no sooner gone than Barbara came in.

Jake felt sick. He always felt sick when he saw her, but this morning was worse than usual because of what she wore.

'Kimmy's almost ready,' she said.

'Fine,' he muttered, staring at Barbara and wondering what the hell she was trying to do.

She wore a blue silk kimono. Its front was open, showing a long V of bare skin all the way down to the sash at her waist. The glossy fabric shimmered from the motion of her breasts. Turning away from Jake, she crossed the living-room. The kimono was very short. At the far side of the curtains, she reached high to pull the drawcord and the garment lifted above the pale curves of her buttocks. The curtains skidded open. She lowered her arms, and the fabric drifted down.

'Real cute,' Jake said.

Whirling around, she glared at him.

Jake smiled. His mouth felt rigid. His chest ached.

'Problem?' she said.

His smile died. 'You're some piece of work, woman.'

'You better believe it.'

'What're you trying to pull?'

'I'm not trying to pull a thing, darling. Do I take it that you don't approve of my attire? It's an early birthday present from Harold. Isn't it heavenly? And it *feels* so scrumptious.' Staring at Jake, she smiled lazily and half shut her eyes. Her hands started high and glided downward, caressing the kimono. They made small circles, rubbing the fabric against her breasts. 'Scrumptious,' she whispered.

'If only Harold could see you now.'

'So what if he did.' She squirmed slightly as she kept on rubbing her breasts. Her motions had loosened the front of her kimono, widened the opening. It was open all the way down.

'For godsake!' Jake hissed.

She smirked. 'Turning you on?'

'I get turned on better scraping dog shit off my boot.'

Her eyes went wide. Her face coloured. Her back went stiff. She tugged the kimono together. 'You bastard.' Her voice trembled when she said it. Her chin started to shake.

Astonished, Jake realized she was about to cry.

She pivoted away from him. 'Kimmy!' she shouted. 'Get your ass down here!'

'Barbara!' Jake snapped.

'Fuck you.' She hurried from the room.

Jake stayed on the sofa, stunned and angry and confused. What the hell had just happened?

Normally, when he came to pick up Kimmy, Barbara acted as if he were a visiting peasant: haughty, sarcastic, delighted by the opportunity to rub his nose in the lifestyle she had achieved by dumping him for Harold.

What was this, today?

Acting like that with Kimmy and Harold in the house.

Harold had to know she was dressed that way.

What was she trying to prove?

That's pretty obvious, he thought. She was trying to prove she could turn me on.

Look how she flew apart when I put her down.

The gal's got a major-league problem.

Off the deep end, or she wouldn't be pulling that kind of stunt.

Troubles with Harold?

Oh, wouldn't that be a shame.

Golly, I'm so sorry. It breaks my heart, you slut.

The harsh thoughts made Jake feel a little guilty. He told himself that he had loved her once, that it was wrong to wish misery on her.

What about Kimmy? If Barbara and Harold were having problems, she could certainly be affected. He didn't want that. If Kimmy had to live with her mother – and there was no real alternative as long as Jake remained unmarried – then he wanted her to be in a home where there was love and happiness.

The situation was only tolerable as long as he could be sure that Barbara was taking good care of her. If this morning was any indication, however, Barbara was losing her grip.

Maybe it's nothing, he told himself. Just a fleeting aberration. Tomorrow's Barbara's birthday. She would only be twenty-seven, but he remembered her saying, when she hit twenty-one, that it was all downhill from there. She apparently believed it, too. Each year, after that, she had fallen into pits of depression around birthday time.

That must be it, he decided.

Flaunts her stuff in front of her ex-husband to prove to herself that she's still got something to flaunt.

And he smashes her down.

Shit.

At least it was good to know that her bizarre behaviour was nothing more serious than the birthday blues.

If that was what it was.

'Hi, Daddy!'

He stood up, suddenly feeling good as Kimmy came towards him, smiling. As always, after going days without seeing her, he was amazed by her beauty. A gorgeous four-year-old kid with big blue eyes and a great smile, she couldn't go anywhere without people taking a second look.

Harold stood in the entryway, holding her overnight bag. Kimmy had Clew, her tiny toy kitten, clutched in one hand. She raised her arms, and Jake picked her up and kissed her. 'How's my baby!' he asked.

'I'm not a baby, I'm a little girl.'

'Oh, well excuuuuuse me.'

Leaning back and grinning, she poked a finger against a button of Jake's shirt. 'You have a spill, Daddy.'

'I do?' He looked down.

Kimmy darted her finger up and poked his nose.

'Oow! Y'got me!'

Laughing, she sucked on her forefinger. Her eyes were eager with mischief. A Wet Willy was on its way.

'Oh no you don't,' Jake said, forcing her away before she could twist the wet finger in his ear. She giggled and tried to hold on, but he freed himself and put her down.

Not in front of Harold, he thought.

Then he wondered, with a tug of pain, if she ever gave Wet Willies to Harold.

'Let's get the show on the road,' he said.

He reached down his hand. Kimmy took a firm grip on his forefinger and led the way.

'You two have a good time,' Harold said as they approached him. He gave the overnight bag to Jake. His smile looked strained. 'You'll have her back tomorrow?'

Jake nodded.

They left. It was good to get out of the house. He smiled down at Kimmy.

Her smile was gone. 'Don't I get to stay by you tomorrow?'

'Not this time. Tomorrow's Mommy's birthday.'

'I know that.' She gave him an annoyed look. She did not approve, at all, of being told what she already knew. Clearly demeaning.

'Well, you want to be there for her party, don't you?'

'I s'pose.'

'It'll be fun.'

He opened the passenger door for Kimmy, and lifted her onto the safety seat. While he strapped her in, she tucked Clew into the top of her OshKosh B'Gosh bib overalls so the tiny grey head poked out like a kangaroo in its mother's pouch.

Then she stuck her forefinger into her mouth.

'Oh no you don't!'

'Yes I do!'

Jake grabbed her wrist, but let himself be overpowered. The wet fingertip pushed into his ear and twisted. 'Eaah! You got me!' Before she could get him again, he ducked out of the car.

He hurried around and climbed in behind the steering wheel.

Kimmy was ready to bestow another Wet Willy. She strained to reach him, but it was no good.

'Saved by the car seat,' he said.

'C'mere.'

'Not a chance. Think I'm dumb?'

'Uh-huh,' she said, nodding.

'Wiseacre.' He pulled into the street. 'So, what would you like to do today?'

'Go to the moojies.'

'The moojies it is. Anything special you want to see?'

She made an eager face with her eyes wide and her brows high. '*Peter Pan*.'

'We saw *Peter Pan* last week.'

'I really really want to see *Peter Pan* again.'

'Sure, why not. Maybe this time the croc will gobble up Captain Hook . . .'

Gobble up.

Ronald Smeltzer.

Could've gone all day without thinking about that.

'Can we eat at McDonald's?'

'No.'

'Daddy!' She shook her fist at him, grinning over the tiny knuckles.

'Well, if you insist.'

'Daddy, can I talk to you?'

'Sure. Isn't that what we've been doing?'

She braced an elbow on the padded armrest of her seat, and leaned towards him. She looked serious. 'There isn't any such thing as crocodiles, is there?'

'What makes you think that?'

'Well, because it's just a moojie.'

'That doesn't mean they don't exist.'

'Dracula and werewoofs and the mummy aren't really real, you said so, so crocodiles aren't real, are they?'

'Gotcha worried, has it?'

'This is not funny.'

'Crocs are real, but I wouldn't worry about them.'

'I do not want to get eaten.'

Jake felt as if he'd been kicked in the stomach. 'Well, you'll just have to keep your eyes open. If you see a croc waddling your way, toss it a fruitgum and run. It'd much rather eat fruitgums than you.'

'I'm not so sure.'

Chapter Seven

With a fresh cup of coffee, Dana Norris returned to her table at a corner of the student union. She read the poem again, wrinkled her nose, and sighed.

Why couldn't this guy write stuff that made sense?

'Salutations.'

She looked up and found Roland standing in front of her table. Roland the Retard.

He wasn't actually retarded – brainy, in fact, but nobody would guess by looking at him.

His black slicked-down hair was parted in the middle like Alfalfa of the old Our Gang films. The style, he liked to explain, was his tribute to Zacherle who used to host a late-night horror show on television.

Today he was wearing a bright plaid sports jacket and one of his assorted gore-shirts. The skin-coloured T-shirt featured a slash wound down its midsection with a bright array of blood and guts spilling out.

'May I join you?' he asked.

'I'm trying to study.'

Nodding, he pulled out an orange, moulded plastic chair and sat across the table from her.

Dana looked down at her book. 'What the hell is a force in a green fuse?'

'Sounds like a slimy wick to me.'

'You're a big help.'

Roland leaned forward, elbows on the table. 'Did you hear what happened out at the Oakwood Inn?'

'Why don't you go away and get yourself something to eat? You look like . . .'

'A cadaver?' he suggested.

'Exactly.'

'Thank you.' He grinned. His big crooked teeth looked like a plastic set you might buy at a joke shop the day before Hallowe'en.

Dana didn't know how Jason could stand to room with this guy, much less be friends with him.

'So,' he said, 'I guess you didn't hear.'

'Hear what?'

'About the massacre.'

'Ah. A massacre. That explains the gleam in your eyes.'

'It happened right outside town. There's that old restaurant, the Oakwood Inn. This couple came up from LA planning to open it again. The place had been closed for years – apparently shut down after several of the patrons turned toes up when they ate there. Food poisoning.' He wiggled his thin black eyebrows. He looked absolutely delighted. 'So last night they were in the place fixing it up and the husband went totally berserk and blew off his wife's head with a shotgun. Then a cop showed up and blew away the husband.'

'Just your cup of tea,' Dana said.

'Outrageous, huh?'

'Too bad you couldn't have been there to enjoy it.'

'Yeah, well, those are the breaks. I drove out there this morning, but the cops have it all blocked off.' He shrugged. 'The stiffs were probably gone by then, anyway.'

'More than likely.'

'I sure would've liked to get a look inside, though. I mean, maybe it hadn't been cleaned up yet. Can you imagine the mess it must've made, a gal catching a twelve-gauge in the face? Pieces of her brains and skull sticking to the walls . . .'

'You're revolting.'

'Anyway, I thought I'd go back later. Maybe the cops'll be gone by then. Do you mind if I borrow your Polaroid?'

Dana stared at him. She felt a rush of heat to her face. 'What makes you think I've got a Polaroid?'

'I just know. How about it?'

'That shit. He showed you the pictures, didn't he?'

'Sure. We're roomies.'

Her mouth was dry. She lifted her coffee mug with a shaky hand and took a drink. She should've known that Jason wouldn't keep his word. Who else had he shown them to? Everyone in the dorm? She'd wanted to burn the things, but Jason had promised he would hide them, never to show them to another soul.

She could just see Roland the Retard drooling over them.

'How about it?' he asked. 'Can I borrow the camera?'

'I'm gonna kill that shithead.'

Roland giggled. 'If you do, let me watch.'

On second thoughts, Roland probably hadn't drooled – hadn't even found the photos particularly interesting since they showed no entrails or severed limbs. Unless he supplied all that with his sick imagination. Which seemed more than likely.

'Have you seen a shrink about this problem of yours?' Dana asked.

'A shrink? A *head*-shrinker? Do you know how they do that, by the way? First, they split the scalp so they can peel it off the skull, then . . .'

'Knock it off.'

Roland's mouth snapped shut.

'What is it with you? I know you're Jason's roommate and buddy and I'm supposed to be nice to you and treat you like a human being, but he's not here so forget that shit. What is it with you, huh? I'm curious. Either you're totally deranged, which I doubt, or this whole obsession with blood and guts is some kind of game. If it's a game, it's something you should have outgrown at least five years ago.'

During her outburst, Roland had taken his elbows off the table and pressed himself into the chair. He looked stunned. His tiny eyes were wide open, his mouth hanging down.

'Do you know *why* you're this way?' Dana continued. 'Well, I've got an idea on that subject. It boils down to this – you're scared.'

Roland glanced over his shoulder, apparently to see who might be within earshot. Nobody was at the nearby tables.

'You're scared that nobody will know you exist if you don't go around acting like a weirdo. This way, people notice you. They don't *like* what they notice, but they do notice you. That's number one. Number two is, you latched onto this blood and guts crap because it makes a joke out of what scares you more than anything – death. You make a mockery out of pain and death to keep it from being real because the real thing has you terrified.'

Dana stopped. She leaned back in her chair, folded her arms beneath her breasts, and glared at him.

'You're crazy,' he muttered.

'People were really truly killed out at that restaurant last night,' she said, forcing herself to speak in a calm voice. 'It was real – if what you told me is true.'

'Yeah, it—'

'Real, Roland. Not one of those splatter movies you love so dearly. And it's got you scared pissless, so you have to defend your fragile psyche by trivializing it.'

'You're a regular Sigmund Freud.'

'The truth is, you probably drove out there in the full expectation that you'd be turned away by the cops. You knew you wouldn't get to see the bodies – or the brains sticking to the walls. The only reason you went out there was so you could brag about it. You make it part of your weird-guy act and it gets you attention, it isn't so real any more, isn't so scary.'

'That's not true.'

'You creep, you're scared of your own shadow.'

'I am not. I *wanted* to see the bodies. It's not my fault the—'

'A coward, Roland. You're a coward.'

'I would've gone in if—'

'Sure. If the cops hadn't shooed you off. I'll bet. As a matter of fact, I *will* bet. A hundred bucks. Imagine the neat T-shirts and masks you could buy with a hundred bucks.'

A corner of Roland's mouth curled up. 'You're betting me a hundred dollars I won't go inside the restaurant?'

'I sure am.'

'You are nuts.'

'Have you got a hundred to put against mine?'

Roland hesitated.

'Didn't think so.'

'That's a pile of money.'

'I've got a deal for you. If you lose, you don't have to pay me a cent. You drop this gore crap. You stop wearing those stupid T-shirts and start acting like a human.'

He frowned. 'I don't know. That's . . .'

'Trying to worm out?'

'No.'

'How about it?'

'All I have to do, to win, is go inside the restaurant?'

'At night,' Dana added.

'No sweat.'

'You go in tonight, and you stay *all* night. Alone.'

His smile started to slip.

'As for my Polaroid, you may take it along.'

'How are you going to know if I stayed all night? I mean, I could sneak out. Not that I *would*, but . . .'

'I'll be right outside in my car. And who knows, maybe I'll come in to check on you from time to time just to make sure you're still there.'

'You've got a deal.'

'I'll pick you up at nine behind your dorm.'

Chapter Eight

'So maybe I was wrong,' Helen said.

'Huh?' Alison asked.

'You haven't given *King Lear* a glance in the past half-hour, just been staring at the phone.'

'I thought he might call,' she said.

'So did I. Maybe we misjudged him. I figured him to make a grand play for you, but . . .'

'I think his grand play is to ignore me.'

59

Celia, lying on the sofa, pulled the stereo headphones off her ears and said, 'Am I missing something?'

'Alison's getting anxious.'

'So call the guy,' she advised.

'I can't do that.'

'She can't do that,' Helen repeated. 'She's laid down the terms. The next move is up to Evan.'

Groaning, Celia eased her feet off the sofa and sat up. 'You don't want to just sit around all day hoping he'll call,' she told Alison. 'You need to do something to take your mind off him. I need to get out, myself.'

'Try going to your two o'clock,' Helen said.

'That seminar's the shits. Besides, it's been three weeks since I last cut a class. I need a break. Especially after yesterday.'

'We *told* you you'd be sorry,' Helen said, 'signing up for a Friday afternoon class.'

'Take a hike.' She looked at Alison. 'How about we go over to the mall?'

Alison liked the idea. 'Are you up to something like that?'

'A walk'll do me good, get the kinks out.'

'How about it, Helen?' Alison asked. 'Want to come along?'

'Nah.'

'Come on,' Alison urged her. 'You're turning into a hermit.'

'I had three damn classes this morning. How does that make me a hermit?' She got up and went to the window. 'Anyway, it's going to rain.'

'What's a little rain,' Alison said.

'Besides, I'd have to change back into something.'

'Aw, go as you are,' Celia told her.

Helen turned around and looked down at herself as if considering Celia's suggestion. She was wearing a house dress that looked like an old tablecloth, complete with food stains. She fastened a snap that had come loose between her heavy breasts. 'I guess, if I keep my raincoat on . . .'

'Get serious,' Celia said.

'I'll just stay here.'

'No, come on,' Alison said. 'You don't want to spend all afternoon cooped up in the house. If you wear your raincoat, nobody'll know what you've got on. The dress isn't so bad, anyway.'

Helen looked at Celia.

'I don't care. Wear whatever you want. Let's just get going.'

'I'll just be a minute,' Alison said.

As she headed for the hallway, she heard Celia say, 'For godsake, at least put on some underpants. You fall on your ass, you'll be flashing beaver.'

Helen's response, if any, was silent.

Smiling, Alison began to climb the stairs to her attic room. The staircase had barely enough light to see the steps, so she ran her hand along the banister as she hurried to the top. Her room was not much brighter than the staircase. Not bothering with a lamp, she stepped over to the single window and looked out.

Pretty gloomy out there, all right. A storm was certainly on the way, but she guessed that it might hold off for a while.

It'll probably start up, she thought, just in time to catch me walking to Gabby's.

She could get a ride from Evan. He'd be glad to . . .

She remembered. The hollow ache came back.

What have I done?

It's okay, she told herself. It's okay. If he's through with me over something like this, fine.

She crossed the small room to her dresser and took out her blue jumpsuit. The one-piece velour outfit would feel soft and cosy, perfect for this kind of weather. Getting into it would be the problem. She had turned the heater off before leaving for her morning classes, and the room was chilly.

As fast as she could, she jerked her flannel shirt over her head, flipped off her slippers, tugged her jeans down her legs, kicked the jeans away, stepped into her jumpsuit and pulled it up. Shivering, she thrust her arms into the sleeves. She raised the zipper to her neck, and sighed with relief as the chill was shut out.

Quickly she put on a pair of wool socks and stepped into her Nikes. Then she snatched her windcheater from the closet, grabbed the strap of her shoulder bag, and hurried downstairs.

Helen, waiting in her sou'wester and boots, looked ready for a typhoon.

'Ahoy,' Alison said.

'We're *waiting* for you, Celia!' Helen called from somewhere inside her rain-gear.

'Patience,' Celia called from her room. 'I'm a crip, remember?' A few moments passed and she came out clutching a snap-brim cap in her teeth while she adjusted her sling. She had changed into a bulky cable-knit pullover that she'd bought on a trip to Ireland. Her pants were loose-fitting corduroys with deep pockets, cuffs tucked into snakeskin boots.

'You look smashing,' Alison told her.

'Smashed up is more like it,' she said, taking the cap from her teeth and flipping it onto her head at a rakish angle.

'Where's your raincoat?' Helen asked.

'My raincoat is a poncho. I'm not gonna fool with it.'

'You'll get soaked.'

'If it rains, which I doubt, you'll stay dry enough for the three of us.'

A cool wind hit Alison when she opened the door. She fastened the snaps of her jacket. Halfway down the stairs, she looked back. Celia was using her good hand to keep the cap on her head. 'Are you going to be warm enough?'

'You kidding? This is an Aran sweater.'

'Whatever you say.'

Helen, higher on the stairs, turned up the broad brim of her rain hat. Her face appeared, and she smiled as if pleasantly surprised to find herself in the company of others.

Three steps from the bottom, Alison leaped. Her bent knees absorbed the impact.

'Gimme a break,' Celia called.

Grinning, Alison walked backwards. 'This is neat weather,' she said. 'Invig—'

'Look out, now.'

Something prodded her spine.

Celia started to laugh.

Whirling around, Alison found a knotty cane levelled at her belly. At the cane's other end stood Dr Teal, a grocery bag in his free hand. He swung the cane back, resting it on his shoulder. As he looked at the three, his eyebrows lifted, crinkling his forehead. 'Setting out, I see. A fine day for an excursion.'

'A blustery day,' Alison told him. He was a man who appreciated allusions.

'Keep a sharp eye out for Eeyore's tail,' he said.

'Want a hand with the groceries?' Alison asked.

'Thanks for the offer, but I must not keep you from your expedition. Proceed!' He stepped off the cobblestones into the wind-bent grass, and made a sweeping gesture with his cane.

Alison stepped past him and turned around. Celia tipped her cap to the professor.

'You, my dear, have looked better.'

'I got a little banged up.'

'I'm very sorry to hear it.'

'You oughta see the other guy.'

Shaking his head, the old professor patted her gently on the shoulder as she passed him.

'Say-hay,' Helen greeted him.

'Say-hay.' He leaned close to her and said something Alison couldn't hear. Then he walked around the stairway, stopped at his side door, and propped his cane against the wall.

Alison walked a little further, then waited for the others to catch up. 'What'd he say?' she asked Helen.

'I don't know, some nonsense. That guy's battier every time I see him.'

'But what did he say?' Alison persisted.

' "Let the albatross live." Whatever that's supposed to mean.'

'I think,' said Alison, 'he was saying he liked your outfit.'

As she reached the sidewalk, she saw a man on the next block. He was leaning into the wind, clutching his tan jacket round him. He had light brown hair like Evan. Alison felt her heart quicken. She squinted, trying to see him better.

They'll just have to go on without me, she thought. They'll understand.

He's come back to me. In spite of the ultimatum.

She'd almost given up hoping, but Evan must've decided to try the new arrangement.

She was glad she was wearing the jumpsuit. Of all her outfits, it was Evan's favourite. The zipper down the front drove him wild.

As she walked towards him, she popped open the snaps of her

windbreaker and lowered the jumpsuit zipper a few inches.

She could take him to the house. It would be warm and cosy, and they would have the place all to themselves until Celia and Helen got back.

Not such a great idea, she thought. It'd be asking for trouble.

On the other hand, it would be a good test. If Evan could resist temptation under those circumstances . . .

He was closer, now.

He didn't look so much like Evan, any more.

He turned away at the corner, and his profile was all wrong – his nose too long, his chin too weak.

'That guy looked a little like Evan,' Celia said.

Alison shrugged. She felt cheated and empty. 'Evan can take a flying leap,' she muttered.

The warmth of the enclosed shopping mall felt good. Alison's windbreaker was light, so she wasn't bothered by keeping it on, but she pitied Helen. The poor gal must feel stifled under that heavy raincoat.

Don't feel too sorry for her, Alison thought. She could've put on decent clothes if she hadn't been so lazy.

The three wandered along the concourse, close to the left side. While Celia and Helen looked into shops, Alison scanned the other shoppers. Many of them were students. One of them might be Evan.

At Contempo Casuals, Celia stopped and gazed at the mannequins near the entrance. 'I want to check it out,' she said, and they entered.

Helen took off the huge floppy hat. Her round face looked moist and florid.

She opened the top buckle of her coat.

'Better stop there,' Celia warned. 'They'll sound the slob alarm.'

'Eat it,' Helen said. But she left the lower buckles alone.

They followed Celia to the rear of the store, where she began looking at negligees.

'You're not getting *another*,' Helen said.

'Oh no?'

'What've you got, twenty of them? And the rate you go

through guys, none of them gets a chance to see more than one, anyway.'

'Jealous?'

Helen just shook her head.

Celia took her time studying the selection, lifting various negligees on their hangers and inspecting them, pondering, putting them back. She went about the task one-handed, so after a while Alison began to help by returning the rejected garments to the crowded racks. At last she found one she seemed to like. She turned to Alison, holding it up. 'What do you think?'

It was a backless nightie, very short, of glossy royal blue. It had spaghetti straps for tying behind the neck, and an open, plunging front. The cups were wisps of blue gauze.

'Figures you'd pick a thing like that,' Helen said.

'Looks fine to me.' Alison wondered if there was another one just like it. If Evan saw her in something like that . . .

Forget him.

'I wouldn't get it,' Helen said.

'Of *course* you wouldn't.'

With one side of her lip curled up, Helen flicked the sheer gauze. 'You don't want that. And I'm not talking modesty here. I realize you're far beyond such things.'

'Then what *are* you talking?'

'That colour, it'll make your titties look sick. You want to look like you've got blue boobs and purple nips?'

Celia raised her eyebrows. She looked at Alison.

'I hadn't thought of that,' Alison admitted.

'See if they've got the same thing in black,' Helen suggested.

'Good idea.' She smiled. 'Thanks.'

'Though, if you ask me, you'd be better off putting your money in potato chips.'

Alison held the blue nightie until Celia, searching the rack, came up with a black one in the same style. 'Great,' Celia said. 'Perfect.'

Alison hooked the hanger over the rail, then unhooked it and looked again at the garment. The blue was deep and bright and shiny. She caressed the fabric. It felt slippery, and clung to her hand. She wondered how it would feel on her naked body, and how it would look. She had never owned anything like this. She raised her eyes. Celia and Helen were both staring at her. She grinned.

'Blue boobs,' Helen warned.

'I can live with it,' she said.

Celia smiled. 'A little something just in case Evan comes through?'

'What happened to your vow of chastity?' Helen asked.

'This has nothing to do with it,' Alison said.

'Oh no?'

As they left the shop with their purchases, Alison offered to carry Celia's bag.

'Yeah,' Helen said. 'Take it off her hands. Something like that, it must weigh a ton.'

'Maybe you should've bought one,' Celia told her.

'Ready to go?' Helen asked, ignoring the remark.

'We just got here.'

She curled her upper lip. There were sparkles of sweat above it. She must be suffering, Alison thought, trapped inside that heavy raincoat.

'Maybe we should go,' Alison said.

'I just want to be fair to you guys,' Celia explained. 'Poor Helen needs to ogle the puppies and hit the doughnut shop, and you want to check out the bookstore, don't you?'

'It doesn't matter,' Alison told her. 'I think one of us is melting.'

'I'm all right,' Helen said, though clearly she wasn't.

Celia grinned. 'That perked you up – doughnuts, maple bars, bear claws, chocolate eclairs . . .'

'I could sure use a Coke,' she admitted.

They headed across the concourse towards the wing of the mall where the food stands were located.

'Salutations,' someone said from behind them.

They turned around.

Alison saw that it was the weird kid. Though she didn't know his name and had never spoken to him, she had noticed him frequently around the campus. He was impossible not to notice, the strange clothes he wore and the way he parted his hair in the middle. Right now, he was wearing a garish sports jacket and a T-shirt with a gash spilling blood and entrails printed on its front. He was clutching a bag from Spartan Sporting Goods.

'You're Celia Jamerson, right?' he asked. 'I saw you in *The Glass Menagerie*. You were great.'

'Thanks,' Celia said.

'You probably don't remember me.'

'You're Jason's friend, aren't you?'

He grinned, his thin lips stretching away from big crooked teeth. 'I'm his roommate, Roland. Anyway, I was just wondering if you're okay. What happened, were you in an accident?'

'I had a little mishap on my bike.'

'Gosh, I'm sorry.' His gaze travelled sideways to Alison and slid down her body, then returned to Celia. 'I hope it wasn't serious,' he said.

'Well, thank you. I'll be all right. How's Jason?'

'Oh, he's fine. He'll be trying out for the spring play. I know he's hoping you'll be in it.'

'I don't know. Auditions are next week. I'm pretty banged up.'

'That's awful.' He looked again at Alison. She felt an urge to pull her jacket round her. 'Anyway, I'd better get going. Hope you're feeling better.'

'Thanks,' Celia said. 'See you around.'

He turned and walked away.

Alison realized she had been holding her breath as if afraid of inhaling a disease from the guy.

'What a dreamboat,' Helen said.

'A nightmare boat,' Alison muttered. 'I feel like I need a bath.'

'He sure looked us over.'

Alison hadn't seen him looking Helen over, but she kept her mouth shut.

Celia shrugged. 'It was nice of him to be concerned about me.'

'Play your cards right,' Helen told her, 'maybe he'll ask you out. How'd you like to model your new nightie for him?'

'Gimme a break.'

With Helen in the lead, they walked towards the food area. Alison still felt a little squirmy. Though there wasn't much similarity between them, Roland somehow reminded her of Prince Charming, the crazed, filthy man she'd seen yesterday afternoon at Gabby's.

They stopped at one of the refreshment stands. Helen ordered a Coke and hot dog. Alison and Celia each ordered Cokes. They found a vacant table in the middle of the concourse, and sat down.

Poking her straw through the plastic lid of her drink, Alison could almost see Roland leering at her. 'What a creep,' she muttered.

'He gives new meaning,' said Helen, 'to the expression "nasty slimy yuck".'

Celia grinned. 'Yeah, but his roomy's not half bad.'

'He the guy who played the gentleman caller?' Alison asked.

'That's the one.'

'If he's so wonderful,' Helen asked, squeezing a thick trail of mustard across her hot dog, 'how come you haven't added him to your list?'

'For godsake, he's a *freshman*.'

'Shouldn't let a little thing like that stop you.'

'You kidding? I'd never live it down, it got around I was seeing a freshman. Besides, he's already going with some gal.'

'So,' Helen said, 'it's not that he's a freshman. Just that somebody else has her claws in him.'

'Gimme a break. He'd drop her like a hot spud if I gave him the ol' look.'

Helen took a big bite out of her hot dog. Mustard dribbled down her chin. Wiping the mustard off with the back of a hand, she said to Alison in a muffled voice, 'Don't you just adore modesty in a person?'

'Hell,' Alison said, 'she's probably right.'

'Not that I intend to give Jason the ol' look,' Celia pointed out. 'Like I said, he's a freshman.'

Helen licked the mustard smear off the back of her hand. 'Maybe you could date him incognito. Wear Groucho glasses.'

'He's got to have a personality defect,' Alison said, 'if he pals around with that weirdo.'

Celia grinned. 'Can't judge a person by his roommates. Shit, look at *mine*.'

Chapter Nine

Roland waited alone. He wished Jason were here, not off in Weston for his sister's wedding. They could talk about the bet, make jokes. It wouldn't be nearly so bad.

It wouldn't be happening at all if Jason were here. Dana wouldn't have crapped on him.

The bitch.

She'd always despised him, he knew that. But she never let it show much until today.

She was probably annoyed because Jason left without her. They always went to the movies on Friday nights; then parked somewhere to screw around.

But not tonight.

No fun and games with Jason tonight, so take it out on Roland.

He stepped to the windows.

It was raining like shit out there.

A car came in off Spring Street, its headlights making shiny paths on the pavement of the parking lot. Roland's stomach twisted. As the car neared the rear entrance to the dorm, however, he saw that it wasn't a Volkswagen.

The clock on his desk showed a quarter to nine. If Dana was on time, she wouldn't be here for another fifteen minutes.

Fourteen.

His stomach stayed tight.

That bitch, why is she doing this to me?

Did it have to do with the Polaroids? That's when she went haywire, after she realized he must've seen them.

Crouching at Jason's desk, Roland slid open the bottom drawer, lifted out a stack of *Penthouse* and *Hustler* magazines, and pulled out the envelope. He took it to his desk. Sitting down, he turned on his gooseneck lamp. He removed the ten photos from the envelope and spread them across his desktop.

Two of them were over-exposed.

Another shot, this one a real close-up apparently taken from between her knees, was blurry. Jason must've been so excited he forgot to adjust the distance setting. But he'd tried again and got it right.

Yeah, Dana probably wasn't very happy at all that I got a look at these.

Roland unsnapped the case on his belt and pulled out his folding Buck knife. He prized open the blade. Touched its point to the glossy surface between her thighs. 'How do you like *this*?' he whispered in a shaky voice. He felt an urge to shove the knife in, but didn't dare. Jason would know he was the one who'd done it.

Pressing the flat of the blade against his chin, Roland stared down at the photos.

What if I gave them to her? Maybe she'd let me off the hook.

If I try that, she'll know I'm scared.

I'll spend the night in that fucking restaurant and I'll make a hundred bucks. A cinch. Might even be fun.

Fun. Like hell.

But he didn't have any choice. If he backed out, Dana would tell everyone he's a chicken and a phoney.

Maybe I can find a way to get back at her.

He slipped the photos into the envelope.

The faint beep of a car horn made him flinch. He stood up, saw his reflection in the window, and turned off the lamp. Looking down through the darkness, he saw a VW beetle at the kerb. It was Dana's, all right. It had that banner on the aerial.

Roland pushed open the glass door and jogged towards her car. He hunched himself over as if the rain were a heavy weight. His shoes slapped water off the pavement. He wore a dark stocking cap and a windbreaker. A sleeping bag was clutched to his chest.

Dana leaned across the seat to open the door for him.

After climbing in, he dropped the sleeping bag to the floor between his feet, pulled the door shut, and struggled out of a small backpack.

'A beautiful night for your adventure,' Dana said.

'Yeah. Too bad there's no thunder and lighting.' He chuckled. He sounded nervous.

Dana pulled away from the kerb and headed across the parking lot. 'You'll have to give me directions.'

'Take a right on Spring. I'll let you know when to turn off.'

She stopped at the parking-lot exit, waited for a few cars to swoosh past, and turned onto Spring Street. The rain was coming down hard. She leaned forward, trying to see better.

Roland was silent.

He usually talked non-stop.

'Scared?' Dana asked.

'Yeah, I'm scared. Your wiper blades aren't worth shit.'

'Tell me about it,' Dana muttered. Instead of sweeping the water aside, they seemed to smear it and leave trails across the windscreen.

'I didn't come out tonight to get killed in a car wreck.'

'I know. You came out to get killed in a haunted restaurant.'

'Haunted. That's a good one.'

'Don't you think so? Aren't you the guy who told me and Jason that ghosts happen when people get croaked too fast?'

'Maybe,' he said.

'Sure. We were walking back from that midnight show of *The Uninvited* and you said a ghost gets started when someone doesn't know he's dead yet. His spirit, or whatever, thinks he's still alive. Isn't that how you explained it?'

'Well, that's a theory, anyway.'

'These two people got *blown away* last night. Can't be much more sudden than that. So their ghosts must be hanging around, don't you think?'

Roland didn't answer.

'My camera's in the back seat. Maybe you can get some snapshots of them.'

'Make a left at the traffic light,' he muttered.

Dana checked the rearview mirror. The road behind her was dark, so she slowed. A pickup truck approached from the front. She squinted against the glare of its headlights. It sped by, spray from its tyres splashing her door and window. She made the turn, then took a deep breath. The road ahead was dark except for a few streetlights. There were houses on both sides. She knew that the road led out of town, but couldn't remember a restaurant along the stretch.

'You don't believe in ghosts,' Roland said.

'Ah, but you do. Or is that just part of your act?'

'They don't scare me.'

'Ever seen one?'

'No.'

'Not yet, huh?'

'If ghosts exist, they're harmless. They can't do anything to you.'

'Such as cut your throat or something?' Dana asked, glancing at him and grinning.

'They wouldn't be able to hold a knife. Or anything else, for that matter. They don't have any substance. All they can do is appear.'

'And turn you into a raving lunatic.'

'Only if you're scared of them.'

'Which you aren't, of course.'

'There's no reason to be.'

'Who are you trying to convince?'

Roland said nothing.

'The gal got her head blown off, right?' Dana said. 'So does that mean her ghost won't have a head, either?'

'I'm not sure.'

'I thought you were supposed to be an expert.'

Dana saw no more houses ahead. On both sides of the road were fields, barren except for scattered trees. 'Where *is* this place, anyway?'

'We're almost there.'

'Seems like a queer place for a restaurant, this far out.'

'The turn-off's around the next bend. You'll want to go right.'

'I don't know much about these things,' Dana said, 'but I'd bet the babe's ghost is missing its head. Just a guess, you understand.'

'You'd better slow down.'

There were headlights near the crest of the hill far ahead. Her rearview mirror was dark. She eased down on the brake but couldn't see the side road. 'Where?'

Roland pointed.

It was a narrow low space that looked more like a driveway than a road.

Dana slowed her car almost to a stop. As she turned, the headlights swept across a large darkwood sign. She tried to read the sign's carved words, but they were a blur through the water streaked and splattered on her windscreen. The wipers beating back and forth were no help – just another distraction. The headlights left the sign. Squinting, Dana saw the falling rain, the shiny trails her headlights made on the pavement, and land rising on both sides of the road.

'Have you got the money?' Roland asked.

'In my purse.' She grinned at him. 'Not that you'll be getting it.'

'I'll get it, all right.'

'I'd be surprised if you last ten minutes.'

'You're going to come in at dawn, right?'

'Wrong. We'll both be back in town snug in our beds before midnight.'

'I mean, just assuming I don't chicken out. Which I won't. You'll come in at dawn?'

'Just come out.'

'You want to see inside the place, don't you?'

'No.'

'Well, come in anyway.'

'No way.'

The sides of the road were gone, and Dana realized she had entered the parking area. She kept driving straight ahead. At first she couldn't see the restaurant. Then her reaching headlights found its stairs, its porch and door. The pale band of a Police Line ribbon was stretched across the porch posts at the top of the stairs. The door was cross-hatched with boards.

Dana stopped directly in front of the stairs and killed the headlights. 'Whoops,' she said. 'Where'd the restaurant go?'

'How am I supposed to get in?'

Dana bent over, head against the steering wheel, and reached down between her knees. Her fingertips combed the gritty floor mat until they found the tyre iron. She picked it up and gave it to Roland.

'You thought of everything,' he muttered.

Twisting around, Dana knelt on her seat and got the camera for him. 'Take some good ones,' she said. 'Especially of the gal. No head. Should be nifty.'

Roland put the camera into his pack. Leaning forward, he swung the pack behind him and struggled into its shoulder straps.

He hugged the sleeping bag against his side and gripped the tyre iron. 'How about turning on the headlights till I'm inside?' he asked.

'Why not.' The lights tunnelled into the darkness. 'Have fun.'

'You'll come in for me at dawn,' he said. It was not a request.

'I'm not going inside that place.'

'I think you will.' He opened the door and climbed out. Standing in the rain, he leaned inside. 'I've got the pictures with me.'

'Give them here,' Dana snapped.

'You may have them in the morning. If you *don't* come in after me, you'll never see them again. But everyone else will.'

'You shit!'

He slammed the door.

When he was in front of the car, Dana blasted the horn and he jumped. He turned around. Glared at her. Then curled his lip above his crooked teeth and turned away. At the top of the stairs, he broke the police ribbon and stepped to the door. He started to prize the boards off.

Dana, furious, watched him. Her heart was beating fast, her breath hissing through her nostrils. She saw herself rush up behind Roland and slam his head against the door until he was senseless. Then she would search him and find the pictures.

But she didn't move.

With her luck, the creep would probably hear her coming.

In her mind she saw Roland whirl around and lay open her head with the bar.

She wouldn't put it past him.

He's a fucking wimp, she thought, but he's not exactly stable.

She saw him drag her body into the restaurant.

The thoughts began to frighten her.

Roland got the door open. He lifted his sleeping bag off the porch floor, glanced back at Dana, then went inside. The door swung shut.

Dana shut off her headlights.

Leaning across the seat, she locked the passenger door.

She reached for the ignition key, intending to turn the engine off. But she changed her mind, shifted to reverse, and slowly backed the car away. She considered leaving. It would serve the shit right, getting stranded out here. If he realized she was gone, however, he might decide to spread out his sleeping bag on the porch. He had to spend the night inside. That was the bet. That was the punishment, the price he had to pay for being such an asshole.

And for looking at the pictures.

He has them *with* him.

Dana, suddenly realizing she might be dangerously close to the rear of the parking area, hit her brakes. The car jolted to a stop. She put on the hand-brake and killed the engine.

When her eyes adjusted to the darkness, she found that she could see the restaurant. It was about fifty yards ahead of her, a low dark shape the width of the parking lot, black beneath its hooded porch.

It looked forbidding.

And Roland was inside.

Dana smiled. 'You'll have a *real* good time,' she muttered.

When Roland closed the restaurant door, he stood motionless and scanned the darkness. He could see nothing. He heard only his own heartbeat and quick breaths and the sound of the rain.

There's nothing to be afraid of, he told himself.

His body seemed to believe otherwise.

He knew what he wanted to do. He wanted to drop the sleeping bag, take off his pack, and get his hands on the flashlight. But he couldn't move.

Go ahead and do it.

He was sure it would be all right, but part of him knew with absolute certainty that something was hunched silent in the dark nearby. Aware of his presence. Waiting. And if he should make the slightest move, it would come for him.

The quiet whinnying of Dana's car engine broke through his fear. He turned around and opened the door. The Volkswagen was backing away.

She's leaving?

The thought alarmed him at first, then filled him with relief. If she actually drove off, he wouldn't need to stay inside. Spend the night on the porch, maybe. Keep a lookout and make sure he was back inside when she returned.

If she returned.

And if she didn't come back in the morning, the hike back to town was only a few miles and he'll still win the bet.

The car didn't turn around. Near the far end of the parking lot, its red brake lights glowed briefly behind it.

It had stopped.

The engine went silent.

Roland's hopes died. Dana wasn't leaving, after all, just putting some distance between herself and the restaurant. She must've been nervous about being close to it.

He watched for a while, but the car didn't move again.

Leaving the door open for a quick escape, Roland dropped his sleeping bag to the floor. He took off his pack and removed the flashlight. With his back to the doorway, he thumbed the flashlight switch. The strong beam shot out. He whipped it from right to left. Shadows jumped and writhed, but no foul shape was lurching towards him.

Roland allowed himself to breathe. He wished his heart would slow down. It felt like a fist punching the insides of his chest.

He shut the door and sagged slightly against it. He locked his knees to keep them from folding under him. The kneecaps began to flutter with a spastic, twitching bounce as if they wanted to jump off.

Roland tried to ignore them. Aiming the flashlight ahead, he took several steps until he could see around the corner of the wall. The wall extended down the right side of the main dining-room. Something just beyond the corner caught his eye. He held his breath until he identified the objects as a step ladder, lamp and vacuum cleaner. On the floor near them were a toolbox, some jars and bottles and rags. He moved the beam away from them.

A bright disc at the far end of the room startled Roland, but it was only his own light reflecting off a window. He wasn't alarmed when his light hit the other windows.

Except for the clutter near the one wall, the dining-room was empty. He swept his beam back across it, to the wall ahead of him, and to the right. A few yards away was the corner of an L-shaped bar counter. The shelves behind it were empty. There were no stools in front of the counter. A brass footrail ran its length.

Turning slightly, Roland played his beam over the space between the bar counter and the front wall of the restaurant. A card table stood near the wall. Bottles and a few glasses gleamed with the light. There were two folding chairs at the table.

Crouching, he shone his flashlight beneath the card table.

He stood up. Beyond the table, at the far end of the room, was an alcove. A sign above the opening read, 'Restrooms'.

Roland moved silently forward until he could aim his light into the space behind the counter.

Returning to his backpack, he took out two of the candles he had purchased that afternoon. He went to the table and lit them. He let the wax drip onto the table, then stood the candles upright in the tiny puddles. He stepped back. The two flames gave off an amazing amount of light, their glow illuminating most of the cocktail area.

Comforted somewhat by the light, Roland walked past the table. He noticed batwing doors behind the bar, probably to give the bartender access to the kitchen.

The kitchen.

Where the killings happened.

The areas above and below the doors were dark. He didn't shine his light inside. Instead, he entered the short hallway to the restrooms. A brass sign on the door straight ahead of him read, 'Ladies'. The door marked 'Gentlemen' was on the right.

He needed to check inside each, but the prospect of that renewed his leg tremors and set his heart sledging again. He didn't want to open those doors, didn't want to face whatever might be lurking within.

It'll be worse, he told himself, if I don't look. Then I won't know. I might get a big surprise later on.

He took the flashlight in his left hand, wiped the sweat off his right, and gripped the knob of the ladies' room door. The knob wouldn't turn. He tried the other door. It, too, was locked.

For a moment, he was glad. He wouldn't be opening them. It was a great relief.

Then he realized that the locked doors didn't guarantee that the restrooms were safe. Probably the doors could still be opened from inside.

He shone his light on the knob of the men's room door. It had a keyhole. A few times in the past, he had got into toilets simply by inserting a pointed object into the lock hole and twisting. He pulled up the leather flap of his knife case.

The snap popped open.

Christ, it was loud!

Whoever's behind the door . . .

Calm down.

. . . heard it.

There's nobody inside the goddamn john.

Roland stared at the door.

He imagined a sudden harsh rap on the other side.

Gooseflesh crawled up his back.

Leaving his knife in its case, he backed away.

The candlelight was comforting.

He picked up the folding chairs one at a time and carried them to the entryway beneath the restrooms sign. Back to back, they made a barrier that would have to be climbed over or pushed away. He placed a cocktail glass on the seat of each, near the edge. If the chairs moved, the glasses should fall.

Pleased with the device, Roland returned to the card table. He picked up one of the bottles. It was nearly full. With a candle behind it, he saw that the liquor was clear. He turned the bottle until he could read its label in the trembling light. Gilby's Vodka.

Great.

He twisted off its plastic cap, raised the bottle and filled his mouth. He swallowed a little bit at a time. The vodka scorched his throat and ignited a fire in his stomach. When his mouth was empty, he took a deep breath and sighed.

If he drank enough, he could numb himself to the whole situation.

But that would make him more vulnerable.

One more swig, then he recapped the bottle.

Crouching over his pack, he lifted out Dana's camera and folded it open. A flashbar was already attached to the top. He stood up and took another deep breath. It felt good inhaling, filling his lungs. They didn't seem tight like before. In fact, he realized that he was no longer shaking. There was a slightly vague feeling inside his head. Had the vodka done this?

Back at the table, he set down the camera and took one more swallow.

Then one more.

Picking up the camera, he went to the end of the bar. He lifted the hinged panel, tipped it back so it would stay upright, and stepped through the opening. He stopped in front of the batwing doors. Beyond them was darkness.

The kitchen.

'Anybody . . .' He almost said 'here?' but that word wouldn't come out. He wished he'd kept quiet. His fear had come back with the sound of his voice, a tight band constricting his chest.

He raised the flashlight above the doors. Its beam spilled along the kitchen floor, shaking as it moved.

He smelled the blood before he saw it. He knew the odour well, having collected some of his own in a mayonnaise jar and smeared it over his face on Hallowe'en to gross out the guys in the dorm. His blood had smelled just this way – metallic, a little like train rails.

His light found the blood. There was lots of it, all over the floor about halfway across the kitchen. It looked brown.

There were pale tape outlines showing the positions of the bodies.

This is getting real, he thought.

Shit.

This is getting very real.

He'd made a big mistake. He had no business here. He was a dumb-ass kid intruding where he didn't belong.

He lowered the flashlight. Backed away. Felt someone sneaking up and whirled around. Nobody there. He hurried to the other side of the bar.

I don't need this. I don't need to prove anything. I don't need Dana's money.

Near the door, he dropped to his knees and stuffed the camera into his pack.

Take pictures. Sure.

He stood, lifting the pack by one strap and hooking a finger of the same hand through the drawcord of his sleeping bag.

Shit, the candles.

The bundles swinging at his side, he rushed to the card table.

As he puffed one candle out, he spotted the chairs he'd set up to block the hall to the restrooms.

Leave them. Who cares.

He blew out the other candle. Followed the beam of his flashlight to the door. Opened the door.

The night breeze, smelling of rain, blew against his face.

He stared through the downpour at Dana's car – a small dark object waiting at the far edge of the lot. The plastic banner on its aerial waved in the breeze.

I'd be surprised if you last ten minutes.

The bitch, she'll never let me live this down. She'll tell everyone. I'll be a joke.

Roland kicked the door shut.

'*I'm staying!*' he yelled. '*Fuck it!*'

He stepped close to the bar. He unrolled his sleeping bag, took off his cap and jacket, and sat on the soft down-filled bag.

I should've done it like this in the first place.

Shouldn't have snooped around.

Should've done it the way I'd planned.

Reaching deep into his pack, pushing aside the candles and camera, he touched steel.

The handcuffs rattled as he pulled them out.

He snapped one bracelet around his left wrist, the other around the brass footrail of the bar.

Flashlight clamped under his left arm, he aimed it at the card table and gave the handcuff key a toss. It clinked against one of the bottles and dropped onto the table.

Out of reach.

We'll see who chickens out, he thought.

We'll see who lasts the night.

Chapter Ten

It was almost quitting time, and the rain outside Gabby's showed no sign of letting up. Alison backed away from the window. She was glad that she'd borrowed Helen's rain-gear; she would get drenched if she'd worn her windcheater to work.

Not if Evan picks me up, she thought.

Fat chance.

Who knows, maybe he'll surprise you. After all, he showed up last night when you didn't think he would.

Alison went to the table that had just been vacated. She dropped the tip into her apron pocket and began to clear off the dirty plates and glasses.

If he cares at all about me, she thought, he'll pick me up. He knows it's pouring outside and I'll have to walk home in it unless he gives me a ride. Coming to my rescue about now would go a long way towards getting back on my good side. He has to know that.

After wiping off the table top, she lifted the heavy tray and carried it into the kitchen.

Maybe he'll show up, she told herself. And if he does, maybe he'll be in for a surprise.

Before leaving the house that afternoon, Alison had tucked her toothbrush and her new nightie into the bottom of her flight bag. Then she had taken them out. She would have no use for them even if Evan should make an appearance. After all, she hadn't changed her mind about sleeping with him. It was silly to prepare yourself for something that just wouldn't happen.

But she thought about last Friday night. He had come into Gabby's after the movie let out at the Imperial, sipped a beer while he waited for her to finish the shift, and they had walked back to his apartment. She hadn't expected to spend the night. It was so wonderful, though, that she couldn't force herself to leave and they had made love almost till dawn. It was her first whole night with him.

81

If they could just have another night like that . . .

We won't, she told herself. Too much has changed.

But she went ahead and put her toothbrush and nightie back into the bag. You never know. Maybe, somehow, everything would suddenly be right again.

She *wanted* it all to be right.

As she unloaded the dirty dishes in the kitchen of Gabby's, she imagined Evan coming for her. 'I just couldn't stay away from you any longer,' he would say. 'I tried to stay away and punish you, but I couldn't. I've given it a lot of thought, Alison. Sure, I'd like to make love with you. I'd like nothing more, because it makes us part of each other as if, for a little while, we're both one person. But I can live without that if I have to. The main thing, really, is just to *be* with you. I would be happy just looking into your eyes, just hearing your laughter, just holding your hand.'

And just maybe she would go back to his apartment, after all. While he waited on the sofa, she'd close the door to his bedroom and slip into the negligee . . .

'Al!'

Startled, she turned around. Gabby, standing at the grill, was looking over his shoulder at her. 'Go on and get out of here. Have a good weekend.'

'Thanks,' she said. 'You too.'

At the rear of the kitchen, she scooped her tips out of the apron and into her bag. She struggled into Helen's heavy raincoat, put on the strange hat, and lifted the bag. 'See you Monday,' she called, and pushed her way through the swinging door.

The table that she had just cleared off was no longer deserted.

Evan sat at its booth.

His arm was around Tracy Morgan.

More-organ Morgan, Mouth-organ Morgan, also known as Tugboat Tracy for reasons that had always been unclear to Alison.

Alison felt herself shrivel inside.

Evan, as if sensing her presence, looked around at her. His glasses were spotted with rain. One side of his mouth twitched upward.

Alison rushed for the door, shouldered it open, and lurched into the pounding rain.

She looked sideways.

Behind the lighted window, Evan watched her and calmly stroked Tracy's long auburn hair.

Chapter Eleven

Roland had purchased the handcuffs that afternoon at Spartan Sporting Goods for $24.50.

He had wanted to buy the cuffs when he first saw them a few weeks ago. Staring through the display case at the shiny bracelets, he'd been excited by thoughts of what he might do with them. Not that he would ever do such things. Still, just owning them would be nice, the same way it was nice to own a few knives even if you didn't actually plan to run around carving up women with them. He'd bought the Buck knife that day. It wasn't embarrassing, buying the knife, because people bought knives for camping, fishing, hunting. But if you're not a cop, why do you need handcuffs? What would the salesperson think? It would be like buying a pack of condoms.

Roland had never bought condoms, even though he wanted them. And he hadn't bought the handcuffs, either.

Until today.

When Dana challenged him to spend the night in the restaurant, he immediately remembered the cuffs and he knew how to win the bet. The cuffs would guarantee it. His courage, or lack of it, would be irrelevant once he had anchored himself to something in the restaurant. No matter what, he would win the bet.

With a hundred dollars and his reputation riding on the bet, he had returned to the store. He could feel himself blushing as he peered through the counter glass.

'Can I help you with something?' asked the clerk.

Roland kept his eyes down. 'I'd like to see the handcuffs.'

'Black or nickle finish?'

'Nickle.'

Crouching, the man slid open the back of the counter and reached inside. He was heavy-set, his brown hair long around the sides of his head as if to make up for what was lacking on top. He put the cuffs on the counter.

Roland picked them up. They felt heavy.

'Grade A tempered steel. The links'll withstand a direct pull of twelve hundred pounds.'

Nodding, Roland tugged the bracelets. The connecting chain snapped taut. 'Fine,' he said. 'How much are they?'

'Twenty-four fifty. Interested in a case?'

'No, I don't think so.'

'Anything else? We've got a sale on the Navy MK.3 Combat knife, regularly forty-nine ninety-five. A real beaut of a knife. Like to see one?'

Roland shook his head. 'No, this'll do it.'

'Cash or charge?'

That was all there was to it. No embarrassing questions, no snide remarks. Relieved, Roland left the store with his purchase.

And spotted Celia. Now, there was a gal he wouldn't mind trying the handcuffs on. That other gal, too – the one in the jumpsuit. Looking at that one, he could see himself cuffing her hands behind her back and pulling down that zipper all the way past her waist.

Oh, yes. Either one of those gals. Cuff them, and they'd be at his mercy.

But he hadn't bought the cuffs for that. He would never have the guts, anyway.

I'm not crazy, he had told himself.

He'd bought the handcuffs only because of the bet. With them, nothing could prevent him from winning ... as long as the restaurant had a secure fixture to which he could fasten one bracelet. It was sure to.

A door handle. A pipe. Something.

A brilliant idea.

Sitting in the darkness cuffed to the bar rail, however, Roland wasn't quite so sure the idea was brilliant. What if something happened and he *had* to get out?

Like a fire, for instance.

Good thing he had blown out the candles.

The place isn't going to burn down, he told himself. Don't worry about it.

He couldn't help worrying about it.

Suppose Dana started the place on fire to drive him out so he'd lose the bet? No. She's not that crazy. A little crazy. That time at the movies when he reached across to get the popcorn from Jason and accidentally brushed her breast with his arm, she dumped her Coke on his lap. Once when they went to the drive-in, she made him get in the trunk of Jason's car so he could sneak in without paying, then she had talked Jason into leaving him there for almost an hour.

She really hates my guts, Roland thought. But she won't burn the place down. That was too crazy even for Dana.

Probably.

What she might do is leave.

No, she wants the Polaroids. She'll come in for them.

That doesn't mean she'll give me the key.

When she finds me cuffed here, she might just take the photos and go. Or worse.

Roland's mouth went dry. A cold hand seemed to clutch his stomach.

I'll be at her mercy.

Oh, shit, what'll she do to me?

It wasn't a question of *whether* Dana would do something to him – it was a question of *what*.

You've got all night to wonder about that one.

Why didn't I think of that before I cuffed myself to this fucking rail?

He jerked his left hand. The steel clattered and the edges of the cuff dug painfully into his wrist.

A twelve-hundred-pound pull. That's what the salesman said it would take to break the links.

Roland felt along the floor at his side. He touched the flashlight, picked it up, and shone it at the card table. The bottles glinted in its beam. The key was up there, out of sight.

The table was eight or ten feet to his left.

With his cuffed left hand he slid the bracelet along the rail. It made an awful metallic scraping sound that sent a shiver through him. But it did move. By sliding it, he would be able to move sideways until he was close to the table. Then maybe he could hook a foot around one of the table legs and drag the thing over to him – and get the key.

Worth a try, he thought.

What about the bet?

No problem.

Roland grinned.

Just let me get the handcuff key, I'll stay. A cinch.

A cinch because he realized that the restaurant no longer frightened him much. What really frightened him was knowing that Dana, at dawn, would come in and find him handcuffed.

I'll get that damned key, he told himself.

He squirmed sideways off his sleeping bag, his back rubbing the smooth wood of the bar counter, his left hand scooting the cuff along the brass rail with that awful grating noise. A noise that made his teeth ache. A noise that tormented him like the scrape of fingernails down a blackboard.

He stopped to rest.

The silence was soothing.

Just a little more distance to go, and . . .

Roland heard a sound.

It was a soft thump such as a rope might make dropping from a height onto the hardwood floor.

It came from . . . where?

Off to the right.

Roland's flashlight was aimed in the general direction of the table. The bright centre of the beam shook.

He listened. He heard his heartbeat and the rain and nothing more.

What could *make* a sound like that?

A snake? A snake flopping off the bar?

His skin suddenly crawled with goosebumps.

How could a snake get in here?

Hell, the place had been deserted for years. Maybe it fucking *lives* here.

Or Dana sneaked it in. She might do that. Pick one up at a pet shop.

The bitch.

Dana bought a snake to scare him out, and Roland bought cuffs to keep himself in.

If she bought the thing, it's harmless. They don't sell poisonous snakes. Do they?

Roland needed to see it – to see what it was, and *where*.

Maybe the light'll drive it off, he thought.

He swung the beam sideways, planning to check the floor to the right. It passed in front of him and had already moved on before he quite realized that he'd seen something between his feet. The beam jumped back to it.

Roland lurched. The back of his head thumped the bar. Urine sprayed his thigh, filled his jeans as he jerked his legs back.

The thing was fast. It squirmed like a sidewinder going for his right foot.

But it wasn't a sidewinder.

It wasn't a snake.

Roland lifted his right foot off the floor, away from its head, and shot his left at it. His heel caught the thing and sent it skidding and flipping away. It came straight back at him.

It had slimy yellow flesh webbed with red and blue veins. Its eyes had the dull grey look of phlegm. Its head – or mouth – made wet sucking noises as it flattened, then spread open.

Roland raised both legs as high as he could. He was still urinating, his stream hitting the inside of his jeans and splashing back, showering his genitals and running down his buttocks. He kicked down hard with his right heel, but missed the thing and flung his leg high again.

It didn't try to leap for his upraised foot. Instead, it darted forward and bit the back of his leg just to the right of his groin.

Roland's throat constricted, ready to emit a cry of agony and horror.

But he felt no pain.

Only a hot tingling pressure that sent a delicious shiver through his body.

He grabbed the thing, but didn't try to tug it off. Instead, he held it gently. It felt warm and powerful. Soon it was gone, leaving a hole the size of a quarter in the leg of his jeans.

And in his leg.

The wound didn't bother Roland.

He opened his waist button, lowered his zipper, and curled onto his left side. He slid his hand inside the seat of his jeans. He wore no underpants. The denim was sodden against the back of his hand, and the skin of his rump was wet.

The creature moved inside him, just beneath his flesh. With a hand pressed to the mound it made, he could feel it sliding along. His skin sank into place again after it had passed. He felt it turn towards his spine. Bending his arm behind him as much as possible, he caressed it through his skin until it was too high up to reach.

He put his hand to the back of his neck in time to feel the skin rise beneath his palm. Moments later, the thing stopped moving.

A sudden jolt hit Roland – pleasure so fierce it made him squirm and moan for release.

Chapter Twelve

Alison hung her dripping raincoat and hat on a rack near the door of Wally's Saloon. Fortunately the restrooms were just off to the side; she could change out of her waitress costume without having to pass through the crowd of drinkers.

In a toilet stall, she took off the uniform. She took off her slip and bra. Crouching, she removed her jumpsuit from her flight bag. Beneath it was her negligee. The sight of the royal blue fabric made Alison ache as if all her insides, from throat to bowels, were being squeezed and wrung.

That bastard. Oh, that bastard.

Screw him. Who needs him.

She stepped into the jumpsuit, pulled the soft fabric up her legs, pushed her arms into the sleeves, and raised the zipper.

Then she stuffed her bra, slip and waitress costume into the bag, and left the stall.

She leaned close to a mirror. Her short hair was matted down somewhat from the rain hat. She ran her fingers through it, shook her head, and it looked okay. Her eyes were still a little red from the crying she'd done after leaving Gabby's. The hike through the rain, however, had left her cheeks with a rosy glow.

The jumpsuit clung to her breasts. Her nipples made the fabric jut. She wondered if she should put her bra back on. Did she really want to go into the bar this way?

Hell, why not? Give the guys something to look at.

Besides, the soft warm fabric felt good against her bare breasts.

She trembled as she slid the zipper down. In the mirror, she saw the pale skin below her sternum throbbing from her heart-beat.

She stared into her eyes.

Are you really going to do this? she wondered.

Damn right. Two can play this game.

This is crazy.

No it's not. Evan doesn't want me, somebody else will. It'll serve the bastard right.

But the zipper really was too low. If she had to bend over, everyone in the vicinity would get an eyeful. So she raised it a couple of inches, then left the restroom, the flight bag swinging at her side.

As usual, Wally's was crowded and noisy. It was the university's watering hole, so she recognized most of the patrons. She greeted a few friends on her way to the bar. Some asked where Evan was, and she answered, 'Busy.' Which was, she thought, the plain truth.

She dodged Johnna Penson as the girl backed away from the bar with a beer pitcher. Johnna saw her and grinned. 'Hey-ho, what's up?'

'Not much.'

'Where's lover-boy?'

'Scared to come out in the rain. You seen Celia?'

'Just missed her. She took off with Danny Gard and some other guy. See ya.' Johnna squeezed past Alison.

Alison stepped up behind a guy who was waiting to order.

She realized that she had expected Celia to be here. The

support of a friend would've been welcome. On the other hand, she could just imagine Celia's reaction. 'You don't want to do it, pal. It isn't you. You're hurting, but you aren't gonna solve anything by putting out for the first guy smiles at you. Believe me, you'll regret it.'

So what if I regret it?

You just want to pay him back, she thought. You're stooping to his level.

Maybe I'll just have a beer or two, and go home.

Who you trying to kid?

We'll just see what happens, okay? Any objections?

The man in front of Alison sidestepped out of the way, and she moved in against the bar. 'A mug of draught. No, make it a pitcher.'

She set her flight bag onto the counter and dug out her purse while the bartender filled her order. After paying, she slung the strap over her head to free her hands, picked up the pitcher and frosty mug, and turned away.

Moving through the crowd was an ordeal. Alison nodded, smiled, said 'Hi' to people she knew, said 'Excuse me' to strangers, squeezed between them trying not to bump her drink or theirs, and finally found a deserted table near the front wall. It was a small round table with two chairs. She put down her load and sat facing the mob.

No sooner had she filled her mug and taken a sip than a man walked towards her, smiling nervously.

That sure didn't take long, she thought.

Her heart thumped faster as he approached. She had seen him around campus, but didn't know his name. He was tall and lean, with a boyish face and a scrawny, pale attempt at a moustache.

Not wanting to appear interested, Alison lowered her gaze to her beer.

I'm not so sure about this, she thought.

'Excuse me?' he said.

She looked up. Smiled. Said, 'Oh, hi.'

He patted the back of the unoccupied chair. 'Anyone sitting here?'

She shook her head.

'Mind if I borrow it, then?'

Feeling foolish, she shook her head again.

'Thanks a lot,' he said.

Alison watched him carry it to a nearby table, where he joined a couple of friends. Her face burned.

'Terrific,' she muttered.

All he wanted was the goddamn chair.

And now I'm without it, so if some guy *does* come along he won't have anywhere to sit.

I ought to get out of here.

Can't leave all this beer behind.

Give the pitcher to someone, make a gift of it.

Pour it over that dummy's head.

Instead, she drank what was in her mug, refilled it, and warned herself not to guzzle. This whole deal, she thought, is iffy enough without getting smashed. Take it easy.

She sipped slowly.

At the far end of the room, just beyond the dance floor, a huge television screen was suspended from the ceiling. It showed music videos, the volume so high that it could drive you mindless if you were near the speakers.

The noise had never seemed to bother Evan. It had driven Alison nuts, but she'd suffered with it, time and again, just to keep him happy. He loved to watch her dance – always looked as if he wanted to reach out and tear her clothes off.

What the hell am I thinking about *him* for?

What if he shows up?

Alison looked towards the entrance.

Suppose he shows up with Morgan the Organ-grinder and sees me sitting here alone like a fucking wallflower. Wouldn't that be cute?

One more good reason to make a quick exit.

She refilled her mug.

Better take it easy.

Alison looked again at the video screen. Now a hairless woman wearing a loincloth and skimpy top of leopardskin was twisting and writhing to the music. She had shiny blue skin (same colour as my nightie, Alison thought, the one that Evan, the shit, will never be lucky enough to see me in). The gyrating blue woman had a snake around her leg. Its head vanished behind her thigh, then reappeared against her groin. The snake slid higher, angling towards a hip, its thick body rubbing her through the loincloth as she writhed in apparent ecstasy.

Lord, Alison thought.

She took a sip of beer, her gaze fixed on the screen.

The snake curled around the woman's bare torso, circling higher. Its head came out beneath her armpit. It moved slowly across her breasts. Its tail was still flicking across her left breast when the head showed up beside her neck. The woman, squirming and rubbing her sides and belly (in lieu, Alison thought, of where she'd be rubbing if the producers weren't worried about taking a final step out of bounds), turned her face towards the head of the snake and pursed her thick shiny lips.

'Excuse me?'

Alison flinched.

A young man was standing in front of her, just off to the side. She was surprised that she hadn't noticed his approach.

'Sorry if I startled you,' he said.

'It's all right.'

'That's quite a video, huh?'

She felt herself blush. Her mouth was dry. She took a sip of beer. 'Pretty far out,' she said.

'Are you with someone?'

'Uh, no.'

'Mind if I join you?'

He didn't look familiar to Alison. He appeared more mature than most students, and better dressed in his slacks and white crewneck sweater. His black hair was neatly trimmed. Instead of a beer, he had a cocktail in his hand – probably a martini.

She pegged him for a law student.

'Some guy made off with the other chair,' she said.

'No problem.' He wandered away. A few moments later he came back with one and sat across from her. 'I'm Nick Winston,' he said, and offered his hand.

'Alison Sanders.' She shook his hand. 'Law student?' she asked.

'How'd you guess?'

'You have that look.'

'Old, you mean?' he asked, grinning.

I prefer older men, she thought. But she stopped herself from saying it. 'Just more together than the rest of us,' she told him.

'You a psych major?'

'What makes you think so?'

'You have that look,' he said.

'Neurotic?'

'Introspective.'

'Nah, I'm not introspective, just depressed.'

'And what, may I ask, could cause a beautiful, obviously intelligent young woman like you to be depressed?'

' "I see myself dead in the rain." '

'Ah, an English major.'

She smiled. 'Right.'

'Do you really?'

'What?'

'See yourself dead in the rain?'

'Nope. Just felt like spouting some Hemingway.'

'Don't you find his outlook rather juvenile?'

Her appreciation of Nick Winston slipped a notch. 'What do you mean, juvenile?'

'Well, in particular, his portrayals of women. They're like the fantasies of an adolescent. Maria, for instance.'

'I love that sleeping bag scene.'

Nick raised an eyebrow. 'Well, now.'

Alison found herself blushing again. 'I just mean, I think it's very romantic.'

'Romantic, perhaps, but idealized to a ludicrous extent. Have you ever experienced intercourse in a sleeping bag?'

'Maybe.'

'Ah, we're being coy.'

Alison shrugged, and took a drink. When she looked again at Nick, he was gazing into her eyes.

This is certainly progressing apace, she thought.

What the hell am I getting into?

'If you *have*, I'm sure you found it confining and the ground very hard and the entire experience barely tolerable.'

I didn't find it that way at all, she thought. But that's my business, Nick old sport.

'I find a king-sized bed to be the ideal setting for such encounters, don't you?'

'I thought we were discussing Hemingway.'

'And so we are. I believe that I was explaining my theory that the sleeping-bag scene in *For Whom the Bell Tolls* presents a false, idealized view of—'

'I think it's nice.'

The corners of Nick's lips curled up. 'I don't think it would be so nice in a rainstorm.'

'If you had a tent . . .'

'Unfortunately, I have neither a tent nor a sleeping bag. I do, however, have a Trans Am which could transport us in comfort to my apartment.'

'Where, no doubt, you have a king-sized bed.'

He lifted his glass and took a sip, staring at Alison over the rim. She felt that the stare was probably well practised. Setting down his drink, he leaned forward. He folded his arms on the table and gazed steadily into Alison's eyes. 'As a matter of fact, yes, I do have a king-sized bed. Whether or not we use it, however, is entirely up to you.'

'Thanks.'

'I realize that we've just met, and I would understand a certain hesitancy on your part to indulge in . . . intimacies. I certainly wouldn't want you to feel any pressure from me in that regard.'

'I don't know, Nick.'

You don't know? she asked herself. Isn't this exactly what you were looking for?

Maybe, maybe not.

'I'll drive you over to my place. We'll have a drink or two to take off the chill, listen to some good music. Nothing more than that, unless, of course, you insist.'

'I see. You'll be a perfect gentleman.'

He shrugged elaborately. 'Of course, if you would rather not.'

'I didn't say that.'

'Ah, but you have your doubts.'

'I'm not exactly in the habit of rushing over to a guy's apartment after I've known him for about five minutes.'

'I'm not exactly in the habit of *asking* after five minutes.' He took another small sip of his cocktail. He set it down. He gazed into her eyes. 'To be quite honest, Alison, there's something . . . special about you. I felt it the moment I saw you sitting here . . .'

'Gaping at that erotic video,' she added.

'It wasn't that. It's just that, when I saw you, it was as if we weren't strangers, as if I'd known you for a very long time.'

I doubt it, she thought.

Might've been a good line, except that it sounded so trite.

Trite or not, what if he actually meant it?

'I want to know you better,' he said.

'I don't . . .'

'A couple of drinks, that's all. We'll listen to music, we'll talk. We'll get to know each other. What've you got to lose?'

Right, what? Good point.

'If you're afraid I might *attack* you, or something . . .' He shook his head, smiling at the ridiculous suggestion.

'It isn't that.'

'What, then?'

'I don't know.'

'Then let's give it a try. We owe it to ourselves.'

'Give me some time to think about it. Meanwhile, I've got to use the john. I'll be right back.'

In a pig's eye, she thought.

She left the table, taking her flight bag with her. Unfortunately, she really *did* need to use the toilet. The homeward hike would take a good fifteen minutes. In her condition, she'd never make it without exploding.

She rushed into the restroom. Her jumpsuit made matters difficult, but eventually she finished and left the stall.

She stepped to one of the sinks. Slowly, she washed her hands.

You *could* go with him, she thought. Isn't that why you came here tonight?

Her heart pounded so hard that it made her chest ache.

Forget it. Grab the rain duds and pull a disappearing act.

In the mirror above the sink, her eyes looked wide and frantic.

She dried her hands on a paper towel, then walked to the restroom door. She opened it.

Nick stood in front of the coat rack, wearing a clear plastic slicker and a tennis hat. He smiled when he saw her. 'All set?' he asked.

Oh, God.

Nodding, she pulled Helen's rain-gear off the hanger. Nick held the heavy coat while she struggled into it. She put on the hat. Nick pushed open the door, and she stepped outside. The rain was still coming down hard.

Nick took hold of her hand.

They walked across the parking lot, Nick leading her around puddles.

At the passenger side of his car, he released her hand and bent over the door to unlock it.

'Nick,' she said.

'Yeah,' he called without looking back.

'I don't think so.'

'What?' He forgot about the door. He whirled around and scowled at her. 'What did you say?' he asked over the noise of the storm.

'I'm not going to your place. Not tonight. Thanks for asking, though. I'm sorry.'

'Got a car?'

'What?'

'A car. Did you drive here?'

'No.'

'Get in, then. I'll drive you.'

'I told you . . .'

'I heard, I heard. To your place. You don't want to walk in this mess.' Turning away, he bent over and unlocked the door. He opened it for her.

Alison hesitated.

'Get in or don't. It's up to you.'

'Okay. Well. Thanks.' She climbed in, and Nick shut the door. She took off the rain hat and opened the coat.

Now what? she wondered.

Nick slid in behind the wheel and started the car. He looked across the darkness at her. 'A long time,' he said, 'since anyone's tried to ditch me.' He sounded amused, not angry.

'I'm sorry. It's been a bad night.'

'My fault,' he said. 'I picked up on your reluctance, but I persisted, anyway. I should have backed off, I realize that now.' He turned on the headlights and windscreen wipers, and backed the car out of its space. 'I suppose I can lay some of the blame on conditioning. So often, women play games. They make a show of pretending not to want whatever, while in point of fact they *do* want it.' He drove slowly towards the road. 'Apparently they take some sort of bizarre delight in watching men struggle to win their consent.'

'I guess that happens,' Alison said. 'I suppose I've done it myself. It isn't always a game, though. Sometimes you just don't know what you want. You could go either way.'

Nick glanced at her. 'Is that how it was with you, tonight?'

'Pretty much.'

He stopped at the edge of the parking lot. 'Which way?'

'Right.'

He waited for a car to pass, then swung onto the road. 'Therefore, you're suggesting that a different approach on my part might have succeeded.'

Alison smiled. 'Could be.'

'I should've played hard to get.'

'Maybe.'

'Damn it,' he muttered. 'I'm always striking out.'

Alison found herself liking him better. Without the cool posing, he seemed like a different person. 'Maybe next time at bat,' she said, 'you'll do better.'

He sighed.

'A left at the next corner.'

He nodded. After making the turn, he said, 'Anyway, I'm glad we met. Even if I did make a mess of things.'

'It's not your fault. It's me.'

'No. You're terrific. God knows, the way I was acting *I* wouldn't have gone off with me.'

'You can let me out here,' she said.

He swung his car to the kerb, stopped it, and put on the handbrake. Leaning forward, he peered out of her window. 'You live in that house?'

'Upstairs. With a couple of roommates. Thanks a lot for the ride.'

'No problem. I'm glad we . . . had this chance to talk. God only knows why, but it makes me feel a little better about things.'

'Me too.' Leaning towards him, Alison slipped her fingers behind his head. His head was a dim blur in the darkness, moving closer. She pressed her mouth gently to his, then eased away. 'See you around,' she whispered. 'Okay?'

'Okay.'

'You in the student directory?' she asked.

'Yeah.'

'Me too. You going to call?'

'You bet.'

Then Alison was out of the car and striding through the rain. She knew that she had almost stayed. She was glad that she hadn't. She felt lonely and hurt, but strong. She had lost Evan. Maybe she had made a new friend tonight, but that didn't matter as much as knowing that she had won against herself.

It would be good to get inside the house where it was lighted and dry.

Chapter Thirteen

Dana, cramped in the back seat of her Volkswagen, woke up again. This time it was her right arm that had fallen asleep. Before, it had been a leg, a buttock, a foot. No matter what her position, one part or another of her body got its circulation cut off.

Right now, she was lying on her side with her knees bent, using her right arm for a pillow. The arm had no feeling at all. With a struggle, she managed to sit up. She shook her arm, grimacing as the numbness became an aching tingle. The tingle was like a thousand stabbing needles. But soon it went away and her arm felt almost normal.

She reached to the floor and picked up her travel clock. Pushing a button on top, she lit its face. The digital numbers showed 2:46 a.m.

The alarm had been set for 3:00 a.m.

She wouldn't be needing the alarm.

When she'd set it, she hadn't realized she would be waking up every fifteen or twenty minutes.

She flicked a switch sideways to deactivate the alarm, and put the clock down.

The rain still pounded down, making its endless rumble hitting her car. Apparently it wasn't about to quit.

Might as well go ahead now, she thought.

She began to shiver.

It'll be fabulous, she told herself.

She didn't want to go out in the rain. But this was too good an opportunity to miss, and she'd already gone to so much trouble. What's a little rain?

I'll get soaked.

But I'll scare the hell out of Roland.

Besides, he had stuck it out this long. Left alone, he might very well make it till morning.

Dana didn't want to lose the bet.

The money was no big deal, but the whole idea was to humiliate and destroy Roland. If he didn't come running out of the restaurant in terror . . .

I'll do it.

She struggled into her plastic poncho, flipped up the hood to cover her head, and left the car. She shut the door quietly.

The rain pattered on the plastic sheet as she stepped to the front of her car and opened its trunk. She slipped the screwdriver and knitted cap into her pockets, and clutched the five-pound sack to her belly underneath the poncho to keep it dry. Then she closed the trunk and headed for the restaurant.

If Roland is watching from a window, she thought, I'm sunk.

That wasn't likely, though. If he was awake at this hour, he was probably hiding in a damn closet – and scared out of his mind.

But not half as scared as he'll be in a few minutes.

Dana crossed the parking lot at an angle.

She was pleased with herself. She'd made a pretty good show of being afraid of the restaurant, so Roland would never suspect a trick like this.

At the corner of the lot, she waded through some high grass to the restaurant wall. The grass was wet, soaking through her running shoes and the cuffs of her jeans.

She stayed close to the wall. She headed towards the rear, ducking under windows.

There were no doors along this side of the restaurant. At the back, however, she found one. The upper portion had four sections of glass.

Dana crept up the wooden stairs and pressed her face to one of the panes. Dark in there. A lot darker than outside, but patches of the counters and floor were pale grey with light from the windows.

She knew that she was seeing the kitchen. This was where the killings had supposedly taken place.

She couldn't see Roland.

The kitchen wouldn't be at the top of his list of places to spend the night. Anywhere *but* the kitchen.

Dana set the sack down between her feet. She tried the knob. When it didn't turn, she began to work her screwdriver into the crack between the door and its frame directly across from the knob.

She widened the gap. Splinters of wood broke off. She kept digging and prizing. At last the lock tongue slipped back and she carefully opened the door.

Picking up the sack, she entered the kitchen. The sounds of the storm were muffled when she shut the door. The fresh air also went away. There was a heavy, unpleasant odour.

Motionless, she listened. Water dripping onto the floor from her poncho, nothing else. Except her heartbeat.

Roland won't hear that.

He obviously wasn't in the kitchen. The rain pounding on the roof provided enough steady noise to cover any sounds Dana might make.

As long as she was careful.

Very slowly, she pulled the poncho over her head. Its plastic made quiet rustling sounds. She lowered it to the floor.

Listened.

Then balanced on one foot at a time while she pulled off her shoes and socks.

She realized that she was gritting her teeth and trembling.

Excitement, not fear.

Poor Roland, he'll have a cardiac arrest.

Wouldn't *that* be a pity.

Dana unbuttoned the waistband of her jeans and lowered the zipper. Thumbs under the elastic of her panties, she drew down both garments at the same time and stepped out of them. Then she pulled her sweatshirt off.

She took a deep, shaky breath.

This'll be quite a treat for you, Roland old pal. You wanted to look at the bod, you'll get it. The *real* thing, this time, not some fucking snapshots.

Hope you enjoy it.

Squatting, Dana folded open the sack. She scooped out a handful of flour. It seemed almost iridescent. She spread the powder over her skin from shoulder to shoulder. Streams of it trickled down her breasts. Coating her left arm, she noticed that her skin was covered with goosebumps. She filled her other hand and covered her right arm. Then she scooped up flour in both hands and spread it over her chest and belly. Her nipples were stiff. Touching them sent warmth down her body. She rubbed flour over her thighs, hands gliding, feeling her gooseflesh through the thin layer of powder, feeling her slick wetness when she patted the flour between her legs. With her hands full again, she coated her feet and shins and knees.

Then she straightened up. Shoulders to feet, she was white except for faint areas where the flour had been rubbed thin from the way she had squatted. She dug more powder from the sack, spread it over her thighs and hips and belly, and emptied her hands by swirling the last of the flour over her breasts.

She looked down at herself again.

Some ghost.

Roland wouldn't know whether to get a hard-on or a heart attack.

The floor around her feet was dusted white.

Dana wrung her hands, trying to get the flour off them. They remained white. She reached back and rubbed them on her buttocks. That got most of it off.

Turning towards her pile of clothes, she bent from the waist to avoid smearing the powder, and pulled her knitted cap from the pocket of her jeans. It was navy blue, but it looked black in the darkness. Holding the cap away from her body, she felt for the eyeholes she had cut that afternoon. When she found them, she pulled the cap over her head, drew it down to her chin, and tucked her dangling hair up the back of it.

Dana wished she could check out the effect. Maybe tomorrow night. Do it again, only in Jason's room. He had a full-length mirror. Maybe have *him* spread the flour on her. And she would do the same for him. And then they'd make it.

Only one problem, Jason might not be overjoyed that she had paraded in front of Roland bare-ass naked.

He should complain, the shit. He's the one showed Roland the Polaroids.

Dana took a trembling breath through the wool cap.

Time to get going and give Roland the thrill of his life.

She started across the kitchen. After a few steps, one of her feet landed on something sticky like paint that hadn't quite dried.

Her nose wrinkled.

Hadn't they cleaned up the mess from last night?

She sidestepped and got out of it, but her foot made quiet snicking sounds each time she lifted it off the linoleum.

With her back to the kitchen windows, she couldn't see much. Blind man's buff.

Hands out, she finally touched a wall. She made her way slowly along it, and found a door. When she opened the door, a cool draught wrapped her skin. Something wasn't right about this. Clutching the doorframe, she slipped her right foot forward and felt the floor end.

Stairs?

Maybe a stairway leading down to the wine cellar, or something. Roland might be down there.

Not a chance.

Dana shut the door and continued following the wall. Soon she touched another doorframe. Reaching past it, she felt wood. Ribbed wood. A louvred door of some kind.

Moving in front of it, she gently pushed. The hinges creaked slightly.

That's okay. Let Roland hear it. Give him something to think about.

Holding the door open, she stepped through. Her side hit something that squeaked and wasn't there any more, then bumped her again from armpit to hip. Even without being able to see, she knew what must have happened: they were double swinging doors, and she'd only opened one side before trying to go through.

Roland *must* have heard that.

Give him a little more?

She considered moaning like an anguished spirit. Maybe spirits don't moan. Besides, he might figure out who it is.

Dana stepped through the doors, eased them shut, and stood motionless.

It was a big room.

Roland might be here. Might be looking at her now. Frozen with terror.

This is it.

Dana's heart pounded furiously. Tremors of excitement shook her body. Drops of sweat slid down her sides, tickling.

Several windows along the three walls let in hazy grey light, but vast areas of the room were black.

Dana looked down at herself through the fuzzy holes of her cap. The flour gave her skin a dull grey hue, not the glow she had wanted. But good enough. Maybe better, in fact. Bright enough to let her be seen, but only dimly.

What you can't quite see – that's what is really scary.

So how does a ghost walk? she wondered. They probably don't. In movies, they generally swoop through the air. But zombies, they kind of stagger around with their arms out.

Dana lifted her arms as if reaching for her next victim and took long stiff-legged strides towards the centre of the room.

Shit, this isn't a zombie walk, it's Frankenstein.

Frankenstein's the scientist, stupid, not the monster.

Yes, Roland.

She stopped strutting and changed her gait to a slow, lurching stagger.

Perfect.

So where the fuck are you, Roland? If you're too scared to scream, let's at least have a few gasps or whimpers.

Crouched in a corner, wetting your pants?

Dana slowly turned around, searching for his huddled shape in the grey near the windows, trying to find him in the black areas.

He isn't here, she decided. Even if I can't see him, he for sure would've seen me by now. He would've *done* something – yelled or maybe run for it.

Dana turned towards the front of the restaurant, lowered her arms for a moment to smear the sweat rolling down her sides, then raised her arms again and shuffled forward.

Over to the left, the room branched out. Dana saw a vague shape that might be a bar.

He's probably hiding behind it.

She took a few steps in that direction and a rush of excitement stopped her.

Roland's sleeping bag.

Mummy bag.

One dark puffy end of it was barely visible in the gloom from the front window.

I can't see him, but he can see me. If he's looking this way. If he's awake.

For a few seconds, Dana couldn't force herself to move. She stood there, shaking and breathless, feeling as if her legs might give out.

This'll be good, she thought. This'll get him. The shithead'll wish he'd never been born.

Go for it, she told herself.

She lurched towards the sleeping bag. Her legs felt like warm liquid, but they held her up. She let out a low moan.

That'll get his attention.

When she stopped moaning, she heard him.

He was taking quick short breaths.

Awake, all right.

She stood over him, no more than a yard away, peering down but still unable to see anything in the darkness. No, maybe that was a face – that oval blur. If so, Roland was sitting up.

Bending at the waist, she reached towards him.

A shriek blasted her ears.

Every muscle in Dana's body seemed to jerk, snapping her upright, hurling her backwards. She waved her arms, trying to stay up, then fell. The floor pounded her rump.

A light beam stung her eyes.

She shielded her eyes with a hand. 'Take it out of my face.' The beam lowered. She pulled off her cap. The light was on her chest, moving from one breast to the other. It dropped, streaking down her belly and shining between her legs. She threw her knees together, blocking it. The light returned to her breasts. She covered them with one arm and used the other arm to brace herself up. Her chest heaved as she struggled to catch her breath.

'So,' she gasped, 'did I scare you . . . or what?'

In answer, the light tipped downward. Roland was sitting on top of his mummy bag, his legs stretched out. The lap of his faded blue jeans was stained dark.

Dana grinned. 'You wet your pants.'

'I wanta go,' Roland said in a shaky voice.

'Hell, you already *went*.'

'You won, okay? You won. Let me loose.' He turned his light towards a nearby card table with bottles on top. 'The key's up there.'

'Key?'

The beam moved again, this time to his left hand. It was cuffed to a metal rail near the bottom of the bar.

'Holy shit,' Dana muttered.

'My insurance. That's how I knew I'd win.'

'You *cuffed* yourself?'

'Get the key, okay?'

So that was why Roland had insisted that she come in at dawn to get him – so she could unlock the handcuffs.

'Where are the Polaroids?' she asked.

'In my pack.'

'Give me the flashlight.'

Roland didn't argue. He lowered it to the floor and pushed. It skidded towards her feet. Dana sat up, stretched forward, and grabbed it.

Getting to her knees, she shone the beam on Roland. His gaunt face, dead pale, looked even more cadaverous than usual. Squinting, he turned away from the glare.

She aimed the light at his crotch.

'Peed your fucking pants,' she said. 'Did you really think I was a ghost?'

'I don't know,' he mumbled.

Dana chuckled. Then she crawled to the pack, searched it, and found an envelope. Inside the envelope were the photographs. She flicked through them, counting. All ten were there. She set the envelope on the floor and took her camera from the pack.

'What're you doing?' Roland asked.

'Just recording the moment for posterity.' Standing up, Dana faced him and clamped the flashlight between her thighs, aiming it so that the beam lit his wet jeans. She raised the camera to her eye. 'Say "cheese".' She took three shots, the flashbar blinking bright. 'Now take off your pants.'

He shook his head.

'Want me to leave you here?'

With his one free hand, Roland opened his jeans and tugged them down to his knees.

'You don't believe in underpants?'

Dana snapped three shots, then gathered up the photos that had dropped to the floor. She tucked them inside the envelope and put the envelope and camera into his pack. She put her stocking cap in with them, swung the pack up and slipped her arms through the straps.

She shone the beam on Roland, who had pulled up his pants and was zipping the fly. 'Adios.'

'Unlock me,' he said, squinting into the light.

'Do you think I'm nuts?'

'I went along with it. You promised. Now come on.' He wasn't pleading. He sounded calm.

Dana thought about it. She really wanted to leave him here. But that would mean coming back tomorrow or sending Jason over to set him free. Also, he would end up winning the bet. A hundred bucks down the toilet.

'I don't care about the pictures,' he said. 'You can keep them.'

'Mighty big of you. I'd like to see you just *try* to take 'em off me.'

'Then what's the big deal? Get the key.'

'Maybe. Stay put while I get dressed.'

'Very funny.'

She left him there. With the aid of the flashlight, her return to the kitchen was easy. Her foot had left smudges of blood on the linoleum. She wrinkled her nose at the sight of the mess she had stepped in.

Using the wool cap, she began to brush the flour off her body.

The gag had certainly worked.

Scared the hell out of Roland.

Wet his pants.

Funny how he hadn't tried to hide that, just flashed the light down there to show her the damage as if it was nothing.

In fact, he'd been awfully calm about letting her take the pictures. Even pulled his pants down without much protest.

After having the headless ghost come at him, everything else must've seemed easy.

Maybe he's in shock, or something.

Probably is.

On top of which, he's scared shitless I'll drive off and leave him. He knows he damn well *better* cooperate. Without the key, he's stuck and he knows it.

Dana shone the light down at her body. Most of the flour was off, but her skin was still dusted white. She would need to take a shower when she got back.

After dressing, she slipped the envelope containing the photos into a rear pocket of her jeans. She pulled the poncho over her head and picked up Roland's pack.

The open bag of flour remained on the floor.

Her dorm room was without a kitchen, so she had no further use for the flour. She left it, and returned to the cocktail area.

Roland still sat with his back against the bar and his legs stretched out. He looked as if he hadn't moved at all while she was gone.

'So,' Dana said. 'I guess you're ready to leave.'

He nodded.

'I don't want pee on my car seat.'

'I'll sit on my sleeping bag.'

'I've got a better idea. How about if you walk back to campus?'

'It's raining.'

'Yeah, you can use the shower.'

'Just give me the key.'

Dana stepped to the table. 'I knew you wouldn't last out the night,' she said. The small key to the handcuffs glinted. She picked it up. 'The cuffs were a pretty neat idea, though. You would've won for sure if I hadn't come along. But you lost, all right. I always knew you were a chicken. I guess you knew it, too, or you wouldn't have cuffed yourself in. Huh? You *knew* you didn't have the guts to stick it out.'

She twisted the cap off a bottle of vodka. The key was small enough to fit through the bottle's neck. She dropped it. The key made a quiet splash. A moment later it clinked against the bottom. She screwed the cap back on and tightened it with all her strength.

'Do yourself a favour,' she suggested. 'Drink your way down to the key. It'll help take the sting out of your hike.'

Dana tossed the bottle onto his lap.

At the door, she smiled back at him and said, 'Cheers.'

The door bumped shut. Roland, in the darkness, clamped the bottle between his legs and twisted the cap off. He tugged his T-shirt up. Dumped vodka onto his belly until the key fell onto his bare skin. Flung the bottle away. Peeled the key off his belly and unlocked the cuff at his wrist.

Dana, walking quickly through the rain, was only a few yards from her car when she decided that Roland had probably succeeded, by now, in removing the handcuffs. It would still take him a while to gather up his sleeping bag. She glanced back, anyway.

Roland!

He looked crazy sprinting towards her, his head thrown back and his mouth wide, his arms windmilling as if he were trying to swim, not run.

In his right hand was a knife.

Dana raced for the car.

She thought, that was damn quick of him.

She thought, what's he doing with that knife?

Where are my keys?

In the ignition.

Lucky. No fumbling.

She grabbed the door handle and pulled. The force of her pull ripped her fingers from the handle and she remembered she had left the car by its passenger door.

She whirled around.

Roland was almost upon her.

'Okay, look, you can ride back with me!'

He stopped. His lip curled up.

'Hey, Roland, come on.'

He clutched the front of her poncho, jerked her forward, and rammed the knife into her belly.

Roland pulled the knife out. He shoved Dana backwards, keeping his grip on the poncho, and lowered her to the pavement. She sat there, moaning and holding her belly.

Roland sat on her legs.

He punched her nose and she flopped back. Her head thumped the pavement. She didn't lose consciousness, but she didn't struggle. Rain fell on her face. She blinked and gasped for air.

Straddling her, Roland plucked the front of the poncho away from her body, poked his knife through it, and sliced the plastic sheet open to her throat.

'Plea . . .' she gasped.

He cut open the front of her sweatshirt and spread it apart.

Rain sluiced away the blood on her belly, but more blood poured from the gash. Her chest rose and fell as she panted. Roland stared at her breasts. Then he pulled his knife away.

Bending low, he stretched up his arms. He held her breasts. They were wet and slippery, warm beneath the wetness.

He kissed the gash on her belly.

He sucked blood from it.

Dana shrieked and jerked rigid beneath him when he bit.

She stayed alive for a long time. It was better that way.

Her heart still throbbed when Roland tore it from her chest cavity.

He was almost full, so he didn't eat much of it. He stuffed what was left into her chest, then crawled to her head.

He scalped her, cracked open her skull with the tyre iron, and scooped out her warm, dripping brain.

The best part.

Chapter Fourteen

Just after sunrise, Roland returned to campus. He left Dana's car in the lot behind his dorm, and hurried into the lobby. He rushed upstairs, along the quiet corridor, and got inside his room without being seen – lucky since he was naked except for his windcheater.

He dropped his backpack onto the floor, then took off his windcheater and inspected it for blood. He'd been very careful with it, knowing that he would need to wear it back to the dorm after getting rid of his other clothes.

They were with Dana, stuffed inside his mummy bag and hidden in bushes about ten miles south of the restaurant.

The windcheater, inside and out, looked spotless. He dropped it over the pack, then checked himself. The rain had done a good job cleaning him. Though all his fingernails had blood caked under them, he looked fine otherwise.

Roland put on his robe, gathered what he needed for his shower, put the room key in his pocket, and hurried down the corridor.

The restroom was silent. He made sure the toilet stalls were vacant, then unloaded his shower kit onto a bench in the dressing area of the shower room and approached the sinks. They had mirrors above them. Taking off his robe, he looked over his shoulder. At the back of his leg was a crust of dried blood in the shape of a circle where the thing had chewed its way into him. From there, a bluish bruise extended upward, angling across his right buttock to his spine, then straight up his back to the nape of his neck. His hanging black hair, he thought, was long enough to cover the neck area when he was dressed.

He stepped closer, shivering as the cold edge of the sink met the back of his legs. Turning sideways, he twisted his head around. He could see a slight hump at the back of his neck. It continued to about halfway down his spine.

Roland fingered the distended skin behind his neck. The lump felt much larger than it looked. He stroked it. The thing writhed a bit, and gave him a mild tingle of pleasure – only a hint of the ecstasy it had bestowed when he had fed it.

Worried that someone might come through the door, Roland draped the robe over his shoulders and returned to the dressing area. He dropped his robe onto the bench, gathered up his washcloth, soap, shampoo and toothbrush, and entered the shower room.

The hot spray felt wonderful on his chilled skin. He lathered himself and scrubbed. He washed his hair. After rinsing, he found that much of the blood was gone from under his fingernails. But not all of it. He used his toothbrush to get rid of the rest.

Back in his room, Roland stood in front of the built-in bureau and combed his hair forward as he always did before parting it down the centre. This time he parted it on the left. It made him appear more normal. Good. He no longer cared to draw attention to himself by looking weird. He wanted to blend in with the student body. At least until it was time to find a new van and hit the road.

No. Too soon.

You'd attract more attention if you suddenly changed.

For now, do everything the same as always.

Roland nodded and moved his parting to the centre where it belonged.

He put on a clean pair of jeans and socks, then a yellow T-shirt with bloody bullet holes printed across its front as if he'd been stitched by a machine-gun. The T-shirt, however, let too much show. He put on another shirt over it – a black sports shirt with a collar high enough to conceal the back of his neck.

Roland yawned. He ached to sleep. Plenty of time later for that. Just a couple more items . . .

He removed the handcuffs and key from his pack, and hid them under some socks in his bureau.

Then he took out the envelope with the photos. The envelope was smeared all over with bloody fingerprints.

'Not too cool, Roland old man,' he whispered.

He opened it. The photos weren't stained. He separated them, slipped the shots of Dana into a fresh envelope, and returned them to Jason's drawer.

He flipped through the remaining photos and grinned. Dana

would've been pleased by the way they turned out. Roland in his pissed jeans. Roland naked from the waist to knees. She would've had fun with these, using them to humiliate Roland.

Roland?

Me.

He frowned, puzzled that he had been thinking of himself by name.

After tearing the photos and envelope into tiny pieces, he returned to the restroom and flushed them down a toilet.

Back in his own room, he stretched out on his bed and slept.

The door bumped shut, waking him. Sitting up, he rubbed his face while Jason tossed an overnight bag onto the other bed and hung up his suit.

'How was the wedding?' Roland asked.

'Not bad. The groom's a real dummy, but that's her problem. Man, did I tie one on.' He sat on his bed and made a sour face. 'What gives, anyway?'

'Huh?'

'I saw Dana's car in the lot.'

'Yeah.'

'Where is she?' Jason lowered his head slightly. 'Hiding under the bed? You been slipping it to her?'

'Oh, sure.'

'So what's her car doing out there?'

'It's a long story.'

'So? Spill it.' Jason opened his bag, removed a pint flask, and took a swig. 'Hair of the dog,' he muttered.

'She's probably all right,' Roland said.

'Yeah? What do you mean, probably?'

Roland got up. He found the newspaper story about the killings at the Oakwood Inn, and handed it to Jason. 'Read this.'

Waiting, Roland glanced at the clock. Almost noon. He'd been asleep for nearly six hours. He felt good.

Jason looked up. 'Yeah? What's this got to do with Dana?'

'We went over there last night. To the restaurant.'

'For dinner?' He looked at the paper. 'Who opened it?'

'No, it wasn't open. It was deserted, locked up.'

'Then what were you doing there?'

'Dana got this thing into her head about me not having any guts. She dared me to spend the night in the restaurant. She bet me a hundred bucks I wouldn't.'

A grin spread over Jason's face. 'Yeah, that's Dana all right. I was gone, so she figured she'd use the opportunity to stick it to you.'

'She doesn't like me much.'

'Sure she does. She just gets a kick out of tormenting you, that's all.'

'Well, whatever. Anyway, I said I'd spend the night there, and that I had more guts than she did.'

'Wrong move, buddy.'

'So the way it turned out, we both went into the place. The deal was, whoever chickened out first and split would lose.'

Jason shook his head slowly. 'Christ, and to think I missed out on all this. So what happened, you turned tail, she stayed, and you drove her car back here?'

'There was more to it than that.'

Jason took another drink from his flask.

'Around midnight, we heard a noise. Kind of a bumping sound. Scared me shitless.'

'Yeah, I bet it did.'

'I was ready to get the hell out, and Dana told me to go ahead and kiss the hundred bucks goodbye. So I stayed. She went exploring to find out what made the noise.'

Jason began to look concerned. 'You let her go off alone?'

'I *told* her not to.'

'You could've gone with her.'

'Anyway, the thing is, she didn't come back. I stayed by the front door, near the bar. I heard her wandering around. After a while, she called out and said she'd found the wine cellar. I guess she went down there. I waited a long time, Jase, but she didn't come back.'

'So you ran off and left her?'

'No. Not then, anyway. I went to the kitchen. It was . . . that's where those two people got killed. There was blood. Lots of it.'

'You must've felt right at home,' Jason muttered. There was no humour in his tone. He sounded annoyed and worried.

'It was pretty disgusting. Anyway, I found an open door with stairs leading down to the cellar. I shone my flashlight down, but I couldn't see her. Then I called her name a few times. She didn't answer. Finally I started to go down. I was pretty damn scared, but I'd made up my mind I *had* to find her. I'd just gone down a couple of stairs when I heard someone laugh. It was a real quiet, nasty laugh. *That's* when I got the fuck out of there.'

Jason's mouth hung open. He gazed at Roland with wide, bloodshot eyes.

'I ran out and got in the car. She'd left the keys in it. I thought I'd go for the police, and then I realized it must've been Dana who'd laughed that way.'

'Did it sound like her?'

'God, who knows? When I heard it, I thought it sounded like a man. Then I got to thinking, and I was sure it must've been Dana. She did it to scare me off. You know? To win the bet. So I was sitting in her car and she'd won the hundred bucks by pulling that stunt and scaring me off, so I got kind of pissed at her and I figured it'd serve her right if I just took off with the car and left her there. So that's what I did.'

'Jesus.'

Roland shrugged. 'It's just a few miles out. I figured, let her walk. She's probably back at her dorm by now.'

Jason got up without another word and left the room. Roland went to the door and watched him stride down the corridor – heading for one of the pay phones near the exit door.

Roland sat on his bed and waited. His story had sounded quite convincing, he thought. He forced his smile away in time to greet Jason with a sombre face.

'I talked to Kerry. Dana isn't back yet. She sounded pretty worried.'

'Maybe Dana got a late start. Like I said, it's a few miles. If you want, we could drive out that way and give her a lift.'

'Let's go.'

Jason's car was low on gas, so he said they should take Dana's Volkswagen. He told Roland to drive. Then he settled in the passenger seat and shut his eyes. 'Tell me when we get there,' he said.

He wished he'd taken it easy on the booze yesterday. All that champagne at the reception, then dinner with his folks – cocktails, more champagne, brandy afterwards. Great fun at the time, but now he had a headache and his stomach felt as if he'd been eating rotten eggs. And his body seemed to buzz.

Should've skipped the whole deal, he thought. Could've been here last night instead, making it with Dana. Then none of this would've happened.

What'd those two think they were doing, going out to some damn empty restaurant like that?

Easy to figure. Dana wanted to mess with Roland's head. Never could stand the guy. As for Roland, he probably had some fancy hopes of putting it to her. Lotsa luck on that one, pal. You were the last guy on earth, you wouldn't stand a chance. Hates your guts, pal.

What if he tried and she told him to fuck off and he went ape and nailed her?

The thoughts made Jason's heart pound harder, sending jolts of pain into his head.

Roland might be a little peculiar, he told himself, but the guy wouldn't pull something like that. He might want to, but he didn't have the guts. Especially not with Dana.

But it could've started with a small disagreement. Dana turned mean, lashed out at him with that tongue of hers. Next thing you know, Roland strikes back.

If he hurt her, I'll kill him.

Jason rubbed his temples. He remembered a talk with Roland, late one night in the darkness of their room when they were both lying awake.

Part of the conversation forced its way into his mind.

Jason: 'If you could fuck any girl on campus, who'd it be? Aside from Dana.'

Roland: 'I don't want to fuck Dana.'

'Jason: 'Oh, sure.'

Roland: 'Jeez, I don't know.'

Jason: 'Just one. Who'd it be?'

Roland: 'Mademoiselle LaRue.' His French teacher.

Jason: 'You're joking. She's a bitch.'

Roland: 'She's a real piece.'

Jason: 'She's a bitch. What are you, a glutton for punishment?'

Roland: 'First I'd tie her up. I'd throw the rope over a rafter or something, so she's hanging there. Then I'd take out my knife and cut off all her clothes. When she's all naked, I'd start cutting on her.'

Jason: 'Pervert. I said "fuck" not "torture".'

Roland: 'Oh, I'd get around to that. Eventually. But I'd want to have some fun with her first.'

Jason: 'Fun? You are warped, man. Definitely warped.'

Just a fantasy of his, Jason told himself. The guy's a chicken. He'd never actually try to *do* anything like that, not with Mademoiselle LaRue or Dana or anyone else. All just talk.

Better be.

He opened his eyes and looked at Roland.

'Almost there,' Roland said. 'I've been watching the road. Surprised we haven't run across her walking. But you know, she could've been getting back about the time we started out. Maybe we just missed her.'

Or maybe she's at the restaurant, tied up and hanging from a rafter, stripped and cut up . . .

'She better be all right,' Jason muttered.

'God, I hope so,' Roland said. 'I keep thinking about that laugh I heard in the cellar. I mean, suppose it *wasn't* Dana?' His lips pulled into a tight line. He looked in pain. 'If anything happened to her, it's all my fault. I should've gone down there. I should've.'

Ahead, on the right, was a sign for the Oakwood Inn. Roland slowed the car and swung onto a narrow road in front of the sign.

'What if someone was down there?' he said. 'Like a pervert or something, and he got her? Maybe he hangs around the place, just waiting for people to come along . . .'

'You've seen too many of those splatter movies,' Jason told him.

'That kind of thing happens, though. In real life. Look at *Psycho* and *Texas Chainsaw Massacre*. They were both based on real life, on that Ed Gein guy in Wisconsin. Know what he used to do, he used to *dress up* in the skins of his victims – wear 'em like clothes.'

'Hey, come on. I don't want to hear this.'

'All his neighbours thought he was a real neat guy because

he'd bring them gifts of meat. What they didn't know, the meat was human.'

'For Christsake, cut it out.'

'I'm just saying it's not just in the movies. Weird shit happens.'

Roland stopped the car in front of the restaurant. He turned off the engine. He frowned at Jason. 'Wish I'd brought my knife,' he whispered. 'I mean, there's probably nobody in there, but . . .'

'Wait in the car if you're scared.' Jason threw open the door and climbed out. He walked straight to the porch stairs. He took them two at a time.

Bad enough, he thought, without Roland talking about that stuff and acting like he's scared some nut might be hiding in the restaurant.

In front of the door, Jason hesitated. Nobody's in there, he told himself. Except maybe Dana.

She'll be standing inside, hands on her hips and a smirk on her face. 'So, my ride is here at last. Took you dummies long enough. If you thought I was gonna *walk* back, you were nuts.'

She won't be in there.

Maybe her body. Hanging naked, all cut up.

She's probably back on campus by now.

She'll get a big laugh when she hears about this. Our rescue mission.

She won't get a big laugh. She'd dead.

Jason looked over his shoulder. Roland was coming, so he waited. He rubbed his sweaty hands on his jeans. He tried to take a deep breath, but there was a hard tight place below his lungs that wouldn't let them expand enough.

Roland climbed onto the porch. Crouching, he picked up a board with nails at both ends. There were several such boards lying around. Apparently they'd been used to barricade the door. 'Why don't you get one?' Roland whispered.

Jason shook his head. He didn't need a weapon unless he believed there was danger inside; he didn't want to believe that.

He pushed on the door. It swung open. Cool air from inside breathed on him, raising goosebumps. He took a single step forward.

Enough light entered the restaurant through the doorway and windows for him to see the cocktail area to his right, the big dining area to his left. He stepped towards the dining-room. It looked empty except for a ladder, an open toolbox, some cans and jars, a vacuum cleaner and broom, all clustered near its right wall. Nothing moved.

'Dana!' he called out. His voice sounded hollow, as if he'd yelled the name into a cave.

No answer came.

Did you really expect one? he thought.

He looked to the right. On the floor in front of the long bar was an empty vodka bottle. Had Dana and Roland been drinking? Maybe they both got drunk. Maybe that's how it started.

He could ask Roland about the bottle. But he didn't want to hear his voice again – didn't want anyone else to hear his voice again.

With Roland at his side, he walked into the dining area. Along the wall beyond the ladder was a double door – the kind that saloons always had in Westerns. He pushed through it, and entered the kitchen.

The linoleum floor had footprints, maybe a dozen of them, rust-coloured stains made by a bare left foot. A small foot. Dana's foot? The tracks began at a dried puddle of blood near the far side of the kitchen and became fainter as they approached the place where Jason was standing.

Near the blood puddle was a sack of flour. The floor directly behind the sack was coated with the white powder.

'What's all this?' Jason whispered.

'The blood's from those two who were killed Thursday night.'

Christ, he thought, don't the cops clean it up? If they don't, who does?

'What about the flour?'

'It was here when we came,' Roland answered in a voice as hushed as Jason's.

'The footprints?'

'I don't know.'

'They weren't here?'

'I don't think so.'

'Was Dana wearing shoes?'

'Sure. Anyway, she had shoes on last time I saw her.' Roland pointed with his board at an open door. 'The cellar's down there.'

Jason walked slowly towards it, rolling his feet from heel to toe so he wouldn't make any noise, though he knew that anyone down there – anyone alive – would've heard him call out Dana's name and maybe even heard the quiet conversation in the kitchen.

He peered down the steep wooden stairway.

Dark as hell down there.

He hoped that the restaurant had electricity, then recalled that there'd been a lamp and vacuum cleaner with the ladder and things in the other room. He flicked a switch on the wall beside the door. A light came on below.

'Want me to stay up here and keep watch?' Roland whispered.

'Keep watch for what? Come on.'

He started down the stairs. The steps groaned under his weight. He pictured breaking through one, falling. Worse, he pictured someone hiding behind the stairway, grabbing his ankle from between the boards.

Partway down, he stopped and ducked below the ceiling. From here, he could see most of the cellar. Straight ahead were several sections of empty shelves, some made for holding wine bottles and others apparently intended for the storage of other restaurant supplies. Off to the left was a vast area with pipes running along the ceiling, a furnace near the far wall.

No Dana.

No one else.

That he could see.

He rushed to the bottom, got away from the staircase and looked back. Nobody behind it.

His tension eased a little. Even though the cellar had plenty of places where someone might be hidden, he doubted that anyone, alive or dead, was down here.

Just me, he thought. And Roland.

Nevertheless, he began to search. Roland stayed behind him as he walked through the aisles between the shelves.

Roland. Behind him. Carrying that board with the nails in it.

And I'm probably the only one who knows he was here last night with Dana.

If it *was* Roland who . . .

He could almost feel those nails piercing his skull.

He turned around. Roland, with the board resting on his

shoulder, raised his eyebrows. 'You want to take the lead for a while?' Jason whispered.

Roland's lip curled up. 'Thanks anyway.'

'I'm going first, I ought to have the weapon.'

'Could've got one for yourself.'

'Don't give me shit.'

'What'll *I* use?'

'Don't worry about it, huh? Anything happens, I'd be better with that thing than you.'

Roland's eyes narrowed. For a moment, Jason half expected Roland to swing the thing down at him. Wouldn't dare, he thought. Not with me facing him. Knows he wouldn't stand a chance. I'm bigger, stronger, quicker. By a long shot.

'Guess you're right,' Roland said, and handed the board to him.

They resumed the search. Now that he had the weapon, Jason wondered about himself. He must've been crazy to think that Roland might try to kill him.

The kid's more scared than me about being down here.

He didn't lay a finger on Dana.

He's sure, in that twisted mind of his, that some maniac right out of a slasher movie was down here last night and did a number on Dana.

What if he's right?

No, please. Nobody got her. She was down here alone, she did that laugh herself to scare Roland off, she's probably back at the dorm by now.

She's dead, whispered Jason's mind.

But he didn't find her body in the cellar. He didn't find a pool of blood. He found none of her clothes. He found no signs of a struggle. He found nothing at all to indicate that Dana had ever been in the cellar, much less murdered there.

He was glad to get out of the cellar. He shut the door and leaned against it.

'What do you think?' Roland asked.

'I don't know.'

'Why don't we get out of here?' Without waiting for a reply, Roland walked to the rear door of the kitchen and swung it open. He stopped. 'Hey.'

'What?'

'Take a look at this.'

Jason hurried over to him. Roland was fingering the edge of the door. The wood on its outside, near the latch, was gouged and splintered. 'Someone broke in,' Jason said.

'Not me and Dana. We came in the front way.'

'Christ.'

Roland whispered. 'There *was* someone else.'

Jason tossed the board aside and went through the doorway. Beyond the rear of the restaurant a vast, rolling, weed-covered field stretched to the edge of a forest.

He stepped down from the porch. He walked through the tall grass and weeds of what had once been a lawn. The edge of the lawn blended in with the start of the field, only different in that the lawn was flat and the field began with a small rise. He climbed the rise.

Roland came up behind him and stood at his side while Jason shielded his eyes against the sunlight and scanned the area.

'What now?' Roland asked. 'Search in the weeds?'

'I don't know.' There were acres and acres, and then the forest. The idea of trying to find Dana out there seemed overwhelming and futile.

If she's in the weeds, he thought, she's dead.

'Maybe the guy has a place in the woods,' Roland said. 'A shack or something, you know? That Ed Glein I was telling you about . . .'

'We'll never find her,' Jason said.

'Maybe . . .' Roland didn't continue.

Jason looked at him. 'Maybe what?'

Roland shrugged. 'It's probably a dumb idea. But if we go back to campus and she still hasn't shown up and we figure maybe she really did get snatched by some kind of a nut . . .'

'Then we'll go to the police.'

'Hell, shit, they'll think *I* had something to do with it. Man, I was the last one with her last night. They'll blame *me*, and then we'll never get the guy that did it. I mean, she might still be alive. If some crazy guy got her, maybe he's keeping her alive. Maybe he doesn't want to kill her till after he's done . . . messing with her. You know?'

'Guy sounds a lot like you,' Jason said.

Roland gave a nervous laugh. 'Yeah. Takes one to know one. Shit, though, I'd never *do* anything like that. I just think about it, you know? But that gives us an advantage, right? I can like imagine what he might do. And that's why I've got this idea.'

'What idea?'

'How to get him. And how to find Dana.'

'Yeah? Let's hear it.'

Chapter Fifteen

'How you doing, fella?'

'Just fine,' Jake said into the phone. He didn't feel fine at all, he felt depressed. As soon as he hung up, he would be taking Kimmy back to her mother. 'Did Steve get in?'

'Sure did. He wants to talk to you. Hold on a sec.'

Moments later, Steve Applegate came on the line. 'Jake? I finished up on Smeltzer. I want you to get over here.'

'Find something interesting?'

'Interesting? Yes, I'd say interesting. How soon can you be here?'

'Fifteen, twenty minutes.'

'Higgins should be in on this.'

The Chief? 'What is it?'

'Whetted the curiosity, have I? Well then, you'd better get moving. I'll phone Higgins.' Without another word, he hung up.

Jake put down the phone.

Kimmy was huddled down in a corner of the sofa, watching television. The Three Stooges. Curly saluted his nose to block a two-fingered eye jab from Moe, then went, 'Nyar-nyar-nyar!'

'Hon,' Jake said, 'we'd better hit the road.'

'Do we have to?'

'You giving me back-talk?' he snapped. 'Huh?' He rushed over to Kimmy. Eyes wide, she clamped her arms to her sides. Jake pushed his fingers under them, digging into her ribs. She laughed and writhed. 'I'll teach you! Sass me, will you?' Rolling on her back, she kicked out at him. The sole of her Rose Pedal shoe pounded his thigh. 'Owww!' Clutching his leg, he staggered backwards and fell to the floor.

Kimmy grinned down at him from the sofa. 'That's what you get,' she said, 'when you mess with She-Ra.'

'Jeez, I guess so. You discombobulated me.'

She waved a fist at him. 'Want some more?'

'No, please.' Jake stood up. 'Anyway, we really do have to go.'

The joy went out of her face. 'Do we have to?'

'I'm afraid so, honey. Mommy's expecting you, and besides, I have to go to work.'

'I'll go to work with you, okay?'

'I don't think so.'

'I won't make the siren go,' she assured him, looking contrite and hopeful. 'Really I won't. Can't I go with you?'

'I'm sorry, honey. Not today. Besides, I won't be using the siren car.'

'I want to go with you, anyway.'

'You wouldn't want to go where I'm going. I have to see a guy who's toes up.'

'Oh, yuck. Really?'

'Yep.'

She made the kind of face she might have made, Jake thought, if somebody stuck a plate of beets under her nose. 'Well don't touch him,' she advised.

Stopping behind BB's Toy, Jake got out and opened the passenger door for Kimmy. She watched him with sombre eyes. When the safety harness was unsnapped, she didn't throw the straps off her shoulders in a hurry to climb out. She just sat there.

'Let's see a smile,' Jake said. 'Come on, it's Mommy's birthday. She'll want to see a smile on that mug of yours.'

'I don't feel good.'

'Are you sick?'

'I am not happy.'

'Why not?'

'You're making me go away.'

'I'm sorry.'

'No you're not.'

Jake lifted her out of the car seat. She wrapped her arms and legs around him. 'You'll have a good time today,' he said as he carried her towards the house.

'No I won't.'

'And I'll be back on Friday and we'll have two whole days together like we're supposed to.'

Kimmy squeezed herself more tightly against him. He could feel her begin to shake, and he knew that she was crying. She didn't bawl; she cried softly, her breath making quiet snagging sounds close to his ear.

'Aw, honey,' he whispered. And struggled not to cry himself.

Jake swung his car into the lot beside the Applegate Mortuary. The town of Clinton wasn't large enough to justify a city morgue, but Steve, whose brother took care of the funeral parlour side of the business, had spent twelve years as a forensic pathologist with the Office of the Medical Examiner in Los Angeles – resigned in a huff when his boss was fired for mismanagement – and had come back here to practise in his hometown.

Clinton didn't do a booming business in autopsies, but there were apparently enough to keep Steve happy. An autopsy was required for everyone who died as the apparent result of an accident, of suicide or homicide, under any kind of circumstances in which the death was not pretty much expected by the deceased's physician. An autopsy was also required for every corpse headed for the crematorium instead of the grave. With all that, even a small peaceful town like Clinton provided quite a few opportunities for Steve to practise his art.

Three new customers Thursday alone, Jake thought as he climbed from his car. Steve must think he's back in LA.

Jake entered through a rear door that opened into Betty's office. She looked away from her typing, smiled when she saw him, and swivelled her chair around. 'Been a while, Jake.' Tipping back her chair, she folded her hands behind her head – a posture that seemed designed to draw Jake's attention to her breasts. Betty's job didn't require her to face the public, so she was allowed to dress as she pleased. She was wearing a T-shirt with the slogan 'Make My Day'. It clung nicely to her full breasts. Her nipples pointed at Jake through the fabric.

'Looking good,' he said.

'Natch.' She stared at his groin. He didn't look, himself, but he could feel a warm swelling down there.

'Well,' he said, 'Steve's waiting for me.'

'No hot hurry. Higgins isn't here yet.' She looked up at his face. Her eyes widened a bit. 'So what's the story?'

'What story?'

'Got a new friend?'

Jake shook his head.

'Taken a vow of celibacy?'

'Just busy, that's all.'

A smile tilted her mouth. 'Well, if you ever happen to get unbusy, I just bought a rubber sheet for my bed and I've got a great big bottle of slippy-slidy oil we can rub all over each other. You oughta just see how it looks on me in candlelight.'

Jake could imagine. He pursed his dry lips and blew through them. 'I'll keep it in mind,' he said.

'Just in case you find some free time on your hands.'

'Yeah.'

She nodded. Again her gaze lowered to his crotch. 'I'd be glad to take care of *that* for you right now, if you'd like. Plenty of empty rooms around here. How about it?'

'You're kidding.' He knew she wasn't. 'We're in a morgue,' he reminded her.

'Just the place for taking care of stiffs, and I'm looking at one.' She rolled back her chair and stood up. She was wearing a short black leather skirt. Her bare legs were slender and lightly tanned.

'This is crazy,' Jake muttered. He felt shaky inside. Was he really going along with this?

Then the rear door opened and in stepped Barney Higgins, Chief of the Clinton Police Department. Betty rolled her eyes upward. She turned to Higgins. 'Hi-ya, Barn.'

'Hey, Betts.' The small wiry man winked and snicked his tongue. 'What's that y' got in yer shirt?'

125

'Your guess is good as mine, Barn.'

'Where'd you pick 'em up? I'd like to order a set for the wife.' He laughed and slapped Jake's shoulder. 'Let's get a move on, I got a hot poker game back at the house.' He turned to Betty. 'Where's the Apple, down in his butcher shop?'

'B-1,' she said. 'Have fun, boys.'

Leaving her office through a side door, they started down a flight of stairs towards the basement. 'You get a good look at that gal?' Barney asked.

'Sure did.'

'Prime. Ooo. How'd y'like playing some hide-the-salami with a prime thing like that? Yeah!'

'She's a knockout, all right.'

At the bottom of the stairs, Jake pulled open a fire door. Directly across the corridor was B-1, the autopsy room. His stomach fluttered as he stepped over to it and opened the door. From the room came a high whining buzz like the sound of a dentist's drill.

Steve Applegate, a cigar stub clamped in his teeth, squinted down through the smoke at what he was doing. Whatever he was doing, it involved the head of a naked woman who was stretched out on one of the tables. And it involved the small buzz-saw that was making such a racket.

Jake chose to watch his shoes as he walked across the polished linoleum floor.

The saw went silent.

'Who y'got there?' Barney asked.

'Mary-Beth Harker. A probable cerebral aneurism.'

'Joe Harker's girl?'

'That's right.'

'Aw, shit. Shit. When'd it happen?'

'Last night.'

'Shit. She's not, what, eighteen, nineteen?'

'Nineteen.'

'Shit. That's his only daughter.'

Jake felt cold spread through him like a winter gust. Kimmy. God, what if it was Kimmy? How could a man go on living if something like that happened to his kid?

He turned away and walked towards another table. The body

on this one was covered with a blue cloth. 'This Smeltzer?' he asked without looking around.

'That's Smeltzer, Ronald. I'll get to Smeltzer, Peggy, later today.'

I killed this guy, he told himself, wanting to feel the guilt, wanting it to come and take away the terror of imagining Kimmy dead. I killed this guy. He's dead because of me.

His mind began to the replay. Fine. Smeltzer raising his head, tearing a flap of skin from his wife's belly, turning in slow motion to reach for the shotgun.

'I've never seen anything like this,' Steve said, pulling Jake out of the memory. He drew back the cover.

Smeltzer was facedown. Jake's bullets had left five exit wounds on his back and splayed open the side of his neck.

'Good shooting,' Barney commented.

Jake was looking at the gash that ran down from the nape of Smeltzer's neck down his spine, over his right buttock and down his right leg to the outer side of his ankle. The raw bloodless gash was bordered by about half an inch of blue-grey skin. 'What's this?' Jake asked.

'Something of a puzzle,' Steve said. With the tip of his cigar he pointed at the quarter-sized ankle wound. 'Know anything about it?' he asked Jake.

Jake shook his head.

'When I stripped him down this morning, I found it along with the haematoma – that discoloration you see there. Frankly, I didn't know what to make of it. A bruise is usually caused by a blunt trauma that breaks capillaries in the skin. So I asked myself what could've hit this man in such a way as to follow the curves of his body like this.'

'Something flexible,' Jake said.

'A whip,' Barney suggested. 'Maybe a hose.'

'That occured to me. The problem is, the epidermis showed no evidence of injury, which you'd expect if the man had been struck by that kind of instrument. And the ankle wound made me suspicious. So I made an incision at the wound and followed the track of the haematoma to his neck. What I found was a two-centimetre separation between the fascias and—'

'Spare me the jargon, huh?' Barney said.

'Along the entire length of the bruise, the connecting tissue between the skin and underlying muscle was no longer connected. It was as if an approximately inch-wide area of skin had been forcibly raised from the inside.'

'What are you gettin' at?' Barney asked.

'Something entered this man's body via the ankle wound and burrowed its way up to his neck.'

'Y'mean like somethin' *alive*?'

'That's just what I mean.'

'Balls.'

Steve tapped some ash off the end of his cigar. It dropped into a gutter at the foot of the table. 'I found considerable trauma to the brain stem. Appears that it had been chewed into.'

Jake stared at the corpse. 'Something tunnelled up his body and bit his brain?'

'That's sure the way it looks.'

'Jesus,' Jake muttered.

'Okay,' Barney said. 'So where's it at, this *thing*?'

'Gone.'

'Gone where?'

'After this man was deceased, it chewed through the posterior wall of his oesophagus, travelled down to his stomach, chewed through the stomach wall and made a bee-line for his colon. Chewed through that, and exited through the anus.'

'You gotta be kiddin'.'

Steve punched his cigar dead in the metal gutter. Then he bent down and picked up a pair of boxer shorts that had been turned inside out. The seat was smeared with faeces and blood.

Barney wrinkled his nose.

Steve picked up a pair of blue jeans, also pulled inside out. Down the right leg was a narrow trail that diminished as it neared the cuff. 'Kidding?' he asked.

Barney shook his head slowly from side to side.

'What could've done something like this?' Jake asked.

Steve shrugged. One side of his mouth stretched upward. 'An ambitious snake?'

'Yer a festival a laughs,' Barney said.

'I haven't the faintest idea what did this, but it appears to have been something *shaped*, at least, like a snake.'

'I never heard a snakes doing shit like that.'

'Who has?' Steve said.

'Smeltzer was alive when this thing got in him?' Jake asked.

'Definitely.'

'How can you tell?'

'The amount of subdural bleeding and the quantity of blood on his right sock. I'd guess, from the degree of coagulation of his ankle wound, that this thing got into him within probably minutes prior to his death.'

'And it left his body after his death? How do you know that?'

'Again, the amount of bleeding. Very little in the areas that it chewed through on the way out.'

'Fuckin' *Twilight Zone*,' Barney said.

'So what do you make of it?' Jake asked.

'I couldn't say.'

'We're talking, here,' Jake said, 'about a guy who blew off his wife's head and started to eat her. And you're saying that, like minutes before he went at her, this snake-thing burrowed up his leg and bit him in the brain?'

'That's sure the way it appears.'

'And after I shot him, it . . . took off.'

'Didn't see it, did ya?' Barney asked.

'I didn't stick around long. I took a quick look through the restaurant to make sure there wasn't a third person. Then I headed back to my car to call in. I must've been gone close to fifteen minutes. I guess that gave it time to get out.'

'The poop-shoot express,' Barney said.

'It might still be in the restaurant,' Jake suggested.

'I already searched around here,' Steve said, 'and the van that brought him in. Didn't want that thing sneaking up on *me*.'

Barney sidestepped, reached over, pinched a leg of Steve's white trousers and lifted. 'I already checked that, myself,' Steve said. He raised both cuffs above his socks.

Barney crouched for a close look, then turned to Jake. 'How 'bout you?'

'I took three showers after . . .'

'So y'got hygiene. Lift your pants.'

Jake drew them up to his knees. Barney squatted beside him, took a long look, then slid Jake's socks down around his ankles.

129

'Okay, so now we know you guys aren't gonna start munchin' on me.'

Jake nodded. 'So I'm not the only one who thinks this snake-thing made Smeltzer go haywire.'

'It don't make sense, but it makes sense.'

'I'm afraid I have to agree,' Steve said. 'It sounds like madness, but the possibility is certainly there . . . some kind of creature that sustains itself through a symbiotic relationship with its human host. A parasite. But it doesn't simply take its nourishment from its host, it – somehow controls his eating habits.'

Barney smirked. ''Less Smeltzer was in the habit a eatin' his wife.'

'So we're talking here,' Jake said, 'about a snake-like creature that burrows into a person, takes control of his mind, and compels him to eat human flesh. That *is* what we're talking about here, right?'

'Can't be,' Barney said. 'Last time I looked I wasn't nuts.'

'If there's another way to interpret this situation,' Steve said, 'I'd be more than eager to hear it.'

'Yeah. You guys are figments a my fuckin' nightmare.'

'Neither of you, I take it, has ever heard of a similar situation?'

'You gotta be kiddin'.'

'I've heard of cannibalism,' Jake said, 'but never anything about a snake or whatever that gets inside you and turns you into one.'

'Gentlemen, I think we've got a situation.' Steve slipped a fresh cigar from a pocket of his white jacket, stripped off its wrapper and bit off its end. He spat the wad of leaf into the table gutter. He licked the whole cigar. Then he poked it into his mouth and lit up.

'I drove over to Marlowe yesterday, at the request of a colleague, Herman Willis. Thursday afternoon, the nude body of a twenty-two-year-old female was found. It had been buried in a field just east of Marlowe. Might never have turned up, except a kid happened to be out playing in the field with his dog. The dog found the grave. The kid ran home for a shovel, apparently thinking he had stumbled onto a buried treasure. He dug for a while, then ran home yelling.'

'Musta gave'm a good turn.'

'Here's the interesting part: the body had been eaten. Quite a lot of the skin had been torn off, portions of muscle devoured . . .' The cigar in Steve's hand was shaking. 'She had bite marks all over her body. Some were just enough to break the skin, others took out chunks of her. Her torso had been ripped open. Her heart had been torn out and partly eaten. Her head . . . she had been scalped. Her skull had been caved in with a blunt instrument, possibly a rock. Her brain was missing.'

'Holy fuckin' mayonnaise,' Barney muttered.

'Willis had never seen anything like this. I think he called me in more for moral support than for my professional opinion. At any rate, the teeth marks and the saliva samples we took from the wounds indicated that her assailant was human.'

'Yer sayin' she was a victim of this thing.'

'Of someone "occupied" by this thing.'

'When was this person killed?' Jake asked.

'Wednesday, around midnight. Willis was able to pinpoint the time of death pretty accurately, based on her stomach contents. She'd been seen at a local pizza at eight that night. The degree to which the pizza had been digested . . .'

Barney flicked the back of his hand against the hip of the body stretched in front of him. 'So, where was Ronald Smeltzer Wednesday night?'

'I don't think Smeltzer did it,' Jake said. His heart was beating fast. 'That van, the one that tried to run down Celia Jamerson, was coming from the direction of Marlowe. Thursday afternoon. Someone, some*thing*, got out of the van alive. There was blood on the pavement behind the rear door. I followed the traces into the field, but couldn't . . .' He shook his head. 'Where the van crashed was only a few hundred yards from the Oakwood Inn. Suppose what I tried to follow was this snake-thing and it found its way to the restaurant, got into Smeltzer that night?' Jake turned to Steve. 'You got that John Doe from the van?'

'This way.'

They followed Steve out of the autopsy room, down the corridor, and into a room with a dozen refrigerator compartments. He checked the drawer labels, then slid one open. The body that rolled out was covered by a sheet. Jake was grateful for the aroma of Steve's cigar, though it wasn't enough to mask the odour of burnt flesh and hair.

'If you'd prefer not to see this,' Steve said, 'I think I know what we're looking for.'

Jake, who had seen the charred corpse hanging out of the windscreen of the van, wasn't eager for a close-up view. But he didn't want to look squeamish in front of Barney, so he kept quiet.

'Let's see'm,' Barney said.

Steve drew back the sheet. Jake stared at the edge of the aluminium drawer. Though he didn't focus on the body, he saw it. He saw a black thing vaguely shaped like a human.

'I'll have to turn him over,' Steve said.

'Manage?' Barney asked, sounding reluctant to help.

'No problem.'

Jake swung his gaze over to Steve and saw that he was wearing surgical gloves. He watched Steve bend over the body. He heard papery crumbling sounds. He heard himself groan.

'Guy's a real flake,' Barney muttered. 'Fallin' apart over ya.'

Steve grinned rigidly around the cigar in his teeth. Lifting and pulling, he wrestled the black lump onto its back. When he had finished, the front of his white jacket looked as if someone had rubbed it with charcoal.

'Jake, you were right.'

Jake let his eyes be guided by Steve's pointing finger to the grey knobs of spinal column laid bare from the nape of the corpse's neck to midway down its back.

'Looks like the thing was positioned the same as in Smeltzer,' Steve said.

'Only didn't take a sneaky way out,' Barney added.

'With all this damage, it's hard to be sure exactly what happened, but it appears that the thing made an emergency exit by splitting open the skin all the way up.'

'Must be awfully strong,' Jake said, 'to do that.'

'Yeah,' Barney said. 'And to open the back door a the van.'

'The impact probably popped the door open,' Jake told him.

'Yeah, maybe.'

'I'll take a mould of this man's teeth and draw a blood sample,' Steve said, 'and make a run over to Marlowe. I'll call from there and let you know if it's a match, but I'd be willing to bet on it.'

'Call me at home,' Barney told him. 'I got a hot poker game goin'.'

'If this *is* the guy who killed the woman in Marlowe,' Jake said, 'it pretty much clinches our theory.'

'I think we can assume it's clinched.'

'Yeah,' Barney agreed. 'So we got us a snake that gets in 'n' turns guys into cannibals. Y'believe it?'

Jake stepped away from the corpse. He leaned against the wall of drawers, scooted sideways to get a handle out of his back, and folded his arms. 'The thing killed on Wednesday. It tried for Celia Jamerson on Thursday afternoon, then started to go for Peggy Smeltzer on Thursday night. That looks like maybe it goes for a new victim daily.'

'Give us this day our daily broad,' Barney said.

'This is Saturday. I wonder if it got someone yesterday.'

'Can't do it on its own,' Barney said, 'or it wouldn't be climbing inta guys.'

'We'd better check out everyone who was at the restaurant Thursday night, everyone who's come into contact with Smeltzer's body.'

'Y'got yourself a job. Get on it. Do whatcha can on yer own, we'll see where it gets us. Nobody knows but us three, we'll keep it that way. Folks hear about this thing, they'll go apeshit. Yer our task force, Jake. Stay on this till we got it nailed. Report t'me.'

'What about Chuck?'

'I'll reassign him till yer done. I want y'workin' alone. That's the only way we're gonna keep this quiet.'

'Are you sure we *should* keep this quiet?' Steve asked. 'If people are aware of the danger, they'll take precautions.'

'They'll go apeshit. Or they'll say *we* got loose screws. Or both.'

'I'm aware of that, but . . .'

'Keep yer drawers on, Apple. We don't nail this down in a day or two, we'll let the whole suck-head world in on it. Okay? Y'can hold a press conference. But let's take a crack at it before we start tellin' folks they're on the fuckin' menu.'

133

Chapter Sixteen

Alison didn't know why she was here. She had left the house after lunch and started walking with no destination in mind, just the desire to be alone and to be outside.

The wandering had taken her down Summer Street, within sight of Evan's apartment. She'd finished with him, but she gazed across the street at his building as if to punish herself. She saw two windows on the second storey that belonged to his rooms. The shades were open. Was he inside? Was Tracy Morgan with him? Was he alone and would he see her passing by and come after her?

He didn't come after her.

Alison had walked on, feeling empty.

Not knowing why, she ended up here – in the woods above Clinton Creek. The creek was swollen and rushing. It washed around islands of rock. Occasionally it carried along tree limbs, casualties of last night's storm.

Alison made her way carefully down the steep embankment. At the water's edge she noticed a familiar flat-topped rock. During her years in Clinton, especially when she was a freshman and such an emotional wreck, she had spent a lot of time on this very rock. Standing on it, sitting on it, sometimes with her bare feet in the water. She used to think of it as Solitary Rock. It was where she always came to be alone when she was feeling low.

She had forgotten about it. She had been down here several times over the past few months, had probably seen Solitary Rock and maybe even stood on it without remembering that it used to be so special.

Now she remembered. She stepped onto it and sat down, drawing her knees up and hugging them against her body.

This is nice, she thought. No wonder I used to come here all the time.

She heard a car cross the bridge, a sound much like that of the rushing water. She looked towards the bridge, but it was hidden by trees beyond the bend in the stream. She looked the other way and saw only the stream sluicing around a rocky curve. The slopes on both sides were heavy with bushes and trees. She saw no one, but wondered if there were couples concealed in nooks among the foliage or rocks, making love.

It was just around that bend where she and Evan . . .

It was a secluded, sunlit pocket with waist-high rocks on both sides and the stream at one end. A dense bramble at the other end sheltered them from anyone who might be looking down the slope. They could've been seen from the opposite embankment, but nobody ever went over there. They sat on the blanket that Evan always kept in the trunk of his car. They ate sharp cheddar on Ritz crackers. They drank white wine from Alison's bota, squeezing the bag to squirt it into their mouths, into each other's mouths, laughing when they missed. When her blouse was soaked, she took it off and lay back on the blanket. Evan, kneeling between her legs, spurted the cool wine onto her neck and chest and breasts. It trickled down her skin, tickling. The laughter had stopped. He aimed at her nipples, the thin stream of wine hitting and splashing off one, then the other. Then he licked her. He made a puddle of wine in the hollow of her navel, and as he lapped at that he opened her jeans.

That had been Sunday afternoon. A week ago tomorrow.

How could things have gone wrong so fast?

Don't idealize it, she told herself. It had been great – fun and thrilling and then incredible. But not quite right. You only planned on a picnic by the stream. You never intended to make it with him, not there where anyone could show up and find you at it. But when he soaked your blouse with wine, you knew what he wanted and you went along with it. For Evan, not for yourself. Because you didn't want to disappoint him. And that is not the best of all possible reasons.

Hell, she thought, it sure didn't bother you much at the time.

Shortly afterwards, though.

If there *are* regrets, you soon feel them, before you even have time to get your clothes back on. If there aren't regrets, you know that, too. There had been times when Alison felt right afterwards. Not recently, though. Not with Evan. Maybe not since Jimmy the summer after high-school graduation.

Jimmy. It was missing him, more than anything else, that had brought her so often to Solitary Rock during her freshman year. Especially after the letter that began, 'I will always cherish the memories of what we shared together, but . . .' But she was eight hundred miles from Jimmy and he'd fallen for Cynthia Younger in his world civilization class.

Sitting on Solitary Rock with the sun warm on her head and back, Alison didn't feel the loss of Jimmy. She had finished with the pain and bitterness a long time ago. Instead, she inspected the memories of Jimmy and the way her life had gone since then.

The guys she had dated. The guys she had been serious about. The ones she had slept with.

Four of those, she thought, but only three if you don't count Tom and you shouldn't count Tom because that was only once and we were drunk. So three after Jimmy – Dave, Larry and Evan. And it hadn't been really right with any of them.

Good, but not right. Not wonderful. Not without those regrets sneaking in.

She wondered how she would feel about Nick Winston, the guy she'd met last night at Wally's. Thinking about Nick, she felt no eagerness to see him again. Probably a nice guy, but . . .

Her rump was starting to hurt. She changed positions, lowering her legs and crossing them. Leaning back, she pressed her palms against the rock and braced herself up. She lifted her face into the sunlight. The heat felt wonderful. She imagined going now to the secluded place where she had been with Evan, taking off her clothes, and feeling the sun all over her body.

No way, she thought.

But she leaned forward and pulled her skirt up high on her legs. She unbuttoned her blouse, lifted its front, and tied it around her ribs. Then she leaned back again, bracing herself on stiff arms. That was better – feeling the sun on her chest and belly and thighs. The sun, and the mild breeze.

So I've struck out a few times in the man department, she thought. It's not the end of the world. I'm twenty-one, not bad to look at. No reason to let this stuff get me down. I'm better off without Evan, better off alone than getting stuck with a guy who isn't exactly right. Hold out for the one who *is* right and don't lie to myself when one isn't. That's the main thing.

Later, when Alison left, she didn't return to Summer Street. She felt peaceful, and had no need to tease or punish herself by passing by Evan's apartment. She walked the length of the wooded park. She saw a few strolling couples. She spotted lovers leaning against a tree deep in the shadows, and felt only a moment of sorrow.

At the house, she found Celia asleep on the sofa with her headphones on. The quiet tapping of a typewriter came from the closed door of Helen's room. She stepped to the door and knocked. 'Yo,' Helen called.

She opened it. Helen scooted her chair back, turned it around, and looked at Alison from under a transparent green visor.

'Anything exciting happen while I was gone?'

'Just Celia bitching about her aches and pains, though I don't believe I would call that exciting.'

'Any calls?' she asked. Why do I care? she wondered. I don't. But she felt a letdown when Helen shook her head.

'Nary a one. Your public must be otherwise occupied.'

'Just as well.'

'I thought you were finished with Evan.'

'I am. I was just curious, that's all.'

'Celia got a call from Danny Gard, wanted to go out romping with her tonight. You should've heard her pissing and moaning.' Helen scrunched her face. ' "No, I can't. No, I wasn't just fine last night, I was in aaaagony. Maybe next week. Maybe next month. No, it's not you, it's meeee. I'm in pain. I can hardly moooove." '

'Celia isn't really going to stay home on a Saturday night,' Alison said.

'Nah. She's just waiting for a better offer. I guess she didn't have a great time with him last night.'

'He's a gross character. Last time I saw him, he was at Wally's engaged in a belching contest with Lisa Ball.'

'He's a Sig,' Helen said, as if that explained it.

Alison nodded. 'His idea of a high time is lighting farts.'

Grinning, Helen asked, 'You know that from personal experience?'

'I've heard him pontificate on . . .' The sudden jangle of the telephone stopped her words. She felt herself go tight. 'I'll get it,' she muttered, and hurried into the living-room.

Don't let it be Evan, she thought.

Her hand trembled as she picked up the phone. 'Hello?'

'Celia?'

Thank God. 'Just a moment, please,' she said. Celia, still on the sofa, had her eyes closed. The music from the headset had probably covered the blare of the ringing phone. Alison wondered if she was asleep.

Helen appeared in the doorway of her room. She raised her bushy eyebrows.

Alison covered the phone's mouthpiece. 'It's for Celia.'

'A guy?'

'Yeah.'

'Find out who it is.'

'Who may I tell her is calling?' Alison asked.

'This is Jason Banning.'

'Thank you. Just a moment.' She covered the mouthpiece again. 'Jason, the actor, that scuzzball's roommate.'

'The freshman.'

Nodding, Alison set down the phone and hurried to the sofa. She nudged Celia's shoulder. The girl frowned and mumbled and kept her eyes shut. Alison lifted one of the muff-like speakers off her ear. 'Hey, snoozy, you got a wakeup call.'

'Huh?'

'You got an admirer on the phone.'

A single eyelid struggled upward. 'Huh? Who is . . . ?'

'Jason.'

She raised her other eyelid. Her gaze slid sideways to Alison. 'Jason? Jason *Banning*?'

'That's the one.'

'Be damn,' she mumbled.

'Want me to tell him you can't come to the phone?'

'Eat my shorts.' She pulled the headset off and slowly sat up, groaning. 'God, I'm death warmed over.'

Alison brought the phone closer. She placed it on the coffee table and handed the receiver to Celia.

'Hi, Jason,' Celia said. She sounded cheerful and friendly and in tip-top shape.

Alison looked at Helen. Helen shook her head and chuckled.

'Yeah, some bastard ran me off the road . . . No, not too bad. I'm not too pretty to look at, but . . . Well, that's just 'cause you haven't *seen* me . . . Oh? Well, I wouldn't mind seeing you, either . . . Tonight? . . . No, I don't have any plans that I can't get out of . . .'

Helen, still shaking her head, swivelled her eyes upward.

'That'd be great. What time? . . . Okay. Great . . . Terrific. See you then.' She held out the phone, and Alison hung it up for her.

'Are you sure you're up to a date?'

'He's taking me to the Lobster Shanty, I'm up to that.'

'Decent,' Alison said. The Lobster Shanty was the finest restaurant in Clinton.

'That should be a real thrill,' Helen said, 'going out with a freshman.'

'A *gorgeous* freshman,' Celia amended.

'Robbing the cradle.'

'Floss your butt.' She lay down again on the sofa and crossed her ankles. 'Besides, he's twenty-one, same as us.'

'Sure.'

'He is.'

'What'd he do, flunk three times?'

'He worked after high school. Modelled, did commercials, that sort of stuff.'

'What about his girlfriend?' Alison asked. 'I thought you said he was going with some gal.'

'Yeah, he was. Guess he saw the error of his ways.'

'Maybe he likes to date cripples,' Helen suggested.

'Wants to use her for a base,' Alison said.

'Wants to slide in,' Helen added.

'You two are a riot.'

'We're just jealous,' Helen told her. 'We just wish *we* could go to the Lobster Shanty with a freshman.'

'I'll call him back,' Celia said. 'Maybe he can set up one of you guys with Roland.'

'I'm not selfish, Alison can have him.'

Celia turned her head on the cushion and smiled at Alison. 'We'll make it a double date, just like junior high.'

'Pardon me while I heave.'

'I realize Roland probably isn't as handsome and worldly as

Evan, but hey, it's Saturday night, you don't want to sit around alone on a Saturday night, do you?'

'Besides,' Helen added, 'he's obviously got a good case of the hots for you.'

'A case of the hards,' Celia said.

'Way he was eyeing you yesterday . . .'

'Stripping you with his eyes . . .'

The talk made Alison feel squirmy. 'I'd really like to double with you, Celia, but I happen to know that Roland has other plans. He's got this *ménage à trois* scheduled for tonight.'

Helen snorted.

'Chortle chortle,' Celia said.

Alison eyed Helen. 'She thinks I'm joking. Don't you find it a trifle *peculiar* that Jason, who has never before asked Celia out – in spite of her beauty and wit – should invite her to dinner the very *day* after her chance encounter at the shopping mall with his roommate, Roland?'

Helen stroked her heavy lower lip and nodded. ' 'Tis passing strange.'

Celia smirked. 'Tell you what, Roland shows up for dinner, I'll give him my house key and tell him I got two horny roommates just dying for a piece of him.' She winked at Helen. 'And I'll advise him to bring chips.'

'So what do you think?' Celia asked.

Alison, on the recliner, set her yellow highlighting pen into the gutter of the Chaucer text she had been studying for the past two hours, and looked up. 'Not bad.'

The bandage was gone from Celia's brow. Tied around her head was a blue silk scarf that concealed the abrasion. The scarf was knotted over her left ear, and its ends hung almost to her shoulder. She wore big hoop earrings.

'You look like Long John Silver,' Alison said.

'Cute, huh?'

'Matter of fact, you look great.'

'You'd never know I was damaged goods, would you?'

'Just by your reputation,' Helen said, coming in from the kitchen with a stein of beer and a can of peanuts. She held the can towards Celia.

'No thanks, I'm saving all my room for dinner.'

'Where's your sling?' Helen asked.

'I'm not going to the Lobster Shanty with a goddamn sling on my arm.' She lifted the arm stiffly away from her side. 'I've got an Ace bandage on the elbow. And both knees.'

'I'm surprised you have an outfit that'll cover them,' Helen said.

'It's the best I could do.'

The blue gown had sleeves to her forearms and its skirt reached well below her knees, covering her bandages but not entirely hiding them. They showed, Alison noticed, because of the way the glossy fabric clung to every inch of her. She appeared to wear three bandages beneath the gown, and nothing else.

Celia looked down at herself. 'I would've preferred something that showed a little in front,' she said, fingering the neckband at her throat.

'Cellophane might show more,' Helen said, and dropped onto the sofa. 'Peanut?' She tossed one to Alison. Alison snatched it out of the air and popped it into her mouth.

'This is a problem,' Celia said, 'but I don't know what I can do about it.' She turned sideways and took a step. Her right leg, bare to the hip, came out of a slit in the gown. The knee was wrapped with a brown elastic band. 'I tried taking off the bandage, but the knee *really* sucks without it.'

'You could try a body stocking,' Alison suggested.

'Har!' Helen blared.

'The thing is,' Alison said, 'he knows you were hurt. There's no big deal if he happens to see your bandages.'

'He'll see them all anyway,' Helen said, 'once you throw your dress on the floor.'

'She won't throw her dress on the floor,' Alison said. 'Roland'll hang it up for her.'

'Real cute. What time is it?'

Helen checked her wristwatch. 'Six twenty.'

'Good. He's picking me up at ten to seven. I think I'll have a little . . .'

'I'd want to get drunk too,' Helen said, 'if I was going out in public wearing that.'

141

'You went out in public wearing this,' Celia said, 'the public should get drunk.' She grinned at Alison. 'Get you something?'

'Thanks. Whatever you're having.'

Celia went into the kitchen.

'God, she looks fabulous,' Helen whispered. 'I looked ten per cent as good as her . . .' She shook her head and sighed. 'Life's tough, then you die.'

'Let's send out for a pizza after she's gone.'

Helen raised her thick eyebrows. 'Well, maybe life ain't so tough.'

A few minutes later Celia returned, carrying a tray with her left hand. Two tumblers were balanced on the tray. 'Double vodka gimlets,' she announced as Alison took one of the glasses.

'You're going to be polluted before he even gets here,' Helen said.

'Just a little something for what ails me. Besides, *he's* driving.' She set the tray carefully on the table, then lowered herself onto the sofa and lifted her glass.

Alison took a sip. The drink was very strong. She frowned at Celia. 'Are you sure about tonight?' she asked.

Staring into her glass, Celia shrugged one shoulder. 'I'm not going to call off my life just because some bastard racked me up.'

'Maybe you need some time.'

'Sit around and think about it?'

'I think it hit you pretty hard.'

'You're telling me?'

'Emotionally, I mean.'

'Alison's right,' Helen said. 'You can't just pretend it didn't happen. You almost got killed and that guy died. It's pretty heavy stuff.'

'I'm handling it, okay? What're you trying to do, ruin my appetite?' She took another drink. 'I'll be fine. And I'll be a lot finer after a couple of drinks and a lobster dinner with a nice guy who likes me and happens to be a hunk even if he is a freshman. I appreciate your concern, but knock it off, okay? I'm fine.'

'It's a good drink,' Alison said. 'Pretty soon, we'll both be fine.'

'Yeah, but I'll be with a charming gorgeous man and you'll be with Helen. Eat your heart out.'

'Hey,' Alison said, 'you're depressing me.'

A peanut bounced off her forehead and plopped into her drink. It floated on her vodka. She picked it out. Grinning, she flicked it into her mouth. The salt was gone. She fished an ice cube out of her glass and studied it.

'Hey, no,' Helen pleaded. 'Come on, you could hurt somebody with that.'

'You're right. What could I have been thinking?' She tossed it at Helen.

Squealing, Helen hunched her shoulders and twisted in her chair. She flinched when the cube dropped onto her lap. Her hand jerked. A foamy tongue of beer slurped over the edge of her stein and flopped onto her breast. 'Yeee-ah!'

'Whoops,' Alison said.

'Golly,' Celia said. 'Maybe I'll phone up Jason right now and call it off. I can see that it'll be a lot more fun around here tonight.'

Helen clamped the peanut can between her knees. Scowling down, she plucked the wet fabric away from her skin. She was wearing the same faded, stained, shapeless dress that she had worn yesterday when they went to the mall. Or a different one, Alison thought, that looked the same. She had several. They were hard to tell apart. She sniffed a fistful of the wet cloth. 'A definite improvement,' she said.

'They're gone,' Alison called from her recliner.

Helen's bedroom door eased open and she looked around as if to make sure the coast was clear before venturing out. Satisfied, she approached Alison. 'So, how was he?'

'He looks like an aftershave commercial.'

'Huh.' Helen ran the back of a hand across her nose. 'He's probably a jerk. Every guy she goes out with is a jerk, you ever noticed that?'

'I don't know,' Alison said.

'They are. Someday, she's going to be sorry.'

'I hope not.'

'You go out with enough jerky guys, sooner or later . . .'

'What kind of pizza we going to get? Salami, sausage?'

'I got some menus in my desk.'

'Get 'em.'

Chapter Seventeen

Jake was still trembling when he climbed out of his car. With the flashlight in his left hand and the machete clamped under his arm, he stepped to the trunk. The point of the key missed the lock hole a few times before he managed to fit it in. He turned the key. The trunk opened. He put the machete and flashlight inside, next to the can of gasoline, then slammed the trunk shut.

On the front porch of his house, he clutched his right hand with his left to hold it steady and got the key into the door lock. Inside, he engaged the deadbolt. He slipped the guard chain into place. Though evening light still came in through the windows, he made a circuit of the living-room and turned on every lamp. Along the way, he found himself checking each window and looking behind the furniture.

'Nerves of steel,' he muttered.

In the kitchen, he hit the light switch. He checked the windows and back door to make sure they were secure. Bending at the waist because his leather pants were too tight for squatting, he opened a cupboard and took out a bottle of bourbon. A drop of sweat fell from his chin and splashed the toe of his boot.

Stepping to the sink, he yanked a yard of paper towel off its roll. He mopped his face and wet stringy hair.

Then he filled a glass with bourbon. He took a few swallows and sighed as the liquor's heat spread through him.

He carried the glass down the hallway, turning on lights as he went, and entered his bedroom.

He turned on his bedroom light. He looked around. The curtains were shut. The closet door was open, just as he had left it. Taking another drink, he stepped past the closet and looked in. He wandered to the other side of his bed. He had an urge to get down on his hands and knees and peer under the bed.

Don't be a jerk, he thought. You're home now. This isn't the goddamn Oakwood Inn, this is home and there's nothing under your bed except maybe some dust bunnies.

Besides, it'd be too much effort in this outfit.

After taking another swallow of bourbon, Jake set his glass on the dresser. He unzipped his leather jacket and pulled it off. His blue shirt, dark with sweat, clung to his skin. He tried to open the buttons, but his fingers shook badly so after getting the top buttons undone he yanked the shirt up and pulled it over his head.

He unbuckled his gunbelt, swung it towards the bed and let go. The holstered revolver bounced when it hit the mattress. He stared at it while he opened his pants and tugged them down to his knees. Sitting on the bed, he popped open the leather strap and slid the revolver free. He placed it close to his right leg, then bent down and pulled his boots off. His socks felt glued to his feet. He peeled them off. He slid the tight pants down his calves and kicked them away.

In the lamplight, his legs were shiny with sweat. Their hair was matted down. He rubbed the clammy skin of his shins, turned his legs and looked behind them.

There were no quarter-size holes.

Hell, of course not. Nothing could've got through the boots and leather pants. Not without me knowing it.

Jake stood up. His rump had left sweat marks on the pale blue coverlet. He drew down his sodden shorts and stepped out of them.

Okay, I'm a jerk, he thought.

Picking up his revolver, he dropped to his knees and elbows. He lifted the hanging edge of the coverlet and peered into the dark space under his bed.

A pair of eyes looked back at him.

He yelped. He jabbed the gun barrel towards the eyes. He almost pulled the trigger before he realized he was looking at Kimmy's Cookie Monster doll.

Stretching out an arm, he pulled it from under the bed. He pressed it to his cheek.

God almighty, what if I'd shot it?

Just a stuffed animal, he knew that. But, like all of Kimmy's dolls, it was somehow more. It was part Kimmy, as if she had breathed some of her own life into it. He could hear her say in a low and grumbly voice, 'Me want *Cookie*!'

Jake had a tight lump in his throat.

'Close call, Cookie,' he whispered.

He pushed himself to his feet. With the chubby blue doll in one hand and his revolver in the other, he headed for the door. He planned to put Cookie Monster back into Kimmy's bedroom. Then he changed his mind. He set it on his nightstand next to the telephone.

Barbara's side of the closet still had her full-length mirror on the outside of the door. He swung the door shut and looked at himself.

You'd know if it got you, he thought.

Maybe it can make you forget. If it can turn you into a cannibal . . .

There were no wounds on his legs. His scrotum was shrivelled and his penis looked as if it wanted to disappear. He slipped a hand between his legs, checking on both sides of the tight sack and behind it. He prodded his navel, and shivered as he imagined his finger going in all the way. But his navel was okay. The rest of his front appeared all right, thought the knife scar under his right nipple looked a little more white than usual.

He turned around. He looked over one shoulder, then the other. He probed between the sweaty cheeks of his rump.

You're all right, he thought, unless the damn thing went up your butt. Couldn't have done that, though, without going through the leather pants, and the pants didn't have any holes.

Satisfied that the thing hadn't invaded him, Jake took another drink of bourbon. The glass was almost empty. He carried it, along with his revolver, into the kitchen. After refilling the glass, he opened a drawer and took out a large clear plastic freezer bag.

He wondered if he'd flipped his lid.

Nobody will ever know about this, he told himself. It makes you feel better, so do it.

Some kind of cop, scared as a kid.

He slipped his revolver into the bag and pinched the zip-lock top shut along its seam.

Jake locked himself into the bathroom. He searched the floor, the walls and ceiling, the sink, the tub. Then he turned on the shower. He had a couple of drinks while he adjusted the heat of the spray, then set the glass on the toilet seat and climbed into the tub. He slid the frosted glass door shut.

The built-in soap dish had a metal bar above it for holding a washcloth. He slipped the barrel of his bagged revolver between the bar and the tile wall, wiggled the weapon until he was sure it wouldn't fall, then picked up the soap and began to wash himself.

The strong hot spray felt good. Jake told himself that he couldn't be much safer: the door was locked, he'd checked the bathroom, he was shut behind the shower doors, and his revolver was within easy reach. Nothing could get him.

Then he noticed the sudsy water swirling down the drain.

Gooseflesh crawled up his back.

Don't be crazy, he told himself. There's a metal drain basket down there, nothing could come up.

He dropped to his knees. His fingertip went into the drain only as far as the first knuckle before it touched the obstruction.

Okay. No problem.

Your only problem, pal, is your head.

Two hours alone, searching that damned restaurant.

If it was going to get you, it would've got you then.

It didn't come home with you. It's probably already found a new home – in whoever broke into the restaurant between Thursday night and this afternoon. Some lucky bastard is running around with the thing up his back, looking for a meal. *Give us this day our daily broad.* Good old Barney, he can joke about it. He should've gone in there. He might be worried about drains, himself.

Jake stayed in the shower until the water started turning cold. Then he climbed out, dried himself, had another drink of bourbon and took the revolver out of the bag. In his bedroom he combed his hair and put on a robe. He carried his drink and revolver into the living-room. Sitting on the sofa, he crossed his legs to keep his feet off the floor. He rested the gun on his lap. Then he swung the telephone over from the lamp table and dialled Barney's home.

Barney answered by saying, 'Higgins.'

'It's Jake.' His voice sounded all right. 'Did Applegate get back to you?'

'Sure did. Y'were right on the John Doe from the van. Perfect match on the teeth 'n' blood type. How'd it go from yer end?'

'I checked out everyone who was at the crime scene Thursday night. Nobody was carrying.'

'How'd y'make sure?'

'Strip searches.'

'They musta liked that. Tell'm why?'

'Damn near. I said Smeltzer had a parasite infestation. They were pretty cooperative.'

'Coulda told'm I'd ordered a circumcision survey.'

Jake ignored the remark. 'After I finished with them, I went out to the Oakwood. Somebody's been in there. The front and back doors had both been forced. I found a bag of flour on the kitchen floor.'

'A bagga what?'

'Flour. Like you use for cooking. You know.'

'Somebody makin' cookies?'

'I doubt it. No oven. There were some footprints, too. Somebody had stepped in the blood and left tracks. A bare foot. About a size seven. And somebody had polished off a bottle of vodka the Smeltzers had left out in the bar area.'

'What d'ya make of it?'

'Maybe a derelict. The size of the footprint, though, makes me think a girl was in there. Maybe a couple of kids from the college had themselves a party.'

'But no sign a old Sneaky Snake?'

The skin on Jake's thighs and forehead seemed to go stiff and tight.

'Y'looked, didn't ya?'

'I looked. I spent more than two hours looking. I checked every inch of that place.'

'No luck, huh?'

'I didn't find it . . .'

' 'M I hearin' a but on the way?'

'Yeah. But.' He felt breathless, a little dizzy. He sat up straight and filled his lungs. 'Down in the cellar, behind the stairs, I found half a dozen eggs.'

'Eggs?'

'Yeah.'

'Like chicken eggs?'

'No, not like chicken eggs.'

Barney whistled softly into the phone. 'Like *its* eggs?'

'I . . . yeah, I think so. They were clear. Like . . . almost like jelly beans, but soft. Red, but clear. I could see inside them. And each of them had a little . . . like a little worm.'

'You puttin' me the fuck *on*, Corey?'

'Little grey worms.'

There was a long silence from Barney. Then he said, 'Where're they, these eggs?'

'Still there.'

'You *left* 'em!'

'I stomped them flat.'

'You crazy? Shit!'

'What was I supposed to do, bag them for evidence?'

'We coulda had tests run, found out . . .'

'I know. I know that. I . . . I freaked out a little, Barney.'

There was another long silence. 'Y'all right?' Barney asked in a soft voice.

'I'm managing.'

'Yer not a guy loses it.'

'Oh, I can lose it pretty good.'

'I shouldn'ta had y'go in there alone. I'm sorry. Y'gonna be okay?'

'Sure.'

'Y'mashed the little fuckers.'

'Yeah. I'm sorry.'

'Well, maybe just as well. Guess we don't wanta be takin' any chances.' Jake heard him sigh. 'So momma wasn't there, huh?'

'I think . . . it could be anywhere, but there's a good chance it went out of that place with whoever it was that broke in.'

'The party kids.'

'It's just a guess.'

'No idea who they were?'

'Just that one was probably a female, and I don't imagine she went in that place by herself. Probably with a guy. We might lift prints off the door handles and vodka bottle. I bagged the bottle, so we might as well check it. But I don't think that'd get us much of anywhere. We've got three thousand students at Clinton U., about five hundred more at the high school, print cards in our own files on maybe two dozen.'

'How 'bout strip-searchin' every kid in town? I'll help y'out 'n' do the gals myself.'

'Yeah, sure. I almost wish we could. That or print them all, it's about the only way we'd find the thing.'

'No guarantee the woocha got one a the kids, anyhow,' Barney said.

'Woocha?'

'A bad-ass whatchamacallit. Coulda gone off 'fore the kids showed. Gotta move in mind?'

'Not really. Maybe stake out the Oakwood. I'm pretty sure the thing's gone, but there's always a chance that the kids might return.'

'Slim t'none. Y'better get some rest. Our woocha got into someone, maybe it'll fly the coop and be outa our hair. It sticks around, then we'll have us a missing person or a dead body next day or two, and maybe we'll get lucky.'

'Either way,' Jake said, 'we'll have to go public with it.'

'Y'had to remind me,' Barney muttered.

'If I didn't, Applegate would.'

'Yeah. We talked it over when he called. We're gonna hold off till noon Tuesday. Then it's press conference time if we haven't nailed it. You, me 'n' him, we'll be instant celebrities – the three stooges that panicked the nation. Oh, what fun. We better get that fucker by then.'

'I hate to just wait around.'

'No point wastin' yer time, you haven't got any leads. Just sit tight, try t'get yer mind off it.'

'Yeah.'

After hanging up, Jake finished his bourbon. He went into the kitchen to start dinner, and was peeling a potato over the sink when he realized that he had left his revolver on the sofa. He didn't go after it. For some reason, his jitters had gone away.

Maybe it was the bourbon. More likely, it was talking to Barney – talking about the thing and its eggs, and about the break-in. Especially about the break-in. He had no doubt, any more, that the creature had found a new host. It wasn't slithering around, looking for a chance to sneak up on him. It wasn't ready to lurch out of the garbage disposal in a burst of potato peelings and bite his neck.

It was up the spine of a kid who'd gone looking for fun in the wrong place.

Jake wondered if the kid was getting hungry.

Chapter Eighteen

'It was a loverly dinner,' Celia said as they left the Lobster Shanty. 'And you are a loverly person.'

'My pleasure,' Jason said.

She swept an arm around his back and pressed herself against him and kissed him. They were standing in the light beneath the restaurant's portico, but the parking valet was nowhere in sight. Neither was anyone else. Jason held her, feeling the wet heat of her mouth, the soft push of her breasts, her belly flat against his belly. He was getting hard. He knew she could feel it. She squirmed, rubbing him. He slid a hand down her back. There was only smoothness through her gown, not even a band at her waist. He caressed the firm mounds of her rump.

He thought about Dana and felt guilty. I'm doing it for you, he told her.

For me, right, he could almost hear her say. You're turned on, you bastard.

So who's going to tell on me? he asked himself. Dana might even be dead.

Don't think that. Jesus.

A car pulled into the restaurant's driveway, so they parted. Holding Celia's hand, Jason led her to the sidewalk. 'Would you like to go somewhere?' he asked.

'Sure thing.'

'I know a nice secluded place.'

'The secludeder, the better,' she said, bumped his side,

staggered, turned her ankle and said, 'Ow! Shit. Hang on.' She kicked off her high heels. Keeping her knees straight, she bent at the waist to pick up her shoes. Jason stared at the way the gown clung to her buttocks. Thoughts of Dana prevented him from stroking her. Celia straightened up, holding her shoes. 'Tough enough, walking in these things if you're sober.'

'You mean you're not sober?'

'Not entirely,' she said, speaking the words slowly and precisely. 'Nor am I entirely polluted.' She made a lopsided grin. 'Are you entirely polluted?'

'I am *un peu* polluted.'

They arrived at his car. He opened the passenger door, helped Celia in, then went around to his side. The overhead light came on when he opened the door. Celia's left arm was hooked over the seatback, drawing the gown taut across her breast. Her nipple made the glossy fabric jut. Her left leg had found its way through the slitted side of her gown. Except for a flesh-coloured elastic band wrapping the knee, it was bare to her hip. The fabric draped her inner thigh. I'll get a nice shot, Jason thought, if that little bit of gown moves slightly further to the right.

Celia grinned as if she knew what he was thinking. 'Are you getting in, or what?'

'Yeah.' He sat down behind the steering wheel and pulled the door shut. The light went off. He fumbled the key into the ignition and started the car.

Celia's hand found the back of his neck. It rubbed him. 'You tense?' she asked.

'A little, I guess.' He pulled away from the kerb.

'How come?' she asked, massaging his neck muscles. 'You aren't nervous about me, are you?'

'I think it's excitement more than nerves,' he said.

'Mmmm.'

But it's nerves, too, he thought. Christ. It hadn't gone the way he'd planned. He'd planned to get her smashed, and that part of it had worked fine; she was plenty loaded. But he hadn't planned on feeling anything. He was to play a role in the melodrama cooked up by Roland to save Dana. That's all. Act a part. Act interested and affectionate while he plied her with fine food and plenty of booze until she was plastered mindless and totally helpless.

She's just the way I want her, he told himself.

But I'm not.

It had started to go wrong the moment he saw her and thought, Dana never looked this good. Feeling like a traitor, he had tried to push the thought out of his mind. All through the evening, however, he compared the two and found Dana the loser. Celia was far more beautiful than Dana. She seemed to listen, to care about what he said. She wasn't conceited. She was wittier than Dana, sometimes breaking him up, but even her sharpest remarks seemed good-humoured and without the malice that made Dana's sarcasm a little ugly. She had a warmth, a softness, that was totally alien to the other girl.

While they ate, he had found himself more and more attracted to Celia. And he felt poisoned by guilt. He was betraying Celia by using her this way; he was betraying Dana by wanting to trade her for Celia.

'That light's . . .'

Red, he thought. But it was too late to stop, so he sped on through the intersection.

Celia's hand went away from his neck. 'You'd better concentrate on your driving,' she said. 'If you get stopped in your condition . . .'

'Yeah.' For the next block, he watched the rearview mirror.

'Are you all right?'

'Yeah.'

'Something on your mind?'

'You.'

'Me. I know, you're overwhelmed by my cheauty and barm.'

Jason smiled. 'Right, your cheauty and barm.'

'And dizzy with anticipation.'

'You're very perceptive.'

'But what is it, really? I mean, has it got something to do with Dana?'

Jason felt a jump inside his chest.

'You two were going at it pretty hot and heavy, and suddenly she's out of the picture and I'm in. Do you want to talk aboud . . . about it? I mean, this isn't some kind of a ploy to get back at her or make her jealous or something, is it?'

A ploy, all right.

He was thankful for the darkness hiding his hot face which was probably scarlet.

'It's not that at all,' he said. 'We broke up, but she didn't dump me. I dumped her. I just couldn't stand her any longer, she's such a bitch. I don't know what I ever saw in her in the first place.'

Sorry, Dana, he thought.

Eat shit, he imagined her snapping. You meant every word of it. I was never anything to you but snatch. But fair's fair, you were nothing to me but a hard cock.

He turned onto Latham Road.

'I finally realized,' he said, 'that I was missing a lot. I mean, a relationship needs to be more than screwing.'

'Two entirely different things,' Celia said.

'I don't know. I want to at least *like* the person I'm with, and it was getting so I didn't even want to be around her. She was hard and crass and mean . . . not like you. You're really a sweet person.'

'Yeah, I'm an angel.'

'Compared to her, you are.' So why am I taking you out there? I don't owe Dana a damn thing. Besides, she might already be dead (I almost hope . . . No!) and I shouldn't be talking about her like this, thinking about her like this – even though it's the truth.

I've got to do what I can for her. I owe her that much.

It's a stupid plan, anyway. It'll never work.

So if nothing happens, I take Celia home and she never has to know she was bait.

And if it works, fat chance, nobody gets hurt anyway. We nail the guy, he takes us to Dana . . .

Takes us to her body, hanging naked from a rafter, mutilated and dead . . .

But nothing will happen to Celia, either way.

Take her someplace else. Forget the whole thing. A motel, maybe. That'd be nice. Don't do this to her.

'Just up ahead,' Celia said, 'is where that guy tried to run me down.'

'Do you want a look?'

She shook her head. 'I don't even like being this close. My bike's still there. I haven' even gone back for it.'

'Should we pick it up? We could put it in the back seat.' Say yes, he thought. We'll get the bike, we'll forget about the Oakwood.

'Iss too messed up. Even if it could be repaired, I wouldn't want it anyway. I'll ged a new one if I ever want to go riding again.'

'You sure?'

'Yeah.'

Jason slowed down, flicked the arm of the turn signal, and swung the car onto the narrow road leading to the Oakwood Inn. He looked at Celia. She was staring at him.

'Where're we going?' she whispered.

'There's a parking lot. It'll be good and deserted.'

'This's where those people got killed Thursday night.'

He nodded. 'Yeah. I read about it. If you'd rather go someplace else . . .'

'No.' That was all she said. She didn't explain.

'I think we won't have to worry about being disturbed,' Jason said. 'Nobody'll come out to a place like this after what happened.'

'Maybe for the thrill.'

The road flared out. Jason steered to the right. He drove in a circle, watching his headlights sweep around the parking lot. There were no other cars. The beams met a corner of the restaurant and moved across its dark front, flashing off the windows. When they lit the door, he stopped.

'Go closer,' Celia whispered.

'Are you . . . ? Okay.' He let the car roll forward almost to the porch stairs. Then he stopped it, turned off the engine and put on the hand-brake. He left the headlights on.

Celia leaned forward, a hand against the dash, and peered through the windscreen. 'Weird,' she whispered.

'What?'

'Being this close to where it happened. Get the lights, okay?'

He pushed the knob.

Celia stared through the darkness. 'Think we could get in?' she asked.

So easy. She *wanted* to go in. Let's do it, get it over with.

'I don't know,' Jason muttered.

'Scared?' she asked. Her voice sounded a little shaky.

'Yeah. Aren't you?'

She didn't answer. She eased back into her seat. Looking at Jason, she lifted his hand and placed it on her bare thigh. 'Can you feel the gooseflesh?'

He moved his hand lightly up her leg. Yes, he could feel the gooseflesh. She must've shaved, but the nubs of hair were standing and just a bit bristly along the top of her thigh. He curved his hand down the inner side. There, the skin was smooth, incredibly smooth and soft. The fabric brushed the edge of his palm. Another inch, he thought, maybe two . . .

She'll let me, I know she will.

No. You can't mess around with her, not if you're going ahead with it.

So forget the plan. It's a dumb plan.

What if Dana's alive, maybe being kept somewhere, being raped and tortured by some maniac, and this is her only chance? You can't just write her off.

Damn it, what'll I do?

He took his hand away from Celia's leg. 'Yeah,' he said, 'gooseflesh. Are you scared or cold?'

'I got the willies,' she said. Jason could see the white of her teeth. 'You think that's racist? The willies?'

'Why would it be racist?'

'Wasn' Willy a black guy in the old movies, like in the thirties? He'd get in a haunted house and go all buggy-eyed and shaky?'

'Gee, I don't know.'

'I think tha's where the expression came from. The willies. But don't hold me to it. Wherever it came from, I got 'em.'

'I've got just the thing,' Jason said, 'for getting rid of the willies.'

'Not sure I wanna get rid of 'em. Kind of *like* the feeling. Y'know? I'm shivered inside. It's almost sexual.'

'Well, maybe this'll make you feel even more . . . shivery inside.' Huddling down against the steering wheel, he reached under the car seat and pulled out a bottle of champagne.

'Well now,' Celia said. 'That's what I call class.'

He nodded, and began to peel the foil off the top of the bottle.

The champagne had been Roland's idea. Insurance, Roland had called it. Fill her up with bubbly, you won't have any trouble at all getting her inside. With any luck, she'll pass out. You can carry her in.

It was insurance that Jason didn't need.

156

But he wanted time to think, to decide.

If we do go in, he told himself, it'll work better if she's totally smashed.

As he twisted the wire seal, Celia turned away from him. Reaching across her body, she used her left hand to roll the window down. She faced him again. 'You can shoot the cork out my window.'

'Don't want to hit you with it.'

'On a good day, I could catch the cork in my teeth.'

'This isn't a good day?'

'It's dark and I'm a trifle tipsy. So try to miss me.'

Jason pulled off the wire basket, clamped the bottle against his chest, and began to twist the knob of cork. It squeaked quietly. He aimed well in front of Celia's face and gave the cork a final turn. With a hollow pop, it shot past her nose and sailed out of the window. He heard her laugh as he rushed the erupting bottle to his mouth, spilling foam down his hand and shirt. He gulped the airy froth and choked.

'You okay?'

A few moments later, he was okay. He took a sip of the champagne, then passed the bottle of Celia. She raised it high and tilted back her head. He watched her throat work as she swallowed. With a sigh, she passed the bottle back to him. 'That's good stuff,' she said.

She faced Jason, sitting sideways and sliding her leg onto the seat. Her knee touched the side of his leg. The inner side of her thigh was turned upward. He followed the pale skin with his eyes and glanced at the patch of shadow beneath the edge of her gown. Then he raised the bottle. He took one swallow, closed his lips and pretended to drink more before handing the bottle back to her.

'Still feeling shivery?' he asked.

'Yessiree. More'n ever.' She took a drink. 'Bring any cheese and crackers?'

'Afraid I didn't think of that.'

'Maybe there's some in there,' she said, and nodded towards the Oakwood. Then she took another drink. 'It *is* a restaurant.'

'You can't be hungry.'

'Hungry, all right.' From the way she said it, Jason knew that she wasn't talking about food. She looked over the seatback. 'That's a blanket there,' she said.

Jason nodded.

'Grab it and follow me.'

Before he could object, Celia slid her leg off the seat, turned away from him, and opened her door.

'Hey, what're you doing?' he asked as she climbed out.

'I've gotta go in there.'

'Are you nuts?'

'Yup.' She swung her door shut.

Jason threw his door open and jumped out. Over the roof of the car he saw her standing in the moonlight, her back arched, the bottle high as she drank from it.

'I don't want to go in there,' he said.

She lowered the bottle. 'Come on, it'll be a trip.'

'It might be dangerous.'

'The blanket,' she said. She waved the bottle at him, then walked unsteadily, limping slightly and weaving, to the porch stairs.

Jason grabbed the blanket off the back seat and hurried after her.

She waited for him at the door of the Oakwood. After taking a drink, she handed the bottle to him. 'Ladies first,' she said in a trembling whisper. Then she opened the door. Taking hold of Jason's elbow, she led him inside and shut the door. 'Oh God, dark in here.'

'I've got matches,' Jason whispered. His heart was sledging.

'We don' need no steenking matches,' she said with a Mexican accent.

'Don't you want to see wh . . . ?'

'I like zee dark.' Her left arm went around Jason. He let the blanket fall. He put his arms around her, the champagne bottle in his right hand pressing against her back.

She felt warm, but her body shivered. When they kissed, he realized that even her chin was trembling. Her tongue went into his mouth. Her right hand caressed his rump while her left untucked the back of his shirt and went under it and roamed his back.

He eased his mouth away from her. Her face was a vague pale

shape with black holes instead of eyes and a mouth. He didn't like seeing it this way. 'I've gotta get rid of the bottle.'

'Polish id off.'

'I don't want any more.'

'Give.' He brought it to the front. Her hand covered his, then took the bottle. A moment later, he heard her swallowing. He reached through the darkness to the area below her dim face. One hand found a shoulder, the other an armpit. Once he knew what he was touching, he had no trouble locating her breasts. He took them in his hands. Celia stopped swallowing and moaned. She took a quick breath when he gently squeezed her stiff nipples.

The champagne bottle thunked the floor, startling Jason. He flinched. Celia gasped a sharp 'Ah!'

'I'm sorry,' he whispered.

'Never mind.'

A hand pressed the front of his pants. He squirmed against it, aching. He felt a small pull, then heard his zipper clicking downward.

He wished he could think. He wanted her. But not here. He wanted to get her out of here, but he wanted to feel her cool fingers on him and he wanted to put his hand through the open side of her gown and follow the smooth warm skin of her thigh upward. And then we're naked and we spread the blanket and it's not supposed to be this way. It's not the plan.

We're here now, we should go by the plan.

She didn't reach in. She tugged at his belt instead. He could hear her breathing heavily as he rubbed her breasts.

'Wait,' he gasped in a husky whisper.

'Wha'?'

'I've gotta use the john.'

'Lemme have the matches. I'll ged the place ready.'

'I'll need one to find the john.' He took the matchbook from his pocket, peeled out a match and struck it. The brightness hurt his eyes. Celia squinted against the glare.

He gave the matchbook to her, then headed for the alcove at the far end of the bar where the restrooms were located, He stepped around the card table. The match was hot on his fingertips, so he shook it out. Hands in front of him, feeling the air, he made his way slowly forward.

Behind him, a match snicked. He hurried the rest of the way to the alcove, then looked back. Celia was standing midway between the front door and the corner of the bar, straddle-legged, looking down at the blanket. She staggered and almost fell when she bent over to pick it up. With one hand she shook the blanket open. Very slowly, she raised the match to her face and puffed it out. She vanished.

Jason stared into the darkness, waiting for another match to flare. It didn't happen. Finally he turned around and felt his way along the wall. He found the door to the men's room. He turned the handle, stepped inside, and flicked the light switch.

Roland, sitting on the toilet, grinned up at him.

Chapter Nineteen

'How's it going?' Roland whispered.

Jason shook his head.

Roland pointed at his open fly. 'I assume, from that, that you're not alone.'

'She's here.' He pulled his zipper up and fastened his belt. Then he leaned back against the restroom door. He took a deep breath. He rubbed his face. 'I've got my doubts, Ro.'

'What do you mean?'

'She's a nice girl. This seems like a rotten way to use her.'

'You want to help Dana, don't you?'

'Of course. I wouldn't be here if I didn't. But it's a stupid idea, anyway. What are the chances that the guy'll come back tonight?'

'He was here last night,' Roland pointed out. 'And he made a good catch. So why shouldn't he come back and try for another?'

'It's crazy.'

'When he comes, we'll nab him.'

Jason shook his head. Pushing himself away from the door, he stepped to the sink and turned on a tap. 'Don't want her hearing us,' he said.

'Where is she?'

'Over near the front door. She was spreading the blanket.' Jason splashed water onto his face, wiped himself dry with the front of his shirt, and stepped backward until he was leaning against the door.

'Did you get her soused?' Roland asked.

'She's demolished.'

'Great.'

'I feel like a shit.'

'Nothing's going to happen to her.'

'If the guy comes . . .'

'We'll nail him. And he'll take us to Dana.'

'Celia, she'll know I used her if the guy really shows up.'

'What do you care? She can't do anything about it. It's not like you kidnapped her or something, she came here of her own free will.'

'She didn't plan to get used for bait.'

'Tough toenails. So maybe she'll be pissed. But you'll find Dana. It'll be worth it, right?'

'I guess.'

Roland stood up. 'We'd better get out there,' he said, and turned off the tap. 'Don't want our madman running off with her while we're in here gabbing about it. You go over to her, but be quiet about it. Don't say anything. If this is going to work, she needs to conk out.'

'She was pretty wired when I left her.'

'Turned on?'

'Yeah, and jittery.'

'If she's awake, fuck her. That'll calm her down. Soon as she's asleep, get back here. She won't be much of a decoy if you're right there with her.'

'I don't know,' Jason muttered.

'You don't know what?'

'This whole thing. Maybe I'll just take her home.'

'Don't be a jerk.'

'Ro, she's *nice*. I like her.'

'Just going to let Dana turn in the wind?'

Jason twisted his face as if he had a gut-ache. That phrase got him, Roland thought – turning in the wind. 'I'll see how it goes,' he muttered.

Roland waved him away from the door, then flicked off the light and slowly turned the knob. The latch disengaged without a sound. The hinges were silent as he eased the door open. He grinned. He'd thought of everything. Earlier, after popping open the lock with a simple twist of his knife point, he had sprayed oil on the latch and knob and hinges.

His bare feet were silent on the hardwood floor. He could hear Jason's footsteps behind him, but they weren't very loud. Running a hand along the wall, he found the entryway and stopped beneath it.

Jason put a hand on his shoulder.

The light in the bathroom had messed up Roland's night vision. Except for grey areas near the windows, everything looked black. He listened, but heard only his own heartbeat and Jason breathing close to his ear. Jason sounded like he'd just finished a sprint. His breath smelled of liquor.

Roland turned sideways, his back to the edge of the entryway. He found Jason's shirt and gave it a slight tug. Jason stepped past him and started through the room.

Going great, Roland thought.

He hoped that Celia was still awake. He hoped that Jason would fuck her. If that happened, he'd sneak up close and have a ringside seat. Nothing to see, but plenty to hear. And he'd be able to imagine the rest. He'd looked her over good yesterday at the mall – her and her friend, the cute one.

Could've been that one tonight. But this was fine. This was great. The date gimmick might not have worked on Celia's friend, and he liked the date gimmick. The bait-date. What a laugh. People were such damned fun to manipulate. Mess around some with their heads, they'll do whatever you want.

So how's it going, Jason old pal? Ready to pork her?

Pork.

Roland laughed softly, caught himself at it, and pressed his lips together hard.

He heard quiet footfalls.

Jason was coming back.

'She's zonked,' Jason whispered.

Shit. So much for the good-time show. 'Great,' Roland said.

'So where do we hide? We should probably get closer. Maybe if one of us waits behind the bar?'

'Good idea.'

'You got the handcuffs?'

'Right here.' Roland patted a front pocket of his jeans.

'What about my hammer?'

Roland didn't answer.

'You had it when I dropped you off.'

'I'm thinking.'

'I'm not gonna jump the guy bare-handed.'

'Must've left it in the john,' he said. 'Yeah.'

'Well, go find it. Christ.'

Roland made his way back to the restroom. He entered and quietly shut the door. He turned on the light. The claw hammer was propped against the wall beside the toilet. He had placed it there, out of sight, intending to return for it once Jason realized he was without a weapon.

He picked it up. It still had a price sticker on its handle. They had bought it that afternoon at a hardware store for Jason to use against the fabricated maniac.

Roland pushed its wooden handle under his belt.

He popped open the snap of his knife case, removed the knife, and folded out the blade. It made a quiet click as it locked into place.

Facing the restroom door, Roland flipped off the light. He opened the door. 'Jase?' he asked in a loud whisper.

'Find it?'

'Yeah, but come here.'

He listened to the shuffle of Jason's shoes on the floor.

'What?'

'Come in here a minute, we've got to talk.'

Jason stepped inside and shut the door. 'What is it?'

'I'm getting scared.'

'Oh, for Christ . . .'

'No, really.' He reached out with his left hand, found Jason's shoulder, and gripped it. 'I never really believed the guy'd show up, but I don't know any more. What if he does, and we can't handle him? I mean, he might kill us all.'

'Calm down, Ro. My God. There's two of us, and we'll have the element of surprise, and besides which, he isn't gonna show up anyway. We'll try it for a couple hours, then I'll take Celia home and . . .'

Roland punched the knife into Jason's belly. The impact slammed him against the door. Roland twisted the knife hard, pulled it out and shoved it in again. His wrist was grabbed. He jerked the knife out, freeing his bloody hand from Jason's grip. Before he could strike again, a blow to his chest knocked him backwards. He staggered through the darkness and started to fall. The edge of something – the sink? – pounded his rump. His feet slid forward on the wet tiles. He was going down. Throwing back his arms, he caught the sink with both elbows and braced himself up as he struggled to get his legs under him. His feet kept sliding away.

The light came on.

He saw Jason on his knees, a shoulder against the door. The wall around the light switch was smeared with bloody hand-prints as if Jason had found it essential to get the light on, to *see* what was happening. He turned his head and looked at Roland. His face was the colour of dry ashes. His eyes were bugged out, his mouth so wide open that the corners of his lips had split and blood trickled down the sides of his chin.

Most of the floor between Jason and Roland was coated with a spreading red puddle. Roland, legs stretched out, had his heels in it. Still braced up, he bent his knees and drew in his legs until they were directly beneath him. Carefully, he stood up. With his left hand on the sink, he held himself steady.

Jason clutched the doorknob and started to get up. His feet slipped away. He landed on his rump with a quiet splash of blood.

Roland switched the knife to his left hand. He pulled the hammer from his belt and started forward slowly, not daring to lift his feet, sliding them instead, skating over the slippery tiles. Jason gaped at him and raised a hand to ward off the blow. Roland swung, hammering the back of his wrist. The arm flopped aside. He brought the hammer down with all his strength on top of Jason's head. It went in only half an inch. Lifting it, he saw a quarter-size indentation with matted hair inside. Blood began to fill the hole. He pounded once more, trying for the same place. The hammer, slightly off target, nicked a half-moon of skull off the edge of the original hole, smacked up a quick spray of blood and sank in deep.

Roland left the hammer embedded. He slid himself backwards to admire his work. Jason was seated on the floor with his back against the door, his legs stretched out, his arms hanging at his sides. His pants and the lower half of his shirt were sodden with blood. His pouring head hung forward, chin against his chest. He wore the hammer like a weird party hat.

Though Jason didn't move, the amount of blood spilling out from under the hammer meant that he wasn't dead yet.

Some folks don't die easy, Roland thought.

The thought surprised him. After all, Jason was only his second victim, and Dana hadn't been a problem.

But he *knew* there had been others – some who'd been very tough to kill. No big mystery, he told himself. The memories of the other kills had to be coming from his friend. Smiling, he rubbed the bulge on the back of his neck. He felt it squirm a bit, and a small wave of pleasure washed through him.

Get on with it, he thought.

He skated closer to Jason. Hanging onto the doorknob, he squatted and slashed open Jason's throat.

He stood up, tugged the hammer free and jammed its handle under his belt. He closed his knife and pushed it into its leather case. But he didn't bother to snap the case shut. Digging a hand into a front pocket of his jeans, he took out the handcuffs.

Jason's weight was against the door. He tumbled onto his side when Roland opened it.

Roland flipped off the light, stepped out, and shut the door.

At first his feet were slippery against the floor. But they became less slippery with each step. He stopped beneath the entryway to wait for his eyes to adjust to the darkness.

As he stood there, he felt a few tentative beats of pleasure. They came from his friend. Hints of the maddening ecstasy it would blast through him just a few minutes from now. Licking his dry lips, he wondered why it hadn't given him a good zap for wasting Jason.

He wondered, then he knew. Jason had simply been in the way – an obstacle, not the real target. You just get a little boost for taking him out, the biggy is saved for when you deliver Celia.

Makes perfect sense, he thought, and was rewarded with a small thrill.

You don't know, he thought. Shit, maybe you do, maybe you do. This is just my thing. I've always wanted to pull this kind of stuff, just never had the guts till you came along. I don't need your zaps to get a charge out of it.

But the zaps are great.

Oh yes, oh yes. And I'll get one soon.

His heart was thudding, his mouth dry, his breath trembling, his penis growing hard.

It was almost time. He could see a few things, now, in the darkness: the vague shape of the card table with some bottles and glasses on top, the long flat surface of the bar counter and a corner of something dark – maybe Jason's blanket – caught in a spill of grey light from a window.

He couldn't see Celia.

She had to be there. Asleep on the blanket.

He couldn't hear her, either. Just his own heart and breathing.

She's there unless she heard us in the can, he thought.

We didn't make much noise. Jason hardly made a sound. There hadn't been anything to hear except maybe a couple of thuds. If she was good and plastered, she should've slept through all that.

Roland touched his knife case. The flap was loose. Beneath it, the brass butt of the knife handle felt gummy. He left the knife inside its case. He wouldn't be needing it for a while.

He only needed the cuffs.

On the seat of his jeans, he wiped as much blood as possible off his hands.

He held one bracelet in his right hand, letting the other dangle by its chain, and started forward.

His bare feet snicked each time he lifted one off the floor. With each step, his heart pumped harder, his breath grew more raspy. Sweat stung his eyes and trickled down his sides. He walked with a slight stoop to ease the pressure of his erect penis against his jeans. He grinned. He felt like this now, and he wasn't even getting any new surges from his friend. Those were yet to come.

He halted at the foot of the blanket. He still couldn't see Celia. *What if she's gone!*

Then he heard her. She was taking long slow breaths.

Roland crouched. He reached out carefully until his hand met the blanket. He felt something through its softness – probably a leg – and realized that Celia must have covered herself after lying down.

On his knees, Roland moved to her side. He searched with one hand for the edge of the blanket, found it and lifted it. As he uncovered her, she mumbled something but didn't awaken.

He could see her now, in spite of the darkness. She was naked, and enough light found her skin to give it a vague, dusky hue. She lay on her back. Her legs were slightly apart, bare except for darker wrappings at her knees. Her right arm, inches from Roland's knee, lay against her side. The wrapped elbow was bent slightly, and her hand rested with curled fingers just above the jut of her hipbone. Her other arm was high, elbow pointing off to the side, hand beneath her head for a cushion.

Roland stared at the small patch of darkness between her legs. She didn't have a bush like Dana. She must trim herself down there, he though.

He gazed at her breasts. They were dim mounds, tipped with darkness. They rose and fell slightly as she breathed.

With his left hand, he reached forward and touched the nearer breast. It was so smooth. It felt like velvet. The nipple, too. But the nipple seemed to squirm under his touch, rumpling and rising stiff.

Celia's breathing changed.

'Hi there,' she whispered in a groggy voice. 'Wha' took you so long?'

Roland squeezed her breast, then took his hand away.

Oh God, he ached! He was getting surges now, waves that pounded through him, shaking him.

'Jason?' Celia asked.

'Jason's not here. Jason . . .' and Roland suddenly shrieked, 'HAD SOME DYING TO DO!' He grabbed her wrist and snapped a cuff around it.

In an instant, before Celia could begin to struggle or scream, he whipped the other cuff around his own left wrist.

Chapter Twenty

Alison woke up. There was sunlight on her bed. The warm breeze drifting through her open window smelled of flowers and grass. A raucous bird was squawking as if annoyed by the pleasant chirping of its neighbours. The bells of a church, somewhere in the distance, pealed a tune. Alison imagined a congregation singing along – 'In the sweet, bye 'n' bye, we will meet on that beautiful shore . . .'

Feeling good, she stretched beneath her sheet. Then she slipped the sheet aside and was surprised for a moment to see that she was wearing her new blue negligee.

She had planned to save it for a special occasion. Maybe last night had counted as one, somehow.

She remembered coming up to her attic room after playing Trivial Pursuit and watching *The Howling* on television with Helen, remembered sitting at her desk and staring at the snapshots of Evan pinned to her bulletin board, feeling empty and alone, wondering about him. He was probably making it with Tracy More-organ Morgan. The bastard. Wishing for a way to hurt him, she had taken down all the photos and started to rip one into tiny pieces. The snapshot showed her holding Evan's hand. Celia had taken it two weeks ago on the lawn behind Bennet Hall. Evan was wearing a T-shirt with the logo 'Poets do it with rhythm'. He had a silly look on his face because Celia, instead of telling them to say cheese, announced, 'Say, "I am a cunning linguist." '

By the time Alison had ripped the photo apart and watched its tiny bits float down into the wastebasket, she was in tears. She couldn't bear to destroy any more, so she had made a neat stack of the rest, put a rubber band around them, and dropped them into the top drawer of her desk.

Hurting, she had taken off her clothes and opened her dresser. She had planned to wear one of her ordinary nightgowns, but the new one, blue and glossy, caught her eye. There was no reason to save it, no one to save it for. She might as well enjoy it. So she put the negligee on, sighing as it slid over her skin. She wiped her eyes and gazed at her reflection in the mirror. Her breasts were plainly visible through the gauzy top. She shrugged so that one of the spaghetti straps slipped off her shoulder. Eat your heart out, Evan, she thought. You'd go ape if you ever saw me in this, but you never will. Tough luck, shithead.

The memories brought back some of last night's pain, stealing pleasure from the good feel of lying on the sunlit bed with the breeze sliding over her.

Alison got up and went to the window. It looked beautiful out there. She needed to *do* something, find a way to enjoy herself. Sundays had been fine before Evan, and they could be fine again.

This would be a great day for a long walk. Go to Jack-in-the-Box for one of those crescent rolls with cheese, sausage and egg inside. Forget about studying, pick up a brand-new paperback at the newsstand – a good juicy thriller. Later on, head over to the quad with the book and a radio and spend a couple of hours lying in the sun. Or go to the park for your sunbathing, go down by the stream. You'd have privacy there. But the quad was bound to be lively on a day like this. Depends. Would you rather be alone or have company and maybe meet someone? There'd be a lot of guys at the quad. Just decide when the time comes.

She crossed the bedroom, enjoying the way the negligee clung round her. She felt pretty fine again.

What was that Hemingway story? A kid, probably Nick Adams, went to bed at night feeling awful because he had broken up with his girlfriend. Saw her with another guy? The thing of it was, the last line. He went to bed feeling rotten, and the next morning he was awake half an hour before he remembered that he had a broken heart.

Great stuff.

Nick Winston didn't know what he was talking about, dumping on Hemingway.

Maybe drop by Wally's tonight. Maybe Nick'll be there.

Do I really want to see him again?

She peeled the negligee over her head, folded it neatly, and placed it in the dresser drawer. She rolled deodorant onto her armpits. A bath would be nice. Save it for this afternoon when you're finished lying out.

She put on panties, went to her closet and slipped a sleeveless yellow sundress over her head. Then she stepped into sandals. She took her shoulder bag from the dresser top and left her room.

At the bottom of the attic stairs she entered the bathroom. She used the toilet, washed, brushed her teeth, brushed her hair, and hurried out.

She found Helen sitting cross-legged on the living-room carpet with the newspaper spread in front of her, a box of powdered doughnuts on the lap of her rather tattered pink nightgown, and a mug of coffee on the floor near one knee. 'What-ho,' Helen greeted her, looking up.

'Morning.'

'You're looking perky.'

'Perk perk. And how are you this fine morning?'

'Fine, is it?'

' "God's in his heaven, all's right with the world." '

'Hey, what's with you, a midnight visitor sneak into your room?'

'No such luck.'

Helen lifted the box off her lap and held it towards Alison. 'Doughnut?'

'Thanks anyway. I'm going to hike over to Jack-in-the-Box and get a sausage crescent. Want to come along?'

Helen shook her head, cheeks wobbling. 'I don't think so. I'd have to get dressed.'

'You could just throw on your rain-gear.'

'Har.' She bit into a doughnut, crumbs and white powder falling onto the exposed tops of her breasts and between them.

'Celia up yet?'

Helen shrugged. She chewed for a moment, then took a drink of coffee. 'Celia may or may not be up, but wherever she is or isn't up, it isn't here.'

'She didn't come back?'

'It would appear that she found a more suitable abode of the night.'

'That bodes well for her.'

Helen rolled her eyes upward. 'Spare me.'

'So she and Jason must've hit it off,' Alison said.

'Not necessarily. They could've been in a traffic accident.'

Alison ignored the remark. 'I just hope it turns into something.'

'No doubt it turned into an orgy.'

'No, I mean it. She likes to pretend she enjoys going through one guy after another, but she only got that way after Mark dumped her.'

'Yeah, that's when she started screwing around.'

'It'd be nice if she'd get really involved with someone.'

'But a freshman?'

'He must have something going for him,' Alison said, 'or she wouldn't have spent the night. She almost never stays over with a guy.'

Grinning, Helen said, 'Think they stayed in his dorm room with el weirdo, Roland? Wouldn't that be the height of funzies?'

'The height of vomitus.'

'Maybe Roland joined in. A big beef sandwich with them as bread and Celia as the meat.'

'You're a very disturbed person, Helen.'

'Think about it.'

'I'm sure they didn't go to Jason's room. Not if that disgusting yuck was going to be there. They probably shacked up in a motel, or maybe they just parked someplace.' Or rolled out a sleeping bag in a field, she thought, like Robert Jordan and Maria. The warm night would've been fine for that.

'When she gets back,' Helen said, 'I'm sure she'll tell us all about it.' With that, she stuffed the remaining chunk of doughnut into her mouth and picked up the comic section.

'See you later,' Alison said.

Helen nodded.

Alison stepped to the front door and pulled it open. On the wooden landing stood a glass vase filled with yellow daffodils. An envelope was propped against the vase. She stared at the bright flowers, at the envelope. Frowning, she stroked her lips.

They're probably not for me, she thought.

But her heart was beating fast.

Crouching, she lifted the envelope. Her name was written on it. Hands trembling, she tore open the envelope and pulled out the papers inside. They fluttered as she unfolded them.

Three typed pages. Signed at the end of the last page by Evan.

Dearest Alison,

I am loathsome scum, a worm, a maggot. You would be perfectly justified in spitting on this missive and flushing the flowers down the nearest toilet. If you are still reading, however, let me tell you that you certainly could not detest me more than I detest myself.

There is no excuse for my behaviour of Friday night. It was childish and vile to show up at Gabby's with Tracy. What can I say? I was blinded by the pain of your rejection, and I desired to punish you. It was a foolish, contemptible gesture. Let me assure you, however, that the manoeuvre backfired. As much torment as I may have caused you, I caused myself more.

Let me also make it clear that I have no interest in Tracy. The sole reason I invited her out was to rub her in your face and, hopefully, to make you jealous. I do not care for her at all. Though you may find this difficult to believe (due to her well-deserved reputation and your opinion that I have nothing on my mind except sex), we did not indulge in any intimacies whatsoever. I even avoided a goodnight kiss when we parted.

I spent last night alone in my apartment, miserable, wanting to be with you but too ashamed to telephone or come over and see you. I thought about you constantly, remembering how you look and the sound of your voice and the way you laugh. I thought about the many good times we shared, and no, not just the sex (though I couldn't help thinking about that, also – especially how it feels when we are so sweetly joined, as if we are one). I even spent some time gazing at your photographs in the school yearbooks, but it was unbearable to look at frozen images of your face and know that I had possibly lost you forever.

When I slept, I dreamed of you. I dreamed that you came into my room and sat down on the edge of my bed and took hold of my hand. In my dream, I began to weep and tell you that I was sorry. I said that I never meant to hurt you, that I loved you and would do anything for your forgiveness. You said nothing, but you bent down and kissed me. I woke up, then, and I was never so sorry to wake up from any dream. My pillow was wet with tears. (I realize that all this must sound maudlin, but I want you to know everything, no matter how embarrassing it may seem in the light of day.)

Right now, it is three in the morning. I got up, after that dream, and sat down at my typewriter to let you know how I feel. I am sure it is too much to hope for easy forgiveness. The dream was a fantasy, the wishful thinking of a tormented mind. I realize that my treatment of you was rash and abominable, and that you probably prefer never to see me again. I wouldn't blame you at all.

If you wish to have nothing more to do with me, I suppose I will learn to live with it. I suppose I will have no choice, short of shuffling off these mortal coils with a bare bodkin. (Forget I said that; I don't believe I am that desperate, though morbid thoughts along those lines have crossed my mind.)

Perhaps I won't deliver this to you. Perhaps I'll burn it, I don't know.

I miss you, Alison. I wish that I could make everything right again, that I could turn time backward to Thursday afternoon when I started all this stupid, disgusting behaviour. But life doesn't work that way. You can't just make the bad things go away, no matter how much you may want to. (There, I'm so distraught that I've ended my sentence with a preposition – now I *know* I'll burn this.)

I love you.

I hope that you don't hate me.

I am miserable without you, but it's all my own fault and I know that I deserve the misery.

If this is the end, it is the end.

Have a good life, Alison.

All my love,

Evan

Alison's mind felt numb. She folded the letter, slipped it inside the envelope, and picked up the vase of daffodils. She carried it into the house, nudging the door shut with her rump.

'What's the deal?' Helen called.

Alison shook her head. She didn't trust herself to speak; her voice would shake and she might cry.

'Well, all *right*, flowers. Told you he'd see the light.'

She climbed the stairs to her room, placed the vase on her dresser, and sat on her bed. She pulled the pages out of the envelope and read them again.

He wrote about a dream. *This* was like a dream. She almost couldn't believe that he had written such a letter. The anguish in it, the desperation. Even a threat, in the *Hamlet* allusion, of suicide – which he was quick to retract but which remained, nonetheless.

Alison told herself that she ought to be delighted. Isn't this what she had wanted; to have him repent and plead for her to take him back? But she wasn't delighted. The letter was almost disturbing. Could she mean that much to him?

Did she *want* to mean that much to him?

He sounded almost obsessed.

Alison lay down on her bed, the letter pressed to her belly, and stared at the ceiling. She kicked off a sandal, heard it thump the floor, then kicked off the other. She felt exhausted, as if she had just come back from an endless walk. She took a deep breath. Her lungs seemed to tremble as she exhaled.

You wanted him back, didn't you? Well, he's yours. If you want him.

You'll have to do something.

Something.

Evan's probably sitting in his apartment, staring at the telephone, waiting, wondering if you sneered when you read his message, or if you wept. And very possibly thinking he had been a fool to open himself up that way.

It's cruel to make him wait.

I should go downstairs, right now, and call him. Or walk over to his apartment. Make it like his dream. Don't say anything when he opens the door, just kiss him.

Don't make it that easy on him.

Maybe I don't want to go back to him at all.

What should I do? Maybe pretend I didn't get the flowers and note, go along as if nothing happened.

Alison lay there, wondering. She felt stunned, confused, hopeful but a little bit frightened.

She pulled the pillow down over her face. The dark was nice. The soft pillow felt good.

Later, she thought. I'll do something about it later.

Chapter Twenty-one

Roland couldn't understand. He had taken off the cuffs before pushing her down the cellar stairs, and he hadn't put them back on because she was beyond struggling and he needed both hands free. So how come, now that he was done, he was suddenly cuffed to her again? It didn't make sense.

He knew that he hadn't attached the manacles again.

Had *she* done it? No. Huh-uh. She's dead.

Then how?

He felt a tingle of fear.

As he dug into the pocket where he kept the key, he wondered vaguely why he was wearing clothes at all. Hadn't he left them upstairs?

The key wasn't there.

Don't worry, you'll find it. You've *got* to find it.

Fighting panic, he searched every pocket. The key was gone.

This can't be happening to me, he thought.

Fortunately, he had turned on the overhead light before following Celia into the cellar. The bulb cast only a dim yellow glow, but it should be enough. Getting to his knees, he scanned the concrete floor. The area surrounding them was pooled with blood. Could the key be *under* the blood? He began to sweep his free hand through the wet layer.

Out of a corner of his eye, he thought he saw Celia grin.

175

No.

He looked directly at her. She was scalped, her skull caved in (and brain gone, don't forget that), her eyes shut, her face a mask of blood, and she was *grinning*.

Her eyelids slid up.

'YOU'RE DEAD!' he shrieked.

Her jaw dropped. Her tongue lolled out. The handcuff key lay near the end of her tongue.

He reached for it.

Celia's teeth snapped shut on his fingers. Crying out in agony, he jerked his hand back. The stumps of three severed fingers spouted blood.

In horror, he watched her chew his fingers.

The cellar suddenly went dark.

He heard the stairway creak.

'Who's there?' he yelled.

No answer came, but Roland knew who was there. He knew. He began to whimper.

'Leave me alone!' he cried. 'Go away!'

In a mocking sing-song, a voice in the darkness chanted, 'I don't *thinnnk* sooo.' Dana's voice.

'Youuu are go-ing to diiie noww,' sang Jason.

The voices came from high on the cellar stairs, but something grabbed the front of Roland's shirt (Celia's hand?) and tugged him. He toppled forward. Onto her. Her legs locked around him. Her hands (why wasn't one cuffed to him any more?) clutched his hair and forced his face down. Down against her face. She pressed his mouth against her mouth. She huffed. Into Roland's mouth gushed the mush and splintered bones of his half-masticated fingers.

He started to choke.

And he woke up, gasping for air. For a moment, he thought he must still be in his dream.

But the bulb still glowed from the cellar ceiling. He wasn't on top of Celia's body; he was sprawled on the concrete floor beside it. Quickly, he lifted his hands. Though they both trembled violently, neither was cuffed and he still had all his fingers.

He glanced towards the cellar stairs. Nobody there. Of course not.

Just a nightmare.

As Roland sat up, his bare back came unstuck from the floor.

He looked around and picked up his knife, but he didn't see the handcuffs. Then he remembered leaving them upstairs with his clothes.

He groaned as he struggled to his feet. His body felt tight and chilled. His muscles were sore. It had been madness, allowing himself to fall asleep down here. What if he had slept through the night?

He was confident, however, that he had only been asleep for an hour or two. There would still be plenty of time to sneak away under cover of darkness.

He climbed the cellar stairs as quickly as his stiff muscles permitted, and opened the door. The brightness of day stung his eyes. He cowered, shielding his face. Sickened, he saw himself shrivel and crumble to dust like a vampire. He wanted to turn away from the light, rush down into the comforting gloom of the cellar.

But the warmth felt good. As he stood hunched in the doorway, the deep chill seemed to be drawn out of his body. As the chill diminished, so did his panic.

Major fuck-up, he told himself. Not the end of the world, though.

Consider it a challenge.

Right.

He looked down at himself. His naked body was crimson and flecked with gore.

A challenge.

He was no longer cold, but he felt shivery inside as if he might start to cry.

If anybody sees me like this . . .

I'll figure out something.

Oh God, how could I have fallen asleep? How could I have slept till *morning*?

He rubbed his sticky face, let out a trembling sigh, and stepped to the kitchen's batwing doors. Before opening them, he scanned the dining area. He listened. Satisfied that he was alone in the restaurant, he pushed through the doors.

Near the front, along with the step ladder, vacuum cleaner,

toolbox and cans of cleaning fluids, he found several rags and old towels. The few rags were filthy, but two of the towels seemed reasonably clean. He took them with him.

He stepped to a window and looked out. His heart gave a sick lurch when he saw the car in the parking lot.

Just Jason's car.

He turned away from the window. His shirt, pants and handcuffs were on the floor near the rumpled blanket. Celia's neatly folded gown lay on top of the bar counter.

Roland picked up his T-shirt. It was one of his favourites, orange with the slogan 'Trust me' printed beneath a colourful, monstrous face. It was stiff with dried blood. He was about to throw it down when an idea came to him.

Why not *wear* his bloody clothes? He could probably walk right up to his dorm room in them. With his reputation, anyone seeing him would just assume it was another gag.

But he might be seen on the way back to campus. Townies didn't know about his reputation for bizarre behaviour.

Muttering, 'Shit,' he threw the shirt down.

He knew that he could wash the blood from his hair and body. No problem there. But he needed clothes. Jason's, he knew, were even worse off than his. Only Celia's gown was bloodless. No way, he thought. Talk about conspicuous.

If he'd had any brains, he would've stripped before he opened up Jason.

He felt trapped.

There *must* be a way out. Think!

Where there is a problem, there is a solution. There has to be.

Problem. I can't leave here in bloody clothes. I can't leave here naked. I can't wear Celia's gown.

Why is it a problem? Because if I'm seen by the wrong people, I might get arrested.

Solution?

Obvious. Don't get seen. Stay here. Until say three o'clock in the morning.

Somebody might come. Like that guy yesterday.

Roland shuddered.

That guy yesterday.

That guy *knew*.

Roland had been inside the restaurant no more than ten minutes when he heard a car and rushed to the window. Out of the car stepped a man in boots and leather clothes, a man wearing a gun on his belt and carrying a machete. The sight of him sent an icy surge along Roland's spine. Memories filled his mind of other men, in other times, dressed in protective garments and carrying sharp weapons: axes, scythes, sabres, long-bladed knives. Other men who knew, just as this one did.

Confused and terrified, Roland had fled out of the rear door and hidden in the field behind the restaurant. Lying in the weeds, he had waited until his panic subsided. Then he had crept through the field, keeping low, working his way around the restaurant until he could see the parking lot.

Who *was* this man?

A cortez.

What the hell is a cortez? Roland wondered, and his mind suddenly reeled with images of carnage: bearded soldiers with swords and battle-axes slaughtering Indians beneath a blood-red sky. In the background stood a strange pyramid. As quickly as the images had come, they were gone.

That Cortez, Roland thought. My God. He remembered reading an article in *National Geographic* a few years ago. His parents had a subscription, and he always used to look through the magazines for pictures of bare-breasted natives. But this one article had caught his attention, and he'd read it. All about the Aztecs, how they not only offered the hearts of their victims as sacrifices to the sun god, but also how they ate the captured warriors. The greatest delicacy was the brain, and it always went to the high priests.

The writer of the article theorized that primitive cultures such as the Aztecs turned to cannibalism because they required protein and had no cattle. He was wrong, Roland realized, and grinned. Boy, was he wrong. The Aztecs had friends up their necks.

And Cortez, with his conquistadors, made mincemeat out of them.

So that's why this guy who went into the restaurant with the machete is a Cortez. One who knows, and therefore threatens the existence of my friend – and me.

Lying in the field, Roland understood why he feared the man

so much. The man should be killed, but he felt no urge to attempt it. Better to remain hidden.

After the man finally left, Roland entered the restaurant. He climbed down the cellar steps. Finding a gooey smear on the concrete behind the stairway, he trembled with rage and sorrow at what the Cortez had done.

I'll get him, he thought.

No, he's too dangerous. Better to get far away from one who knows. Leave town.

Not tonight, though. Stay tonight for Celia.

What about her girlfriend? I want that one, too.

We'll see.

She would be worth a little risk, he thought. He remembered how she had looked when he saw her at the mall – that lovely, innocent face, that jumpsuit with the zipper down the front, the way the fabric hugged the mounds of her breasts.

His friend gave him a quick hot surge of pleasure.

Roland came out of his reverie and found himself standing over the blanket and bloody clothes. His penis was stiff, but it shrank quickly as he once again confronted his plight.

If he stayed here to wait for darkness, he would be risking a return of the Cortez.

I'll think of something, he told himself.

He straightened the blanket, tossed his T-shirt and jeans and Celia's gown into its centre, rolled it up and carried it into the restroom. The air in there was heavy with odours of blood and faeces. He shook open the blanket, the clothes falling out, and spread it over Jason's corpse.

The sink had a mirror above it. Except for pale skin around his eyes as if he had worn goggles last night, Roland's face was painted with blood that had dried and turned a shade of red-brown. Locks of hair were glued to his forehead. A bit of something clung to one eyebrow. He picked it off, but it adhered to his finger. He flicked it with his thumbnail and watched it stick to the wall under the mirror.

He turned the tap on, bent over the sink, and began to clean himself, using one of the towels as a washcloth. He didn't like the noise of the splashing water. It deafened him to other sounds. A car could drive into the parking lot, someone could sneak up behind him . . . He shut the water off. As he listened, he straightened enough to see himself in the mirror. His face and neck were clean.

He turned the tap on again and resumed washing himself, this time standing back from the sink, flooding the towel with warm water and slopping it against himself. The water spilled down his body, sluicing off blood. He rubbed his skin vigorously, wrung the pink residue from the towel, wetted the towel again and repeated the process. Soon he was standing in a shallow pool of water and blood but the front of his body was almost spotless.

He shut off the tap, listened, fought an urge to venture into the bar area for a glance out of a front window, and turned the water on again. He began the task of washing his back. This was more difficult.

Restaurants ought to have showers, he thought, for occasions like this. He grinned.

When he supposed he must've got most of it off, he splashed across the floor until he was standing almost at the restroom door. There, he looked over his shoulder. He was far enough from the mirror so that it reflected his back all the way down past his rump. The green-yellow bruise ran down his spine and angled across his right buttock, but he saw no blood.

He used the other towel to dry himself. Now that he was clean and dry, he was very careful not to slip on the puddled tiles. He skated slowly along as he worked at his few remaining chores.

After draping the towel over one shoulder, he spent a few minutes at the sink washing his knife and handcuffs. He retrieved his shoes and socks from the space behind the toilet. He carried them, along with the knife and cuffs, to the restroom door. He opened the door and tossed them onto the hardwood floor outside.

Crouching beside Jason's covered body, he flung the blanket aside and took the car keys from a pocket of Jason's trousers. His hand got bloody again doing it, and he sighed. He found Jason's wallet in a rear pocket, removed the student ID and the driver's licence. After making sure nothing remained in the wallet to identify its owner, he flushed the cards down the toilet.

He picked up his jeans. In the dorm yesterday he had removed everything from his pockets that could be used to identify him.

(The Skidrow Slasher, he knew, had been caught because the idiot had lost his wallet, driver's licence and all, on a hillside while fleeing from a break-in.) He took the handcuff key from the right front pocket and was about to toss the jeans down again when it occurred to him that they didn't look too bad.

They were wet from lying on the floor. They were matted with blood. But they *were* blue jeans.

He spent a while at the sink, scrubbing them with hot water and wringing them out. When he shook them open, he found that the stains were not especially noticeable.

He left the restroom with them. Leaning against a wall by the door, he cleaned his feet. He stepped into the damp clinging jeans and pulled them up.

You're in business, pal.

A warm sunny day like this, nobody would think twice about seeing a guy shirtless. And nobody except the Cortez would react to the bruise up his back.

Roland put on his shoes and socks. He folded his knife shut and slipped it into the case on his belt. He stuffed Jason's car keys, the handcuffs and their key into a front pocket of his jeans.

All set.

He was about to leave when he remembered that he had left the spray-can of oil in the restroom behind the toilet. It would have his fingerprints.

Fuck it, he thought. I've already got my shoes on. I'm not going back in there.

His prints were probably all over the restaurant. Big deal.

The area in front of the bar looked okay. There were some smears on the floor, but no large quantities of blood. He pulled the towel off his shoulder, spent a few moments scrubbing the area, then tossed the towel behind the bar. He picked up the empty champagne bottle and set it on the card table.

Was he forgetting anything?

Probably.

Who cares? Even if someone finds the bodies today, it'll take a while to identify them. They won't have a clue as to who did this until they've figured out who Jason and Celia are. By then, I'll be on the road.

Roland shut the front door behind him, saw Jason's car, and

went back into the restaurant. He walked quickly around the corner to the dining area, crouched and opened the toolbox. There were several screwdrivers inside. He took out the largest and went outside again.

It took only a few minutes to remove both licence plates from Jason's car. He took them to the edge of the parking lot and sailed them into the weeds.

Then he returned to Jason's car. He opened the trunk, looked inside, and shut it. He opened a back door and looked along the seat and floor. Fine.

He climbed in behind the steering wheel. The warmth of the car felt good. On the floor in front of the passenger seat was Celia's purse. He opened it and found her wallet. Rather than taking time to search it, he stuffed the entire wallet into a back pocket of his jeans. He found her key chain and pocketed it. Then he inspected the rest of the purse's contents, making sure that nothing remained to identify its owner.

He searched the car's glove compartment. A registration slip gave Jason's name, so he put it into his pocket.

That appeared to be it.

Unless he had missed something, Jason's car was now stripped of everything that might lead to a quick identification of its owner or last night's passenger.

Roland drove away from the Oakwood Inn.

Yesterday afternoon he had parked Dana's VW beetle on a residential street and hiked the final mile or more to the restaurant. Now he drove back to the place where he had left her car. It was still there, along a lengthy stretch of kerb between two expensive-looking ranch-style houses. Across the street, an oriental man in a pith helmet was rolling a power mower down a couple of boards leading from the tail of his battered pickup truck. Otherwise, the neighbourhood looked deserted.

Roland turned down a side road and parked near the far corner. He stuffed Celia's purse under the front seat. Then he pushed down the lock buttons of all the doors and climbed out.

He strolled back to Dana's car. It was unlocked, just as he had left it. Feeling around beneath the driver's seat, he found Dana's keys. The engine turned over without any trouble, and he drove away.

You did it, he thought. You pulled it off.

He let out a deep sigh, rolled down the window, and rested his elbow on the sill. The warm air came in, caressing him.

He liked this neighbourhood. Finding himself in no hurry to return to campus, he drove along the peaceful streets. The homes around here must cost a pile, he thought. Inside, they were probably nicer than any he had ever known.

Not now, but someday, I'll take care of a family and spend a few days in a really nice house like one of these. Do it over a holiday when the father won't be expected at work and the kids don't have any school. Really live it up.

Ahead of him, a girl stood at a corner. A real beauty, no older than four or five. Her blonde hair, blowing in the breeze, looked almost white. She wore a pink blouse and a lime-green skirt that reached only halfway down to her knees. A Minnie Mouse purse hung from her shoulder by a strap.

Even though Roland had a stop sign, the girl waited without attempting to cross in front of him.

She was alone.

A hot beat coursed through Roland.

Slowing the car as he neared the stop sign, he looked all around. He saw nobody, just the girl.

No, he thought. This was crazy.

Take her back to the Oakwood.

It's too risky.

But he was breathless and aching and he suddenly didn't care about the risk.

He eased closer to the kerb, stopped, and rolled down his window.

The girl's eyes widened. They were very blue.

'Hi,' Roland called to her. 'I'm sorry to bother you. I'll bet your parents told you never to talk to strangers, but I'm lost. Do you know where Latham Road is?'

The girl frowned as if thinking very hard. Then she raised her right arm. In her hand was a small dingy toy. It looked like it might be a kitten. She shook the kitten towards the east. 'That way, I'm pretty sure,' she said.

'What's your kitty's name?' he asked.

'Clew.'

'He's cute.'

'Clew's a she.'

'I had a kitty named Celia. Celia had beautiful green eyes. What colour are Clew's eyes?'

'Blue.'

'Would you let me pet her?'

'Well . . .'

'I'm feeling awfully sad, 'cause my kitty, Celia, got run over yesterday.'

The girl's face clouded. 'Did she get killed?'

'I'm afraid so.'

'Was she all mooshed?'

'Yeah. It was awful.'

'I'm sorry.'

'I'd feel a whole lot better if you'd let me pet Clew. Just for a second, okay?'

'Well . . .'

'Please? Pretty please with sugar?'

She shrugged her small shoulders.

Oh, beautiful and young and tender.

Roland pulsed with need.

Chapter Twenty-two

Jake, driving his patrol car along the streets of Clinton, felt helpless. This was getting him nowhere.

Earlier he had taken the vodka bottle to headquarters, dusted it for prints, lifted some good latents with cellophane tape and fixed them onto a labelled card. He had then spent a while comparing the prints with those of juveniles and the few college students in the department's files. He had expected no match, and he had found none.

Nothing to do, now, except spin your wheels and wait. Either the creature with its human host had gone off seeking greener pastures in a different jurisdiction, or they were still in the area and would strike again. So it came down to waiting for a missing person report, or for a body to be found.

By then, it would be too late for someone.

But we might get lucky.

Jake hated the waiting. He wanted to *do* something. But what? Where do you start when you've got nothing to go on?

The Oakwood Inn.

In spite of the warmth inside his patrol car, Jake felt a chill on the back of his neck.

No reason to go back out there, he told himself once again. You searched the place thoroughly yesterday.

The thing left its eggs.

Yeah, but . . .

Yeah, but . . . yeah, but. Face it, Corey, you know you ought to be out there, should've probably been there all last night staking the place out, you just let Barney talk you out of it because you're scared shitless of going back.

There's nothing to *find* out there.

Sure, keep telling yourself. You're doing nothing now but wasting time. The thing left its eggs in that place. Maybe it'll go back to them.

I don't *want* to. Besides, I'm not dressed for it and I haven't got the machete.

That's no excuse, he told himself. The thing isn't slithering around, it's in someone. Probably.

There's no point. It won't be there.

If it won't be there, what're you scared of?

Even as Jake argued with himself, he was circling a block. He returned to Central Avenue, turned left, and headed in the direction of Latham Road.

Okay, he thought, I'll check the place. Won't accomplish anything, but at least I'll have done it and I can stop condemning myself.

He started to drive past the campus. A lot of students were out: some strolled the walkways; others sat on benches beneath the trees, reading or talking; a couple of guys were tossing a

Frisbee around; quite a few co-eds were sprawled on blankets or towels, sunbathing in bikinis and other skimpy outfits.

Jake pulled into the kerb and stopped.

Hardly a back among the whole bunch, males and females alike, that wasn't bare.

Through the broad gap between Bennet Hall and Langley Hall, he could see into the campus quad area. Even more students were gathered there – most of the men shirtless, nearly all of the women in swimming outfits or halter tops.

Jake considered leaving his car and wandering among the students. Sure thing, he thought. In uniform.

Go home and change into your swimming trunks. Then you could blend in, check them out, ask a few questions.

It didn't seem like a bad idea.

Anything to avoid going out to the Oakwood?

Whoever has the telltale bulge up his (or her) spine won't be showing it off. Maybe not, but that narrows the field. He'll be one of the few wearing a shirt.

If he's out here at all.

You'd have nothing to lose by conducting a little field investigation.

You're procrastinating. Move it.

Jake sighed, checked his side mirror, then swung away from the kerb.

I'll come back in my trunks, he decided, as soon as I've checked out the damn restaurant. Nothing better to do, and who knows? I might learn something.

When he turned onto Latham Road, he began to tremble. His heart quickened. The steering wheel became slippery in his sweaty grip.

He wished Chuck were with him. Some company would be nice, and his partner's banter always had a way of keeping the mood from getting too heavy. Barney shouldn't have reassigned Chuck. What difference would it make, anyway, if one more person knew what was going down?

Why the hell can't *Barney* be riding with me? Who does he think I am, the Lone-fucking-Ranger?

Calm down.

Try to think about something pleasant. Like what? Like

Kimmy. And how you were cheated out of being with her yesterday? Great. Pleasant thoughts. You had to work yesterday, anyway.

After today, you only have to go four days and then it'll be Friday and she'll be with you. Four days. Seems like forever. And what if all this crap is still going on?

We're letting it all out of the bag on Tuesday. After that, it won't be on my shoulders any more. Anything still going on by Friday, someone else can handle it.

Jake glanced to the right as he drove past Cardiff Lane. On the way back, maybe he would make a detour past the house. Not much chance of seeing her, though. If she was outside, she'd be in the back yard behind the redwood fence.

Maybe I could drop in. Barbara hates surprise visits, but she shouldn't begrudge me this one. After all, I gave up my rightful time yesterday so Kimmy could be there for her birthday.

Maybe give Kimmy a ride. Not much traffic along here. Let her turn on the siren and lights. She'd love that. Tell her, 'Don't turn on that siren.' She'd get that look on her face and reach for the switch.

Jake's smile and good feelings faded as he spotted the sign for the Oakwood Inn. He turned onto the narrow road. Kimmy, he thought, would like this road with its rises and dips. If he took it fast, the car would drop out from under them after each crest and she'd get 'fluffies'. This was one road, however, that he would never take her on. Not a chance.

At the top of a rise, Jake saw the restaurant and felt something similar to a fluffy himself – a sinking sensation in his stomach. But there was no fun about this one. This one made him feel sick and didn't go away. It got worse as he drove closer to the restaurant.

The parking area was deserted.

What did you expect, he wondered, a frat party?

Something like that. He had hoped, he realized, to find at least one car on the lot: the car belonging to the guy (or maybe girl) who had the thing up his back. Go in and maybe find him down in the cellar kneeling over the smear of demolished eggs.

Just a faint hope. He hadn't actually expected that kind of luck.

He stopped his car close to the porch stairs. He wiped his sweaty hands on the legs of his trousers. He stared at the door.

Nobody's here, he thought. What's the point of going in?

To see if anything has changed since yesterday. Maybe someone was inside after you left.

Jake rubbed a sleeve across his lips.

You made it this far, he told himself. Don't chicken out now. Just take a quick look around and get out.

He tried to swallow. His throat seemed to stick shut.

At least go in and get a drink. You can use the kitchen tap.

He saw Peggy Smeltzer sprawled headless on the kitchen floor, Ronald tearing the flesh from her belly. He saw the way the skin seemed to stretch as Ronald raised his head.

Just do it, he thought.

He levered open the driver's door and swung his left leg out. As he started to rise from the seat, the car radio hissed and crackled.

Sharon, the dispatcher, said in her flat voice, 'Unit two, unit two.'

He picked up his mike and thumbed the speaker button. 'Unit two.'

'Call in.'

'Ten-four.' Jake jammed the mike onto its hook.

The Oakwood has a phone, he remembered. But he'd tried to use it Thursday night and it hadn't been connected. It wouldn't be working now.

'Too bad,' he muttered.

He shifted to reverse and shot his car backwards away from the restaurant.

He had passed a Shell station about two miles back on Latham. It had a pay phone.

He swung his car around and sped out of the lot, feeling as if he'd been reprieved but tense, now, with a new concern. The message from headquarters could mean only one thing: a new development in the case. Any other matter was to be handled by Danny in unit one.

He floored the accelerator. The car surged over the road, flying off the rises (some real fluffies for you, honey) and hitting the pavement hard on the downslopes.

You're flying, he thought. Flying away from that damned place. But towards what? Maybe towards something worse.

He braked, slowed nearly to a stop at the junction with Latham, made sure no cars were approaching, then lunged out.

A car ahead. He gained on it quickly, so he activated the siren and lights. The car pulled over and he raced past it.

Seconds later, Jake spotted the service station. He slapped a front pocket of his uniform trousers to make sure he had change. Coins jangled. Of course he had change. He'd made sure before leaving home, knowing that he would need to phone Barney if he got a 'call in' message. The procedure seemed excessive to Jake, but Barney had insisted that, for the sake of keeping a tight lid on the matter, the car radio was not to be used.

For some reason, Jake had expected to get through the day without needing the coins.

I was wrong, he thought.

At least the timing was good.

Shit. Someone probably turned up dead, and all you care about is getting saved from the Oakwood.

He whipped across the road, cut sharply onto the station's raised pavement, and mashed the brake pedal to the floor. The car lurched to a stop beside the pair of public phones. He killed the siren, rammed the shift lever to Park, left the engine running, and threw open the door. He fished a quarter from his pocket as he ran to the phones.

The phone on the right had a scribbled 'Out of Order' note taped to its box.

He muttered, 'Shit.' He grabbed the handset of the other phone and listened to the earpiece. A tone came out, indicating that this instrument was operational. Because of the tremor in his hand, he knew he would have trouble poking the quarter into its slot. So he jammed the coin to the metal plate, as close as he could come to the slot on the first try, and skidded it sideways, pressing its edge hard against the flat surface until it dropped in. The sound of a ding came through the earpiece.

He dialled as fast as he could.

The phone didn't finish its first ring before Barney answered. 'Jake, it might be nothing. I don't want you jumping to conclusions.'

Barney didn't sound right. His voice seemed stiff and tightly under control, and he wasn't pronouncing his words like a thug.

This is bad, Jake thought. Very bad.

I don't want to hear this!

'Barbara phoned in. She's concerned about Kimmy. Apparently Kimmy has been missing since about thirteen hundred hours.'

Jake looked at his wristwatch. For a moment, he had no idea *why* he was looking at it. Then he realized that he wanted to know what time it was. Two thirty-five. Kimmy had been missing for . . .

'Jake?'

He didn't answer. Kimmy had been gone for . . . thirteen hundred was one o'clock, right?

'She probably just wandered off,' Barney said. 'You know kids. There's no reason to think this has anything to do with . . . the other matter. Jake?'

'Yeah. I'm on my way.'

'Keep me posted.'

Jake hung up. In a numb haze, he returned to the patrol car. He started to drive.

Kimmy.

She's all right, he thought. She has to be all right. Just wandered off. Maybe got lost.

He saw Ronald Smeltzer in the kitchen, down on his knees, teeth ripping flesh from the belly, but it wasn't Smeltzer's wife being eaten, it was Kimmy. Shrieking, 'No!' he blasted the man dead.

She's all right. Nobody got her. She just took a walk or something.

Gone more than an hour and a half.

He saw Harold Standish open the door, playfully stick up his hands and say, 'Don't shoot.' Jake shoved his piece against Harold's forehead and blew out the fucker's brains. Barbara came running. She wore the blue silk kimono. She cried out, 'It's not our *fault!*' Three bullets crashed through her chest. Then Jake stuck the barrel into his mouth and pulled the trigger.

That's how it's gonna play, assholes, he thought. That's just exactly how it's gonna play if anything happened to Kimmy.

Better calm down.

Fuck that.

You bastards, why weren't you *watching* her!

He swung onto the driveway behind BB's Toy, resisting an urge to slam into it. Then he was out of the car, striding towards the front door.

His right hand was tight on the walnut grips of his Smith & Wesson .38. He flicked off the holster's safety strap.

What am I doing?

He pulled his hand away and clenched it in a fist.

The door of the house opened before he could ring the bell. Barbara, pale and red-eyed, threw herself against him and wrapped her arms around him. He pushed her away. She looked surprised, hurt, accusing.

'Okay,' he said, 'how'd it happen?'

Barbara shook her head. 'I don't know.' Her voice was whiny. 'She was sitting on the front step. We'd come back from brunch. At the Lobster Shanty. And she was pouting all the way home 'cause I wouldn't let her have ice-cream. She'd already *had* chocolate cake, I didn't want her to make herself sick. Don't *look* at me that way!'

'Sorry,' Jake muttered, glaring at her. He wasn't sorry. He wanted to grab the front of her blouse and smash her against the door jamb. Ice-cream. Kimmy wanted ice-cream and Barbara had to play Boss Mommy and tell her no and now she's gone.

Barbara sniffed. She wiped her nose with the back of her hand. 'So Kimmy was pouting and she plonked herself down on the stoop and said she wouldn't come in. So I left her there. I mean, you know how she gets. What was I supposed to do, drag her in by the ears? So I left her. I figured she'd come in in a couple of minutes. But then when she didn't, I came out to get her and she was gone. I'm *sorry*, all right? God, she's my daughter, too!'

'We can put on her tombstone, "Mommy wouldn't let me have ice-cream." '

'You shit!' she cried out. She swung at Jake, fingers curled to claw his face.

He caught her wrist and clamped it tight. When he saw her other hand flashing towards him, he gave her wrist a quick twist and she dropped backward. Her rump hit the marble floor of the foyer. Clutching her face, she rolled onto her side and curled up.

Jake stepped inside, kicked the door shut, and stood over her. 'Where's that dickhead you married?'

'He . . . looking for Kimmyyyyy.'

Jake stared down at her. She was sobbing so hard that her whole body shook. 'Hope you're happy. Wasn't enough for you to run out on me, you had to . . . did you want her dead, is that it? I'm sure she was in the way a lot, always underfoot. Well, now maybe you won't have to put up with her any more. You'll like that.'

Barbara curled up more tightly.

Why don't you just kick her a few times? Jake thought.

He suddenly felt sick.

What am I doing? he thought. Kimmy's out there and maybe she'll be okay if I get to her in time and I'm standing here tormenting this woman I used to love.

He felt as if a terrible blackness had cleared away from his mind.

Crouching, he put a hand on Barbara's bare shoulder. She flinched. 'Hey, come on,' he said. 'I'm sorry.'

She kept on sobbing.

'You couldn't have known,' he told her, stroking her upper arm. 'I know you love Kimmy. I know you'd never do anything to hurt her.'

'I'll . . . kill myself,' she gasped.

'Kimmy'll be all right. She was upset, she probably decided to run away from home. You know kids.' Jake realized he was echoing Barney's empty platitude. 'Maybe she went to a friend's house.'

Barbara shook her head. 'We . . . no. Called everyone.'

'She'll be all right. I'll find her. I promise.'

'You think . . . someone took her.'

That was exactly what he thought. Someone took Kimmy – someone with a beast up his back. 'Let's not jump to conclusions,' he said. 'I'm sure Kimmy's fine. Did you check everywhere in the house? She might've come in when you weren't looking, and . . .'

'Everywhere. Her room, closets . . . everywhere.' Barbara rolled onto her back. She wiped her wet cheeks with open hands, then let her arms flop to the floor. She stared at the ceiling. She was no longer sobbing, but she struggled to catch her breath. Her green blouse had come untucked in front. Her short skirt was twisted around her thighs. She looked as if she had been the victim of a recent assault, except that she wasn't bruised and bloody. Not where you can see it, Jake thought.

He took hold of her hand, and gently squeezed it.

She glanced at him, then quickly shifted her eyes away. 'We looked all around for her,' she said. 'I walked around to all the neighbours. Nobody saw her. Harold went out in his car.' She sniffed. She used her other hand to wipe her eyes again. 'I kept thinking he'd come back any minute with Kimmy. I kept praying. But he came back without her. That's when I called the police. Barney talked to me. He . . . he was very nice. I always thought he was such a jerk, but he was very nice.'

'What was Kimmy wearing?'

'A short-sleeved blouse. Pink. A green skirt. Pink socks and black shoes. And . . . that necklace you gave her. The one with the snap-together beads. And she had Clew. And her Minnie Mouse purse. She kept Clew in the purse while we ate, and she snuck some pieces of cracker into the purse . . . for Clew.' Barbara's voice trembled. 'She looked so . . . so beautiful.'

'I'll be right back,' Jake said.

In the living-room he placed a call to headquarters. Barney said that he had already contacted all the off-duty officers. They were on the way to help in the search. Jake gave him a description of Kimmy. 'We're all pulling for you,' Barney told him. Jake thanked him and hung up.

Barbara was still on the floor of the foyer, but now she was sitting up, knees raised, arms wrapped around her shins.

Jake crouched beside her. 'In a few minutes,' he said, 'the whole department will be out looking for her. We'll find her. Don't worry, okay?'

She answered with a bleak nod.

'I'll bring her back to you.'

She lowered her forehead against her knees.

Chapter Twenty-three

Alison felt herself becoming more nervous as she approached home. She had hoped that Evan would show up while she was sunbathing on the grassy quad and save her from the necessity of calling him. It would have been so much easier, that way.

Naturally, he hadn't put in an appearance. He'd probably spent the whole afternoon in his apartment, waiting for his phone to ring.

I've got to call him right away, Alison thought as she climbed the outside stairway. The longer I put it off, the worse it will be.

At the top of the stairs, she found the door standing open. She stepped inside and took off her sunglasses.

On the television screen was some horror movie with a teenage girl running through the woods, chased by a maniac. Helen was asleep on the sofa, wearing only a white bra and panties. The panties were so old that the fabric had torn away from the elastic waistband at one hip and drooped, showing a crescent of skin that looked like uncooked dough.

Alison went over to the television and turned it off.

'Hey, what're you doing?'

'I thought you were asleep.'

'Just resting my eyes.'

Alison turned the TV on again and stepped out of the way.

'The door was wide open,' she said. 'Good thing I'm the one who came in, and not some nut off the street.'

'Had to get some breeze. In case you didn't notice, it's hotter than a hooker's twat in here.'

'Any calls?'

'You mean lover boy? Nope, he didn't call. I suspect that's intended to be your move.'

'No doubt,' she said, the knot in her stomach seeming to tighten. 'Celia back yet?'

'Guess she just can't get enough of that freshman meat.'

'She call or anything?'

'Nope.'

Alison frowned. 'I hope she's all right.'

'She must be raw, by now.'

'This is a long time to be gone.'

'Maybe it's love. Isn't that what you wanted for her?'

'Sure,' Alison said.

'Any minute, she'll come limping in. So, you gonna give Evan a buzz, or what?'

'I think I'll get cleaned up first.'

'Keep putting it off, he'll forget who you are.'

'Oh, I don't think so.' With a smile, Alison turned away. She went up to her room, grabbed her robe, and trotted down the stairs again.

In the bathroom, she hung her robe on the door and took off the oversized shirt she had worn as a cover-up. Her bikini was damp with perspiration and stained by suntan oil. Since she might want to wear it again before laundry day, she left it on when she stepped under the shower.

The hot, pelting spray felt good. She turned slowly beneath it. As her bikini became wet, its thin fabric clung to her. She liked the way it hugged her breasts and groin and rump, so she left it on while she shampooed her hair. With sudsy hands, she rubbed the bikini to clean it.

Tonight, she thought, the hands on me will be Evan's.

What happened to the celibacy?

We'll see.

If you go at it with him, you'll be back where you started. You'll never find out if there's anything more.

I'll try to hold off.

Rinsing the shampoo from her hair, Alison thought, it's like going to a party where you know there'll be drinking. You have to make up your mind, before you start out, that you won't get drunk. If you just go unprepared, it sneaks up on you, one drink leads to another, and before long you're blotto.

Or before long, as the case may be, you're naked and he's slipping into you.

Which might not be all that bad.

Alison untied the wet cords of the bikini top and peeled the clinging fabric off her breasts. She held it up close to the nozzle.

The spray caught it and tugged at it. After a few moments she turned her back to the shower, wrung out the excess water, and draped the top over the curtain rod.

She didn't think that she had burned, but with the bikini top off she could see that her skin had a slight pink hue that looked as if it had been sprayed on, leaving a well-defined line that angled across the tops of her breasts. On the other side of the line, her skin looked bleached.

Real cute, she thought. Boobs like bugging eyes.

I don't think Evan will complain.

Evan ain't gonna see them, is he?

You'd better decide.

Later. If I try to decide now, it won't bode well for abstinence.

She untied the cords at each hip. The triangle of fabric in front was so small that the weight of the hanging cords was enough to pull it down. She plucked the seat away from her buttocks and the garment came off. She rinsed it, wrung it out, and hung it on the rod beside her top.

Alison picked up a slippery bar of soap and began to lather her body.

If you see Evan tonight, she thought, he'll expect you to come across. Nice phrase, come across.

Too bad you're not here right now, Evan old pal. There wouldn't be much of a fight. Hell, there wouldn't be *any* fight. You might be the wrong guy, but you'd do in a pinch. Just catch me any time after I've been lying out in the sun for a while.

Maybe the sun's an aphrodisiac. Or maybe it's the feel or smell of the oil. Or maybe it's just that you're sprawled out almost naked, and the sun is hot on your bare skin and you can feel it through your bikini and sometimes a breeze comes along, caressing you.

I ought to write a paper on it for Dr Blaine next time he asks for a descriptive passage. Give the guy a hard-on. He'd put it in *me* if I gave him half a chance. Horniest prof I've ever seen.

Let's not disparage horny.

But let's get over it before we make the big call to Evan.

How's about the old cold shower trick?

Thanks, I'd much prefer to stay horny.

But the house was hot. If she didn't force herself to undergo

197

the torment of a cold shower, the sweat would pop out as soon as she had dried herself, and she'd stay dripping for a long time.

Laughing a little, Alison turned the hot-water tap. The spray became cool, then chilly. She clenched her teeth. She felt goose-bumps rise on her skin. She stood rigid with her back to the cold shower, buttocks flexed tight, fists pressing her cheeks. After a while, the cold deluge didn't feel so bad on her back. She turned around and shuddered. Finally, she lowered her head into the spray. She felt as if someone had dumped a pitcher of iced water on top of her.

When she climbed out, the towel felt wonderful. She hugged it to her body, savouring the warmth and softness. As she started to dry her hair, a knock on the door made her flinch.

'Telephone,' Helen called.

Alison felt as if her breath had been knocked out. 'Who is it?'

'It's Helen, who do you think?'

'Very funny. Who's on the phone?'

'Three guesses.'

'Oh, Jesus,' she muttered.

'Wrong. One down, two guesses to go.'

'Tell him I'll be right there.'

'I could tell him you'll call back.'

'No!' Alison draped the towel over her head and rushed to the door. She jerked the robe off its hook and put it on. The velour clung to her wet body. Helen stepped out of the way as she hurried into the hall.

'Slow down. I'm sure he isn't going to hang up on you.'

Alison rubbed her hair with the towel a few more times on her way towards the living-room. She rushed the rest of the way hunched over, sweeping the towel up and down her legs. She was a little breathless by the time she reached the telephone.

'Hello?'

'Hi,' Evan said. In that one word, Alison heard a tension and weariness that seemed completely unlike him.

'How're you doing?' she asked, trying to keep her own voice calm in spite of the tremor she felt inside. Water drops ran down the backs of her legs. She sat down in a chair. Her robe blotted some of the trickles.

'I'm okay, I guess,' Evan answered after a pause.

'I was planning to call you in about five minutes,' she said. 'The flowers are lovely.'

'I'm glad you like them.'

She tried to think of what to say about the letter. Her mind seemed hazy. She rubbed her wet thighs with the towel. Helen came in from the corridor, grinned and made an O sign with her thumb and forefinger, then went into her room and shut the door.

The silence stretched out.

I've got to say something about the letter, Alison thought.

'I suppose you read my . . . apology.'

'Yeah.'

'What do you think?'

She felt as if the air was being squeezed from her lungs. Arching her back, she managed to take a deep breath. 'I don't know,' she said.

'I was such a jerk. About everything. I should've respected your decision. I was just . . . hurt and confused. But that's no excuse. There is no excuse.'

'Temporary insanity?'

He gave a feeble laugh.

'I'll come over, if you want.' Alison could hardly believe she had said that. There had been no decision. At least not a conscious one.

'Really?' He sounded alive again. 'Tonight?'

'What time?'

'Oh God, Alison. I can't believe it.'

'We'll see how it goes.'

'It'll go great. I promise. How about five?'

'Okay.'

'I'll make us something terrific for dinner. I'll pick up some champagne. It'll be great. You're incredible, did you know that?'

'I don't want any hassles, though, okay? We'll just have a friendly dinner and talk and see how it goes.'

'I've missed you so much.'

Alison's throat tightened. 'I've missed you, too. A lot. See you at five.'

'Would you like me to pick you up?'

'No. Thanks anyway. I think I'll walk over. I need to stop by Baxter Hall for a second.'

'The freshman dorm?'

'I just need to talk to someone. Don't worry, I haven't thrown you over for a freshman. Or for anyone else, as a matter of fact.'

'Well, that's good to know. Not that I'd blame you, after the way I treated you.'

'No more apologies, all right? Let's just start out, from right now, with a clean slate. All that other stuff is water under the bridge, or over the dam, or wherever the hell the water is supposed to go.'

Like down your chest, she thought, and slid the towel over her wet neck and breasts.

'That's fine with me,' Evan said.

'Okay. See you in a while.'

'If you can make it over sooner than five, that'd be fine.'

'We'll see.'

'Take it easy, Al,' he said.

'Yeah. You too.'

She hung up the phone, leaned back in the chair, and pulled her robe together. A moment later, Helen's door opened. 'Did you catch all that?' Alison asked.

'Catch what?' Helen asked. 'So what's the verdict?'

'I'm going over for dinner tonight.'

'Well, say hey! Score one for love and true romance.'

'I don't know about that, but I'm going.'

'What was that about Baxter Hall?'

'You *were* listening.'

'No. Who, me? But I couldn't help catching a word here and there. You think Celia's over at Baxter?'

'I don't know. But I guess I'll drop by and check things out. She's probably not there, but maybe someone knows what's up.'

'Gonna drop in on Roland?'

Alison wrinkled her nose. 'He's Jason's roomy. If anyone knows where they are, he should.'

'That'll be loads of fun.'

'Yeah, fun like the dry heaves.'

'You could phone instead. The next best thing to being there.'

'It's on the way.'

Helen lowered her bushy eyebrows. 'You don't think anything's wrong, do you?'

'I'm starting to get a little worried, aren't you?'

'Celia's a big girl.'

'She's been gone a long time.'

'You want me to go with you for moral support?'

'You'd have to get dressed.'

Neither of them smiled.

'It's all right,' Alison said. 'I can handle it.'

'Well, don't let him get you alone. Stay out of the room.'

'Yeah, I'll keep that in mind.' She pushed herself up from the chair. 'I'd better get a move on.'

Alison went up to her room. Sitting at her desk, she pulled open the drawer and took out the photographs of Evan.

We used to have great times together, she thought as she looked at the pictures. Maybe it isn't over. Maybe this will be a new start, and everything will be wonderful from now on. Let's hope so.

But don't count on it.

She pinned the photos onto her bulletin board and stared at them.

In one, he was holding her hand.

In another, they were kissing.

In a third, they were seated on a blanket on the grass beneath an oak tree. Evan looked very pleased with himself. Though the photo didn't show it, Alison remembered that his right hand was inside the rear of her shorts and panties, pressed tight against her rump.

Not long after that one was taken, they had gone to his apartment and made love on the living-room floor. It was the only time they ever did it with Alison on top. She sat astride him, leaning forward and bracing herself up with stiff arms, Evan fondling and squeezing and sucking her breasts as she squirmed on him, impaled.

The memory of it sent a warm shimmer through Alison.

You have to get through tonight without any of that, she told herself. Even if it's only tonight. One night without sex, no matter how much you both might want it. Otherwise, you'll never know if there's more.

Sex is like the knot that's been holding us together, she thought. I've got to untie it, just once, just to see whether we come apart.

Just to see if there's another knot in the rope binding us to each other – a knot like love.

Chapter Twenty-four

Jake drove past the elementary school where Kimmy would be attending kindergarten next fall if . . . don't think it, he warned himself. To die before she even . . .

Stop!

He rubbed his forehead. He felt so damn tired. If only he could somehow make all this go away.

When they'd met briefly at headquarters to organize the search, the other six men had all been full of assurances but their eyes gave them away. They expected the worst, and except for Barney they didn't even *know* the true scope of the danger.

Jake saw a blonde girl on a swing of the school playground. His heart lurched. He hit the brake.

From this distance, the girl looked a lot like Kimmy. A man was standing behind the swing, pushing her. She wore blue jeans and a white T-shirt. Kimmy was supposed to be dressed in a pink blouse and green skirt.

But Jake remembered a news story about a girl who'd disappeared in a shopping mall. Her mother alerted security. The mall exits were immediately sealed. And the girl was recognized by her mother when the abductors tried to take her past the guards. Only she no longer looked like a girl. After grabbing her, the two men had rushed her into a restroom, thrown her dress into a waste bin, put her into jeans and a boy's shirt, cut her hair short and put a baseball cap on her head.

The guy pushing the girl on the swing . . .

Is her father, Jake thought.

Maybe, maybe not.

She *was* about Kimmy's size, with pale skin and hair that looked almost white.

The man pushed her higher and higher. When she flew forward, her hair streamed behind her. When she swung back, it blew across her face.

Watching the man and girl, desperately hoping, Jake slowly cruised to the next street. He turned left. He was closer now, and she still might be Kimmy.

Don't kid yourself, he thought.

At the next street, he turned left again. The swing set was ahead, just beyond the sidewalk and behind a chain-like fence. Jake could only see the back of the girl.

Please.

He drove past the swings. Looking over his shoulder, he saw the girl surge forward, down and up. As the hair blew away from her face, Jake's hopes fell apart.

He sped away.

Okay, it wasn't Kimmy. But I'll find her. I will. Or one of us will. Including Harold and Barney, eight men were searching for her.

One of us . . .

Where are you, honey? Where?

Jake was at least a mile from the house. Surely she wouldn't have wandered this far. But he had been up and down every street and alley, working his way outward in an ever widening circle.

A long time has gone by. She certainly *could* have come this far.

He turned down an alley that ran through the centre of the block. Near the far end of the alley, a red Pinto pulled over to the side. A lanky man in a plaid shirt climbed out. His hand went to his face, and he tugged on his long nose.

The man was far away and out of uniform, but the nose-pull gave him away. Mike Felson.

Of course, Jake thought. I'm in Mike's search sector.

Mike didn't seem to spot the cruiser.

He walked towards the closed door of a garage and past the garage and lifted the lid off a trash barrel. He peered into the barrel. He put the lid down, stepped to the next trash can, and took off its lid.

Jake groaned. Hugging his belly, he pushed his forehead hard against the upper rim of the steering wheel. He couldn't stop groaning. He raised his head a few inches and pounded it down on the wheel. Then he did it again.

Chapter Twenty-five

Roland snapped his chequebook shut. At the start of the semester his parents had given him $350.00 in addition to the cost of tuition, room and board. Whatever was left after buying text-books could be used for incidentals such as entertainment, extra food, clothing (knives and handcuffs, he thought, grinning) and so on. He had $142.55 left in the account.

In the morning he would withdraw it from the bank and use it for escape money.

It didn't seem like a whole lot.

Roland got up from the chair, stepped over to Jason's desk, and sat down. He found Jason's chequebook in the top drawer. He flipped through the cheque stubs until he found the last total Jason had entered, then worked his way forward, subtracting the approximate amounts of the several cheques Jason had written since then. It looked as if Jason had close to $400.00 left in the account.

A goodly sum.

Roland would have to practise Jason's signature . . .

You dumb shit, you flushed his driver's licence down the toilet at the Oakwood. Remember? Not only that, you didn't even take whatever cash he had in his wallet.

He wondered if Celia had any money in her purse.

He had left her purse in Jason's car.

Go back and get it?

No, too risky.

Bending down, he pulled open the bottom drawer of Jason's desk. He lifted the *Penthouse* and *Hustler* magazines, removed the envelope containing the snapshots of Dana (why not take those along as a souvenir?) and searched under a few more magazines until he found Jason's stash. The money was folded in half and fastened into a packet with rubber bands.

Roland took it out. Though its thickness was encouraging, he discovered that most of the bills were ones. Still, the total came to $87.00.

He carried the money and envelope over to his desk, and stuffed the cash into his wallet.

On the corner of his desk stood a framed eight by ten photograph of himself. He'd had it blown up from the negative of a picture taken at Hallowe'en. It was a great shot, showing him wrapped in a vampire cape that he'd rented for the occasion. His plastic fangs were bared. His mouth and chin were smeared with blood.

Roland patted the envelope of Polaroids and grinned as an idea came to him.

He slipped his photo out of its frame. He removed the Polaroids of Dana from the envelope. Then he took scissors and glue from his drawer.

He snipped Dana apart.

A fine, fine way, he thought, to while away the time.

He glued pieces of her to the vampire photo. Soon his leering face was surrounded by floating body parts.

A work of art, he thought when he had finished.

I ought to name it.

Call it 'Private Dreams'.

He grinned, enjoying the pun.

As he picked up the scraps, someone knocked on his door.

Roland's heart kicked.

Quickly he slipped the photo into his desk drawer. 'Who is it?' he asked.

'Alison Sanders. I'm Celia Jamerson's roommate.'

'Just a second,' he called. His pulse beat fast. Celia's roommate. One of the girls who'd been with her at the mall? What if this is the great-looking one who'd been wearing the jumpsuit?

Quickly he grabbed his jeans and put them on. Crouching, he closed the suitcase on the floor and pushed it under his bed. He rushed to the closet, took out a sports shirt and slipped into it. With trembling fingers he fastened a couple of the buttons before opening the door.

It *was* the jumpsuit girl and she looked even better than Roland remembered. She must've been out in the sun since then, for her face had a glow that made the white of her eyes and teeth striking. Even in the shadows of the corridor, her hair shone like gold. She wore a powder-blue blouse with short sleeves. It was buttoned close to her throat. At her shoulders the straps of a bra were faintly visible through the fabric. Pockets covered each breast. The blouse was neatly tucked into the waist of billowy white shorts with rolled cuffs midway down her thighs. She wore knee socks that matched her blue blouse, and bright white athletic shoes. In one hand she held the strap of a leather purse. The purse swayed, brushing the side of her calf.

'Why don't you take a picture,' she said. 'It lasts longer.'

Cal Taber chose that moment to walk past her. He laughed at Alison's remark, looked over his shoulder and said, 'Save some for me, Roland.'

Roland flipped him a finger.

'Real cute,' Alison muttered.

'Sorry. Some of these guys are such pigs. You want to come in?'

'Here's fine. Do you know where Jason and Celia are?'

Try the Oakwood Inn, he thought. Frowning, he shook his head. 'I don't know. The last I saw of Jason, he was taking off from here to pick her up. He planned to take her to the Lobster Shanty.'

'You haven't heard from him since then?'

'No.' He wondered if Alison always wore her blouse buttoned that high. He imagined slicing off each button with his knife and spreading open the blouse.

Alison's eyes narrowed. Mind-reader? Roland wondered. 'So you don't have any idea where they might be?' she asked.

'Well, not really. Maybe. I don't want you thinking I'm a snoop, but . . .'

'Don't worry about what I think.'

'Well, yesterday afternoon I noticed that Jason had a couple of telephone numbers on his desk. He wasn't around and I was a little curious, so I called the numbers. You know, just for the hell of it. One was the Lobster Shanty. When I called the other number, I got the registration desk of a motel in Marlowe. I guess Jason was thinking about taking her there.'

'Why all the way to Marlowe?'

'You'd have to ask Jason. I don't have any idea. He did take an overnight bag with him when he left.'

'It still seems pretty strange that they'd be gone this long.'

Roland smiled. 'They must be having a good time.'

Alison didn't look amused.

'I'm sure there's no reason to be worried. They'll probably be back pretty soon – unless they decide to stay over another night.'

'Yeah,' Alison muttered. From the look on her face, she wasn't convinced.

Shit, Roland thought. I should've told her Jason had phoned and *said* they'd be staying over.

He could call Alison later and tell her that. But would she believe him?

It doesn't matter.

She won't be with us long enough to cause any trouble.

'I wouldn't worry,' he said, 'unless they don't get back tomorrow morning. Jason has a ten o'clock. I'm sure he'll be back in time for that.'

Alison nodded. 'Will you call me if Jason gets in touch? I probably won't be there, but you can leave the message with Helen. Do you have something to write down my number?'

'It's in the student directory, isn't it?'

'Yeah.'

And so is the address. 'I'll call if I hear from them.'

'Thanks.' She turned away.

Roland watched her walk down the corridor, the loose fabric of her white shorts pulling lightly across her buttocks with her strides. She began to twist around for a glance over her shoulder, so he stepped back and closed the door.

He rushed over to his bed and stepped into his shoes. He tied them. He felt under his hanging shirt-front and touched the knife case on his belt, then patted a pocket to make sure he had his room key.

By the time he opened his door again, Alison was out of sight. He pulled the door shut and raced down the hall. He bounded down the stairs.

'Slow down, jerk-off,' Tod Brewster warned as Roland dodged him and his girlfriend on the landing.

'What a dip,' he heard the girl say.

Three steps from the bottom, he leaped.

Through the glass doors ahead he saw Alison outside. She was on the walkway alongside the dorm's north wing.

Roland waited in the lobby until she disappeared around the corner. Then he followed.

He stayed a distance behind Alison as she headed through the centre of the campus. She took the walkway along the western side of the quad. Some guys were playing touch football on the lawn. In spite of the late hour, several girls were scattered about, most of them wearing bikinis, some reading, others apparently asleep, some talking in small groups, a few watching the football game. Here and there, couples were sprawled on blankets. One couple was tangled in an embrace. One girl, alone near the walkway, had her top unfastened and was braced up on her elbows, engrossed in a book, and Roland slowed down to stare at the pale exposed side of her breast. He felt a stir of arousal.

I wonder who she is, he thought.

Forget it. You've got other plans for tonight, and you're hitting the road as soon as you're done. No time for this one, even if you did know who she is.

Things are getting too hot around here.

If you really wanted to play it safe, you'd leave right now and forget about Alison.

Oh, I can't do that. No way.

Alison first, then I'll take off.

Though it's a pity to leave all this behind.

Don't let it worry you. The world is full of delicious young flesh.

At the far end of the quad, Alison turned to the left and made her way through the shaded area between Doheny Hall and the Gunderson Memorial Theatre. She walked directly to the street. Then she crossed it.

Roland watched from behind a tree until Alison rounded the

corner of the block. Then he rushed to the other side of the street. When he reached the corner, Alison was no more than twenty yards ahead. If she turned around now ... He quickly backstepped and ducked behind the shrubbery bordering the lawn of the Alpha Phi Sorority House.

He waited for a few moments, then peered around the bushes. Alison had stopped midway down the block. She was gazing at something high and off to the side. She raised the strap of her purse onto her shoulder. Her back arched and she seemed to take a deep breath. She touched the top button of her blouse. Her hand dropped to the bottom of the blouse and felt around as if to make sure she was tucked in. Then she left the sidewalk.

Roland hurried forward.

He spotted her. She was inside the courtyard of an old apartment building with ivy vines on walls of rust-coloured brick. As he watched her, she climbed a flight of stairs to a balcony that ran along the upper storey. She walked past two doors, and stopped in front of the third.

Instead of knocking or opening the door with a key, she backed away from it and leaned against the wrought-iron railing of the balcony. Her head lowered. For a while, she didn't move. Then, stepping away from the railing, she lifted an arm and twisted around as if trying to see the back of her shorts. She swiped her seat briskly a couple of times. Finally, she stepped to the door and knocked.

A man opened the door. He was bigger than Alison, probably six feet at least. He wore slacks and a clinging knit shirt. Even from this distance, Roland could see that he was powerfully built. He had a flat belly, a big chest, a thick neck and bulging upper arms.

This was not a guy to mess with.

The man backed out of sight, and Alison entered the apartment. The door swung shut.

Now what? Roland wondered.

Go up and give it a try?

Don't be stupid.

Wait till she leaves, and nail her while she's walking home?

If the guy's any kind of gentleman, he'll walk her home. Besides,

I want her inside somewhere so I won't have to worry about intrusions.

I'll want a long time alone with her.

Go on back to the dorm, he decided, and look her up in the directory.

Yeah.

Roland rubbed his sweaty, trembling hands on his shirt.

'Hurry home, Alison,' he whispered.

Then he hurried away.

Chapter Twenty-six

Jake saw a blonde girl on a tricycle behind the chain-link gate at the end of a house's driveway. She wore a white blouse.

Kimmy?

He could only see her back.

What would she be doing here, riding a trike? Maybe this is a friend's house. Barbara said she'd phoned all of . . .

The right front of the patrol car tipped upward. Jake forced his eyes away from the girl. He jammed the brake pedal down, but not in time, and his car slammed into the trunk of an oak. The impact flung him forward. The safety harness locked, caught him across the shoulder and chest, and threw him back against his seat.

The girl, hearing the crash, looked over her shoulder.

She wasn't Kimmy.

Smoke or steam began rolling out from under the hood. Jake turned off the engine. He released the harness latch. Trembling, he opened the door and got out to see what had happened. He shook his head. He couldn't believe it.

While watching the girl, he'd let the car turn. Its right front tyre had climbed the corner of the driveway and he'd smacked into a tree on the grassy stretch between the kerb and the sidewalk.

He staggered to the front of the car. It was hissing. The white cloud pouring through the caved-in grill and around the edges of the hood smelled wet and rubbery. He didn't need to open the hood to know what had happened: he'd ruptured the radiator.

Dropping onto the driver's seat, he reached for the radio mike.

'Thanks for the lift,' he muttered, and climbed out of unit one.

'Grab some rest before you start looking again,' Danny suggested.

'Sure.' He swung the door shut. The cruiser pulled away.

Jake walked up the driveway towards his Mustang, digging into a pocket for his keys. He felt exhausted and sick. His head throbbed. He needed badly to urinate. On wobbly legs, he turned away from the driveway and crossed his lawn to the front door.

He let himself in. Though it was dusk outside, the house was dark. He turned on a light in the living-room.

After using the toilet, he swallowed three aspirin. He rubbed the back of his stiff neck. In the medicine-cabinet mirror, he looked as bad as he felt. His hair was untidy. His red eyes seemed strangely vacant. His face had a greyish pallor. Under his arms, his uniform blouse was stained with sweat.

He washed his face, then went to his bedroom. He started to take off his damp clothes.

You thought it was bad yesterday. You thought searching the Oakwood was bad.

You didn't know the *meaning* of bad.

He peeled off his wet socks and underwear and left them on the floor. He took fresh ones from his dresser, knew he would probably fall if he tried to step into them, sat down on his bed, put on the fresh underwear, then the socks. Groaning, he stood up again. He went to the closet for a clean shirt. He slipped into it, tried to fasten a button, and gave up. He took a pair of brown corduroy pants off their hanger and carried them to the bed. Sitting down, he pulled them up his legs.

Yesterday was nothing, he thought. Yesterday it was your goddamn imagination working overtime.

211

He remembered checking under his bed for the snake-thing and almost blasting Cookie Monster.

Me want Cookie!

His eyes burned and tears blurred his vision.

He turned his head to the nightstand where he had placed Cookie after coming so close to putting a bullet between its bobbly eyes.

The doll was gone.

Jake *knew* he'd left it there.

He checked the floor around the nightstand. Then he was on his feet, all the weariness and pain washed away by a cleansing surge of hope, on his feet and pulling up his pants and rushing from his room and across the hall and hitting the light switch and finding Cookie Monster on Kimmy's bed, snug against the side of Kimmy's neck, held there by her tiny hand.

Then Jake was on his knees, his arm across her hot back, his face against her shoulder.

'Barbara, she's here. She's fine.'

'Oh my God!' For a long time, Barbara said nothing more. Jake listened to her weeping. Finally she found enough control to ask, 'Where is she?'

'Here. At my house.'

'Where did you *find* her?'

'Right here. I came back to get the car, and . . .'

'That's impossible. It's *miles*.'

'A little more than three, I guess.'

'Oh, damn you! Why didn't you look there *first*!'

'I thought about it. I just . . . it seemed . . . it's so far. I didn't even think she'd know the way, much less walk that far. I still can hardly believe it. But she's here.'

'Do you have any idea the *hell* I've been going through?'

'It's over, now. She's safe.'

'Let me talk to her.'

'She's asleep.'

'Wake her up, goddamn it!'

'In a while.'

'NOW!'

'Calm down. I have to call headquarters and get the search

212

called off. Then I'll wake her up. She's probably starving. I'll get her something to eat, and bring her over to you in an hour or so. Have a drink or something. Get hold of yourself. I don't want you all hysterical when she shows up.'

'Hysterical? Who's hysterical? I had her dead in ditch some-where and all the time she's off paying a fucking surprise visit to her fucking daddy!'

'I have to call headquarters,' he repeated. 'We'll be along in a while.' Then he hung up.

When he had made the second call, he returned to Kimmy's room. She was still sleeping.

Jake knelt beside her and stroked her head. Her hair was damp. He put a hand on her back. Her skin was very hot through the fabric of her blouse. He felt the rise and fall of her breathing. She snored softly.

Jake tickled the rim of her ear. Without waking up, she rubbed the itch with Cookie Monster's furry blue head.

He smiled. He had a lump in his throat, but he was better now. Earlier, he'd fallen completely apart. She had slept through all that, fortunately.

Hell, the kid could sleep through almost anything.

With a hand on her shoulder, he gently shook her. 'Wake up, honey,' he said. He shook her again. 'Hello. Anybody home? Kimmy?'

She moaned and rolled onto her side, her back to Jake.

'Armpit attack,' he said, and wiggled his fingers under her arm.

Twisting away, she buried her face in the pillow.

'Butt attack!'

She reached back and slapped his hand off her rump, then rolled and faced him. 'That's not nice,' she protested.

'So sorry. Want to go to Jack-in-the-Box?'

'Can I have nachos?'

'Sure. Let's go.'

'You don't have to rush me.'

'If we don't get out of here fast, Mommy might show up and take you home, and you won't get the nachos.'

Kimmy sat up. Searching under the pillow, she found Clew. 'Is Mommy mad at me?'

'I wouldn't be surprised. We were both terribly worried about you. What you did was very dangerous.'

'I was very careful.'

'Come on.' He took her hand. She hopped down from the bed, looked back at Cookie Monster as if considering whether to bring him along as well, then let Jake lead her across the room.

'Can I stay here tonight?'

'I don't think so. Mommy will want you at home.'

'Isn't this my home, too?'

'Sure it is.'

'Don't you want me to stay with you?'

'I'd love it. But this wouldn't be a good night for it. Besides, I'm on a very important case.'

'Somebody toes up?' she asked, and grinned at him.

'That's right.'

Outside, Jake lifted her into the car and strapped her into the child seat. He hurried to his side of the car, started the engine and turned on the headlights. As he backed out of the driveway, he told Kimmy, 'We looked all over town for you. The whole police department was looking for you.'

'Does that mean I'm in trouble?'

'I don't think we'll put you in jail this time. First offence. If you ever do it again, though, I'm afraid it'll be slammer time. Why'd you do it?'

'Mommy wasn't being nice.'

'Because she wouldn't let you have ice-cream?'

'No, 'cause she socked me.'

'What do you mean, socked you?'

'Gave me a knuckle sandwich. Right here.' She bumped Clew's small grey head against her upper arm. 'It really hurt. You're not suppose to hit little girls, you know.'

'So you ran away because she hit you?'

'*You* never hit me.'

'That's only because I know you'd pound me if I ever tried.' He smiled at her, but blood was seething through him.

Kimmy never lied.

That bitch had punched her.

Didn't even have the guts to admit it.

'So you got mad because she hit you, and you decided to

pay me a visit? How did you find my house? And how did you get in?'

'Oh, I knew where it was. You left a window open.'

'And you walked all the way?'

'Sure. My foots got tired, though.'

'There were a lot of people looking for you. I'm really surprised that none of them found you.'

'Well, you see, I hid. I'm a good hider.'

'What did you do, duck into the bushes every time a car came along?'

'Sometimes there weren't no bushes. I got behind trees and cars.'

'Very clever,' Jake said.

'Well, you see, I got scared about the man with the cat. He didn't have a cat, for real, 'cause it got smooshed, but he wanted to pet Clew and I ran away.'

'What?' Jake asked. My God, he thought, somebody *had* tried to pick her up.

'Daddy, you should've listened the first time. I do not repeat.'

'I was listening,' he assured her. 'You said that a man wanted to pet Clew.'

'Only that was just a story. He was going to grab me and take me in his car.'

Jake's heart pounded. 'Did he tell you that?'

'No.'

'Then what makes you think he wanted to grab you?'

'You can't fool She-Ra.'

'When did this happen?'

'Today.'

'After you left Mommy's house?'

'Well, of course.'

'He was driving a car?'

'Yes.'

'And he stopped near you while you were on the way to my house?'

'Yes.'

'What did he say?'

'I already told you.'

'Press rewind.'

215

Kimmy made a buzzing sound. 'Okay, all done.'

'What did the man say?'

'His cat got smooshed by a car and he felt sad. I don't think it really did, though. Do you?'

'I don't know.'

'I wouldn't let him pet Clew. I ran away.'

'Did he drive after you?'

'Well, you see, I ran to a house.'

'That was very smart. And what did he do?'

'He drove away fast.'

'What did he look like?'

'Are you going to put him in jail?'

'I might.'

'Good.'

'But I need to know what he looks like, or I won't be able to find him.'

'Maybe you should shoot him. I think that might be a good idea.'

'How old was he?'

'I don't know.'

'Was he younger than me?'

'Yeah, but he was a grown-up.'

'Did he look old enough to be a student at the college?'

Kimmy shrugged. 'He was kind of the same as George.'

George was the boyfriend of Sandra Phillips, who used to babysit for Kimmy before the marriage broke up. At that time, George was a senior in high school.

'What did he look like?'

'Well, he didn't have a shirt on.' In a sly voice, she added, 'I saw his beeps.'

'Did you see his back?' And did his back have a bulge, Jake wondered, as if he had a snake under his skin?

Kimmy shook her head.

'What colour was his hair?'

'Black.'

'How about his eyes?'

'I don't *know*,' she said, sounding a bit impatient. 'Are we almost at Jack-in-the-Box?'

'Just a couple more blocks. Was he skinny, fat?'

'Oh, skinny.'

'Did he wear glasses?'

'Nope.'

'Sunglasses?'

'Daaaaddy.' She sighed heavily. 'I'm tired of this.'

'You want me to shoot him, don't you?'

'Well . . .'

'What kind of car was he driving?'

'Oh, that's easy. It was just like Mommy's.'

'A Porsche?'

'What's a Porsche?'

'Mommy's car that Harold bought her.'

'Oh, that. Huh-uh. It was like her old car. Maybe it *was* her old car!'

'Was it exactly the same? The colour and everything?'

'Yeah. Only it had a thing on it.'

'What kind of a thing?'

'A pointy flag.'

'What colour was it?'

'Red-orange.'

'Like your red-orange crayon?'

'Well, of course.'

'Where was this flag? Was it glued to a window, or . . .'

'It was on that thing.' Kimmy pointed through the window at Jake's radio antenna.

'That's great, honey. That'll be a real help. Anything else you can remember about the guy or his car?'

'I don't think so. His cat's name was Celia. Only I don't think he really had a cat, do you? I think it was just a story to make me let him pet Clew and grab me. I bet he wanted to do something bad to me. Only I outsmarted him, didn't I?'

'You sure did, honey.'

Moments later, Jake swung the car into the crowded lot of a 7-Eleven.

'Hey, you promised Jack-in-the-Box.'

'I need to make a call.' The parking spaces close to the public telephone were taken, so he had to settle for a spot near the far end.

'Are you going to call Mommy?'

'Nope. Want me to?'

'No!'

'I'm calling the police.' He unbuckled Kimmy. She scurried down from her high seat and followed Jake out of the driver's door. Taking hold of her small hand, he led her across the parking lot. 'I'm going to tell Barney all about the creep in the Volkswagen.'

Kimmy's eyes widened with excitement. 'Really?'

'Yep. We're gonna nail that guy.'

'Can we eat before we nail him? I'm starving.'

'We'll eat as soon as I'm done calling.'

'Well, make it snappy, buster.'

Chapter Twenty-seven

Roland parked Dana's Volkswagen at the kerb halfway down the block and climbed out. He walked back past two houses. In the glow of the streetlight he checked the address he had copied from the student directory: 364 B Apple Lane.

He was on Apple Lane. The porch light of the house across from him revealed the numbers 364 on the front door.

The B on the address undoubtedly meant that Alison had an apartment on the property, either in a different section of the house or in a furnished annexe at the back.

Light shone through windows on the ground floor and upstairs. Whoever lives in the main part of the house, Roland thought, must be home. I'd better keep it in mind.

A walkway led straight to the front door, but flagstones curved away to the right.

Roland cut diagonally across the lawn. Stepping onto a flagstone at the corner of the house, he saw a wooden stairway to the second storey. A door at the top of the stairs was lighted by a single bulb. The railing up there was decorated with potted plants. Girls would have plants like that, he thought.

Near the bottom of the stairs a mailbox was mounted on the house wall. Roland stopped beside it. The address on the box was 364 B.

Slowly, he began to climb the stairs.

Hearing voices, he stopped and turned around. The sound came from an open window. Though the window overlooked the stairway, it was far to the side so he couldn't see in. He listened for a few moments. The voices had a flat quality – and background music. They came from a television.

So Helen is here, just like Alison said.

Watching the tube.

Alone?

She might have a boyfriend visiting.

Possible. I'll have to be careful, Roland thought.

At the top of the stairs, he removed a plastic bag from the front pocket of his jeans. It was a sturdy translucent wastebasket liner he had taken from his dorm room while planning tonight's activities. Confident that the noise from the television would prevent Helen from hearing such quiet sounds, he unfolded the bag and puffed into it. The bag expanded with his breath.

He took out the keys he had removed from Celia's purse, chose the one that appeared most likely to be the door key, and slipped it silently into the lock. He bit the edge of the bag to free his other hand. Then, using both hands, he slowly turned the key and knob. He eased the door open.

The sound from the television increased. He smelled a pleasant odour. Popcorn.

From where he stood with his face pressed to the gap, he could see only a corner of the living-room. No one was there.

He swung the door a little wider and sidestepped through the opening.

He saw the top of her head above the sofa back. Her hair was in curlers.

The furniture arrangement made it easy. If the sofa had been placed flush against the wall, he wouldn't be able to sneak up behind her. But the sofa had a wide space behind it, apparently so people could cross the room without passing in front of anyone who might be sitting there.

Roland considered shutting the door. He decided not to risk making a sound that might disturb her, and left it standing open a few inches.

He took the bag in both hands. Holding it open, he began to walk slowly over the carpet. A slight breeze stirred the bag.

This'll be a cinch, he thought.

Unless there's a guy lying on the sofa with his head in her lap.

Then he was close enough to see that nobody else was there. On the cushion beside Helen rested a big white bowl of popcorn. She reached into it and scooped out a handful. She was wearing a red bathrobe. Her legs were stretched out, feet resting on top of a low table in front of the sofa. The robe hung open, revealing thick white thighs.

Too bad she's such a pig, Roland thought. This would be much more pleasant if she looked more like Celia or Alison.

No thrill in this.

He raised the bag.

Something thumped off to the side.

He looked. The door had blown shut.

Helen looked too, her head turning enough to see the door, then turning more and tilting back. Her eyes bugged out when she saw Roland. Half-chewed popcorn spewed from her mouth, some spattering the inside of the bag as he swung it down over her head.

She lunged forward. Roland flung an arm across her face to hold the bag in place. Hugging her head, he was dragged over the back of the sofa. She reached back and tore at his hair. Pain erupted from his scalp.

Helen's shoulder slammed the top of the coffee table. Roland's side hit the surface, knocking her drink out of the way. She squirmed and kicked. Her wild struggle scooted Roland along the table. Its other end flew up. He dropped to the floor, Helen smashing down on top of him.

Pinned beneath her writhing body, Roland clutched the bag tight to her face. With his other hand, he jerked open the snap of his knife case.

No! No blood!

He threw his free hand across Helen. Her robe had come open. He grabbed a breast and twisted it. She squealed into the plastic over her mouth. Letting go, he pounded a fist down hard into her belly. Again. Her body flinched rigid with each blow. Then she seemed to quake. He heard heaving noises. The bag pulsed warm and mushy against his hand and he realized she was vomiting. He fought an urge to pull his hand away. He pressed the bag even more tightly to her mouth. Convulsions racked Helen's body. She twisted and bucked on top of him, finally throwing herself off.

He rolled with her, but lost his grip on the bag. Vomit slopped out onto the carpet. Her hand slipped in the mess when she tried to push herself up. Roland scrambled onto her back. She was choking and gasping beneath him. But breathing, at least enough to stay alive. As he straddled her and reached for the bag, she tugged it off her head.

Roland wrapped his fingers around her slippery neck and tried to strangle her. As he squeezed her throat, Helen pushed herself up. She got to her hands and knees. Whimpering, she began to crawl. Roland rode her. His fingers weakened. He felt a tremor of fear.

Letting go, he scrambled off Helen's back. He staggered a few steps, got his balance, then rushed at her and kicked the toe of his shoe up into her belly with such force that she toppled onto her side. She hugged her belly and sucked breath. She had lost her glasses. Her face was scarlet where it wasn't smeared with vomit.

Roland danced back and forth, looking for the best target. He wondered for a moment what one of those mammoth breasts might do if he punted it. That wouldn't be lethal, though, and he needed to finish this business. She had already proved herself almost too much for him.

He aimed a kick at her throat.

It missed, but knocked her jaw crooked and threw Helen onto her back.

Roland jumped, bringing his knees up high and shooting his feet down, stomping her crossed arms and belly with all his weight. Breath exploded out of her and she half sat up. Roland bounded off her.

Whirling around, he kicked the side of her head.

221

Her arms flopped onto the floor.

He kicked her head again for good measure.

Then he retrieved the plastic bag. He sat on the soft cushions of her breasts, pulled the bag down over her head, and held it shut around her neck.

As he sat there, he hoped Alison would be spending a long time at her boyfriend's apartment. It would take a long time to clean all this up.

The pig had made a real mess.

Chapter Twenty-eight

They had nearly finished eating and Alison grew uneasy about what might happen once they left the table. To postpone the moment, she asked for coffee. Even got up to prepare it.

Don't worry so much, she told herself. So far, everything has gone fine. Reasonably fine.

She had been terribly nervous on her way to Evan's apartment, had even come close to backing down. But somehow she found the courage to knock on his door.

She had half expected Evan to look wild-eyed and desperate. If he'd been that way when he wrote the letter, however, he'd had time to recover. The man who opened the door seemed composed and cheerful. Perhaps a bit too cheerful.

'Ah, *la belle dame sans merci*,' he greeted her. 'Make that *avec merci*.'

'That's better,' Alison said.

'Come in, come in.' He didn't try to hug or kiss her. He backed into the apartment, smiling. 'You look terrific.'

'You don't look so bad, yourself.'

'You got some sun.'

'I was over at the quad for a while.'

Evan lifted a glass off the table in front of the sofa. It was empty except for a few ice cubes that had melted down to nuggets. 'What could I get you? How about a margarita? We're having Mexican.'

'Great.' Alison took a deep breath, relishing the aromas that filled the apartment.

'I'll just be a minute. Make yourself comfortable.'

He walked past the bookshelves that lined the wall, stepped around the table in the small eating area, and disappeared into the kitchen. The table had been cleared of the typewriter and piles of books and papers that usually covered it. Places had been set. In the centre of the table stood a single red candle with a tapered tip and a wick that had never been lit.

Alison heard the blender whine.

She stepped over to an armchair and sat down.

The gulf between the chair and the sofa, in this small room, looked enormous.

This is no way to start things fresh, she thought. Evan's not contagious.

So she moved to the sofa. On the seat of a folding chair straight ahead was an oscillating fan. It swept a mild warm breeze back and forth. The moving air felt good on her damp face. She leaned forward. The top button of her blouse pressed against her throat. She unfastened it. Arching her back, she reached around and plucked the clinging fabric away from her skin.

It hadn't been *that* hot outside, she thought.

Nerves. Confronting Roland, then coming here.

It can only get better, she told herself.

What makes you so sure?

It's already better, she thought. I'm done with Roland, Evan seems all right, and the fan feels terrific.

Alison looked around the room. She had been here so many times before. Nothing looked different, yet nothing seemed quite the same. This might have been a movie set cleverly made up to *look* like Evan's apartment, and she was an actress in the role of Alison – a role she didn't quite know how to play.

Need a script, she thought. That'd certainly help.

Evan came in with a margarita in one hand and a bowl of

tortilla chips in the other. After placing them on the table in front of Alison, he returned to the kitchen. He came back with a bowl of red salsa and another margarita. He put them down, then sat on the sofa beside her.

Beside her, but about two feet away. A good sign, Alison thought. He isn't going to pretend that everything is like it used to be.

They lifted their drinks. 'To new beginnings,' Evan said. They clinked their glasses and drank.

Alison asked how his dissertation was coming along. He spoke with enthusiasm about its progress, his hopes of developing his study of flight imagery in *Finnegan's Wake* into a full book that could gain him recognition as a Joyce scholar and help ensure tenure a few years down the road. While he talked, Alison dipped chips in the salsa, ate them, and drank. Occasionally she made comments or asked questions.

When Evan finally lapsed into silence, Alison asked if he had heard, yet, from any of the universities to which he had applied for teaching positions. He gave her a strange look. 'You mean since Thursday?'

'Seems like longer,' Alison said.

'Seems like weeks. God, it's good to have you back.'

Not all the way back, she thought. Not yet. I'm here, but I'm not back.

Evan took the empty glasses into the kitchen. While he was gone, Alison dipped another chip into the salsa, cupped her hand beneath it in case it dripped, and ate it.

Better stop gobbling these things, she thought, and licked a smear of red sauce off her fingers.

Evan came back with the glasses refilled.

Alison was already feeling somewhat light-headed from the first margarita. Drink this one more slowly, she cautioned herself. Keep at it with the booze and chips, you'll be bloated and drunk by dinnertime.

'You build a mean margarita,' she said.

'Wait'll you try my enchiladas.' He sat down beside her.

Beside her, and only about one foot away, this time. That's okay, Alison thought. We *are* closer than we were when I got here.

Still not like we used to be, but getting better.

'What have you been doing with yourself?' he asked.

'Not much.' She didn't want to tell him that she had spent the past few days thinking about him, often with bitterness, sometimes with longing. 'I went to Wally's one night,' she said.

'Any luck?' he asked.

'I wasn't there for that,' she said, and took a drink. 'Saw this far-out video. A woman dancing with a snake. Have you seen that one?'

'I've caught it on MTV. Blue Lady doing "Squirm on Me".'

'Pretty far-out,' Alison said again.

'Erotic.'

'Helen and I played Trivial Pursuit last night. I landed on the Art and Literature spaces whenever I got the chance. I wiped the floor up with her.'

'Sounds like your Saturday night was better than mine.'

This keeps straying into areas I don't like, she thought. 'I must've gained five pounds. Between the two of us, we polished off a bag of potato chips and a bag of taco chips. Not to mention a six-pack. If I keep spending Saturday nights with Helen, I'll start to look like her.'

'Impossible. You could gain a hundred pounds, you'd still be beautiful.'

'Oh, sure.'

'Your momma could beat you with an ugly stick from now till doomsday, you'd never look like Helen.'

Alison laughed, then shook her head. 'Come on, she's my best friend.'

'I didn't start it.'

'She's a great gal. It's not her fault she looks the way she does.'

'If she cared, she could fix herself up.'

'Not by much,' Alison said, and immediately regretted it. 'I mean, there's only so much that a hairstyle and make-up and clothes can accomplish. Shit, I don't mean it that way.'

Evan was grinning, laughing softly. 'No, of course not.'

'Anyway, we had a great time. Then today, I took a long walk and I picked up a copy of the new Travis McGee and spent most of the afternoon with that. MacDonald's great to read when you're lying out in the sun.'

'What were you wearing?'

'My white bikini.'

'Ah.'

She took another drink. The second margarita was getting low. 'I like all the MacDonalds,' she said. 'MacDonald, John D.; Mcdonald, Gregory; McDonald, Ross; McDonald, Ronald.'

'I love how you look in the white bikini.'

'Is dinner almost ready?'

'Ah, I'll check. Shall I get refills while I'm out?'

'Not for me, thanks.'

'No problem. Champagne with dinner. I promised champagne, remember?' Leaving his own empty glass on the table, he stood up. He walked slowly as if being careful not to weave.

Alison wondered how many drinks he'd had before she arrived.

Don't worry about it, she told herself. Just make sure *you* don't get looped.

She settled back against the sofa and sighed.

So far, so good, she told herself.

She sighed again. It felt good to sigh. She felt pleasantly lazy and light. A great burden had been lifted from her. She was with Evan again, and it was working out fine.

Pretty fine.

He didn't get my McDonald joke.

Too busy thinking about me in my bikini.

Who can blame him?

She laughed softly and closed her eyes.

'Hey, Sleeping Beauty.'

She opened her eyes. The room was dark except for the glow of a single candle. The candle was on the table in the dining area. Food was on the table.

Evan was standing above her. 'I understand it is traditional,' he said, 'to awaken the princess with a kiss. However, I showed remarkable restraint and took no advantage of your somnolent condition.'

Alison sat up. 'How long was I asleep?'

'Oh, perhaps an hour.'

'Jeez.' It didn't seem possible. 'I'm sorry.'

'No need to apologize. You're beautiful when you're asleep. Or when you're awake, for that matter.'

'I hope dinner isn't ruined.'

'I'm sure it'll be fine. In fact, it's just now ready.'

'Do I have time to use the john?'

'Help yourself.'

She made her way through the darkness and down a short hallway to the bathroom. Though she was embarrassed about falling asleep, the rest had left her feeling refreshed. She turned on the light. She used the toilet. At the sink, she cupped up cold water with her hand and took a few drinks. She studied herself in the mirror. Her eyes looked a little pink. Her hair looked fine. The middle button of her blouse had come undone. She fastened it, then washed her hands and left the bathroom.

The kitchen light was on. The enchiladas on her plate were steaming and looked wonderful. Evan pulled out her chair for her and she sat down. He filled her glass with champagne. Before taking his seat, he switched off the light.

'Remember our spaghetti dinner?' he asked. 'You were wearing your good white blouse and claimed you didn't want to spill on it so you took it off?'

'Evan.'

'You were so lovely in the candlelight. Your golden glowing skin, your dusky nipples.'

'Stop it.'

'Sorry,' he muttered. He lowered his head, cut into an enchilada with his fork, and began to eat.

Alison's appetite was gone, but she took a bite. She had a hard time swallowing, and washed the food down with champagne.

For a while, they both remained silent.

This is lousy, she thought. What was the real harm in what he'd said? They had a wonderful time, that night. It shouldn't be a crime to remember it, to mention it.

'Good grub,' she said.

He looked up from his plate. 'Try some sour cream on it.'

'Don't mind if I do.' She spooned a large glob of sour cream onto her enchiladas. 'It was a good thing, too,' she said, 'that I took off my blouse. I slopped all over myself that night.'

She saw Evan smile. 'On purpose, I believe.'

'Yeah. I'm not, after all, a slob.'

'No, indeed.'

They returned to eating. Now the food tasted fine. The cool sour cream added a tangy flavour to the enchiladas. She drank more champagne, and Evan refilled her glass.

'You're really a terrific cook,' Alison said.

'I have my specialities. One of them is chocolate mousse pie, but I think we should save it for later. Give us time to digest all this.'

'Maybe we should take a walk when we're done,' Alison suggested.

He said, 'Maybe.' He didn't sound thrilled by the idea. 'I've got a tape of *To Have and Have Not* I thought you might want to look at on the VCR. Hemingway. Bogart and Bacall. You know how to whistle, don't you?'

'I'd like that,' Alison said. 'I haven't seen it in years.'

'I thought y'might like it, tweet-hot,' he said, flexing his upper lip.

He would turn it on and sit with her on the sofa. Soon his arm would be around her.

We'll be right back where we started before Thursday in Bennet Hall, before the ultimatum, before his date with Tracy Morgan, before the flowers and letter.

And maybe that's not such a bad thing, Alison thought. Why fight it? What's the point?

But what were the last three days all about if you give in tonight? You won't have learned anything.

Sure. You'll have learned that, no matter what, it all comes down to fucking.

It shouldn't have to be that way, damn it.

She pushed her fork under the small portion that remained of her dinner.

Running out of time, kiddo.

She chewed. She swallowed. She drank the rest of her champagne.

Evan lifted the bottle. 'Polish it off?'

'No thanks.'

He emptied the bottle into his glass and quickly drank the last of the champagne.

'I could use some coffee, if you have some.'

'Sure, no problem.'

* * *

Evan carried two mugs of coffee into the living-room and set them on the table in front of the sofa. Then he crouched and slipped his tape of *To Have and Have Not* into the VCR on the shelf below his television. When he started to get up, he stumbled. He staggered a few steps, found his balance, and grinned over his shoulder at Alison. 'I meant to do that,' he said.

He's pretty polluted, she thought.

He walked carefully into the kitchen. While he was gone, Alison pushed herself off the sofa and turned on a lamp. As the lamp came on, the kitchen went dark.

She was seated again by the time he wandered in. He had a loose-jointed, swaying walk. He had a bottle of whisky in one hand, a can of whipped cream in the other. 'How about Irish coffee?' he asked, and dropped heavily onto the sofa beside Alison.

Beside Alison, no more than three inches away.

'I think I'll take my coffee straight,' she said.

'Fine. Do not let it be said that I attempted to ply you with liquor. When all is written and the story told, let it not be reported that Evan attempted to cloud the fair lady's mind with spirits, opiates or sorcery.'

'You're bombed,' Alison said.

'I'm . . . semi-bombed.' Talking out of one side of his mouth in a fairly good impression of W.C. Fields, he said, 'She was a gorgeous, delectable blonde and she drove me to drink; it's the only thing I'm grateful to her for.'

Alison took a sip of her coffee. 'Barf, and I'm on my way home.'

'Barf and the world barfs with you . . .' But he left the whisky on the table. He took a drink of coffee. Then he turned on the movie.

Alison sat on the edge of the sofa, leaning forward, until her mug was empty. Then she settled back against the cushion. She slipped out of her shoes, propped her feet on the edge of the table, and stared between her knees at the television.

She couldn't follow the movie. Her mind was on Evan. She sensed that he was paying no attention to the movie, either.

He was slumped beside her, his legs stretched out beneath the table, his left arm not quite touching Alison but so close that she thought she could feel the heat of it against her arm. His hand rested on his thigh.

The lighted red numbers of the VCR's digital clock showed 9:52.

We've been sitting like mannequins, Alison thought, for almost twenty minutes.

She had an urge to shift her position. But she didn't move. A move might trigger something.

This is crazy.

She lowered her feet to the floor, sat up straight, and stretched, arching her back. She rolled her head to work the kinks out of her neck.

Evan said, 'Here.' He reached up with one hand and began to massage her neck.

The fingers felt good plying her stiff muscles. Alison turned her back to Evan, sliding a leg onto the cushion.

Now it starts, she thought.

Both Evan's hands were on her shoulders and neck, rubbing, squeezing, caressing. They eased the tightness. Alison closed her eyes and let her head droop. The massaging hands made her feel weak and lazy.

They worked on the bare sides of her neck, beneath her collar. Nice. Why not nicer?

Alison unfastened a button. Evan's hands moved outward from her neck, kneading her skin, widening the bare area. Alison felt something loosen and realized, vaguely, that her middle button had popped open on its own. Evan tried to spread the blouse more. It pulled at her. She tugged, untucking it, and it rose and opened, exposing her shoulders.

She swayed under the soothing motions of Evan's strong hands. She felt powerless to lift her head or to open her eyes or to protest when, soon, he slipped the bra straps off her shoulders.

His hands no longer massaged, but glided over her bare skin, caressing her from neck to shoulders.

He stopped for a moment. The sofa cushion moved slightly under Alison and she guessed that Evan was changing his position. Getting onto his knees? Yes. From the sound of his breathing, he was higher now. He stroked her shoulders, eased his hands under her blouse and inside the sleeves to caress her upper arms, then slid his hands out and down, down over her collarbones, down her chest, going away instead of touching her through the filmy fabric of her bra, and opening the last buttons.

He slipped the blouse down her back. Alison's wrists were trapped in the sleeves, but she made no effort to free them.

For a while, his hands roamed her back and sides. Then they unfastened her bra. Evan kissed the side of her neck. He nibbled, making her squirm. Her heart quickened, desire pushing away the lazy weak feeling. He caressed her sides. His hands moved beneath her arms, slipped under her bra, and lightly cupped her breasts. Her nipples stiffened, pressing into his palms.

Reaching back, she rubbed his thighs through the soft fabric of his pants.

He squeezed her nipples.

A hot tremor pulsed through Alison. She caught her breath. She reached higher, intending to caress his penis through his pants, but she found it rigid and bare. Her hand flew from it.

He chuckled softly. 'Surprise,' he whispered.

How long had he been that way, his penis secretly exposed while he caressed her? It seemed wrong, deceitful, almost perverted.

But he rubbed and squeezed her breasts and what did it matter if he jumped the gun a bit? He saved me the trouble, Alison thought. She reached up and stroked him.

Then she turned around. Evan was on his knees. As he opened his belt, Alison removed her hands from the sleeves of her blouse.

She glanced down at herself. Her bra hung like a flimsy scarf above the tops of her breasts. She began to sweep its strap down her left arm and saw a smudge of red on the white translucent fabric of one rumpled cup.

She stared at the red stain. It looked like a smear of the salsa they'd been dipping their chips into before dinner.

I must've spilled . . .

It's on my *bra*.

In the bathroom after waking up, she had found the middle button of her blouse unfastened.

After waking up.

Evan, naked from waist to knees, lifted his knit shirt to pull it over his head. It was covering his face. Alison jabbed a fist into his belly. Air whooshed out of him. He folded at the waist. Alison flung herself off the sofa just in time to avoid being struck by his crumpling body.

She rammed her feet into her shoes.

Behind her, Evan was gasping for breath.

'You shit,' she muttered. Shaking with rage, she shoved her bra into her handbag. 'You filthy shit, you felt me up while I was asleep!' She whirled around to face him. He was on his knees, his forehead pressed against the sofa seat. 'Really stinks. Really stinks!' She thrust a hand down the sleeve of her blouse. 'It's *sick* is what it is!'

'I'm sorry,' he gasped.

'You rotten bastard.' She struggled to find the other sleeve, then shoved her arm through and slung the purse strap onto her shoulder. With palsied fingers, she tried to fasten her blouse as she rushed to the door.

'Alison!'

She jerked the door open and glanced back at Evan. He was still on the sofa, his ass in the air.

'Don't go!' he called. 'Please!'

She stepped out and slammed the door.

Chapter Twenty-nine

I got him good, Alison told herself as she hurried along the sidewalk. I got him real good.

Oh, sure you got him good. Maybe he'll have a sore gut for a while, maybe even a bruise, but by morning he'll be almost as good as new and you won't.

How could he *do* a thing like that?

How could I sleep through it?

He probably just slipped his hand in for a quick feel, nothing more.

Yeah, sure thing. A feel here, a feel there.

If he'd cleaned the goddamned salsa off his hand, I never would've been the wiser. What the fuck was he doing, *eating* while he groped me?

Alison heard an engine. Headlights brightened the road on her left. A car moved slowly ahead of her, close to the kerb. 'I'm sorry!' Evan called through the open passenger window. 'Please, can't we at least talk?'

She kept walking.

Evan's car stayed beside her. 'At least let me drive you home. We can't leave it like this.'

'Oh yes we can.'

'I didn't *do* anything!'

'Oh no?' Alison strode across the grass and stepped off the kerb. Evan stopped his car. She crossed in front of its headlights and went to his door. The window was down. She clutched the door and peered in at him. 'You didn't do anything? How do you figure that, huh? What do you call grabbing my tit, not to mention whatever else you might've grabbed?'

'I didn't *know* you were asleep, damnit! I came back from the kitchen and sat down with you, and you *looked* at me. You opened your eyes when I sat down, and gave me this look as if everything was okay, and I put my arm across your shoulders. You didn't tell me to get lost, so I thought you *liked* it. I thought everything was okay again. That's when I put my hand in your blouse. I didn't know you were asleep. You didn't *act* asleep. My God, you *moaned* when I . . . touched you.'

'I don't believe you,' Alison muttered. But her outrage had turned to confusion.

What if he's telling the truth?

She lowered her head. Her grip on the car door seemed necessary to hold her up.

'I thought you were awake. I never would've done those things if I didn't think you were awake.'

'What things, exactly?'

'You really don't remember any of it?'

'You did more than . . . touch my breast?'

233

'Yes.'

Alison groaned.

'You seemed to like it.'

'Christ.'

'You were breathing hard, you were kind of writhing . . .'

'My God, I don't . . .'

'Then suddenly you *snored*. I couldn't believe it. I mean, I was in shock. I still couldn't believe you'd been sleeping the whole time, but I thought *what if you were*! I mean, what if you suddenly woke up and found me all over you? So I buttoned up your blouse as fast as I could, and decided I'd better pretend the whole thing never happened unless you brought it up first. Which you didn't.'

'It was just going to be your dark little secret.'

'It was a mistake, Alison.'

'Yeah, uh-huh.'

'I'd planned to tell you about it, but not until later. I figured that, once everything was patched up between us, it'd be safe to tell you about it. Hell, you probably would've thought it was funny.'

'A riot.'

'I can certainly understand your being upset. I mean, I know how it must look. But look at it this way: if you hadn't noticed that sauce on your bra, we'd be making love right now. Wouldn't we?'

'Probably,' she admitted.

'So what I did . . . it wasn't actually bad, the timing was just off. If it'd happened before last Thursday or after tonight, it wouldn't even be an issue.'

'Murder isn't a fucking issue if you put a bullet through someone's head a minute after he's already dead.'

'What the hell does murder have to do with anything?'

'I'm just making a point. About timing.'

'I've said I'm sorry, Alison. I've explained that it was a mis-understanding. I thought you were awake.'

'Did *I* start to undress *you*?'

He didn't answer.

'Wouldn't that be the standard procedure if I'd been a participant in your little grab-fest?'

'I thought you were just relaxing and enjoying it. Like the way you just relaxed and did nothing while I was giving you the massage.'

'Sure,' she said. She felt so tired.

'I just want you to understand. I want you to come back with me. Everything was going so great, Alison. We owe it to ourselves to give it another try.'

'No.' She shook her head slowly from side to side. 'Huh-uh. It's over. It's done.'

'We'll talk about it tomorrow, all right?'

'Goodnight, Evan.' She pushed herself away from the car door, staggered backward a few steps, and rubbed her face.

'Tomorrow,' Evan said.

'Get out of here,' she muttered.

He drove away slowly.

Alison stood in the street for a while. Finally, she willed herself to move. She shuffled her feet along the pavement and managed to step over the kerb. She was still several blocks from home. She felt drained. Instead of continuing down the sidewalk, she wandered onto the grass. Soon the cool dew soaked through her shoes. She wanted to lie down, to shut her eyes and forget, but not on the wet grass. She went to a concrete bench that surrounded the trunk of an oak near Bennet Hall.

At the far side, where she couldn't be seen from the road, she lay down on the bench. She folded her hands beneath her head and let her legs hang off the edge of the circular seat. She closed her eyes.

This is fine, she thought. If Evan comes around again looking for me, he'll never spot me over here.

The concrete hurt the backs of her hands and her shoulder-blades, so she used her purse for a pillow and folded her hands on her belly. That was much better.

Something skittered noisily among the leaves overhead. Squirrels, she thought.

She wished she had a sweater. A blanket would be better. If she had a blanket, maybe she would just stay here all night.

Evan's got one in the trunk of his car. His make-out blanket. Shit, he got a lot of use out of it with me.

Never again.

Thought I was awake. Sure he did.

The chill of the concrete seeped through the back of her blouse and shorts and seemed to seep into her skin. She felt a cool breeze sliding over her bare arms and legs. It stirred her hair. It smelled moist and fresh.

Her attic room would be hot.

Another good reason not to move.

I couldn't move if I wanted to, Alison thought. And I don't want to.

Fuck it all. Fuck everything.

Okay, not the squirrels unless one lands on my face. And not Mom and Dad. And not Celia and Helen. And not pizza. Or John D. MacDonald or Ronald McDonald.

That shit didn't even get my joke.

Fuck him. Fuck Evan Forbes. And fuck Roland Whatever and how about Professor Blaine because they both look like they want to rip my clothes off? And who else? How about all of them? How about every man everywhere? Helen's right, they're nothing but walking cocks looking for a tight hole.

Okay, just most of them.

Alison realized she was gritting her teeth and shivering. She wrapped her arms across her chest.

Stick around here, she thought, and they'll find you in the morning like the frozen leopard on Kilimanjaro. They'll stand around you in awe and say, 'What's she doing here?' And some asshole will probably stick his hand in your blouse. Can't let a little thing like rigor mortis stand in the way of a cheap feel.

You're going nuts, Alison.

She rubbed her face. With her arms no longer hugging her chest, the breeze slid over her and stole the warmth from the skin beneath her blouse.

Her attic room would be hot, her bed soft.

Enough of this.

She got to her feet and started for home.

The second-storey windows were dark, but the light at the top of the stairway had been left on. Alison, still shivering, hurried up the stairs and unlocked the door. She stepped inside. The warmth felt wonderful.

Helen must've been burning incense. In spite of the breeze coming in through the open windows, a faint pine odour still hung in the air.

No light came from the crack beneath Helen's bedroom door. Alison had expected Helen to be waiting up, eager for an account of the night's events. It must be after eleven, though. With an eight o'clock class in the morning, she had probably decided to forget her curiosity and turn in.

By the dim light from the windows, Alison made her way into the corridor and entered the bathroom. She washed her face. She brushed her teeth. She used the toilet.

Standing in the bathroom doorway for a moment, she got her bearings, then switched off the light and angled across the dark hall to the staircase. She climbed the stairs slowly, gliding a hand up the banister.

Her room at the top, illuminated by a grey glow from its single window, seemed almost bright after the blackness of the staircase. Its open curtains trembled slightly in the breeze. At this distance, Alison couldn't feel the breeze at all. The room felt stifling, even worse than she had expected.

No middle ground, she thought. You're either shivering or sweating.

She lowered her purse to the floor, out of the way so she wouldn't trip over it if she needed to make a late trip to the toilet.

Then she took off her blouse and dropped it to the floor. She unfastened her shorts. She drew them down, along with her panties, and stepped out of them.

The room was still uncomfortably hot, but she could feel a hint of the breeze on her bare skin.

With a glance over her shoulder, she stepped backward to the door of her closet and leaned against it. The door banged shut. She flinched and caught her breath, shocked as much by the support giving way behind her as by the sharp noise.

She took a deep, trembling breath.

She bumped the door with her buttocks. *Now* it was shut all the way.

The smooth painted wood felt cool on her skin. Braced against it, she raised one leg and pulled off her shoe and sock. Then the other.

At the dresser, she opened a drawer and moved her hand across the clothing. Her fingers slipped over the filmy fabric of the new negligee. It was lighter than the others, and would feel fine on a night such as this. She took it out, carried it past the end of her bed, and stood in front of the window.

The faint breeze drifted in, roaming her skin. Not long ago, the cool air had chilled her to the bone. Now, it felt wonderful. It curled around Alison's thighs, slipped between her legs, caressed her belly, slid over her breasts and beneath her arms. She dropped her negligee. She placed her hands high on the window frame and spread her legs and closed her eyes.

The soft touch of the breeze moved over her.

Chapter Thirty

After hearing the toilet flush, Roland counted slowly to sixty. He made the count again and again. Then his mind wandered. He pictured Alison in her attic room, taking off her clothes, getting into bed. In his fantasy she wasn't covered by a sheet. She wore only a pyjama jacket. He saw himself standing over her, carefully unfastening the buttons as she slept, spreading open the jacket. Her skin looked like ivory in the dim light from the window. He reached down to touch her and suddenly she was obese, she was Helen and she was dead, and she grinned up at him. He lurched, bumping his forehead against the box-springs.

He lowered his head to the floor.

And held his breath, listening, half expecting Helen to moan or turn on the mattress above him, awakened by the jolt.

Don't be ridiculous, he told himself. She's dead as shit.

But I'm right under her.

He listened and heard nothing. Helen's eyes were open,

though. He could see them open. She knew he was under her bed.

Roland must've spent hours in the narrow space only a couple of feet beneath her corpse. It seemed unfair that his mind should start turning against him now, when the wait was almost over.

He still heard nothing.

But Helen was listening as she gazed with dead eyes at the ceiling, and *she* could hear Roland under the bed – his quick heartbeat and shaky breath.

'You're dead,' he whispered.

Helen rolled over, got to her hands and knees, ripped open the mattress with crooked fingers and tore out great clumps of stuffing. Then she was staring down at him through the mattress tunnel. She bared her teeth. She snarled and thrust her hand down the hole, clawing towards his face.

It isn't happening, he told himself.

But he trembled and gasped. He had to get out. He felt as if spiders were scurrying over his body. He scooted sideways over the carpet, but stopped just beneath the side of the bedframe. Helen was waiting up there. Waiting to grab him when he emerged.

With a stifled whimper, he thrust himself into the open and rolled clear. He sat up. In the dim light from the window, Helen was a motionless mound beneath the covers of her bed.

Watching her, Roland got to his feet. He kept his eyes on her as he sidestepped to the bedroom door. He opened the door, stepped out, and pulled it shut. He backed away from it.

No longer in the presence of the body, his fear slowly subsided. He felt angry and embarrassed for letting his imagination torment him.

Why, he wondered, had his friend allowed him to lose control that way? Certainly, it could've stopped the horrid thoughts – given him a nice zap to remind him of Alison. Did it enjoy his suffering? Or did it simply not care?

He touched the bulge at the back of his neck.

I'm doing it all for you, he thought.

Then he felt ashamed. This was his friend who had turned his secret fantasies into reality, who had led him into a new life even more bizarre and thrilling than his most lurid dreams. The fear was his own fault. He had no right to blame his friend.

As if stirred by the reassurance, or perhaps only to remind him of what lay ahead, his friend sent a small tremor of pleasure through Roland.

Had enough time gone by? He wanted Alison to be asleep before he went up to her. Otherwise she might cry out. Her window had been open when Roland went exploring after he'd finished cleaning the mess in the living-room. She wouldn't have closed it; the house was still too hot. With the window open, a scream might be heard by someone outside or even by the people who lived downstairs.

Roland needed to catch her asleep. Then there would be no scream or struggle.

He went to the sofa, sat down, and waited.

He savoured the waiting. Last night with Celia had been incredible. But Alison had stunning beauty along with an innocent, alluring quality that Celia lacked. She would be . . . overwhelming.

It *would* be like a dream.

All night with her.

But he needed to wait. Settling back in the sofa, he folded his hands behind his head and stared at the dark screen of the television. He called up an image of Alison in the mall wearing the jumpsuit with the zipper up the front that he longed to slide down. She'd had a bag in her hand. So had Celia. He wondered what they had bought that day.

Roland grinned. Whatever they'd bought, it cost plenty. It cost their lives and Helen's too. If he hadn't seen them at the mall . . .

He would've chosen someone else, not the Three Musketeers.

Big enough to share with a friend.

His stomach growled.

Desire pulsed through him. Roland writhed, gasping, until it faded.

Okay, he thought. I get the message.

Leaning forward, he pulled off his shoes and socks. He pulled off his shirt and spread it on the top of the table. Standing, he slipped the knife from its case and placed it on the shirt. He removed his handcuffs from a front pocket of his jeans. Digging into the other front pocket, he took out a smashed and flattened roll of industrial tape.

He touched the handcuff key dangling across his chest by a thin chain.

His hands shook badly as he peeled off a six-inch strip of the broad metallic tape and sliced it off the roll with his knife. He stuck one end of the tape to his chin. It hung down like a strange beard.

He lowered his jeans and stepped out of them.

This time there would be no problem of blood on his clothes. He would leave them down here and put them on again after showering. He would be clean when he left the house.

I'm learning, he thought. I'm getting good at this.

He sat on the sofa again, picked up his jeans, and pulled the belt out of its loops. He put the knife case back onto the belt, then stood and buckled the belt loosely around his waist. He folded the knife. He slipped it into the case.

Now he would have both hands free for cuffing her and taping her mouth.

He liked the feel of the cool belt and the weight of the knife against his side.

A naked savage.

Drape a cloth over the belt, and he would have a loincloth.

Better like this, he decided.

He slid a hand down the length of his engorged penis, then picked up the cuffs. He stepped around the end of the sofa. His feet were silent on the carpet. He heard only his thudding heart. He began to tremble. With each step, the tremors grew. He wasn't cold; he wasn't frightened. He was shaking with excitement, with delicious shivers of anticipation.

At the bottom of the staircase, Roland shifted the cuffs to his left hand. He curled his right hand over the railing. Slowly, he began to climb.

The staircase was black. But a patch of grey showed at the top.

A step creaked under his weight.

He stopped and listened.

His throat was making an odd dry clicking sound with each heartbeat. He swallowed, and the sound went away.

He began climbing again. After a few more steps his eyes were level with the floor of the attic room. The blanket lay heaped on the floor at the foot of the bed. The top sheet hung off the side of the mattress, almost at the end, but still on the bed ready to be pulled up in case Alison should grow chilly in the middle of the night.

Roland was still too low to see Alison. He climbed. The bed seemed to descend, and there was Alison, sprawled on her back.

He crouched until he could no longer see her. Staying low, he made his way up the final stairs. On elbows and knees, he crawled over the carpet. He stopped close to the side of the bed.

He listened to Alison's soft slow breathing until he was certain she was asleep. Then he stood and looked down at her.

She was bathed in a glow of moonlight. Her nightie seemed glossed with silver except for the areas over her breasts. There it had no sheen but it was transparent. He could see the creamy skin of her breasts, the dark flesh of her nipples.

Roland licked his dry lips.

He could almost feel the nipples in his mouth, almost taste them.

Alison's pillow rested crooked against the headboard as if she had found it too hot under her head, and shoved it away. Her face was turned towards the window. A few wisps of hair curled over her pale ear. Her left arm was extended towards Roland, her hand at the very edge of the mattress, palm up, fingers curled. Her other arm lay close to her right side. Her long bare legs were spread, feet tilted outward. The moon-silvered nightie clung to her thighs.

He bent over, caressed the slippery fabric between her legs, pinched a bit of it and lifted it, drawing it gently upward.

A hot surge suddenly ripped Roland's breath away. He shuddered with an agony of need, tugging briefly at the gown before it slipped from his fingers. Alison moaned. Her head turned.

Roland, quaking and fogged but somehow alert in spite of the ecstasy, made a quick grab for her left hand. He slapped the cuff around its wrist. Her arm jerked, yanking the other cuff from Roland's grip. Gasping, she rolled for the other side of the bed.

He grabbed her shoulder and hip, stopping the roll, pulling until she was on her back again. He threw himself onto her. He straddled her hips. She bucked and writhed beneath him. He caught her right hand as it lashed at his face. He pressed it to the mattress. He tore her tight left hand away from his throat and forced it down. She flung her head from side to side. She crashed a knee into his back. Roland grunted from the impact.

He jerked her cuffed hand down, pinned it under his knee to free his right hand, and punched her hard in the face. She jerked rigid beneath him, then stopped struggling. She made soft whimpering sounds as she gasped for air.

Roland peeled the tape off his chin. He pressed it across her mouth. The sounds of her breathing changed to a frantic hiss as she sucked air through her nostrils.

He should cuff her other hand now.

But Alison wasn't fighting any more, and he could feel the mounds of her breasts between his thighs. He put his hands on them. The fabric felt like netting. Her skin was hot beneath it.

He no longer heard Alison's hissing struggle for air.

She was silent.

Roland squeezed her breasts.

Her right hand rose off the bed slowly. Suspicious, he watched it. It pressed his hand more tightly to her breast and held it there. She squirmed a little and moaned.

My God, Roland thought. What's going on? Does she *like* it?

Her hand moved upward, caressing his arm, curling gently over his shoulder. She stroked the hair on the side of his head. She stroked his cheek.

The shriek drove spikes into Alison's ears. Her wrist was grabbed and forced down and her thumb popped out of his eye socket with a wet sucking sound. He didn't try to hold her. He clapped a hand to his face and swayed above her.

Alison thrust his knees upward. He tumbled onto the mattress between her legs. She rammed her feet against him, turning him and shoving him away, then kicked a leg high over his body and flung herself off the bed.

She ripped the tape from her face as she backed away. In the moonlight, Roland's naked body looked grey and cadaverous. He was writhing, clutching his face, digging his heels into the mattress and thrusting his pelvis up as he squealed.

Alison whirled around. She grabbed the railing and rushed down the dark stairway. At the bottom, she tried to call out to warn Helen but her voice came out like a choked whisper. She ran through the hallway, rounded the corner, threw open Helen's door and slapped the light switch.

'Helen!'

Helen, under the covers, didn't move.

Alison hurried towards her. 'Quick! We gotta . . . Roland's upstairs . . . attacked me!' She jerked the covers down and Helen stared dull-eyed through crooked glasses. Her face was torn, scraped and swollen. Her chin had a crust of dried mess. Alison squeezed the dull grey-blue skin of her shoulder.

'Helen!' She shook the shoulder. Helen's head wobbled slightly. Her huge breasts quivered. 'Helen, come on!'

Alison let go of the shoulder. The skin stayed dented where her fingers had been.

Numb, Alison backed away.

He'd killed Helen.

No. This was some kind of a sick joke. Helen isn't dead. Not Helen. It's a joke.

She's dead.

Alison backed through the doorway. She looked towards the dark hall. '*YOU BASTARD!*' she cried out.

And heard quick thuds of footfalls on the attic stairs. They triggered a blast of white-hot fear that sent Alison running to the door. She flung it open, lunged outside, slammed it and fled down the stairs. The painted wood of the steps was wet with dew and slippery under her bare feet so she slowed down, dreading a fall that might give Roland a chance to catch her. Four steps from the bottom, she leaped. She dropped through the chilly night air, her nightgown billowing up, and landed staggering over the flagstones and grass.

She looked back. Roland wasn't on the stairs. Stepping sideways, she saw that the door at the top was still shut.

She hurried past the stairs to Professor Teal's door. His kitchen was dark beyond the glass panes. She tried the knob. The door was locked, so she pounded the wood hard, shaking it. 'Dr Teal!' she shouted. Then she yelled, '*Fire! FIRE!*' She hammered the door. The kitchen was still dark. With a flick of her right hand she caught the dangling cuff, clenched it in her fist like a knuckleduster and smashed the glass. She reached in, being careful not to rip her arm on the pointed blades of glass, and turned the knob. With the door ajar, she eased her arm out.

She glanced towards the stairway. Still no Roland.

She shoved the door open. The glass shards on the floor clinked and scraped as the bottom of the door swept over them. Clinging to the door jamb, Alison swung herself inside and stretched out a leg as far as she could before placing her foot down. She felt no glass under it. With her weight on that foot, she pivoted and found herself clear of the door. She bent over, fingered its edge, and whipped it shut.

A sudden light blinded Alison.

Squinting, she whirled around.

Under the entry, cane raised like a club, stood Dr Teal. His white hair was untidy. He wore baggy striped pyjamas. Frowning, he blinked and his mouth started to move.

'Turn off the light,' Alison commanded in a sharp whisper.

He didn't ask questions. He hit the light switch.

Alison turned away from him and stared out of the door windows.

Still no Roland.

'He killed Helen,' she said. 'He . . . I hurt him but he's up there.'

'Oh my dear God.'

Alison heard a quiet clatter. She looked over her shoulder. Dr Teal's cane was clamped between his knees. He held the pale handset of the wall phone and spun the dial. 'Police emergency,' he said, his voice as firm and vibrant as if he were standing at the lectern in a hall packed with enthralled students. He waited a few moments, then said, 'We have bloody murder at 364 Apple Lane, and the cur is among us. Get here immediately.' He hung up the phone.

'Come away from the door,' he ordered.

Alison backed away, unwilling to take her eyes from the windows. She halted when the professor's hand curled gently over her shoulder.

'It's all right now, darling. He won't hurt you. The police will be here shortly, I'm sure.'

245

'He killed Helen,' she said. Her voice came out squeaky and tears filled her eyes.

Professor Teal patted her shoulder. 'Stay here.' He slipped past her. He walked towards the door, his cane swinging at his side like a nine-iron. Glass crunched under his slippers. He eased the door open.

'Maybe you shouldn't do that,' Alison whispered.

Ignoring her, he leaned outside. His head turned, tilted back. Then he brought his head back through the opening and looked around at Alison. 'You say that you injured him?'

'I . . . gouged one of his eyes.'

'Bully for you. Perhaps you incapacitated the rotter. I'll bash his head to pulp if . . . what about Celia?'

'She's not home.'

'Thank God for that.'

'I don't know. I'm . . . I think maybe he got her last night.'

'Dear God, no.'

'She went on a date with his roommate and she never came home.'

'Two of my girls. Two of my sweet, darling . . . oh, he shall pay dearly, dearly . . .' Professor Teal threw the door open wide and stepped out.

'No!' Alison yelled.

She ran after him, leaped the area of broken glass, and came down on the flagstone outside the door. Professor Teal was already at the bottom of the stairway. 'Wait inside,' he told her.

'Wait for the cops!' Alison cried out. 'Please!'

Ignoring her, he began to trot up the stairs. Alison darted beneath the stairway, reached between two of the steps, and grabbed the old man's ankle.

'Unhand me!'

'He'll kill you, too!'

'We shall see about that.' He tried to shake his foot free.

Alison almost lost her grip. She wrapped her other hand around the man's bony ankle and hung on.

Brakes screamed. Through the gap in the stairs, Alison saw a squad car lurch to a stop, red and blue lights spinning. A man raced around the front of the car. He pulled a pistol from his holster as he ran straight over the lawn towards Alison.

'You win,' the professor said.

She didn't trust him. She kept her grip on his ankle until the policeman jangled to a stop, crouched, aimed at him and shouted, 'Freeze, cocksucker, or I'll blow your fucking brains from here till yesterday!'

'He's not the one!' Alison yelled.

She stepped out from under the stairway.

Professor Teal turned around slowly. 'I am the owner of this house,' he said. 'We have every reason to believe that the killer is upstairs.'

'Who'd he kill?'

'My roommate,' Alison said. 'And he tried to get me.'

'Is he armed?' asked the burly policeman.

'I don't know. Not that I saw.'

'He's still up there?' Without waiting for an answer, he started up the stairs. Professor Teal stepped out of his way and came down as the officer continued to the top.

Alison went to the professor's side and put an arm around his back.

'Silly old bear,' she said.

He smiled sadly.

They both flinched as a gun blast shocked the night. Alison's head jerked sideways. She saw Roland at the top of the stairs, arms out. The policeman flopped backwards over the rail, yelling with alarm, flapping through the air. His yell stopped short when he hit the ground. For a moment he seemed to be performing a weird headstand, legs kicking at the sky. Then he toppled. He lay on his back, twitching. He had a knife in his chest.

Roland, at the top of the stairs, turned slowly. He was no longer naked. He wore jeans and an open shirt. The left side of his face was shiny with red from his empty socket, red that dribbled onto his shirt and chest. With zombie-like slowness, he lifted his left hand to study it with his one eye. The policeman's bullet hadn't missed Roland completely. Alison saw that his forefinger was gone entirely. His middle finger dangled by a strip of flesh, swinging like a pendulum. He clutched it with his other hand, tore it loose, and sailed it down at Alison like a blunt dart. It dropped into the grass at her feet.

He began to descend the stairway.

Professor Teal pushed Alison away and stepped almost casually to the foot of the stairs. He raised his cane overhead, prepared to strike when Roland came into range.

Alison rushed towards the policeman. He looked dead. She pictured him falling. Had he been holding the revolver? She didn't know. But it was not in either of his hands. She scurried around his body, trying to find the gun.

Where *is* it!

She looked towards the stairway in time to see Roland leap. He dived from high above Professor Teal. The old man, cane overhead, swung it down at the flying body. It missed Roland's head and broke across his shoulder. Roland slammed the professor to the ground.

Alison jerked the knife from the policeman's chest, whirled and ran at the sprawled, struggling men. Roland hammered the professor's nose with a fist. He rolled off. He was on his back, pushing himself up with his right arm. He raised his shot hand as if signalling Alison to halt.

Alison flung herself onto him. He fell back. He tried to push her away, fingers and stumps thrusting at her face. She drove the knife down hard. Roland squealed. Then his right hand clubbed her ear. Stunned by the impact, she felt herself being shoved off him. On her side, she saw Roland grab the knife handle. The blade had pierced his left nipple, but it hadn't gone deep. A rib must've stopped it. Roland yanked the knife free.

His ravaged hand reached for Alison.

She rolled, scurried to her feet, and ran.

She ran for the street.

The dewy grass was slippery, but she ran all out, sprinting, flinging her legs out with long quick strides, pumping her arms. The loose cuff on the end of its chain whipped across her knuckles, her forearm, sometimes lashed her side or breast.

She heard Roland gasping and whimpering behind her. Not very far behind her. She didn't dare to look.

Faint white plumes puffed from the exhaust pipe of the police car.

One foot pounded the sidewalk. The other foot landed in grass at the other side. She sprang from the kerb, rushed past the front of the car. Turning, she glanced over her shoulder. Roland hit the hood belly-first and slid across it, teeth bared, ruined hand reaching for her, knife clenched in his other hand. Alison spun away from the reaching hand. Its two fingertips grazed her belly. Stumbling backward, she grabbed the handle of the driver's door.

She jerked open the door, leaped inside, and slammed it shut while Roland was squirming off the hood. The window was open. She started to crank it up. Roland stumbled towards her. The glass slid higher. He stabbed. His knife blade pounded the window and skittered down with a grating whine like fingernails on a blackboard.

Alison released the hand-brake.

Roland opened the door.

Alison cried out, 'No!' How could she *not* have locked it?

She rammed the shift lever to Drive and stomped the gas pedal to the floor.

The car surged forward.

Roland yelled.

The door bumped against its frame.

Alison swerved away from the kerb to miss a parked Volkswagen.

She looked at the side mirror.

Roland was sprawled facedown on the pavement, half a block away.

Chapter Thirty-one

Jake entered the dispatcher's cubicle, nodded a greeting to Martha, who looked back at him with grim eyes, and turned to the girl.

She was sitting on one of the moulded plastic chairs that belonged in the waiting area outside the cubicle and must've been brought in so she wouldn't have to wait alone. She held a plastic coffee cup in both hands. The left side of her face was red and puffy. She wore Martha's old brown cardigan over a blue nightgown. She looked up from her coffee as Jake approached.

'I'm Jake Corey,' he said. 'I'm in charge of the investigation.'

She nodded.

'Would you like to step this way?'

She glanced at Martha, who nodded that it was all right. Then stood up.

Jake held the door open for her. She walked stiffly, staring down at her coffee as if concerned about spilling. Though she must've been about twenty years old, she had the look of a hurt and frightened little girl.

Jake pulled the door shut and stepped to her side.

'Where are we going?' she asked.

'Just over here.' He gestured towards Barney's office. 'We can't talk about this in front of Martha.'

She walked beside him.

'Are you all right?' he asked.

'Yeah.'

He opened Barney's door and flicked the switch. Overhead fluorescent lights came on. He followed the girl into the room. 'Sit in the chief's seat,' he told her.

'Behind the desk?'

'It'll be more comfortable.'

She stepped around the desk, set her coffee cup on the blotter, and sat down. The stuffed chair bobbed and squeaked. She rolled it forward as if to take shelter behind the big protective desk. Her hands curled around the sides of the cup.

Jake sat on a folding chair across from her. 'You're Alison?'

'Yes. Alison Sanders.'

'Dr Teal told me what you did. You're a very brave young lady.'

'Is he all right?'

'He's fine. He's very upset, of course.'

'The policeman, is he dead?'

'Yes.'

'I'm sorry,'

'So am I,' Jake muttered.

'You didn't get him, did you.' It wasn't a question.

'Not yet. But we will.'

'It was Roland,' she said in a steady low voice. 'I don't know his last name, but he lives in room 240 of Baxter Hall on the campus.'

Jake took a notepad from his shirt pocket. He quickly scribbled the name and room number. 'Was he a friend of yours?'

She shook her head. 'I've only seen him around. He's a freshman.'

'Do you have any idea why he might have . . . done this?'

'I don't know.' Alison rubbed her forehead. 'He was somehow involved in . . . his roommate took Celia out last night. That's Celia Jamerson. She was living with . . .'

'Celia Jamerson?' Jake asked, surprised. He saw the slim girl sitting by the road, scuffed and bleeding, holding her tremulous arm. 'A van tried to hit her Thursday?'

Alison nodded. 'She went out with Roland's roommate last night and she didn't come home. I went over to the dorm this afternoon to ask Roland about it. That was the only time I ever really talked to him. He said they'd gone to some motel in Marlowe, but I didn't really believe him.' She met Jake's gaze with weary, knowing eyes. 'I think Roland killed her. Maybe he killed Jason, too. That's the roommate. Maybe Jason's in on it, but . . . I don't think so.'

'What happened after you spoke with Roland?'

'I went over to a friend's house. We had dinner. Then I walked home. The place was dark. Helen's door was shut. I thought she'd gone to bed, but . . . I guess she must've already been killed. I guess Roland must've been hiding somewhere. I went up to my room and went to sleep. He woke me up. He got a handcuff on me. And he put tape on my mouth. He was naked. I thought that what he wanted to do was, you know, rape me. I mean, I'm sure that *is* what he wanted to do, not just kill me, or he wouldn't have bothered with the cuffs and tape. Anyway, we fought and I . . . I blinded him in one eye.' Her right hand left the coffee cup. She lifted her thumb and stared at it. 'I washed,' she muttered. 'Martha let me wash up. She found a key that opened the cuff. And gave me her sweater. She's very nice.'

'You said that Roland was naked.'

'He had a belt on. That's all.'

'Did you notice anything peculiar about his appearance?'

She looked at Jake and raised her eyebrows. 'You mean like a tattoo or birthmark or something?'

'Did you get a look at his back? Or feel it?'

'I don't think so. Why?'

'I just wonder if he had any kind of a bruise or bulge down his spine.'

'I don't know. Not that I noticed. Why?'

'It's a long story. I'd rather not get into it right now. After you gouged his eye, what happened?'

'I got away. I ran downstairs and went to warn Helen. But she was . . .' Alison caught her lower lip between her teeth. She shook her head.

'Then you went outside?' Jake asked.

'Yeah. I went down and broke into Dr Teal's kitchen, and he came out to help.'

'Okay, fine. He's filled me in from there, up to the point where you ran for the patrol car.'

'That's about all, then. Roland almost got me, but I drove away and . . . he was lying in the street the last time I saw him. I drove here to the police station and told Martha what happened. She sent a car and ambulance to the house and phoned someone.'

'She called the chief. He phoned me, and I went over. Could you describe this Roland?'

'He's . . . eighteen, I guess. Skinny. About five-seven. Black hair. He's minus his left eye and two fingers of his left hand, and he's got a knife wound on his left nipple.'

'He won't go far in that condition.'

'I guess not.'

'Did you notice if he had a car?'

'I don't know. There was a VW beetle on the street by the house. I almost hit it with the police car. It might not have been his, but . . .'

'A yellow beetle with a banner on its aerial?' Jake asked. He felt excited. He felt sick.

'I don't know about the banner, but I'm pretty sure the car was yellow.'

'My God,' he muttered.

'What?'

'It *was* him. He tried to pick up my daughter this afternoon.'

A corner of Alison's lip curled up. 'Your daughter?'

'She ran away from him.'

'Jesus. She's all right, though?'

'Yeah, fine. It threw a scare into her, but she's fine.'

'How old is she?'

'Four and a half. She lives with her mother.' Jake wondered why he added that. He stood up. 'It's time I got after the guy, Alison. Do you have a place to stay?'

'The house,' she said.

'I don't think so.'

'Well, Professor Teal has a spare room downstairs.'

'The odds of Roland showing up are slim to none, I think, but until he's accounted for . . .'

'You mean I need to disappear for a while?'

'Just to be on the safe side.'

'I don't know. I guess I could check into a motel. I don't have my purse, though.'

'You're welcome to stay at my place. I'll be out, anyway.'

'Thank you, but . . .'

'It's comfortable. There's food and drink in the fridge. And that way, I'll know where you are and I won't have to worry about you.'

She gave a small, slightly crooked smile. 'You'd worry about me?'

'Yes.'

'That's nice,' she whispered.

Jake felt his face redden. 'Well, you're also our main witness.'

Alison picked up the coffee cup. It was still full.

They left Barney's office and returned to the dispatcher's cubicle. 'Alison will be coming with me,' Jake said.

Alison set the cup on Martha's desk. 'Thanks for the use of the sweater,' she said. 'And for helping.'

'No problem, honey,' Martha said.

Alison started to unbutton the sweater.

Martha held up a hand. 'You keep that on, you'll catch a chill.' Grinning, she added, 'And you don't want to give Jake any ideas. Not that he's not a perfect gentleman . . . You can just send it back to me when you're done with it.'

Alison thanked her again.

They left, and went outside to Jake's car. Alison climbed into the passenger seat. Walking around to the driver's door, Jake scanned the area. He saw no cars moving on the nearby streets. He saw no parked Volkswagens. He got in and started the engine.

'You didn't notice anyone behind you on the way over, did you?' he asked.

'No. And I was looking. I was afraid he might come after me.'

'The shape you left him in, he's probably not coming after *anyone*. He might very well be dead or dying by now.'

'I hope so,' she muttered.

'I'd like to find him alive,' Jake said. Find him dead, he thought, and you probably won't find the damn snake-thing. It's got no use for a dead man. The fucker'll pull a disappearing act and turn up in someone else and you'll be back to square one.

Jake watched the rearview mirror as he drove. The road behind him appeared clear, but Roland could be staying far back with the headlights off.

Jake turned onto a side street, killed his lights, and swung to the kerb. 'We'll wait here for a while,' he said.

'Fine.'

He shut off the engine. He smiled at Alison. 'I'm sure we're not being followed. This is just a precaution.'

He glanced at her bare legs. Her negligee was very short. Her open hands rested on her thighs as if to hold it down. An awareness came to Jake, suddenly, that he was alone in the car with a very attractive young woman who was no doubt naked except for the skimpy nightgown and Martha's sweater. And he was taking her to his home. The awareness gave him a warm feeling that threatened to become more than that.

Watch yourself, he warned. The last thing she needs is to get the idea that you're getting turned on.

Turned on? Forget it, Corey.

He rubbed his sweaty hands on his pants, and checked the side mirror. 'Looks all right,' he said.

Though he felt sure that Roland wasn't tailing them, he decided to take a roundabout route to his house. He knew that he should make the trip as fast as possible, drop her off, and start searching for Roland.

But he wasn't eager to find Roland.

And he wasn't eager to get rid of Alison.

She was very quiet. Jake wondered what was going on in her mind. Nothing pleasant, probably. She'd gone through hell tonight. Most people never have to face such an ordeal. If they do, they often don't survive to cope with the emotional trauma.

'Things must look pretty bleak,' he said.

Alison turned to him. 'I'm alive,' she said. 'I feel pretty lucky.'

'It took a lot more than luck.'

'I don't know if I deserve it, though. I mean, why me? This must be how people feel when they survive an airline crash. Kind of guilty that they're still alive . . . when so many others aren't.'

'I suppose so,' Jake said. 'Do you have classes tomorrow?'

'I'll probably cut them. I don't think I could handle sitting in a classroom.'

'That's probably best. I hope this will all be over by then, but if it's not I won't want you going anywhere. You and I will be the only ones who know where you are, and I'd like to keep it that way until further notice, okay? That's the only way we can be certain you're secure.'

'No one to tell,' she said.

'What about your parents?'

'They're in Marin County.'

'You could call them if you want.'

'No reason to stir them up. They'd go hysterical on me.'

'Any boyfriends?' Smooth, Jake thought. Slipped it right in. He felt vaguely ashamed of himself.

'We broke up,' she said. 'Tonight, as a matter of fact. It's been a banner night.' After a few moments of silence, she added, 'I should probably phone him in the morning, let him know I'm okay.'

'Fine. Just don't tell him where you are.'

'Fat chance of that.'

Jake saw his house just ahead. He decided to circle the block before taking Alison in. Just as a precaution, he told himself.

'You don't think someone *sent* Roland over?' she asked.

'No, nothing like that. He could get to someone, though. If nobody knows where you are, nobody can tell him.'

'There's more to this than you're letting on, isn't there?'

Jake hesitated, then answered, 'Yes.'

'And it has something to do with Roland's back.'

'You're sharp,' Jake said, smiling at her.

'Must be pretty bad, if you're afraid to tell me.'

'It's a long story,' Jake said. 'And we're almost home.'

'Maybe it's something I should know.'

Jake didn't answer. He steered around the final corner, checked once more to be sure there was no Volkswagen in sight, then swung into the driveway of his house.

Alison held the hem of her negligee to prevent it from sliding up as she scooted off the car seat. Jake shut the door after she was out. He walked backward across his yard, a hand resting on his holstered gun, his head turning slowly, eyes scanning the neighbourhood as if he expected Roland to charge out of the darkness.

He didn't seem nervous, though. Just careful. Alison felt safe with him. She didn't like knowing that he would leave just minutes from now.

He opened the house door. Alison followed him inside. The lights were already on, the curtains closed. The warmth of the house felt good after the chill outside.

'Just make yourself at home,' Jake said. 'The kitchen's over here.'

He led the way. Alison began to unbutton her sweater, but stopped when she realized what she was wearing under it.

Jake turned on the kitchen light. 'There's food, soft drinks, beer in the refrigerator. Help yourself.' He pointed at a cupboard. 'Hard stuff in there, in case you get the urge.'

'What's your daughter's usual bedtime?'

'Oh, Kimmy's not . . .' He laughed softly. 'What's your hourly rate?'

'In my prime, five bucks per hour. For Kimmy, no charge.'

'That's good, since she isn't here.' They left the kitchen. 'Sofa,' he announced, walking in front of it. 'Where I'll stretch out when I get back. Television.' He bent over the coffee table, picked up the remote control, and turned the TV on and off, demonstrating. He smiled a bit self-consciously.

Alison followed him to the bathroom. He flicked on its light. 'Fine if you want to take a bath or shower or something,' he said and blushed slightly.

'I could use one.'

'There're towels and stuff in the closet here.'

He nodded as they passed a dark doorway. 'Kimmy's room. Her bed's a little small for you.' He opened the door of a linen closet and pulled folded sheets and a pillow case down from the shelves. Then he stepped into his room. He turned the light on. The bed was unmade. Alison guessed that he had been sleeping when the call came tonight.

He walked over to the bed. 'Want to give me a hand with the sheets?' he asked.

'I'll take care of that,' Alison told him.

'Well . . .'

'No problem,' she said. 'It'll give me something to do after you're gone.' It was a small lie. She had no intention of taking his bed, forcing him to sleep on the sofa when he returned from hunting down Roland.

Jake set the sheets and pillow case on the end of the bed. He entered his closet. When he came out he was holding a shotgun. 'Have you ever fired one of these?' he asked.

Alison nodded. 'I've gone duck hunting with Dad a few times. Hell, *more* than a few times.'

He handed the shotgun to her.

It was a bolt-action .12 gauge. She opened the bolt enough to see a shell in the chamber, then closed it.

'There're three more in the clip,' Jake said.

'Okay.'

'Keep it close to you. Just don't shoot me when I come back.' Alison smiled.

The colour suddenly drained from his face.

'What is it?'

'Maybe that wasn't such great advice.' He sat on the end of the bed and frowned up at her. 'I want you to brace the bedroom door shut before you turn in. If I try to force my way in, use the shotgun.'

'Are you crazy?'

'I don't expect anything like that to happen, but . . . When you come out in the morning, keep me covered if I'm here and have me take my shirt off. Then take a good look at my back. If there's a bulge going up my spine as if I've got a snake under my skin, blow me away. Try to hit the bulge. If you don't nail the thing, it'll probably come out as soon as I'm dead and it might come after you.'

She stared at Jake.

He meant it.

'Jesus Christ,' she muttered.

'*Invasion of the Body Snatchers*,' Jake said. 'But it's for real. This snake-thing was up the back of the guy who tried to run down Celia. It got into Ronald Smeltzer over at the Oakwood Thursday night just before he blew off his wife's head. And now I'm pretty sure it's in Roland. It's some kind of parasite that takes control and turns people into killers. It's conceivable that it might get into me when I catch up with Roland. I certainly don't intend for that to happen, but . . . do us both a favour and blast me if I come in with the thing. And try to kill it, too. Or at least make sure it doesn't get close to you.'

Alison was numb.

Jake stood up. 'You okay?'

She stared at him.

He stepped close to her. He put his hands on her shoulders. 'I'm sorry. I had to tell you.'

The weight of the shotgun pulled her arms down.

He lifted it away from her, took her gently by one elbow, and led her down the hall to the living-room. He guided her to the sofa. She sank onto it. He propped the shotgun beside her, went away, and came back.

'Maybe this will help,' he said. He placed a mug of beer with a white frothy head in her hand. He ripped open a bag of potato chips and set it on the cushion so it rested against the side of her thigh. She smelled the pleasant aromas of the beer and chips. From the odour, she knew that the chips were sour cream and onion flavour.

A favourite of Helen.

She looked up at Jake.

He managed a thin smile, but his eyes were sad. 'Everything will be okay,' he said. Then he crouched in front of her. 'Alison.'

'Huh?'

'You look pretty stunned.'

'I'll be all right,' she heard herself say. 'In a while.'

'What I just told you, it's a secret. Right. At least until Tuesday. Then we'll be going public with it.'

'Nobody will believe it.'

'But you do.'

'I wish I didn't.'

Jake put a hand on her knee. 'Get a good night's sleep.'

She pressed a hand on top of his. 'Watch out,' she said. 'Come back safe.'

Chapter Thirty-two

The second-floor hallway of the dorm was deserted. Only a few of the overhead fluorescent lights had been on for the night, giving a cool, desolate illumination that added to Jake's uneasiness. Bands of light showed beneath some of the doors. Jake heard music coming from one of the rooms and the sound of a shower from the bathroom.

He stopped in front of Roland's door. No light came through the gap at its bottom. Taking out his wallet, he spread the bill compartment and removed a thin plastic case. He slipped the lock pick and torque wrench from the case.

The burglary tools were a gift from Chuck, who had provided lessons for the price of a six-pack.

Jake had never quite planned to use them for an illegal entry. Nevertheless, he'd carried them in his wallet for the past two years, mostly to please Chuck but also telling himself they might come in handy if he ever locked himself out of his house. Lately, he'd picked the house lock several times for Kimmy because she got a kick out of it.

The recent practice paid off. In less than a minute, the lock of Roland's door clicked and Jake eased the door open half an inch.

He put away the burglary tools.

He didn't expect Roland to be in the room. He'd found no yellow VW in the dorm parking area and Roland must know that Alison would say where he lived. But the guy was hurting. He might go to ground anywhere, even in his own room.

Jake drew his revolver, stepped against the wall for cover, and shoved the door. It swung open and bumped to a stop. He listened and heard nothing.

Reaching around the doorframe, he found the switch plate.

Light spilled into the hallway.

He lunged into the room.

Saw no one.

The room had a linoleum floor with a tan fringed rug spread across the centre. Jake saw no blood on the floor or the rug.

There was a bed along each of the long walls. One bed was made, one wasn't. Beyond the head of each stood a desk with a straight-backed chair. The far wall had shelves partway up, then windows to the ceiling.

Jake swung the door shut.

He was standing between two wooden partitions which he guessed were the sides of twin closets.

If Roland was in the room, he was hiding. Under a bed or inside one of the closets.

Keeping his back to the door, Jake dropped to his hands and knees. Both of the beds had suitcases under them. That left the closets.

Jake got to his feet. He rushed forward and spun around, sweeping his revolver from one closet to the other. The sliding doors of both were open. Which left half of each closet out of sight.

Jake stepped to the one on his left, ducked, and peered in beneath the hanging clothes. Nobody there. He sidestepped to the other closet. The hangers were empty, giving him a good view through the dim enclosure.

Satisfied that the room was safe, he holstered his revolver.

If this was Roland's closet, where were the clothes? Had Roland already been here, packed up and fled? It hardly seemed likely that someone in his condition would return for his clothes before taking off. And there was no blood.

Remembering the luggage. Jake crouched beside the nearer bed and pulled out the suitcase. It wasn't latched. He opened it. The case was stuffed with folded clothing. The T-shirt on top was printed with a message. He lifted it, shook it open, and read, 'GHOULS JUST WANTA HAVE FUN'.

Jake put down the shirt and pushed the suitcase back under the bed.

Obviously Roland had been planning a trip.

Planning to get out of town before the heat came down on him. Planning, maybe, to travel the roads like the John Doe in the van, killing whenever the opportunity presented itself, leaving a trail of half-eaten bodies in shallow graves.

But he hadn't come back for the suitcase.

Not yet.

He won't be back, Jake decided. He's blind in one eye, maybe brain-damaged from Alison's thumb, and less two fingers thanks to Rex Davidson's bullet. He's got a stab wound in the chest, though it sounded as if that might be superficial. At the very least, he has to be in shock and weak from blood loss. The last thing he'll be concerned about is picking up his suitcase.

If he's concerned about anything, at this point. If he's not already dead.

Jake sat on the edge of the bed. On the wall across from him was a poster of the actress Heather Locklear. He stared at her slender bare legs and his mind drifted to Alison.

Maybe leaving her alone wasn't such a good idea.

She's safe, he told himself.

You can't be sure of that.

Maybe go back.

The best thing you can do for her is nail Roland. Before he dies and the damned snake-thing gets into someone else.

On a shelf below the poster stood a framed portrait of a family. The young man in the photograph was probably Roland's roommate, Jason, the guy who'd disappeared with Celia.

Maybe Roland has a photo of himself, Jake thought. He glanced over his shoulder. The wall was covered with grim pictures that looked as if they'd come from magazines. Most of the subjects weren't familiar to Jake, but he recognized one that showed Janet Leigh in the shower scene from *Psycho*. Another was Freddy, the killer who wore a battered fedora and a glove with long blades on its fingers in *Nightmare on Elm Street*. There was a hideous fat guy holding a chainsaw overhead. There was a group of decomposed zombies, one munching on a severed arm.

Jake shook his head. The snake-thing had certainly chosen itself a compatible host. Coincidence?

He remembered that he was trying to find a photo of Roland. Knowing what the guy looked like would help.

He stood and wandered to the end of the room. The desktop was clear except for a bottle of glue and a pair of scissors. Dropping onto the chair, Jake slid open the middle drawer and stared.

He'd found his photo of Roland.

He felt sickened by it.

Body parts floated around the leering face: numerous breasts, torsos, buttocks, vaginas and a few arms and legs.

These were not cut from magazines. They had the thickness of snapshots.

The only part of the girl's anatomy not cascading around Roland's head was her face.

Maybe Celia Jamerson, Jake thought.

A drop of sweat fell onto Roland's left eye. Jake blotted it with his sleeve, then wiped his face.

He lifted the photograph out of the drawer. Beneath it lay its frame.

So Roland hadn't slipped it back into the frame after finishing his project.

The wastebasket was midway between the two desks, close to the wall. Jake crouched over it. The bottom of its white plastic liner was littered with scraps. He upended the wastebasket, sat on the floor, and searched.

Most of the shots didn't include the girl's face. The photographer, obviously, had been more interested in views of her lower areas – all of which had been snipped out, usually leaving the limbs intact.

Jake found three pictures showing the girl's face. The face in all three belonged to the same girl.

She wasn't Celia.

She wasn't dead. At least not at the time she posed. She

smirked; she licked her lips. In one, she sucked her middle finger.

Jake slipped a view of the girl's face into his shirt pocket. He scooped up the remaining scraps and dumped them into the wastebasket.

In the morning he would get a search warrant. The room would be photographed and gone over, inch by inch, every item studied and catalogued, every surface closely inspected and checked for prints, the whole area vacuumed for stray bits of hair, fabric and other particles that might incriminate Roland.

Jake took the eight by ten with him, and left.

After leaving Baxter Hall, Jake cruised the streets around the campus, looking for the yellow Volkswagen beetle with the banner on its aerial, not really expecting to spot it, wanting to return home and make sure that Alison was safe but knowing that his duty was to search.

First the streets near the campus, then the Oakwood Inn.

He dreaded the thought of driving out there and entering the dark restaurant. The longer he prowled the streets, however, the more certain he became that the Oakwood was where Roland must've gone. The damned creature seemed to have an affinity for the place. And that was where it had left its eggs.

Jake knew that he was procrastinating.

He turned onto Summer Street, which bordered the campus on the north.

What I'll do, he thought, is go home and get into my gear before heading out there. I'm not going to the Oakwood without my boots and leathers. Roland might be dead. The thing might be loose.

And that'll give me a chance to see Alison.

He wondered if she was asleep yet.

He glanced down a side street, spotted a Volkswagen at the kerb, and hit the brakes. He checked the rearview. Clear behind him. He backed up, stopped, and gazed at the car.

It was parked beneath a streetlamp, but the light above it was dead, leaving it in darkness. Jake couldn't make out the colour of the VW.

But it had a banner on the aerial.

This is it.

Heart thudding, he turned. He drove straight for the car. His headlights pushed towards it, lit it.

Yellow.

Someone was in the driver's seat.

Jake gazed through the windscreen, stunned.

The man in the VW didn't move. The left side of his face looked black in the glare of the headlights.

This had to be Roland.

Jake opened his door. He crouched behind it, pulled his revolver, and took aim. 'Step out of the car!' he yelled.

Roland didn't move.

Jake repeated the command.

Roland remained motionless. He was dead, unconscious or faking.

Jake stepped away from the door. Keeping his handgun pointed at Roland, he walked slowly forward. He tried to watch Roland through the windscreen, but found his gaze drawn downward to the pavement.

He wished he had his boots on. His ankles felt bare in spite of the socks.

He remembered the machete in the trunk of his car. Halting, he considered going back for it.

The front bumper of the VW was no more than two yards in front of him. He stared at the darkness beneath it.

Glanced at Roland.

The right eye was open. It seemed to be watching him.

This guy is dead.

The fucking snake might be *anywhere*.

Like under the car, just waiting for me to get close enough.

The skin prickled on the nape of Jake's neck.

He backed away, sidestepped at the rear of his car, and dug into his pocket for the keys. He found the trunk key. He fumbled it into the lock and twisted it. The trunk popped open, blocking his view. He snatched out the machete and rushed clear.

Roland hadn't moved.

Jake saw nothing squirming towards him on the pavement.

With the machete in his right hand, the revolver in his left, he hopped onto the kerb and approached the passenger side of the VW until he was near enough to see that the windows were rolled up. Then he dashed to the middle of the street. The windows on the driver's side weren't open, either.

Whether Roland was alive or dead, the snake-thing was still in the car. Probably. Either inside Roland or writhing around loose, trapped.

Jake stepped close to the driver's window and peered in. He glimpsed the gaping hole where Roland's left eye should have been and quickly looked away from it.

Roland reclined in the seat, the front of his shirt bloody, his head tipped back slightly against the headrest. His position prevented Jake from checking the back of his neck.

The headlights left the lower areas of the car's interior in darkness. If the creature was on the seats or floor, Jake couldn't see it.

There was only one way to find out whether it was still up Roland's spine: open the door, shove him forward, and look.

No way.

Not a chance.

Jake holstered his pistol. Watching Roland, he walked backward to his car, slid in, and took a pack of matches from the glove compartment. He got out. He backstepped to the trunk and picked up the can of gasoline.

He poured gas onto the kerb beside the VW, onto the pavement behind the car and near its driver's side, then past the front to the kerb again, completing the circle. Then he splashed the car, dousing it with the pungent liquid and running trails out to the surrounding gas. Finally he crouched and flung gas into the space beneath the undercarriage.

He stopped when the can felt nearly empty. He wanted to save some gasoline, just in case.

He capped the can. Hurrying into the road, he stepped over the wet path of the circle. He set the can down behind him, squatted, struck a match, and touched it to the stained pavement.

A low, bluish flame with flutters of yellow and orange stretched out in both directions. It met intersecting paths and rolled towards the car.

Jake picked up the can and backed away. By the time he reached the far side of the street with it, the car was a blazing pyre. He could feel its heat warming his clothes and face. The fire lit the night, shimmering on the leaves of nearby trees, glowing on the walls and windows of the apartment house beyond it, shining on the hood and windscreen of his own car.

A car parked behind the VW seemed to be safely out of range.

He wondered if he should move his own car.

Or himself.

Hissing, popping sounds came from the fire. Then a sharp crack made Jake flinch. He heard glass crash on the pavement.

'Christ,' he muttered.

He rushed forward until the wall of fire stopped him. Shielding his eyes, he squinted through the flames at the wide wedge-shaped gap in the driver's window.

Nothing came out.

As he watched, flames enveloped Roland. They crawled up from below, sweeping up his face and igniting his hair. Jake gagged as the face blackened and bubbled. Then dense smoke covered the horror.

Jake heard distant shouts of 'Fire!'

He heard more windows burst.

Then he was rushing around the car, brandishing his machete, peering through the blaze at one broken window after another. Smoke poured from the openings. But nothing else came out.

Not yet.

The car's gas tank went up with a muffled boom. Jake staggered back as heat blasted against him. A spike of glass flew past his cheek. Another stabbed his thigh. He pulled it out. The car was still rocking from the impact.

Now it was an inferno.

The fucker's cooked, Jake thought. Cooked. It's a goner.

For the first time, he noticed a few people watching from the other side of the street. He turned around. More were on the lawn in front of the apartment house. He took a step towards two young men, probably students. One wore a robe, the other wore only boxer shorts. Both men backed away. No wonder, Jake thought. I'm not in uniform, I've got this machete.

'I'm a policeman,' he shouted. 'One of you guys call the fire department.'

'I already called,' said a brunette in pyjamas. 'I hope nobody's *in* that car.'

'Nobody alive,' Jake said.

'How'd it start?' asked the guy in the boxer shorts.

Jake shook his head. Then he turned away. The fire was still blazing. Several of the spectators from the other side of the street were inching forward for a better view.

When Jake rushed into the road some of them backed off and one young couple turned and fled, the woman shrieking. Apparently they had missed the news that he was a cop. Or couldn't bring themselves to trust a guy, cop or not, who was running at them with a machete.

'Everybody stand clear,' Jake yelled. 'The fire department is on its way.'

'Somebody's in the car!' a man shouted, pointing.

'Get back,' Jake warned.

A woman turned away, hunched over, and vomited.

'Everybody move back, back to the sidewalk. There'll be fire trucks coming in.'

One couple ignored his warning. They were standing over Jake's gas can, frowning at it and muttering to each other. The girl wore a pyjama jacket. The guy wore pyjama pants. The girl crouched and reached towards the can.

Oh, shit, Jake thought. 'Don't touch that!' he snapped. 'It's evidence. The arsonist might've left prints.'

Clever, he thought.

Dumb asshole, why didn't you put the can back in your truck?

As the girl backed away, Jake slipped the blade of his machete through the can's handle, raised it, and carried the can towards his car.

No point leaving the thing in sight. The fire boys might not be so easily fooled, and he would have a rough time trying to explain why he torched a vehicle with a suspect still inside.

The gas can and machete were locked safely in his trunk by the time he heard the sirens.

The firemen rushed the car with chemical extinguishers. Blasting flames out of the way, they pulled Roland's carcass off the seat and dragged it into the road. Two firemen fogged it with their extinguishers, then left it there and joined those trying to knock down the car fire.

Jake looked at the corpse. It was still smoking. It was a charred, featureless hulk that hardly resembled a human being. If he hadn't watched the body being removed from the car, Jake wouldn't have been able to tell whether it was face up or face down. He knew it was face up. But it had no face. Or ears. Or genitals. The surface was a black crust flecked with frothy white from the extinguishers. Fluids leaked from cracks in the crust.

When the honking blasts of the extinguishers went quiet, Jake heard the sizzling sound that came from the body. It sounded like a rib roast.

It didn't smell like one.

Jake stepped back, struggling not to vomit.

A fireman showed up and spread a blanket over the body.

Smoke rose from under the blanket.

Jake kept watch.

The fire was out, the car a smouldering ruin, by the time the coroner's van arrived. The men stayed inside the van, smoking cigarettes, waiting, as instructed, for Applegate to show up.

Soon Steve arrived in his Lincoln Continental. He climbed out, wearing a warm-up suit and carrying a doctor's bag. He joined Jake. 'What's going on?'

'This is our man,' Jake said, nodding towards the covered corpse. 'Earlier tonight, he killed a girl and tried to nail her roommate. He killed Rex Davidson. There's a good chance he had our snake-thing up his back when he did it.'

'Oh, terrific,' Steve muttered. 'Let me guess: you want a little on-the-scene exploratory surgery to determine whether it's inside him.'

'Good guess,' Jake said.

'Shit.'

Steve went to the van and spoke to the men through its open window. They climbed out.

Wearing gloves, they uncovered the body and lifted it into a body bag. They zipped the bag. One man retrieved a stretcher with folding legs from the rear of the van. They hoisted the bagged remains onto the stretcher, rolled it to the van, and pushed it in.

'Is this a solo job?' Steve asked Jake. 'Or do I get the pleasure of your company?'

'I'll stick with you.'

'Good decision. Congratulations. Have a cigar.'

Once the cigars were lit, Jake followed Steve into the rear of the van. He pulled the doors shut. The lights remained on. The smoke from the cigars drifted into vents in the ceiling.

Steve knelt on one side of the body bag, Jake at its end with his back to the doors. He drew his revolver.

'Yes,' Steve said. 'I was about to suggest as much.'

'The thing's probably dead,' Jake whispered. 'If it's in him at all.'

'If it remained between the spine and the epidermis, I would agree with you. But just suppose, when the situation heated up, it took a trip into this fellow's stomach? It passed through Smeltzer's stomach, so obviously it has no problem with the acids.'

'This guy must've cooked for fifteen minutes,' Jake pointed out.

Steve raised an eyebrow. 'Charred on the outside, rare in the middle. That's how I prefer my steaks.'

Jake squinted at Steve through his rising cigar smoke. 'So if the thing went deep, it might be all right?'

'Very likely fit as a fiddle.'

Jake muttered. 'Shit.'

Cigar clamped in his teeth, Steve opened his satchel and pulled on a pair of surgical gloves. He slid the zipper down the length of the body bag.

In spite of the van's ventilation system and the aroma of the cigars, the stench that rose from the burnt corpse choked Jake. His eyes filled as he gagged, but he watched the bag's opening and held his revolver steady.

Steve seemed unaffected. He bent over the remains. With the tip of a gloved finger, he prodded a blackened crater a few inches above the groin. 'Was this fellow shot?' he asked, his words slurred by the cigar in his teeth.

'Just in the hand.'

'This might be the creature's exit.'

'Couldn't the fire have made that?'

Steve shrugged. He pushed with his finger. The charred surface in the centre of the crater crumbled, and his finger went in deep. He wiggled it around. 'Nope,' he said. He pulled his finger out.

Then he grabbed the far side of the body bag, lifted and pulled it towards him. The corpse rolled out, bumping face down onto the stretcher. Black flakes fell off it.

Jake switched the revolver to his left hand long enough to wipe his right hand dry on his trouser leg.

Steve spent a while looking at the back of the corpse. Then he took a scalpel from his satchel. He turned his eyes to the barrel of Jake's revolver. 'Try to miss my hands if we have a sudden visitor. They mean a lot to me.'

'What about that exit hole on the other side?'

'If that's what it is.'

'Great.'

'Ready?'

Jake eased his forefinger over the trigger. 'No, but go ahead.'

Steve pressed the blade of the scalpel to the nape of the neck, pushed it in, and slid it downward.

'Jesus,' Jake muttered, watching the crust of skin crumple at the edges of the incision.

Nothing came bursting out.

Steve brought the blade again to the back of the neck. He inserted its point into the slit and poked around. 'I think we may be all right,' he said. He grinned at Jake. 'Just watch it don't come popping out his arse.'

'Thanks.'

Setting the scalpel aside, Steve used both hands to spread open the incision. The outer layer of black cracked and flaked off with a sound like dry leaves being crushed. Steve dug in with all the fingers of his right hand. After probing inside the wound for a few moments he said, 'The thing was here, all right. I can feel a definite separation of the lower epidermal layer from the muscle fascia.'

Picking up the scalpel again, Steve ran the blade the rest of the way down the spine. He did more exploring with his hands.

'Yep,' he said.

'So it was in him, and now it's gone,' Jake said.

'That's how it looks. Took a powder through the stomach hole. That's my professional opinion. Of course, the thing *might* still be inside him . . . lying low, so to speak. Won't know that, for sure, until I've done a full autopsy. I'll get the boys to bag him up again. We'll keep him in cold storage and I'll call you over so you can ride shotgun when it's time for the big event. Though, as I said, I'm almost sure it's not in him at this point.'

'If it's not,' Jake said, 'the thing is either ashes inside his car or else . . . it's not.'

'And looking for a new home,' Steve said.

'Or already found one,' added Jake.

Chapter Thirty-three

The ringing of a bell woke Alison up. She raised her face off the pillow and turned her head. After a moment of confusion, she realized that she was lying on the sofa in Jake's living-room. The lamps were on. No light came through the curtains, so morning wasn't here yet.

The bell rang again.

She threw back the sheet and sat up. A strap of her negligee hung off her shoulder. She brushed it back into place.

The front door was open a few inches, the guard pulled taut.

Jake, she remembered, had warned her to barricade herself in the bedroom. Not wanting to take his bed from him, she had chosen to sleep on the sofa. She had heeded his warning enough, however, to fasten the door chain to prevent him from entering while she slept.

'Who is it?' she asked.

'Jake.' A belt with a holstered revolver swung through the opening and dropped to the floor. 'I'll step away. Bring the shotgun, unchain the door, then back off and keep me covered.'

'Just a minute.' She lifted the sweater off the coffee table and slipped into it. She fastened the middle button to keep it together across her breasts. The shotgun was propped against the table. She picked it up and went to the door.

She pushed the door shut. She glanced down at herself.

The negligee was *awfully* short.

Her face heated.

He's seen me in it before, she told herself. Hell, he's seen me in nothing else.

She slid the guard chain to the end of its runner, let it drop, and opened the door.

Jake was standing on the lawn. He shook his head. 'That's no way to cover me.'

Shrugging, Alison lifted the butt of the shotgun off the floor. She clutched the weapon in both hands. But she didn't aim at him. She backed away.

Jake entered the house and shut the door. A miasma of unpleasant odours came in with him. Though more than two yards in front of him, Alison smelled gasoline, cigar smoke, sweat and a disgusting, sweetish stench that she couldn't recognize.

Jake's face and clothes were smeared with soot. One leg of his tan trousers was torn at the thigh and matted with dry blood.

'What happened to your leg?'

'Flying glass. No big deal.' He untucked his shirt, undid the buttons, and took it off. Then he turned around.

Alison stepped closer. The odours got worse, but his back looked fine. She reached out with her left hand and ran fingers down his spine. She felt no bulges. His skin was cool and damp. 'Except for the stink,' she told him, 'you're fine. What happened?'

Jake turned to face her. 'I found Roland. He's dead. He was already dead by the time I found him.'

Alison nodded. She suddenly felt sick, and didn't know whether it was the godawful odours from Jake or learning that Roland had died. *I* killed him, she thought.

It's good that he's dead.

I killed him.

It was self-defence. He deserved to die after what he did to Helen . . . what he did, maybe, to Celia.

'Gouging his eye?' she muttered.

'He had a bad stomach wound when we found him. I suspect that was the finishing touch.'

'A stomach wound? So it wasn't me who killed him?'

'Wasn't you.'

'Thank God.'

'I'd better take a shower before you pass out on me. You're looking a little green around the gills.'

She nodded. 'What *is* that odour?'

'I found Roland in his car parked on a side street near the campus. I didn't want to take a chance of the . . . remember that snake-thing I told you about?'

'I don't think I'm likely to forget that.'

'Well, I doused Roland's car with gasoline and torched it. With him in it.'

'Christ.'

'The idea was to burn the snake-thing. Afterward, I had the coroner cut Roland open to see if we could find it.' Jake shook his head. 'Wasn't in him. We think it left from his stomach. That's what made the wound that probably polished him off. It knew that Roland was on his last legs, wouldn't be any more use.'

'It broke out of him . . . like that monster in *Alien*?'

'Something like that. We're hoping Roland was inside the car when it happened. All the windows were rolled up. So if the thing was trapped in the car, it almost has to be dead. I searched the rubble afterward. Couldn't find any trace of the thing, but that doesn't mean much. Might've been nothing left but a heap of ashes.'

'It might be dead, then, or it might not?'

'We're going to assume it's alive until we know otherwise.'

'And if it *is* alive?'

'Then it'll try to find someone else to get in, and we're pretty much back where we started. I'm sorry. I wish I could tell you the whole mess is over.'

'But maybe it is.'

'I'd bet a month's salary that the damned thing is dead. But I won't bet your life on it.' He rubbed the shirt across his face, smearing sweat and soot. 'I'd better take that shower now.' He stepped past Alison and headed for the hallway.

When she noticed the sound of the water running, she realized that she hadn't moved since Jake left. She dragged the shotgun over to the door and propped it against the wall. She attached the guard chain.

The disgusting odours still filled the room. In the kitchen, she searched until she found candles in a drawer. She lit three of them, dripped wax onto paper plates, and stuck them upright. She brought the candles into the living-room and placed them on the coffee table.

Sitting on the sofa, she leaned back and propped her feet on the table between two of the candle plates.

She wondered if Jake would come back into the room after his shower. Maybe they could have a drink together.

He'd been through a nightmare of his own, tonight: burning Roland, watching while the coroner cut him open. That one odour, the really bad one . . .

And he apologized to me for not having better news.

Maybe he won't like seeing the candles. They might remind him of what happened earlier.

Alison sniffed. The nasty odours seemed faint. She puffed out the candles and carried them back into the kitchen. Then she went to the front door. She opened it enough to peer out, then shut it again, removed the guard chain, and swung the door wide.

The breeze smelled wonderful. It blew her hair. It felt cool and good on her body. She opened the sweater. The breeze caressed her through the negligee, moved up her bare legs. It felt just as fine as before, when she was standing naked at her bedroom window, and then it stopped feeling fine as the memory surged in of waking to find Roland above her. Moaning, she swung the door shut. She leaned against it, head on her crossed arms.

'Alison?'

She turned around. Jake was standing in the hallway entrance, wearing a robe.

'Are you all right?' he asked.

'Not very. How about you?'

'Better.'

'I was just letting some fresh air in.'

She saw his gaze stray downward, then back to her face. *Just in time to catch my blush,* she thought.

'I guess I'd better hit the sack,' Jake said. 'Don't you want to trade places? I'm sure my bed would be a lot more comfortable for you.'

'The sofa's fine. Really.'

'It's up to you.' He rubbed his chin. 'Well, see you in the morning, Alison. Sleep tight, huh?'

'Yeah. You too.'

He turned away. Alison looked down at herself. You sure gave him an eyeful, she thought. He noticed, too, but he didn't get funny. That's good. Would've been awkward if he'd decided it was some kind of an invitation.

Was it some kind of an invitation? she wondered. How come I didn't bother pulling the sweater together before I turned around? He probably thinks I did it on purpose.

I bet that's why he ran off so fast. He came in, maybe to spend a while talking, saw me like this, and decided he'd better beat a quick retreat.

Scared him away.

Don't flatter yourself, she thought. He left because he's had a long, rough day and he's tired. Probably didn't care, one way or the other, about me and my nightie.

She took off the sweater. Standing there, she folded it slowly and watched the hallway.

Jake was probably in bed already.

Alison moved quietly through the room, turning off lights. There was no need for the lights now that Jake was here.

It felt good, knowing that he was in the house, only a few seconds away.

Alison lay down on the sofa and pulled the sheet up.

He didn't have to rush off like that, she thought. We should've talked for a while.

She imagined herself walking down the dark hallway to his room. Asking if he was asleep. Telling him that she didn't want to be alone, not just yet.

Why not crawl into his bed while you're at it? Sure. You just dumped Evan because he wasn't interested in anything but making it and you're hot to jump in bed with a guy you hardly know.

I am not. I wouldn't do that. Why am I even *thinking* about it, after all that's happened tonight?

What do you *want* to think about – Helen?

She saw Helen on the bed, glasses crooked . . .

The image clenched her with cold tight fists. She lurched up and gazed through the darkness, gasping.

* * *

When Jake woke up, his room was bright. He squinted at the alarm clock on the nightstand. Almost ten o'clock. But what day was this? Monday.

He rolled onto his belly and pushed his face into the soft warmth of the pillow.

Need to get up, he thought. Need to – what? Go back to where you found Roland, check around, talk to people. What for? See if they saw anything. A snake in the grass.

Shit. It seemed pointless.

Need to do something, though. Need to make sure the thing's dead, is what. 'Cause if it's not dead, Alison . . .

She's here. Sleeping on the sofa.

And me in my bed. What virtue. Congratulations, Corey. Missed your big chance.

It would've been wrong. Taking advantage.

I know, he thought. Don't I know. Fell asleep last night telling myself just how wrong it would be . . . and how nice. Even if we'd done no more than hold each other, it would've been fine.

He remembered how small and vulnerable she had looked sitting behind Barney's desk, holding onto the coffee cup as if it were a talisman that would keep harm away. And sitting in the car, that nightie barely covering her legs. And when he came out after the shower and her sweater was open.

Jake's penis was pushing uncomfortably against the mattress. He rolled onto his back to relieve the pressure.

Real nice, he thought. The knight in shiny armour has a hard-on. Sorry about that, Alison.

Alison, a pretty name. Alison Sanders.

He wondered if she was still asleep. It would be nice to see her sleeping on the sofa, probably looking peaceful like a little kid. He couldn't go sneaking in and watch her, though. What would she think if she woke up?

Go in and make a pot of coffee. Take a cup to her.

We'll sit for a while, talking. Alison will be all sleepy, her hair tousled. Maybe she'll have the sheet wrapped around her so neither of us will have to be embarrassed about her nightgown.

Take your robe to her. That way, she'll know your intentions are honourable.

Jake pulled the sheet aside. He rolled off the bed and stood up. He was shirtless, and wearing his pyjama pants. Though his erection had diminished, the front of the pants still bulged somewhat. He headed for the dresser, planning to put on his pyjama jacket before venturing from the room, and stopped abruptly at the foot of his bed.

Alison was asleep on the floor.

She lay curled on her side, a pillow under her head, her bare feet protruding from the sheet that covered her to the shoulders.

Jake stared down at the girl, bewildered by her presence. Unless she had walked in her sleep, she must've come here on purpose, needing the comfort of being close to him. She must've been suffering, alone in the other room. Needed a friend. And sneaked in here and made her bed on the floor to be near him in secret.

I should've stayed up with her, he thought. I should've realized.

He crouched in front of Alison. Wisps of hair hung over the side of her face. Her mouth was open, its lower corner buried in the pillow. The peaceful way she looked in her sleep reminded Jake of Kimmy.

But Kimmy never had a swollen discoloured jaw and cheek like Alison.

A bruise on her arm, though. She'd shown it to him when they got to Jack-in-the-Box last night.

Should've given Barbara a bruise for *her* arm.

Ever hurts Kimmy again, it'll be a court order. How could the bitch slug her own daughter like that? How could *anybody* slug a girl like Kimmy?

Or a girl like Alison?

The guy who did that is dead. A hunk of burnt meat.

Deserved it, the bastard. Pounded Alison, tried to rape and kill her.

Reaching out, Jake lightly brushed the hair upward from the puffed and purple side of her face. He slipped it behind her ear.

'Good morning,' Alison said, her voice quiet and husky. She turned her head, rolling back slightly until her rump touched the edge of the box-springs. She smiled lazily up at Jake – but with only the right side of her face. The punished left side didn't move much.

'I didn't mean to wake you,' Jake said.

'You didn't. I've been awake for a while.'

'Playing possum, huh?'

'A little bit. Mostly too ruined to move.'

'Hard floor,' Jake said.

'Least of my problems. I feel like I've been hit by a Mack truck.'

'You *look* like you've been hit by a Mack truck.'

The right side of her lip curled up, baring some teeth. 'That bad, is it?'

'Not that bad. You look pretty fine, all things considered. Did you sleep well down here?'

'Not bad, all things considered. You snore, you know.'

'Sorry.'

'It was nice. Kept me reminded you were there.'

'If you . . . I would've stayed on my own side of the bed, you know. Kept my hands to myself. Especially if I didn't wake up.'

She smiled slightly with the working half of her face. Then the smile faded and she studied his eyes. 'We'll never know,' she said.

'We'll never know. Could you use some breakfast?'

'Sure.'

'You can wear my robe. It's on a chair by the door.'

'Thanks.'

Jake stood up and went to the dresser. He took out his pyjama jacket. With his back to Alison, he put it on and fastened the buttons. Then he turned around.

She was sitting cross-legged, the sheet spread over her lap and knees. She hugged the pillow to her breasts. 'If you've got something more elaborate in mind than Trix or Fruit Loops, I'd be glad to make it. I might as well do something useful.'

'I'll have you know I'm a pretty fair cook. I haven't burnt anything . . .'

Since last night, he thought.

'I trust you,' Alison said. 'But I'll help. What's a woman for?' she asked, a gleam of something that might have been mischief in her eyes.

'I'll pick you up a toothbrush. Do you need anything else?'

'I could use some clothes,' Alison said, and took a drink of coffee. 'I feel like a convalescent, wandering around in my nightgown . . . and your robe.'

'I could go over to your place and pick up some things,' Jake said.

'How long are you planning to keep me here?'

'As long as possible.'

She raised an eyebrow.

'Tonight, anyway,' Jake told her.

'It was Roland who was after me,' she said. 'Not that I have anything against sticking around – you've got a nice floor. But he's dead, and he's the one who wanted to get me. So even if that snake-thing is still alive, there's no reason to think it would try to find *me*.'

'I hope you're right. But it was in the driver of the van when he tried to run down Celia, then it was in Roland when she disappeared. Maybe that's just a coincidence. On the other hand, maybe it's the creature that chooses the targets no matter who it's in.'

Alison curled up her lip. She could've done without that theory. 'So I just have to lay low until you find the thing.'

'Until it's accounted for, one way or another.'

'Okay.'

'I'm sorry.'

'Did you know that you spend a lot of time apologizing for stuff that's not your fault?'

'Sorry.' He grinned.

Alison liked his grin. She hadn't seen much of it. 'When you get back, am I supposed to keep you covered again and look at your back?'

'Yep.'

'At least it's a good excuse to get your shirt off.'

Jake took a last drink of coffee, set down his cup, and rubbed his mouth with a napkin. 'I'd better get going.'

They left the table. Alison walked ahead of him to the front door. 'Don't you wear a uniform?'

'Usually.'

'I'd like to see you in it, sometime. Bet you look dashing. The fuzz.'

'I crashed the patrol car yesterday,' he said.

'That was careless.'

'Yeah. Wouldn't look right, I think, driving around in uniform in my own car.'

'What time will you be back?'

He shook his head. 'I have no idea. It'll depend on how things go.'

'Well, should I make supper for you?'

'I don't want you starving. Say if I'm not back by seven, why don't you go ahead and eat without me.'

'Okay.'

He stepped past Alison and opened the door.

'Watch yourself,' she said.

'You too. If there's any kind of trouble – you see someone suspicious hanging around, anything like that – call the station and ask for Barney. He'll be there, and he knows the whole story.'

'All right.'

'You know where everything is?'

'I'll be fine, Jake. Don't worry.'

Nodding, he hesitated in the doorway as if reluctant to leave. Then he started to turn away. Alison touched his arm. He looked into her eyes. She stepped against him, embracing him, tilting back her head. Jake put his arms around her. Holding her gently, he kissed her mouth. When his lips went away, he cupped the back of her head. She pressed her face to the side of his neck.

'I'd better get going,' he whispered as he stroked her hair.

'I know.' Alison squeezed him hard, then stepped back. 'See you later,' she said.

He stared at her. He kissed her once more, then turned away.

Alison stood in the doorway, watching him until the car moved off down the road. Then she shut the door and locked it. She slid the guard chain into place.

She leaned against the door, closed her eyes, and let herself go back to linger a while with the feel of his body against her, the feel of his lips on her mouth.

Chapter Thirty-four

After filling Barney in on all that had happened the previous night, Jake returned to his car. He tore off the additions Roland had made to his photograph. He felt guilty about damaging evidence, but Roland was dead, there would be no trial, and he didn't want to show the picture around with the naked body parts surrounding the guy's head. Once they were removed, he drove out to the place where he had burned the Volkswagen.

The car had been towed away, leaving only black smears and ashes. Jake searched there first, spreading the ashes with his shoes. He wasn't sure what he hoped to find. The thing's charred body? The tiny remains of its skeleton, if it had one?

When he finished there, he wandered around the area looking at the pavement, the grass strip between the kerb and sidewalk, the sidewalk. Thursday, the thing had left some blood on the pavement of Latham Road behind the burning van and in the weeds on the other side. Today, there was nothing to see.

Jake told himself that the creature had probably died inside the Volkswagen. Maybe he should go over to the yard, later on, and sift through the remains of the car's interior. In the poor light last night, he might easily have missed something. Besides, he'd been tense and eager to get home. He needed to make the search again, thoroughly and in daylight.

Picture in hand, he headed for the apartment house on the corner to begin the door-to-door enquiries.

Alison hung up the telephone after explaining to Gabby that she wouldn't be able to work for the next few days. He'd heard on the radio about the killings in the night and her narrow escape, so he was sympathetic and said she should take off as much time as she needed.

She had another call to make. This one wouldn't be so easy. It was necessary, though.

She misdialled and hung up before the ringing started.

Her stomach hurt. Her heart pounded. The pulsing of it made her face throb. Sweat slid down her sides. She stood up, took off Jake's robe, sat again on the sofa, and dialled Evan's number.

His phone rang once.

'Hello?' He sounded tense.

'Hi. It's me.'

'Alison. My God. Are you all right?'

'You heard about last night?'

'Of course I heard about last night. Christ. Are you all right?'

'I'm a little beat up, but I'm okay.'

'My God, I couldn't believe it. You could've been killed. I've just been sick ever since I heard about it. I didn't even go to my classes. You should've called.'

'I did call. Just now.'

'I've been through hell.'

'I'm sorry. It hasn't been a picnic for me, either.'

'Who was it? Who did it?'

'A freshman named Roland.'

'Some guy you know?'

'I'd met him a couple of times.'

'Was he after *you*, or what?'

'I guess so.'

'What for? I mean . . .'

'I guess he wanted to rape and kill me.'

'Jesus Christ. Did he . . . touch you?'

'He didn't rape me.'

'Thank God for that. You, what, fought him off?'

'Yeah.'

'Christ, it's my fault. I should've been there. If you'd let me drive you home . . . you shouldn't have left, you know. That business was just a mistake, like I said. You should've stayed at my place, last night. None of this would've happened.'

'Would've happened to Helen, regardless,' she said. 'And even if I'd spent the night with you, I would've gone home sooner or later.'

'You should've stayed.'

'Well, I didn't.'

'Where are you now?'

'I'm safe.'

'Well, I know you're safe – the guy's dead, right? They said on the news he got killed in a fire.'

'Yeah.'

'So where are you?'

'I'm not supposed to tell anyone.'

'That's stupid. Who told you that?'

'A policeman.'

'Well, shit. What's the big idea?'

'He thinks I might still be in some danger.'

'I don't get it. The bastard's dead, right? So where's the danger?'

'I'm going to do as I'm told.'

'Since when?'

'Don't be a creep, Evan.'

'I need to see you.'

'You can't.'

'Alison. We have to talk.'

'We *are* talking.'

'Face to face.'

'I'm not up to a confrontation.'

She heard him sigh. For a long time he said nothing. Alison finally broke the silence. 'I just wanted to let you know that I'm okay. I figured I owed you that.'

When Evan spoke again, he sounded weary. 'I honestly didn't know you were asleep last night when I . . . touched you. I love you, Alison. When I think what almost happened to you last night, it kills me. Please, I need to see you. Please. Tell me where you are. I'll come over and we'll talk. Just talk, I promise.'

'I'll call you in a day or two.'

'No, please. Alison, I'm so wasted. I didn't sleep at all last night. I can't do anything except think about you. I promise I won't give you any trouble. I just need to see you, to be with you for a while. I'm begging you.'

Alison shut her eyes and leaned back against the sofa cushion. This was worse than she'd expected. Evan sounded miserable, desperate.

It's my fault, she thought. I've done this to him.

'I guess we could meet somewhere,' she finally said. 'How about Wally's?'

Evan said nothing.

'That all right?'

Alison heard a faint sound of ringing. 'Someone at your door?' she asked.

'Yeah,' Evan whispered. The ringing came again.

'You'd better see who it is.'

'I don't care,' he whispered. 'It can't be you, so I don't care.'

'I'll hang on.'

'I can't go to the door. I'm not wearing anything. I just got out of the shower.'

The bell rang again.

'Probably just a salesman, anyway.' After a few moments, he said, 'Okay, he's gone.'

'I was saying we could meet at Wally's.'

'That's awfully public.'

'That's the idea. I don't want any hassles.'

'Christ, Al. Okay. Wally's. What time?'

'What time is it now?'

'About noon.'

'I'll need some time to clean up and walk over there.'

'I can pick you up.'

'Thanks anyway. How about one-thirty?'

'Okay. I'll buy you lunch.'

'Fine. See you then.' She hung up.

She didn't want to see Evan.

Some things, she thought, you have to do.

It won't be so bad.

It'll be awful. I'll have to tell him it's over, tell him face to face and make him understand it's final.

It'll be awful, but it won't last forever. Then it will be ended and I'll come back here and Jake will show up, sooner or later.

Jake.

Just keep thinking about Jake, and the rest won't be so bad. He'll be here tonight.

This is getting nowhere, Jake thought. At more than half the doors he tried, nobody responded. The missing occupants, he supposed, were either in class or at work.

Of those people he spoke to, several had been out to watch last night's spectacle, but many claimed ignorance of the entire affair. None admitted to knowing the identity of the young man in the photograph, though three were pretty sure they had seen him on campus at one time or another. Nobody had seen anything, last night or today, that looked like a snake. Nobody had seen or heard anything strange except for the uproar over the car fire.

It seemed pointless, but Jake didn't give up.

He had gone to every door of every apartment building on this side of the block except the one at the corner. Unlikely, he thought, that anyone so far from the scene had noticed anything. But he might as well check, anyway, before crossing the road and trying the other side.

At the first two apartments on the ground floor, nobody came to the doors. At the third, he heard music inside. He rang the bell.

A woman in her late twenties opened the door. She was as tall as Jake, with a terrycloth headband around her black hair, thick eyebrows that almost met in the middle, prominent cheekbones, full lips, a jutting jaw, and broad shoulders. Her breasts strained the fabric of a top that looked like two red bandannas knotted together. Her belly was tanned and flat, striped with a few runnels of sweat. Her hips had the breadth of her shoulders. Instead of pants, she wore something that reminded Jake of a pirate's eyepatch – a black strap that slanted down from her hips, a black satin triangle not quite large enough to cover her hairless pubic area.

'I'm sorry to bother you,' Jake said. 'It's police business.' He held his wallet open.

She glanced at the badge, ignored the ID card, and licked some sweat from the corner of her mouth. 'Come on in out of the cold,' she said.

He stepped into the apartment. In spite of the fan and open windows, the heat seemed worse than outside. The woman turned away, and Jake watched her walk to the stereo. A slim black strip clung to the centre of her buttocks, leaving the flawless cheeks bare. They flexed as she walked.

She seemed as casual about her attire as if she were wearing a three-piece suit. Jake wished she would put on something to cover herself.

The woman reduced the volume of the stereo, and turned around. 'Want some iced tea?'

'No thanks.'

'I'm Sam. Samantha Summers. Maybe you already know that.'

He shook his head. 'Jake Corey,' he told her. 'I'm making enquiries around the neighbourhood about a situation last night.'

'So you're not here to bust me, huh?'

'For what?'

Her heavy lips curled into a smile. 'I'm sure I wouldn't know. Corrupting the staid mentality of minors?'

'You've been doing a lot of that?'

'Some might say so. I'm an associate professor of philosophy at the university.'

Jake thought, you're joking. Then he thought, why didn't *I* ever have a prof like this?

'Maybe I'll sign up,' he said.

'Do that. I'll help open your mind to the imponderables.'

'I could do without imponderables.'

Sam sat on the carpet in front of him. She lay back, folded her hands behind her head, and began doing sit-ups. Her legs were spread. She touched an elbow to the opposite knee, lowered her back to the floor, curled upward and touched the other elbow to the other knee. 'How can I help you?' she asked without pausing.

You could help by stopping *that*, Jake thought. 'Did you see this student last night?' he asked, and held the photo of Roland above her knees while she sat up three times. He tried to keep his eyes on the back of the picture.

'Dracula,' she said.

'He thought he was, maybe. He's dead.'

Sam stopped. She took the photo from Jake and crossed her legs. 'Dead?'

'He killed at least two people that we know about. Maybe more. When I found him last night, he was dead.'

'Well, I saw him. It was sometime after one o'clock. Maybe as late as two.'

'Are you sure?'

'He's not a person I'm likely to forget. He used to get on my nerves following me around campus. His name's something like Rupert or . . .'

'Roland. Where did you see him?'

'I was out running. I run five miles every night.'

'At one o'clock?'

'I like the night.'

'Where was he?'

'Just up the block. A young man was helping him into his car.'

The words hit Jake like a blow to the stomach.

'He seemed pretty out of it. I assumed he was drunk. I see a lot of that around here. Students don't appear very adept at holding their liquor.'

'And somebody was with him? Do you know who it was?'

Her thick eyebrows lowered. 'I don't know his name. I do know that he's a graduate student in the English department with a teaching assistanceship.'

'Do you know where he lives?'

Sam shook her head. She handed the photo back to Jake.

'I have to find him right away. It's urgent.'

'Was he in on the killings?'

'I doubt it. But Roland was . . . carrying a disease. I need to get to this guy before he infects someone.'

'If I had a school yearbook.'

'You don't have one?'

'Afraid not.'

'Will you be here for a while?'

'I'll stick around.'

'I'll be back in fifteen minutes.'

Professor Teal didn't come to the door, so Jake hurried around the side of the house and climbed the stairs. He broke the Crime Scene ribbon, used his lock picks, and let himself inside.

Any of the three girls, he thought, might have school yearbooks. But he remembered, from his quick inspection of the house last night, that an entire wall of the attic room was lined with bookshelves. It must be Alison's room, he thought; she had mentioned running downstairs to warn Helen.

At the top of the attic stairs, Jake stared at the disordered bed. This is where it happened, where she woke up and struggled with Roland, where her mauled body would've been found if . . . oh, she nailed the bastard good. Hard to imagine that the same girl he found curled at the foot of his bed this morning could be savage enough to inflict such damage on someone.

Her purse was on the floor beside Jake's feet. I should get it for her, he thought. And maybe some clothes.

There were clothes scattered on the carpet near the purse: white running shoes half covered by knee socks, a rumpled blue blouse, a bra with wispy transparent cups, white shorts with panties still inside them as if she had pulled both down at the same time.

Jake picked up the purse and stood there, staring at the clothes. Less than ten minutes ago, he'd been with Sam. Astonishing Sam in her bandannas and patch. But she hadn't affected Jake a fraction as much as the sight of Alison's discarded clothing on the floor.

For godsake, he told himself, this is no time to get turned on.

Reluctantly, he looked away. He went to the bed, set the purse down, and searched the shelves. In seconds, he found three yearbooks – slim volumes that stood inches taller than most of the other books. He pulled them down. The cover of each was embossed with the title, *Summit*, and the year. The most recent had last year's date. Jake scowled. He wanted the current edition. Then he realized that the *Summit* covering this year probably hadn't been issued yet.

The guy better have been enrolled last year, he thought.

He tossed the books onto the bed.

On his knees, he reached under the bed. He found a suitcase and pulled it out.

You shouldn't do this, he told himself. You should get the books over to Sam.

It'll just take a minute. If I don't, I'll have to make a special trip.

You just want to go through her things, whispered a small voice he didn't like very much.

He carried the suitcase to Alison's dresser, set it on the floor, and opened it.

In the top drawer of the dresser were nightgowns, panties and bras. He grabbed a handful of panties, trying not to think about them, and put them quickly into the suitcase. He was tempted not to get any bras for her, felt guilty about that, and took out two for the suitcase. In the next drawer he found socks, pantyhose, slips. He took socks. There were sweatshirts, T-shirts, gym shorts and a jumpsuit in the next drawer. He took a T-shirt, a pair of red shorts and the jumpsuit. The bottom drawer held sweaters. He didn't bother with them.

From her closet he selected a sleeveless sundress, two blouses and a pair of faded blue jeans. Then he went to the pile of clothing on the floor. He wanted to see her in the white shorts. He picked them up and shook them until the panties dropped through a leg hole. He watched the panties flutter to the floor. He was proud of himself for not touching them. With the shorts in one hand, he gathered up her shoes and returned to the suitcase.

Anything else she might need? he wondered, and scanned the room.

He saw the bulletin board on the wall beyond her desk. Snapshots were tacked to it.

She won't need those, Jake told himself. Get going.

But he wanted to look at them, wanted to look at Alison.

He walked over to the desk. Most of the photos showed Alison, but she was with a guy. The same guy. In one, he was pushing her on a swing. In another, they were sitting on a blanket in the shade of a tree. Another showed them kissing.

Jake's stomach hurt.

The guy was handsome, in spite of his glasses, and he looked in good shape.

This is what I get for snooping, Jake thought.

He felt better, however, when he remembered Alison saying she had broken up with her boyfriend last night.

This guy had been dumped.

Good riddance.

Jake hefted the suitcase, picked up Alison's purse and year-books, and rushed downstairs.

After soaking in the bath for nearly an hour, Alison felt a little better. The hot water had soothed her tight muscles. It had done nothing, however, to take away the deeper tightness, the cold sick feeling that seemed to grip her insides.

If only there was a way to turn off her mind.

Or change channels. Get rid of the bad shows starring Roland and Helen and Celia and the dead policeman and Evan. Turn to the Jake channel. The Jake show was comforting, sometimes exciting. All the others hurt.

Alison stepped out of the tub, dripping, and began to dry herself with a soft towel.

Everything would be much better if she could just avoid seeing Evan.

You have to go. You have to finish it.

I don't have any clothes.

Alison wanted that for an excuse, but she'd had plenty of time to consider the problem and find a solution.

She hung the moist towel over a bar, and left the bathroom. The air in the hallway felt cool. In Jake's room the windows were open. A nice breeze came in.

She went to the closet, took out a plaid shirt and put it on. Buttoned, it resembled a dress. A short, loose dress to be sure, but it would have to suffice. She rolled the sleeves up her forearms. Then she found a belt and fastened it around her waist.

On the inside of Jake's closet door was a full-length mirror.

The shirt didn't look that much like a dress. It looked like a man's shirt. She pulled at it, rearranging the tucks to make it hang more smoothly.

Returning to the bathroom, she brushed her teeth, using a finger smeared with Jake's toothpaste.

Finally she went into the kitchen. On the wall beside the telephone was a notepad and pen. She tore off a sheet and took it to the table.

'That's him,' Sam said.

Jake's heart slammed in his chest. 'Are you positive?'

'I got a good look at them both. There's no doubt about it. He's the one who was helping Roland into the car.' She slid a finger across the page of photographs and stopped it beneath the name. 'Evan Forbes.'

Alison's dumped boyfriend. The man in those snapshots on her bulletin board.

No need to worry, Jake told himself. They'd split up.

But she'd said she should call him, let him know she's okay.

What if she tells him where she's staying?

'I need to use your phone.'

'Help yourself.'

Jake dialled his home. He listened to the ringing.

Come on, pick it up. Come on, Alison. Answer the damn phone!

It rang fifteen times before he hung up.

'Do you have a directory?'

Sam rushed from the room. She ran back, clutching a telephone book, and thrust it at Jake.

He flipped through the pages. Forbes was listed. Jake recognized the address: the apartment building in front of which he'd found Roland's car parked last night. He'd already been there, knocking on doors.

'Thanks, Sam.'

He ran.

He kicked the door. With a splintering crash, it flew open.

The carpet at his feet was crusted with dry blood.

Chapter Thirty-five

Alison walked the L-shaped parking lot of Wally's, looking for Evan's car. It wasn't there. Nor was it parked along the street.

She had left the house at one o'clock, giving herself half an hour to reach the bar. Though she didn't have a wristwatch, she guessed that the walk must have taken no more than fifteen or twenty minutes and that she was early.

To make herself as inconspicuous as possible, she wandered out of the parking lot and headed for one of the elms alongside the street. The grass felt soft and cool under her bare feet. The shade felt good. Leaning back against a tree trunk, she took a deep, shaky breath. She was trembling badly.

She could *see* her legs trembling. They were out in front of her, knees locked to brace her against the tree, thighs pressed together. From the bottom of the shirt to her kneecaps, her skin shimmied over the fluttering muscles. As she watched the shaking, a corner of her shirttail was lifted by a puff of breeze. She swept it down and held the shirt-front flat against her thighs. Her open hands felt tremors through the fabric.

Just calm down, she told herself. There's no reason to be so jumpy. I'm just going to have a talk with Evan. It's not like I'm about to get my teeth pulled without benefit of anaesthetic.

Maybe Evan's already inside. He might have walked over. I could stay here fretting for an hour while he's inside drinking and thinking I stood him up.

Well, I'm not going in. Bad enough I had to walk over here dressed this way – undressed this way. At least I didn't run into anyone I know.

But even at this hour, Wally's was bound to be loaded with students and Alison was bound to know many of them.

As if to prove her theory, a station wagon slowed in front of the parking-lot entrance and started to turn. She spotted Terri Weathers through the passenger window. Luckily, Terri was looking the other way. Alison quickly sidestepped, circling to the other side of the tree.

I should have stayed home is what I should have done.

She heard the car crunch over gravel and stop. The doors bumped shut. She heard footsteps heading away, then the windy sound of another approaching car. Her head snapped to the left. Coming up the street was Evan's blue Granada.

It swung to the kerb in front of her, and stopped. Leaning across the seat, Evan opened the passenger door. 'You're early,' he said.

Both hands holding the shirttails down, she climbed into the car. The seat upholstery was hot against her bare rump. Raising herself, she swept the shirt down beneath her. She kept her eyes away from Evan.

'What are you *wearing*?'

'All I could find.'

'What is that, a guy's shirt?'

She faced Evan. His hair was neatly combed and he was dressed for the heat in a glossy Hawaiian shirt, white shorts and sandals. He looked good except for his sallow skin and blood-shot eyes. The eyes had a feverish glaze. Alison didn't like the way they stared down through his glasses, studying her.

'Take a picture, why don't you.'

'I could use a drink,' he muttered.

'Let's stay here. I really don't feel like going inside. It'll be noisy, and . . .'

'Aren't you hungry?'

'People will ask questions. About last night. You said it was on the radio.'

'Terrible,' he said. 'Last night.' He peered at her face. 'You got beat up pretty good.'

'Yeah.'

'You look great, though.'

'Sure.'

'You do. A bruise hath no power to diminish the beauty of so sweet a flower.'

'Thanks.'

'Let's at least get something to eat, okay? We can go someplace that has a drive-up window, so you won't have to worry about meeting anyone.'

'Couldn't we just talk here?'

'I'm famished, Al. Really. I haven't eaten all day.' He gave a grim smile. 'I didn't have any appetite. But I'm feeling a lot better now. You being here. I feel like I've been brought back from the dead.'

'I guess it's all right if we pick up something,' Alison told him.

'Great.' He started to drive.

The front door of Jake's house wasn't chained. He stepped inside, sensing that Alison was gone.

He called her name as he hurried through the rooms. In the bathroom he found his bathrobe and Alison's nightgown hanging from a hook. In the kitchen he found a note. It was on the table, folded in half to stand upright:

Dear Jake,

I had to go out for a little while to see my old
boyfriend. I know I was supposed to stay here, but he
needs to see me. I'm sure it will be okay, since I'm
meeting him at Wally's. There will be plenty of other
people around, so please don't worry.

I'll probably be back before you see this, but thought
I'd leave a note anyway just in case you dropped by early
and wondered what happened to me.

Please don't worry.

I'll be back as soon as possible. Believe me, the sooner
the better.

This was just something I had to do.

Alison

Cold and numb inside, Jake lurched to the kitchen phone and
dialled directory assistance. He got the number for Wally's, called,
and asked for Alison Sanders to be paged.

'She doesn't seem to be here,' he was told after a long wait.

He hung up and raced for his car.

The note didn't say what time she had left for Wally's. Maybe
only a few minutes ago. Maybe hours ago. If she'd walked, she
might still be on the way over there. Jake tried to take her most
likely route. He scanned the sidewalks for pedestrians.

Evan might have picked her up, he thought. No, the note said
she was *meeting* him at Wally's. So she walked. Unless she got a
friend to pick her up.

That could be it. She called a girlfriend, asked the girl to bring
over some spare clothes and give her a lift to the bar. Maybe the
friend will stay with her.

Alison's not *at* Wally's.

So maybe she's still on the way over.

Please.

She might've been there and left. By now she might be on her
way home.

Stupid wishful thinking. Evan has that fucker up his back and
he isn't going to let Alison get away.

Maybe Evan's not the guy she went to see.

He is. But maybe he doesn't have the thing in him.

Then what was that blood on his apartment floor? Roland, half dead, must've staggered up to Evan's door. When Evan opened up, the thing burst out of Roland's belly and nailed him. It took control, got Evan to haul the dead or dying Roland down to the VW. Sam saw them, just thought Roland was plastered.

Why no blood on the sidewalk?

The thing's clever. Maybe it got Evan to bandage the wounds before carrying Roland out. The fire took care of the bandages.

Evan's got it, all right.

And Evan's got Alison.

Evan handed Alison the bags containing their soft drinks, cheese-burgers and French fries. She held them on her lap, glad to have more than her shirttails for covering.

In spite of his frequent glances in that direction, he'd acted all right during the drive over. Alison's jitters had subsided, though she still dreaded telling him that she wouldn't go with him after today.

She would postpone that moment for as long as possible.

Evan pulled away from the drive-up window. Instead of turning in front of the restaurant to circle around to its parking area, he continued ahead and swung onto the road.

'Aren't we going to eat in the lot?' Alison asked.

'That'd be kind of dreary. Let's drive someplace nice. We can have a picnic.'

'Evan.'

'Don't worry. I'll be a perfect gentleman.' He smiled at her. A corner of his mouth trembled. 'No more touchy-feely, not unless you start it. I'm a slow learner, but I finally got the message. I've put our relationship in too much jeopardy already. Here you are, convinced I'm some kind of a sex fiend. Well, I'm not. You'll see. From now on, it's hands off. Consider me a eunuch.'

Too late for that, Alison thought.

'I came so close to losing you, last night. My boorish behaviour, then . . . the attack on you. I had to face how much you mean to me, what it would be like if I never saw you again. I love you so much, Alison. I'll never again do anything to make you doubt me.'

'We'll see how it goes today,' she said.

'A test. I've always passed my tests with flying colours.'

Alison settled back against the seat. She believed him. The lunch would go smoothly. He would make the sacrifice today, knowing this was his last chance. Be a good boy, and there would be plenty of future opportunities to make up for it. So he thought.

He's no mind-reader. He doesn't know that, regardless of how wonderfully he might behave, this is it.

By the time he finds out, it'll be over.

He steered onto Latham Road.

'Where are we going?' Alison asked.

'Just out of town a little way. We'll have a picnic, all right? Just like old times. Except no fooling around.'

'What'll it be?' asked the bartender.

'I called earlier about Alison Sanders,' Jake said.

'Right. She wasn't here.'

'Do you know her?'

'Not the name. Maybe if I saw her . . .'

Shaking his head, Jake started to turn away.

'You said Alison Sanders?'

Jake faced a slim young man who was seated on the barstool beside him, nursing a martini. He looked rather old to be a student. 'Do you know her?'

'I met her a few nights ago. Are you a friend?'

Jake showed the man his badge. 'I'm also a friend. I need to find her fast. She said she was coming over here today.'

'Well, she was here. Around one-thirty or a quarter to two. I was just arriving. In fact, I'd come here in hopes of seeing her.' He shrugged. 'She was with someone else. I just caught a glimpse of her getting into his car.'

'Did you see who she was with?'

'I wasn't looking at the driver.'

'Did you tear your eyes away from Alison long enough to notice the car?' Jake asked, not bothering to hide his annoyance.

'A dark blue four-door. I'm not good with cars. I do know that it wasn't a compact. It had a rather squarish shape along the lines of a Mercedes. It wasn't a Mercedes, of course.'

'Licence number?'

'I didn't notice. Nothing suspicious was going on, why would I look at the licence plate?'

'Did you see the car leave?' Jake asked.

'It was still sitting at the kerb when I came in here.'

'This was about one forty-five?'

'Give or take.'

Jake checked his watch. Ten past two.

Rushing out of Wally's, he squinted against the sudden glare of daylight and ran to the street. He looked both ways. He saw no blue car.

He leaned sideways against a tree trunk.

Twenty fucking minutes.

If he'd just been quicker.

Groaning, he rammed his elbow hard against the trunk.

Evan slowed the car. As he started to turn, Alison glimpsed a sign on the other side of the narrow road.

The Oakwood Inn.

He's taking me to the Oakwood.

Alison felt herself sinking, going down and down, dropping into an abyss.

It's happening, she thought. Oh dear Jesus, it's happening. It *is* the thing that wants me.

I took care of Roland. I can take care of Evan.

Jesus, I'm going to die.

Maybe Evan just picked this place by accident, just took the first side road that looked interesting.

'Look at that,' he said, 'a restaurant.'

Alison nodded.

'Looks like we're the only ones here.'

'It's closed,' Alison said. Her voice came out a whisper. 'It's where those people were killed.'

'Really?' He sounded surprised. 'Well then, I guess nobody will mind if we use the parking lot.' He steered towards the front of the restaurant.

Alison lifted the bags of food off her lap. Leaning forward, she set them on the floor between her legs.

Evan stopped the car no more than a yard from the porch stairs. 'So this is where it happened,' he said. 'I wonder if we could get inside. It'd be kind of fascinating, wouldn't it? Explore the scene of the crime?'

'Maybe after we eat.' She faced him. She stared into his intense, bloodshot eyes.

'What's wrong?' he asked.

'I've been so rotten to you, Evan. All my dumb nonsense. Not wanting you to . . . It all seems so stupid and petty, now. I mean, I was almost killed last night. That sort of thing, it makes a person . . . it made me take a long look at what's important and what isn't. All that really matters is caring for another person. Loving another person. So why have I been putting us both through all this . . . this shit? Will you forgive me?' She put a hand on his shoulder.

'You're kidding,' he said, and let out a tiny, nervous laugh. 'This part of the test or something . . . ?'

'Forget all that. There's no test. I want it to be like it was between us.'

'Really? Really?'

She eased him closer. Clear of the steering wheel, Evan turned to her. She kissed his mouth. She put her arms around his back.

The bulge beneath his shirt felt huge.

Her whimper of despair must have sounded passionate to Evan. He clasped a hand over her breast and squeezed. His other hand moved up her thigh. She opened her legs. Shuddering as he stroked her, she muttered, 'I've missed you so much, missed the feel of you.' She caressed his shorts. His penis felt hard and big. He squirmed as she fondled it. His breathing was ragged. 'I'll get the blanket, darling. It's in the trunk?'

He nodded.

Alison pulled the key from the ignition. 'Bring the food,' she said. 'We'll eat afterward.'

'You're something else,' he said.

'I was such an idiot. I never should've screwed things up between us. But that's over.' She climbed from the car.

She stepped behind the trunk.

Through the rear window, she saw Evan lean over to pick up the food bags.

She whirled and flung the car keys with all her strength towards the weeds at the side of the lot.

Then she sprinted over the hot pavement, heading for the road out.

It was like last night, running from Roland, but this time there was no police car nearby as a goal. Alison could only hope to stay ahead of Evan, to reach Latham Road. Maybe, there, someone in a passing car would stop and help her.

She wasn't even out of the parking lot yet.

She pumped her arms. She flung her legs out. Her bare feet slapped the pavement. She knew she was moving fast. She could feel her hair flying behind her, her shirttails flapping.

She could hear Evan's shoes pounding behind her.

He had chased her before, always in fun, always catching her easily. But she had never run from him like this. She felt as if she had never run so fast in her life.

Now she heard not only his shoes but his huffing breath.

He's gaining on me!

Tucking her chin down, she pistoned her arms and tried to hurl out her legs even faster than before.

She made it past the parking-lot entrance, onto the road that led to Latham.

Evan was close behind her.

'Leave me ALONE!' she yelled.

He smashed her between the shoulderblades.

Alison plunged forward in a crazed dance of flinging arms and wild legs. Then she was off her feet. She slammed the pavement, hit it with palms and knees. It knocked away her arms and legs. It punched out her breath. She skidded to a stop. She couldn't get air and her skin burned, but she started to scurry up again.

Evan kicked an arm out from under her. She landed hard on her side. Evan grabbed the numb arm and pulled.

He lifted her. He swung her over his shoulder, turned around, and headed back across the lot.

Chapter Thirty-six

Jake sat in his car in the parking lot of Wally's, his forehead against the steering wheel.

Don't just sit here, he told himself. Go after her, damn it!

Sure thing. Go where?

I don't want her to die!

Try Evan's apartment.

He wouldn't take her there. Not enough privacy for what he has in mind.

Eating her.

God!

Think!

The apartment is out. He'd take her someplace secluded, where he wouldn't have to worry about neighbours hearing anything, where he could work on her secretly for a long time. A field, maybe, or an abandoned building.

And which abandoned building would that be, you dumb asshole?

You could've been there by now!

Evan's shoulder bounced against Alison's belly as he rushed up the restaurant's porch stairs. He stopped in front of the door. One of his arms went away from Alison, but the other stayed clamped like a tight bar across the backs of her knees, pinning her legs against his body.

He got the door open and carried her inside. The door banged shut. He took a few steps, then bent at the waist to unload her. Alison felt herself start to fall. When she flopped off his shoulder, she reached up fast and clutched the back of his head. For a moment, she held herself up. Then Evan knocked her arm away. He kept her legs pinned until her back slammed the floor. Her head snapped down and hit the hardwood.

Evan bent over her. He tore open the shirt, spread its front, and stepped back. He stared down at her. His mouth hung open. He was panting for air.

Alison lay there, stunned from the blow and straining to breathe. She wanted to close the shirt. She couldn't lift her arms.

'Beautiful,' he gasped. 'Gotcha now, huh? Beautiful, deceitful cunt.' He suddenly flinched. Squeezing his eyes shut, he grimaced. His back stiffened and he writhed as if possessed by a terrible ecstasy. He swayed and moaned. Saliva dribbled down his chin. He rubbed his penis through the bulging front of his shorts.

Alison gazed up at him.

He was out of it, caught up in his frenzy.

Now, she thought vaguely. Before he comes out of it. Move!

She found the strength to roll over. She thrust her burning hands and knees against the floor and pushed herself up.

Evan grabbed her ankles. He yanked her legs straight. Her belly slapped the floor. Still holding her ankles, he crossed them and twisted them savagely. Alison flipped onto her back.

'Oh, you're not going anywhere. No party without you.' He took a step backward. He wiped his slippery chin with the back of a wrist. Then he unbuttoned his shirt. He shrugged it from his shoulders and it fluttered to the floor.

He wore a patch of gauze and tape just to the left of his naval. A band of purple skin at the edge of the patch angled across his belly and around his side.

On his belt was a black case. Alison watched his hand move to the case. He popped open its flap. He slid out a folding knife. He prised out the blade. It locked rigid with a metallic click. Staring down at Alison with half-shut eyes, he licked a flat side of the blade. 'Do I taste Celia? Yes, I believe I do. A saucy wench, but tender.' He lapped the other side of the blade.

Crouching, he leaned over Alison. The blade was cool and wet on her thigh. He turned it over and wiped the other side on her skin. With a flick of his wrist, he nicked her. She flinched. 'Aw, did that hurt? For shame. Poor, poor Alison.' He rubbed her cut. The back of his hand came up smeared red. He licked it and sighed.

Alison felt blood trickle down her inner thigh.

Evan stood up. Twisting at the hips, he threw the knife behind him. It thunked the floor. 'Plenty of time later for that,' he said. 'Gotta ream you with something else, first.'

He opened his belt buckle. He unbuttoned the waist of his white shorts and lowered the zipper. The shorts dropped around his ankles. He was wearing brief red underpants. The front jutted with the push of his erection. He slid his thumbs under the elastic at his hips.

Alison lashed out with her foot, catching his left shin. Evan staggered backward, arms waving, feet tangled in the shorts. He started to fall.

Alison flung herself over. She shoved at the floor, got to her hands and knees and scurried up, staggering. In front of her was the bar. She threw her hands against its edge to catch herself. She spun around. Evan had freed himself of the shorts. He was crouched. He sprang at her.

Alison lunged to the right. Straight ahead was the main dining area. Straight ahead, at the end of a long stretch of bare floor, was a window. Crash through it? *That* might kill her. But better the window than Evan. Too far, anyway. Evan was already too close behind her, shoes thudding the floor, breath hissing.

She dodged around the corner.

Had a moment to see the clutter on the floor: cans, rags, toolbox, vacuum cleaner, ladder. A moment to wonder if she could leap clear.

Evan hit her.

His head pounded her rump. His arms wrapped her thighs. His diving tackle drove her forward and down.

She cried out as her body crashed. Cans overturned. One stayed under her hip. Another pushed at her belly. The edges of the open toolbox dug into her chest. Her left breast was inside the toolbox, pressing cool steel.

Evan squirmed off her. He pulled her by the ankles. As the edge of the toolbox scraped the underside of her breast, she hooked her left arm around the box. It skidded along the floor.

Evan stopped dragging her. He clutched her hips. Growling with effort or rage, he lifted her off the toolbox, swung her sideways, and dropped her. Falling, Alison hugged her belly and turned her face away from the floor. The impact wasn't as bad as she expected.

For a few moments, nothing happened. Alison lay there, gasping.

Evan was nearby, but out of sight as long as she didn't turn her face the other way.

She heard him move closer.

A hand curled over her right shoulder. Another hand hooked her right hip. They tugged at Alison. She rolled onto her side, rolled onto her back. And kept rolling, opening the arms folded across her belly as she came up onto her left side, facing Evan who crouched on the floor naked, who was staring at her breasts and not at her right hand, not at the screwdriver she'd taken from the toolbox.

She rammed it into him.

It hit him just under the sternum. It punched in deep. The force of the blow sent him tumbling backward. Knees in the air, he stared bug-eyed at the ceiling. His mouth was a rictus of agony. He made whiny sucking noises, struggling to breathe. A palsied hand pulled the screwdriver. It's blade started to slide out, but was still deep inside him when his hand gave a spastic jerk, wrenching the screwdriver sideways. His body lurched, heels driving against the floor, thrusting his pelvis higher and higher as he yanked the blade the rest of the way out.

Alison had begun to get up while she watched his contortions. She was still on the floor, turned his way, braced on a stiff arm, drawing in her legs, when Evan freed the screwdriver and hurled himself over, twisting, trying for her. She lurched back. Evan's arm swung down as his side struck the floor. The tip of the screwdriver buried itself in the wood an inch from her hip.

Alison scooted further away. Turning over, she crawled towards the toolbox. She watched over her shoulder and saw Evan yank the screwdriver from the floor. He was flat on his belly, writhing.

She took a claw hammer out of the box.

Evan till squirmed on the floor.

She crawled back to him. His twitching arms and legs shuddered against the floor as if he were trying to push himself up.

'Stay down,' Alison gasped. She raised the hammer overhead. 'Stay down or I'll bash your fucking skull.'

She stared at the bruise that curled around from his side to his back. The discoloured skin over his spine, all the way to the nape of his neck, bulged out almost an inch.

It's that *thing*, Alison thought.

She remembered Jake's warnings.

If Evan dies, the thing will come out.

And come after me.

Well, he's not dead yet.

The screwdriver dropped from his hand. He tried to pick it up again, but his jumpy fingers flicked it and sent it rolling.

Alison got to her feet. She was trembling badly and her legs threatened to give out. Ready to fall, she staggered backwards to the ladder, dropped the hammer, and grabbed one of the upper rungs to hold herself up.

Evan still writhed on the floor, but not so much any more.

She would need to go around his body to reach the front door. He was in no shape to stop her now. She let go of the ladder, took a single step and flinched rigid as blood exploded from the nape of Evan's neck.

The creature surged up through the red spray, sliding out of Evan, darting across his shoulderblade, dropping to the floor, streaking towards Alison's feet.

She lurched backward. Bumped the ladder. Got a heel onto its first rung. Grabbed the side rails behind her with both hands and climbed. The ladder wobbled. She was only two steps up by the time the creature reached the foot of the ladder. Gazing down at the monstrosity, she moved one rung higher, then clung there, gasping.

The creature slowly circled into a coil.

It resembled a snake, but with its slimy undulating flesh, the thing looked more to Alison like a two-foot length of intestine. Where Evan's blood had rubbed off, it was pale yellow and webbed with veins.

One end of the thing rose from the centre of the coil. Not a head so much as an opening. A garden hose with teeth. The opening flattened shut, and Alison saw the dull grey globs of its eyes.

The eyes seemed to gaze up at her, seemed to *desire* her.

Alison's skin crawled. She glanced at herself. The open shirt hung off one shoulder. She had never felt so naked, so exposed, so vulnerable. She ached to button the shirt and clamp a hand between her legs but she stood there frozen, clutching the sides of the ladder.

The creature stretched upward, uncoiling, and half its length dropped onto the ladder's bottom rung. Its lower end squirmed and flipped. In an instant, the entire length of the creature was stretched along the aluminium step.

Whimpering, Alison climbed higher.

As Jake's car shot over the crest of the road, he saw the Oakwood parking lot. A blue car was parked near the restaurant's front door.

Let me be in time! Please!

His car flew and dropped, pounding the downslope.

Let me be in time! his mind shrieked. Please.

It had taken so damn long! He'd driven as fast as he could, sped through intersections without regard for red lights or stop signs, barely avoiding collisions twice. But it had taken so long!

Five minutes? Closer to ten.

Oh, God, please. Let her be all right!

The thing kept coming. It kept *coming*.

Alison climbed higher, but so did it. And it seemed to get better at swinging itself from one rung to the next.

Alison sat on the head step, at the ladder's peak, and clutched its edges and stared down between her knees.

She was sobbing. The thing was a vile jaundiced blur through her tears.

It flopped onto the next rung.

With a whine of despair, Alison carefully let go of the edges and stood up. She climbed backwards, arms out for balance. One step, then one more. Then she was standing on the very top of the ladder. She teetered as it wobbled from side to side. When the motion eased, she spread her feet apart and bent her knees just slightly to keep herself steady.

Peering down, she watched the creature mount the rung where her feet had been only seconds earlier. One more, and it would be on the step below the top. From there . . .

Alison heard the roar of a car engine.

A car! It was coming here! It had to be!

Somehow, Jake had figured out . . . God, I hope it's Jake! He'll burst through the door in the nick of the time and blast the fucker to hell.

Brakes squealed.

The corner of the wall blocked her view of the front door.

'*HELP!*' she yelled.

Then she looked down.

The creature was already on the next step. The ring of its mouth flattened shut and its grey phlegm eyes seemed to peer up between her legs as its head rose.

Alison leaped.

She kicked her right leg far out, shoved off with her left foot hoping to knock the ladder over, and dropped. She fell for a long time. Fell towards Evan's sprawled body. Her feet hit the floor. Her knees folded. She tumbled forward, outflung hands slapping Evan's back. Her left hand slipped on the blood. As she smashed down on him, something flopped onto her back.

Something long and squirmy.

Rushing up the porch stairs, Jake heard a wild scream.

He threw open the door.

The restaurant seemed dark after the brilliant afternoon sunlight. He snapped his head from side to side. He saw no one, just a knife standing upright, blade embedded in the floor near his feet. But he heard someone sobbing. Then quick footfalls.

He whirled to the left, swinging up his revolver. Alison charged around the corner. Her face was twisted with panic. She clawed the air with one hand as if reaching for Jake. Her other arm was up, elbow high beside her head, hand behind her back. Her open shirt followed her like a fluttering cape as she ran.

Jake lunged sideways to get a clear shot past Alison, but nobody chased her around the corner.

'It's on me!' she cried out. '*In* me!'

She twirled around in front of Jake. The thick yellowish thing at the small of her back whipped from side to side like a grotesque misplaced tail.

Jake dropped his gun. He clutched Alison's shoulder to hold her still. With his left hand he caught the flipping creature and tugged. His hand slipped off its slimy yielding flesh. He caught it again. Wrapping his hand around it, he felt it moving deeper into Alison. He clenched it in his fist and yanked. Alison shrieked in agony and staggered backward. The creature didn't come off.

'*NO!*' Jake shouted.

He threw Alison to the floor. He jerked the shirt from her shoulders and flung it aside, then dropped onto her writhing body. Sitting on her buttocks, he tore the knife from the floor.

He grabbed the beast, wrapped his left hand around its flaccid slippery body and pulled it taut. The length of it stretched and thinned, but it kept moving into Alison. The lump under her skin was three inches long and growing longer.

He stabbed Alison in the back.

She yelped, went rigid, dug fingernails into the floor.

The tip of the blade entered the tunnelling front of the bulge. Jake was careful not to stab deep. Half an inch, no more. Blood and a thick yellow syrup flowed from the gash. He drew the blade down, splitting Alison's skin until it parted at the hole, then tore the creature from her back.

'*GOT IT!*' he yelled in triumph.

Alison, crying, rolled onto her back and looked up through her tears as Jake leaped to his feet. In one hand was the bloody knife. In the other was the beast. He whirled around, swinging it overhead like a whip. Yellow stuff flew from its ripped body. He lashed it against the wall near the door. It left a dripping smear. He swung it high and whipped it down against the floor. He stomped it with one foot, then with both feet, jumping up and down on the thing until it was mashed flat.

Bending over it, he scraped it up with the edge of the knife. He carried it through the door.

'Jake?'

He didn't answer.

Alison pushed herself up. She crawled to the doorway, wincing as pain swarmed from her ripped back. She grabbed the frame and rose to her knees. Holding on, she watched Jake run to the rear of his car, the flat thing swaying and dripping at his side.

She was hurting and still frightened. She felt blood streaming down her back and buttocks, running down the backs of her legs. She didn't want to be left alone.

Take care of *me*, Jake. I need you.

Shit, she told herself, don't be a baby. He saved your ass. Let him finish whatever he's doing.

He took a red can of gasoline from the trunk of his car. He carried the mashed carcass a few yards, dropped it, and doused it with gas. He emptied the can onto it. A puddle spread over the pavement.

'Wait!' Alison called. She pulled herself up, grabbing the shirt and hugging it to herself. She staggered onto the porch.

Jake waved her away, but she shook her head.

Setting down the gas can, he rushed towards her. He leaped onto the porch and put an arm around her back. 'Alison,' he said.

She held onto him. With Jake bracing her up, she climbed down the stairs. He led her to his car. She leaned against the driver's door, then slid down it and squatted as Jake hurried over to the wet patch on the parking lot. He struck a match and touched it to the gasoline.

As the pale flames rose, he came back to Alison. He squatted beside her. She put a hand on his knee. He looked at her. 'What happened to Evan?'

'I killed him.'

Jake nodded, and turned his gaze towards the fire.

Greasy black smoke swirled up from the remains of the creature. Alison heard sizzling, popping sounds. When a breeze tore away the shroud of smoke, she glimpsed a bubbling black smear on the pavement.

Jake curled a hand behind Alison's head, and softly stroked her hair.

They watched until the fire burnt out.

Chapter Thirty-seven

Jake bent over the bed and kissed her. He stroked the back of her head. 'Nighty-night, honey. Do you want a record on?'

'Not now,' Kimmy said, arching an eyebrow. 'We are not ready. We're busy.'

'Busy, huh? Well . . .' He leered at her ear and licked his lips. 'Some mayo,' he muttered.

'No!' She hunched up a shoulder. She pressed Clew to her ear. 'No earwich. I mean it.'

'But I'm hungry.'

'You're going to have popcorn. And you'd better save me some.'

'We'll see.'

She turned to Alison, who was sitting beside her on the bed. 'I'll get saved some, won't I?'

'Sure,' Alison said.

Kimmy gave Jake a haughty look. 'Alison will make sure of it.'

Grinning, Jake said, 'Goodnight, honey,' and left the room.

Alison lifted the open book off her lap. 'Now, where were we? Let's see, Pooh and Piglet were tracking the Woozle through the snow.' She started to read, but Kimmy placed a small hand on the page, covering the paragraph. She looked up into Alison's eyes.

'Are you going to be here all the time?' she asked.

'I don't know.'

'Well, all your stuff's here.'

'Yeah, it is.' Alison put a hand on the girl's back. 'As long as my stuff's here, I guess I'll be here. Do you think that's okay?'

'I think so,' she replied, frowning and nodding. ' 'Cause you know, I like how you read. You read a lot better than Daddy. And you know what else? When Daddy used to take me to the moojies and I had to go pee . . .' She covered her mouth and tittered. Pressing a tiny shoulder against Alison, she tilted her head back and took her hand away and whispered, 'He made me go in the wrong john and there were men peeing in the sinks! It was so gross!'

'In the *sinks*?'

'Yes!'

'Well, I guess I'd better not let him take you to the moojies any more without me.'

'No more without you.'

Alison closed the book. 'Now, I'd better let you get some sleep. We need to get up bright and early for the zoo.'

'Think we'll see a Woozle?'

'One never knows about Woozles.' Alison stood up. She slipped the book onto the shelf while Kimmy crawled between the sheets.

Alison tucked her in, then knelt beside the bed. Kimmy tucked Clew into the top of her nightgown. 'Gonna say your prayers?' Alison asked.

Kimmy grinned. 'No, you. Do that one you told me. The spooky one.'

'Maybe you should do a nice one. I don't want to be a corrupting influence.'

'I want the spooky one,' Kimmy insisted.

'Well, all right.' Alison shut her eyes and folded her hands on the mattress. 'From ghoulies and ghosties and long-leggity beasties and things that go bump in the night, oh Lord deliver us.'

'Neat,' Kimmy said.

'Sleep tight.' She started to get up.

'You forgot to kiss me.'

Alison bent over Kimmy. The girl's arms wrapped around her neck, pulling her down with a tight hug. From the force of it, Alison expected a hard, mashing kiss. But Kimmy's lips pushed against her mouth with such lingering tenderness that tears came into her eyes. 'See you in the morning, sweetheart,' she said as she stood up.

'Don't forget to save me some popcorn.'

'Never fear. Do you want the record on?'

'Side two.'

Alison flipped the record and turned on the stereo. She dimmed the lamp on Kimmy's table, looked back at her with Clew tucked into the neck of her nightgown and one arm around Cookie Monster, waved, and left the room.

At the entrance to the living-room, she saw Jake on the sofa. A huge bowl of popcorn rested on the cushion beside him. There were two glasses of cola on the table at his knees. Instead of joining him, she went into the kitchen. She took one of Kimmy's cereal bowls from a drawer. It had Charlie Brown and Snoopy on it. She carried it into the living-room, bent over the large bowl and started scooping popcorn in.

'Boy, she's got you well trained,' Jake said.

'My word is my bond.' She carried Kimmy's serving into the kitchen, left it on the counter, and returned.

She'd been hot in her robe. Jake watched as she took it off. She was wearing a red jersey nightshirt she had bought that day at the university store. 'What do you think?' she asked, turning in front of him.

'Nice. Though I have a certain attachment for your blue negligee.'

'It brings back some bad memories.'

'Not for me.'

'Then I'll wear it once in a while.' She lifted the popcorn bowl and sat down beside Jake. The nightshirt was very short. She felt the sofa upholstery against her bare skin. Her stomach fluttered. For an instant, she was sliding into the seat of Evan's car, the shirttails too short to cover her buttocks.

'What's the matter?' Jake asked. He was so quick to notice the slightest changes in her moods.

'A little flashback.'

'I'm sorry.'

She smiled at him. 'It's not *your* fault.'

'I just hate to see you upset.'

'I know.' She set the popcorn bowl on her lap. It felt warm against her bare thighs. 'It's just that you look so woebegone when you sorry me. Have some popcorn.'

He dug in a big hand and took out a fistful.

'What did you rent for tonight?'

'*Halloween* and *The Hills Have Eyes*.'

'Fantastic!'

'I bet you've already seen them.'

'Of course,' Alison said.

'They do have such things as comedies at the video store.'

'They're not nearly as much fun.'

Jake grinned, shook his head, and tumbled some popcorn into his mouth. 'Amazing,' he said, after chewing for a moment. 'It really doesn't bother you, watching this kind of thing? After what happened?'

'The movies are pretend.'

'I'd think *they* might give you flashbacks.'

'They do. Sometimes. But all kinds of things do. It's only been three weeks.'

'Three great weeks,' Jake said.

'Yeah.'

311

She watched Jake munch some more popcorn. She took a handful, tossed some into her mouth, and flinched. 'Ow!'

Jake looked at her, startled.

'It's too damn hot to eat.'

Now he looked perplexed.

Alison lifted the bowl off her lap, leaned forward and set it on the table. 'I think we'd better let it cool off for a while, don't you? We don't want to burn our tongues while we watch the movies.'

'Oh. Right.' Jake blushed a little.

Alison pulled the nightshirt over her head. Facing him, she began to open the buttons of his pyjama jacket. He swallowed the remains of his popcorn. He stared into her eyes. His gaze roamed downward, lingering on her naked body.

Alison watched his hands move slowly towards her until his fingertips trembled against her breasts. The hand that had held the popcorn felt grainy with salt, and slippery. 'Whoops,' he whispered. He took the hand away and rubbed it on his pyjama pants, leaving an oily smear.

The oil and butter on Alison's breast gleamed in the lamplight. 'You'd better lick it clean,' she said.

He did.

As his tongue lapped and swirled, Alison slipped the jacket down his arms. She gasped and arched her back when he sucked.

Then his mouth went to her mouth and his arms went around her.

Alison fell sideways against the sofa back and stretched her legs under the table. Jake pushed his tongue into her mouth. She tugged the waistband of his pyjamas. The snaps popped open and she pulled at the pyjamas until he was bare against her, smooth and hard.

His tongue left her mouth. He kissed her lips, her chin, the side of her neck. His hands roamed, caressing her shoulderblades, gliding down, curling over her buttocks, moving up again.

They stayed away from the middle of her spine.

Gently clutching his hair, Alison eased his head away and looked into his eyes. 'You never touch me . . . *there*.'

His eyebrows lifted slightly.

'Where *it* was.'

'I guess not,' he whispered. Alison could feel his penis shrinking against her thigh.

'Does it disgust you?'

'No. God, no. Nothing about you disgusts me.'

'It was in me.'

'Nothing's in there, now. I watched the doctor clean the wound, and . . .'

'But you're afraid to touch me there.'

'No, I'm not.'

'Scared you'll catch something?'

'I don't want to hurt you.'

'It's healed. All but the scar.'

'You want me to touch it?'

'Not if you don't want to.'

'It isn't that,' he muttered, looking miserable.

'What is it?'

'I did it to you. I stabbed you, cut you open. I hurt you, and when I see the wound or touch it, it all comes back how you cried out and jumped and dug your nails into the floor. It all comes back how much I hurt you.'

'You mean it's guilt, just guilt?'

'You might say that.'

'Dipshit, you saved my life.' Alison pressed her cheek to his and held him tight. 'I look at it in the mirror. It's special, Jake. It's you cutting into me and taking out the nightmare.'

The tips of Jake's fingers trembled against the flesh of Alison's wound. They gently followed the length of it. They tickled and she squirmed.

'Does it hurt?'

'No. Does this?'

Jake moaned.

'Let's knock off all this small talk,' Alison said. 'The popcorn's getting cold and we've still got a double feature to watch.'

'What am I,' Jake asked, 'the coming attraction?'

Alison laughed and swung a leg over his hip.

Resurrection Dreams

Senior Year

Chapter One

That had to be Steve Kraft. It was Kraft's blue Trans Am, the one his dad gave him when he threw six touchdown passes against the Bay last fall. So that had to be Steve, all right.

The way his head looked reminded Wes of when you've got a marshmallow on a stick and you're trying to toast it to a nice golden tan and the bastard goes up in flames.

You blow out the fire. Then you go to pull the marshmallow off the stick. The stiff crust slips right off like a shell, and the white gooey centre stays on the stick.

Maybe Steve's face would slip off like that if you . . .

Wes twisted away from the car's blazing wreckage and doubled over. 'Watch it!' Manny danced backward to save his shoes as Wes started heaving.

'Whatcha tryin' to do,' Manny asked, '*gross me out?*'

Wes heard him laughing and wondered how anyone – even Manny – could find something funny about Steve Kraft piling into the bridge's wall and burning like a marshmallow.

Then Manny patted his back. 'Should've lost it on Kraft, old buddy. Maybe you could've put him out.'

Wes straightened up. 'That's really sick,' he muttered.

'Hey, the guy was an asshole.' Manny took a swig of the Old Milwaukee he'd been drinking when they stopped to check out the fire. He passed the bottle to Wes.

Wes drank some, washing the sour taste of vomit out of his mouth. 'Maybe we better get outa here,' he said. 'Cops show up, they'll know we been drinking. 'Specially Pollock. He'll give us real shit.'

'Fuck Dexter Pollock,' Manny said. Standing in the middle of the road, he swung his head from side to side as if searching for the police chief. 'Any car shows up, we'll just . . .' His head jerked hard to the right. His mouth dropped open.

319

Wes looked.

The girl was halfway across the bridge, sprawled over the top of its low concrete parapet.

Wes *thought* it was a girl. He couldn't be sure, since her head was out of sight. But she looked as if she might be naked, and Steve Kraft wouldn't have had a naked *guy* in his car.

'I think she's bareass,' Manny said. His voice sounded hushed, secretive. 'Come on.'

They walked slowly toward her. Wes felt his heart drumming. His mouth was dry. He took another drink of beer.

'Bet it's Darlene,' Manny said.

'Yeah.'

Manny rubbed his mouth. 'Not a stitch on. No wonder Kraft piled up.'

The firelight fluttered and rolled over the bare skin of her back and rump and legs. Her left leg hung toward the walkway. The other was up on top of the wall as if she intended to climb over and leap into the creek.

'What's she doing?' Wes whispered.

'Lost a contact lense?' Manny suggested, and let out a short, nervous laugh. 'Not a stitch,' he said again.

That wasn't quite true, Wes realized. Now that he was closer to the girl, he could see that she wore white socks and white tennis shoes. Around her left ankle hung a pair of panties that looked glossy in the russet firelight.

'Think she'll be glad to see us?' Manny asked.

Wes didn't bother to answer. He suspected that Darlene would rather see just about anyone except Manny. She, like all those snob cheerleaders and most of the other kids in the senior class at Ellsworth High, thought Manny was the scum of the earth.

Manny called out, 'Hey, Darlene, don't jump! It's not that bad. Stevie's a goner, but *we're* here.'

She didn't move.

'Maybe she's hurt,' Wes said.

'Can't be hurt too bad, she came this far. Darle-e-e-ne.'

As they hurried closer, Wes looked back at the blazing car. Flames flapped through the space where the windshield belonged. He faced forward. Manny was already beside the sprawled girl. 'Hey, you don't suppose she got thrown all the way . . .'

'Not a chance.' He slapped the girl's rump. It jiggled slightly, but she didn't flinch or yelp. He leaned over her. 'Hey, Wes,' he said. 'I think I know what she lost off the bridge.'

Wes didn't like the high, strange sound of Manny's voice. 'What?'

'Her head.'

'Quit joking around.'

'Look for yourself.'

West sidestepped past Manny, and looked.

Her left shoulder rested on top of the wall. The right was beyond the edge, drooping over the ravine, her arm hanging straight down.

Wes *knew* her head had to be there, just this side of the drooping shoulder, but he sure couldn't see it.

'No,' he said. 'It's there.' On that side of the wall, there was no light from the fire. That's why he couldn't see Darlene's head.

'Bitch got herself decapacitated.' To prove his point, he gave the body a tug.

Wes yelped and lurched backward as it came toward him. It rolled off the parapet, dropped, and hit the sidewalk at his feet.

'See?' Manny said, stepping out of the way so his shadow left her.

Wes saw, all right. He saw a stump of neck between her shoulders.

'That's Darlene, all right,' Manny said. 'Nobody's got a set like that.'

'I don't think we oughta be looking at her,' Wes said. 'You know? She's dead.'

'Yeah, I imagine she is.' Manny squatted down for a better view.

Wes felt angry at Manny, disgusted with himself. He knew it was wrong to look, but he kept staring at her.

'Ever see one before?' Manny asked.

'Just Steve.'

'Not a stiff, a naked babe.'

'Sure,' he lied.

Manny moved a hand up her thigh.

'Hey, don't.'

'Check her out, man. This is as close as a loser like you's ever gonna get to a babe like this.'

321

'For godsake, get your hand off her.'

'Wish we had more light.' Manny started to pull her leg sideways.

Wes booted him in the shoulder and he tumbled over.

'Hey!'

'Don't mess with her. Just leave her alone!'

'Fuck you!' Manny leaped to his feet and whirled toward Wes. His fists were clenched at his sides.

Wes realized he still held the beer bottle. 'Stay back!' he warned. 'I'll bash you! I swear, I'll bust your head open!'

He raised the bottle like a club, and chilly liquid spilled down his arm.

'You think you can take me, man? I'll take that bottle and shove it up your tight ass.'

'I don't want to fight you,' Wes said.

'Damn straight, you don't.'

Wes tossed the bottle. It flew over the low wall where Darlene had been sprawled. A few seconds later, it hit the stream with a soft splash.

'Okay?' he asked. 'Okay?'

'Okay.' Smiling, Manny patted his shoulder. Then he smashed his knee up into Wes's stomach. Wes dropped to his knees. 'Now we're even,' he said, and took Wes by the arm and helped him up. 'Don't know why you wanta act like such a dumb fuck. Come on, let's check her out. Isn't every day you get a chance like this.'

Wes, bent over and holding his stomach, fought to suck air into his lungs and shook his head.

'Just don't mess with me, then.'

Manny turned away and crouched over the body. And shot up straight as headlights glowed in the distance.

They ran. They ran away from Darlene's body and through the heat near the blazing Trans Am, into the cooler air beyond it. They flung themselves into Manny's car.

Manny started the engine. He looked at Wes and grinned. 'Tough luck,' he said. 'Coulda been a kick.' Then he swung his car into a tight U-turn, and they sped toward town.

Chapter Two

When her clock blared Monday morning, Vicki set the snooze alarm to give herself another ten minutes. She stretched, rolled over, and pushed her face into the warm pocket of her pillow.

This was usually one of her favourite times of the day, a time to snuggle in the cosy warmth of her bed and let her mind roam.

Today, however, she felt uneasy, even a little frightened.

She knew it was because of what happened to Steve and Darlene.

It gave her a cold feeling inside.

She didn't feel sorry for them. Not exactly. After all, they had done it to themselves if it was true what Cynthia'd said. *No one* does seventy on River Road. And if they were really nude when they hit the bridge, that was even worse. They'd been speeding and screwing around. It was no better than suicide.

Besides which, neither of them was any great shakes as a human being. Steve may have been a hunk and he *was* a pretty good quarterback if you happened to care, but he was also so conceited it made you want to throw up. Darlene was not only conceited, but she used her looks like a weapon to torment half the guys in school.

Vicki knew she wouldn't miss either one of them.

But they were dead.

Dead.

It made her feel *really* cold inside.

Lying here thinking about it wasn't making it any better.

She got up and shut off the snooze alarm. She stretched, hitched up her drooping pyjama pants, and stepped to her bedroom window.

Looked beautiful out there. The sky was clear and pale blue. Off in the distance, Mr Blain was on his dock, squatting down to untie his outboard.

The warm morning breeze stirred Vicki's pyjamas. The light fabric caressed her skin.

She heard the hum of insects, birdsongs and the cackle of a loon. A butterfly dipped past her window.

She thought how wonderful it was, and then thought about how Darlene and Steve would never see another morning.

She pictured Darlene in a dark narrow coffin, trapped under six feet of dirt. That seemed worse, somehow, than getting cremated like Steve.

She started to wonder whether she'd rather be cremated than buried. If you could feel the fire . . .

Shivering, she turned away from the window. She went to the closet and put on her robe and told herself as she hurried from her room that they're both in heaven. She wasn't real sure about Heaven, but it beat thinking about them being just dead forever.

In the hallway, she smelled coffee. She wondered how anything that smelled so good could taste so bitter.

Dad was at the breakfast table with his coffee. Mom, at the stove, looked over her shoulder as Vicki walked in. 'You want your egg fried or scrambled?' she asked.

'Fried, I guess.'

It all seemed so normal.

'Morning, Pops.'

'I'll *Pops* you!'

She bent over, put an arm around his shoulders, and kissed his cheek. He hadn't shaved yet.

She'd heard somewhere that whiskers kept growing for a while after a man's dead.

He patted Vicki's rump.

He's going to die someday, she thought. Mom, too.

Knock if off, she told herself. They're only thirty-eight, for godsake.

She gave him an extra squeeze, then straightened up and looked at her mother. Mom was breaking an egg into the skillet. She wore the blue robe Dad gave her two Christmases ago.

If I go around hugging everyone, Vicki thought, they'll figure I'm going weird.

So she sat in her usual chair and took a drink of orange juice. Dad watched her.

'Did you sleep all right?' he asked.

'Sure.'

'Bad dreams?'

She shrugged.

'We heard you talking in your sleep last night,' Mom said from the stove.

'Really? Did I say anything spectacular?'

'Just jibberish,' Dad told her.

Mom said, 'You sounded pretty upset.'

'I don't know. I don't remember.'

'If you're upset about something . . .'

'I'm fine, Mom. Really.'

'Like missing your period,' Dad said.

Vicki felt her face go hot. 'Very funny.'

'So that isn't the problem, I take it?'

'Not hardly.'

Mom brought the plate over. The fried egg rested on a slab of toast, the way Vicki liked it. There were two strips of bacon. While she cut up her breakfast and mixed it all together, Mom poured more coffee into Dad's cup. She gave herself a refill and sat down.

'It was a lovely service yesterday. You really should've gone with us.'

'Would've helped get it out of your system,' Dad said.

'My system's just fine, thank you.'

'Your science project could've waited,' Mom told her. 'You still have all week before the fair.'

'I didn't like it hanging over my head. Besides, Darlene's parents were your friends, not mine.'

'They asked about you,' Mom said.

'Great,' she muttered. She got a piece of bacon onto her fork, stabbed the tines through a chunk of eggwhite and yolk-sodden toast, and stuffed them into her mouth. They didn't taste as good as usual.

Thanks for ruining my breakfast, folks.

'Well,' Dad said, 'it was your decision.'

'Mine, but wrong.'

'It would've been nice if you'd gone,' Mom said.

'Fine. Next time any kids get themselves wiped out doing seventy while they're screwing, I'll be sure to attend their funerals.'

Mom's face turned scarlet.

Dad raised his eyebrows and looked somewhat amused.

'That's a terrible thing to say.'

'I'm sorry, Mom.'

'If you could've seen her poor parents . . .' Mom pressed her lower lip between her teeth. There were tears in her eyes. 'Their only daughter . . .'

'I know. I'm sorry.'

'All I could think about was how I'd feel if that had been you.'

Now Dad's eyes were red.

'It wasn't me.'

'It could've been.'

'Sure, it could've been. Yeah. If I looked like Darlene and was head cheerleader and had all the guys drooling all over my body and had a red-hot boyfriend who thought it was cool to see how fast he can drive on a narrow road while I'm doing God-knows-what to him. Could've been me. Right! But I'm not a knockout and guys like Steve Kraft don't know or care that I exist and the only guy who does care is too timid and smart to drive like a maniac and if he ever did I'd pull out the damned ignition key and make him eat it.'

She stopped. She nodded her head once, hard, and jammed another bite of food into her mouth.

'So there,' Dad said. He still had wet eyes, but his mouth wore a tilted smile.

Mom's mouth hung open. She looked a trifle stunned and bewildered, but at least the weeping had stopped.

Dad got up from the table. 'Unfortunately, I have a living to earn. Now, don't you ladies launch into any tirades without me, okay?'

He stepped behind Vicki's chair and put his hands on her shoulders. 'You are too a knockout,' he said.

'Right. Sure.'

Mom nodded in agreement. 'You shouldn't belittle yourself, honey. You're a very attractive young woman – and very bright. Your father and I are both very proud of you. There's no reason in the world why you should ever feel the least bit jealous or envious of someone like Darlene.'

'I don't envy her, that's for sure.'

'Good,' Mom said. She didn't get it.

Dad did. He kissed the top of Vicki's head, muttered, 'Beast,' and left.

The rest of breakfast tasted just fine.

Getting things off your chest, she thought, must improve the appetite.

'Alice is here,' Mom called a few moments after Vicki heard the doorbell.

'I'll be out in a minute.' She finished tying her white Nikes, bounced up from the bed, and slung her book bag onto her back as she hurried from her room.

It was good to see Ace. It was always good to see her, but especially this morning.

'I know,' Ace was saying to Mom. 'It's a terrible tragedy.' She nodded a greeting to Vicki. Her face looked solemn. 'It's especially terrible for her loved ones.'

'Awful,' Mom said. Though she was Vicki's size and Vicki hardly considered herself a shrimp, she seemed small and fragile beside Ace.

Nearly everyone did.

Alice 'Ace' Mason was the tallest girl in the senior class, but plenty of boys had more height than she did – and most of them seemed smaller in her presence.

Imposing, Vicki thought. That's what she is.

And, at the moment, posing.

She turned sorrowful eyes to Vicki and said, 'I suppose we'd better get going. Have a nice day, Mrs Chandler.'

Vicki gave her mother a quick kiss on the cheek, then followed Ace outside. They reached the sidewalk. They were halfway down the block when Ace looked at Vicki with bright mischievous eyes.

'Where's your black threads, Vicks?' she asked in her usual brash voice.

'Where're yours?'

She snorted. 'Black panties, hon.' She took a long stride and swung her rump in Vicki's direction.

She wore white shorts that hugged her buttocks. A dark triangle and narrow waistband showed through the material.

'They really are black.'

'You can see them?' She twisted around and looked for herself. 'Well shitski.'

'Sexy, too.'

'Ordered them special. Want me to get you some?'

'Right. What happens when Mom does the wash?'

'We'll get her some, too. Drive your dad crazy with lust.'

'Please.'

'We order now, you'll get them in time for the dance.'

'Thanks anyway.'

'Give Henry a treat.'

'As close as Henry'll get to my underpants, I could be wearing polka-dot boxer shorts.'

'Poor guy. I can see he'll be having a memorable night.'

'How was your weekend?' Vicki asked, hoping to get away from the subject of Henry.

'Caught some rays. Aunt Lucy was her usual kick in the head. Wish I'd been here, though. Missed out on all the excitement. Your mom says you blew your chance to see Darlene get planted.'

'Couldn't go. No black panties.'

'We'll fix that. How about she was giving him head when they wiped out?'

'You're kidding. Where'd you hear that?'

'Thought it was common knowledge.'

'Nobody told me.'

Ace halted on the deserted sidewalk, looked all around as if to make sure nobody was within earshot, then bowed her head toward Vicki. 'Did you hear she was butt-naked?'

'Yeah. Cynthia called me Saturday morning. She overheard her mother on the phone with Thelma Clemens. She said Steve got burnt to a crisp and Darlene got thrown through the windshield – and how she was naked and how her head got . . . cut off.'

'That's all?' Ace asked.

From the gleeful look in her eyes, Vicki knew a major detail was missing from Cynthia's verson. 'What?' she asked.

'Well, I talked to Roger last night and his brother's best pals with Joey Milbourne. Joey's supposed to be the guy that found her head. It was way on the other side of the bridge under some bushes? Well, he's the biggest jerk-off ever to wear a badge, next to Pollock, and maybe he just made this up so he'd have a good story to tell, but he told Roger's brother that when he found Darlene's head . . .' Ace stopped talking and looked around again.

'Come *on*.'

'You sure you haven't heard this?'

'Quit goofing around and tell me.'

'She had Steve's dick in her mouth.'

'*What?*'

Ace bared her teeth and chomped them together.

'Holy shit,' Vicki muttered.

'When she bit it, she really *bit* it.'

Vicki cracked up and shoved Ace away from her.

'What a way to go!' Ace blurted through her own laughter.

'Makes me hurt,' Vicki gasped.

'You ain't even *got* one.'

'Well, if I did . . .'

'He came and went.'

'Ace, Ace!' She wiped her eyes. 'Stop it!'

'At least Darlene got a last meal.'

'Knockwurst!' Vicki squealed. 'Hold the sauerkraut!'

'More of a hot dog from what I heard. More of a *cocktail weenie*.'

'Oh, God. Stop it, Ace.'

'*Me?*'

Later, Vicki felt miserable with guilt. It was bad enough to feel no particular sorrow about the demise of her classmates. It seemed unforgivably gross to have joked and laughed hysterically about it.

During fourth period study hall, she passed a note to Ace. The note said, 'He went to St Peter without his.'

Ace read it and snorted.

Mr Silverstein, who had been busy grading papers, jerked his head up. 'Miss Mason, would you like to share with the rest of us?'

'Nah, I don't think so.'

'Is that a note I see clutched in your hand?'

'Nothing in my hand,' Ace told him. 'See?' She blatantly stuffed the note into her mouth, and held up both hands as she began to chew.

The performance drew applause from about half the kids in the room. Mr Silverstein shook his head. He frowned at Ace as if debating whether to pursue the matter, apparently decided not to risk it, offered a lame, 'Well, let's all try to keep it down; this is a study hall, not a sideshow,' and went back to grading papers.

Ace removed the sodden ball of paper from her mouth. She tossed it at Melvin Dobbs, who was sitting in the next row over, two desks up. It stuck to the back of his neck. Vicki tried to hold back her laugh. The air blew out her nose.

Normally, she felt a certain amount of sympathy for Melvin. He was a weird kid, odd enough to make himself the target of choice for everyone in the mood to cause trouble. Vicki wished Ace had thrown the spitball at someone else, but she couldn't help laughing.

Melvin flinched when the wet glob struck his neck. He sat up straight, picked it off his skin, then carefully plucked the wad open and studied it.

Oh great, Vicki thought.

Melvin turned around. He stared at Ace with his bulgy, half-shut eyes. Then he balled up the paper. He sniffed it, licked his thick lips, and stuffed the paper into his mouth. He chewed it slowly, smiling a bit and rolling his eyes as if really savouring the taste. Finally, he swallowed.

Vicki managed not to gag.

When the bell rang, she joined up with Ace.

Ace rolled her eyes, imitating Melvin. 'You see him chew it down?'

'I almost lost my breakfast.'

'That guy is *strange*.'

In the hallway on their way to the cafeteria, they saw Melvin ahead of them. He was walking stooped over, pumping vigorously with one arm while his other arm hung straight down with the weight of his briefcase. His pink shirt was untucked in the rear. It draped the seat of his gaudy plaid shorts.

'Got another piece of paper?' Ace asked.

'What for?'

'Maybe he'd like a second helping.'

Just then, Randy Montclair took a long sideways stride, cutting in front of Ace, and swatted the back of Melvin's head. 'Fucked up my appetite, you pig,' he said, and gave the kid another whack. Melvin cowered, but kept walking.

Randy had been in study hall. Obviously, he'd watched Melvin devour the spitball.

Doug, his buddy, skipped along beside him, laughing. 'Give him another!'

'Scum.' Randy slapped Melvin again.

'Knock it off!' Vicki snapped.

Still pursuing Melvin, he glanced over his shoulder. His lip curled out. 'Butt out.'

'Just leave him alone.'

Ignoring her, he backhanded Melvin's low head.

Vicki shrugged out of her book bag. Holding it by the straps, she swung it at Randy. The loaded satchel slammed into his shoulder. He staggered sideways, knocking into Doug. They almost went down, but not quite.

Then they were facing Vicki.

They didn't look happy.

'Just leave him alone,' she said. 'All right?'

Scowling, Randy waved a fist in front of her nose.

'Oh, I'm so scared.'

But not much. Not with Ace beside her.

'If you weren't a girl, I'd knock your face in.'

Doug looked as if he might echo his friend's remark, but he glanced at Ace and kept his mouth shut.

'Take a leap, guys,' Ace said.

Randy's scowl dissolved. He looked up at Ace. 'Just tell Vicki to keep her nose outa my business.'

Ace raised her eyebrows. 'I didn't hear the magic word.'

Randy muttered something inaudible and stepped out of the way, shoving Doug as if all this were somehow Doug's fault.

Vicki and Ace left them behind.

'Thanks,' Vicki said.

'You owe me a Ding-dong.'

'Only Twinkies today.'

'A Twinkie will do just fine. You all of a sudden Melvin's bodyguard or something?'

'It was my note he ate.'

'It was my spit.'
'It makes him your blood-brother,' Vicki explained.
'Gawd! Get a lobotomy, girl!'

Chapter Three

On Saturday morning, Vicki's father helped load her science project into the trunk, and drove her to the Community Center.

The Spring Science Fair was one of the town's frequent events like the Antique Show, the Gun Show and the Handicrafts Show that seemed to exist mostly for the sake of giving the residents of Ellsworth something unique to do on their weekends.

Most of the other shows brought in merchants and visitors from out of town, which was good for the motels and restaurants. But not the Science Fair. It was a showcase for the efforts of the local kids, who had to attend and demonstrate their creations if they wanted a passing mark in their school science classes. The kids and teachers got in free. It was $2.00 a head for everyone else, and it seemed that nobody in the entire town could bear to miss it.

Not only because most of the kids participating had a whole slew of relations, but because things never failed to go wrong and provide the folks with gossip – which seemed to be their chief recreation.

'Just think,' Dad said, 'this is your last Science Fair.'

'And not a moment too soon.'

It would be her twelfth – one a year since first grade. In the early years, she'd enjoyed the fair and looked forward to it almost gleefully. Her first project had been a chicken egg and a 100-watt lightbulb to warm it up. Later on, she'd made an electro-magnet with a nail and a dry-cell battery.

'Remember your volcano?' Dad asked. He, too, was apparently remembering the good old days.

'God, that was a disaster.'

When Vicki was in sixth grade, she'd made a terrific-looking volcano out of plaster of Paris and stood it on a platform concealing a dry chemical fire-extinguisher. Every now and then, she gave the extinguisher a honk, shooting a white cloud out of the volcano's crater. The volcano actually *trembled* each time she triggered an eruption. But when the judges showed up, she wanted to give them an eruption to remember so she kept the lever down. The horn blared. All around, people cringed and covered their ears – then vanished behind the wall of white cast out by the extinguisher. The volcano shuddered. It all looked just great – what Vicki could see of it through the fog – until her hand slipped and the horn lost its perfect positioning beneath the crater and the powerful discharge blasted out the front of her volcano throwing plaster at the judges like shrapnel.

'You were the hit of the show,' Dad said.

'At least I didn't kill anyone.'

'I'd like to have seen a reprise of that. You could've resurrected the volcano for your final project.'

'Now that I'm a big girl,' Vicki told him, 'I don't get quite the same joy out of humiliating myself.'

Joy. She remembered the way she had cried afterwards. Everyone for godsake *clapping* hadn't made it any better.

'Displaying the parts of a dismantled rat,' Dad said, 'doesn't have half the flair of blowing up a volcano. Though it does have a certain gross-out potential.'

'I figured I might as well do something useful this year.'

'Just give you a few more years, you'll be cutting up cadavers.'

'Don't remind me.'

'Maybe you should go into law.'

'I'd rather heal people than screw them.'

Laughing, Dad swung the car into the parking lot of the Community Center. Though it was still early, most of the parking spaces near the open doors of the arena were already taken. Parents and kids were busy unloading tables and projects from cars, vans and pickup trucks. Dad drove as close to the door as he could get, which was a good distance away, and parked.

They went around to the trunk. When Dad opened it, the pungent aroma of formaldehyde swelled out. Vicki reached in. She picked up the dissection tray. The surgical gloves and implements she planned to use for her procedure were inside the tray. She handed it to her father, and lifted out the bottle containing the rat she would be dissecting during the course of the fair. With that securely clamped under one arm, she took out the wooden display case in which the parts of a previously 'dismantled' rat were carefully mounted and labelled.

'Hiya, Vicki.'

The voice sounded familiar, but she couldn't quite place it. She turned around.

'Melvin.'

His wide head was tilted to one side, and he blinked and smiled as he rubbed his hands together. 'Use some help?' he asked.

'Good man,' Dad said. 'So, they gave you a day off, huh?'

'Yep.'

'Think they can get along without you?'

He rolled his head around.

'Guess your father'll have to pump the gas himself, huh?'

'And wipe the windshields, too,' Melvin added.

Dad slipped the card table out of the trunk and handed it to him.

'Don't you have your own project to set up?' Vicki asked.

'Done it already,' he said.

Dad shut the trunk, and the three of them started across the parking lot toward the arena. Melvin walked in the lead, balancing the table on top of his head.

He hadn't spoken a word to Vicki after the incident with Randy Montclair in the hallway on Monday. Though she hadn't relished the prospect of a conversation with him, she'd expected at least a word of thanks. Finally, she had decided that he was probably unaware of what she'd done. That didn't seem so likely, now. Offering to help carry her project was apparently his way of showing appreciation.

When he reached the door, he slid the table off his head, held it against his chest with both hands, and sidestepped through the entrance.

Vicki and her father followed him. The area set aside for the high-school seniors was at the far end. She spotted Ace, who looked busy unloading a carton onto a table. Melvin knew enough to head for the big girl. He lowered the card table in the open space beside Ace's display. When she said something to him, he darted a thumb over his shoulder. Ace saw Vicki approaching, and nodded.

Melvin folded out the legs and set the table upright.

'Thanks a lot for the help,' Vicki told him.

A corner of his mouth slid up. He nodded and blushed and turned away. A few shambling steps took him to the other side of the space that had been left open for a walkway between the two rows of projects. He slipped a tattered paperback book out of a rear pocket of his baggy shorts, then sat on a stool facing the girls, and began to read. The book was *Frankenstein*.

'Want me to help you set up?' Dad asked.

'No, that's all right. Thanks.'

'Okay. We'll be back later. Have fun.'

He said goodbye to Ace, then walked away.

Vicki set her bottled rat on the table.

'I see you brought your lunch,' Ace said.

'You've got the bread, cheese and beverages. We'll have a feast.'

Ace's bread and cheese, neatly arranged atop her table, were coated with mould. She also had jars of coffee, red wine and apple juice. Each jar looked as if someone had dumped in a handful of fuzz from a vacuum-cleaner bag. A pair of hand-lettered posters, joined together with tape, listed mould's beneficial uses.

'You'll get a blue ribbon for sure,' Vicki said.

'Eat my shorts.'

Vicki went ahead with her preparations. She opened her wooden display case and propped it up near the back of her table. Then she emptied her dissection tray and put on surgical gloves. She started to open the jar containing the formaldehyde and rat.

'Spare me, would you?' Ace said. 'The thing doesn't start for half an hour. Wait'll you've got an audience, for godsake.'

Vicki shrugged. 'Why not?' She put the bottle down and pulled the gloves off.

Ace was busy unfolding the two chairs she had brought from home. She set them up side by side with the backs to their tables. Both girls sat down.

Melvin, across from them, glanced up then resumed reading.

'What do you suppose *he's* got?' Ace asked in a quiet voice.

'Maybe he made that megaphone.'

The megaphone rested on the floor beside his stool. It didn't look homemade.

Behind him was an enclosure the size of an outhouse: a framework draped with blue bedsheets.

'What've you got in there?' Ace called over to him.

He raised his head and grinned. 'It's a surprise.'

'You got another car engine this year?'

'Maybe.'

'Come on, be a sport and give us a peek.'

'You'll see. I gotta wait for the right time.'

'When's that?'

'Not till the judges show up.'

'You're kidding.'

He shrugged his round shoulders. 'It's kind of a one-shot deal,' he said, and went back to reading.

'Turkey,' Ace muttered.

Vicki and Ace talked about other things for a while. When Ace's boyfriend, Rob, showed up, Vicki left her seat and wandered over to Henry's display. Not because she especially wanted to visit with him. But he was the closest thing Vicki had to a boyfriend, and he *was* taking her to the senior dance next week so she felt it would be weird of her to ignore him.

She found him seated at his computer, hunched over the keyboard, avidly pecking out commands that made Humphrey dance and wink though nobody seemed to be watching the performance.

Humphrey was a marionette, about three feet tall, decked out in a top hat and tails. He did his numbers beside Henry's computer, and looked somewhat as if he'd been impaled on the plastic pipe that ran from the control box to his rump.

'Howdy, Humphrey,' Vicki said.

The marionette waved to her and gave his legs a couple of spastic kicks.

Henry, seated on a swivel chair, swung around and looked up at Vicki. Behind his glasses, his eyes were wide with eagerness. They always seemed that way, as if Henry were perpetually on the verge of making a startling announcement.

'How're things?' Vicki asked.

'Oh, fine.'

'Nifty outfit,' she said. Henry wore a bow tie and black dinner jacket. His outfit was identical to Humphrey's, though Henry wore no top hat. His hat rested on the table beside his keyboard, ready to be donned when the spectators started wandering by.

'You look very lovely this morning,' he said.

'Thanks.' Vicki wasn't especially pleased by the compliment. A day rarely went by that Henry didn't make a similar comment. But she'd never seen him really look her over. The words just came out like a programmed response to her arrival – as if he realized he ought to feign some interest in her physical appearance.

We've really got a red-hot romance cooking here, she thought.

But she supposed it was her fault as much as Henry's. Their relationship had started on an intellectual level when they'd been teamed up as lab partners in physiology last year, and neither of them had made any effort to get physical. They had gone out together at least a dozen times, and never even kissed. It was as if neither of them had bodies.

Vicki sometimes wondered what might happen if she should embrace him and kiss him hard and squirm against him, really let him know she was a woman, not just a discussion partner. Henry might suddenly turn into a lusting animal.

The idea didn't have much appeal.

So she'd done nothing to change the nature of the relationship – such as it was. She liked Henry, and he did fine in the role of boyfriend until something better might come along.

Which didn't seem too likely in the immediate future.

Of all the guys she could think of, there was not a single one who really interested her.

Thanks to Paul. When he moved away, it all fell apart.

She realized that Henry was talking to her. 'What?' she asked. 'My mind was wandering.'

'Did it wander someplace interesting?'

Someplace empty, she thought.

'No,' she said. 'What were you saying?'

'I thought that perhaps we might meet during the lunch break. We should discuss our plans for next Friday.'

'Sure. That'd be fine.' She glanced at her wristwatch. 'Well, it's about time for the fun to start. I'd better get back to my rats.'

'*Ciao*,' Henry said, and swivelled around to face his computer. His fingers fluttered over the keyboard, and Humphrey waved and winked.

Vicki walked back toward her table. Ace and Rob were standing in front of the chairs, facing each other, holding hands. Ace was nodding as she listened to him. Though three inches taller than Rob, she somehow always seemed less imposing when they were together, as if his presence transformed her into someone more feminine and vulnerable.

Vicki didn't want to intrude on the intimacy she sensed. She turned to her table and picked up her surgical gloves.

She wished she hadn't thought about Paul.

Sometimes she went for days at a time without thinking about him.

Her parents had called it 'puppy love', which seemed like a way to make her feelings for Paul sound less important. Vicki had thought of it as love, and still did. When she'd been with Paul, she'd felt special and beautiful and full. Whether they were just sitting together in class, or holding hands in a movie, or spending a whole day exploring the woods or swimming or boating on the river, each moment seemed golden.

But his father was a Master Sergeant in the Marines. Paul showed up at Ellsworth High in the fall of Vicki's sophomore year. They met at once and fell in love and had just that school year and the following summer. Then new orders came down, and Paul left with his family for a base in South Carolina.

They'd had almost exactly one year together. It had been over so fast.

It was as if the best part of her life ended when Paul went away. 'You'll get over it,' her parents had said. She supposed she did get over it. In a way. More like getting used to it. The loss seemed always there, deep inside, a shadow that made every day a little less bright – a loss that would rise to the surface every time she was reminded of Paul.

A time like now.

Pulling on her gloves, she felt a hollow ache in her chest.

No point in getting yourself all upset, she thought. Hell, I'll probably meet some terrific guy at college in the fall.

Sure.

She unscrewed the lid of the jar, lifted out the rat with tongs and placed it on the dissection tray.

'That's *really* disgusting,' Ace said. 'Barforama.'

'Your mould is appetising?'

Ace watched over her shoulder as she pinned the rat's paws to the waxy bottom of the tray.

'What's Rob up to?' Vicki asked.

'He's taking me to the drive-in tonight.'

'What's playing?'

'Who cares?' Ace said, and let out a couple of cheery snorts.

Vicki alternated between exposing the vitals of her rat and sitting on the chair to chat with Ace, whose project was a display with no performance. They spent a lot of time watching Melvin ward off curious spectators wanting to see what was hidden inside his enclosure of bedsheets.

He explained that it was a 'one-shot deal' and that they should be sure to hurry back when he made the announcement with his megaphone.

'He's sure getting *me* curious,' Vicki said.

'Maybe he's got a guillotine in there and he'll do us all a favour and lop off his ugly head.'

'You think he's got the brains to make a guillotine?'

'If he had any brains, he'd be dangerous.'

Vicki was beginning to look forward to lunch by the time the four judges reached the project next to Melvin's. She checked her wristwatch. A quarter till twelve. At noon, there would be an hour-long break. Some of the parents, she knew from past Science Fairs, would have tables set up just outside the doors with beer and wine for the adults, soft drinks, hot dogs and pizza and tacos – all kinds of good stuff. Though she wasn't especially eager to spend the lunch hour with Henry, she was definitely hungry. Her mouth had been watering all morning because of the formaldehyde, which simply did that to you even if you were bent over cutting up a dead rat.

Ace patted her knee. 'The moment, ladies and gentlemen, is upon us.'

The judges stopped in front of Melvin. He climbed off his stool, picked up the megaphone, and flipped a switch. A high piercing whine stabbed Vicki's ears, then faded.

'Attention, everyone,' Melvin announced, his voice sounding tinny and loud. 'Come one, come all. Come and see Melvin's Amazing Miracle Machine.' As he spoke, he swayed from side to side and rolled his head. 'You don't want to miss it. Nosirree.'

'What a moron,' Ace whispered.

He *did* have a rather moronic look on his face, which wasn't all that unusual for Melvin.

Spectators were beginning to come over.

'Come and see it,' Melvin went on. 'The Amazing Miracle Machine. Hurry, hurry. Step right up. You've never seen anything like it. You don't want to miss it. Come one, come all.'

Mr Peters, the principal and head judge, stepped up to Melvin and said something – probably telling him to get on with it.

Melvin nodded, put the megaphone to his mouth, and said, 'The show is about to begin!'

By now, a substantial crowd was gathered in front of Melvin's display. Vicki followed Ace's example, and stood on the seat of her chair. From there, she had a fine view.

Melvin set his megaphone on the floor beside his stool. He stepped to a corner of his enclosure, hooked back one of the sheets enough to let him slip through, and vanished.

Nothing happened.

Everyone waited. More people showed up. There were murmured questions, heads shaking.

Mr Peters checked his wristwatch. 'We haven't got all day, Melvin,' he said.

'Is everybody ready?' Melvin finally called out. His voice sounded flat without the amplifier.

'*Do* it, doufuss,' Ace yelled.

A few people turned and looked up at her, some laughing, others frowning.

'And now – Melvin's Amazing Miracle Machine!'

The sheet across the front of the framework fell to the floor.

People gasped and went silent.

Vicki stared. For a moment, she didn't understand what she was seeing. Then, she couldn't believe it.

Surrounding Melvin and his 'project' were coils of razor-edged concertina wire. A poster at the rear proclaimed, 'I AM THE RESURRECTION AND THE LIFE.' In the centre, on a platform at least a foot high, rested a wheelchair.

In the wheelchair sat the corpse of Darlene Morgan. She wore the cheerleader outfit in which she had been buried: a pleated green skirt, a golden pullover sweater with a raised green E on its chest for Ellsworth High.

Her neck was wrapped in bandages to hold her head on. Her head was tipped back, her mouth hanging open. Her eyes were shut. Her face looked grey.

Between her feet was a car battery, jumper cables clamped to its posts. Melvin raised the other ends of the cables overhead and bumped the clamps together. Current flashed and crackled.

Vicki, stunned, felt herself swaying. She grabbed Ace's arm to steady herself.

Somebody started to scream. Then everyone seemed to be yelling or shrieking.

'My God!'

'Stop him!'

'What's he *doing*?'

'Melvin, for godsake!'

'Do something!'

Instead of trying to stop Melvin, the people at the front of the group were backing away.

Melvin went on with business as if he were alone.

He clamped a jumper cable to each of Darlene's thumbs, then leaped aside, shouting, 'RISE! RISE! COME ON, BITCH, RISE!'

Darlene didn't rise. She just sat there. The battery charge seemed to have no effect at all.

'I COMMAND YOU TO RISE!' Melvin yelled. He rushed behind the wheelchair, grabbed its handles and shook it as if trying to stir her into action. 'COME ON! GET UP!'

Darlene shimmied and swayed. Her head wobbled. She didn't get up.

'UP! UP! I COMMAND YOU!'

Mr Peters leaped over the tangle of concertina wire.

Melvin jerked the handles ups. The wheelchair tipped forward, hurling Darlene from her seat. Mr Peters yelped as the body tumbled at him. He ducked under it.

Darlene flopped onto him. Her head came off, rolled down his back, and dropped face-first into the razor wire.

Melvin gave the screaming crowd a big, idiotic grin.

Homecoming

Chapter Four

You'll be living here, Vicki told herself. You can't avoid him forever, so you might as well go ahead and get it over with.

There was enough gas left to reach Ace's, so she didn't absolutely have to stop. But that would leave the U-Haul with an empty tank and she needed to drive forty miles to Blayton tomorrow once she finished unloading at the new apartment Ace had found for her.

Maybe the Arco station at the other end of town would still be open. It used to close down early, but its hours might've changed.

Just go ahead and stop at Melvin's, she thought.

Though she was still at least a mile from the Ellsworth city limits, the decision made her heart thud faster. The steering wheel felt slick in her hands. Cool trickles slid down her sides all the way to the waistband of her shorts. She wiped a hand on the front of her blouse, then fastened the two top buttons she had opened earlier to let the air in.

Maybe he won't even be on duty, she thought. He could've hired a kid, or someone, to run the place. God knows, he could afford to.

He shouldn't have come back to Ellsworth. What was he, a glutton for punishment? He'd been an outcast even before he flipped out at the Science Far, and nobody was ever likely to let him forget the Darlene Morgan business.

When Ace told her on the phone last year that Melvin had returned, she'd been so appalled that she had given a lot of thought to changing her own plans. As much as she looked forward to returning to Ellsworth once she finished her residency, the idea of living in the same town as Melvin made her queasy. Maybe he was 'stable', maybe he would never do anything crazy again, but she knew that every time she saw him she would remember his Amazing Miracle Machine.

Still, Ellsworth was home. Even though her parents had moved to Blayton during her first year at medical school, it was Ellsworth that she longed for: the quiet, familiar streets of her childhood, the shops she used to visit, the woods and river, her friends. It was where she had been carefree and happy and where she had fallen in love.

Knowing that Melvin Dobbs had returned there after his release from the institution took away some of the town's nostalgic glow.

It might have been enough to make Vicki change her plans about returning. Except for one thing.

A $25,000 loan from Dr Gaines, offered to Vicki, and accepted, on the condition that she return to Ellsworth and help him in his family practice until the loan was paid back. A great deal, especially since she had always hoped to practise in Ellsworth. And she'd looked forward to working with Charlie Gaines, a charming old guy she liked a lot.

Her obligation to the doctor removed any real possibility of avoiding Ellsworth, where she wanted to live anyway, so she had resigned herself to an eventual encounter with Melvin.

The encounter had been eventual a year ago.

Now, it was imminent.

Vicki felt sick.

Calm down, she told herself. It's no big deal. He's not going to *do* anything to me.

Rounding the bend in River Road, she saw the lighted service station ahead. There was Melvin standing slouched in front of a car, apparently writing its licence plate number on a credit card receipt.

The way he was dressed, he might have looked ridiculous. He wore a baggy, bright Hawaiian shirt, plaid Bermuda shorts and dark socks that sagged around his ankles. But he didn't look ridiculous; there was nothing funny about it. Vicki doubted that anything about Melvin, however odd, could ever strike her as amusing.

Her courage faltered.

Go to the Arco tomorrow, she thought.

But that would only postpone the inevitable. Better to face a nasty situation than to put it off and keep dwelling on it.

She slowed down, let out a shaky breath and swung off the road. The car was pulling away from the full-service island. She started for the self-service pumps, then changed her mind. This would be bad enough without having to get out of the truck. Especially the way she was dressed. So she drove to the full-service area and shut off the engine.

Melvin hobbled over to her window, peered in, and tipped his head to one side. His lower eye narrowed. Up close, his face looked heavier than she remembered. Uglier, too. His eyes seemed bigger and farther apart, his black eyebrows bushier, his lips thicker. His long hair was combed straight back over the top of his head, and slicked down.

'I know you,' he said.

'Vicki Chandler. How are you doing, Melvin?'

He leaned closer. He'd been eating garlic. 'Vicki. Gosh.' His head bobbed and he smiled. 'Last time I saw you, you was standing on a chair looking green.' He chuckled, puffing his garlic breath into her face.

She wondered if it was a good sign that he could talk about that day, laugh about it.

'Well,' she said, 'I was a little shocked.'

'I guess you wasn't the only one.' He winked. 'That was the whole point, you know.'

'The whole point?'

'Giving Darlene a jump-start like that. Shoot, you don't think I thought it'd work, do you? No way. Only a crazy person'd think it'd work. Dead's dead, know what I mean?'

'Sure looked like you were trying,' Vicki said, astonished that he was discussing this with her, explaining himself.

'Put on a good show, didn't I?'

'Why'd you do it?'

'Got tired of being pestered. You remember how the kids used to pester me. You was always nice. You was about the *only* one didn't used to talk mean or knock me around. I figured it this way. I figured they was always after me on account of me being kind of different, so what I'd do, I'd shock their pants off and they'd be so scared of me they'd leave off.' He sniffed, and rubbed his nose. ''Course, I learned my lesson. I shouldn't of done it. Made me look like a crazy person.'

You *are* a crazy person, Vicki thought. Or at least you *were*.

'I'm sorry about your parents,' Vicki said.

'Thank you. They was pig vomit.'

'I could use a fill-up, Melvin. Unleaded.'

'They left me sitting pretty, that's about all the good I can say for them. Want me to check under the hood?'

'No, that's all right.'

He left the window, and Vicki took a deep breath.

Whatever they did to him in the institution, she thought, it sure hadn't changed him much.

In the side mirror, she saw him remove the gas cap and insert the nozzle of the pump. Then he came back to her window.

'You here for a visit, or what?' he asked.

She was surprised he didn't know. On the other hand, people probably didn't spend a lot of time chatting with him. 'I'll be working at Dr Gaines's office.'

'What'll you do there?'

'I'm a physician now.'

'A doctor?'

'Yeah.'

'No fooling. I got no use for doctors. Messing with people, you know?'

'I guess you've seen your share of them.'

'None as pretty as you, that's a fact.'

'Thanks,' she muttered.

'You married?'

'Not yet.'

'Saving yourself for me?' He laughed and rubbed his nose. 'Just a joke. I like to make jokes, sometimes. I used to have the orderlies and nurses cracking up. The patients didn't laugh much, they was too doped up. They didn't do much but drool.' He laughed at that one.

Vicki heard the gas pump click off.

'That be cash or charge?' he asked.

'Cash.'

He went away. While he was gone, Vicki lifted her handbag off the passenger seat and took out two twenties. Her hand was shaking badly, and the bills fluttered when she held them out the window to Melvin. He wandered off to get change.

Almost over, she thought. It wasn't so bad.

Wasn't so good, either.

When he returned, Vicki rested her wrist on the window sill to keep her hand from trembling. He counted the coins and bills into her palm.

'I'm real glad you're back,' he said.

'Thanks.' She tucked the money into the pocket of her blouse, and saw Melvin watch her do it.

'Hope you'll come around again anytime you need a fill-up.'

She nodded.

'Don't *you* be scared of me. Okay?'

'I'm not scared of you, Melvin.'

'Sure you are. They *all* are. Shoot, I'd go out of business if it wasn't for strangers passing through. Way folks around here act, you'd think *I'm* the one that killed Darlene. I never hurt her. All I just did was dig her up and play a little prank. But I don't want you scared of me. Okay?'

'Fine,' she said, forcing a smile. 'So long, now. I'll see you around.'

He stepped away from the side of the truck. Vicki started the engine and pulled forward. She swung the truck onto River Road.

You could almost feel sorry for the guy, she thought.

The same way you could almost laugh at his peculiar appearance and mannerisms.

Except she didn't find him amusing or sympathetic.

Pig vomit. That's what he called his dead parents. You can't feel sorry for a guy who'd say such a thing. Or for a guy who'd pull such a sick stunt with Darlene.

Sure, kids gave him a hard time. But that was no excuse. A lot of people get teased and don't go out and dig up a dead girl and put on a show with her body.

And he asked if I was *saving myself* for him.

Ace came to the door in a bright yellow nightshirt with Minnie Mouse on the front, and threw her arms around Vicki. Stepping back, she said, 'God, it's been a while.'

'Three years next month since my last visit,' Vicki told her.

'It's a shame the way you've aged.'

'You and the horse you rode in on.'

She grabbed up Vicki's suitcase and led the way through the house. 'How was the trip?'

'Endless.'

'We'll have a few snorts.'

'Sounds good.'

Ace swung the suitcase onto the bed in the guestroom. Then they went into the kitchen. 'Vodka and tonic?'

'Great.' Vicki sat at the table. 'Where's Jerry? Or shouldn't I ask?'

'Gave him the boot.'

'You're kidding. Everything was fine when we talked.'

'Well, a lot can happen in a week. He popped the big one Wednesday night. Can you imagine? The alimony and child support he's forking out, and he wants to marry me? That's a laugh. I'd be supporting him, the damn free-loader.'

She brought the drinks to the table, and sat down across from Vicki.

They raised their glasses.

'To living hard,' Ace said, 'dying young, and having a great-looking corpse.'

'Charming,' Vicki said. But she drank to it. Then she said, 'So you turned Jerry down?'

'I tossed him out on his bald ass.'

'Seems rather harsh.'

'He was no prize, anyway.'

'You're awfully picky for a gal in the springtime of her spinster-hood.'

Ace gave her the finger.

'Can't be many left.'

'Hon, there's plenty of fish in the sea. I've got no trouble hooking them. The problem is, I can't seem to land a keeper.'

'Jerry sounded pretty good to me.'

'This from the gal who dated Henry Peterson.'

Vicki rolled her eyes. 'Don't remind me. So what else has been going on?'

They talked and drank. It was after 3 a.m. when they quit.

Vicki staggered into the guest room. She sat down beside her suitcase on the bed, and flopped backward. Coins spilled out of her blouse pocket. They rested on her chest, and fell off her shoulder when she swung her legs up to remove her shoes and socks. She tugged down her shorts and panties, and kicked them away. Opening the buttons of her blouse, she noticed that her fingers were a little tingly. She would have to sit up to take the blouse off. She supposed she *could* sit up, but she didn't look forward to the attempt. To postpone it, she plucked the folded bills out of her pocket and let them fall onto the bed behind her shoulder. Then, moaning, she pushed herself up. She stood, slipped her blouse off and let it fall to the floor.

She dragged her suitcase off the bed. As it fell, she swung it around, stumbling as it pulled at her. She steered the case down to the carpet and knelt in front of it. There was a knotted rope around its middle because one of the clasps was broken. She picked at the knot. It felt hard and tight. Working at it made her fingernails hurt.

Her nightgown was inside. Along with her toothbrush and toothpaste. She wanted them.

But not that much.

She crawled to the bed, pushed herself up and saw the scattered coins and bills.

The gas change.

Can't just leave it there, she thought. It'd end up on the floor.

So she bent over the mattress, bracing herself up with one arm, and swept the money into a pile. She closed her hand around it. Stepping back, she saw that she hadn't missed any. But one bill, caught only by a corner, fluttered loose on her way to the dresser. It brushed her thigh and swooped between her legs like a flying carpet. Her left hand made a snatch for it. And caught it.

Pretty darn good, Vicki thought. What speed! What agility!

She dumped the handful of money onto the bureau, then placed the captured bill neatly over the top of the pile.

Something was scribbled across it with a red pen.

Vicki lowered her head and squinted at the writing.

'MELVIN DROP DEAD AND DIE YOU SICK FUCK.'

In her dream, Vicki was sitting in darkness. She didn't know where, only that it was someplace bad to be. She wanted to get out fast. But she was bound to the chair. She felt ropes around her

351

ankles, wrapping her wrists, criss-crossing her torso like bandoliers.

Gotta get out of here, she thought, close to panic. Haven't got much time. He'll be here any second.

She struggled to free herself. The ropes rubbed against her bare skin, but didn't come loose. Then she realized that her bound hands, resting on her lap, weren't fastened down. She raised them to her mouth. Her teeth found the bundle of knots. She bit at the first knot and tugged it open, but there was another knot beneath it. She tore that one loose with her teeth, only to find still another knot waiting.

She started to whimper.

He's getting closer.

When the lights came on, she knew it was too late for escape.

She was seated in the middle of the Community Center arena.

The clamour of a banging door reverberated through the empty auditorium.

He's coming!

She saw him.

Melvin. He walked toward Vicki from a distant corner, pushing a wheelchair. In the wheelchair sat Darlene. She should've been wearing the letter sweater and pleated skirt of her cheerleader outfit. Instead, she wore Vicki's white nightgown.

So that's where it went.

I'll have to throw it away, Vicki thought. *I sure can't wear it after it's had a dead person in it.*

Darlene looked very dead. Grey and withered. Even worse than she did for real.

This is a dream, she suddenly realized. *This isn't happening.*

But it sure seemed to be happening, and Vicki wondered if she only *thought* she was dreaming.

She started biting the knots again, got another one open as Melvin rolled the wheelchair closer, but there was still another knot below it.

Melvin kept coming. Did he plan to ram her?

Eight or ten strides away, he stopped it.

The white bandage around Darlene's neck appeared to be the same fabric as the nightgown. Through its diaphanous layers, Vicki could see a bloodless, horizontal gash across the girl's throat.

Let's wake up now. Come on.

'You're looking lovely tonight,' Melvin said, tilting his head and nodding.

'Cut it out. Go away.'

'Have you saved yourself for me?'

'No.' She realized she was whimpering again. 'Leave me alone. Please. Just go away.'

'Be mine, darling, and I'll give you everlasting life.'

'No.'

'You'd like that, wouldn't you? To live forever?'

'I don't know.'

'Look at Darlene. Look at the face of death.'

Oh, Jesus, Darlene's left eyelid bulged, slid up a bit, and a white *worm* squirmed out.

It's time to wake up, damn it!

'Don't you believe that I can give you life everlasting?'

'No.'

Melvin, leering, raised high the black rubber handles of jumper cables. 'Get this!' He bowed and swung the cables down over Darlene's shoulders. The clamps opened like jaws. They snapped shut on Darlene's nipples. Vicki heard a crackling buzz. The girl twitched and shimmied. White smoke began to roll out of her mouth. Blood welled out of her nipples around the teeth of the clamps and soaked the nightgown. Blood seeped into the fabric wrapping her neck. Her eyelids lifted. She had eyes, not empty sockets, and the worm was gone from her cheek. She blew out a puff of smoke. Smiling, she opened the clamps and tossed the cables back over her shoulders, where Melvin caught them.

Darlene rose from the chair. She took a few steps toward Vicki. Then, she snapped her body straight and planted her fists on her hips.

'Still think I can't?' Melvin asked.

Darlene, standing rigid, clapped her hands.

Clap–clap–clap–clap.

She shot a fist into the air.

'WE GOT PEP!'

Her other fist darted up.

'WE GOT STEAM!'

She danced and twirled.

'WE ARE THE GIRLS ON MELVIN'S TEAM!'

Shouting, 'TEAM,' she leaped high, threw back her head, kicked her legs up behind her and flung her arms high. Vicki heard a ripping sound. Darlene's head went back farther and farther, the bandage splitting, her throat opening like a mouth. Her head dropped out of sight. It appeared behind her kicking legs. It thumped against the floor. She came down, her right foot landing on her face. Balance lost, she stumbled backward. As she fell into the wheelchair, her head rolled toward Vicki.

'NO!'

Melvin laughed.

The head rolled closer and closer.

Its mouth closed around Vicki's big toe and began to suck.

Yelping, she lurched up.

The bedroom was full of sunlight.

Chapter Five

Melvin looked up as headlights swept across the office windows. They belonged to a Duster that pulled up to the self-service island.

There was someone in the passenger seat.

Melvin peered through the window. Looked like it might be a gal, but he couldn't tell for sure.

He'd been waiting for a gal. He needed one.

His heart started thumping hard.

He folded his *Penthouse* shut and slipped it into the desk drawer.

The driver climbed out and walked around the rear of his car to the unleaded pump. He was a tall, skinny guy, probably in his early twenties. That meant the gal – if it was a gal – might be a young one.

Too bad she had to be with him. He looked like a hard case, the way he wore that T-shirt with the sleeve cut off, and those blue jeans hanging low and those cowboy boots.

You can't be too picky, though, Melvin told himself. It wasn't often a gal would drive into the station by herself, especially not this late at night. The last one to do it had been Vicki, three nights ago.

He'd planned to use her till he saw who she was. She would've been just right, coming along at that hour, and all alone. But she was a local, and people were probably expecting her, so it wouldn't have been smart even if she hadn't been someone he liked so much.

I'll just go out and take a look at this one, he thought.

He started to stand up, but the passenger door opened. He settled down in his chair again.

The passenger was a gal, all right. She swung her long, slim legs out of the car, stood up, and said something to the guy. Her hair was short, so it didn't hang down her neck at all. She wore cut-off blue jeans, and a white tube top that only stayed up because its elastic was hugging her around the middle. It left her midriff bare. Its upper edge was straight across her chest, high enough to cover her breasts completely. Her breasts looked like tennis balls and had been cut in half and stuffed under the stretchy fabric.

Pretty small, but right there. One good tug on that tube top . . .

He rubbed the back of his hand across his mouth.

The gal shrugged at something her friend said, then started walking straight for the office. She didn't look where she was going because she had her head down and was searching inside her shoulder bag.

Her cut-offs hung very low. When she entered the office, Melvin saw that she had a small red rose tattooed midway between her navel and right hipbone. Its stem disappeared down the front of her shorts.

He raised his eyes before she looked at him.

She didn't have much of a face. Too long and narrow, with crooked slabs of teeth and an upper lip that wasn't long enough to keep her gums out of sight.

Though she looked at Melvin, she didn't appear to see him. Her face didn't change at all. It just turned away, and she started inspecting the munchies inside the vending machine.

Typical bitch. Plenty of them did that. Acted like he wasn't here.

You're no prize, yourself, you horse-face slut.

She reached out and dropped coins into the machine, then pressed a couple of buttons. Melvin saw a package of barbeque-flavoured potato chips drop from a clamp. It thumped into the trough and the girl bent down to take it out. The seat of her jeans was frayed just below the right pocket, and pale skin showed through the loose threads. She straightened up, turned around and left the office.

Instead of heading back to the car, she walked past the window and rounded the corner. Looking for the restroom.

Making it easy for me, Melvin thought.

The guy, done filling his tank, came to the office. He stood in front of Melvin and dug some bills out of his jeans.

'Be needing anything else?' Melvin asked. 'Got a sale on wiper blades.'

'I don't see any rain,' the guy muttered, plucking bills out of his hand and tossing them on the counter.

Melvin stood up. First, he checked the windows. Then, he glanced at the computer, saw that he was owed $12.48, and picked up the money. A five and eight ones. 'That makes fifty-two cents back to you,' he said.

'You can count.'

'Sure can.'

He stuffed the bills into the left-hand pocket of his Bermuda shorts, reached into his other pocket, brought out a canister of tear gas and sprayed the guy in the face.

Got him right in the eyes. He squeezed them shut and grabbed his red face and staggered backward, bending over and going, 'Uhhh uhhh uhhh.' He was on his knees by the time Melvin cleared the counter. The kick caught him in the ear and knocked him onto his side.

Melvin heard the faint sound of the toilet flushing, so he stomped the guy's head against the floor a few times. That seemed to do the trick. Maybe didn't finish him off, but at least he was out cold. Melvin grabbed him by the boots, dragged him around behind the counter, and sat down.

The gal probably could've seen him as she walked past the

window, but she was busy using her teeth to rip open her package of potato chips. She didn't give the window even a glance. She just walked back to the car, got into the passenger seat, and shut the door.

Probably figuring her friend had gone to take a leak.

Her friend, Melvin noticed, *had* taken a leak. The front of his jeans was soaked pretty good. He was also taking a leak out of his left ear, but that was blood. It dripped into a little puddle on the linoleum under his head.

The gal sat in the car, eating.

After a while, her head turned. She must be starting to wonder what was taking the guy so long. He wasn't coming, so she went back to her chips.

Melvin opened the bottom drawer of his desk. He pulled out a box of plastic wrap, stripped off about a yard of the cellophane, and tore it free. He checked the gal. She wasn't looking. He lifted his shirt, held it up under his chin, and spread the filmy plastic sheet against his belly. It clung to him. It went most of the way around his back. He let his shirt fall, covering it.

Then he put the box away and watched the girl.

Finally, she climbed out of the car. She stood beside the open door, frowned toward the corner of the building, and brushed her hands on her shorts.

Melvin guessed her patience had lasted about as long as the potato chips.

She headed for the corner of the building. Just to make sure she wouldn't look into the window and spot the guy on the floor, Melvin stood up and stared out at her. She caught a glimpse of him, and did as he expected – she looked the other way. He kept gazing at her, turning around when she reached the corner, and she kept looking elsewhere until there was no more window between them.

This was working out just fine.

Melvin figured she would come back into the office when she couldn't find the guy in the restroom, but he preferred to take care of her out back where he wouldn't have to worry about anyone driving past the station or stopping in for a fill-up.

He hurried out of the office and around the corner. Walking

alongside the building, he heard her knocking. Then her voice. 'Rod? What're you doing in there?'

He reached the rear corner and stepped past it.

She was facing the men's room door. She knocked on it again. 'Rod, you either answer me or I'm coming in.'

Melvin stood motionless. She hadn't noticed him.

'All right for you, I'm coming in.' She turned the knob and pulled the door open. The light had been left on inside. She stood in the glow of it for a moment, then stepped through the doorway.

As the door swung shut, Melvin started moving. When it was completely closed, he ran.

He jerked it open and rushed in.

The gal whirled around, letting go of the toilet stall's door.

This time, she didn't try to avoid his eyes.

Pretty hard to ignore me now, Melvin thought.

'Get out of here,' she said. Her voice was high-pitched. She didn't seem angry, yet, just surprised and confused as if she couldn't believe he'd blundered into the restroom with her. '*I'm* in here. Get out.'

'You're in the men's,' he said, and smiled.

'I know that. I was looking for someone.'

'Rod's in the office.'

'Okay.' She flapped a hand sideways, gesturing for him to step out of the way.

Melvin didn't move.

Her head turned a bit as if she figured that glaring at Melvin from the corners of her eyes, instead of straight on, was somehow more intimidating. 'You'd better just let me by.'

'Gonna tell Rod on me?'

She tipped her head back and kept staring at him. 'I'm warning you.'

With a shrug, Melvin stepped aside. He swept an arm toward the door.

'That's better,' she said. She walked toward the door, watching him with narrow eyes, looking sure of herself and eager to tell Rod about this creep who'd given her a hard time in the john. As she passed Melvin, she turned her face toward the door. She reached out and grabbed the knob. She pushed and the door opened.

Melvin snatched her hair and jerked. She yelped. Her hand, still on the knob, slammed the door as she flew backward. He swept a foot out from under her, gave her hair another yank and let go and watched her go down. Her back slapped the tile floor and she skidded.

Before she could start to get up, Melvin dropped onto her chest. Her breath whooshed out. Her eyes bugged. Her face went bright red. She squirmed, but her arms were pinned under Melvin's knees.

He lifted his shirt, peeled the cellophane away from his skin, folded the plastic film to double its thickness, and stretched it taut across her face.

With his hands clamped to the sides of her head, he had a good view through the clear plastic. Her face was distorted, eyelids stretched sideways so she looked oriental like a robber in a stocking mask. Her nose, mashed down, had a white tip. The flattened lips of her wide mouth were pale. The disk of cellophane over her mouth crackled as she sucked and puffed. It fogged up.

She bucked and twisted and writhed under Melvin, but he rode her like a bronco.

Her tongue thrust into the plastic, making it bulge. Though the film didn't break, it stretched and formed a bubble. When she drew in her tongue, the bubble snapped into her mouth. It puffed out with a soft whupping sound, then was sucked in again. And she bit it. She caught it between her big crooked front teeth and worked her jaw back and forth – grinding it, chewing it. Her tongue pushed a hole through the plastic, darted back into her mouth, and she loudly sucked air into her lungs.

The air came out screaming.

Melvin slapped a hand across her mouth. That muffled the noise, but he doubted his ability to suffocate her with the hand. Especially the way she was flinging herself and shaking her head. The screaming soon stopped, but she kept breaking the seal and breathing.

Shit! He hadn't wanted to damage her. The cellophane usually worked.

She lurched violently, almost throwing Melvin, and suddenly

her teeth found the edge of his hand. Before he could jerk it free, she bit. He felt her teeth sink into his palm, saw them break the skin on the back of his hand and go in. He heard himself cry, 'YEEEOOOW!' as pain bolted up his arm.

It took four punches with his left fist to her temple, each punch jarring her head and tearing his right hand, before he got it out of her mouth.

She was still conscious, her head rolling from side to side.

Melvin peeled the plastic wrap off her face.

Her eyes were half shut. She was moaning.

The side of her face was red from the punches, and starting to swell up.

Damn it.

Now she was marred.

She wouldn't have been pretty, anyway, Melvin consoled himself, but he hated the idea of leaving her bruised. After all, the bruise would probably be permanent.

Maybe some make-up.

She was stirring a little more.

With his left hand, Melvin grabbed the hair on top of her head. He lifted her head and gave it a bounce off the floor.

That settled her down.

He wrapped some plastic around his hand, partly to hold in the blood and partly to give himself a firm hold. Then he picked up the other end and stretched an unbroken section of the cellophane across her nose and mouth.

If at first you don't succeed . . .

This time, she didn't fight it.

Chapter Six

Vicki pressed the ten-minute snooze button on her alarm clock and snuggled down with her face in the pillow.

It's Wednesday, she thought. Charlie'd be heading out to the golf course, so this would be her first full day alone at the clinic. She felt a little nervous about that, and told herself to relax. Nothing was likely to come up that she couldn't handle – certainly nothing to compare with some of the emergencies she'd had to face during her residency at Good Samaritan.

Like Rhonda Jones. That was about the worst. Rhonda was brought to the ER by a truck driver who found her wandering along the highway, eyes slashed and both hands cut off by some maniac who'd raped her. One of the nurses actually fainted at the sight. Vicki, applying tourniquets and setting up the IV, kept a clear head and thought to herself at the time that she should be grateful to Melvin Dobbs and his Amazing Miracle Machine. Because, after seeing him try to jump-start Darlene and watching her head fall off, even the horrible mutilation of Rhonda Jones couldn't shock her senseless.

I don't believe I'll thank him, she thought.

Saving yourself for me?

She remembered that she'd dreamed about him again last night, and woke up gasping at around 2:30 with her nightgown soaked. She hadn't been able to remember the nightmare, but supposed it was pretty much the same as the one she'd had at Ace's house. She sure remembered that one.

She'd had dreams about Melvin every night since coming back. Three times, they'd caused her to wake up. She supposed the brief encounter with him at the gas station had done a number on her subconscious. The nightmares, bad as they were, didn't trouble her much except while she was in the midst of them.

After all, she was used to nightmares.

Following the Science Fair, she'd had them constantly for about two months. Then they'd become less frequent. Eventually, they'd dwindled down to one every two or three months, except when something disturbing came up to trigger a new series.

These would undoubtedly peter out, just like the old ones. Until that happened, she would just have to live with them.

She preferred the old nightmares. Those had pretty much been replays of the real event, lacking the weird variations present in the recent dreams. And in those, she'd been an observer, not a participant. Now, it seemed that Melvin's perverse stunt was *directed* at her.

All my fault, she thought. I shouldn't have stopped at his place for gas.

Vicki sighed. So much for enjoying a few extra minutes snuggling in bed. She reached out, shut off the snooze alarm in time to prevent it from blaring, and got up.

She made her way through the darkness to the bathroom. After using the toilet, she returned to her bedroom and put on the running clothes that she had arranged on the chair the night before. She slipped a thin chain over her head. It held the apartment key and a police whistle. She dropped them down the front of her T-shirt.

The corridor outside her rooms was dimly lighted. She walked silently, and pressed a hand against her chest to stop the jangling of the key and whistle.

She didn't like this corridor. Not late at night, and not at 5 a.m. It gave her the creeps.

All corridors gave her the creeps when she was by herself in a quiet building. You name it, she thought: school, dormitory, hospital, office building, apartment house. Just something about a deserted hallway when everybody else is either gone or asleep – or supposed to be.

A feeling that, if you make any noise, someone might just throw open a door and jump out at you.

This particular corridor was L-shaped so Vicki had to step around a corner before reaching the lobby and front entrance. She didn't much care for that corner.

But she stepped around it without hesitating.

The landlord's door was open.

Oh, great.

She cast a glance as she walked by, and sucked in a quick

breath. Dexter Pollock was standing motionless just inside the doorway, wearing a bathrobe, bare-legged, staring out at her. She twisted her mouth into a smile of greeting, muttered, 'Hi,' and kept walking.

'Word with you,' Dexter said.

Dandy.

He didn't come out of the doorway, so she had to go back to him. He stood there with his hands tucked into the pockets of his robe. His legs looked very pale in the faint light. He was a big man, well over sixty now and gone to fat, but when Vicki had been a girl he was chief of the Ellsworth Police Department, and she suspected that he still had the soul of a tyrant. She could kill Ace for choosing an apartment building that was *owned* by this man.

She leaned against the far wall of the corridor to keep the maximum distance from him, and crossed her ankles. He was known to be a lech. She was very aware of her bare legs – and his. She supposed he was probably naked under the robe.

'Early in the day to be going out,' he said.

'I suppose it is.'

'Still dark out there.'

'It's almost dawn.'

'You're a good-looking young woman.'

She didn't say anything. His words made her feel squirmy inside.

'Didn't your folks ever caution you about going out alone in the dark?'

'Sure they did.'

'I know they did. Your folks are fine people.'

'Thanks.'

'You think they'd approve, you going out at this hour and dressed in your skimpies?'

'I do it when I visit them. They don't seem to mind.' Then she added, 'I'm dressed fine,' 'though she wished at the moment that she was wearing her warm-ups instead of the T-shirt and flimsy shorts.

Dexter's eyes were pale blurs, but Vicki saw his head lower and rise as he inspected her. 'You're a rape,' he said, 'looking for a place to happen.'

363

'I have to get going,' she told him, hating the weak sound of her voice. You oughta tell him to shove it, she thought. She pushed herself off the wall and turned away from him.

'I'm still talking to you, Miss Chandler.'

'*Doctor* Chandler,' she said.

'Be that as it may. You have some respect and listen to me.'

She turned to him, frowning.

'You been away, so you're likely not on top of the local situation, and besides which, it's been kept pretty quiet. Nobody wants to get folks stirred up. Thing is, there's been half a dozen young women in this county vanish without so much as a trace being found of them. That's just in the past eight or ten months. And that's just the ones that got reported missing. Might be plenty more we don't even know about. So you'd best keep that in mind and think twice before you go off gallivanting at all hours in your underwear.'

'Thanks,' she said. 'I'll be extra careful. May I go now?'

'Do what you want.'

She pushed herself away from the wall and walked away, forcing herself not to hurry. As she reached the lobby, she glanced back. Dexter had stepped into the corridor. He was facing her.

She pulled open the glass door and stepped outside. The summer morning was warm, but she was trembling.

Thanks a real lot, pal, she thought.

His news about the disappearances was a little disturbing, but not much. She'd never kidded herself into thinking that Ellsworth was completely safe. No place was safe, especially for women.

What she found upsetting was Dexter ambushing her that way.

Had he been waiting for her? How did he know she'd come by?

Creep.

She liked to do her warm-up exercises on the broad stoop of the apartment building. But Dexter might just wander into the lobby and watch her through the glass, so she trotted down the stairs and started along the sidewalk.

She wondered if he would make a habit of waiting for her.

There was no way to leave the apartment without passing his

door. The only other exit, conveniently located at her end of the corridor, would trigger an alarm if she tried to use it.

She came to the corner, and looked back. At least Dexter hadn't followed her. The sidewalk, grey in the glow of the streetlights, was deserted except for a cat sitting near the end of the block, rubbing a paw across its face.

Before starting to warm up, Vicki turned completely around and scanned every direction.

I always check, she told herself. Nothing to do with Dexter's warning.

Satisfied that no one was lurking nearby, she began bending at the waist and touching her toes.

I'm not going to put up with him, she thought. I'll just have to find a new place. Such a pain, though, moving.

Even with Ace's help, it had taken hours to unload the U-Haul and carry all her stuff into the apartment. And both of them with hangovers. Torture. She wasn't eager to repeat the process.

She sat down. The concrete felt cool through her shorts. She straightened out her legs, bent forward and grabbed the toes of her running shoes.

Give it some time, she told herself. Maybe Dexter won't make a habit of bugging me. He had his say. And I went out in spite of it.

But Vicki suspected that his 'say' was nothing more than an excuse to stop her, ogle her, and test his powers of intimidation.

Acts as if he's still the police chief.

He'd always been a jerk. Most of the kids in town used to despise him. He didn't just make them toe the line, he seemed to enjoy giving them grief. He probably picked on kids because he was such a coward when it came to adults.

The stories had it that he'd let his partner, Joey Milbourne, get beaten half to death by a couple of lumberjacks from the Bay who got drunk in the Riverfront Bar. He ran off and locked himself in his patrol car instead of giving Joey a hand.

But he sure was the tough guy, a regular Dirty Harry, when it came to a teenager snowballing a car or knocking a baseball through somebody's window or parking by the river to neck.

He even gave Ace a bad time the night of the senior dance, which made Vicki especially glad they hadn't double-dated.

According to Ace, she was butt-naked in the back seat of Rob's Firebird, going at it hot and heavy, when Dexter shined his flashlight through the window. He opened the door and ordered them both out of the car. He didn't even allow them time to put their clothes on. Ace snatched her gown off the floor as she crawled out, and held it against herself while Dexter brow-beat them about fornication and the possibility of getting themselves killed by a wandering lunatic. About the time he was threatening to run them in for indecent exposure and phone their parents, headlights appeared up the road. Ace dropped her gown and put her hands on top of her head. 'Guess you wanta frisk me,' she said. Dexter grabbed up her gown and shoved it at her and yelled, 'Get outa here, you crazy bitch!' And she and Rob scampered into his car and peeled away while the other car was still approaching.

Vicki got to her feet, brushed off the rear of her shorts, and started running.

Anyone other than Ace, she thought, would've been too humiliated from an experience like that to ever look Dexter in the eye again. So what does she do? She rents me an apartment from him.

When Vicki had found out, over vodka and tonic that first night at Ace's house, that Dexter Pollock was the owner, she'd said, 'Are you out of your mind?'

'I told him it was for you,' Ace said, 'and he dropped the rent ten per cent.'

'I hope you're kidding.'

'He said he figured it'd be handy having a doctor in the building.'

'I'm not a plumber, for Pete's sake.'

'Probably wants you to look after *his* plumbing.'

'Ha ha. Jesus.'

'He's not such a bad guy. He mellowed out some, after his Minnie kicked over.'

'You've sure got a short memory, Ace. You forget all about senior dance night?'

'Nope.' She grinned. 'Neither's he. Poor old fart goes red as a pimple every time he looks at me. The truth is, I scare him shitless. He thinks I'm nuts.'

'Because you dropped your dress in front of him?'

'Partly that.' Ace stirred her ice cubes with a finger, smiling down into her drink. 'You wouldn't remember those skimpy black panties I bought mail order?'

'You wanted me to order some.'

'Those are the ones. Well, day after my run-in with Dexter, I mailed 'em to his house with a note. Said, "Dear Dex, Keep these as a souvenir of our ecstasy. Love and kisses, Honey Pot." '

'You didn't.'

'Wanta bet? And I personally saw Minnie take the envelope out of the mailbox the next morning.'

'Mean.'

'He's lucky that's all I did,' Ace said, her amused exterior cracking for just an instant and letting out the bitterness. Then she was grinning again. 'Poor jerk hasn't pestered me since.'

I oughta do something like that, Vicki thought as she rounded a corner and headed for Center Street. Make him think I'm crazy, so he'll leave me alone.

Or threaten to set Ace on him if he gives me any more grief.

Better just to move out and find a new apartment.

Give it a couple of weeks, though, see how it goes.

She leaped off the curb at Center Street and looked to the right. The downtown business area of Ellsworth was grey in the pre-dawn light. A few cars were parked in front of the shops, but no one was about.

Light spilled onto the sidewalk from the windows of the bakery a block away. On other mornings, she had run in that direction. She knew the bakery was the only place open. Though she couldn't smell the doughnuts from here, she remembered the delicious aromas and how they made her mouth water when she passed by.

It was sheer torture to run through those sweet smells and not stop in.

She decided to avoid that particular agony this morning, turned her back to the shops of the town, and headed north. She passed the dark windows of Riverfront Bait and Tackle, then left the walkway and ran through the grass of the long municipal park that bordered the river. A soft mist hung over the water. She saw a few boats far out, the silhouettes of fishermen sitting motionless with their poles. Somewhere, a loon cackled. She heard the distant putter of an outboard, but couldn't spot the moving boat. It was probably out behind Skeeter Island.

The ground sloped down toward the public beach and playground. She shortened her strides, wary of the dewy grass, and almost reached the bottom before her right foot slipped. Gasping, she saw both her feet fly up. She landed on her rump, tumbled backward, and dug her heels into the grass to stop her skid.

Brilliant, she thought.

She had that strange tightness in the throat familiar from other times (not very many and mostly long ago) when she'd fallen on her butt – a sensation that was like an urge to laugh and cry at the same time. It faded after a few seconds. Vicki told herself to get up, but she continued to lie there, panting for air. She felt the cool dew through her shorts and panties. The slide had pulled her T-shirt halfway up her back. The grass against her bare skin made her feel itchy, and it was the itch that soon convinced her to sit up.

She reached behind her with both hands and scratched. She was mildly allergic to grass. The itch would probably keep bothering her until she got back to the apartment and took a shower.

The back of her shirt was sodden. She had to peel it away from her skin before she could lower it. Then the wet fabric clung to her. She stood up, bent her arms behind her, and kept on scratching as she walked toward the beach.

She left the grass. Her shoes sank into the sand. At the water's edge, she was about to continue her run but spied a stick floating just offshore. It was about two feet long, and would make a wonderful back-scratcher. Since her shoes and socks were already wet from the dew, she went ahead and waded into the river. The chilly water rose around her ankles. She crouched, snatched up the stick, reached behind her back with it, and sighed as she scratched herself through the damp T-shirt.

The sky in the east was lighter now. Soon, the first rays of sunlight would break through the trees across the river.

She remembered the time she watched the sunrise with Paul. That was only a week before he went away. Late in the night, they had both crept out of their houses. They met and spent hours roaming the woods north of town, holding hands and talking quietly. It was a sad, sweet time. Long before dawn arrived, they found themselves here at the beach. They sat on the swings for a while. They silently climbed to the top of the slide and sat up there, his arms around her. Then they slid down together and wandered to the shore.

Vicki let the stick fall from her hand. She stared at the diving platform floating on oil drums a distance offshore.

They left their shoes and socks on the beach, that morning, and swam out to it. They sat on its weathered planks, shivering in their wet clothes. Then they lay down and hugged each other and the chill went away. It was as if she and Paul were the only people in the world. They kissed so long and hard that their faces were red around the mouth when the sun finally came up.

Remembering it, Vicki felt a hollow ache.

So many people, later in life, claim they have no regrets, say they'd do nothing differently if they had a chance to go back. But Vicki had a major regret. It filled her with sadness whenever she thought about that morning with Paul on the diving raft. If she had it to do over again, she would've made love with him there before dawn on the gently rocking platform. She had opened her wet blouse for him, and he had fumbled open her bra and lifted it up around her neck and caressed her breasts. That was far more than they had ever done before. It seemed daring and wonderful. Paul had never seen or touched a girl's breasts before, and he was the first to look at Vicki's and touch them. His hands never strayed below the waistband of her jeans, and she never touched him down there though she could feel him while they embraced and squirmed against each other. She thought about it, but the idea of actually taking off their pants and *doing* it seemed huge and grown-up and terrifying. So it didn't happen. When the sun started to rise, they untangled and sat up. Even as she fastened her bra and buttoned her blouse, she felt a peculiar emptiness. Something – she wasn't quite sure what – had been missed or lost. She wept as she watched the sun come up over the river, and Paul put an arm around her back and said, 'This was the best night of my life, Vicki. I love you so much. I'll always love you, no matter what.'

'I'll always love you, too,' she said.

Standing in the river's shallow water, Vicki sniffed and wiped her eyes. Should've done it, she thought. Would've been so beautiful.

Those are the breaks, she told herself.

She turned away from the raft. Head down, she waded ashore. She was in no mood to continue her run. She scratched her back. She decided to return to the apartment and take her shower and get rid of the itch.

It'll be an interesting day, she told herself, trying to shake loose the mood of gloom. Charlie's golf day. I'll be in charge.

So who cares?

Her feet made sloshing sounds inside her soaked shoes.

She wiped her eyes again.

'You okay?' a man called.

The voice stunned her.

She looked up.

Near the far corner of the beach, where the playground equipment stood, a man was perched at the very top of the slide. Paul? Had some strange twist of fate lured him back to the beach at dawn, all these years later? It seemed impossible, but she hurried toward him, staring, her heart pounding wildly.

It can't be Paul, she told herself. If he'd moved back to town, Ace would've told me.

Maybe Ace doesn't know.

Maybe he just arrived.

He seemed about the right age. His hair was the same sandy blond colour as Paul's. He looked bigger, though. Paul had been slim, whereas this man had broad shoulders, a muscular chest and arms. Maybe Paul filled out, she thought.

Then she was close enough to see the features of his face, and her hopes collapsed.

Paul might've grown big and strong, but his face couldn't have changed this way. The man's eyes were farther apart than Paul's. His nose was larger, his mouth wider, his chin more prominent. Even his ears were different: they were bigger than Paul's, and lay close to the sides of his head.

Silly to think he *could* be Paul, she told herself.

'Are you all right?' he asked when she stopped near the foot of the slide.

'I guess so.' She felt cheated. And violated; she'd thought she was alone, but this man had been spying on her. 'What're you doing up there?' she asked.

'Seemed like a nice place to watch the sunrise.'

'Been up there long?'

'A while.'

She wondered if he'd seen her fall.

'I have to get going,' she muttered.

'See you around,' he said.

Vicki turned away and ran toward the road.

Chapter Seven

The little red light at the back of the HotTopper went off, letting him know that the stick of butter had melted. Melvin's right hand was bandaged and still painful from the bite, so he used his left hand to unplug the device, aim it down at the popcorn and squirt. The butter sprayed out as if from the shower nozzle, turning his popcorn golden. He sprinkled salt, shook the bowl, then sprayed more butter and sprinkled more salt.

He carried the bowl of popcorn into the living-room, placed it on the table in front of his sofa, and returned to the kitchen. He filled a glass with ice, took it out to the living-room, then went into the kitchen again and removed a two-litre plastic bottle of Pepsi from the refrigerator. He carried that into the living-room.

He sat on the sofa. He filled his glass. On the television, David Letterman was introducing a Stupid Human Trick. Melvin pressed the Play button on his remote. Letterman vanished.

Melvin grabbed a handful of popcorn and started to munch.

His video camera, mounted near the ceiling of the basement

371

laboratory and aimed downward at a forty-five degree angle, gave him a great view of the work table and the area around it.

Elizabeth's naked corpse lay stretched on the work table, strapped down with leather belts. The belts secured her wrists and ankles to the table top. Another belt crossed her throat. Another crossed her chest, just below her small breasts.

Melvin watched himself step in front of the camera and smile up at it.

'Handsome devil,' he muttered, and ate some more popcorn.

The Melvin on the screen wore a glossy robe of red satin purchased by mail order from a sporting goods company that made such robes for boxers. He rubbed the back of his bandaged hand across his mouth, then said, 'Tonight, we'll be trying a method from page 214 of *Hizgoth's Book of the Dead*. My subject will be Elizabeth Crogan of Black River Falls.' He stepped back and swept an arm toward the corpse on the table behind him.

Turning away, he stepped to a cluttered cart next to the table. The back of his robe read, 'The Amazing Melvin,' in swirling golden letters.

Melvin's hand trembled as he lifted his glass off the table. He took a drink of Pepsi, set it down, and watched himself bend over an open book on the cart.

Checking the recipe.

He picked up a mayonnaise jar and raised it towards the camera. 'The blood of three bats killed under the full moon,' he explained. He unscrewed the lid and stepped over to Elizabeth. Holding the jar in his right hand, grimacing at the pain, he poured some blood into his cupped left hand, and spread it over her face. When her face was red-brown with the syrupy fluid, he waved the jar over the rest of her body, spilling trails of blood onto her neck and arms and chest, her breasts and belly, her groin, and down the tops of her legs to her strapped ankles. He set the bottle aside. With his left hand, he rubbed the blood, smoothing it over her skin.

Melvin let his handful of popcorn fall back into the bowl. He gazed at the television. His heart was pounding, his mouth dry.

He spent a long time spreading the blood on Elizabeth. Then he stepped away and disappeared from the screen.

Melvin heard splashing water while he cleaned his hand in the wash basin.

Every visible inch of the girl's body was painted. His fingers had left streaks and swirls.

Maybe should've turned her over and done the back, he thought.

He took a drink of Pepsi. The glass was slick in his buttery, shaking hand.

Melvin came back, stared at the body, then stepped over to the cart and checked the book again. He raised another jar towards the camera. Pieces of this and that hung suspended in a cloudy white liquid. 'Milk of goat,' he said. 'Eye of cat, tail of newt, henbane and mandragore, spider legs, ashes of a dead sinner. Brought to a boil at midnight.'

He opened the jar, set it down beside Elizabeth's head, then slipped an aluminium funnel into her mouth. Standing behind her head so his body wouldn't block the camera's view, he poured the substance into the funnel. It made soft, slurpy sounds. After a while, it began trickling from the corners of her mouth. Little bits of things rolled with the liquid down her cheeks.

The jar was only half empty.

He frowned at it, glanced into the funnel, then stepped sideways. With his good left hand, he shoved down hard on her belly. Stuff gushed out of her mouth. The funnel overflowed, spilling onto her face and neck. He let up, and the funnel began to drain into her. He pushed again, let up, pushed, let up. Soon, the funnel was empty. He picked up the jar and dumped more in. It went down for a while, then started backing up again. He glanced at Elizabeth's stomach, which was beginning to look bloated.

Shrugging, Melvin set the jar aside. It was nearly empty. He took the funnel out of her mouth. Goop poured from its spout as he cast it away. Her open mouth was full. A dark lump floated in the middle on the milky pond.

Melvin took another handful of popcorn and filled his mouth. He watched himself wink at the camera as he returned to the cart.

He studied the book again, then addressed the camera. 'Three candles, midnight black.' One at a time, he lighted the wicks, dripped pools of black wax onto the body, and placed the burning candles upright in the wax. When he was done, a candle stood in the tangled hair of her pubis and the other two rose from her breasts.

Melvin bent over the book, slipped handwritten papers out from under the top page, and read aloud.

'Master of Darkness, I, your servant, do humbly beseech you. I have prepared the earthly remains of Elizabeth Crogan in the manner prescribed. She has been annointed with the blood of the bat; she has consumed the Nectar of Hizgoth; the candles of the Black Triumvirate are burning at the three corners of the luminex. Her remains are in readiness. I beseech you, send me the soul of Elizabeth Crogan that she might join me in the service of your realm.'

Melvin, listening to his voice, refilled his glass with Pepsi, took a drink, and ate more popcorn.

On the screen, he kept on reading.

Finally, he came to the end. 'This I ask in the name of the Black Triumvirate.'

He stepped around the cart. Standing beside the body, he plucked the lower candle from its bed of stiff wax, and plunged it, flame first, into her mouth. The Nectar of Hizgoth spilled down her cheeks. He tossed the extinguished candle aside, then dunked each of the remaining candles into the Nectar.

Stepping behind Elizabeth's head, he raised both arms high. Blood had soaked through the bandage on his right hand, and trickled down his wrist and forearm. He shut his eyes. He mumbled, 'Come on, babe.'

He looked down at her.

Nothing.

Melvin stopped chewing his mouthful of popcorn. He leaned forward, staring at the body, half expecting its eyes to open, its head to turn. He'd been there; he knew she wouldn't move. But he could almost *see* it happening.

'Come on, come on,' he said on the television.

Then Melvin lowered his arms, dug a Kleenex out of his robe pocket, and mopped the dribbles of blood off his right arm and wrist. Looking up, he glared into the camera.

He bent over the corpse, thumbed up an eyelid, and gazed at the eye.

The lid stayed open when he released it.

He stepped around to the side of the table. He shook her shoulder. Her head, with its single open eye, wobbled from side to side, slopping out the white Nectar.

He bent over and pressed an ear to her chest.

His face came up. He scowled at the camera. The left side of his face was smeared with bat blood.

'Didn't work,' he said to the camera in a calm voice. Then he yelled, 'SHIT!' and hammered his fist down between her breasts. Nectar erupted from her mouth. He pounded her again and again, using both hands, crying out in pain as he punched her with his wounded hand.

Melvin scowled as he watched. He didn't much enjoy seeing himself in the throes of his disappointment and rage and agony. He especially didn't like the way he'd lost control. He picked up the remote and pressed the Fast-Forward button.

In fast-forward, he *really* looked like a lunatic punching her, shaking her, prancing around the table waving his arms as he silently shouted, cuffing her some more, rushing offscreen and reappearing with a mirror that he held under her nose, scowling at the mirror, hurling it away in disgust. As he scurried up onto the table, Melvin pushed the Stop button.

The basement laboratory vanished. On the screen, a cute gymnast in leotards did the splits on a balance beam while she talked about the 'safe, sure feeling of confidence' she got from using Lite-Days Mini-Pads.

Melvin shut the television off. He finished the Pepsi in his glass.

He turned sideways on the sofa and looked at Elizabeth Crogan sitting there next to him, leaning back against the cushions, hands folded on her lap, legs stretched out, feet propped up on the table and crossed at the ankles. She didn't look too bad. He'd cleaned her up after last night's experiment, had even bandaged her broken skin, applied make-up and brushed her hair.

'Still dead?' he asked.

She didn't move. She just stared at the blank television.

'Last call for a come-back,' he said.

Nothing.

'Speak now, or forever hold your peace. I'm gonna bury you. Want me to bury you?'

Nothing.

'Okay. You had your chance.'

He took a last mouthful of popcorn. Chewing it, he slung the body onto his shoulder and headed for the garage.

Chapter Eight

Dexter was waiting for her, that morning, when Vicki passed his door. It came as no big surprise. She had dressed in a warm-up suit.

'Good morning,' she said and kept on walking.

'Hold on, there.'

She turned around, but didn't approach his door. Dexter stepped out into the corridor.

'Come here. I won't bite.'

Maybe you won't bite, she thought, but you're still a creep. She took a couple of steps towards him, anyway.

He wore his faded blue robe. His hands were stuffed in its pockets. 'You gonna keep going out in the dark, no matter what I say.'

'I need to get my exercise.'

'You kids always think it can't happen to you.'

'I don't think that at all,' Vicki told him. 'But I'm not about to spend my life hiding. Besides, who's to say I'd be safe in my room? An aeroplane could crash on the building.'

'That's about as dumb a remark . . .'

'It's nice that you're concerned about my safety,' she said. She doubted that he *was* concerned about that. More than likely, it was just a convenient subject. All he really cared about was stopping her for a talk and a look. 'I appreciate it,' she said. 'But I wish you'd quit bothering me about this business. I've gone running in places a lot more dangerous than Ellsworth, and I'm still around to talk about it. Nothing you can say is going to change things. So how about just letting it drop? Okay? I'm in no mood for lectures at this hour in the morning.'

Dexter raised his thick eyebrows. A corner of his mouth turned up, but he didn't look amused. 'Aren't you the feisty one.'

'I don't appreciate getting hassled by you every time I try to go out.'

'Hassled? I'm just giving you some friendly advice. You want hassle, just wait till some lunatic throws you down in the dark while you're out there running your little butt off, and sticks his peter in you.'

Heat rushed to Vicki's face. She felt her heart slamming. 'That's what you'd like to do, isn't it?'

Dexter's face darkened. 'You don't talk to me that way.'

'I'll talk to you any way I please.'

He grinned, baring his upper teeth. 'You been taking smart-mouth lessons from your pal, Ass?'

She went rigid and glared at him. 'I'm outa here. You can rent your damned apartment to somebody else.'

'Hey, now, you can't . . .'

'Just watch.' She whirled away from him and headed for the lobby.

'Bitch!'

She pushed through the door and rushed for the sidewalk.

After her stretching exercise near the end of the block, she ran. The running quieted her outrage. She decided that the blow-up with Dexter had been a good thing. She might have stayed on at the apartment, otherwise, and tried to put up with him. Moving would be a drag, but not nearly as bad as suffering more encounters with that son of a bitch. She would make some calls from the office, later on. With any luck, she'd be able to find a new place today. Move out in a few days. The last of Dexter Pollock.

When she reached Central Street, she headed north and ran through the park. But starting down the slope towards the beach, she looked towards the playground equipment. Someone was sitting on one of the swings.

The guy from yesterday?

Just a vague shape in the darkness, but he seemed to be about the same size as the man who had watched her from the slide.

What's he doing, *waiting* for me?

First Pollock, now this guy.

Sorry to disappoint you, mister.

Wary of slipping again on the dewy grass, Vicki waited until she reached the bottom of the slope. There, she turned to the left and ran towards the sidewalk.

You ought to be flattered, she thought, that he came back this morning. Yeah? Who says that's why he did it? He was in the park yesterday without knowing I'd show up. Maybe he just likes to sit over there and watch the sunrise.

But he would've said something if I'd tried to run by.

What's so bad about that?

He didn't seem like such a bad guy. He might even be very nice.

You'll never know if you don't give him a chance.

Not today, folks. Not after Dexter.

Though she felt a little guilty about it, she didn't turn around and go back to the stranger. She reached the sidewalk bordering Central, and kept running north.

She wondered if he'd noticed her on the slope, seen her turn away and known the change of course was for no other reason than to avoid an encounter with him. She hoped not. He might think she was afraid of him, or simply stuck up.

It's not that, she thought as if apologising to him, explaining herself. It has nothing to do with you. You seem like a nice guy. I'm just in a foul mood, that's all.

If he's there tomorrow . . . ?

Cross that bridge when we come to it.

The sky was growing pale as Vicki ran past the junction where Central ended just north of town and became River Road. The sidewalk ended with Central. Usually, she turned around here and headed back for the apartment. Not today. She was in no hurry to return and possibly face Dexter again.

She stayed close to the edge of the road and listened for traffic, ready to bolt onto the dirt shoulder if she should hear a car coming up behind her.

There were only a few homes out this way, mostly cottages close to the shore with private docks in the rear. When the road curved away from the river, the homes vanished. Vicki felt as if she were alone on a woodland trail. A paved trail, but shadowed by trees and silent except for the forest sounds of birds and insects and leaves rustling in the breeze. The sweet, warm aromas seemed even more wonderful than those from the bakery on Central Street.

Vicki felt great. But hot. Thanks to Dexter. She should've been wearing her lightweight shorts and T-shirt, not this warm-up suit. She hadn't even thought to put the jacket and pants on *over* her regular outfit. Once she was clear of Dexter, she could've dumped the warm-ups behind some bushes near the stoop. She wished she'd thought of that. But she came out wearing only a bra and panties under the heavy clothes.

The road was deserted, so she slid her zipper down almost to her waist. Air poured in, cooling the sweat on her chest and belly. Much better.

She considered leaving the road. The forest had plenty of footpaths, and she used to know all of them like friends. She could find a place to leave her warm-ups.

Right, and run in your undies.

The idea was tempting, but she turned it down. After all, what if she met somebody on the trails? Slim chance of that, but she didn't want to risk it.

Even dressed, it might not be such a hot idea to go into the woods alone.

She rounded a bend in the road. Her stomach went tight. Ahead was the bridge over Laurel Creek. In her jarring vision, she saw the low stone wall that Steve Kraft had hit. Her mind filled with images of Darlene in the wheelchair, Melvin clamping the jumper cables to her thumbs, Darlene tumbling onto the back of the principal and her head dropping onto the razor wire. Then her nightmare version swarmed in: *Have you saved yourself for me?* and *I'll give you life everlasting;* the worm in Darlene's eye; the teeth of the cable clamps biting into the girl's nipples and how she bloomed smoke and rose from the chair and went into the cheerleader routine that ended in a leap with her head falling off; the head rolling towards Vicki, rolling.

God, I shouldn't have come out this way.

She turned her back to the bridge and ran from it.

After Elsie Johnson left the office, Vicki had a free hour before the next scheduled appointment. She opened the *Ellsworth Outlook* to the classified section and began searching for an apartment. She found three ads that looked promising, and made two calls before Thelma knocked and poked her head in. 'Melvin Dobbs just walked in,' she said. 'He doesn't have an appointment, but he'd like to see you. Apparently, he's injured his hand.'

Melvin.

'Is Charlie back from his house call?'

'Afraid not. Would you like me to tell him you're busy?'

'No, that wouldn't be right. I'll see him.'

Thelma shut the door.

Vicki stood up. Her legs felt a little shaky. Maybe because of the longer run this morning, maybe because she dreaded facing Melvin. She couldn't blame her goosebumps on the run. Rubbing her arms, she stepped to the office door. She removed her white jacket from its hanger, put it on over her sundress, and buttoned its front.

I should've stayed in bed today, she thought.

Entering the corridor, she saw that the door of Examination Room B was shut. That's where Thelma would've put Melvin. She hesitated in front of the door.

The more I see of him, she told herself, the less he'll spook me.

She wasn't sure she believed that. After all, it was seeing him at the gas station that apparently triggered her fresh round of nightmares.

She opened the door and stepped into the room. Melvin was seated, shoulders hunched and legs dangling, on the end of the paper-covered examination table. He looked as if he'd dressed up for the occasion. Instead of his gaudy shirt and shorts, he wore a blue dress shirt and slacks. His right hand, resting on his thigh, was wrapped with gauze and adhesive tape.

'Good morning, Melvin.' Her voice sounded steady. 'You have a problem with your hand?'

He squeezed an eye half shut and bobbed his head. He raised the hand towards her. 'It got bit.'

'Oh? You have a run-in with a dog?'

'A scum-sucking kid. I went to give a credit card back to his old man, and the little shit took a bite out of me. I think it's infected.'

Nodding, Vicki took scissors off the instrument tray. She held his hand and began to snip the bandage. 'When did this happen?'

'I guess about three days ago. I figured it'd get better, but it just keeps hurting.'

'Well, let's see what the damage is.' She finished cutting through the bandage. The bottom layers of gauze were glued to his wound with pus and blood. She soaked a cotton ball with alcohol and used that to loosen the grip of the sticky fluids. At last, she was able to peel the last of the gauze away. She swung the lamp closer, held his hand beneath its powerful light, and inspected both sides.

'That's a pretty nasty bite he gave you,' she said.

The teeth had left shallow, crescent-shaped wounds on the back of Melvin's hand. There were similar wounds, but deeper, on his palm. The kid must've snapped at Melvin, caught the edge of his hand, and bit down very hard. The area surrounding the injuries looked slightly red and swollen.

'It might not be a bad idea to get some x-rays of this. Just to rule out the possibility of a fracture. We don't do that here, but I could refer you to a radiologist over at Blayton Memorial.'

'No x-rays. You kidding?'

'Oh, they're harmless, Melvin.'

'Sure. They're so harmless, how come they can cause a spontaneous abortion if a foetus gets zapped?'

His question surprised Vicki. How could he know such a thing? Give him some credit. He's not as stupid as he seems. 'That's fairly rare,' she said. 'And you're not a foetus.'

'Just the same, nobody's gonna zap me with no radiation.'

'Does your hand seem to work all right? Any loss of motion in the fingers?'

'They move okay. They're just sore. Whole hand feels sore.'

'Well, you're right about it being infected.'

'Gonna have to amputate?' Melvin asked.

'Oh, not today. I don't think there's much to worry about. I'll just clean and dress the wound for you, and give you a prescription for some antibiotics. Human saliva's a regular cesspool of bacteria. You would've been better off if a dog *had* bit you.'

He grinned up at her. 'Been a dog,' he said, 'I'd of brought you its head so you'd give it the rabies test.'

The words made a cold place inside Vicki.

'The kid's old man almost knocked *his* head off.'

She started to clean the wounds. 'Did you get their names?'

'On the credit card.'

'His family really should have to pay for the medical care.'

'I got insurance. I'm not gonna mess with going after them.'

That was refreshing. Most people were ready to sue over the slightest injury. In this case, a lawsuit seemed more than justified. She could understand, though, how someone with Melvin's history might prefer to avoid stirring up trouble.

'You should try to avoid using this hand,' she said. 'Do you have somebody to help you out at the station?'

'I got Manny Stubbins helping me out.'

'That's good. You definitely don't want to be pumping gas or changing tyres or anything like that. Has the pain been bothering you much? Have you had trouble sleeping?'

'Some.'

'Have you taken anything for it?'

'Just aspirin.'

'And that's helped?'

'I guess.'

'Well, I could prescribe you something for the pain if it's really bad. Some Darvon or Valium. But I'd prefer not to. You'd be better off sticking with aspirin or Tylenol, as long as that's helping.'

'Yeah, I don't want no dope. Turn me into a zombie. Had enough of that in the looney-bin.'

Vicki started to apply a fresh bandage.

She could feel Melvin staring at her. Almost done, she told herself. A few more minutes, and he'll be gone.

'Much as I generally hate doctors,' he said, 'it's sure nice coming to one as pretty as you.'

'Thanks.'

Saving yourself for me?

'You got a piece of this?' he asked.

'A piece of what?'

'The clinic here. You a partner, or something?'

'No, I just work here.'

'You oughta have a practice of your own.'

She managed a smile. 'Yeah, I could go for that. But it costs a lot of money to start up a practice. Besides, I wouldn't want to go into competition against Dr Gaines.'

'How come?'

'He's a nice man, and he's done a lot for me. If it weren't for him, I probably couldn't have made it through medical school.'

'What'd he do, pay for it or something?'

This is getting awfully personal, Vicki thought.

Though the subject made her uncomfortable, she realized she was the one who had brought up Charlie's helping her. And what did it really matter if Melvin knew?

'He gave me a pretty good loan,' she said. 'My parents helped out, and I had scholarships and I worked part of the time, but without . . .'

'So you're here because you owe him?'

'Well, I'm here because I want to be here. It's not just the loan. I'm sure I'll stick around, even after it's paid back.'

'How much do you owe him?'

'That's between me and Dr Gaines.'

'Just asking,' he muttered. 'Didn't mean to make you mad.'

'I'm not mad.'

' 'Cause I could help you out, you know. I'm pretty rich.'

'Well, thanks. I'm fine.' She finished bandaging him, turned away, and scribbled out a prescription. Her hand trembled as she wrote. Just great, she thought. He wants to give me money. What next?

'I want you to get this filled,' she said, giving the slip to him. 'Take the tablets three times a day. And change your bandage every night. If your hand doesn't get better, come back and we'll have another look at it.'

'So, we're done?'

'Yep.'

Nodding, he hopped off the examination table. Vicki stepped into the corridor ahead of him.

'Thanks for fixing me up,' he said.

'Any time.'

Tilting his head sideways, he narrowed an eye and peered at her. 'You're awful nice to me,' he said. 'I'm gonna be nice to you.'

She forced herself to smile. 'Have a good day, Melvin.'

He lurched up the corridor, stopped at the door to the waiting-room, looked back over his shoulder and winked at her. Then he was gone.

Chapter Nine

A few minutes before five that afternoon, Melvin slid into a booth at Webby's Diner and ordered a cup of coffee. As he sipped it, he kept watch through the window.

From there, he had a fine view of the Gaines Family Medical Clinic across the street. He could see not only the front entrance, but also the small parking lot along the side of the building.

After a while, Dr Gaines came out. He went to a white Mercedes in the lot, and drove away. That left a green Plymouth station wagon, a yellow VW bug and a white Dodge Dart. The bug, he knew, belonged to Thelma the receptionist. Vicki had driven into town in a U-Haul. She might've bought a car, but neither the wagon nor the Dart looked new.

She hasn't got much money, he reminded himself. Not if she had to borrow from Gaines. So she probably couldn't afford a new car. Maybe she doesn't have any car at all. Or maybe she bought a used one, or she borrowed one.

While Melvin was thinking about this, a pregnant woman left the building. She drove away in the Dart. That left the wagon. It didn't seem like the kind of car Vicki would drive.

Beggars can't be choosers, he thought.

While the waitress was refilling his coffee mug, a man came

from the wrong direction, carrying cans of paint, and opened the tail gate of the station wagon. He must've been in Handiboy, next door to the clinic. When the paint was loaded, he drove away.

That left only Thelma's VW.

Melvin frowned.

Maybe he'd missed Vicki.

Or she's still in there, but doesn't have a car. Or has a car, but walked. She might only live a few blocks away.

At twenty after five, the front door of the clinic swung open and Vicki stepped out. Melvin stared. He rubbed the back of his hand across his mouth. She looked beautiful. He liked her more in the white doctor jacket she had worn that morning; it was a stiff, formal costume that somehow made Vicki seems all the more soft and vulnerable, as if she needed to wear it for protection. But she looked just fine without it, too. Without her shell. She wore a yellow sundress that had no sleeves at all. Her legs looked very bare below the swaying skirt.

As she walked away, Melvin snapped a quarter tip onto the table. He headed for the door, forcing himself to move slowly so he wouldn't arouse the suspicion of the waitress or Webby behind the counter. He knew they were watching him. *Everyone* always watched him, except for strangers in town who didn't know what he'd done.

Outside, the heat of the afternoon closed around him. He squinted across the street. Vicki was halfway up the block, walking fast. His car was parked at the curb. It'd be stupid, he thought, trying to follow her with the car. Unless he got in and went after her and asked if she'd like a lift. Would she accept a ride from him? Maybe. But she might wonder how come he happened to show up just then.

He decided to follow her on foot.

He stayed on his side of the street, and didn't hurry.

On the next block, Vicki entered Ace Sportswear.

'Getcha something spiffy in the way of a bikini? Give you our sawbones discount.'

'Not today.'

'Well, then, fuck you. Get outa here.'

A young woman was standing nearby. She whirled around and gaped at Ace.

'Jennifer,' Ace told her, 'do me a favour and throw this gal out.'

Jennifer's mouth fell open. Her face went bright red. She looked no older than seventeen or eighteen.

'Oh, don't get your shorts in a knot, hon. This is my old bud Vicki Chandler.'

The girl rolled her eyes upwards. 'I thought you'd flipped out. I mean, Jesus hunchin' Christ. I mean, shitski, I never heard you take off after a *customer* like that.'

Vicki grinned at Ace. 'You been giving speech lessons around here?'

'What do you mean? Hey, how do you like Jen's outfit? Spiffy, huh?'

The girl wore a black and white striped dress that looked like an umpire's shirt. It wasn't much longer than a shirt, either. The belt was a loose silver chain with a silver whistle that hung against her left thigh. She wore white knee socks and black running shoes.

'Unusual,' Vicki commented.

'Guys love it. Has the sports motif, the little girl motif . . .'

'The nightshirt motif,' Vicki added.

'Hottest item in the store,' Ace said. 'When I get my new shipment in, I'll give you one. It drives the guys wild.'

'You ready to go?'

'Been waiting for you.' To Jennifer, she said, 'Things stay slow, you can close up early. So long.'

'Nice meeting you, Jennifer.'

'You, too,' the girl said.

They left the shop and walked around the corner to Ace's car. Hot air poured out against Vicki when she opened the passenger door. She rolled the window down before climbing in. The sun had been burning down on the seat. She winced, feeling scorched, and shoved herself up and hooked her elbows over the seatback to keep her rump off the searing upholstery.

'You okay?' Ace asked.

'Medium well,' Vicki said.

Ace sat down on a beach towel folded neatly on the driver's seat. 'Sorry about that, hon. I've got another towel in the trunk.'

'Any burn ointment?'

'Want to stop in at the clinic?'

'I'll live. I guess.' Vicki lowered herself slowly. It didn't hurt so much, this time. She sighed.

'Where to?' Ace asked, starting the car.

'The first place is on George Street. Near the church.'

Ace made a right onto Central. 'Oh, looky there.' She swung her thumb to the left.

Vicki leaned forward, peered past her, and saw Melvin. His back was turned. He was facing the display window of Johnson's Pharmacy, scratching his cheek with his left hand.

It was odd to see him. Vicki felt as if time had gone haywire. He'd left her office about seven hours ago, hadn't he?

'He was in this morning,' she muttered.

'I know. You told me on the phone. Going senile?'

'Weird.'

'What's weird? After seeing you, he probably got inspired to buy some condoms.'

'Oh, charming. Thanks.' Vicki looked over her shoulder and tried to spot Melvin through the rear window. The angle wasn't right. She couldn't see him.

'It's not uncommon, you know, for patients to fall in love with their doctors.'

'It's not uncommon for doctors to perform frontal lobotomies on wiseass friends.'

Ace glanced down at her breasts. 'Think I need one?'

'What?'

'That operation. On my frontal lobes. They look fine to me.'

Vicki ignored that one. She dug into her handbag and took out the folded paper on which she'd written the address of the two apartment buildings they planned to visit.

'I really am sorry about Pollock,' Ace said. 'That piss-bag. I'm gonna have a few words with him.'

'Please don't. I just want to get out of that apartment and be done with him.'

'Dirty old fart.'

'I just hope I can get into one of these places fast.'

'I wouldn't count on moving in tonight. I tell you what, we'll stop by your room after we've checked these places out. You can pack up whatever you'll need, and stay with me till they let you move in.'

'It's a deal.'

'Great. We'll have us a blast.'

Melvin supposed they might've seen him as they drove by, but he guessed it didn't matter much. After all, he was right in front of the drugstore, and Vicki *had* given him a prescription. He'd gotten it filled that morning, but Vicki wouldn't know that.

When the sound of Ace's Mustang faded, he turned around and spotted it heading north on Central. He kept an eye on it as he rushed back for his car.

It turned left on George Street.

He reached his car, made a U-turn, and went left on George. The red Mustang wasn't in sight. 'Shit!' He punched the steering wheel. With his right hand. And cried out in pain.

When the agony subsided, he muttered, 'Okay, it don't matter.' He really wanted to find out where she lived, but he'd just have to try again tomorrow. And the next day, if tomorrow didn't work out. It shouldn't be hard. He knew he would find out, sooner or later.

Coming to an intersection, he glanced both ways. No sign of Ace's car.

He kept heading west on George Street, figuring he might as well stick with it for a few more minutes.

On the next block, he found the red Mustang parked at the curb in front of a two-storey brick apartment house. No sign of the girls.

He stared at the building.

That's gotta be it.

He drove on.

That night, a little before ten, Melvin parked around the corner from the apartment house. His heart pounded fast as he walked towards the entrance. The pounding made his right hand throb.

He needed a new gal. He wouldn't use Vicki for that, though. Someday. Once he got it right. But it'd be awful to mess up with her and have to bury her like the others. She'd just have to wait.

In the meantime, he'd settle for looking at her.

He stopped at the door. Peering through its glass, he saw a small, dimly lighted foyer with a panel of mailboxes on the wall. On the left was a narrow stairway to the second floor. To the right of the stairs, a corridor stretched the length of the building. He saw no one.

He tried the door. It opened, which was hardly surprising. In Ellsworth, nobody gave much thought to security.

He stopped up to the mailboxes. There were a dozen, each labelled with the apartment number and name of the renter. The first box had an extra label that read 'Manager'. Melvin moved his finger down the row, touching each name label.

No Chandler.

But the name on the card taped over the mail slot for 4 had been scratched out with a blue pen.

That's gotta be Vicki's, Melvin decided.

She'd only been here a few days, probably hadn't bothered to put her name up yet.

The hardwood floor of the corridor creaked under his shoes. He winced at the noise. But he didn't have to go far. Apartment number 4 was the second door on the right. As soon as he spotted it, he turned around and hurried outside.

He crossed the lawn. At the corner of the building, he found a narrow lane of grass. Light spilled out from the windows of apartment number 2, slanting down and casting a glow on the hedge that bordered the property. Melvin ducked below those windows, and made his way through the darkness to the windows of number 4.

He peered through the glass. The curtains seemed to be open, but the room beyond was so dark that he could see nothing.

Either Vicki had already gone to bed, or she was away somewhere.

If she'd gone to bed, he wouldn't get to see her unless maybe she woke up to use the john, or something. Not much chance of that.

He wondered if he should stick around, just in case she was out.

He didn't want to waste the night, though. It'd be worth waiting for, if he knew for sure that she'd come in pretty soon. Just spying on her would be great, and even if she shut the curtains there might be a gap so he could see her undress.

But she might already be asleep.

And maybe this wasn't her apartment. After all, her name wasn't on the mailbox.

Waste tonight, he thought, and it'll just be that much longer before you can *do* things with her.

I'll try again tomorrow, he decided. I'll come earlier.

He crept away, ducked under the lighted windows of the neighbouring apartment, then thought he might as well take a peek. Slowly, he rose from his crouch. The curtains were open. The woman on the reclining chair looked familiar. He couldn't place her at first, then realized she worked as a check-out girl at the Riverside Market. Melba, that was her name.

A fat pig.

She was sitting there, leaning back in the chair with her feet propped up. Her hair was in rollers. She wore a beige bra and panties. She held a paperback book in front of her face, so she couldn't see Melvin. An open bag of taco chips rested between her legs, and a can of Diet Pepsi rested on the lamp table within easy reach.

She looked like a bloated, bulging wad of raw dough.

Melvin considered killing her. She was repulsive. At the store, she acted like a snot.

It'd be nice to kick her swollen belly till she puked up blood.

Don't be dumb, he told himself. You don't want to mess around with someone you won't use.

He wouldn't be able to get her body out to the car, even if he wanted to.

Besides, he'd have to touch her to kill her. He could just *feel* his fingers sinking into that puffy white skin.

Melvin ducked down below the window, and headed for the street wishing he hadn't looked at Melba. He wished it had been Vicki sitting in that chair. Vicki, for sure, wouldn't wear cruddy beige undies. Maybe red. Maybe black.

He imagined her sitting there in nothing but her white doctor jacket. It was unbuttoned, hanging open.

He climbed into his car, and began the forty-mile drive to Blayton Memorial Hospital.

Chapter Ten

A little after midnight, they started coming into the hospital parking lot. The area was brightly lighted. Melvin, sitting low in the driver's seat, watched them through the windshield.

There were both men and women. Some wore street clothes, but others were dressed in white. He supposed they were doctors, nurses, lab technicians, orderlies, janitors, all ready to head home now that their shift had ended.

Melvin settled on a tall, slim gal in a white dress. Probably a nurse. At this distance, he couldn't see her face too well. But she had short blonde hair like Vicki, and her figure looked good. She looked better than any of the others.

She walked with a stocky woman who was likely another nurse, and a man in overalls. The three of them stopped beside a van. They chatted for a while. Melvin heard the quiet sounds of their voices, but he couldn't make out what they were saying. The man soon climbed into the van. The two nurses stayed together as they passed several cars in the area of the lot reserved for staff. Then, the slim one climbed into a VW Rabbit and the stocky one kept walking.

Melvin backed his car out of its space, joined the small line of other vehicles waiting to exit the lot, then rolled onto the street and swung to the curb. Peering over his shoulder, he watched the Rabbit VW turn onto the road.

It turned right, just as he had.

A good omen, he thought.

The Rabbit passed him. He quickly moved out behind it, then eased off his accelerator and let himself drop back a ways. No point in hugging the gal's tail, even though she probably assumed he was just another hospital employee heading home.

She might not be easy to get.

The ones who stopped at his gas station were always easy. A couple of those, he just did them while they sat in the driver's seat, all set to pay him for the gas. Some, he followed them into the john and took care of them there. Others, they'd stop at the full-service island and he'd make a slice on the fan belt while he was under there checking the oil. After they drove off, he would shut the station and head up River Road in his tow truck. He'd find them stranded on the roadside a couple miles out of town, and they'd think it was a miracle that he'd happened to show up. Easy.

But this was a lot different. He wasn't sure how to handle it.

He'd given the matter considerable thought while he was waiting in the hospital lot. He knew how he *wanted* to get her. He wanted to just follow her home, wait till she was inside, then sneak in and take her by surprise. That way, he would have all the privacy and time he might want. For all he knew, though, the gal might be married or staying with her parents or have a roommate. In fact, he had to admit that it was most likely she *didn't* live alone.

He could go in and get her, anyway, but he wasn't sure he wanted to bother with that.

The other choice was to nail her before she got home. Either figure a way to stop her on the road or try to get her after she parked, while she was on her way to the door. Those methods would only work if nobody else was nearby.

Just play it by ear, Melvin told himself.

The Rabbit turned left. Melvin followed. He checked his rearview mirror. None of the cars behind him made the turn. The road ahead was empty, with only a few houses in sight up ahead. He knew this road. It led to Cedar Junction, eight miles west of Blayton. Soon, there would be a long stretch through farmland before the outskirts of Cedar Junction. If she just doesn't pull into one of these driveways . . .

She didn't.

Headlights appeared in the distance, so he held off. The lights drew nearer. He squinted against their glare. A pickup whooshed by, and the glare was gone. Melvin watched the taillights in his rearview. When they were tiny red specks, he swung across the centre line and stepped on the accelerator. He gained on the Rabbit, sped past it, then eased back onto his side of the road.

Nothing ahead except the moonlit road and fields.

He studied the Rabbit in his rearview mirror. It seemed to be about three car lengths behind him.

Melvin grinned at his craftiness. He knew he could've swerved into the car's path while he was passing it, but a weird manoeuvre like that would've put the woman on guard. This way, she might not be suspicious at all until it was too late.

He braced, left hand tight on the steering wheel, arm locked straight, pressing himself against the seatback and the headrest.

And jammed down on the brake pedal.

His tyres grabbed the pavement, skidded and shrieked.

The Rabbit bore down on him.

He heard its squeal.

His car lurched with the impact. Not much of a jolt, really, but enough. He heard no breaking glass, so he doubted that either car had been damaged.

He swung onto the dirt hard shoulder of the road, and stopped. The Rabbit moved slowly past him, both its headlights still working. For a bad moment, he feared the nurse might keep on going. But she turned her car onto the shoulder and stopped a few yards in front of him.

Her door opened. As she climbed out, Melvin slumped against the steering wheel. He heard the quick scrape of her shoes on the road. The sounds stopped beside him. He slowly sat up straight, shaking his head.

'Are you all right?' the woman asked. Her voice was trembling.

'I guess,' he muttered. He rubbed the back of his neck.

She was standing close to his door, bending down to look in at him. He wished he could see her better, but the light was too faint. What he could see looked good. He guessed she was in her early twenties. Her white dress had a name tag over the left breast, but he couldn't read it.

'What happened?' she asked. 'Why did you stop?'

'Something . . . ran out in front of me. Maybe a cat. I don't know. It all happened so fast. Guess I should've gone ahead and hit it.'

'I'm so sorry. I shouldn't have been following so close. Did you hit your head?'

'I don't know.' He rubbed his forehead. 'I'm all right, I guess.' He turned off the engine, and took out the keys with his bandaged right hand. He slowly opened his door and stepped out onto the road. Pretending to ignore the woman, he wandered to the rear of his car.

'I don't think there's any damage,' she said as she followed him.

The tail and brake lights glowed red.

'Don't look like it,' Melvin mumbled. 'I got a flash in the trunk. I'd better get it.'

'I'll give you my name and number,' the woman said. 'If there are any problems, I'd be more than happy to pay.'

He unlocked the trunk. Its lid swung up.

'We don't have to get the insurance companies involved, do we?' she asked. 'I'd rather take care of this just between us, if it's okay.'

'Sure,' he said.

'Great.' She sounded very relieved.

Melvin took the flashlight out of his trunk. He turned it on, and shined it on the woman's hands as she searched her purse. She found a pen and notepad. He watched her hands shake as she tried to hold the pad steady and write on it.

'You may develop some stiffness in the neck,' she said as she wrote. She sounded a lot like Vicki talking about his bite. 'That wouldn't be at all uncommon in a situation like this. But if you'll come to the hospital and ask for me . . .'

'Fine,' Melvin said.

'I'll see that you're taken care of. We have a fine physical therapy department.'

'Okay.'

She tore a page off the pad. It fluttered as she gave it to him. He held it under the flashlight beam. Her name, Patricia Gordon, was scribbled in shivery ink. Beneath the name was a telephone number. Melvin tucked the paper into his shirt pocket.

As she slipped the pad into her purse, he aimed the light at her face.

She squinted and turned her head.

Not bad-looking at all. A cute little nose. Freckles. Sandy-coloured hair sweeping across her forehead.

The name tag read, 'Patricia Gordon, RN'. The dress had a

zipper down the front. It was low enough to show a small wedge of bare skin below her throat.

'Could you . . . ?' she started to say, but her breath exploded out as Melvin rammed the flashlight into her belly. Pain bolted up his own right arm. He cried out and dropped the flashlight at the same moment Patricia doubled. He drove his knee up into her so hard she was lifted off her feet. Before she could fall, he wrapped his arms around her waist. He hoisted her and flung her into the trunk. She landed on her back, legs in the air. The slamming trunk lid knocked her legs down. The trunk latched.

Melvin picked up the flashlight with his left hand. He thumbed the switch back and forth a couple of times, but the light was dead.

The red rear lights gave enough brightness for him to check the area behind his car. While he looked around, he heard bumps and muffled shouts from the trunk.

The purse, he decided, must've gone into the trunk with Patricia. It had been on a shoulder strap. He didn't see anything on the pavement or ground.

He walked over to her car. The engine was still running. He opened the driver's door, leaned in, pulled out the ignition key and punched off the headlights with a knuckle. When he shut the door, the car rested in darkness.

He wiped the door handle with the hanging front of his shirt.

Back at his own car, he removed the key from the trunk lock. Patricia shouted, 'Let me out of here! You can't do this!'

'Wanta bet?' he muttered.

He climbed into his car, made a U-turn, and drove away.

He knew he might be leaving his tyre tracks on the dirt shoulder of the road. He thought about going back and rubbing them out. Someone might come along, though. He'd been lucky to take care of Patricia without another car showing up. Tomorrow, he'd send Manny away and put different tyres on his car, get rid of these. Easy.

At home, Melvin parked inside his two-car garage. He used the remote control on his dash to lower the door. As it rumbled down, he climbed out of the car.

This was the first gal he'd brought home alive.

Exciting, a live one in his trunk. But a little scary, too.

He stood at the rear of his car and stared at the trunk.

What'm I gonna do with her now?

During the long drive, he'd had plenty of time to consider the problem. But he hadn't come up with any great ideas. It was a toss-up between killing her immediately and keeping her alive for a while. It might be fun if he didn't kill her right away. He could tie her up and fool around with her. On the other hand, he was eager to try a new method on her. That, after all, was the reason he took her.

I'm not a goddamn rapist, he told himself.

Besides, how would he tie her up without hurting his bad hand? She was bound to put up a fight. He'd either have to gas her or pound the daylight out of her. Then, if she wasn't out cold, he'd have to hide her face with something. He sure didn't want her *looking* at him while he screwed her. All that contempt in her eyes. Gals nearly always had contempt in their eyes when they looked at him. She would, for sure.

But if he held off till after he killed her and brought her back, she'd be so grateful she'd do anything to please him. Hell, she'd love him.

He went into the house. He came out with his Colt .44 revolver and a green, double-ply plastic trash bag. He shoved the folded bag into a front pocket of his pants. Holding the revolver in his left hand, he unlocked the trunk. The lid rose.

Patricia lay curled on her side, hands covering her face. She was sobbing quietly.

'Climb out,' Melvin said. 'I'm not gonna hurt you.'

'Don't hurt me,' she said through her hands.

'Told you I won't. Come on.'

She got to her hands and knees inside the trunk, never once looking at him. Her back shook as she wept. A string of snot dangled from her nose, swaying. Slowly, keeping her head down, she climbed out of the trunk. She stood with her back to Melvin, and hunched over and held onto the car.

'What are you going to do to me?'

'Just don't try nothing, you'll be okay.'

He pushed the revolver under his belt, took the trash bag out of his pocket, and shook it open.

'What's that?'

'Nothing. Just a bag. You're gonna wear it so you don't see where we're going. Stand up straight, arms at your sides.'

She followed his orders. Melvin spread the bag apart, slipped it over her head, and pulled it down her body. It covered her almost to the knees. He took off his belt and made a loop by slipping one end through the buckle. He dropped the loop over her head. The plastic bag crackled as he pulled, closing it around her neck. He left enough slack in the belt so she could still get air.

'Can you breathe okay?' he asked.

Her covered head nodded. Melvin heard her sniffle.

'It's not too tight?'

'No.'

'Okay, face me.'

She turned around. Melvin shook the belt sideways and watched the buckle slide around to her front. He walked backward, leading her across the garage to the side door of the house. He led her into the house, through the kitchen to another closed door. Opening the door, he said, 'Stairs. Be careful.'

'Where're you taking me?' she asked in a high, whiny voice.

'The basement.' Melvin grinned. 'That's where you're gonna stay till they come up with the ransom.'

'Ransom?'

'Sure. What did you think, I was gonna murder you or something?'

'All you want's money?'

''Course.'

Melvin switched on the basement light. Turning his back to the stairway, he took a careful step down. His left hand held the belt. His right hovered over the banister. Patricia hesitated on the top stair. 'Go ahead and hold the railing,' he said. 'I don't want you to fall and hurt yourself.'

She hitched the plastic bag up around her waist, reached out and clutched the wooden rail.

Melvin stayed two stairs below Patricia, and watched her as they descended. She took slow, careful steps. Her shoes and stockings were white. He hated those white stockings.

They'll be the first to go, he decided.

'Who's supposed to pay for me?' she asked. She didn't sound so upset any more.

'You tell me.'

'I have some savings.'

'How much?'

Melvin reached the floor of the basement. Patricia stepped down the final two stairs. When the banister ended, she pulled the bag down as far as it would go, apparently preferring to be covered and out of sight.

'I've got about eight hundred,' she said. 'Will that be enough? You can have it all.'

'Eight hundred?' Melvin stepped behind her. 'Sure. That sounds fine.' He wrapped the belt around his left hand.

'Well, good. Then that . . .'

He jerked the belt. Patricia stumbled towards him as the loop shut, cinching the trash bag tight around her neck. He lurched out of the way. Her rump hit the concrete floor. He scrambled backward up the first three stairs, keeping the belt taut, dragging her until she lay against the steps. She kicked and squirmed. She worked the bag up her body, freeing her arms, and clutched the choking belt.

Melvin frowned. He wanted to suffocate her, not strangle her. He didn't want marks on her throat. So he gave the belt some slack. She yanked on it. Melvin released his grip. The belt uncoiled from his hand and flew past her feet.

She took a noisy breath and sat up. Her hands plucked at the top of the bag, trying to pull it off her head as if it were a stubborn jersey.

Melvin dropped down behind her. Sitting on the next stair up, he forced Patricia's arms down and wrapped his legs around her, pinning the arms to her sides. Then, he bent over her head and hugged the bag against her face.

When she was dead, he took off her white stockings first.

Chapter Eleven

Vicki flinched awake, gasping. She rolled onto her side, hushed the clamour of the alarm clock, and flopped onto her back. She stared at the dark ceiling. She was breathless, her heart slamming, her head throbbing with pain.

She couldn't recall the nightmare, but it must've been a doozy. No doubt featuring Melvin.

She lifted an arm out from under the sheet, and rubbed her forehead. It felt hot and damp. When she rubbed her scalp, she found her hair drenched.

Coming down with something? she wondered. Felt like a hangover. Though she'd stayed up late last night in the kitchen with Ace, she'd had nothing to drink except Coke. Probably just a bad case of nightmare.

Though Vicki's breathing and heart rate seemed to be normal again, she still had the headache. And she felt leaden.

Forget about running this morning, she thought. Just take some aspirin, try to go back to sleep, and hope you can shake the headache.

She brushed the sheet aside. Moaning with the effort, she sat up. From the feel of the warm breeze on her skin, she knew that something was wrong. She looked down. Her left breast was bare. The bodice of the nightgown hung below it. Thinking that the spaghetti strap must've slipped off her shoulder, she ran a hand up her arm. The strap wasn't there.

Must've pulled loose.

She swung her legs off the bed and turned on the lamp. Squinting against the brightness, she lifted the pocket of lacy fabric over her breast. At its edge was a ragged notch.

Vicki scowled at it.

She stood and peeled the damp nightgown off her body. She caught the dangling cord. At its tip was the small patch of fabric torn from the front.

'Good God,' she muttered.

Normal tossing and turning couldn't have done this, no matter how feverish her sleep had been.

She stepped over to the closet door and looked at herself in the full-length mirror. The strap had left a thin red mark on the top of her left shoulder.

Someone had grabbed the nightgown and ripped it from her breast. Someone, she thought. Guess who.

Unless her room had been invaded during the night by a roaming molester, or Ace was a closet lesbian, Vivki had torn the nightgown herself. The other two possibilities seemed remote. Ace had never shown any inclination towards sexual contact with Vicki. Even if she *was* interested, she was hardly the type to sneak around copping feels. As for a stranger visiting the room, who was likely to come in and do no more than expose one of her breasts?

Vicki felt certain that nobody could've given the nightgown a yank like that without waking her up. It must've hurt, the cord abrading her shoulder that way.

She'd done it herself, probably in the throes of the nightmare.

And that frightened her.

She'd been assuming that the nightmares would taper off. Instead, they seemed to be getting worse.

What's next, sleep-walking?

She tossed the nightgown across a chair, opened the closet door and put on her light, satin robe. Then she made her way through the hall, past Ace's open door, and entered the bathroom. After using the toilet, she took a bottle of aspirin out of her overnight bag and washed down three tablets with a glass of water.

Back in the bedroom, she shed the robe, re-set her alarm clock for eight and turned off the lamp. She stretched out on the bed. The damp, cool sheet felt good against her bare skin. The breeze from the open window roamed over her. She rubbed the back of her stiff neck, folded her hands beneath her wet hair and gazed at the ceiling, wondering if she would be able to fall asleep – wondering if she dared.

She dreamed she was on the diving raft with Paul. The sun hadn't come up yet, and a heavy mist hung over the river. She could see nothing beyond the edges of the platform. 'I love you so much,' she said.

'I'll always love you,' he told her.

She felt a terrible ache of emptiness and longing. 'I want this morning to be special, something we can always have and always remember, even if we never see each other again.'

He took her into his arms and kissed her. Vicki began to weep. 'What's wrong?' he asked.

'You'll be going away.'

'I'll come back. Someday, I'll come back to you.'

'Do you promise?'

'Cross my heart and hope to die.' He crossed his heart. Then Vicki began to unbutton his shirt. 'What're you doing?'

'We're going to make love.'

'Here?'

'Nobody can see us.'

Soon, they both were naked. Vicki lay on her back. Paul, stretched out beside her, braced up on an elbow, slid his hand softly over her skin. 'You're so beautiful,' he said.

She curled her fingers around his penis.

Moaning, he climbed onto her. He knelt between her spread legs. He kissed her breasts. 'You're awful nice to me,' he said. But it wasn't Paul's voice. 'I'm gonna be nice to you.' He licked her nipple and Vicki grabbed him by the hair and jerked his head up. Melvin grinned at her.

She started to scream. Melvin slapped a bandaged hand across her mouth. 'I'm gonna be *real* nice to you.'

'No, please!' Somehow, she was able to speak in spite of his hand.

'It's okay. See?' He held a foil-wrapped condom above her face.

'No!' she cried out. 'Please!'

'Get on with it, would you? We haven't got all day.' Someone else was with them on the raft.

Vicki turned her head.

Dexter Pollock was kneeling beside them. He took off his robe. He was naked except for a gunbelt, and a police badge pinned to his chest. Trickles of blood ran down his breast from the pin holes made by the badge.

'Hey!' someone yelled from a distance. 'What's going on out there?'

The mist lifted. Across the water, far up the beach, was a man sitting atop the playground slide.

Dexter drew his revolver and fired. The man toppled backward and fell to the ground behind the slide's ladder.

Melvin, kneeling above her, now had jumper cables in his hands. He touched the clamps together and sparks exploded from the sharp copper teeth.

Vicki, yelping, clutched her breasts and lurched upright in bed. The room was bright with sunlight. The clock showed 7:50. In ten more minutes, the alarm would've gone off. She wished it had. If the alarm had blared, the sudden waking might've shocked the dream from her memory.

Every detail remained vivid.

Her headache seemed to be gone, but her neck muscles felt like iron.

Ace opened the door and peered in. 'You okay?'

Vicki nodded. She pulled the sheet up to cover herself.

'You yelled.'

'Had a nightmare.'

'You look like death warmed over and pissed on.'

'Thanks. Feel like it, too.'

Ace came in. She was holding a mug of coffee. Her hair was in curlers. She wore her Minnie Mouse nightshirt. Its front bobbed and swayed as she walked. 'Here,' she said, 'take this.' She handed the mug to Vicki. 'You need it more than me.'

Vicki sipped the hot coffee. She sighed.

Ace sat on the edge of the bed. 'Must've been a sweetie of a nightmare.'

'Started off just great. Then Melvin and Pollock showed up.'

'I would've yelled, too.'

'Jesus.'

'You're dripping.'

'I know. That's twice in one night.'

'Same dream?'

Vicki shrugged. 'I don't remember the first one. I've been having these damn things ever since I got into town.'

'Every night?'

'I think so.'

'Your psyche must be a wreck.'

'It's being around Melvin again. He's in all of them, coming after me. At least the ones I remember.'

'Subconsciously, you desire him.'

'Oh, right. Take a leap.'

'Hope they aren't premonitions.'

Vicki sneered at her.

Ace patted her leg through the sheet. 'I know just what'll fix you up, hon. A boyfriend, that's what you need. Fall in love, that'll take your mind off the Amazing Melvin.'

'Right.'

'Barring that, maybe a shrink.'

'It may come to that.'

For just a moment, Ace's concern showed in her eyes. Then she smiled. 'You'll be fine,' she said. 'I'll throw some breakfast together.' She stood up.

'While you're throwing, I guess I'll take a shower.'

'Better take two,' Ace told her, and left the room.

After a long, cool shower, Vicki put on a clean T-shirt and shorts. She found Ace in the kitchen, making a stack of pancakes to go with the sausage links sizzling on the skillet. She leaned over the sausages and sniffed them.

'Maybe I'll just stay with you. The hell with a new apartment.'

'If you think I'd mind, you're crazy.'

'We've already established I'm crazy.'

'I've got no use for that guest room.' She grinned over her shoulder at Vicki. 'When I have guests, that ain't where they sleep.'

Vicki poured more coffee for herself, and filled Ace's mug on the table. 'I don't know,' she said. 'It might be fine for a few days, but . . .'

Ace hoisted an arm and sniffed her armpit. 'Like roses,' she announced. 'So what's the problem? My breath offensive?'

'I'd just be in your way.'

'It'd help me out. Not that I'm hurting or nothing, but you could make a small contribution toward your food and lodging. I'd charge a hell of a bunch less than Agnes Monksby. You'd have the run of the house instead of just some little apartment, no landlady or creepy tenants to deal with, not to mention you'd have a nice yard for sunbathing . . .'

'Not to mention a cook,' Vicki added.

'Yeah, well that's not necessarily part of the bargain, hotshot. We'd take turns on that kind of shitski.'

'I don't know, Ace. I already told Agnes I'd take the place.'

'I didn't see any money change hands.'

'Well . . .'

'Call her up and tell her you changed your mind.'

'I wish you'd mentioned this yesterday, before we talked to her.'

'Yesterday, I didn't think you'd go for it.'

'What makes you think I'll go for it today?'

Ace looked at her and raised an eyebrow. 'You're having all those nightmares, for one thing. You don't want to be waking up in an empty apartment. You need to have a friend around. I'm it. Least till you find some guy who'll fuck you silly and make you forget about Melvin. And I'll help you find the guy, too. I'm not without contacts. In the meantime, tell Monksby you changed your mind. We'll go over to Pollock's after work and get the rest of your stuff.'

The idea of staying here appealed to Vicki. It would almost be the same as having a home of her own. Ace was such a close friend she was like family, and it appeared now that she might be upset if Vicki refused her generosity.

Also, there were the nightmares. They seemed to be getting worse, and Ace was right about the comfort of having a friend under the same roof.

If it doesn't work out, she thought, I can always find a new place later.

'Are you sure you don't mind having me around for a while?'

'Would I ask you if I minded?'

'I mean, I don't want you doing it out of pity or . . .'

'Don't be a pain in the crack.'

After breakfast, she got ready for work. Ace offered to give her a lift.

'You don't open for another hour,' Vicki said.

'It'll only take me five minutes to run you over to the clinic.'

'Thanks. I think I'll walk, though. I missed my workout this morning.'

'Yeah. You'd better walk. Turn into a fat slob, we won't be able to foist you off on some charmer, I'll be stuck with you forever.'

'Right.'

'Stop by the shop after you're done, we'll go over and get your stuff.'

'Great. See you then.'

Vicki left the house. Though the morning was hot, the trees shaded the sidewalk and there was a hint of mild breeze. She felt good. Her headache was gone. Her neck still seemed a little stiff, but that was a minor irritation.

It was a major relief to know that she would be living with Ace. And tomorrow was Saturday. The clinic remained open on Saturdays, but Charlie had given her the weekends off. She could spend the day relaxing, settling in. She looked forward to it.

Her good mood lasted until the clinic came into view and she spotted Melvin Dobbs sitting on the stoop. His hair looked slicked back and oily. His eyes were hidden behind mirror sunglasses. He wore a shiny red Hawaiian shirt decorated with blue flowers, plaid Bermudas and black socks. His Oxfords gleamed in the sunlight.

As Vicki approached, he raised his bandaged hand in greeting, and stood up.

'Good morning, Melvin.' Though she felt shaky inside, her voice sounded calm. 'How's the hand?'

'About the same.'

She could see that he hadn't changed the bandage. If she mentioned it, however, he might ask her to apply a fresh one.

'You look real pretty,' he said.

'Thanks.' She felt a little sick. The reflecting sunglasses prevented her from seeing the direction of his gaze. The neckline of her sundress wasn't so low that it revealed even the tops of her breasts, but she suddenly wished she'd worn something that covered her better.

Armour would do nicely.

'Did you want to see me about something?' she asked.

He nodded. He rubbed the back of his left hand across his thick lips. 'You got a car?'

'No, not yet.'

'Didn't think so. You came in with that U-Haul, and you rode off with Ace yesterday. I was over at the drugstore when you left. You oughta have a car.'

'Well, I'm saving up for one.'

'Come on.' He stepped past Vicki, waved a hand for her to follow, and shambled to the corner of the building.

As she walked toward him, his left hand slipped into a pocket of his shorts and came out with a key ring.

Oh, no.

Parked in the clinic lot beside Thelma's VW bug was a bright red Plymouth Duster.

'Melvin.'

'Like it?'

'It's very nice, but . . .'

'Yours.' He held the keys toward her.

She didn't reach for the keys. She shook her head and rubbed her moist hands on her dress. 'What do you mean?'

'You can have it.'

'I can't accept a car from you.'

His head bobbed. 'Sure you can. I got no use for it.'

'I still can't.'

'I painted it up special for you.'

'That's very sweet of you, but . . .'

'You're my friend. You been real nice to me. You oughta have a car.'

'Melvin.' She sighed. 'That's very thoughtful of you, and I appreciate it, but a gift like that . . . I can't. Really.'

'Okay. Okay.' He was grinning. Vicki wished he would stop grinning. 'Figure it's a loan, then. You can just borrow it off me till you save up and get a new car of your own. How's that?'

'I really don't need a car, anyway, Melvin. I live close enough to walk.'

'Sure you need one. You got this one.' He took a lurching step forward, thrusting the keys at her.

She clasped her hands behind her back, shook her head.

'No. Please, Melvin, I don't . . .'

His bandaged hand darted out. A fingertip hooked out the top of her dress. He dropped the keys down her front. She felt them tumble between her breasts and skitter down her belly. The belt at her waist stopped their fall.

Shocked, she stared at Melvin.

He sidestepped around her, grinning. As he hurried away, he looked over his shoulder. 'When you don't need it no more, just let me know.'

'Melvin!'

'Any trouble with it, come by the station.'

'You can't leave it!'

He vanished beyond the corner of the Handiboy building.

Vicki plucked the front of the belt away from her body. The keys dropped, brushing against her panties, hitting the pavement between her feet with a jangle.

She crouched and picked them up.

Two keys, one for the ignition and one for the trunk, on a small steel loop connected to a plastic disk that read, 'Dobbs Service Station, 126 South River Road, Ellsworth, Wisconsin.'

She considered chasing Melvin and hurling the keys at him.

She looked at the car.

A nice little car, fire-engine red.

How could he do this to me!

Chapter Twelve

Melvin got melted cheese on his bandage as he reached into the bowl beside him on the couch. He poked the coated nacho chip into his mouth, licked the cheese off the tape, and started to chew. Then he pressed the Play button on his remote control. The McDonald's commercial vanished from the television screen and he saw himself in the basement laboratory, wearing his red satin robe, gazing up at the camera.

'Tonight,' he said, 'we'll try a method from page 621 of *Curses, Spells and Incantations* by Amed Magdal, translated from Coptic by Guy de Villier. My subject will be Patricia Gordon of Cedar Junction.' He stepped away from the camera and swept an arm toward the work table. Stretched out on the table, wrists and ankles belted down, was the naked cadaver of the nurse.

Melvin took a drink of Pepsi as he watched himself approach

the cart and check the open book. The Melvin on the television looked up, frowning. 'I don't like this one much,' he said. 'I don't want to mark 'em up. But I'm gonna do it anyhow. If it works, it works.'

He lifted an Exacto knife off the cart, stepped over to the body, and pierced its skin just above the public mound. Slowly, he began to carve a curving line. In the trail of the blade, blood seeped out. Not much. She had been dead for more than an hour before he began the procedure. When he withdrew the blade, the strip of blood formed a circle nearly twelve inches in diameter on Patricia's abdomen. He stepped back, inspected it, rubbed his mouth, winked at the camera.

Bending over the corpse again, he carved an inverted pyramid inside the circle, large enough so that each of its points met the edge. This was to become the 'Face of Ram-Chotep'. So far, it looked pretty much like the diagram in the book. He nodded, and cut eyes into Patricia's skin just within the upper points of the triangle.

Then he cut the mouth – a deep slash just above her navel four inches in length.

Melvin watched himself return to the cart, pick up a chunk of root from the 'Tree of Life', stick it into his mouth and start to chew. Recalling its bitter taste, he took a drink of Pepsi. He remembered thinking as he chewed the root to paste that this better be the real thing. The Shop of Charms in San Francisco had charged him $150.00 per ounce, and that included the twenty per cent 'favoured customer' discount. It was the most costly item in the store's catalogue. He'd ordered ten ounces, just to have it in case it worked.

While he chewed the root, he picked up a threaded needle.

He returned to Patricia. He poked the needle into her thigh, just to have it handy. What's one more wound? he'd thought at the time.

Bending over the corpse, he spread the edges of the 'Mouth of Ram-Chotep', pressed his own mouth against the gash, and used his tongue to thrust the masticated root inside.

When he took his mouth away, the green glop began to ooze out. He stuffed it back in with his fingers, and kept stuffing while he used the needle and thread to sew the wound shut.

Finished, he stepped back. The slash, now cross-hatched with stitches, really did resemble a mouth.

As he returned to the cart, Melvin lifted the bowl of chips onto his lap. He ate, watching his image on the screen but paying little attention to the gibberish he was reading from the book.

He'd had little hope for this method. It seemed too simple, requiring almost no preparation at all – just the cutting and the masticated root. No bat's blood or eye of newt. No ashes of a dead sinner, which was good since his father's urn had been depleted from other tries and the Shop of Charms didn't carry that particular ingredient.

But the incantation was in the original language. That seemed like a plus. In so many of the other books he'd used, the chants had been translated, which seemed like a good way to ruin the whole process.

Melvin had a cheese-covered chip almost to his mouth when the reading ended. He let it fall into the bowl, and watched himself return to the table.

He stood on the far side of the corpse so he wouldn't block the camera's view.

'Okay, babe,' he muttered, 'do your stuff.'

Slowly, the lines of blood forming the Face of Ram-Chotep began to widen. Trickles started to roll down the slopes of her body. They streamed across the Face, slid down her sides.

Melvin whirled toward the camera, leaped and shot his fists into the air. 'ALL RIGHT!' he yelled. 'ALL RIGHT!!!' He pranced around, whooping and waving his arms, and froze with one foot high as a loud inhaling noise came from Patricia. She sounded like a drowning woman coming up for a breath. He bent over the table. Her eyes were open. They jittered this way and that, spotted Melvin and stared at him as she wheezed.

He patted her shoulder. 'I saved you,' he said. 'I brought you back. Me. You were dead and I brought you back.'

She frowned. She looked as if she didn't understand.

'You died,' Melvin told her. 'Do you remember dying?'

Her head shook slightly from side to side. She was no longer huffing for air. She lay there, motionless except for the slow rise and fall of her chest, and stared at him. If she was in pain, it didn't show. She simply seemed confused.

'Don't worry, huh? You're all right, now. I worked my magic on you, and made you live again.'

She raised her head and looked down at herself. Alarm began to replace the puzzlement on her face.

'The blood's nothing,' he assured her. 'Just part of the magic. The straps, they were just so you wouldn't hurt yourself. Do you want me to take them off?'

She nodded.

'Can you talk?'

Her lips twitched. She made no sounds.

'That's okay. Now, don't move.' He unbuckled the belt holding her left wrist to the table. He lifted the wrist. His fingertips sought her pulse.

Watching, Melvin remembered the strange beat of her pulse. Strong, but very slow. Twelve beats per minute, he'd found out later when he timed it. The slow heart rate, he figured, probably accounted for the cool feel of her.

He stepped down to the end of the table. As he unstrapped her feet, Patricia slowly lifted her hand. She touched the Mouth of Ram-Chotep. She raised the hand above her face. Her fingertips glistened with blood and the green ooze of the chewed root. She licked them clean while Melvin released her right hand.

He looked at the camera and rolled his eyes upward.

Melvin, watching, chuckled at his expression.

Being dead had made her a little weird. Licking the stuff off her fingers had been the first sign of that, but only the first of many.

She started to sit up.

'Lie still,' he told her. She obeyed. Melvin took a moist sponge off the cart. She lay motionless, watching him as he gently swabbed the blood off her body. The Mouth kept leaking. He taped a gauze pad across it, then went back to the shallower cuts. When he was done, the design remained distinct with shiny thread of blood. But the lines didn't thicken or drip. The bandage made the Face of Ram-Chotep look gagged.

Melvin set the sponge on the table beside Patricia's hip.

Her hand felt for it. She found it, lifted it above her face, and squeezed it into her mouth. Pink liquid spilled from the sponge at first, then slowed to a trickle. Stuffing half the sponge into her mouth, she began to suck and chew on it.

'Hits the spot?' Melvin asked.

She grunted.

She stuffed the rest of the sponge into her mouth.

'Hey, that's enough. You can't eat that.'

She didn't hesitate for an instant, just pulled the sponge out and gave it to him.

'Go ahead and sit up,' he told her.

She sat up, crossed her legs, rested her hands on her knees, and looked at Melvin as if waiting for the next order. A few little drops of blood broke away from the lines and crept down her skin.

'Try to say something,' Melvin said. 'What's your name?'

She frowned, shook her head, shrugged. 'What's yours?' she asked.

Melvin saw his back go straight.

'You *can* talk.'

'I guess so.'

She could not only talk, but her voice sounded *normal*.

'What's your name?' she asked again.

'Melvin.'

She smiled. 'That's a nice name.'

Melvin looked at the camera and shook his head.

'What's wrong?' she asked.

'Nothing. Huh-uh. Everything's fine. Jesus.'

He'd felt as if he must be dreaming. This *couldn't* be happening. It was more than he'd even hoped for. He had never really quite believed he would succeed in bringing one of these gals back to life. It was an ambition – hell, an obsession. But even though he'd told himself over and over that he would eventually stumble onto a formula that would work, he'd always doubted he could pull it off.

And if somehow one of them *did* come back, he'd imagined she would be pretty much along the lines of your standard zombie: bug-eyed, zoned out, a regular retard.

Patricia might not be entirely normal, but she was close. Very close.

'Boggles the mind,' he muttered.

'Do I have a name?' she asked.

'You don't know?'

She shook her head.

'What's the last thing you remember?'

'You said, "You don't know?" '

'No, I mean . . . what did you do this morning?'

She knitted her brow. She chewed her lower lip. She shrugged. The shrugging made her breasts rise and fall. 'Nothing, I guess.'

'Do you remember the hospital?'

'Is that where I died?'

'You worked there. You were a nurse.'

She smiled. 'Really?'

'Who's the President of the United States?'

'I don't know. How should I know?'

'Do you know *anything*?'

Her smiled widened. 'You're Melvin.' Her eyes lowered. She lifted his bandaged hand. 'What happened here?'

'Somebody bit me.'

'Can I?'

Melvin thought he heard something. He pressed the Mute button on the remote. The conversation on the television died.

'Mell-vin,' came Patricia's voice.

'Yeah?' he called.

'Melvin?'

He shut off the VCR, moved the bowl off his lap, and hurried upstairs to his bedroom. He switched on the light. Patricia, sitting up in bed, looked worried for a moment, then smiled and combed fingers through her mussed blonde hair. She had been wearing one of his mother's nightgowns, but now it lay on the floor. The rumpled sheet lay across her legs.

'Something wrong?' Melvin asked.

'I woke and you weren't here.'

'I just went downstairs to look at some television.'

The hand in her hair moved down. It curled over her left breast. Staring into Melvin's eyes, she squeezed her breast. Then she circled the nipple with a fingertip. The centre grew and jutted. She pinched the nub between her thumb and forefinger and pulled, stretching it.

'Do you want to play?' she asked.

'Again?' Melvin asked, grinning.

'I like it.' She twisted her nipple and squirmed. 'You like it, too, don't you?'

'I don't like getting bit.'

'I won't.'

'That's what you said last time.'

'I promise.'

'Okay.' Melvin turned toward the door.

'Where are you going?'

He looked around at her. She had let go of her nipple, which was a relief to Melvin. He knew that she seemed oblivious to pain, but it had still made him nervous to watch her pulling and twisting so hard. 'I'll come right back.'

'Can I come, too?' She looked worried again. Clearly, she didn't want him out of her sight. Ever. That morning, she'd actually cried when Melvin explained that he needed to leave her alone. She'd begged to go with him. Finally, he'd locked her in the basement. By the time he returned from taking the car to Vicki, she was hysterical.

This could get to be a real nuisance.

'Just wait here,' he told her.

Frowning, she nodded bravely.

Melvin hurried down the hallway to the bathroom. He took a fresh roll of adhesive tape out of the medicine cabinet, then returned to the bedroom.

While he was away, Patricia had moved the top sheet to the end of the bed and stretched out. Her hands were folded beneath her head.

'Was that quick enough?' he asked.

'I guess.'

He draped his robe across the chair. Patricia, staring at him, licked her lips as he walked to the bed. He climbed onto her and sat across her hips. Her skin was cool under his rump. He felt the tickle of her pubic hair.

The pad of gauze just above her navel had come loose at one end. He tried to lift it for a peek at the wound, but it was stuck to her. He remembered how Vicki had used alcohol to loosen the bandage on his hand. Maybe he would try that. Later.

He touched the pyramid he had carved into Patricia last night, and felt the stiff, thin ridge of a scab.

'I guess you're healing,' he said.

'Is that good?'

413

'Sure.'

She bounced gently a couple of times, thrusting herself up against him. 'Aren't we going to play?'

'In a minute.' He peeled a four-inch strip of adhesive tape off the spool and tore it loose. 'Close your mouth,' he said.

'I won't bite.'

'I know.'

She closed her mouth and smiled. She slipped a hand from beneath her head. It slid down her body and touched him. Her fingers curled around him and lightly slid up and down his shaft while he applied two strips of tape. When he was done, her lips were sealed by the big white X. 'Isn't gonna hold you,' he said. 'But if you make the tape come off, I'm leaving. Understand?'

Patricia nodded.

''Cause it really hurts when you bite.'

Chapter Thirteen

It seemed rather silly to be sunbathing since the lotion would prevent her from getting a tan, but Vicki felt good sprawling on the lounger, the sun hot on her back, the late afternoon breeze sometimes sliding over her.

She supposed she might get *some* tan, in spite of the screening lotion. She hoped so. She wanted to look good in her new bikini, just in case she should ever wear it to the beach.

Could've skipped the sun block, she thought. A little exposure this time of day wouldn't kill me.

But she knew that without the block she would've felt too guilty to enjoy the sunbathing.

Reaching behind her back, Vicki tied the strings of her bikini top. Then she rolled over, folded her hands beneath her head, and shut her eyes.

It had been a fine Saturday.

There may have been nightmares last night, but she'd awakened without any memory of them. Nor had she torn her nightgown in her sleep – because she'd left it off. Smart move, that.

The running couldn't have been much finer. No Dexter Pollock annoyed her on the way out. A mist hung over the town, muffling the streetlights so they looked like glowing balls of cotton. The mist also seemed to muffle sounds, making the morning seem unnaturally silent and peaceful. The heavy air, while not exactly cool, felt less warm than usual. She wore her shorts and T-shirt. No need for a warm-up suit with Dexter out of the way. She ran fast. The air washed over her. Instead of taking her usual route, she ran south so she wouldn't have to see Melvin's car sitting in the clinic lot, wouldn't have to worry about confronting or avoiding the stranger who'd been in the park those other two mornings.

On the way back, she stopped in the bakery and bought doughnuts with money she had tucked into her sock for that purpose. When Ace got up, they pigged out.

Then she went with Ace to the shop. Ace opened up, and Vicki browsed for a long time, and finally bought shorts and a knit shirt and a skimpy white string bikini – all at the twenty per cent sawbones discount.

After that, she returned to the house and spent hours just sitting around, catching up on the medical journals and taking breaks to read a mystery. Ace came home early, leaving Jennifer in charge of the store, and they got into their bikinis to 'catch some rays'.

All in all, a great way to spend a Saturday. Vicki couldn't remember the last time she'd spent such a peaceful, relaxing day.

As she lay there thinking about it, she heard the shower go on. Though she wasn't eager to move, she knew that she would shower after Ace got out. That would feel good. The plan, then, was to linger over a batch of margaritas and fire up the grill and make hamburgers for supper. Then, they would head into town, pick up two or three movies at the video store, and spend the evening in front of the television. Sounded good to Vicki. Sounded perfect.

The telephone rang.

Ace in the shower.

Sighing, Vicki flung herself off the lounge. She raced barefoot across the patio, jerked open the screen door, and rushed through the kitchen to the wall phone. She snatched up the handset. 'Hello?'

'Who's this?' A male voice. Familiar.

'Vicki. Alice can't come to the phone, right now. Would you like to leave a message?'

'Hi, Vicki.' Suddenly, too familiar.

'Melvin?'

'Thought you might be there. How you doing?'

I *was* doing just great. 'Okay. I wish you'd stop over at the clinic and pick up your car.'

'I got no use for it. You go ahead and keep it.'

'I don't want it, Melvin. Honest. I appreciate your gesture. It was very thoughtful, but please.'

'You don't like it? You want a different kind?'

'There's nothing wrong with the car. I just can't accept a gift like that – not even as a loan. Okay? So if you'd just take it away again, I'd . . .'

'I can't. You've got the keys.'

You dropped them down my dress.

'Do you have another set?' she asked.

'Nope.'

'Okay. Then I'll drop the car off at the station.'

'I'm home. You wanta bring it here?'

'I can't do it now, anyway. I'm pretty busy right now. I'll just take it to the station sometime, maybe tomorrow or Monday. Okay?'

'Okay.' He sounded disappointed. 'Vicki?'

'Yes?'

'I'm sorry. I only just wanted to help. I figured you could use a car, you know? I wasn't trying to cause you no trouble. Guess I messed up, huh?'

'No, you didn't mess up.'

'Are you mad at me?'

'No. You were just being nice. I understand that. I just can't go around accepting gifts like that.'

'From me.'

'From anyone. Don't put yourself down, Melvin.'

416

'Why not? Everybody else does.'

'I've really got to go, now. Have a nice evening.'

'You, too.'

'Bye.' She hung up, slumped against the wall, and muttered, 'Why me, Lord?'

Hearing the water shut off, Vicki went to her bedroom. She picked up her robe, sat on the edge of the bed, and wondered what to do about Melvin.

The car business wouldn't be the end of it.

What next? Would he send flowers, ask her for a date?

She wanted nothing to do with him, damn it. But she didn't want to hurt his feelings. God knows, he'd spent his life getting dumped on.

Through the doorway, she saw Ace leave the bathroom. A towel was wrapped around her head. Another, tucked together between her breasts, hung down just far enough to cover her groin.

'Save me any hot water?' Vicki called, rising from the bed and stepping into the hall.

'I took that shower so fast I hardly got my butt wet.'

'Why the hurry?'

'I got me a powerful thirst.'

'Did you hear the phone?'

'One of my myriad admirers?'

'Melvin.'

'No shit?' Grinning, she leaned sideways against the door frame. 'He's tracked you to your lair.'

'You may think it's funny.'

'I think it's love.'

'You'd be smirking out the other side of your face if it was *you* he had the hots for.'

'I wouldn't be smirking at all, hon, I'd be barfing.'

Vicki leaned against the wall, the robe draped over her forearm, and stared at Ace. Ace stared back. Her grin slipped away. 'So what're you gonna do?'

'I don't know.'

'You scared?'

'A little, I guess.'

'Never should've been nice to him. That was your first mistake. You take a loser like that and treat him nice, you're asking for it.

You can afford to be nice to somebody normal, a normal guy isn't gonna blow it all out of proportion and fall in love with you and get crazy. A guy like Melvin, you've gotta either ignore him or treat him bad. That's the only way to play it safe.'

'Yeah, well the damage is already done.'

'Tell me about it.'

'What'll I do?' Vicki asked.

'Tell him to fuck off.'

'I can't do that.'

'Want me to do it for you?'

'No.'

'Don't want him mad at you.'

'It's not that, exactly.'

'I know. You feel sorry for him. That's what got you into this.'

'But how do I get out of it?'

'Short of moving out of town? Well, I know something that worked for me. There was this guy, Blake Bennington. You wouldn't know him, he showed up while you were in med school. A real yuck. He came into the shop one day and I sold him a swimming suit and I thought I'd never see the end of him. Talk about a royal pain. He wouldn't leave me alone. The more I told him to fuck off, the more he wanted to fuck *me*. I just couldn't get rid of him.

'There's this *thing* about guys like that. They think they're in love with you, but they aren't. What they love is their *idea* of you. And that just grows if you keep your distance from the guy. So what you've got to do is get up-close and personal. Shatter the image.

'What I did, I finally let Blake take me out. We went to the Fireside Chalet. I tell you, he thought he'd died and gone to heaven. We're both sitting there in our fancy duds, drinking and having lobster tails, the way he looked at me, you'd think I was Venus or something. So then about halfway through the meal, I laid this gorgeous fart.'

'Oh, no,' Vicki said.

'During dessert, I kind of casually started picking my nose. I actually got out a pretty good-sized booger and wiped it on the edge of my plate. He kept glancing at it. Couldn't keep his eyes off the thing.

'He was down, but not out. He went ahead and took me to his apartment after dinner. He tried to get me out of my dress, and I told him I didn't think he'd better because, after all, my skin rash might be contagious.'

'Gawd,' Vicki said.

'And I told him that even if it *wasn't* contagious, I was pretty embarrassed and didn't want anybody to see my runny sores. And besides which, it was my time of the month and did he really want blood all over everything?'

'Sounds like you laid it on a little thick.'

'He got pretty depressed. We both drank more and more. Finally, I threw up on his coffee table.'

Vicki shook her head.

Ace grinned. 'All this apparently had a subtle but profound effect on the fantasies he'd built up around me.'

'Subtle.'

'He never asked me out again. In fact, he seemed to go out of his way to avoid me.'

'And you think I should try something like that with Melvin.'

'Just a thought. It's a tried and true method. And it's a way to get rid of him without wounding his pride. You don't tell him to take a hike, he decides he *wants* to take a hike. Perfect solution to your little dilemma.'

Vicki pushed herself away from the wall. 'Know something, Ace?'

'Plenty.'

'You're crazier than shit.'

Ace laughed. 'I might be crazy, but I got rid of the guy. Think about it.' She headed for her room.

While Vicki took her shower, she did think about it. She knew she couldn't pull off such stunts as Ace had described. Even if she had the guts, her sense of dignity wouldn't permit it.

But Ace had a good point about idealising.

Melvin doesn't know me. If he thinks he's in love, or something, it's because of fantasies. The more I try to avoid him, the more he'll probably want me.

Spend some time with him?

Ugh!

When she finished her shower, she put on shorts and a T-shirt and joined Ace in the kitchen. Ace had already prepared a batch of margaritas in the blender. The glasses were rimmed with salt, waiting for her arrival. Ace gave the blender another buzz, then filled the glasses with the frothy cocktail.

They went out to the patio and sat at the table.

Vicki sipped her drink. 'Delicious.'

'*And* good for you.'

'I've been thinking about what you said.'

'Gonna barf on Melvin?'

'Hardly. God, I don't really want to do this, but it makes sense.'

'What? Spell it out, Einstein.'

'Meet with him. Not to gross him out, or anything. But I can see a couple of ways it could help. For one thing, it's bound to put a crimp in his fantasy life if he spends some time with the real me.'

'Except the real you is so adorable.'

'Right. I know I'm wonderful, but I bet I don't live up to his image, whatever that might be.'

'Especially if you cut the cheese.'

'The other thing is, even if he isn't turned off by a dose of my adorable self, it still ought to take some of the fuel out of the fire. Just because of access.'

'You gonna give him *access*?'

'People mostly desire what they can't have.'

'Right. Go to bed with him.'

'The more I try to avoid him, the more he'll need to be with me. It's like roots. If a plant isn't getting enough water, its roots keep growing longer and longer.'

'Christ. You go away to school, you come back deep. Roots, for godsake.'

'You know what I mean.'

'Right. You don't want Melvin's root growing longer and longer. So what's the plan?'

'Meet him someplace in public. Have a couple of drinks with him. Just socialize for maybe an hour or so. With you along for moral support.'

'Oh, good. I'd hate to miss it.'

'How about the Riverfront Bar? Tonight?'

'That's about as public as you can get.'

They drank up, and went into the kitchen. While Ace refilled their glasses, Vicki checked the telephone directory. Melvin was listed.

Ace stood there, watching as she dialled.

Through the earpiece, Vicki listened to the ringing. She felt a little breathless. Her heart was pounding, her stomach knotted. After the sixth ring, she began to hope he wasn't home.

Maybe this isn't such a hot idea, she thought.

Maybe try it for another night.

Like next month.

After the tenth ring, Melvin answered. 'Who's this?'

'Vicki.'

'Vicki?' He sounded amazed. 'Hi!'

'I was thinking about the car.'

'Yeah. You wanta keep it?'

'No, but I thought you might want to pick it up. Ace and I are going to be at the Riverfront Bar tonight at about ten o'clock. Why don't you stop in, we'll have a couple of drinks, and I'll give you the keys. Then you can stop by the clinic later on and take the car home with you.'

'Have drinks with you?'

'Sure. It'll give us a little chance to chat.'

'Gosh.'

'Okay?'

'Sure. Sure. Ten o'clock?'

'Right. See you then, Melvin.'

'Sure. See you then.'

Vicki hung up. She let out a deep, trembling breath. 'I must be crazy,' she muttered.

Ace handed a glass to her. 'Crazy, but smart. It may work. Or it may not. Either way, you'll have the joy of knowing you brought joy, however fleeting, into the otherwise drab existence of that young, adoring, demented, shit-for-brains dork.'

Chapter Fourteen

Melvin whistled as he prepared his hamburger.

Whistled 'Everything's Coming Up Roses'.

He couldn't believe his good fortune. Only two nights ago, he had resurrected the dead. Now, this. Vicki had actually invited him out for drinks.

Giving her the car had been a bright idea, after all. Though she was apparently too shy to accept such a gift, she appreciated the offer of it. This was her way of thanking him.

Melvin didn't know how he could stand to wait for ten o'clock.

He turned his hamburger over. Grease sizzled and snapped on the skillet.

It's not *all* coming up roses, he told himself. He wasn't real happy about going into the Riverfront Bar. At that hour on a Saturday night, half the assholes in Ellsworth would be drinking in there.

Nor was he exactly delighted that Ace would be sitting in on the festivities. She wasn't an asshole. She was okay, he supposed. Still, three's a crowd.

If only he could be alone with Vicki, someplace private.

But this was a start. This was a *great* start.

Melvin draped a slab of sharp cheddar over the top of his burger, and put the lid on the skillet. While he waited for the cheese to melt, he spread mayonnaise over his bun. He picked up a knife and was about to saw off a thick slice of red onion when he thought, what am I, nuts?

Onion breath on his first date with Vicki?

No way.

Not that she's gonna kiss me, he told himself.

But maybe she will. Who knows?

He took the lid off the skillet. The cheese had melted and run down the sides of the burger. He slid a spatula under the patty, and lifted it over to his bun. He pressed the top of the bun down on it. Then he turned off the stove, picked up his plate, and sat down at the table.

Patricia, sitting there, smiled at him and stuffed a wad of raw ground beef into her mouth. There wasn't much left of the half pound he'd set in front of her before starting to cook the burger for himself.

Eats like an animal, he thought. Nothing but uncooked meat, and of course there was the jar of bat blood in his laboratory. She'd gulped that down the first night. He doubted that she'd had an appetite for such things before he killed her. It was like the biting, somehow connected with having been dead.

As Melvin ate his hamburger and watched her, a drop of pink juice fell from her chin, joining the other stains on the white front of her T-shirt. The spots were in the middle between her breasts.

Melvin could see the dark of her nipples through the thin shirt.

He never would've guessed he'd get tired of looking at a naked woman, especially one as attractive as Patricia. But there was just so much to see, and seeing it constantly – not to mention 'playing' with her to the point of exhaustion – had finally started to bore him. So he'd given her the shirt this morning and told her to wear it. She obeyed.

Melvin hadn't expected the shirt to turn him on. It was intended simply to spare him from always seeing her naked. But the way he could sort of see through it, the way it took on the shape of her breasts and moved with them, and how it almost wasn't long enough . . . He found a whole new joy in watching her.

They had spent most of the day cleaning house. *Patricia* cleaned, Melvin supervized. House-cleaning was wonderful. It required a lot of motion: walking, reaching, bending, kneeling. The T-shirt bobbed and swayed, and rose and fell mere inches like a stage curtain controlled by a tease. He loved it. He watched, but didn't touch. Finally, unable to stand it any longer, he went ahead and took her. On the carpet of the upstairs hall. With the vacuum cleaner still running, humming beside their heads. He made her keep the T-shirt on. He'd been in such a frenzy that he didn't take time to tape her mouth, and she gave his shoulder a nasty bite. Worth it, though. Out of this world.

He watched Patricia stuff the last of the raw meat into her mouth. Juice dribbled down her chin, spilled onto the shirt.

She was mostly obedient except for the biting. It seemed that she simply couldn't control it.

Can't go on this way, he thought.

Two days, and he already had four bites on his shoulders, another on his upper left arm. Once, she'd come very close to opening his throat.

She always did it to him when he was about to go off, and was too distracted to stop her. The sudden pain of the bites never failed to push him over the edge. He had incredible orgasms. They weren't half as good the few times she didn't bite.

In spite of that, he knew that he couldn't go on letting Patricia sink her teeth into him every time they screwed. The pain of the wounds lasted a long time after the ecstasy was over.

And the wound worried him. In those Romero movies, a single bite from the living dead was enough to turn *you* into one. He tried to convince himself that was a pile of shit, but he couldn't quite get the idea out of his head. Besides, even if that was shit, he knew for a fact that the bites weren't doing him any good. Like Vicki had said, human saliva's a regular cesspool of bacteria.

The antibiotics he'd been taking for the bite on his hand should help with the others, maybe keep him from getting infected, but still . . .

Try screwing her right after she's eaten?

Could try it now, and see if she bites.

But he didn't feel like it. He would be seeing Vicki in just a few more hours.

If he used the method on Vicki, would she turn out the same as Patricia? He didn't especially want that to happen.

Too soon to tell, though.

The smart thing was to try it with a few others, see how it goes, before taking a chance with Vicki.

Maybe they can bite each other, he thought, and smiled.

Patricia smiled back. She lifted her T-shirt, baring her breasts, and used the shirt to wipe her wet lips and chin. 'Do you want to play?' she asked.

'Let's watch television.'

She nodded. She seemed to like television almost as much as playing.

They went into the living-room and sat together on the couch. He gave the remote to Patricia. She spent a while changing channels, then settled for a rerun of *Gilligan's Island*.

Melvin gazed at the show. He didn't even try to pay attention. He imagined how it would be tonight with Vicki. Whenever his mind returned to the present, he glanced at the red numbers of the digital clock on the VCR. How could time possibly pass so slowly?

The shows changed. He fidgeted. He watched the clock.

Finally, it was eight-thirty.

He squeezed Patricia's leg. 'Stay here,' he said. 'I've gotta take a shower.'

'I'll come with you.'

'Stay here.'

She gave him a pouty look, then turned her eyes to the television.

Melvin went upstairs. In the bathroom, he hung his robe on the door. He stood before the mirror and watched himself remove the bandages. His hand was looking better. The swelling and inflammation had gone down. The newer bites on his arm and shoulders didn't appear infected.

But they burned like flaming oil when the hot spray of the shower splashed onto them.

Gritting his teeth against the pain, he shampooed his hair and lathered himself with soap. He was rinsing when he glimpsed a vague, moving shape through the plastic curtain. *Psycho*. Goosebumps crawled up his back. The curtain skidded open and of course it was Patricia standing there, not Norman's mother with a butcher knife.

'Damn it!' he snapped.

She lowered her head as if ashamed. 'I missed you, Melvin.'

'Go downstairs.'

'Don't you like me any more?'

'I like you to obey me.'

She sobbed. She raised her face. Her eyes shimmered with tears.

Melvin sighed. This possessive business was almost as bad as the biting. In a way, it was nice, but . . .

'I'll go,' she said. She turned away. Melvin saw the way the T-shirt curved over her buttocks. He felt a stir.

'Okay,' he said. 'Come on back. Get in here, but leave your shirt on.'

She faced him, grinning, and stepped into the tub. Melvin slid the curtain shut. He stepped back and watched. Patricia seemed to know what he wanted. She stood beneath the spray, turning slowly. As the T-shirt became wet, it hugged her skin and became nearly transparent.

He rubbed her through the fabric. She reached up and held onto the shower arm and smiled at him through the spray. He peeled the shirt up above her breasts. The water made her skin shiny and slick. His fingertips traced the Face of Ram-Chotep, the stitches cross-hatching the Mouth. She squirmed as he slid a hand between her legs. He kissed her nipples, licked them, sucked.

Before he took her, he stuffed his washcloth into her mouth.

Shortly before ten, Vicki and Ace entered the Riverfront Bar. It was dimly lighted, hazy with cigarette smoke, noisy. People spoke loudly to be heard over the juke box blaring Waylon Jennings. Glasses and bottles clinked. Pool balls clacked together on the two tables at the far side. Beeps and jingles came from a row of electronic games.

Vicki spotted many familiar faces on her way across the floor: strange grown-up faces that resembled kids she hadn't seen for nearly a decade, others that looked just the same as she remembered them from all those years ago, several she'd seen during her more recent visits to town, and a few she'd come to recognize during the past week. She didn't spot Melvin. Nor could she find the man from the playground by the river. Some of the people noticed her, nodded a greeting or simply looked perplexed as if they couldn't quite place her. Ace said 'hi,' to some friends, but didn't stop to chat.

They found a deserted booth along the wall. Vicki scooted across the seat and motioned for Ace to slide in beside her. That way, Melvin would have to sit across the table.

'Let's try and get rid of him fast,' Ace said. 'Then maybe we can scrounge up a couple of guys, get something going.'

Vicki shrugged. She was in no mood to scrounge up anyone. She didn't like the smoke or the noise. She would just as soon leave when the meeting with Melvin ended.

A barmaid came. No one Vicki recognized. She wore blue jeans shorts and a pale blue T-shirt printed with 'I'm a Good Sport – I Scored at Ace's.' Her shirt was the same as the one Ace wore.

426

'What'll it be, gal?' she asked.

'Let's have a pitcher of Blatz and three mugs.'

'Comin' right up.' She rushed away.

'That's Lucy. She's from the Bay. Married Randy Montclair.'

The name seemed vaguely familiar to Vicki. Then she remembered. He used to pal around with Doug. Both of them, royal pains. They'd hoisted Henry into a trash bin after school, one day. And Randy was the one who gave Melvin those whacks, just a week before the Science Fair. Vicki, ticked off, had shoved him or hit him or something to make him stop. She wondered, now, if that little show of gallantry may have been what started Melvin liking her. Maybe she had Randy to thank for her present problems with the guy.

Lucy brought the pitcher and mugs to the table. Vicki paid her. While Ace was filling the mugs, Melvin appeared.

'Greetings,' he said. He scooted over the seat until he was directly across from Vicki. He brought a sweet, cloying aroma with him as if he'd been drenched in after-shave.

'You're looking dapper,' Ace said, and poured him a drink.

He wore a shiny Hawaiian shirt and a pink sports jacket. His black hair was slicked straight back. Maybe the smell, Vicki thought, came from hair oil.

Ace slid the mug to him. He winked at her. Then he grinned at Vicki. 'You look real nice,' he said. His gaze wandered down. Vicki had worn a dark plaid blouse, long-sleeved and too heavy for the weather, chosen solely to prevent Melvin from getting even a hint of what was underneath. But the way he looked at her, it might've been transparent. She had an urge to finger the buttons just to make sure they all were fastened. His stare made her feel squirmy. He rubbed his lips with the back of his bandaged hand.

The bandage was fresh and white, as if he'd put on a new one for the occasion as part of dressing up.

'Well,' Vicki said, 'I might as well give you the keys.'

'If you're sure.'

She took them from her purse and pushed them across the table. He put them into a pocket of his jacket.

Vicki lifted her mug. 'Well, here's looking at you.'

They all drank.

'So whatcha been doing with yourself?' Ace asked him. 'Resurrected anyone lately?'

Vicki cringed.

Melvin grinned and bobbed his head. 'Oh, I gave that up. They taught me better in the funny farm.'

'You sure sparked up that Science Fair,' Ace said.

'That's what I had in mind.' He hunched over the table, leered at Ace, then at Vicki. 'Like I told Vicki, I only just did it to give the finger to all the assholes.'

'Guess you managed that, all right.'

Vicki wished they would change the subject. On the other hand, she was rather glad that Ace was sparing her from having to make conversation.

'So how'd you pull it off, anyway? You sneak into the bone orchard and dig her up?'

'Sure. Took a lot of digging, too.'

'You did it at night, I guess.'

'The Wednesday before the fair.' He seemed to enjoy talking about it. He kept grinning and nodding. 'The graveyard gate was chained. I had to get through that with a hacksaw. Then I just snuck in and started digging.'

'Weren't you scared?'

'I didn't wanta get caught, you know. But I weren't scared of no ghosts or stiffs, if that's what you mean.'

'How'd you get her out of the coffin?'

Vicki rolled her eyes.

'Had a pry bar along. It was easy. The hard thing was hefting her up.'

'Dead weight,' Ace said.

'Jesus,' Vicki muttered.

Melvin chuckled. 'She wasn't just skin and bones, you know. She had a build on her.'

'Shit, yes,' Ace said. 'Her tits alone must've weighed in at twenty pounds each.'

'I wouldn't know about that. All I know, she was tough to lug around.'

'If you'd waited a year or two, she might've been easier to carry.'

Melvin laughed with a mouthful of beer and sprayed it back into his mug.

428

'So, did you carry her all the way home?'

'No, no. Would've herniated myself. What I did, I put her in the trunk of my car, then went back and filled in the hole. Didn't want anyone catching on, you know.'

'Yeah, that would've ruined it.'

'Wanta hear a good one? I almost forgot her head. Yeah. See, I left it sitting on this tombstone while I worked on filling up the hole. Then my hands were full, what with the shovel and pry bar and everything. I got back in the car and drove halfway home before I remembered about her head.'

'Dumb you.'

He chuckled. 'Yeah, but it was still there when I went back for it. Hadn't walked off.'

'Or rolled,' Ace added, 'as the case may be.'

'This is really revolting,' Vicki muttered.

Melvin grinned at her.

'So then you took her home with you?' Ace asked.

'Kept her in the basement. My folks, they never went down there. Then Friday night, I drove over and broke into the Center. Had my stuff all set up before sunup, and had the door open and everything by the time people started coming along to set up for the fair.'

'You sure put a lot of effort into your project,' Ace said. 'I tell you, me and Vicki didn't go to half the trouble you did. And I bet they didn't even give you a blue ribbon.'

'Gave me a straitjacket, that's what they did.'

'And well-deserved, too.'

Melvin laughed. He shook his head and wiped his mouth and took another drink of beer.

'Lucy didn't bring us any peanuts,' Ace said. With that, she got up and left.

Oh, great, Vicki thought. She leaves me alone with him. That wasn't part of the deal. Hell, there was no deal. But she knows how I feel about Melvin.

Maybe that's *why* she left. Figured the encounter'll do me more good if she's not here like a security blanket.

No, she just wants peanuts.

Vicki managed a smile. 'How's your hand doing?' she asked.

'Oh, it's getting better. I got a real good doctor.'

'I see you changed your bandage.'

'Took a shower tonight.'

There's a pretty picture.

'Do you ever think about that movie, *Psycho*, when you take a shower?'

'I try not to,' Vicki said.

'We had this gal at the funny farm, they couldn't get her to take a shower. That's 'cause she saw *Psycho* when she was like ten years old. She'd get real ripe after about a week. Then they'd take her into the shower room, a couple of orderlies, and you'd hear her screaming.' With his left hand, Melvin picked up the pitcher. He filled his mug with beer, then poured more into Vicki's mug. 'My mother, she never took showers. She took baths. Do you like baths?'

'Yeah,' she said. 'I do both.'

Great. His mind's on bathing.

'My mother, she used to shave her legs in the tub.'

How does he know that?

He tipped his head to one side and grinned. 'Do you shave in the tub?'

'That's none of your business, Melvin.'

His grin slipped away. 'I'm sorry. Didn't mean to make you mad.'

'Why don't we talk about something else?'

Where the hell is Ace?

'What did you do today?' she asked.

'Oh, cleaned house.'

'That's a huge house. It must be a real chore, having to keep it up.'

'Oh, it's not so bad.'

'You haven't been working at the station?'

'Doctor's orders. I guess I'll go back next week, maybe. Or maybe not. I kinda like staying home.'

Out of the corner of her eye, Vicki noticed someone approaching the table. She turned her head, expecting to see Ace with a bowl of peanuts.

It was Dexter Pollock with a mug of beer.

'Mind if I sit?'

Before she could respond, Dexter slid in beside her. 'That's Ace's seat,' she said.

'Ass won't mind. She's over gabbing with some folks.' He glanced across the table at Melvin, then looked at Vicki. 'You must be hard-up, keeping company like this.'

'Why don't you get out of here,' Vicki said.

'I didn't get a chance to tell you goodbye. Guess I was away when you took your stuff out. I would've lent you a hand.'

'I didn't need a hand. We had some local movers take care of it.'

'We? You and Melvin?' He squinted across the table. 'She move in with you, lover boy?'

Melvin's face flooded with scarlet.

'You're one lucky fella,' Dexter told him. 'She's a nice piece of ass.'

Vicki felt a rage growing inside her.

Melvin glared at Dexter. 'You don't say shit like that.'

'Aw, isn't that sweet.' He smiled at Vicki. 'You got yourself a regular knight in shining armour, that's what you got. Nutty as a nigger-toe, but he's sure full of chivalry. You ever notice, girl, you got a regular habit of attracting crazy folks? You got your bosom buddy, Ass, and now you got your lover boy, Melvin. Both of 'em mad as Hatters. How come you think that is? You got a *smell* or something, draws lunatics?'

She didn't trust herself to speak. She just stared at him.

'You better get outa here,' Melvin warned.

Dexter ignored him. 'Must be your aroma.' He leaned sideways. His shoulder pressed against her. He lowered his head, sniffing. 'Knew it. Seems to come from down farther.' He hunched down, still sniffing. The side of his face brushed against her breast.

Vicki grabbed his hair and jerked his head back and dumped her full mug of beer onto his lap. He gasped and flinched rigid. He stared at her, eyes bulging, mouth open. 'Why, you little cunt,' he muttered. Then he snatched up his own mug of beer and swung it at her. For a moment, Vicki thought he intended to smash the glass into her face. But it stopped short. The beer flew out, stinging her eyes, splashing over her face and ears.

As she wiped her eyes, Dexter snapped, 'Sit down, you fucking maniac. She had it coming.'

'You'll get it for this,' Melvin said.

'Oh, I'm trembling. I'm shaking in my boots.'

'What're you *doing*, you scum-fucking trash heap!'

Ace's voice.

Vicki stopped rubbing her eyes and looked. Dexter was on his feet, face to face with Ace. Almost face to face. She was three or four inches taller. 'I didn't do nothing,' he said. His voice sounded just a bit whiny, as if he were a schoolkid caught in a nasty act by his teacher.

'Looks to me like you pissed yourself.'

'Get out of my way.' He tried to step past her, but she blocked his way. 'I've got no business with you, Alice.'

'I saw what you did. Tell Vicki you're sorry. In fact, apologize to both of them.'

'You gonna make me?'

'I'm going to count to three, turd-face. One. Two.'

He whirled around. 'Okay, I'm sorry.'

'Buy us another pitcher.'

'I didn't *use* your beer, goddamn it!'

'That's not an issue. Just give me five bucks for another pitcher, and we'll forget this ever happened.'

'You're gonna push me too far, you overgrown . . .'

'Overgrown what?' Ace asked.

'Nothing,' he muttered.

Ace snapped her fingers. Dexter took out his wallet, removed a five-dollar bill, and handed it to her. 'Thanks,' she said. 'Now, get out of here.'

Dexter turned away and walked into the noisy, milling crowd.

Ace set the bowl of peanuts on the table. She bent over and used a napkin to wipe a few drops of beer off the red vinyl cushion, then sat down. Smiling from Melvin to Vicki, she cracked open a shell. She tossed a pair of peanuts into her mouth, chewed a few times, and said, 'Can't leave you two alone for a minute.'

'That dirty, toe-sucking pig,' Melvin said.

'Such language,' said Ace.

'You sure took care of him. He acted like he was scared of you.'

'That's 'cause he knows what I'm capable of.'

'I oughta kill him. Stuff he said to Vicki.'

'Well, if you kill Pollock, don't try and jump-start him. Just let him rot.'

'Yeah.'

'I want to leave,' Vicki told them.

'Come on, we've got to get another pitcher.'

'You stay if you want, I'm going home.'

'Do you have to?' Melvin asked, looking disappointed.

'Yeah. I've had enough fun for one night.'

Ace filled the pockets of her shorts with peanuts.

Vicki, Ace and Melvin left the Riverfront Bar together. On the sidewalk outside, Melvin said, 'I'm sure sorry he came along and ruined our time. But it was real nice, anyway. Maybe we can do it again, only I'll pay.'

'We'll see,' Vicki said. 'Goodnight.'

Chapter Fifteen

Dexter stuffed his damp trousers and boxer shorts into the dirty clothes hamper.

That damn bitch, she had no business dumping the beer on me. She's as crazy as her lunatic friends.

I was still chief, I'd run her in for it. See how she likes a night in the lock-up.

Dexter *could* have still been chief of the Ellsworth Police Department. That's what made it so galling. It was his own stupid fault. Nobody forced him out. He'd put in his thirty years and retired at age fifty-two, figuring there was no point in hanging onto a job when he didn't have to. Retirement had looked good. No responsibilities. No Minnie around any more to nag him. Plenty of income, what with the pension and the property. He'd have all the time in the world to do whatever he wanted: fish, play golf, drink, chase the women.

By the time he realized his mistake, it was too late.

He was used to folks turning nervous when he showed up. Watch out, here comes Pollock. Don't fuck with him. Step out of line, he'll bust your ass. They feared him. They respected him.

No two-bit slut would've dared dump a beer on his crotch.

Doctor Chandler.

Reaching into the closet, he unhooked a hanger and took out one of his uniforms. It was still inside a filmy plastic bag from the cleaners in Blayton.

Dexter always took his uniforms to Blayton or Cedar Junction to have them cleaned. If he had them done here in town, people might start to wonder.

He removed the plastic bag and stuffed it into the wastebasket. Then he got dressed: dark blue trousers; light blue shirt with its chief's shield and name plate on the chest, department patch on the shoulder; black socks and spitshined shoes. He strapped his gunbelt around his waist. He slid his nightstick into its ring on the belt, his .38 caliber Chief's Special into the holster. Last, he put on his police hat.

He swung the closet door shut, and stared at himself in the full-length mirror.

Damn, he looked fine.

And felt fine, too.

He'd been in his blues at the Riverfront, no way Chandler would've pulled any shit. Or Asshole, either. Five bucks for a new pitcher of beer.

And I gave it to her.

Not *me*, that other Pollock. She'd asked *me* for five bucks, she'd be one sorry bitch.

Dexter drew his nightstick. He raised its blunt head toward the mirror.

'Five bucks, huh?' he asked. 'How'd you like this shoved up your ass, Ass?'

Oh yeah?

'Yeah!' Club in both hands, he lunged and imagined himself ramming it into Ace's belly, saw her double over, fall to her knees. 'Still feeling tough?' he asked. He saw himself step behind her. With the end of his club, he flicked her skirt up. Her ass was bare. Of course it was. That's 'cause she mailed her fucking panties to Minnie. 'See how you like *this*,' he said, and shoved the nightstick into her anus.

In the mirror, he watched himself crouching, thrusting with the club. He could almost see it going in and out, almost hear Ace squealing.

He stood up straight. 'That takes care of you, I guess,' he told the area in front of his feet. He twirled the stick a few times by its leather thong, then slid it into the belt ring.

He spread his feet and planted his fists on his hips. He glanced at the mirror image of his jutting trousers, and smirked. 'See that, *Doctor*? It gets that way when someone pours beer on it.' He unzipped his fly and freed himself. 'How about licking it clean for me? Huh? You'll like that, won't you?' He slid his fingers around the engorged shaft.

The doorbell rang.

Dexter saw his face go red, his hands quickly trying to force his penis back inside the trousers. Wouldn't go. Heart slamming, he gave up and threw open the closet door. He snatched his robe off the hook and put it on. He tossed his police hat onto the shelf.

He shut the door. In the mirror, he saw that the robe hardly concealed the fact that he was wearing his uniform.

So, there's no law I've gotta open the door.

He glanced at the clock. Almost eleven. Who'd be ringing the doorbell at this hour?

Maybe one of the tenants.

It rang again.

Heart thundering, he hurried from his room. The leather of his gunbelt creaked as he walked. He fumbled inside the robe, got his shrunken penis back inside his pants and closed the fly.

At the door, he squinted through the peephole.

For just a moment, he thought that the young woman standing in the hallway was Vicki Chandler. Then, he realized she was a stranger. Blonde hair like Vicki, but not quite as pretty. She wore a white dress. What was she, a nurse?

The main thing, I don't know her, she doesn't know me.

She rang the bell again.

Dexter slipped his robe off and tossed it over the back of a nearby chair. He opened the door. 'What can I do for you?' he asked.

'Oh, you're a police officer?' She looked glad about that.

'Chief Pollock, ma'am. Is there some kind of trouble?'

'Well, not exactly, no.' She smiled, shook her head, and fingered the hair over her ear. The name tag over her left breast read, 'Patricia Gordon, R.N'. Her white dress had a zipper down the front. It was open enough to reveal a long V of bare skin that ended between her breasts. 'My car broke down,' she explained. 'I was hoping to find someone with a phone, so I could call and have my girlfriend pick me up. Do you have a phone I could use?'

'Sure do. Come on in, Patricia.'

'Thank you. You're very kind.'

He backed away from the door. She entered, and he swung it shut.

'Would you like me to take a look at your car?' he offered. 'What seems to be the trouble with it?'

'Oh, it just died on me.'

'I'd be happy to take a look at it.'

'No, that's all right. I'll worry about it tomorrow. If I can just use your phone.'

Dexter pointed at the telephone on the end table. Thanking him, Patricia sat down on the couch. Her white skirt slid partway up her thighs. She wore no stockings. Her legs looked very bare. She lifted the telephone onto her lap, picked up the handset, and dialled. Dexter took the nightstick out of his belt, placed it on the floor beside his easy chair, and sat down. He tried not to look at her legs.

Sighing, she shook her head slightly. 'Answering machine,' she said. She waited a few moments, then spoke into the phone. 'It's me, Patricia. The damn car broke down again. Call me as soon as you get back.' She checked the plate in the centre of the dial, and read off Dexter's number. Then she hung up. She placed the phone back onto the table. 'Do you mind if I wait?' she asked. 'I'm sure Sue will be back in just a couple of minutes. She probably just went out to buy some cigarettes. She does that all the time. Smokes like a fiend.'

'You're welcome to stay,' Dexter assured her. 'Could I get you something to drink?'

'No, thank you. But you go on ahead. Did you just now get off duty?'

Dexter felt heat rush to his face. He told himself there was no reason to be embarrassed – Patricia had no way of knowing anything. 'Just got back about five minutes before you showed up,' he explained.

'Neat uniform,' she said.

'Thanks. You look good in yours, too. So, you're a nurse. I haven't seen you around these parts.'

'I'm new in town.' Her gaze lowered. Dexter tried to remember if he'd zipped his pants. 'Have you ever shot anyone with that?'

He realized that her gaze was on the revolver.

'Sure. A few times.' He'd fired it many times while on duty over the years, but never *at* anyone. Mostly just in order to scare people shitless. Like drunks, teenagers making out.

'Have you *killed* anyone?'

'Just four times,' he said.

Patricia pursed her lips and blew softly, almost whistling. 'With that gun?' she asked.

Nodding, he patted the holster.

'Let me see it,' she said, patting the cushion beside her.

Holy Toledo, Dexter thought. Got us a live one, here.

He stood up, popped open the snap of the leather guard strap, and drew his revolver. He smiled at Patricia. 'Safety first,' he told her. He broke open the cylinder, dropped the cartridges into his palm, and snapped the cylinder back into place. Stepping toward her, he dumped the ammunition into a front pocket of his trousers.

He sat down on the couch and handed the revolver to Patricia. 'Ooh, it's so heavy.' Her fingertips caressed the six-inch barrel. She curled her fingers around it, slid them up and down the length of it.

Dexter felt himself getting hard as he watched her.

Moaning, she stroked her cheek with the side of the barrel. Her eyes were half shut. She eased herself backward against the cushion, and kept rubbing the revolver on her face.

Dexter shook his head. This was one strange gal. Comes in to use the phone and starts getting cosy with his sidearm.

Like some kind of hot dream.

She slid the muzzle into her mouth, way in, and started working her lips as if she were milking it.

'Jeee-zus,' Dexter murmured.

She slid the barrel out of her mouth. It came out wet. She turned her face toward him and made a lazy smile.

'Are you . . . all right?' he asked.

'Fine.' A mere whisper.

'Guess you sure like that revolver.'

'Yeah.'

'Maybe you ought to get one of your own.'

She smiled. She slid the barrel inside the top of her dress. Dexter saw its bulge moving under the fabric as she ran the barrel over her breast. 'It's so long and hard,' she whispered.

So am I, he thought. God, so am I.

Her other hand lowered the zipper a few inches. With the gun muzzle, she nudged the cloth aside, baring her breast. Her nipple was standing erect. She slid the barrel over it. The steel pressed it flat, then let it spring up again.

'I don't believe this,' Dexter muttered.

Slowly, she swung the revolver toward him. She touched the muzzle to his lips. 'Open up,' she said.

This is nuts.

He opened his mouth and felt the barrel glide in over his lips. Her thumb drew back the hammer.

Jesus, he thought. Good thing I unloaded it.

I *did* unload it, didn't I?

Sure.

Still, having the thing in his mouth like that made the skin go tight on the back of his neck.

Patricia said nothing. Holding the gun in his mouth with one hand, she used her other to unbutton the shirt of his uniform. She tugged at it, and he felt the tails pull up out of his trousers.

She unbuckled his gunbelt.

She unbuckled the belt of his trousers, opened the waist button, and drew the zipper down. He felt himself spring out. Then he felt her fingers.

Man alive, what a gal!

Then the gun was no longer in his mouth. Patricia tossed it. It landed on the coffee table, skidded across a couple of magazines and dropped to the floor.

She went down on him.

Holy fucking Toledo! Dexter threw back his head and spread out his arms and held onto the back of the couch.

She comes in to use the phone.

She takes my gun in her mouth.

She takes *me* in her mouth.

God, what did I do to deserve this?

He moaned and writhed as Patricia's mouth slid up and down, as she sucked.

He'd had head before.

Never like this.

'Oh babe,' he moaned. 'Oh babe!'

Then, he shrieked.

Chapter Sixteen

'At the top of the local news, retired Ellsworth Police Chief Dexter Pollock was brutally slain last night in his Fourth Street apartment.'

Vicki lurched rigid. Coffee sloshed from her mug and splashed the floor between her feet. She stared at the radio.

'A tenant residing in the building, Perry Watts, discovered the grisly scene when he returned from a party shortly after midnight, and noticed that the victim's door was ajar. Mr Watts immediately notified the authorities. Responding officers found the retired chief dead at the scene, the apparent victim of multiple wounds. The nature of the murder weapon has not been disclosed.

'Patricia Gordon, a registered nurse in the employ of Blayton Community Hospital, is being sought for questioning in connection with the murder. Miss Gordon, herself previously thought to have been a victim of foul play, had last been seen when she left the hospital at the end of her shift Thursday night. Her abandoned car was found Friday on Harker Road, three miles east of Cedar Junction. An extensive search failed to reveal any clue as to her whereabouts.

'According to Chief Ralph Raines, who assumed the position of Ellsworth Police Chief following Pollock's retirement, "We have substantial evidence that the missing nurse, Patricia Gordon, was present in the victim's apartment at the time of the murder. Anyone with knowledge of Miss Gordon's whereabouts should contact the authorities immediately. She may be armed, and should be considered extremely dangerous."

'The WBBR news team will keep you informed on all further developments in this shocking and tragic situation. In Ellsworth, today, the Antique Fair continues . . .'

Vicki wiped the coffee off the floor, and left the kitchen. She walked down the hallway to Ace's room. Ace was sprawled on the bed, her face sideways on the pillow, the top sheet down around her feet, her nightshirt halfway up her back. The skin of her legs and back was pink from yesterday's long exposure to the sun. The skimpy seat of her bikini had left a stark white triangle on her rump. Vicki lifted the sheet and covered her.

She sat on the edge of the bed. Blonde hair hung over Ace's face. A few strands were caught in the corner of her mouth. Vicki brushed the hair aside. Ace didn't wake up.

The clock on the nightstand showed 8:05.

Maybe I should let her sleep, Vicki thought. No. She can spend the rest of the day sleeping, if she wants, but I've got to talk to her now.

She gently shook Ace's shoulder, heard her moan, saw an eye open slightly. 'Wha . . . ?'

'Dexter's been killed.'

She raised her head.

'I just heard it on the radio. He was murdered last night.'

'Holy shit.' Ace rolled onto her back. A wrinkle on the pillow had pressed a red, scar-like crease down the right side of her face. 'Murdered? *Our* Dexter?'

'Yeah.'

'Melvin do it?'

'They seem to think it was some nurse. The one who disappeared a few days ago.'

'They get her?'

'They're looking for her.'

'Oh, weird.' She struggled against the mattress, sat up

and leaned back against the headboard. 'Let me have some of that.'

Vicki handed the mug to her. Ace took a few swallows, and sighed. 'That nurse, they figured she'd been nailed by some roving nut-case.'

'I know. Dexter, he'd warned me . . .'

'His little morning lectures . . .'

'Yeah, about the disappearances. Then the latest missing gal turns up in his apartment and kills him. At least, they *think* she killed him.'

'Melvin sure as hell threatened to kill him last night.'

'Is it just a coincidence?' Vicki asked.

'I wonder what makes them think it was the nurse.'

'They found something in the apartment. It sounded as if they're pretty certain she's the one who killed him.'

'Be nice if it *was* Melvin. They could put him away, he'd be outa your hair.'

'It doesn't sound too likely.'

'Maybe he's in on it with the nurse.'

'Oh, sure.'

'You sound like you don't want it to be Melvin.'

'We just shouldn't jump to conclusions,' Vicki said.

'A, he's nuts. B, he threatened to kill Dexter. C, Dexter got murdered. That doesn't sound like jumping to conclusions. Not to me, it doesn't.'

'So how'd he get the nurse to do it?'

Ace shrugged, and drank some more coffee.

'You know how Dexter warned me about all those missing gals?' Vicki asked. 'Suppose *he's* the one who was doing it?'

'Our own local Ted Bundy?'

'Maybe he's the one who abducted the nurse. Maybe kept her tied up in his apartment, or something. Last night, she got loose and killed him. You know, to save herself.'

'Big problem with that theory, Watson. She would've run straight to the cops.'

'Well . . .' Vicki realized that, if she thought about it, she could probably come up with several reasons why the nurse might *not* have run to the cops after killing Dexter. He'd been a cop himself, after all, and . . . That would be stretching it, though. Ace was right. If the nurse had been his prisoner, she would've gone for help the moment she escaped.

'You honestly don't think Melvin had anything to do with it?' Ace asked.

'God, I hate to get him involved if he's innocent.'

'If he's innocent, I'll eat my shorts.'

'I guess we should tell the police what we know, huh?'

'Yer durn tootin'.'

'Oh, boy,' Vicki muttered. 'I've never done anything like that. What do we do, just walk into the station?'

'Hell no. Let them come over here.'

Vicki wrinkled her nose. 'Okay. I guess I'll . . . what, just call them up and . . . ?'

'You want me to do the calling?' Ace asked.

She felt enormous relief. 'Well, I could do it, but . . . Yeah, you want to?'

'Why not.'

'You're a pal. Thanks.'

'Don't thank me, buy me a Ding-dong.' She gave the mug to Vicki. 'I'll call right now, before we come to our senses.' She tossed the sheet aside. Vicki stood and turned toward the door. 'Think I'll try Joey Milbourne at home. Let him get the glory.'

In the kitchen, she checked her address book and dialled. Vicki refilled the mug with coffee. 'Hello, Iris? It's Ace. Joey there? . . . He was? That's great. That's what I want to talk to him about . . .' Ace rolled her eyes. 'No, I didn't call to get the gory details. I *know* something about it. Vicki and I were *with* Pollock last night . . . Fine, you don't want to wake him up, I'll call the station and somebody else can be the one to break the case wide open. I'm sure Joey will thank you for it.' Covering the mouthpiece, Ace whispered, 'Twat.' Then, she nodded. 'Yes, why don't you.' Again, she covered the mouthpiece. 'Going to see if he's awake. He was at Dexter's last night. She's gonna check and see if the phone woke him up.'

Ace took her hand away. 'Morning, hot stuff. Sorry I woke you, but I thought you might want to trot over here and inter-rogate me and Vicki Chandler. We were with Dexter at the Riverfront last night at about ten-thirty and we *know something* . . .

Yes, about the murder . . . Half an hour's fine. See you then, sport.' She hung up. 'You might want to check this guy out.'

'I remember him.'

'He's a hunk. You could do worse.'

'Who's Iris?'

'His mother.'

'He lives with his *mother*? He must be at least thirty-five.'

'Closer to forty.'

'He's that age and lives with his mother, he's got problems.'

'So, who doesn't?'

Vicki ignored that. She filled a mug for Ace, then headed for her bedroom. She had showered after her morning run, and was wearing her robe. She changed into white jeans and a yellow blouse, and went into the living-room to wait for Joey's arrival.

A hunk. Pollock's murdered and we're planning to finger Melvin and Ace is playing matchmaker. The guy lives with his mother, no less. Last thing I need.

Ace came into the room. She was barefoot, wearing paint-spattered cut-off jeans and a baggy sleeveless grey sweatshirt.

'I see you dressed to impress the hunk,' Vicki said.

'Don't want to steal your thunder, hon.'

'Oh, thanks.'

'You could do worse.'

'How come *you're* not after him?'

'I've had my turn.'

'What's wrong with him?'

'Nothing.'

'I'll bet.'

'He's not my type.'

'Oh, but you think he's mine?'

'As we say in the sportswear biz, can't hurt to try it on for size.'

'As we say in the doctor biz, bend over and spread 'em.'

Ace snorted.

A few minutes later, Vicki heard the faint thud of a car door shutting. Then came the quick sound of footsteps on the walkway, then the doorbell. Ace opened the door. The man who entered was as tall as Ace. His light brown hair was cut short, and he had a neatly trimmed moustache. Vicki could see why Ace considered him a hunk: his face was tanned and handsome; his white knit shirt hugged bulging muscles and a flat belly. He looked tightly packed into his faded jeans.

Vicki remembered him as a baby-faced beanpole. He'd grown the moustache and apparently taken up body building since she last saw him.

'Joey, you remember Vicki Chandler?'

'Of course. Vicki, I hear you're working with Charlie Gaines over at the clinic.'

'Just started last week,' she said. 'How are you doing?'

'I could've used a couple more hours of sleep.'

'You'll be glad I woke you,' Ace told him.

'I actually require eight hours to function at top form, so I'm two hours short.'

'Better take a load off before you collapse.'

He arched an eyebrow at Ace. Then, he sat at the other end of the couch and crossed a leg over his knee, which must've been painful in those tight jeans. He rested a clipboard against his upthrust leg. 'Now,' he said, 'I understand that you two were with Pollock last night.'

'At the Riverfront,' Ace said. 'We were there with Melvin Dobbs.'

'What on earth for?'

'He seems to have the hots for Vicki.'

Joey looked at Vicki. The eyebrow went up again.

'I'm not encouraging it,' she explained.

'I wouldn't. He's an odd bird. So, the four of you were drinking at the Riverfront.'

'The three of us,' Vicki said. 'Me, Ace and Melvin. Then Ace left the table to get some peanuts . . .'

'Salted in the shell,' Ace added.

'You should be careful of salt,' Joey said. 'Bad for the cardio-vascular system.'

'While she was away, Pollock showed up and started bothering us.'

'Bothering you how?'

'I'd been a tenant in his apartment building, but he kept pestering me so I moved out. He wasn't very happy about that.'

'Pestering you how?'

'By being his normal lecherous self,' Ace said.

444

'He'd stop me in the hall, make crude remarks, that sort of thing. Supposedly trying to warn me about running early in the morning. He seemed to think I was asking to get myself assaulted.'

'Which is probably what *he* wanted to do,' Ace suggested.

Joey frowned at her. 'The man's dead.'

'That doesn't make him suddenly a saint.'

'His point may have been well taken. There have been several incidents, recently, of attractive young women disappearing without a trace.'

'Like the nurse who turned up at Pollock's last night?' Ace asked.

'I think we're straying from the point here,' Joey said. He looked at Vicki. 'So you were drinking with Dobbs, and Pollock showed up and began bothering you? What time was this?'

'About ten-fifteen, ten-thirty.'

'And his behaviour was abusive?'

'I'd say so, yes.'

'Was he alone?'

'He seemed to be.'

'Did you notice anyone in the establishment wearing a nurse's white dress?'

'No. Not that I saw.'

'Me neither,' Ace said.

'So how does this tie in with the subsequent murder?'

'Melvin threatened to kill him,' Ace said.

Both Joey's eyebrows shot up.

'I *thought* that might get your attention.'

'Exactly what did Dobbs say?'

' "I oughta kill him." '

Vicki nodded agreement. 'Those were his exact words.'

Joey wrote on his clipboard. 'And by "him", he was referring to Dexter Pollock?'

'No, Eddie Rabbit. Of *course* he was referring to Pollock. Why do you think we're telling you this?'

'So, both of you heard him threaten Pollock's life between ten-fifteen and ten-thirty last night?'

'That's right,' Vicki said. 'But we were all upset with Pollock. I poured some beer on him, myself.'

'Why was that?'

'He was getting cute. The thing is, he was being a jerk and Melvin's remark seemed pretty normal, under the circumstances. I could've said the same thing, myself.'

'But you're not a lunatic who'll go out and *do* it,' Ace pointed out. 'What transpired after the altercation?'

'Ace and I went home.'

'What about Dobbs?'

'He left the bar when we did. Right after we got rid of Pollock.'

'So the three of you left the Riverfront together.'

'At about ten-thirty or so.'

'And went directly home – here?'

'Here.'

'What about Dobbs?'

'He came with us and we had an orgy.'

Joey narrowed his eyes at Ace. 'We're talking about a murder investigation.'

'So sorry.'

'Melvin didn't come with us,' Vicki said. 'We don't know where he went afterwards.'

'Was Pollock still in the tavern when you left?'

Vicki looked at Ace. Ace shrugged. 'He might've still been there.'

'I didn't see him leave,' Ace said.

'You both came directly here after leaving the Riverfront? Did either of you leave the house again last night?'

'What, are *we* suddenly suspects?' Ace asked.

'I'm just asking.'

'We watched TV,' Vicki said, 'until about one o'clock. Then we went to bed.'

'Anything else to add?'

'That's about it,' Ace told him. 'So, you going over to question Melvin?'

He slipped his pen under the clamp of the clipboard. 'I'm not sure there's any reason to bother Dobbs about this.'

'What, it doesn't matter that he threatened to kill Pollock?'

'We already have a suspect in this.'

'The nurse,' Vicki said.

'What makes you think she's the one who killed him?'

'Physical evidence at the scene.'

'Such as?'

'I'm not at liberty to reveal the details of our investigation.'

'Bug-squat.'

'I will say that we found a dress in Pollock's apartment. The name tag identified it as belonging to the suspect.'

'So did she leave starkers?'

Joey shook his head.

'Couldn't her dress have been planted to mislead you?' Vicki asked.

'By Melvin, for instance,' Ace said.

'We have some indications that the perpetrator was a female. And we should be able to confirm, today, that it was actually Patricia Gordon who inflicted the wounds. Once we've checked her dental charts . . .' He stopped abruptly and looked annoyed.

'She bite him?'

'I didn't say that.'

'Of course you didn't.'

'Damn it.'

'We won't say anything,' Vicki told him.

'I would appreciate that.'

'If this nurse disappeared Thursday,' she asked, 'how did she end up in Pollock's apartment?'

'We have no idea.'

'He hadn't been . . . keeping her?'

'It occurred to us. But we found nothing to indicate that she'd been there for any period of time.'

'The earlier theory was that she'd been abducted?'

'That's what we'd assumed. It followed the pattern of the other disappearances, at least until she turned up last night and killed him.'

'Don't you think that's pretty strange?' Ace asked.

'Everything about this is strange.'

'But you're pretty sure,' Vicki said, 'that Pollock isn't the one who abducted her, and maybe kept her tied up or something, and she killed him to escape?'

'We didn't find any ropes in the apartment. His handcuffs were in their case on his utility belt. We didn't find anything that looked as if it might've been used as a gag. There weren't any drugs in his apartment that he might've used to render her unconscious. So it certainly doesn't appear that he was keeping the woman against her will. From the latent prints we found, it doesn't even look as if *anyone* had been in the apartment except Pollock.'

'So where was she since Thursday night?' Ace asked.

'When we find her, we'll ask.'

'Maybe you'll find her at Melvin's house,' Vicki said.

Joey looked at her and hoisted an eyebrow. 'You're thinking that Dobbs abducted her Thurday night, kept her, and sent her over to Pollock's last night to make good on his threat?'

'It's occurred to us,' Vicki said.

'Pretty far-fetched. What do you think Dobbs did, hypnotize her?'

Vicki ignored his sarcasm.

'Possibly,' she said. 'I understand it's widely believed that a person can't be forced under hypnosis to do something she would otherwise consider abhorrent, but there are ways around that problem. If the subject is given an acceptable rationale for the behaviour . . .'

'Like he told her Pollock is a ham sandwich,' Ace elaborated.

'I might as well get going,' Joey said. 'This isn't getting us anywhere.'

He started to rise.

'No, wait. Keep out of it for a minute, would you, Ace? This is serious.'

'It's starting to sound pretty half-assed, even to me.'

'Melvin actually *might* have kidnapped that nurse and hypnotized her into killing Pollock for him. If he was able to convince her that Pollock was a threat, that maybe he intended to rape or murder her, then that could provide a sufficient motive to allow her to justify using violence against him. It's been done. I read a case study in a psychology journal that described *exactly* that . . .'

'It didn't go down that way,' Joey said. 'Gordon didn't behave like a gal defending herself. She went well beyond anything that could've possibly been justified by the kind of hypnotic suggestion you're talking about. The savagery . . . You have no idea. And I'm not about to enlighten you.'

'Okay. Suppose we forget the hypnosis angle. What if Melvin was with her in the apartment? Maybe he had a gun, or something, and forced her to attack Pollock.'

Joey shook his head. 'I already explained there was no indication that anyone else was present. Besides, if he was there, why didn't *he* simply shoot Pollock, or whatever, rather than force the woman to do the killing?'

'I don't know. He might've had some sort of weird reason.'

'What I think this boils down to,' Joey said, 'is that Dobbs made a casual remark last night in the heat of anger – a remark that you yourself said was fairly normal under the circumstances – and Pollock just happened to be killed a couple of hours later. From what you've told me, I might just as easily suspect you as Dobbs. After all, you were upset enough to pour beer on Pollock.'

'You could at least go over to Melvin's house and ask him about it.'

'Did anyone other than you and Ace hear his threat against Pollock?'

'I doubt it.'

'I could go over there. I could probably even get a search warrant on the basis of what you told me. Not that I think I'd find anything. But I could do that. And Dobbs would know exactly who put me onto him. Do you want that?'

'Not especially,' Vicki admitted. She'd realized Melvin would probably find out that she and Ace had told on him, but she had pushed the knowledge aside, not wanting to confront it. Hearing her suspicions confirmed by Joey gave her a bad feeling in the stomach.

'I'd be out there in a minute if I thought you were onto something,' he explained. 'But I frankly just don't see how Dobbs could've possibly been involved in this. The nurse killed Pollock. It's as simple as that. The only thing I'd accomplish by confronting Dobbs would be to make him extremely put out with you and Ace. I really can't imagine you want to have someone like him mad at you.'

'We could live with it,' Vicki said.

'On the bright side,' Ace told her, 'it might put a damper on his affection for you.'

Joey's eyebrows went up again. 'I hope you ladies didn't bring me over here because of your own personal problems with Dobbs. Get the cop to roust him . . .'

Vicki felt her face go red. 'Just forget it. We told you what we

449

had to tell you. If you don't want to follow up on it, that's your business.'

'Better go home and catch up on your beauty sleep,' Ace told him. 'Sorry we bothered you.'

Now, his face was red. 'Maybe I spoke out of line . . .'

'I'd say so,' Vicki said. 'We didn't ask you over here to cause trouble for Melvin. He threatened to kill Pollock and we felt we had a duty to report it. That's all. And if you don't think it's relevant, fine. Don't do anything about it. No skin off our noses. In fact, it's a relief.'

'I just don't think . . .'

'We know,' Ace said.

Sighing, Joey rose to his feet. 'If anything else comes up,' he said, 'don't hesitate to contact me. I mean that. But I honestly need more than an idle threat before I can go barging in on someone. This is America, after all. Freedom of speech is guaranteed by the Constitution.'

'Thanks,' Ace said. She gave Vicki a look of concern. 'I guess we'd forgotten that. What fools we've been.' She got up and walked to the door and opened it. 'Thanks for coming by, officer. And thank you for reminding us that we live in a country where personal liberty is thus cherished.'

Shaking his head, he left the house.

Ace shut the door. 'Freedom of speech my lily-white ass.'

'Some cop,' Vicki muttered.

'About as useful as a limp dick.'

'If I were a cop, I'd hot-foot it over to Melvin's with a search warrant.'

'You sound like you're convinced.'

'Oh, yeah,' Vicki said. 'In fact, I don't see how Melvin could've been involved. It *doesn't* make sense. But I'd go out there, regardless. I'd check him out. I'd search his house. I'd want to make sure the nurse *isn't* there. What kind of a cop is Milbourne, anyway?'

'The kind that has a yellow streak up his back. He knows damn well he oughta go out there. He's just too chicken-shit to do it. The question is, are we?'

'You're kidding. You couldn't drag me over to Melvin's. Besides, if the cops can't be bothered . . . It's their job, after all. We did our part.'

'You just want to forget about it, then?'

'I'm not about to play Nancy Drew.'

'Might be fun.'

'Yeah. Like a sharp stick in the eye.'

'You could give Melvin a call, ask him out for a picnic or something. I'm sure he'd be delighted. While you keep him busy, I sneak into the house and have a look around.'

'Great idea. I only see two problems. One, I'm not about to take Melvin on a picnic. Two, what if the nurse *is* in there and kills your butt?'

'We both know she isn't, of course.'

'Right. So what's the point?'

'Good point. Never mind. Let's go over to Blayton, check out the shopping mall, and take your folks out to dinner.'

'Yeah!'

Chapter Seventeen

Thelma's VW bug was in the clinic parking lot Monday morning. So was Charlie's white Mercedes. The red Duster was gone.

Thank God.

With the car gone, the gift taken back, Vicki felt as if Melvin might be receding from her life. It was too much to hope that she was rid of him entirely. But the car had been a link that was now broken.

And yesterday, he'd neither called nor put in an appearance. Of course, Vicki's spent the afternoon and evening in Blayton, so he might've tried while she was away.

Going an entire day without any contact from Melvin, however, made her feel encouraged.

She was very glad that Joey Milbourne had refused to see him about the threat. She and Ace had done the right thing, telling him, if only because they both would've felt guilty keeping the knowledge to themselves, but the more she'd thought about the situation, the more certain she was that Joey had been wise not to act on it. Obviously, Melvin hadn't been involved in Pollock's death. Confronting him about it would've made things messy, and for no good reason.

Very messy, she thought. Melvin would think we'd stabbed him in the back. And he'd be right.

Just have to hope he never finds out we told.

Don't worry, he won't.

Now, if I can get through today Melvin-free. That'll be two days in a row.

With a last look at the empty space in the parking lot, Vicki turned away and entered the clinic. The waiting-room was deserted. Thelma, behind the reception window, raised her head and smiled. 'Morning,' Vicki said. 'Have a nice weekend?'

'Oh, it was too short, I'd say. Aside from that . . . we went to the Antique Fair yesterday. Jim paid good money for a beat-up old Roy Rogers lunch box, which didn't set too well with me, but he said he had one just like it when he was a kid so what the hell. Men are such children, more often than not. Isn't it something about Dexter Pollock?'

'Terrible,' Vicki said. She'd been feeling pretty good. Not any more.

'Lord only knows why that gal did him in,' Thelma said, 'but I bet she had her reasons. Wouldn't surprise me at all, they find out Pollock was up to no good with her. I always figured, if he lived long enough and didn't mend his ways, one gal or another would up and do him in. In my younger days, I had a couple of occasions to slap him down, myself. 'Course, I never killed him. But I might've, I'd had a gun handy. I suspect, if they ever nab that nurse, there're plenty of folks hereabouts who'd like to pin a medal on her. They'd have to stand in line behind yours truly.'

'Well,' Vicki said, 'I wasn't especially fond of Pollock, myself. I doubt if he deserved to get murdered, though.'

'I suspect he deserved it, all right. But it's a shocking thing, anyhow, I guess, that kind of bloodbath happening here in our own town. You want to go in and see Charlie? He said he wanted to see you first thing.'

Vicki felt a small flutter of concern. 'Do you know what it's about?'

Thelma shook her head. 'No idea. But he's got Jack Randolph with him.'

'Who's Jack Randolph?'

'A lawyer.'

Oh, God. What's going on?

Her heart pounded as she stepped through the waiting-room doorway. She walked slowly down the corridor toward Charlie's office.

A lawyer. *Malpractice?* That seemed unlikely. She hadn't seen anyone with a major problem last week. Complications were always possible, of course. But if somebody had a problem . . .

She knocked on the door of Charlie's office. 'Come in,' he called.

She opened the door. Charlie smiled at her from behind his desk. In spite of the smile, he looked confused for just a moment as if he didn't recognize her.

'You wanted to see me?'

The confusion seemed to clear. 'Vicki? Indeed I did. Have you met Jack Randolph?'

'No, I . . .' As she stepped into the room, the man rose from his chair beside Charlie's desk and smiled at her.

'Dr Chandler,' he said.

She knew she was staring at him. She knew she was blushing, that her mouth was hanging open.

The man from the playground. Who'd watched her from his perch atop the slide. Who'd been there the next day, on a swing, as if waiting for her. Who'd shown up, even in one of her nightmares, only to be shot off the slide by Dexter Pollock. Or was it Melvin? She couldn't remember.

'Hello,' she managed.

'Nice to see you again,' he said.

'Oh,' Charlie said, 'you've met?'

'Briefly,' Jack told him.

'Well, good, that's fine. Jack's an attorney, Vicki.'

'Is there some kind of problem?'

'No, no,' Charlie said. 'Take a seat.'

She sat on the chair in front of his desk. No problem, he'd told her. That was a relief, but she still felt confused and tense. And strangely excited by the presence of the man from the playground. She watched him sit down on the other chair.

What's he doing here? she wondered. It must have something to do with me. How did he know where I work?

'Vicki,' Charlie began, 'I've given some thought to your position here. I find that you're an extremely valuable asset, and I'd like to think that you'll stay here in town and possibly even take over the clinic after I'm gone.'

After I'm gone.

He looked the same as usual: his white hair neatly combed, his face ruddy, his blue eyes bright. But Vicki remembered how he'd seemed a bit confused when she first opened the door. 'Are you okay, Charlie?' she asked. 'Is something wrong?'

'No, no.' He waved a hand as if dismissing the thought, then scratched his stomach. 'I suspect I've got a few good years left in me yet. But I am getting on, Vicki. I've spent my life looking after the folks of this town, and I'd like to see you stay here and take over the clinic after I'm gone.'

There, he'd said it again.

'I don't have any plans to leave,' Vicki told him.

'Well, that's good to hear. The thing is, I want to make it worth your while to stay on.' He scratched himself again. 'I'm asking you to be my full partner here at the clinic.'

'Geez.'

'Is that a yes?' Charlie asked.

'Well . . . yes. Of course. I'm just so shocked . . .'

'We'll be fifty-fifty partners.'

'God. I . . .'

'Jack will draw up the papers today.' He looked at Jack. 'And I want you to put in there that Vicki will assume full ownership upon my death.'

Vicki frowned. 'I'm very grateful, Charlie, but . . . Are you sure you're all right?'

'Fit as a fiddle.'

'This is too much. I don't deserve to have you just *give* me your practice.'

'I want it to be in your capable and caring hands. I wouldn't want to trust it to a stranger. I've spent my whole life caring for the folks of this town, and I wouldn't want to see it all fall apart after I'm gone.'

That's three.

He looked at Jack. 'You'll write all that up and have it ready for my signature this afternoon?'

Jack nodded.

Scratching his stomach, Charlie smiled at Vicki. 'There's also the matter of the loan. Let's just call that a gift.'

'Charlie, you can't . . .'

'Sure, I can. No arguments, now.' She saw a tiny speck of blood appear on the front of his white shirt over the place where he'd been scratching. 'You were a young lady with promise, and I always hoped you'd turn into a fine doctor and come back here to take up for me. Lending you that money was just my way of hooking you back. Now that you're here, we'll just forget about it.'

'That's *twenty-five thousand dollars*, Charlie.'

'I've got no use for it, anyway.' He looked again at Jack. 'Maybe you can put that down on paper, too. Make it official that I'm cancelling out the IOU.'

'Fine,' Jack said.

'Charlie. I . . .'

'Now, I won't hear any more arguments from you or I just might change my mind.' He scratched his stomach again. Now, the front of his shirt was marked by a thread of blood nearly an inch long.

'You're bleeding, Charlie.'

'Am I?' He looked down. 'So I am.' He sounded amused. 'Scratched the scab off, I suppose. Those pesky rose bushes. I was pruning them yesterday. Those thorns are treacherous.'

'Would you like me to have a look?' Vicki asked.

'Lord, no. It's nothing.' He slipped a finger inside his shirt, rubbed, took it out and glanced at the smear of blood on his fingertip. Then he licked it. 'I do suppose I'd better head home and fetch a clean shirt.' To Jack, he said, 'Can you have the papers ready for my signature by, say, five o'clock?'

'No problem,' Jack said.

'Fine. I'll be here waiting. You can go on about your business, now, Vicki. I'm delighted to have you as a partner.'

'Well, thank you. Thank you very much, Charlie.'

'My pleasure.'

As she rose from her chair, Jack smiled at her. 'I'll see you later, Dr Chandler.'

At a quarter past five that afternoon, Vicki was at her desk reviewing records from Blayton Memorial about the rotator cuff repair surgery on a patient she would be seeing tomorrow for a follow-up examination. She was having a hard time concentrating. All day, her mind had been drifting back to the incredible meeting in Charlie's office.

She still felt dazed.

A year or two down the road, it might've been different; she had hoped to be offered a partnership, eventually. But not this soon. Not after she'd been here a week. It seemed outlandish, unreal.

Wonderful, but troubling. What could've prompted Charlie to make such a momentous decision so suddenly?

And to cancel the debt?

Vicki had to believe that something was gravely wrong with him. All that talk about 'after I'm gone'. Almost as if he'd just found out he had a terminal illness. He'd claimed to be perfectly fine, but she just couldn't believe it.

He'd seemed cheerful, though.

Someone knocked on her office door. 'Yes?'

The door swung open and Jack Randolph stepped in. 'I have the partnership papers for you to countersign.' He came to her desk and handed the stapled packet to her. 'After you've looked them over, if you'll initial the bottom of each page and sign the final page.'

Vicki stared at the top sheet and shook her head. 'What do you know about all this?'

'Well, the agreement indicates that you'll take a four-thousand-dollar draw each month. At the end of each fiscal year, you'll receive a fifty per cent share of any profits. You'll also assume that portion of any debts incurred by the partnership.'

'Debts?'

'It's nothing to be concerned about. I had an opportunity to look at the books, and the clinic is in fine shape financially.'

'Do you think I should sign?'

'I sure would, if I were you.'

'Why's he doing this? It's so sudden. I just don't understand.'

'You suspect some ulterior motive?'

'Did he say anything to you . . . about his health?'

'Nothing that you didn't hear.'

'It seems so weird. As if he thinks he might be dying, or something.'

'I don't think you should be too concerned about that. Certainly not on the basis of his decisions this morning.'

'Why would he do it, though?'

'I've seen similar behaviour quite a few times with people who come in to have their wills drawn up. They suddenly get an urge, feel they absolutely have to do it right away. Sometimes, it's because they just had a close call of some kind and they suddenly realize they aren't going to live forever. Maybe a friend has just died unexpectedly. Or they're going in for surgery and have a premonition they won't survive it. Sometimes, it's as simple as having a birthday. All of a sudden, they can't let another day go by without having a will. But it's nothing to worry about. Just human nature. I think Dr Gaines suddenly woke up this morning and realized he'd better make you a partner before a safe falls on his head.'

'I hope that's all it is.' She felt at least a little relieved by Jack's explanation. 'Did he seem all right to you?'

'Maybe a bit confused about a few things. Nothing that struck me as especially odd. But I don't know the man. You're probably a better judge of whether . . .'

'You don't know him?' Vicki asked.

Jack shook his head. 'He phoned me this morning. Said he picked my name out of the yellow pages. Which makes it very interesting that I'm here, since he might just as easily have chosen a different attorney. Enough to make a person wonder about such things as fate. I've been wanting to see you again, Dr Chandler.'

All she could manage was, 'Oh?'

'We didn't have much chance to get acquainted, last time.'

'Yeah, I'm sorry about that. You kind of caught me at a bad moment.'

'I'm sure it must've been a shock, realizing you weren't alone.'

'I didn't expect to find someone sitting on top of a slide at that hour. That's for sure. You do it often?'

'Once in a while. I'm an early riser.'

Vicki found herself smiling. 'So you like to leap out of bed and hot-foot it to the nearest playground?'

'Oh, I take my time. I just wander around and sniff the morning and listen to the silence. It's a nice time of the day. I guess you know that. It's one of the reasons I'd like to know you better.'

'Well . . .'

'If you have a fellow waiting at home for you, or . . .'

'No. At least I *hope* not.'

He gave her an odd look.

'It's nothing.'

'How would you feel about having dinner with me tonight? Your new business arrangement calls for a celebration, and the Fireside Chalet seems like just the place for that kind of thing. What do you say?'

'Best offer I've had all day.' All month, she thought. All year. 'Sure,' she said. 'I'd like that.'

'Great. I'll hot-foot it home and make the reservations. Does eight o'clock sound good?'

'Fine.'

She scribbled Ace's address and telephone number onto a prescription pad, tore off the sheet and gave it to him. 'Can you read that?'

'Your handwriting's pretty good, for a doctor.'

'I'm still new at it.' She glanced down at the agreement papers.

'No hurry about that,' Jack told her. 'You should take your time and read it carefully before you sign. Just give it to Dr Gaines before you leave, and keep a copy for yourself.'

'All right.'

'See you at about a quarter till eight?'

Vicki nodded. Jack, backed away, smiling, a look on his face as if he couldn't quite believe his luck. 'Well, see you,' he said.

'See you.'

He went out the door.

Chapter Eighteen

Melvin and Patricia were in the living-room watching television when the doorbell rang. The clock on the VCR read 9:01. 'Now, that's prompt,' Melvin said. 'Wait here.'

Patricia stayed on the couch, but watched over her shoulder as he went to the door. He peered through the peephole. 'It's all right,' he told her. Then he opened the door.

And staggered back as Charlie Gaines threw himself forward and wrapped his arms around Melvin.

'Hey, hey, cut it out,' he said, patting the man's back.

Charlie squeezed him hard.

'Come on, let go, now.'

Charlie released him. Melvin shut the door and locked it. When he turned around, the doctor was wiping tears from his eyes.

'What's wrong?'

'It's nothing. I'm all right. You won't make me leave again, will you?'

'Depends.'

'I did everything like you told me.'

He took Charlie by the arm and led him to the couch. Charlie sat down in the middle. As Melvin sat beside him, Patricia scurried around both of the men and squeezed in between the end of the couch and Melvin. She put her arm across his shoulders. Melvin slid a hand up her bare thigh and under the draping tail of the big blue police uniform shirt she had worn away from Pollock's apartment. 'Charlie and me, we've got stuff to talk over. So just sit quiet.'

Though her eyes looked troubled, she nodded.

Melvin started to take his hand away as he turned toward Charlie. Patricia grabbed his hand and stopped it. 'Let go,' he said in a firm voice.

Pouting, she released his hand.

He faced Charlie, and found the man scowling at Patricia. 'Did you make sure nobody followed you here?'

'I checked very carefully.'

'Good. Were there any problems?'

'No problems at all.'

'Vicki didn't put up a fuss about you giving her the partnership?'

'She suspected I was ill.'

'Shit, you're not ill, you're dead.'

Charlie laughed. 'If this is dead, I don't know what I was worried about all those years.'

'She went and signed the papers, though?'

'Sure did.'

'Where did you leave them?'

'Exactly where you told me to.'

'In the top drawer of your desk?'

'That's right.'

'And you took care of the loan?'

'I did. She tried to talk me out of that, but I told her just what you said and she acquiesced.'

'How much was the debt?'

'Twenty-five thousand dollars.'

Wouldn't even take a car from me, Melvin thought, but didn't bat an eyelash over twenty-five grand and a partnership from the old doctor.

'How'd you find out how much it was?' he asked.

'Thelma gave me the books.'

'Did she suspect anything?'

'Thelma? No, I don't believe she did.'

'And you didn't say anything about me, did you?'

'To Thelma?'

'To anyone.'

'No. Nary a word.'

'What about the lawyer. Did he give you any trouble?'

'He was just fine. He took care of everything.'

Melvin leaned back. Sighing, he put a hand on Charlie's leg, a hand on Patricia's. 'Well,' he said, 'it sure looks good.' To Charlie, he said, 'Did Vicki seem real happy about the whole thing?'

'She appeared more confused and worried than happy.'

'Well, it must've been a pretty big surprise. I guess she'll be real happy once it all sinks in.'

'I don't know how come you wanted to bother,' Patricia muttered.

'None of your business.'

'You've got me. I don't see why...'

'Don't give me any of your shit, or I'll lock you up.'

'Are you planning to revivify Vicki?' Charlie asked.

'None of *your* business.'

'In my personal opinion, it would be a grand plan. After all, she's a lovely young lady.'

Melvin smashed an elbow into Charlie's side. 'Don't you even *think* about her that way.'

He hung his head. 'I'm sorry. I didn't mean to suggest anything untoward. However, it doesn't seem especially fair to me that you should have Patricia and yet I'm without a woman.'

'You're an old man.'

'There may be snow on the roof, but I assure you there's still plenty of fire in the—'

'You're not getting Vicki, so forget it, you old fart.'

'Perhaps a different woman, then. I would certainly be appreciative.'

'This ain't a fucking *dating service!*'

'I'm sorry. It was only a suggestion.'

'Keep your suggestions to yourself.'

'Yes. I will. I'm sorry.'

'Stay here and watch the TV,' Melvin told him. He squeezed Patricia's leg. 'Come with me.'

She gave Charlie a look of triumph, then stood and followed Melvin upstairs. He led her into the bedroom. Her shirt was already unbuttoned. She plucked open his robe, pressed herself against him, and pushed her tongue into his mouth as her hands roamed his back and rump. Soon, he eased her away. 'Get in bed.'

She let the shirt fall to the floor. Its badge hit the carpet with a soft thump. She climbed onto the bed, crawled to the middle, and lay down. Gazing at him, she licked her lips. She caressed her breasts, pulled at the nipples.

'Stop that.'

She folded her hands beneath her head.

'Now, go to sleep.'

'You want to play, don't you?'

'Maybe later.'

'Oh, come on.'

'I have stuff to do.'

'With Charlie?'

'Yeah.'

She frowned and pushed her lips out.

'I'll be back in a while.'

'I bet you're gonna play with Charlie.'

'Fat chance.'

'Sure.'

'I'm gonna kill him.'

That brightened her up. 'Honest?'

'Yep.'

She nodded, smiling, then frowned again. This time, she looked confused rather than pouty. 'He's dead already. How can you kill him when he's dead already?'

'I'll figure a way,' Melvin said.

Though the problem had been lingering in the back of his mind since he first came up with the scheme to use Charlie Gaines, he'd been too busy to worry about the details of how he might go about rekilling the man.

The first order of business had been abducting Charlie. That turned out to be easy with the help of the revolver Patricia had taken from Pollock. He'd simply hiked over to Charlie's house last night, knocked on the door and stuck the gun in his face. The man offered no resistance, since he didn't want to be shot. He drove his car. Melvin sat in back with the muzzle pressed against his head.

Then came the killing of Charlie. He got him down into the basement and held the cocked revolver in his face while Patricia strapped him to the table. Then he suffocated the old man with cellophane. Simple. No problem at all until Patricia climbed onto the table, all set to bite his neck. A whack on the ear put a stop to that.

Then came the matter of bringing him back. That took Patricia's mind off biting him. She was probably so fascinated by the process because she realized that she'd gone through the same treatment, herself. She'd actually begged to help, so Melvin allowed her to chew the Root of Life and tongue the messy glop into the stomach gash. Then he let her do the stitching. Why not? She was a woman, after all, so she'd likely had more experience than Melvin when it came to needles and threads. She did a fine job of it, too. She acted happy and proud while she worked. Only after Charlie revived did she start getting moody.

Training him came next. Since he woke up with amnesia, the same as Patricia, it took all night to prepare him for Monday's tasks. He'd been a quick learner, but Patricia had made a constant pest of herself. Starting with snide remarks about Charlie. 'I don't think he's so special . . . He's awfully old and ugly . . . He's not very smart, is he?' Melvin ignored her, so she tried being seductive. She stripped and tried a variety of poses. She caressed herself, pulled at herself. When Melvin failed to respond, she found a pair of scissors. That was the last straw. Though Melvin didn't want to be bothered, he didn't care to have Patricia mutilate herself. So he took the scissors away, led her up to the bedroom and wasted a precious hour appeasing her. Then he locked her in the room and returned to Charlie.

By eight o'clock in the morning, Charlie seemed ready. Melvin studied the telephone directory, chose a lawyer, and listened while Charlie made the call. An answering machine took the message to meet Charlie at the clinic at nine.

Finally, Charlie drove away. Melvin, exhausted and unwilling to endure another confrontation with Patricia, staggered up to his parents' bedroom and fell onto their king-sized bed. He slept until mid-afternoon, when he was roused by shouts and pounding from his own room.

He found Patricia breathless and blubbering, her face streaked with tears. In her tantrum, she had raked herself with her fingernails. Her thighs and belly and breasts were lined with weals and scratches, some bleeding. A thread of blood had leaked from a corner of the Mouth of Ram-Chotep as if the ancient deity had snaked and dribbled. Her right forearm was tooth-torn and bleeding.

He had left Patricia alone several times before. Sometimes, he returned to find her asleep. Other times, she was weeping. But she had never done anything like this.

'Are you nuts!' Melvin blurted. He drew back a fist, but she looked so pitiful that he couldn't bring himself to strike her. Instead, he eased the sobbing girl against him and held her. 'It's all right,' he murmured.

'You don't love me any more.'

'Yeah, sure I do.'

'You've got *him*, now.'

'I don't care about him.'

'You didn't . . . come back all night.'

'I'm here. You shouldn't go hurting yourself like that.'

'I couldn't . . . help it. You locked me in.'

'I can't be with you all the time. There's a lot of stuff I've gotta do.'

She kept on crying and clinging to him. Melvin stroked her hair. Then, he lifted her and carried her into the bathroom. They stood together beneath the shower. As Melvin gently soaped her wounds, she stopped crying. She peeled the sodden bandages off his shoulders and chest, kissed his bite marks, slid the soap over them, then ran the slippery bar down his body. Staring into his eyes with a look that seemed both solemn and a little shy, she lathered and fondled him.

'I love you so much,' she said.

'I love you, too,' he told her. Watching the spray bounce off her hair and shoulders, seeing the look in her eyes, feeling the slick glide of her hands, he almost believed it.

When they finally went downstairs, it was late afternoon and Melvin's stomach was growling. He knew he'd better start thinking about ways to rekill Charlie, but the old man wasn't due back until nine. So he threw a frozen pizza in the oven for himself. When it was ready, he took a T-bone steak from the refrigerator and gave it to Patricia. He began to eat his pizza. Patricia unwrapped her steak over a plate, then wrung it out like a washcloth. When the plate shimmered with a puddle of red juice, she poured it into a wine glass. She sipped it while she dined. She used a napkin frequently to dry her chin. She was starting to become very tidy about her meals, as if making an effort to improve her manners. When she finished, her blue police shirt was still spotless.

It had crossed Melvin's mind, after dinner, that he should go down to the basement and search the Magdal book for a way to rekill Charlie. But he simply hadn't felt like it. The task of studying the book seemed like too great a burden. So he took Patricia into the living-room and turned on the television and didn't stir from the couch until the doorbell rang.

Now, it was Charlie watching TV. Standing beside the bed, Melvin wondered just how he *would* go about rekilling the man. Just go ahead and do it, he told himself. It'll probably be as easy as it was to kill him in the first place.

'Why don't we just shoot him?' Patricia suggested.

'It has to look like an accident. I think I'll take him out in his car.'

'I can come with you, can't I?'

Here we go again.

'I'd like to let you,' he said. 'The thing is, you've gotta stay inside. The police are looking for you because of the Pollock murder.'

She seemed to shrink with gloom.

'Don't start carrying on, honey.'

'You're going to leave me again.'

'It won't take long.'

'Oh, sure.'

Melvin sat on the edge of the bed. He slid a hand up her leg, feeling the hard ridges of scabs from last night's tantrum. 'If you don't want me to go,' he said, 'I won't.'

'Really?'

'Honest.'

She beamed at him.

'Charlie will have to stay with us, though. That okay with you?'

Her smile faded. 'I don't want him here.'

'Me neither. But I'd have to take him somewhere to get rid of him, and I can't do that without leaving you alone for a little while.'

She seemed to ponder the problem for a few moments. 'How long would you be gone?'

'Half an hour, maybe.'

'That isn't so long.'

'I'd be back before you knew it.'

'Do you have to do it now?'

'I guess not.' He glanced at the clock beside the bed. Nine-thirty. It really was too early. He'd wanted to take care of it right away, get it finished, but there would be far less risk if he waited. The ideal time would be two or three o'clock in the morning.

He didn't know if he could wait that long.

But the longer he put it off, the better.

'I don't have to go for a while,' he said.

'Don't go till after I'm asleep, okay?'

'Okay.'

Patricia rolled over, reached to the nightstand, and snatched up the roll of masking tape. She tore off several strips. She pressed them across her mouth.

Chapter Nineteen

Jack took her by the arm and led her toward his car. 'Thank you so much,' she said. 'Dinner was wonderful.'

'My pleasure. I haven't had such a great time in . . . oh, days.'

'Jerk.' She bumped him gently with her elbow.

'If I'd said "years", you might have thought I was smitten.'

'Smitten?'

'Smote?'

'But you're not?'

'Actually, I am. But I'm not about to admit it.'

He opened the passenger door for Vicki. She climbed in and leaned across the seat to unlock the driver's door for him. Starting to fasten her safety harness, she considered going without it and sitting in the centre, close to Jack. But if she did that, she might appear too eager.

Let him make the first moves, she thought.

Jack had made it clear during dinner that he found pushy women disagreeable. 'I'm all for equal rights,' he'd said. 'I'm all for women having careers if that's what they want. But so many of them these days have this obnoxious "take-charge" attitude that drives me up the wall. It's as if they see everyone else as a competitors and need to keep the upper hand.'

'You prefer your women meek and submissive?' Vicki had asked, in sympathy with his complaint but feeling obliged to put in a word on behalf of the home team.

'I prefer them like you.'

'And how is that?'

'Aside from all your more obvious attributes, you possess the wonderful, rare quality of being able to laugh at yourself.'

'So, you like clowns.'

'I like people who don't take themselves too seriously. My impression of you is that you see life as an adventure, not as a war.'

'Uh-oh, there's a fine distinction.'

'An adventure may be fairly similar to a war in its day-to-day events and hazards . . .'

'Like running, ducking, getting your butt shot off . . .'

'Right. But the difference is in a person's attitude. The warrior sees everything as a battle to be fought and won. The adventurer sees it all as experiences – exciting or scary or funny or sad. The adventurer is moving toward a goal, the warrior toward a conquest.'

'So you prefer the Amelia Earharts of the world as opposed to the Joan of Arcs?'

'Right.'

'They both went up in smoke.'

Jack managed to swallow his mouthful of wine in time to avoid spraying it across the table when the laughter burst out.

Vicki found out later that he'd been married to an attorney who'd decided that having children would put a crimp in her career, only to become pregnant due to a faulty IUD. She terminated the pregnancy against Jack's protests, and Jack had divorced her. Which explained a lot.

'You haven't told me much about yourself,' Jack said as he drove out of the restaurant's parking lot.

'What would you like to know?'

'Have you ever been in jail?'

'Would my ten years on a chain-gang count?'

'What were you in for?'

'*Man*slaughter.'

He looked at her through the darkness. 'Have you been married?'

'Not yet.'

'How many proposals have you turned down?'

'What makes you think there were any?'

'You're fishing for compliments.'

'Three proposals,' Vicki said.

'But you were determined to finish your schooling and embark on your career . . .'

She snapped her head toward him. 'Hey, now.'

'Perfectly understandable.'

'Don't jump to conclusions.'

'I *know* how it is. Marriage and children, if any, were relegated to the good old "back burner". Certainly in the future, you told yourself. Before the good old "biological clock" ran out of time. Thirty – there's a fine age to start thinking about a family. By thirty, you'd be settled in your career and might be able to find time for such secondary matters.'

He sounded a little malicious, mostly disappointed. He had her all figured out, and he didn't like what he'd found.

'Thanks,' Vicki muttered. She felt cold and hard inside.

What did you think, she asked herself, you'd found Mr Right?

This guy must be one hell of a lawyer. Doesn't know a single goddamn thing about it and decides I'm some kind of super-bitch career broad because I didn't marry the first guy that popped the question.

Well, screw him.

When hell freezes over.

Her eyes burned and the taillights of the car ahead went blurry. Her breath suddenly hitched. She turned her face to the side window. She gritted her teeth and willed herself not to sob.

The car slowed. It swung to the curb, and stopped. Vicki wiped her eyes. The houses on the block weren't familiar.

'What'd you stop here for?' she asked.

'You're crying.'

'No, I'm not.'

He put a hand on her shoulder.

'Don't touch me.'

He took the hand away.

'Vicki.'

'Go to hell.'

'Why are you acting this way? For God's sake, all I said . . .'

'Yeah, I sure want to hear it again.'

'I'm *delighted* that you turned down those guys.'

'Delighted, my ass.'

'If you hadn't, you'd be married now and . . .'

'Would you please take me home?'

'Not until . . .'

She opened the door.

'Okay, okay.'

She closed it, and Jack started the car moving again.

'I didn't mean to upset you,' he muttered.

She turned and stared at him. 'Thought I'd laugh it off? Ha ha? The girl who doesn't take herself seriously? I'm supposed to just write it off as another episode in the Adventures of Doc Chandler? Only I'm not an adventurer, am I? I don't fit into that flattering category any more. Now I'm the warrior. The ball-chopping Amazon. Well, you and the horse you rode in on, buddy.'

Jack shook his head as if he couldn't believe she was throwing such a fit.

Vicki slugged him in the shoulder.

'Ow! Hey!'

'Amazons like to do that.'

Jack held his shoulder and kept glancing at her as he drove. He said nothing. Neither did Vicki. At last, he stopped the car in front of Ace's house.

Vicki opened her door.

'Wait.'

'What?' she asked.

'I'm sorry.'

'So am I. But that doesn't make it go away. You don't stick a knife in someone and say you're sorry and presto the wound's gone. It doesn't work that way.'

'It hurt, Vicki.'

'Good. It was supposed to. That's what a punch is all about.'

'Not that. I wanted to believe you were different. I didn't want you to be one of *them*. But . . .'

'You don't know what I am.' She climbed out and slammed the door and ran to the house. As she took out her keys, she heard the car speed away.

She turned around. Jack's car vanished around a corner. She leaned against the door, sank down feeling the cool painted wood slide on her back, came to rest on the stiff prickly brush of the doormat, raised her knees and hugged them.

'Bastard,' she muttered.

She'd *really* liked him.

How could he do that, just suddenly lump me in with his ex-wife and all the bitches of the world because I'd turned down those three proposals?

Shouldn't have told him.

Screw that. I'm not going to lie. If he can't handle it, that's his problem.

I could've explained.

Who gave me a chance? The creep. He didn't wait for any explanation, didn't *need* any, because he knew. Right, he knew. Career comes first, guys, tough luck.

Who needs him, anyway?

Didn't even give me the benefit of the doubt. Didn't even *ask* why I turned them down.

The bristles of the doormat made her rump itch. With a sigh, she stood up. She rubbed her buttocks, then unlocked the door and entered the house.

Ace, on the couch, looked at her and turned off the television with the remote. 'What went wrong?'

The plan had been for Jack to be asked in for drinks – if they didn't go to his place instead – and Vicki would introduce him to Ace, and then Ace would make herself scarce.

The plan had made Vicki nervous and excited all through dinner. She'd imagined how it would go. The tentative first touches, the first kiss, the inevitable moment when Jack would press a hand to a breast. While they ate, while they talked and laughed, the living-room scene played in a back corner of her mind. She saw him sliding the straps of her dress down her arms. She worried about Ace coming into the room. Ace wouldn't do that, but still she was reluctant to go on with this in the living-room. Did she have the nerve to suggest they move to her bedroom? Maybe she should call a halt before it came to that.

Was she sure that she actually wanted to sleep with this man? Yes, she had decided about the time the chocolate mousse arrived

470

at the table. Yes, but it'd be better to hold off. All the more exciting to build up toward it slowly – see him again and again, moving closer each time as if they were taking a long, romantic trip, stopping here and there to enjoy the sights, growing all the time more eager to reach the final destination but savouring each moment along the way.

That's how it should be. Not from first dinner to bed all in the space of a couple of hours, missing out on the small but wonderful joys of the journey.

Jack might not look at it that way, though. Most men didn't. They felt cheated if you didn't go straight to bed with them. Vicki wondered how persistent Jack would be. She wondered if even she would have the willpower to hold off.

As he placed his Mastercard on the small plastic tray with the bill, she wondered if he had a condom. If not, that would settle the problem. She didn't have any (no need, since she hadn't been seeing anyone), and though Ace undoubtedly had a trunk-load somewhere, Vicki certainly had no intention of asking her for one.

She had a diaphragm. She could put it in. But she wouldn't.

It wasn't pregnancy that worried her.

Might get a little embarrassing, but he certainly couldn't accuse her of being a prig or a tease if she called a halt to things for lack of a rubber. Not with AIDS rolling through the country like a plague.

Maybe he carried one, just in case he got lucky.

Well, he didn't get lucky.

Neither did I, Vicki thought.

'We had a disagreement,' she told Ace.

'You're kidding.'

'You don't see him, do you?'

'Well, shit, how'd you manage that?'

'It was easy.'

'He turn out to be an asshole?'

'Not exactly.' Vicki sat down on the couch. She kicked her shoes off, stretched out her legs and rested her feet on the corner of the coffee table.

'Let me guess,' Ace said. 'He's married.'

'Divorced.'

'Ah-ha. And therefore bitter, resentful, suspicious, wary of any involvement because he doesn't want to get hurt again. Who's to say you're not his ex, cleverly disguised?'

Vicki smiled. 'How'd you get so smart?'

'The school of soft knocks, hon.'

'Beneath my clown suit beats the heart of an Amazon career bitch baby-killer.'

'Baby-killer?'

'His ex had an abortion because she decided a kid would mess up her law practice.'

'And Jack wanted the kid?'

'Yeah. So now he assumes I must be the type to pull a stunt like that.'

'Naturally.'

'The bastard.'

'So how was he otherwise?'

'What does it matter?'

'You must've thought he was pretty nifty, or you wouldn't be so upset about this little development.'

'He was okay, I guess.'

'You were crazy about him.'

'Maybe. But . . .'

'Facts of life, hon. Fact one, you're pushing thirty. Fact two, I don't think you're into pimply, vapid teenagers. Fact three, there are no guys out there of a suitable age who aren't carrying some kind of garbage.'

'The good ones are all taken?' Vicki muttered.

'Or *were*. And we know damn well you wouldn't want to mess with the others. You find a guy over about twenty-five who hasn't been married, or at least had a long-term relationship with some gal, he's gotta be totally fucked. One way or another. Take our friend Melvin, for instance.'

'Thanks, I'd rather not.'

'He's available, hasn't been divorced.'

'And I thought I was depressed *before*.'

'I'm trying to cheer you up.'

'And doing a good job of it, too.'

'What I'm getting at, you just aren't going to find a guy who doesn't have a certain load of garbage. If he's available – and isn't totally fucked that he never had a relationship – there has to be a woman in his past who either messed him up or died on him. Either way, you inherit the shit she dumped on him. It goes with the territory.'

'You're so full of understanding, you should go out with him. I'm sure he'd classify you as an adventurer. Just watch out if he asks how many proposals you've turned down.'

'That's the trick question, huh?'

'Was for me.'

'What'd you tell him?'

'Three.'

'Where's the problem? That just shows you're picky.'

'Not to him. The way he sees it, I laid waste to the guys because marriage would conflict with my career goals.'

'Was he right?'

'Good question. Excellent question. He didn't bother to ask it. That's the whole damn reason . . .' Her voice slipped upward. Her eyes flooded.

Here I go again, she thought.

Ace scooted across the couch and put an arm across Vicki's shoulders. Vicki turned to her, held her, wept against her neck. She felt Ace stroking her hair.

She should've been here on the couch in Jack's arms. That was the plan. It was supposed to be Jack, not Ace. They'd be here right now, and she'd be wondering about condoms, and . . . she cried all the harder.

'It's all right,' Ace murmured. 'It's all right.'

'I . . . *wanted* him,' she blurted.

'I know.'

'What's . . . wrong . . . with me?'

'Nothing. Nothing, honey. You're just lonely. It's been too long and you had too many hopes pinned on this guy.'

'The bastard.'

'Look on the bright side.'

'What . . . bright side?'

'You've got me.'

'I know. I know.'

'That was supposed to be a joke, hon.'

'Even so . . .'

473

Ace squeezed her, gently kissed the side of her head. 'We've got each other,' she whispered. 'No joke.'

'I know. God, Ace . . .'

'Just keep your hands off my tits.'

Vicki laughed and choked on a sob.

'Poor thing, you've struck out twice in one night.'

'Bitch.'

Ace eased her away. *Her* eyes were red and wet. Her fingertips stroked the tears off Vicki's cheeks. 'Better?'

Vicki sniffled. 'Yeah. Thanks.'

'So what are you going to do now?'

'Go out and buy a vibrator?'

'Other than that.'

'I don't know.'

'Guess what? Jack's probably not overjoyed by the way things turned out tonight, either.'

'I'm sure.'

'He's probably home alone right now, crying out his own little eyes.'

'I bet.'

'Being a guy, of course, he's more likely getting drunk and crushing beer cans on his face.'

Vicki laughed and wiped her nose.

'Why don't you give him a call?'

'Are you kidding?'

Ace shook her head.

'I don't know.'

'What've you got to lose?'

'What's the point?'

'He's a man. You're crazy about him, or were, till you had this misunderstanding. He's probably breaking a leg trying to kick his ass about all this.'

'Or just grateful he "found me out" and got while the getting was good.'

'So call him up, find out which it is.'

'No. Huh-uh. It's *his* problem. Let him do the phoning if he wants. I'm going to bed.'

Vicki stood up.

'Sure you don't want to wait up for his call?'

'There won't be one.'

'Right. He'll probably drop by, instead. Maybe I'll slip into my nightie, just in case.'

'My friend.'

Later, lying in bed, Vicki stared at the dark ceiling. She heard quiet voices and background music from the television. She heard no ring of the telephone, no doorbell. But she stayed awake for a long time, listening.

Chapter Twenty

'Okay,' Melvin said, 'stop the car.'

Charlie stepped on the brake. The car jerked to a halt, throwing Melvin forward. He slapped a hand against the dashboard to brace himself. Then he opened the passenger door.

'Where y'goin'?' Charlie asked, his words slurred by the martinis he'd been gulping for the past hour.

'Nowhere,' Melvin said. 'Sit tight.' The gasoline inside the doctor's medical bag sloshed as he lifted it off the floor and placed it on the seat. He climbed from the car, shut the door, and stepped around to the driver's side. 'Take off your seat belt,' he said.

Charlie unlatched the safety harness and reached for the door handle.

'No, don't get out.'

'Huh?'

'When I say "go", I want you to push the accelerator all the way to the floor. Drive around the bend as fast as you can, and run into the bridge over the creek.'

'Wha' y'mean, run into it?' He sounded confused.

'Crash against it. As hard as you can. That wall on the side of the bridge.'

'The parapuh?'

'The parapet, right. I want you to hit it full speed.'

The man frowned up at Melvin through the open window and scratched the side of his head. 'Y'wan' me t'crash?'

'That's right.'

'That'd ligely kill me.'

'Nah. Don't be an idiot. You're already dead.'

'Well, yes 'n' no.'

'Do it!'

'Wha' for?'

'Because I told you to. I brought you back to life, I could make you dead again if I want. So do what I tell you.'

Charlie sniffed and rubbed a hand under his nose. 'I don' wanna make you mad.'

Melvin patted his shoulder. 'I'm not mad. I just want you to crash into the bridge. I promise you won't get hurt. I have a real good reason for wanting the car smashed, and I'll tell you all about it on the way home.'

'How'll we ge' home, I wreck my car?'

'We'll walk back to my station, and take the tow truck.'

'Oh. Ogay.' Charlie shrugged, then drew the safety harness across his body.

'You don't need that,' Melvin told him.

'Y'wan' me t'jump clear?'

Melvin sighed. Though he heard no cars approaching, he glanced up and down River Road. 'If you jump out, the car will slow down. I want it to hit full speed.'

'How y'know I won't get hurt?'

'Trust me, Charlie. You're my pal. Besides, I've got big plans for you.'

'Yeah?'

'I'll need your help getting me some more gals. And I'll let you take your pick. You can have one all for yourself.'

'Yeah?'

'Right.' Melvin squeezed his shoulder.

Charlie nodded.

Melvin stepped back. 'Ready, set . . . go!'

The engine roared. The Mercedes shot forward. It was powered by gas, not diesel fuel, so it had great pick-up. It rushed around the bend, out of sight beyond the trees. 'Go go go!' Melvin yelled. He clapped his hands, winced at the pain from his bite, and waited for the night to shake with the noise of the collision.

The crash, when it came, didn't shake the night.

Melvin raced around the bend. The car wasn't a ball of flames, as he'd hoped. It just sat there.

He muttered, 'Shit.'

Charlie, holding his forehead, looked out the window. 'How'd I do?' he asked.

'Fine,' Melvin said. 'Just fine.' He stepped to the front of the car. The concrete wall had bent the bumper on the right side, smashed the grill slightly, dented the front of the hood, and broken the headlight. From the look of the damage, Charlie must've hit the parapet going all of ten miles per hour.

Damned old fart.

Charlie swung the door open.

'Stay in there!'

He shut the door.

Melvin went to him.

Charlie looked out the window. He was pressing a handkerchief to his forehead. 'Aren' we gonna go home, now?'

'In a minute.'

Charlie lowered the handkerchief. His forehead had a nice gash. He looked at the bloody cloth, then pressed it to his mouth and began sucking on it.

'Hand me your bag,' Melvin said.

Charlie searched, found his medical bag on the floor, and lifted it to the window. 'Wha's in here?' he asked, shaking it.

Melvin didn't answer. He opened it, dumped gasoline onto Charlie's lap, then bent down and hurled the remaining gas under the front of the car.

'Wha' y'doing?' Charlie asked. He sounded worried.

Melvin ignored him. He struck a match and touched it to the moist pavement near the tyre. A faint bluish flame rose and spread over the spill. Melvin stood up. He dropped the burning match into the doctor's bag. With a soft *whup*, the satchel filled with fire. He tossed it onto Charlie's lap.

'Hey now!' Charlie blurted as he went up. One of his flaming arms knocked the bag aside. The door started to open. Melvin kicked it shut.

'Stay,' he ordered.

'Wha's the big idea?' Charlie asked, frowning through the blaze. His shirt was on fire. So were his eyebrows and hair. 'Le' me out, 'fore I'm ruined.'

'Stay.'

Charlie rammed a burning shoulder against the door. The door flew open. He swung a leg out. It wasn't burning yet. Melvin hurled the door shut. There was a soft thud as it struck the man's leg. Melvin tried to hold the door shut, but Charlie reached out the window for him. He lurched away from the blazing arms.

The door flew open again. Charlie, afire from the knees up, climbed out of the car and looked down at himself. He started slapping at the front of his tattered, burning pants and shirt. Then he gave up. He planted his fists on his hips and turned his head toward Melvin. He swept a hand across his face a few times as if trying to bat the flames aside to allow himself to see better. 'You're tryin' t'kill me all over again,' he said.

Melvin glanced at the car. Flames were licking up through the cracks around the hood. Before long, a gas line would burn through.

'Get back in the car,' he said.

'Why, I don' imagine I will, y'damn back-stabbin' s.o.b.'

With that, Charlie raised his blazing arms as if reaching for Melvin, and started limping toward him.

Melvin lurched past the old man and ran to the middle of the bridge. Charlie staggered after him.

The front end of the car was now engulfed in flames.

If only Charlie was still inside!

How could it go this bad? Melvin wondered. He never guessed it would go *this* bad.

Melvin backed against the parapet.

The blazing man, arms out like a movie zombie, stumbled closer and closer. He littered the pavement with flaming bits of cloth. His hair had burned away, leaving his head black and charred. His pants and shirt still burned. Flames still fluttered in front of his face. One eye was a bubbling pool. It burst, and fluid streamed down his cheek.

He was on the walkway, only a few steps from Melvin, when the other eye went.

Melvin sprang away from the parapet. He ran out into the road, then rushed Charlie from the side.

His bandaged hand rammed the man's burning shoulder.

Charlie stumbled sideways. The edge of the wall caught his hip. One leg flew up, but Melvin saw that he wasn't going to tumble over the top without some help. So he grabbed Charlie's ankle and shoved it high. The old man, his weight on the broad top of the parapet, squirmed and kicked as Melvin forced his leg higher and higher.

The car exploded.

Melvin felt a hot blast of wind.

With both hands, he thrust Charlie's ankle toward the sky.

Charlie dropped from the wall.

Melvin leaned over. He watched the burning man twirl and somersault and finally belly-flop into Laurel Creek. With the sound of the splash, Charlie went dark.

Melvin sagged on the wall.

It's over, he told himself. It's probably okay, they'll just think Charlie made it out after the crash, but he was on fire so he jumped into the creek to put the fire out. It'll look like an accident, okay.

'Damn back-stabbin' s.o.b.!'

A chill squirmed up Melvin's back.

He cupped hands around his eyes and peered down at the stream. He saw nothing but darkness.

But he heard a quiet splash.

He hurried to the far end of the bridge, stepped off the walkway, and began to make his way down the steep slope. The weeds under his feet were wet with dew. He skidded. He grabbed bushes and saplings to hold himself steady. Halfway down, his feet shot out. He landed hard and slid over rocks and twigs, wincing, gritting his teeth, eyes filling with tears as his back was scratched and gouged. A boulder finally stopped his slide. He lay there with his feet against the rock and took deep, hitching breaths. His back burned and itched. The wetness of his shirt felt good, though. He didn't want to move.

But he knew that he had to get up. He had to find Charlie and finish him off. Fast. People far away might've heard the explosion of the car. Or a motorist might come along.

There was a rock under his left hand when he pushed himself up. It was half buried in the ground. He tugged it loose. It was the size of a softball, but a lot heavier.

He stood, climbed onto the boulder that had stopped him, and crouched. The stream, a few yards below, looked black except for a few flecks of moonlight. He couldn't see Charlie.

Might be anywhere.

A chill of fear spread through Melvin at the thought of the burnt old man sneaking up on him. He told himself not to worry about that.

The old fart's blind. He can't get me.

The thing to worry about was letting him get away. Messed up as he was, he could still talk.

Tell on me.

Melvin climbed down the front of the boulder. He made his way carefully to the bottom of the slope and stepped into the stream. The water was cold. It wrapped him to the knees. The rocks of the stream bed felt slippery beneath his shoes.

He looked under the bridge. Black in there, but light from the other side would've silhouetted Charlie, at least if he was standing. If he wasn't standing . . .

Melvin squatted down. The cold water seized his groin, stole the heat from between his buttocks. It climbed to his chest and made his nipples ache. But he was low enough for the dim glow beyond the bridge to backlight anything more than a few inches above the surface.

A dark lump near the middle made his heart jump. He squinted at it. Charlie's head? Maybe just a rock or the end of a thick branch. Whatever it was, it didn't move. Melvin thought about wading closer to it.

Awfully dark in there.

He felt cold prickles on the back of his neck.

That's not Charlie, he told himself.

Might be.

'Charlie?' he asked. His voice came out husky, not very loud.

No answer.

Melvin stood up and started to turn away from the bridge, but suddenly he didn't have the nerve to turn his back on all that darkness – and whatever was in there. Standing, he could no longer see the thing. He imagined it gliding toward him. He waded backward as fast as he could.

He looked up at the blazing car. It felt good, comforting, to see all that light. He wished he were up there, right now. In the brightness, feeling the warmth.

When he lowered his gaze, he knew it had been a mistake to look at the fire. His night vision was ruined. Before, he could *see*. Not much, but some. Now, except for the fire way up there, he could see nothing at all.

I'm blind, he thought.

As blind as Charlie.

He could sneak up on me easy.

Melvin whirled around and staggered through the water. He knew he should search for Charlie, finish him off somehow, but all he felt now was fear and a need to get away. It seemed best to follow the stream until he was a good distance from the road, then head through the woods and make his way home.

He flinched at the first blast of the fire alert.

It filled the night, loud and piercing, a siren noise that grew and faded and died, then came again.

Even as it roused the volunteers from their sleep, a police car would be speeding toward the bridge.

Whimpering, Melvin started to run downstream. He pumped his knees, but the water dragged at him, held him back. Then his left foot stepped on something that moved under his weight. His foot slipped off it. He stumbled, dropped his rock, gasped and fell. Water splashed up around him. Closed over him. *Arms wrapped his back*.

OH JESUS NO!

He ached to shriek, but held his breath as he was embraced by the thing beneath him on the stream bottom – the thing that had to be Charlie Gaines. It squeezed him hard. It wrapped its legs over the backs of Melvin's legs. Something slithered across his lips. *Charlie's tongue?* Then he felt the edges of teeth against his lower lip and chin. He jerked his head back, heard the clash of the teeth snapping shut.

Tried to bite me!

Just like Patricia.

In that instant, it all changed for Melvin. His stunned horror shattered like a shell that had been enclosing and smothering his mind. He felt the shell burst and fly apart, felt his mind breathe and flex and smile.

Suddenly, he was *Melvin* again, not some whimpering sissy, and the thing embracing him and hugging him and trying to bite him was nothing more than Charlie Gaines. Not a hideous zombie, just an old fart who'd been burnt to a crisp and didn't know when to die.

A charbroiled steak.

With teeth.

And now the teeth were scraping the side of Melvin's neck. Though Charlie clung to him like a frantic lover, the embrace was *below* Melvin's arms. That left his hands free. He clutched the side of Charlie's face. It felt slick and crumbly. His thumb found the empty eye socket. He hooked his thumb inside the hole. Like pudding in there, but the bone was a solid ring and when he jerked it with his thumb, Charlie's head turned with it. He forced the head sideways and down. He grabbed the near side of the face with his bandaged hand. Pressing the head against the bottom, he shoved himself upward. Charlie's embrace wasn't powerful enough to hold him. The arms opened just enough. Melvin's shoulders and head broke the surface. He gasped for air.

The fire alert blared again.

He wondered if anyone had arrived at the fire.

As the noise stopped, he heard a car door slam.

He looked over his shoulder. The bridge was out of sight beyond a bend in the stream. High to the right, the leaves of the trees shimmered with firelight.

He almost screamed as Charlie raked his back, splitting his shirt and ripping his skin. Hissing instead, he let go of Charlie's face, tried to keep it down with the thumb of his other hand, and felt along the stream bottom, searching for a rock. He grabbed one. Charlie released Melvin's legs and shoved at his chest. Melvin went backward, thumb pulling out of the socket with quick suck. Now he was on his knees. Charlie rose up in front of him. Blacker than the stream. Water sprayed Melvin's face. 'Gonna kill you,' Charlie said. His voice had a gurgle to it. 'Back-stabbin' s.o.b.'

Melvin slammed the side of Charlie's head with the rock. The blow snapped his head sideways. Melvin struck again. This time, he felt the skull crush and go soft. Charlie started to flop backward. With his left hand, Melvin caught the back of the old man's head. Holding it above the water, he pounded the rock again into the soft place. It made a wet sound as if slapping mud. He hit it again and again.

Charlie lay limp beneath him, not moving at all.

So that's how you rekill the fuckers. Melvin thought. Bash their brains in.

He heard voices in the distance behind him. There were sirens, but they sounded much farther away than the voices.

He lowered the rock into the water, and let it fall.

He crawled around Charlie. He found both the man's arms, grabbed his wrists, and began wading backward, towing him downstream.

He did it for a long time.

Sooner or later, he knew, they'd find the body. They'd think Charlie had jumped into the stream to put himself out, had cracked his head open on the rocky bed, and been carried downstream by the current.

They'd think that for a while, at least. A good autopsy would change their minds, for sure. He'd read up on such things. Just one whack in the head, and they might figure it happened when Charlie went off the bridge. But Melvin had clobbered him five or six times. They'd know that wasn't any accident.

They'd figure Charlie'd been murdered. Then they'd find samples of Melvin's skin under his fingernails. They'd know he'd been scratched. They might even learn his blood type.

It was sure getting complicated.

Melvin kept towing Charlie downstream.

The only good solution, he finally decided, was to dispose of the body. If they couldn't find it, they couldn't do an autopsy. They might just stick with the theory that Charlie had jumped off the bridge because he was on fire, and gotten himself swept out to the river and lost.

So how do I get rid of it? he wondered.

That one had him stumped.

Even if he was strong enough to carry Charlie around all night, and he doubted he had the strength to pick him up at all, where would he take him?

He kept pulling Charlie along, certain that he would come up with an answer to the problem. He began to ache from the strain of bending over and wading backward with the body.

Finally, he towed it ashore. He held onto one wrist to keep Charlie from drifting away, and sat on the trunk of a deadfall, feet dangling in the stream. After catching his breath, he listened. He heard the murmur of the stream, the breeze stirring the leaves, birds chirping, mosquitoes humming. No human sounds. He guessed that he must be at least half a mile from the bridge. There wasn't much chance of anyone wandering this far downstream. Not for a long while yet.

'What'm I gonna do with you?' he muttered.

'Bah stah s.o.b.'

Melvin squealed.

He flung himself down, hugged Charlie's head to his chest, ripped out broken shards of skull, flung them, dug in, grabbed brains and jerked them out. He squeezed the sodden mass, felt it ooze between his fingers, heard bits of it splash into the stream. He dug in again, pulled out another mushy handful, hurled it away, and scooped out more and threw it.

'Dead yet?' he gasped. 'Huh? Fuckin' pig!'

Charlie sure *seemed* dead, but he'd seemed dead before.

Melvin yanked the man's jaw down. He tugged on the tongue, tried to tear it out by the roots, but his hand slipped off. So he wrenched Charlie around, slammed the back of his head against the tree trunk, held it there and pulled the tongue out as far as he could.

He bent down close to the face. It didn't look much like a face. It looked like charcoal, except for the white teeth and slightly pale shape of the tongue drooping out between them.

Melvin sucked the tongue into his mouth. Drew it in deep. Bit into it, gnashed, and jerked back his head. Moaning, he picked up Charlie's arm and pulled him to the middle of the stream. He let go. The body started to float away.

Melvin opened his mouth. He pulled out the slab of tongue and flipped it into the bushes.

Let them find the damn body.

'That's one dead fucker won't tell no tales,' he said.

Then he waded ashore, entered the woods, and headed for home.

Chapter Twenty-one

'You've been a very bad girl,' Melvin said. 'You were supposed to save yourself for me.'

He was standing beside her bed, frowning down at her. He bent over. Vicki couldn't see what his hand was doing, but a motor hummed and the back of the bed began to rise. A hospital bed? As it lifted her, she saw that she wasn't in a hospital. The bed was in the middle of the Community Center auditorium. And as it lifted, the sheet on top of Vicki began to slide. She tried to grab the sheet. Couldn't. Her wrists were bound to the guard rails of the bed.

The sheet drifted down, falling away from her breasts and the huge mound of her belly.

'You see?' Melvin asked. 'You didn't save yourself for me. I'm deeply disappointed in you, Vicki. I love you. You *know* how I love you. How could you let another man have you? How could you let him *knock you up*?'

Impossible, Vicki thought. A false pregnancy, that's what it is. 'I didn't,' she said. 'It's a mistake.'

'Oh, really?' He thumped her belly with his knuckles. It sounded like a ripe watermelon. 'Who's inside there, huh? I know who it isn't. It isn't Melvin junior. Could it be Jack junior?'

'No. It's nobody.'

'We'll see about that.'

'I *can't* be pregnant. I haven't slept with anyone.'

'I'm sure you didn't *sleep*. You fucked, though. There's the proof.'

'But I didn't! Honest!'

'Liar, liar, pants on fire.'

It *was* a lie, she supposed. But the last time was so long ago. Bart. He was the last. That was almost three years ago. New Year's Eve. They'd both been smashed, she forgot her diaphragm and he didn't use a rubber ('Like wearing a glove') and then her period was late and she was sick with worry, but then it came. It *did* come. The blood poured out and she wept with relief.

She got her period and, besides, that was *three years ago*. Couldn't be Bart junior. No way. And she never *did* it with Jack.

Unless she forgot.

'We didn't,' she said. 'Jack and I . . . we had a fight.'

Maybe we made up, though.

She could see herself on the couch with him. Or was that Ace? No, it was Jack. He slid the straps of her dress down her arms, lowered the bodice, kissed her breasts. 'Not here,' she said. 'Let's go in the bedroom.'

Vicki realized, with some relief, that she was no longer Melvin's captive in the auditorium. Jack was carrying her down the hallway of Ace's house. He took her into the bedroom. He put her onto the bed. He removed all her clothed, then his own.

She writhed against the smooth bare length of his body, kissing him, moaning as he caressed her all over. Then she was on her back, Jack kneeling between her legs. And she thought, he can't. Not without a rubber. But if I speak up, he'll think I don't want his baby.

I want your baby. I don't want AIDS.

He won't believe that.

I can't tell him. It'll all be over if I tell him.

Then Jack had a foil pack in his hands. He was tearing it open.

Oh, thank God.

Oh, Jack, I was so wrong about you.

She raised her hands toward him. She took the condom. She slipped its rubber ring over the head of his penis and slowly unrolled it, feeling his heat and hard thickness through the moist sheath.

Trembling, she whispered, 'I love you. I love you so much.'

'You should've *saved yourself* for me!'

Melvin rammed his arm in all the way to the elbow, jerked it out, and flung the torn-off leg of an infant at her face. 'TELL HIM YOU DIDN'T WANT HIS LITTLE PIGGIE!'

'NO!' she cried out.

Lurched upright and found herself in the bedroom, whimpering, shaking, naked, the sheet bunched at the end of the bed, both her hands clamped tightly between her legs.

Her heart was pounding. Though she panted, she couldn't seem to get enough air. She crossed her legs Indian-style, arched her back, tilted her face up, pointed her elbows at the ceiling, and interlaced her fingers behind her head. Her hair was dripping wet. So was the rest of her body. She felt runnels of sweat trickle down her face, her back, her sides, her chest. Her eyes stung as if daubed with saltwater.

Trying not to think about the nightmare, she let her mind follow a single drop of sweat as it slid past the front of her ear, down her jaw and neck, over her collarbone, onto her breast. It stopped at the tip of her nipple. It hung there, a tiny trembling weight, turning a little chilly, until another bead of sweat came down and joined it. They fell together as a single dollop, made a cool splash on her thigh, and rolled down the side and under it to be blotted out against the bottom sheet.

Soon, Vicki's breathing and heartbeat were nearly normal again. She reached behind her back, found her pillow, and used it to mop her face. Then, she let it drop down through the circle of her arms. She pressed it against the wet chilled skin of her breasts and belly. It felt soft and warm. Cosy. She eased herself down onto the bed. Embracing the pillow gently, she sighed.

She could almost fall asleep again.

And dream?

She turned her head. The clock on the nightstand showed 2:08. Three more hours before time to get up. She'd better go ahead and sleep, or she would be wasted tomorrow.

Maybe she'd finished with Melvin for the night. One good dose of the creep, like that, ought to be enough to satisfy whatever damn corner of her mind was so obsessed with him. It had given her the mandatory nightly horror show.

Now, leave me alone, she thought.

The part of her dream about Jack had been a very nice fantasy. Let's have some more of that – just leave Melvin out of it.

Jack.

He hadn't phoned. He hadn't come by.

The hell with him.

The dream-Jack had it all over the real thing. Didn't give me any grief. Actually had a condom. And I put it on him. Lord. I've never done that. Obviously, I'd like to.

Stroking the pillow, she remembered the feel of him.

And flinched at the sudden wail of the fire alert. It climbed to a shriek, and died. A few seconds later, it came again.

All over Ellsworth, the volunteer firemen were being blasted awake.

Along with everyone else.

Including Jack.

Vicki slid her pillow aside, climbed from bed and went to the window. Bending over, she put her hands on the sill. The warm breeze drifted over her skin. The street beyond the yard was deserted except for a few parked cars.

The noise of the fire alert continued, blaring to a high pitch, sinking and dying out, leaving an empty stretch of silence, then rising again.

Jack has to be awake, Vicki thought. Nobody could sleep through this racket.

She wondered if he was thinking about her, wondered if he regretted the way it had gone. Maybe he only felt relief that he had found her out so quickly.

He's so wrong about me, she thought.

She heard a car engine. Headlights brightened the street. Then a car raced by, a blue light flashing on its dashboard.

One of the volunteer firemen speeding toward the station.

Vicki felt a small pull of guilt.

Here I am, wrapped up in my own petty problem, and someone out there has *real* troubles. A house might be burning down. A car might've crashed. Someone could be injured or dead.

A doctor might be needed.

The ambulance attendants were trained to render first aid at the scene. By the time she could get there, they'd probably be rushing any victims toward the ER at Blayton Memorial.

She wouldn't know where to go, anyway.

Get directions at the fire station, same as the volunteers.

You *might* get there in time to help.

The alternative, she knew, was to return to bed and try to sleep and maybe have another nightmare.

Her heart pumped as if the decision were already made.

'I'm Dr Chandler,' she said through the open window of Ace's Mustang. 'I'd like to help, if I can.'

The man in the driveway of the fire station nodded. 'It's a car fire out on River Road at the Laurel Creek Bridge. You're welcome to head out there, see what you can do.'

She thanked him, backed onto the street, and sped toward River Road.

A car fire at the bridge. Where Steve Kraft piled up, all those years ago. Where he was burnt, where Darlene was decapitated.

Vicki pictured Darlene in the wheelchair, centre stage at the Science Fair, all decked out in her cheerleader suit, neck wrapped to keep her head on – Melvin clamping the jumper cables to her thumbs.

She shook her head as if to jar the image loose, and prayed it wasn't kids in the car.

It probably *would* be kids. Teenagers. Only kids would be up at such an hour, probably drinking beer and hot-rodding it up River Road. They loved to see how fast they could take those curves. Loved to prove they were Big Men.

Big Men risking Death.

Easy to risk it when you don't believe in it. And most teenagers don't. Vicki knew that for a fact. They just didn't believe in death, Not their own. Not even when they committed suicide. Somehow figured they'd go on living, dead or not. The blessing and curse of youth. *They'd be more goddamn careful.*

She swung onto River Road.

She hoped, if this was some kid trying to prove himself, he didn't have his girlfriend along. Or a carload of pals.

Though the road was still empty ahead, Vicki saw red and blue glows flashing through the air, sweeping the pavement, glancing off trees on the far side. She moved her foot to the brake and slowed down. She rounded the bed.

A line of flares crossed the road. Beyond them, both lanes were blocked by cars. In among the cars stood the pump truck. She saw no fire, just a few wisps of smoke, red then blue in the spinning lights of the fire truck and ambulance and police cruisers. Cars and men blocked her view of the wreck.

Striding toward the line of flares was Joey Milbourne. He raised a hand, signaling Vicki to stop. She set her brake. He walked up to her window and bent down. 'Bridge is . . . Vicki?'

'I thought I'd come out and see if I could be of any help.'

'Pull on ahead,' he told her.

She steered between two of the flares, stopped and climbed out with her medical bag.

'I don't think you'll be needing that,' Joey said, nodding at the bag. 'Not yet, anyhow. All we've got so far's the car.'

'No driver?'

'Nobody.'

She left her bag on the seat. Walking with Joey through the cluster of cars, she saw men with lights searching the roadside ditches near the bridge, one wandering into the trees. Another man, head down, was on the bridge and seemed to be studying its sidewalk and parapet. Two more were searching the area beyond the bridge.

'The driver's door was open when we arrived,' Joey said. 'Looks as if he just wandered off. Maybe in shock. Doesn't look like much of an impact, but you never know. He might've cracked his head on the steering wheel. Looks like he was on fire, too. We found some charred cloth on the . . .'

'My God,' Vicki muttered as she saw the burnt-out husk of the car. It was all black except for patches of white left by the chemical extinguishers. The tyres were flat and smoking. The windows had been blasted out. The hood was up. The trunk lid, torn from its hinges, rested atop the car's roof.

In spite of the destruction, the car's size and squared corners were unmistakable to Vicki.

A Mercedes.

After I'm gone.

Tight and sick inside, she rushed toward the rear of the car thinking, it's not Charlie's, can't be, he's not the only guy in the world with a Mercedes . . . just maybe the only guy in Ellsworth.

She crouched at the bumper. Heat radiated off the wreck. The stench of burnt rubber seared her nostrils. Holding her breath, she squinted at the licence plate. The beam of Joey's flashlight found it. In spite of the raised metal, she couldn't make out the numerals through the blackness. She reached out to rub the soot off, scorched her fingers, jerked them back, then slipped her hand inside her T-shirt and, leaning forward, used the fabric like a thin glove to wipe the plate.

It read, 'DOC CG'. 'It's Charlie's car,' Vicki said. 'Dr Gaines.'

'Christ,' Joey said.

'Got something here!' a voice called from the distance.

Dazed, Vicki stood and followed Joey. They headed for the man in the middle of the bridge. Was he the one who called?

490

Charlie killed himself, she thought. My God, he killed himself. That's why he turned everything over to me. He had it all planned. I was right, he was sick. Found out he had cancer? Something. Should I tell? Let them come to their own conclusions.

Dimly, she realized that the man on the bridge was another cop.

'What is it, Chief?' Joey asked.

Chief Raines? Pollock's replacement?

'Look here,' the chief said, and aimed the beam of his flashlight at the top of the parapet. The concrete was smudged with black. 'He must've come out burning, took a header off the bridge.'

'Dr Gaines,' Joey said.

'Charlie Gaines?'

'His car.'

'Shit.'

Both men leaned against the parapet and shined their flashlights into the ravine. Vicki, stepping up beside Joey, gazed down and watched their pale beams slide over the surface of the stream, over the rocks and bushes along its shores.

'Figured he'd land in the water,' the chief said.

'Must've been crazy.'

'I guess, you're on fire, you'll do most anything.'

Hell, Vicki thought, the *fall* will probably kill you. What was that? A line from some movie. *Butch Cassidy and the Sundance Kid*, that was it. This wasn't a fall like those guys took. Maybe fifty or sixty feet. But she'd been down there many times when she was a kid, and the stream was normally about two feet deep.

'I don't see him,' the chief said.

'Me neither,' said Joey. 'Think he could've wandered off?'

'Possible. More likely, the current took him. We'll probably find him hung up a ways downstream.' The chief backed away from the parapet. Some of the searchers were already on their way over. He called in the rest of them. When everyone was gathered on the bridge, he explained that the driver was Charlie Gaines and must've jumped off hoping to douse the flames in the creek. 'He might've survived and made it ashore. So check around in the trees. My guess, though, we'll find him downstream.'

'Think he might be alive?' asked a white-shirted ambulance attendant.

'Won't know that till we find him, will we? Let's get moving.'

The group split up, men heading for the ends of the bridge.

Vicki stayed with the chief and Joey as they walked back toward the wreck. 'I'll go on down and direct the search,' the chief said. 'Milbourne, you stay up here and control the scene. We don't want a bunch of rubber-neckers showing up and mucking around.' He looked at Vicki. 'What's your business here, young lady?'

'This is Dr Chandler,' Joey said.

'I'm Dr Gaines's partner,' she explained. 'I'd like to help in the search.'

His eyes narrowed. 'You do get around.'

What does he mean by that? she wondered.

'I heard the fire alert and thought I might be able to help.'

'She's the one who identified the car as Charlie's,' Joey pointed out.

'I don't suppose you were *with* him tonight?'

'No,' Vicki said. 'I saw him at about five-thirty, just before I left the clinic.'

'You weren't *drinking* with him at the Riverfront?'

'No, I . . .'

'You didn't hear Melvin Dobbs threaten Charlie's life, did you?'

Vicki felt heat rush to her face. 'Oh,' she said, 'terrific. I'm some kind of a nut because I reported a threat on Pollock's life.'

'And now you're here. What is it, some kind of a hobby with you to butt into police business?'

'I'm a *doctor*,' she said, pushing her voice out so it sounded firm, so it wouldn't reveal how timid and bitter she suddenly felt. 'I came out here to offer my assistance in case anyone needed medical attention.'

'Well, pack up your Bandaids and go on home, *doctor*.'

'I'd like to help in the search.'

'I'm sure you would. Thing is, we don't need you down there gumming up the works. So trot on home.'

'He's my *friend*.' This time, she couldn't stop her voice from trembling.

'Milbourne, get her out of here.'

'Yes, sir.'

With that, the chief stepped past Vicki and strode toward the end of the bridge.

'You'd better leave, now,' Joey said.

'He thinks I'm some kind of a *groupie*!'

'He's just upset, that's all. He's under a lot of pressure over the Pollock mess, and to have something like this happen right on top of it . . .'

'Can't I just wait up here till they find Charlie?'

'I'm afraid not.'

'Well, geez . . .'

'Go on home, now. There's nothing for you to do here. I'll notify you as soon as we find him.'

She stopped at the end of the parapet where the front of Charlie's car was tight against the concrete. Peering over the side, she saw Chief Raines on the wooded slope. He was nearly down to the bank of the creek. Other men were roaming the shore, others wading through the water. The beams of their lights swept and darted.

She turned to Joey. 'Why don't you just lend me your flashlight, and . . .'

'Want to get me in trouble with the chief?'

'Damn it, don't be such a wimp.'

Joey grabbed her arm. Not gently. 'Time to move on out, honey.'

He led her toward her car. Lifting on her arm so her feet barely touched the pavement.

'Let go of me!'

He didn't.

When they reached Ace's Mustang, he jerked the door, open, swung her around it and released her arm. It felt hot where his fingers had pressed into her flesh.

Vicki climbed into the car. As she moved her medical bag to the passenger seat, Joey threw the door shut.

'Go,' he said.

She started the car, made a tight U-turn, and sped away. Her heart was thudding. She panted for air. She was trembling with rage and humiliation.

They'd shooed her off like a stray dog.

What's *wrong* with those men?

Joey had been okay until the chief took off after her. Why didn't he stick up for her? That was easy. He's chicken. What didn't make sense was the chief's attitude. He had her all figured

493

out as a nuisance, just on the basis of whatever Joey had told him about their reporting Melvin's threat against Pollock.

What were we supposed to do, keep it to ourselves?

Even if it didn't lead anywhere (and Vicki would bet they didn't bother to check Melvin out), the chief should've appreciated getting any kind of information about the killing. Instead, he seemed to look at it as an intrusion.

A couple of broads trying to tell him how to run his investigation.

So I show up and he dumps on me. I could've helped look for Charlie. I'm another body, damn it. I've got eyes. I'm not blind, even if I am a woman.

That's the crux of it right there, Vicki realized. I'm a woman.

That's why I couldn't help look for Charlie. That's why they ignored the tip about Melvin's threat. I'm just a meddling broad who gets her kicks by butting into *their* business.

Some kind of flake.

What are all the men in this town, woman-haters?

Not Charlie, she thought.

Oh, Charlie, *what happened to you?*

Chapter Twenty-two

She parked the car in Ace's driveway, then went into the house. No lights were on. She left them off, and made her way through the darkness to her bedroom.

She knew there was no point trying to sleep. She would just toss and turn, wide awake, worrying about Charlie and reliving all the rotten things that had happened during the past few hours: the fight with Jack; the nightmare; the horrible scene at the bridge and knowing that Charlie, on fire, had leaped for the creek; and on top of all that, the humiliating encounter with the police chief. Enough to keep her awake for *days*.

She peeled off her sooty T-shirt, took a fresh one from the drawer, and put it on. Then, she looped the chain with the house key and whistle over her head.

Running would help. It always helped.

On her way back through the house, she wondered if she shouldn't stay and wait for Joey's call. He'd promised to let her know, when they found Charlie. But that might be an hour from now. Or never. No point hanging around.

Besides, the news, when it came, was almost sure to be bad.

Vicki stepped outside. On the sidewalk in front of the house, she did her stretching exercises. Then, she ran.

She ran fast, darting her legs far out, pumping her arms, feeling the warm air rush against the bare skin of her face and arms and legs. She had no destination in mind, but when she found herself on Center Street racing northward past the deserted shops, she remembered a few mornings ago when she followed Central to its junction with River Road and turned back at the Laurel Creek Bridge.

She thought, what if I stick to the shoreline? I'll come to the Laurel Creek inlet. I can follow the creek upstream and look for Charlie without anyone interfering.

It hurt to think about Charlie. She wanted to block him out of her mind, to block out everything, to run and, for a white at least, to be free.

But she wondered if she *could* reach the inlet. There was private property along the shore beyond the north end of town. There might be fences blocking her way.

I could swim around them, she thought.

Ahead was the park. She left the sidewalk and ran on the grass. It felt soft and springy under her shoes.

Go down to the beach and follow the shoreline. Might work.

What's the point, though? Charlie wouldn't have *walked* toward the river. If he survived the jump from the bridge, he would've climbed back up to the road. If he's downstream, he got carried there by the current.

I wouldn't find him alive.

The searchers may have already found him.

I owe him a try.

Vicki shortened her stride as she started down the slope toward the public beach. Gazing beyond the sand, she saw the dim shape of a fence stretching down to the water's edge.

I can wade around it, she told herself. I can swim all the way to the inlet, if I have to. It's probably no more than half a mile.

At the bottom of the slope, she picked up her pace. She came to the beach. She raced across the moonwashed sand.

'Vicki?'

She recognized the voice.

Her head snapped to the left.

Jack was speeding down the silvery ramp of the slide. He flew off its end and ran toward her.

Vicki stopped and faced him. He was barefoot and wearing only shorts. He stopped a few steps away from her.

'Early for your morning jog,' he said.

'What are you doing here?'

He shrugged his broad shoulders. 'I don't know. I couldn't sleep. I was just lying in bed, thinking about you. When I heard the fire alarm, I decided to get up. I just wandered for a while, and ended up here. I guess I hoped you'd show up, sooner or later.'

'What for?' she asked. Her heart was thumping. She felt as if she couldn't get enough air.

'Oh, Vicki.' He started to raise his arms toward her, then let them fall to his sides. He shook his head. 'I'm sorry. I was wrong to jump on you. You're not Gloria. You're so different from her that . . . I guess I've still got a lot of anger in me, and for just a minute there I let it out at *you*. I shouldn't have done that.'

'I'm *not* Gloria.'

'I know.'

'I'm not an Amazon career bitch.'

'Partly Amazon, maybe.' As he said that, a corner of his mouth tipped up and he rubbed his right arm just below the shoulder. 'You pack a pretty mean wallop.'

He turned sideways and pointed. His skin, milky in the moonlight, had a faint smudge of darkness like a shadow where she had punched him.

'I did that?' Vicki asked.

Reaching out, she let her fingertips drift over the contusion. The dark area felt slightly warmer than the skin around it.

'I'm sorry,' she said.

'It's all right.'

'I shouldn't have hit you.'

'It was assault and battery, you know. But don't worry, I won't press charges.'

'The cops would love it if you did.' She slid her hand down his arm and took hold of his hand. 'The chief seems to hate my guts. He just gave me the bum's rush. All I wanted to do was help look for Charlie.'

'Charlie Gaines?'

'He's missing. That's what the fire alert was about. He crashed on River Road. They think he was on fire and jumped off the bridge into the creek, but they couldn't find him. I wanted to help and they kicked me out.'

Jack squeezed her hand. 'Why wouldn't they let you help?'

'I don't know. But I thought I might sneak in the back way and search upstream. The inlet's not far from here.' She nodded toward the fence at the boundary of the beach.

'Want some company?' Jack asked.

'I'd like that.'

'Lead on. I'll try to keep up.'

He released Vicki's hand. She whirled away and rushed across the beach. She heard him running behind her. Then, he caught up and ran at her side.

She angled toward the end of the chainlink fence. A sign near the final post read, 'Public Prohibited Beyond this Point.' The water splashed up her legs as she rounded the post. On the other side, she leaped onto the bank and hurried across the back yard of a cottage. The windows of the cottage were dark. Ahead, a pier stretched into the river. An outboard floated alongside it.

Jack caught up to her, then passed her.

She stared at his wide, pale back, at the dark seat of his shorts, at his strong legs pumping out.

And it felt so good to be with him.

Vicki could hardly believe they were suddenly together. It had happened so fast. One moment, she was alone and Jack little more than a bitter memory: the next, he was back and she felt closer to him than *before* their fight in the car.

He was waiting for me, she thought. Hoping I'd show up.

She followed him past the pier, past a small beach, and through a gap in a hedge at the far side of the yard. They came out behind a two-story house with a wooded lawn. A car tire was suspended from one of the limbs. This house had a larger beach area than the cottage they had left behind. A canoe rested, hull up, on the sand. Some distance ahead was a dock with a boathouse on the other side.

Jack turned toward the beach. He came to a stop beside the canoe, crouched down and flipped it over, uncovering a pair of paddles that had been left beneath it.

'What're you doing?' Vicki whispered.

'Let's borrow it. We'll get there in no time, if we take it.'

'Are you kidding? It isn't ours.'

'This is an emergency. They'll understand. Besides, they'll never find out we took it. Probably.'

Vicki glanced toward the house. She could only see bits of it through the trees.

Jack handed a paddle to her. He kept the other for himself, and lifted the prow. Vicki grabbed the stern. The aluminium canoe felt nearly weightless as she hurried behind Jack, rushing it down the beach.

She half expected someone to shout from the house and come running out to stop them. But no one did.

They waded into the river and eased the canoe down. Jack held it steady while Vicki climbed in. As she knelt and dipped her paddle into the water, Jack swung himself aboard.

She looked over her shoulder.

We're getting away with it!

She felt a strange thrill. She'd never stolen anything before.

We're not stealing it, she reminded herself. Just borrowing it. And this is an emergency.

Though she hadn't been in a canoe for years, she used to spend long hours in them exploring the river's shoreline and islands. It felt so familiar: the narrow wooden slats under her knees, the paddle in her hands, the weight of the water against the blade as she swept it back, the sound of the drops spilling away when she lifted the paddle out, the soft rushing lap of the river under the hull as the canoe glided forward.

Jack acted as if he, too, had spent much of his youth in such a craft. He knelt upright, drawing his paddle through the water with smooth, graceful strokes, leaving the steering to Vicki, seeming to know that the job was hers and realizing immediately that she was good at it.

She matched his strokes. Soon, the canoe was speeding over the calm suface of the river. When they were out beyond the end of the pier, she turned them northward.

The air was warm. The river was calm, black except for silvery moonlight sprinkled across its ripples. Vicki saw no boat lights. She heard no motors. There seemed to be no one else on the river. A few specks of light glimmered along the far shore. The stillness and beauty gave her a hollow feeling of regret.

If only she were out here with Jack and no terrible errand. They could paddle out to the middle of the river and let the canoe drift. She would go to him. He would put his arms around her. They would kiss. They would lie down in the bottom of the canoe . . .

Some other night, she told herself. Maybe next week or next month. All of this will be a bad memory, and we'll come out here for no other reason than to be with each other.

She pictured Charlie floating dead in the creek, and felt a hot jolt of guilt.

We're out here for you, Charlie. It doesn't matter about me and Jack.

Not tonight.

She turned her face to the left. They were gliding past the dock of the last house before the woods. In the distance, she saw a point of land. She remembered from long ago that it reached into the river just this side of the Laurel Creek inlet.

Holding the paddle straight down beside the canoe, she twisted its blade against the flow. Water swooshed and bubbled up. The canoe turned. When it was aimed toward the point, she resumed stroking.

Soon, they slipped past the jut of land.

'It's just ahead,' Vicki said.

Jack, nodding, rested his paddle across the gunnels.

Vicki eased the canoe forward. She peered into the darkness of the bushes and trees along the bank, but didn't see the narrow opening until Jack pointed. Sweeping the canoe toward it, she heard the soft rush of the running water. She gave the paddle a final, strong pull.

As the canoe glided closer to the inlet, she scanned the woods. She saw no lights. She heard voices faint with distance.

Either the searchers hadn't yet come this far or they'd already reached the river and turned back.

Jack slipped into the river. It covered him to the waist. Gripping the prow with one hand, he waded ashore and dragged the canoe partway up the embankment near the edge of the creek. He crouched and held it steady for Vicki. Staying low, she scurried to the front. Jack gave her a hand as she climbed out. It was wet. Together, they pulled the canoe farther up the low slope.

'Now what?' he whispered.

'I guess we walk upstream.'

His big hand closed around her forearm. They stepped around a cluster of bushes and entered Laurel Creek. Its rocky bed felt slick under her shoes. As they approached the middle, the water level rose above her knees.

'Too bad we don't have a flashlight,' Jack said.

'I hadn't really planned to do this.'

Side by side, they waded slowly forward. The creek and its shores were dark except for a few flecks of moonlight. Vicki heard the voices of the searchers, but they seemed no closer than before. She couldn't make out the words.

Though she often checked the black path of the creek in front of her, she concentrated on studying the shores. If Charlie's in the water, she thought, we won't have to see him. We'll feel him. This stretch of the creek was so narrow that they wouldn't be able to miss the body. It would strike their legs.

And she prayed that Charlie was not in the water. They were too far downstream from the bridge.

If he's still alive, she thought, he's either on the shore or the searchers already found him.

Her heart gave a sudden lurch as she spotted a pale shape floating toward her. Jack squeezed her hand, then let go. He hurried toward the thing. 'Just a branch,' he whispered.

'Thank God.'

He bent down and pushed it. The branch slid out of the way, scraping against rocks along the shore.

They continued walking up the creek.

While Vicki's eyes roamed the dim shapes of bushes and rocks alongside the stream, she listened for the searchers. Minutes went by when all she heard were birds and insects, an occasional frog, the slurp of their own legs moving through the water.

Then, a voice would come from the distance ahead. Another would usually answer. Then, more silence.

The voices seemed *farther* away then before.

That pleased Vicki, at first. She certainly didn't want to run into any of the men from the chief's party. But she began wondering what it meant.

It could mean, she decided, one of two things: either Charlie had already been found or the searchers had finished hunting downstream.

She hoped that they had turned back because Charlie had been found. Found alive.

But what she believed, in spite of her hopes, was that the men had made their way to the river's edge without finding him. Some time before she and Jack arrived. Once he was in the river, there was no point in continuing the search. The body would be lost. Until it washed ashore somewhere, maybe miles downriver. Or until it decomposed and the gases sent the bloated corpse popping to the surface. So the men had given up and headed back for the bridge.

We might as well quit, she thought.

No. Too soon.

Jack made a quiet, 'Hmm?' He waded to the right. Vicki stayed beside him, peering at the shore, wondering what he'd noticed. He stopped and looked down. Vicki saw the vague shape of a cigarette butt on top of a dark rock.

'My hands are wet,' he whispered. 'Do you mind?'

Vicki shrugged, unsure of what he meant.

He pressed his right hand against the front of her T-shirt. She felt it rub across her belly, and she realized he was using her shirt as a towel because he wore no shirt, himself, and his shorts were damp. He turned his hand over, rubbed the back of it against her, then clenched the shirt in his fist. When his hand went away, she felt the moisture it had left on the fabric. And she still felt his touch like a warm, exciting after-image.

He bent down. He picked up the remains of the cigarette. He rolled it between his thumb and forefinger. 'Fresh,' he whispered. 'Filter's still wet.'

'So the searchers got this far,' Vicki said. It confirmed her suspicions.

'They might've missed him, I guess.'

'They've got lights.'

'Do you want to turn back?' Jack asked, and tossed the cigarette into the bushes.

'I don't know.'

'It's fine with me if you want to keep looking.'

'We'd just be going over ground they already searched.'

'It's up to you,' he said.

'I guess there's not much point.'

'Maybe they found him.'

'Maybe.'

Jack took a step closer to Vicki. He gave her upper arm a gentle squeeze, then kept his hand there. 'I wish there was something we could do for Charlie.'

'We did all we could.'

'He means a lot to you, doesn't he?'

Vicki nodded. 'He helped me so much. I was his patient, you know. He was my doctor when I was a kid. When he found out I was interested in medicine, he kind of took me under his wing. I'd go over to the clinic after school, sometimes, and he'd show me things and we'd talk.'

'I suppose he must be like a father to you.'

'I never needed a father figure . . . have a perfectly good real one, you know? Charlie and I were never even all that close. We were friends, but it was pretty much on a professional level. He was always encouraging me.'

'He must've cared a lot for you,' Jack said, lightly caressing her arm.

'More than I ever suspected. I wish . . .' Her throat tightened. 'I wish I'd paid more attention to him. I should've seen him outside the clinic, had dinners with him, or . . .'

'Does he have a family?'

'He's divorced. He never had children. He was all alone, and I just ignored him.'

'You joined him in his work,' Jack said. 'It sounds as if that's exactly what he wanted all along. I think you fulfilled whatever hopes he had for you. You shouldn't feel guilty for not doing more.'

That's a good way to look at it, she thought. 'He never acted as if he . . . I mean, I went my way and he went his. I don't know what he did when he left the clinic. He had *lots* of money, a beautiful home. He was fairly handsome for a man his age. So I just assumed he was getting along fine. I never worried about him. I hardly gave him any thought at all. I should've.'

Jack caressed the side of her face. 'Do you want to keep looking?'

'I don't think so.'

'We'll go back to town and find out what's happening. For all we know, Charlie's made it through all this. He might be in a hospital room, right now, giving orders to the nurses.'

'That'd be nice,' Vicki said. 'If only it's true.'

They turned away from the shore. Vicki held his hand. Side by side, they waded down the middle of the creek. Though she had no more hopes of finding Charlie, she scanned the darkness anyway.

I should've cared more about him, she thought. I should've made sure he was happy. He wasn't a father figure to me, but was I like a daughter to him? Maybe. Probably. He did what a father does for a daughter: encouraged me, taught me, gave me advice and guidance . . . paid for my schooling.

God, Charlie, I'm sorry.

You fulfilled whatever hopes he had for you.

Did I?

If you're still alive, Charlie. I'll make it up to you. I will.

Soon, she saw the moonlit river through a break in the trees ahead.

'Almost there,' Jack said.

'I'll be glad when we're rid of the canoe.'

'We can go to my place, and I'll drive you over to the bridge.'

'Okay.'

That's the one good thing about all this, she thought. Being with Jack. If only the rest hadn't happened . . .

We'll be together a lot from now on, she told herself, and squeezed his hand.

He looked at her. She wished she could see his face.

They waded forward. As they neared the mouth of the creek, the view of the river widened.

And Vicki saw the canoe.

On the river.

Twenty or thirty feet out.

Drifting away.

Chapter Twenty-three

'Oh no,' Vicki muttered.

'How the hell . . . ?'

She let go of Jack and lurched forward. He grabbed her arm. 'No. Wait here. I'll get it.' He backed away, held up a hand signalling her to stay put, then swung around and hit the creek in a low dive. Water exploded up. Vicki trudged after him, watching him swim through the last of the narrow channel and into the river.

Wait here?

I don't think so.

She glanced at the slope where they had left the canoe. Saw no one. But *somebody* had been there. The canoe hadn't just slipped into the river. Someone had pushed it. And might be nearby.

Goosebumps swarmed over her skin as she searched the darkness of the slope.

She looked at Jack. He was halfway to the canoe.

She threw herself forward, hit the water flat, knifed through it, glided up to the surface and began to swim. Lifting her head, she snatched a breath. She spotted Jack. 'Slow down,' she called.

He stopped swimming. She saw only his head while he waited for her to catch up.

'I would've come back for you,' he said.

'I know,' she told him, treading water. 'I just didn't want to stay there alone. Somebody *did* this, you know.'

'The possibility occurred to me.'

She saw that the canoe was drifting farther away. 'We'd better get a move on,' she said.

They swam for it.

Jack reached the canoe first. He ducked beneath it. Vicki realized he intended to hold the other side of the vessel to keep it steady while she boarded. 'Okay,' he said. 'Climb on in.'

Stretching out an arm, she grabbed the gunnel. She pulled herself forward, lifted herself high enough to seek Jack's fingers curled over the aluminium gunnel, and glimpsed something large and dark lying in the bottom of the canoe.

A man?

'Jaaaaack?' Her voice came out tight and rising.

'What's . . . ?' His head came up. 'Holy Jesus,' he muttered. 'Is it Charlie?'

'I don't know. I can't . . .'

The thing in the bottom of the boat sat up fast and smashed a forearm across Jack's face. Jack flew backward. The canoe rocked toward Vicki as she heard a hard splash. She tried to thrust herself away. A hand grabbed her hair. Yanked her up. For a moment that seemed to last a long time, she hung there, the canoe skidding on its side about to capsize, her scalp burning with pain, her waist against the gunnel, water rushing around her legs as the canoe slid, her gaze on the black moonlit face that *couldn't* belong to Charlie.

Charred. Cracked. Holes where his eyes should he. No hair. One side of the head gaping open as if his skull had shattered. And in the lasting moment, she thought, it's Charlie. Has to be. Alive!

She felt no elation. Just pain and shock and terror.

What's he doing alive with that kind of head trauma?

Why'd he hit Jack? Why's he *doing* this?

Jack might drown!

She swung a fist up to strike at the outstretched arm, but he twisted away and she felt herself rise up and drop forward. The shift in weight made the canoe drop from its wild tilt. It rocked from side to side, the gunnel pressing into her thighs, raising and lowering them. She felt air on her kicking legs, then water, then air again. Her face rested on something that felt cool and wet and crusted. She knew it was Charlie's burnt leg.

With a gurgling sound that might have been a laugh, Charlie shoved her hip. Her legs scooted along the gunnel. She twisted and squirmed, trying to get away from him. He pushed her, turned her as she struggled. At the moment Vicki's legs dropped into the canoe, he threw her onto her back.

She fell sprawling on top of him.

She bucked and writhed. He held her down.

'Charlie!' she gasped. 'Charlie, it's me! It's Vicki! Let go! What are you *doing*?'

He yanked her T-shirt up until it was stopped by her armpits.

Vicki grabbed the gunnels with both hands and tried to pull herself up.

Charlie tore at her bra. The clasp between the cups gave way. She felt his crisp hands close on the bare skin of her breasts.

'No!' she cried out. 'Charlie.'

He answered with a gurgle.

She grabbed one of the fondling hands and pulled it away. Just for an instant. Then, there was a damp crumbling sound, and a husk of burnt flesh slid off in her hands. With a squeal, she flung it away. Charlie's hand clasped her breast again. Now, it felt warm and slick and she knew it was blood and tendon and muscle caressing her.

His other hand went to her belly and moved down. It pushed beneath the waistband of her shorts.

'NO!' She grabbed it.

Teeth clamped down on her shoulder.

She shrieked.

The canoe lurched, tipped onto its port side, and Vicki threw herself that way. The canoe flopped, spilling her into the river with Charlie on her back. His hands stayed where they were. His teeth kept their painful grip on her shoulder.

His weight pressed her downward as if he had no buoyancy at all.

Vicki, with only an instant to react before the water shut over her, had only managed to snatch a little air. Her lungs ached to inflate.

She kicked and flapped her arms, struggling to stop her descent. But Charlie kept sinking her.

His teeth ground into her shoulder.

His one hand slid to her breast and crawled over it like a huge, scabby spider.

The other, inside her shorts, moved to her hip. Fingertips scraped her skin. She felt a quick tug. The thin elastic band of her panties broke.

She grabbed Charlie's wrist with both hands. She jerked it hard, forcing the hand upward. It didn't let go of her panties. The crotch dug into her, but she kept pulling. The fabric split. Charlie's hand came out from inside her shorts and up against her belly. She twisted his wrist, turned his arm away.

Something more than Charlie's weight thrust her down. Slimy weed licked her skin.

She suddenly felt his head jerk. His teeth ripped her shoulder and let go. His clenching hand was torn away from her breast. Shoving his other arm away, she rolled from under him, tumbled through the clinging fronds, started to rise and kicked madly for the surface.

A hand grabbed the back of her right thigh.

NO!

But instead of dragging her downward, it shoved her up and went away.

Her head broke the surface. She filled her burning lungs with air, saw that she was facing the shore, whirled around and spotted the overturned canoe and swam for it as fast as she could. Moments later, hearing a splash behind her, she slipped onto her side and looked back.

'Go!' Jack yelled. He began swimming after her.

She wanted to wait, but she pictured Charlie coming up out of the depths, reaching for her feet. So she raced for the canoe. She slowed down only long enough to grab a floating paddle. Pressing it against her body, she side-stroked using her free arm until she reached the canoe. She held the prow and looked back.

Jack was moving fast.

She swept her eyes over the rippling surface of the river all around him. No sign of Charlie.

Again, she imagined his black, charred body coming at her from below. She fought an urge to scramble onto the canoe's upturned hull.

Jack flung his arms around the other end of the canoe. 'Let's . . . flip her,' he gasped. 'Count of three.'

Vicki let the paddle float beside her. She slipped her hands beneath the submerged point of the prow.

'Ready?'

'Yes!'

'One, two, *three*!'

She hurled the canoe upward, turning it and sinking herself. Underwater, she heard a metallic smacking sound. She bobbed up. Her shoulder bumped the canoe and she winced as pain exploded from the bite. She eased away and looked. The canoe was riding a little low, but upright. She swam to the paddle, made her way back to the canoe, and tossed it inside. It splashed.

'Get in,' Jack said. He held the other side. Just like before.

Vicki peered over the gunnel. The bottom of the canoe was awash with water, but Charlie wasn't there. She flung herself over the side, landing on her back with a splash. When she got to her knees, she saw Jack a distance away.

The second paddle floated several yards ahead of him.

'Don't bother!' Vicki yelled. 'Get back here!'

He kept swimming toward it.

At least he's going in that direction, she thought. Toward the middle of the river. Away from the place where they'd left Charlie.

Vicki picked up her paddle. She swung her head around, first scanning the area near the canoe, then searching the river between her and the shore.

She almost wished she *would* spot Charlie.

Better to see him, even nearby and swimming closer, than not to know where he was.

Vicki hobbled astern on her knees. She leaned forward, slipping her paddle into the water, and drew it back.

Half expecting Charlie to grab it.

But he didn't.

The canoe moved sluggishly forward, turning.

Jack, she saw, already had the other paddle and was coming toward her. She stroked again. The prow swung farther and pointed at him.

'Hurry!' she shouted.

The distance closed.

Still no sign of Charlie.

Jack hurled the paddle into the canoe and flung himself in after it. He scurried to his knees. He jabbed the paddle down into the river and swept it back.

Vicki turned the canoe southward.

Soon, they were rushing over the river. The water inside the canoe slopped this way and that, splashing up Vicki's thighs, sweeping away, coming at her again like a small tide, rolling from side to side.

She paddled as hard as she could. She huffed for air. Every muscle from her neck to her calves felt stiff and heavy. The narrow slats of the floorboards punished her knees. The bite on her shoulder burned. But she dug the paddle deep and jerked it back and stretched forward and rammed it in again. Again. Again.

She didn't speak. She didn't look to see if Charlie was near. She stared at Jack's bent back and blinked sweat out of her eyes and kept on paddling.

At last, they rounded the end of the pier. Vicki steered toward the beach. The canoe sped alongside the pier. The instant it hit the beach, Jack leaped out. He dragged it a few feet up the sand. Vicki jumped over the side. She lifted her end. They ran the canoe to the place where they had found it. When they overturned it, the trapped water slopped out. They tossed the paddles under the canoe.

Vicki in the lead, they dashed across back yards. The water in her shoes made squeeshing sounds, and she was surprised to realize that she still had them on. All that swimming, and she'd been wearing sneakers. Could've gone so much faster without them. But she was glad to have them, now.

Finally, she rushed into the river and rounded the fence at the border of the public beach. She splashed her way ashore.

Safe on the beach, she hitched up her sagging wet shorts, then bent over and held her knees and tried to catch her breath.

Jack flopped onto his back.

'Get up,' she gasped. 'You'll tighten up. Gotta keep moving.'

With a moan, he pushed himself off the sand.

Heeding her own advice, Vicki straightened up. She walked in circles, back arched, head thrown back, hands on hips. Jack staggered backward, watching her. She was suddenly aware of her broken bra hanging loose from her shoulders. She felt one cup like a wadded hanky above her left breast. The other was crumpled beneath her armpit. The way her sodden T-shirt clung to her skin, she probably looked almost naked. She realized that she didn't care.

She only cared that she was away from Charlie. She was safe. Jack was safe.

'What's that on your shoulder?' Jack asked.

She glanced down at her shoulder. The T-shirt there was dark. 'He bit me,' she said.

'Jesus.'

'Are *you* all right?'

'My head hurts,' he said.

She went to Jack. She rested her hands on his sides. 'I was afraid you might drown.'

'I was never out cold,' he said. 'But the boat . . . it was pretty far off when I came up for air. I had a hard time catching up to it.' He moved closer to Vicki. His arms went around her and he eased her against him. She felt the rise and fall of his chest, the thumping of his heart.

'Thank God you're all right,' she whispered.

'Did he hurt you?'

'Not so much. Just the bite.' She squeezed Jack hard. 'It was so *horrible*. He tore my clothes. He . . . *pawed* me.'

'Was it Charlie?'

'Yes.'

'I don't get it. Why would Charlie . . . ?'

'He acted crazy. I don't know. Did you see him?'

'Not really. Just a glimpse.'

'He was . . . all burnt. Third-degree burns.' A tremor passed through her. 'Jack, his skin was . . . incinerated. And he didn't have any eyes. And his head . . . one side was completely caved in. I mean, he should've been *dead*. Nobody could survive that kind of head injury.'

'Apparently, Charlie did.'

'What'll we do?'

'About what?' Jack asked.

'About him.'

Jack was silent for a while. His hands slowly rubbed her back. 'I'm in no mood to tell the search team, that's for sure. He could've

510

killed us both. He *hurt* you. The hell with him. He's probably drowned by now, anyway. Or died of his injuries. Either way, good riddance. Let the bastard wash ashore. Or disappear forever. I don't care. I know he was supposed to be your friend, but . . .'

'That was Charlie, but it wasn't my friend. I *told* him who I was. He went ahead, anyway, and . . . he would've raped me, Jack. That's what he wanted to do. That burnt-up . . . he wanted to *rape* me.'

Shuddering, she pressed her face to the side of Jack's neck. He held her tight for a long time. Slowly, the tremors passed. Vicki's strength seemed to seep out of her. Only Jack's stout body kept her from slumping to the sand.

'Do you think you can walk as far as my house?' he asked.

'I'd rather go home. To Ace's. You'll come with me, won't you?'

'You bet.'

'Good,' she said. She kept her arms around him. 'In a while?'

Chapter Twenty-four

'Would you like a drink, or something?' Vicki asked as she turned on a lamp in the living-room.

'That can wait until you've taken care of yourself,' Jack said.

'I'll hurry.'

'Do you have an old towel for me to sit on?' he asked, plucking at a leg of his damp shorts.

Nodding, she headed for the hallway. She thought how odd it was that Jack had ended up here in the house tonight, after all. She felt a small stir of excitement, but it was blunted by the weariness of her body and the leaden weight in her mind left by the encounter with Charlie.

When she reached the linen closet, she took down her beach towel. She carried it back into the living-room, where Jack waited.

She gave it to him. 'You might want to get out of your shorts,' she said. 'You can wear this, if you want. We haven't got a robe or anything large enough for you. I can put your stuff in the drier a little later.'

'I'm fine,' he told her. 'Go ahead and don't worry about it.'

'Back in a while,' she said.

In her bedroom, Vicki took her robe out of the closet. She found a nightgown in a drawer. Then, she shambled back down the hallway to the bathroom and shut herself inside.

Rump against the door, she bent down. She pulled off her shoes and socks. The shoes had sand in them. Sighing, she staggered to the wastebasket and dumped the sand.

She remembered the car accident during her sophomore year at college. Tim was driving.

One of the guys I didn't marry, she thought.

They were on their way back to campus on a stormy night when a car ran a red light and broadsided them. They'd both walked away from the crash with nothing more than a few bruises. But this is how she'd felt afterward, waiting in the rain for the police to arrive. Her muscles like warm liquid. Her mind dim and out of focus. Exhausted, dazed, hardly able to stand on her feet.

Hands braced on the sink, she leaned forward and peered at herself in the medicine-cabinet mirror. Her damp hair hung in ropes around her face. Her eyes looked vacant. Her skin seemed pallid in spite of the tan. She had a dark smudge on the right side of her face, and wondered vaguely where that had come from.

Stepping back, she glimpsed the way her T-shirt looked. Wet and dirty. Clinging. She had taken a moment, before leaving the park, to reach inside and arrange her bra. Otherwise, Jack would've had an eyeful. Which would've been all right, she supposed. She really didn't care much, one way or the other. Too messed up to care.

She only glanced at the shirt's torn, filthy, blood-spotted shoulder. Then she pulled it up over her head, wincing as the fabric came unstuck from her wounds, feeling the loose cups of the bra fall aside once the shirt was no longer there to hold them. She slipped the straps off her arm, and looked. '*Uh!*'

She flinched rigid. Her hands flew up and stopped, inches from her blackened breasts.

She understood, now, how she got the dirty face and shirt.

She stared down at herself, moaning.

Her chest, both her breasts, her stomach and sides were smeared with dark soot. Hand-prints. Smears. Streaks and swirls left by Charlie's burnt fingers. One broad, black smudge was low on her belly. She knew it didn't stop at the elastic of her shorts.

She lowered the shorts and stepped out of them.

The black stopped just above her pubic hair and swept sideways to her hip. At her hip were a few scratches, red trails in a field of char.

She drew a fingertip across the grimy top of her left breast. The fifth was *greasy*.

That's why it hadn't come off in the river.

It's what you get on your fingers, she thought, if you picked up a grilled steak. One that's well done. One that's been burned to a crisp.

She suddenly gagged. And gagged again and again, her eyes watering as the spasms hunched her over. She didn't vomit, though. She supposed that her medical training, especially her time as a resident in the ER, had pretty much cured her of that. She'd seen such stomach-turning sights, day after day, that they had finally ceased to disgust her.

But *this* disgusted her.

This was *on* her.

When Vicki stopped gagging, she stood up straight, took deep breaths, and wiped her eyes. She felt a little better, now.

Just clean it off and forget about it.

Regular soap, she thought, might not do the job.

Crouching, she opened the cupboard beneath the sink and took out a can of scouring powder. Its label boasted 'grease-cutting action'.

With that in her hand, she stepped away from the sink and looked around. The mirror showed that her back, from just below her shoulderblades to her waist, was nearly as filthy as her front. From lying on Charlie in the canoe, she thought. Twisting herself, she saw that the backs of her legs also bore smudges.

Jack, she thought, may have a long wait.

When she finished drying, she checked her towel. It looked clean. The mirror was fogged. With a corner of the towel, she wiped an area clear. She inspected her shoulder. Charlie's teeth had left a pair of discoloured crescents. Far apart. His mouth, she thought, must've been open very wide. The incisors had broken her skin. Four uppers and four lowers. The edges of the wounds looked ragged.

That's a pretty nasty bite he gave you.

Weird, she thought. I just treated Melvin for a bite, now I've got one.

Must be going round.

She smiled grimly at herself in the mirror.

We've got something in common. We can compare notes on our bites. Sure thing.

She gave no more thought to Melvin as she soaked her wounds with hydrogen peroxide and taped pads of gauze in place. Then she turned her attention to the scratches on her hip. They were minor. She dabbed them with the disinfectant and didn't bother to apply a bandage.

Takes care of that, she thought.

She put on her robe, carried her nightgown into her bedroom, then shut the door and slipped the robe off.

Turning slowly, she studied herself in the mirror. Her wet hair was a tangle. But her body bore no traces of the greasy ash. Her pallor seemed gone, replaced by a rosy hue.

The hot shower had not only brought colour to her skin. She felt as if it had also awakened her, washed the daze out of her mind and turned her exhaustion into a rather pleasant laziness.

She slipped the nightgown over her head. It drifted down her body like the caress of a cool breeze. Its pale blue fabric gleamed in the lamplight.

Quickly, she brushed her hair. She considered blowing it dry, but Jack had already been waiting too long. She put her robe on, and hurried from the room.

She found Jack sitting on the couch. He smiled when he saw her. 'You look fabulous,' he said.

'I sure feel better.' She knew she was blushing. Partly the compliment. Partly the fact that he was wearing the beach towel like a skirt and she doubted that he had anything on beneath it. My idea, she reminded herself.

But her mind was fairly clear, now, and she found herself reluctant to join him on the couch.

'Sorry I took so long,' she said, stopping in front of the coffee table.

'I took the opportunity to clean myself up some. At the kitchen sink.'

He still had the dark smudge of a bruise on his forehead. It must've been coated with soot before he washed. He'd probably had some of the stuff on his hands, too, from when he pulled Charlie off her at the bottom of the river.

'How about that drink?' she asked.

'What are you having?'

She shrugged. 'Why don't we go out to the kitchen? We'll have a look around and see what looks good.'

He stood up, holding onto the towel. When he was on his feet, he tightened the towel's tuck at his hip. 'This is a . . . somewhat compromising attire,' he said, a sheepish look on his face.

Vicki smiled and found herself relieved by his embarrassment. 'What's it compromising?'

'My modesty?'

'I don't know, it covers more of you than your shorts did.'

'Doesn't feel that way,' he said, and followed her into the kitchen.

His blue shorts were spread flat on the counter by the sink. 'I'll go ahead and throw them in the drier,' Vicki suggested.

'Aah, don't bother.'

'You want to climb into damp pants when you're ready to go home? It's no trouble, really.' She pulled the moist leather belt out of the loops and picked up the shorts. Something jangled. 'You'd better empty your pockets,' she said. As she swung the shorts toward Jack, his briefs dropped out of a leg hole. He ducked and made a one-handed grab for them while he clutched the towel at his waist. Missed. Then snatched them off the floor and wadded them. But not fast enough to prevent Vicki from seeing that they were bikini-style and bright red.

Only slightly brighter red than his face.

Amused, Vicki almost said, 'Snazzy.' But that would probably just fluster him more. 'They're only drawers,' she said.

'Yeah,' he muttered, and took the shorts from her. He removed a key case, checked the other pockets, and looked around as if searching for the drier.

'It's out back,' Vicki explained.

'I'll go with you.' He rolled his shorts up, deftly planting the briefs inside so that Vicki didn't get another glimpse of them, and cradled the bundle against his belly.

He's awfully self-conscious about those things, she thought as she opened the back door and stepped outside. The concrete patio felt cool under her bare feet.

I'd sure be embarrassed if *mine* fell on the floor in front of *him*.

A hot sick feeling suddenly pulsed through Vicki as she was hit by the memory of Charlie ripping her panties off.

It's all right, she told herself. It's over.

She felt the grass, wet and soft on the bottoms of her feet, wisps of it sliding between her toes as she crossed the lawn.

We made it out of there. We're at Ace's, now. I'm safe. Jack's safe. Charlie's far away.

She pictured him under the water, a maimed shape blacker than the river's darkness, still searching the depths for her, still clinging to the flimsy torn rag.

Don't think about him, she told herself. It's over.

Over, sure.

You think you had nightmares *before*?

Nightmares, I can handle. It's the real-life shit that's getting hard to take.

She opened the laundry-room door, felt the trapped heat wash over her, and flicked the light on. Jack followed her inside.

'Cosy,' he said.

'Hot as a huncher,' Vicki said, borrowing Ace's language – and with it, some of Ace's bravado. She walked past the enclosure of the spare toilet, past the washing machine and tubs, and pressed a button to open the door of the front-loading drier. Even before she looked inside, she remembered that she had forgotten to take her laundry out. Laughing softly, she crouched down to remove her things. 'I saw yours, now you see mine.'

'Good. I'll feel a lot better.'

Into the laundry basket at her side she tossed washcloths, towels, socks, a sundress, shorts, blouses, her bikini, a skirt, panties and bras of every colour.

When the drum was empty, Jack handed his rolled shorts to her. She shook them open inside the drier, watched his briefs flop out, then shut the door, straightened up, and started the machine.

Jack picked up the basket.

'Oh, you can leave that here.'

'No problem. You just lead the way in case I lose my towel.'

In the kitchen, she took the basket from him and set it on the floor near the breakfast table. Then she opened the cupboard where the liquor was kept. 'What'll you have? The hard stuff's in here. There's beer and wine in the refrigerator, soft drinks . . . I'm having Scotch.'

'Scotch is fine,' Jack said.

As she filled the glasses, she asked, 'Ice?'

'Maybe one cube. Don't want it watered down too much.'

She dropped one ice cube into each drink, and gave a glass to Jack. They went into the living-room. Vicki realized that she was no longer concerned by the fact that he wore nothing but a towel. She sat down beside him in the middle of the couch and turned sideways, sliding one knee onto the cushion. The robe fell away from her thigh. She glanced down. The blue satin of her night-gown was glossy in the lamplight. It was short enough to show a lot of leg. She thought, looks okay to this kid, and didn't bother to adjust the robe.

'Here's mud in your eye,' Jack said.

Vicki leaned toward him and clinked her glass against his. Easing back, she took a drink. The Scotch went down, spreading heat, making her eyes water. 'Oh, that's good.'

'*Hits* the spot,' Jack said. '*Burns* the spot.'

'Ugh, don't mention burning.' She said it half joking, and wished she hadn't.

'Are you going to be all right?'

'I'm feeling better all the time.' She took another drink. 'How about you? That's a mean lump on your forehead. Do you want some ice for it, or something?'

'No, it's fine.'

'Do you have a headache?'

'That's a leading question.' He smiled. 'How about you?'

'My head's about the only thing that doesn't ache. I probably won't be able to *move*, tomorrow.'

'Hate to tell you, it is tomorrow.'

'I'm gonna be wasted.' I'll have to take Charlie's appointments and mine, she realized. Maybe Thelma can cancel some of them.

517

She looked at the digital clock on the VCR. Four-seventeen. 'Geez.'

'I'd better drink up and go, or you won't get any sleep at all.'

'Gonna go home in your towel?'

'My pants should be dry pretty soon.'

'There's no hurry,' Vicki said. 'I mean, I don't want to keep *you* up. Have you got court or something?'

He shook his head. 'Just a deposition at two. I can sleep in.'

'Lucky duck.'

'You must be exhausted, though.'

'I'm not really eager to be alone just now.'

'Neither am I,' Jack admitted. He set down his glass and held his hand out toward Vicki. His fingers were trembling. 'Look at that. I never shake like that.'

Vicki took hold of his hand and squeezed it gently. She brought it down and rested the back of her hand on her thigh. She took another drink while he reached out with his other hand and picked up his glass. He moved closer to her. She felt the softness of the towel push against her knee.

'I'm sorry I got us into that,' she said. 'They *told* me to stay out of it. I should've listened.'

'There was nothing wrong with searching for him.'

'It nearly got us both killed.'

'Nobody could've foreseen that he'd attack anyone.'

'There's been so much weirdness lately. Pollock, now this. And I keep getting into it.'

'You mean the guy who was murdered by that nurse? How were you involved in that?'

'Ace and I were at the Riverfront on Saturday night. Pollock came to our table and caused some trouble. This guy we were with, Melvin, threatened to kill him. Later that night, Pollock *was* killed. We figured Melvin might've had something to do with it, so we talked to a policeman the next day. I guess he thought we should mind our own business, and he told Chief Raines about us, and that's how come I got such a lousy reception at the bridge tonight.' She took a sip of her Scotch, and sighed. 'I guess they don't appreciate civilian interference.'

'Raines likes to do things his own way,' Jack said. 'I've had some run-ins with him, myself. On behalf of my clients,' he added. 'It's been my experience that he's stubborn, narrow-minded and stupid.'

'But otherwise a wonderful guy,' Vicki said.

'From what I've heard, Dexter Pollock wasn't much better.'

'In addition to all the above, he was a tyrant and a lech.'

'Otherwise wonderful?'

'About the best thing that can be said for Pollock is that he's dead.' Vicki grimaced. 'I shouldn't have said that. I mean, I'm sorry he's dead.'

'But not very.'

'Hardly at all.' She changed position, swinging her bent leg down, turning forward, resting her feet on the coffee table and settling into the cushion behind her. Jack scooted closer. He lifted his arm. She eased forward to let him lower it across her shoulders. He didn't touch her wounded right shoulder. Instead, his hand slipped behind it and curled around her upper arm.

'At the Riverfront,' she continued, 'Pollock started sniffing me. Said I must have an odour that attracts crazy people. I dumped my beer in his lap.'

Jack shook his head. 'You *are* a tough broad.'

'You should've heard what *he* called me.'

Jack caressed her arm. 'That's the incident that led to the threat?'

'Oh, he retaliated and flung his beer at me. Right in my face.'

'Good thing he's already dead, the bastard.'

'I'm liking you more and more,' Vicki said. She patted his leg. Leaving her hand on the towel, she took another drink. Her cheeks, she realized, were beginning to feel a little numb.

'So who's this Melvin? Is he just a casual acquaintance, or is he someone I need to worry about?'

'Don't worry about him. That's my job.'

'What do you mean?'

'He's apparently smitten with me, and he's crazy as hell.' She fingered the nap of the towel. 'That's partly what Pollock meant about me attracting weirdos. Melvin's as weird as they come. He gave me a *car*.'

'That doesn't sound so weird.'

'Wouldn't be weird if we were engaged or something. We've never even gone out together.'

'Glad to hear it.'

'He just likes to *do* things for me. Maybe even things like killing Pollock to pay him back for what he did at the bar. Wouldn't surprise me. He doesn't have loose screws, he's *missing* screws.'

'He can't be all that crazy if he's smitten with you.'

'Oh no?' Vicki asked, looking at Jack.

He leaned forward, turning himself, setting his glass on the table as his arm eased Vicki away from the cushion. When she faced him, their eyes locked. She felt him take her glass. He bent away from her, putting it down. Then both his hands were on Vicki's back, guiding her closer. She held his sides, brushed her lips against his, then felt the soft pressure of his mouth. She closed her eyes as they kissed. Her mind seemed to spin slowly – the Scotch and the deep weariness – and she felt herself sinking into the dark, peaceful place where there was only the comfort of knowing Jack was with her, kissing her, and everything was right.

She was on the diving raft with Jack, standing in the darkness, holding him, the raft rocking gently under her feet as they kissed. He lifted her nightgown. She stepped back and raised her arms. As he drew the gown over her head, she closed her eyes. She stood there, trembling, the warm breeze sliding over her skin, and waited for his touch. He kissed her breast. The mouth on her nipple felt crusted and greasy.

NO!

She clutched the charred head and thrust it away from her and staggered backward as Charlie, black and eyeless and wearing a beach towel around his waist, lurched toward her, reaching out. She teetered on the edge of the raft. Windmilled her arms. Then tumbled backwards.

Flinched as she fell, and jerked awake.

She was in bed. Daylight filled the room. Gasping for breath, she sat up. Her heart was thudding. Sweat trickled down her face. Beneath her robe, her nightgown felt glued to her skin. She pulled the robe open as she scooted off the bed. The movement awakened a hot ache in her shoulder, lesser aches in the stiff muscles all over her body. Standing, she shook the robe off. She peeled the damp, clinging nightgown over her head. With a shaky hand, she lifted a corner of the sheet and used it to dry her face.

The clock on the nightstand showed 7:58.

At least I didn't oversleep, she thought.

An hour before she had to be at the clinic.

Charlie.

A chill swept over her body as memories of last night's attack rushed through her mind. She rubbed the gooseflesh that pebbled her arms, and jumped as the alarm clock blared. She lurched to the nightstand and silenced it.

She didn't remember setting the alarm.

Maybe Jack did it.

The last thing she could remember was kissing him. Had she actually fallen asleep while they kissed? What did he do then, carry her into the bedroom and set the alarm so she wouldn't be late for work?

She heard the distant ringing of the telephone. It rang only twice. She went to the dresser. As she pulled a football jersey over her head, she heard footfalls in the hallway. A knock on her door, then the door opened. Ace looked in, grinning. 'Told you he'd call,' she said. 'Bet he's been up all night, kicking himself.'

'You're half right,' Vicki said. She brushed past Ace and hurried to get the phone.

Chapter Twenty-five

'Dr Chandler's with a patient right now,' Thelma said. Though she looked composed, her eyes were red as if she'd been crying recently. 'She's very busy this morning, Melvin. May I schedule an appointment for you?' She glanced down at something on her desk. 'There's an opening next Wednesday at . . .'

'I just want to talk to her for a minute,' Melvin said. 'About this.' He held up the bandaged hand.

'As I explained, she's very busy. Dr Gaines . . . we lost him last night.'

'Lost him?'

'There was a terrible accident up on River Road. He's still missing and . . . we don't hold out much hope for him.'

'I'm sorry. Gosh.'

'So I hope you can appreciate that this is a very difficult time, just now. I've been on the phone all morning, rescheduling appointments to ease the burden for Dr Chandler. So if you'll be patient and give us a few days to sort things out . . .'

Melvin turned around, scanning the deserted waiting-room. 'I don't see anyone,' he said.

'I've just explained to you,' Thelma said, an edge to her voice. 'I'm *cancelling* today's appointments. As many as possible. If you'd like to come back next week . . .'

'I'll just sit and wait. Maybe she can find a minute for me.'

Thelma pressed her lips together and glared at him. But she said nothing. Melvin turned away. He stepped over to an easy chair, sat down, and settled into it gently. The cushion pressed against the furrows Charlie had scratched into his back. They hurt a little, but not much. Compared to all the bites put in him during the past week, the scratches seemed like nothing more than a minor irritation.

But they itched through the bandages Patricia had applied.

He'd found her asleep when he returned from dealing with Charlie. He woke her up. She yelped with alarm and threw her arms around him. 'What happened?' she blurted. 'What'd he *do* to you?'

'Not near as much as I did to him,' Melvin said.

He told her all about it while they went into the bathroom and he shed his damp, filthy clothes. The back of his shirt was split apart. Standing behind him, Patricia ran her fingertips lightly down his scratches, making him squirm. In the mirror, he saw that his face – especially around the mouth – and neck were smeared with the same kind of black grime that had darkened his shirt and pants.

He filled the tub with hot water. He climbed in, and Patricia got in with him. Kneeling behind him, she lathered his back and rubbed it gently with a washcloth. Then, she rubbed harder. 'Ow! Stop that!'

'It doesn't want to come off very good,' she said. He told her to get the Goop from under the sink. It was a lotion that he often used after returning from work at the service station to clean car grease off his hands. She left the tub and came back, with the jar. She spread the slimy lotion over his back. When she rinsed it off, she said, 'It's like magic! Let me do your front.'

She climbed out. Melvin scooted toward the rear of the tub to make room for her. She stepped in and knelt between his legs. Holding the jar in one hand, she peeled the sodden bandages off his shoulders and chest and tossed them onto the bathroom floor.

'You're just so covered with hurts,' she said, a sorrowful look in her eyes as she gazed at his wounds.

'Thanks mostly to you,' Melvin said.

She nibbled her lower lip. 'I'm sorry. I try to be good. I love you, Melvin. I don't *want* to hurt you.'

'I know,' he said. Something seemed to tighten inside his chest and throat. He looked at the trails of scratches remaining on Patricia's breasts and belly from the tantrum she'd thrown last night. Because she'd *missed* him. Most had faded to pinkish lines. Others were dark with thin crusts of scab. He saw that the Face of Ram-Chotep seemed to be healing well except for one corner of the Mouth, which she'd opened during her rage. The bite wound on her forearm was covered with a wet bandage. 'You shouldn't hurt yourself, either,' Melvin said.

'I know. I'm sorry.'

She scooped up a mound of the white Goop with her fingers and spread it over Melvin's face. As he watched her eyes, he wondered about the tenderness he'd lately been feeling toward her. She's dead, he thought. She's nothing but a goddamn zombie.

But *my* zombie. She loves me.

Nobody had ever loved him. Maybe his parents, but that was doubtful, the way they used to treat him. Certainly no girls had ever looked at him with anything but contempt.

Except Vicki, and now Patricia.

Vicki was the only *live* one who was ever nice to him. But it was pretty clear she didn't love him.

She will, he told himself, and closed his eyes. I've just gotta be patient and keep being good to her.

His plans were already bringing rewards. Though Vicki made him take the car back, the gift must've pleased her – she'd asked him out for drinks at the Riverfront. Pretty soon, they'd be having dinners together, maybe going to the show. They would be kissing goodnight. Then, she would start asking him into the house and they'd hug and make out.

He felt Patricia bathing his face with warm water, then swirling the slippery lotion over his shoulders and chest. He imagined her hands were Vicki's hands. Someday soon, they would be. He opened his eyes just a crack, reached out to her breasts, and caressed them. They would be Vicki's breasts, cool and smooth and slick, the stiff nipples pushing against his palms. He felt a swelling rush of desire. If only this was Vicki. Here and now. He'd won her over, at last, and she was living with him, sharing his tub, sliding her hands over his chest, and down, wrapping her fingers around his erect penis.

'You missed me, didn't you?' Patricia's voice.

He opened his eyes. He had left dark hand-prints on her breasts. 'I sure did.'

Her hand moved up and down beneath the water, lightly stroking him.

'Do you love me?' she asked.

'Sure I do.'

'I'm glad you got rid of Charlie. I hated him.'

'I know.'

'You won't make any more, will you?'

'I don't know.'

'We don't need anyone else.'

'I don't want nobody else but you.'

'I love you so much, Melvin.'

She'll never stand for having Vicki around, he thought. She was jealous as hell about Charlie, and Charlie wasn't even a gal. She'll go apeshit when Vicki moves in.

I'll need to get rid of her before then.

Cut off her head? Maybe that'll work.

He felt a hollow ache inside that stole the pleasure from his groin.

Can I do that to her? he wondered. I'll have to.

She's dead anyway, so what does it matter?

It matters, he realized. She loves me and she's good to me and I like her more than I've ever liked anyone except Vicki.

But I'll have to get rid of her.

524

* * *

Melvin heard footsteps. Then a voice. Vicki's voice. Though she spoke too softly for him to understand the words, he could see her through the sliding doors of the receptionist's window. She was standing beside a counter back there, talking to Thelma. Beside Vicki stood an obese woman with hair like a grey helmet.

Vicki looked wonderful. Her blonde hair was golden, her skin a mellow tan, her eyes clear and blue. Her doctor jacket hung open, showing the front of a blue silken blouse that was open at the throat.

Melvin's pulse quickened.

She glanced at him, then faced Thelma again, said a few more words, and walked away. The fat woman stayed by the counter for a while. Then, she opened the door, passed through the waiting-room without glancing at Melvin, and left.

Thelma got up from the desk. She walked around the end of the counter. She turned toward the door.

All right!

She opened it. 'Dr Chandler will see you now.' She held the door for Melvin, then led the way down the corridor to the same room where Vicki had treated his hand last week. 'She'll be with you in a minute,' Thelma said, and left him alone.

Melvin sat on the paper-covered examination table. He took a deep, shaky breath and let it out slowly. His heart was pounding fast. He felt trickles of sweat dribble down his sides.

Then, he heard footsteps. Not the clack of heels like Thelma wore – the whisper and squeak of rubber soles.

Vicki entered the room. Her white coat was buttoned shut, and she had closed the button at her throat.

She's made herself nice and proper for me, Melvin thought. That'll change. One of these days, she'll be as eager as Patricia. I won't be able to *keep* the clothes on her.

He pictured her naked. But she had the Face of Ram-Chotep carved on her torso.

No, it won't be like that. I won't have to do that to Vicki. She'll be alive, and *still* want me.

'Good morning, Melvin,' she said. Though she didn't smile, she didn't look as if she'd been crying. 'Are you having more trouble with your hand?'

'It's still hurting.'

'Shall we have a look at it?'

'I think so,' he said. Last night, Patricia had applied a fresh bandage after the bath. The hand had looked good. But the hand was his excuse for being here, and he wanted Vicki to come over to him and unwrap it.

He held the hand out to her.

She approached, stopping when her thighs were almost close enough to touch his knees. With one hand, she held his hand steady. With the other, she began to peel the tape loose. She smelled clean and fresh, a little like lemons.

'I heard what happened to Dr Gaines,' he said. She stiffened slightly, and the grip on his hand tightened. 'Thelma, she says they haven't found his body.'

'No. They haven't.'

'I'm real sorry for you. I guess he was a good friend.'

Vicki nodded. She seemed distant, withdrawn.

'So, you're running the clinic all on your own, now?'

'For the time being,' she said.

'That's gonna be a lot of work. Maybe you better hire somebody to help out.'

'I imagine I'll have to.' She unwound the last of the tape and peeled off the gauze pad. She turned his hand over, inspecting the wounds on both sides. 'It's looking a lot better,' she said.

'Yeah. Still hurts, though.'

'That's to be expected,' she said, not looking up at him. 'I'll put a fresh dressing on it, and you can be on your way.'

'You're acting like you want to get rid of me.'

'I'm very busy.' She stepped over to a cabinet. There, she opened the shallow metal drawer. She took out a roll of gauze and a tape dispenser. On top of the cabinet, she found scissors. She came back to him and began to bandage his hand. She worked quickly – and not very gently.

'Something wrong?' Melvin asked.

'Everything's just peachy.'

'You mad at me, or something?'

'Mad? I wouldn't say that.'

'What'd *I* do?'

She squeezed the last stip of tape into place, released his hand,

and stepped back. She looked down at the scissors in her hand, then tossed them. They landed with a clatter on top of the cabinet. She stared at Melvin with narrowed eyes. 'What *did* you do, Melvin?'

He felt heat rush to his face. 'What're you talking about?'

'You killed him, didn't you?'

Melvin forced out a laugh. 'Hey, I'm supposed to be crazy, but I don't go around killing people. I'm into resurrection, not murder. *Was* into. Back when I tried to jump-start Darlene. Resurrection, not murder.' He shook his head. 'That's wild. Where'd you ever get an idea like that?'

Vicki didn't answer him. She gazed steadily into his eyes.

'He cracked up his fuckin' car! I didn't have nothing to do with it!'

'Not Charlie. Dexter Pollock.'

'What?'

'You heard me.'

Melvin huffed out another laugh. 'Boy, you've got some imagination on you.'

'Do I?'

'Some nurse nailed Pollock. Everybody knows that. The cops even know who she is. Patricia something. A nurse. Geez. *Me* murder Pollock? That's wild!'

'Is it?'

'Come onnn! You're pulling my leg, right?'

A corner of Vicki's mouth twitched.

'They say *I'm* crazy.'

'You can tell me, Melvin.'

'Are you nuts?'

'Maybe. Maybe I'm nuts to think you meant it, Saturday night, when you said you'd like to kill him. Maybe I'm nuts to think you hated him for what he said – what he *did* to me. Maybe I'm nuts to think you cared enough about me to make him pay for it.'

'*Jesus*,' Melvin muttered.

'Maybe I'm nuts to want to thank you.'

'Thank me?' The words came from him in a hoarse whisper.

This can't be happening, he told himself. It's a trick, or I'm dreaming, or . . .

'I suppose I *am* nuts,' Vicki said.

'I wanted to kill him,' Melvin told her. 'I wanted to tear him to pieces. I *do* care about you. I . . . But I didn't kill him. I shoulda, maybe, but I didn't.'

'Then get out of here,' she said in a tight, hard voice. 'And stay away from me.'

'But . . .'

'You either don't trust me enough to admit it or you were too chicken to kill the bastard for me. Get out!'

Stunned, Melvin hopped down from the table. Vicki side-stepped out of his way. When he was in the corridor, the door slammed at his back.

'I guess maybe I *am* nuts,' Vicki said. She stared down at her lunch, and shook her head.

'Certifiable,' Ace agreed. 'Holy God in a basket, what were you thinking?'

'I don't know. Seemed like a good idea at the time.' She lifted to top of the sesame bun off her hamburger. The broiled patty reminded her of Charlie. Wrinkling her nose, she covered it and pushed the plate away.

'Better eat,' Ace told her. 'A busy gal like you, you've gotta keep your strength up.'

'My appetite's shot.'

'What on earth possessed you to run off at the mouth like that?'

Vicki shrugged. 'I was just feeling so tired. I figured, why not confront him with it?'

'If he did kill Pollock,' Ace said, 'it wasn't such a smart move. I don't care how adorable he thinks you are, if he's afraid you know too much, he might decide to . . .'

'Terminate me with extreme prejudice?'

'You read too many damn books, hon. If that means kill your ass, yeah. He might try something like that to save himself.' She bit into her chilli dog. 'He really might,' she added, her words coming out muffled.

'I know. That occurred to me.'

'Then why . . .'

'By the time I thought of it, I'd already accused him. Since it was too late, then, I changed my tactics and acted as if I would've considered it a favour if he *had* killed Pollock. So he wouldn't think I'm a threat. And also, I thought maybe I might get him to admit it. I don't know whether he believed me or not.'

Ace swallowed her mouthful of food. She wiped chilli off her lips with a napkin. 'That wasn't such a hot move, either, hon.'

'Probably not.'

'No probably. You as much as told him that he failed you by *not* killing the man who insulted you.'

'But he did it, Ace. I know he did. When I said I wanted to thank him for it, he got this odd look on his face.'

'He's always got an odd look on his face.'

'He said, "Thank me?" And I got the feeling he regretted denying it and was really close to confessing. He *wanted* my approval. He ached for it. But he just wasn't quite convinced that I really meant what I said, so he backed off.'

'My pal, Nancy Drew. What's next on the agenda?'

'It wasn't planned, Ace. It just happened.'

'Keep after him, maybe he'll break down and admit it. Maybe just a little more urging. Take him out to dinner tonight, woo him a little, show him you were serious . . .'

The suggestion made something flutter inside Vicki.

What if I tried it? she wondered. I can't! Christ, a date with Melvin? But what if I *could* get him to confess?

Then what? Tell Raines? That jerk wouldn't listen to me anyway. He'd listen to Jack, though. Or we could go to the DA.

Ace, chewing and staring at her, suddenly looked alarmed. 'Hey, I was *kidding*!'

'Don't worry, I wouldn't have the guts.'

'Don't even think about it. Christ! Why did I open my trap?'

'But just suppose I did get him to admit it. They'd have to investigate. They might find real evidence . . .'

'What do you care? Pollock was a pain in the ass!'

'That was no excuse to murder him. He didn't deserve that.'

'Stop it, would you? You're scaring the shit outa me! If he killed Pollock, let the high-and-mighty cops nail him. That's their job, as they've pointed out in no uncertain terms. It's none of your business.'

'It is my business, Ace. He did it because of me – because of what happened at the bar.'

'Horse-squat. He did it because he's a fruitcake. *If* he did it. Maybe he did, maybe he didn't. But you can't hold yourself responsible. Just forget about it. My God, why are we even discussing this? It's crazy. Forget Melvin. Forget he exists. You've gotta look out for number one.'

'From that angle,' Vicki said, 'it makes even more sense. He's never going to leave me alone. Never. He'll just keep . . . *at* me. But if they can get a conviction, he'll be sent away for years. He may *never* get out.'

Ace, with a look on her face as if she were in pain, muttered, 'You're really seriously gonna do it, aren't you?'

'I don't know.'

'You've got a date with Jack, remember? I was standing right there. Seven o'clock, his place. Remember?'

'It'd only take a couple of hours to . . .'

'Well, don't do it without me. He won't try anything if I'm along.'

'He won't confess, either.'

Back at the clinic, Vicki found two patients in the waiting-room. 'I'll start seeing them in just a few minutes,' she told Thelma. She borrowed the telephone directory, and hurried into her office.

Melvin's phone rang three times before he picked up.

'Who's this?'

She squeezed her eyes shut.

'Who the hell is this?'

She pressed a hand to her pounding chest and said, 'Vicki.'

'*Vicki?* Hi!'

'Melvin, I called to apologize. I . . .' She sucked a shaky breath into her lungs. 'I'm sorry about the way I behaved this morning. I was tired and upset, but I shouldn't have . . .'

'No sweat. Honest.'

'Well, I'd feel better if you'd let me make it up to you. Would you like to have dinner with me tonight? My treat. I was thinking about the Fireside Chalet.'

'Yeah? Just you and me?'

'Just you and me.'

'Great. Uh . . . what time you want me to pick you up?'

She'd planned for that one, and had a story ready. 'I need to run over to Blayton Memorial this afternoon, so . . .'

'Want a lift?'

'No, that's fine. I've got Ace's car. It'd be a lot more convenient for me if I just meet you at the restaurant.'

'Yeah, I guess.'

'That way, I can just stop in on the way back from the hospital.'

'Yeah. I guess that makes sense.'

'So why don't we meet at the restaurant at about six o'clock? Is six all right for you?'

'Sure. Great. I'll get dressed up real nice for you.'

'Me, too. See you then, Melvin.'

'Yeah. See you then.'

She hung up. Her heart was racing. Tilting back her chair, she folded her hands behind her head and took slow, deep breaths. I did it, she thought. I actually did it. I'm committed now. I *should* be committed. To an asylum.

But if it works, I'll be rid of him. Maybe for good.

When her calm returned, she looked up Jack's name in the directory. She found two numbers, one for his rooms and one for his office. She dialled the office.

After the second ring, a woman answered the phone. 'Good afternoon, Law Offices of Jack Randolph.'

'Is Mr Randolph in?'

'Who may I say is calling?'

'Vicki Chandler.'

'Just a moment, please.'

Seconds later, Jack said, 'Hi. How's it going?'

The sound of his voice suddenly made her feel a lot better. 'Not as bad as I expected. Thelma cancelled most of the appointments, so it's nothing I can't handle. The thing is, I'll have to be a little late tonight. I should be able to make it over by about nine, if that's all right.'

'I guess I can live with that,' he said. 'We'll eat fashionably late.'

'I'll have to eat before I come over. I've got a dinner engagement.'

'Oh. Okay.'

'It's nothing. I just . . . have to do it. I'll explain when I see you.'

531

'You don't have to explain anything, Vicki.'

'Don't worry, I will. It should be interesting. If I survive.'

'Now I am worried.'

'It just won't be any fun, that's all. I'm not exactly looking forward to it. But we'll be in a public place, and I'm driving myself, so nothing's going to happen.'

'What *are* you doing?'

'I'll tell you all about it when I see you.'

'Vicki.'

'I really can't go into it right now. It's a long story, and I've got a couple of patients waiting. I'll see you at nine, okay? Earlier if possible.'

'Well . . . Fine. See you then.'

'Bye, Jack.'

Chapter Twenty-six

Melvin's heart quickened when he spotted the red Mustang in the parking area alongside the Fireside Chalet.

Vicki had actually come.

All afternoon, he'd wondered about the invitation. Was it for real? Maybe it was just a dirty joke. In school, he'd been the butt of plenty. Darlene Morgan herself had asked him to be her date for the junior prom. But that was right after the movie *Carrie* played for two weeks at the Palace Theater, so Melvin didn't fall for it. There on the phone, right in front of his mother, he told Darlene to eat shit. And always wondered, afterward, if the bitch really would've gone through with the date.

But Vicki was here. She really intended to have dinner with him.

It seemed so incredible.

I knew it would happen, he told himself as he swung into the parking lot.

But not this soon.

Or ever, really.

He realized this was like his experiments. He had *known* he would succeed, but deep inside he'd expected failure. Which made the success all the more sweet.

She knows I killed Pollock for her. That's why she's doing this. It's her way of thanking me.

Unless she wants to get me for it.

Either way, I better not tell her the truth.

He pulled into a space two cars away from Ace's Mustang, and climbed out. He'd been sweating, even in his air-conditioned car. Now, the heat seemed to bake him. His face dripped. Trickles of sweat slid down the nape of his neck and soaked his tight collar. Beneath his sport coat, his shirt was plastered to his back and sides. His underwear was stuck to his rump.

He wanted to look good for her, not like a sweaty pig.

When he opened the restaurant door, cool air rushed out against him. He entered the dimly lighted foyer. Ahead, a gal in old-fashioned clothes stood behind something that looked like a speaker's stand. She was busy talking on the telephone. Looking around, Melvin noticed a sign that read, 'Restroom,' over the entrance to a recessed area. He hurried that way, and pushed through the door marked, 'Gentlemen.'

Instead of towels, it had blowers. He hated those things. Stepping into a stall, he used toilet paper to dry himself. Then, he went to a sink and checked himself in the mirror. He thought he was fine except for his necktie being crooked.

Until now, he hadn't been able to see how he looked in his jacket and tie. To keep Patricia from being upset – she would've thrown a fit if she knew he was having dinner with Vicki – he'd told her that he needed to work at the station tonight. He'd carried his good clothes out to the car earlier, while she was watching television. When he kissed her goodnight and left the house, he was wearing his greasy coveralls. Alone in the garage, he stripped and dressed himself for dinner.

Melvin straightened his tie. He ran a comb through his slicked-down hair, gave himself a wink, and left the restroom.

He walked up to the girl behind the lighted stand. She was a slender brunette, a few years younger than Melvin, and pretty in spite of the expression on her face. She looked at him the way she might look at a pubic hair floating in her soup. 'I'm supposed to be eating with Dr Vicki Chandler,' he said. 'She here?'

'This way.'

He followed her. She walked fast as if trying to get away from him.

The bitch.

He wondered how she'd enjoy having cellophane wrapped around her face.

Then, he saw Vicki. She was seated in a high-backed booth along the wall. She smiled up at him, blushing. He sat across the table from her.

To Melvin, she always looked beautiful. Tonight, however, she was more stunning that he had ever seen her. Her golden hair seemed to float around her face. Her eyes were as blue as the sky on a cloudless summer morning. She wore a single thin gold chain around her neck. Her pale blue blouse, gleaming like silk, was open wide at the throat, open all the way down to a button just lower than her breasts. Between the folds, he could see the shadowed slope of her left breast.

'You look very nice this evening, Melvin,' she said.

'You too. You look great. Gosh.'

'Thank you.' She lifted a half-empty glass and took a drink. When she set it down, a few grains of salt speckled her lower lip. She curled her lip in over her teeth and licked the salt off. 'Would you like something from the bar?' she asked. 'I'm having a margarita.'

'Yeah, that'd be great.'

'I got here a little early,' she said.

'Figured you'd better get a drink in quick before I showed up?'

'Don't be silly.'

A waiter stepped up to the table. Melvin was glad it wasn't the bitch, but he didn't look at the man's face. Instead, he watched Vicki smile up at him and say, 'We'll have two margaritas.'

When the waiter was gone, he said, 'I bet he wonders what you're doing with a guy like me.'

'You shouldn't put yourself down all the time, Melvin.'

'Beauty and the beast.'

'I wouldn't be here if I thought you were a beast.'

'How come you *are* here?'

Her head tilted slightly to one side. 'Because I want to be. I think . . . I haven't been very nice to you.'

'You been okay. You been fine.'

One shoulder shrugged a fraction. Her blouse, Melvin noticed, didn't cling smoothly to it. As if she wore a pad of some kind between the shiny fabric and her skin. Some kind of a female underthing, he supposed. But the other shoulder didn't seem to have it.

'To be honest,' she said, 'I really was a little frightened of you, at first. The night I came into town, for instance. I mean, the last time I'd seen you was the Science Fair and that pretty much freaked me out.'

'Freaked everyone out,' he said.

'But I'm not frightened of you any more. Now that I've gotten to know you better, I've seen that you're sensitive and thoughtful.' Smiling, she shook her head. 'Nobody ever gave me a car before.'

'You made me take it back.'

'But the thought was very generous. And I can understand how . . . It seems like everybody's always dumped on you. So it makes sense if you might feel the only way to gain affection is by giving things to people.'

She *does* understand, Melvin thought. He felt a tightness in his throat.

'You don't have to give me gifts, though. I like you for who you are, not for what you give me.'

'That's . . . real nice.'

The waiter arrived with the drinks. He set them on the table, a small napkin under each glass. 'Would you like to enjoy your drinks for a few minutes,' he asked, 'before I bring the menus?'

'I think we'd like to see them now,' Vicki said. She smiled at Melvin. 'I'm starving, how about you?'

He nodded.

Maybe she's starving, he thought. Or maybe she just wants to hurry things up and get finished and get away from me.

If that's it, why's she here at all?

The waiter handed a menu to Vicki, then gave one to Melvin. 'Would you like a few minutes to look them over?' he asked.

'A couple of minutes,' Vicki said.

He went away.

Vicki didn't open her menu. She set it aside. So maybe she's not in a big hot rush, Melvin told himself as he set his own menu down.

She lifted her margarita toward him. Her hand wasn't steady. The surface of the drink trembled. 'To knights in shining armour and damsels in distress.'

Didn't Pollock say something about knights when we were at the Riverfront?

That's what she's getting at, Melvin thought. She's toasting me for nailing the bastard.

He clinked his glass against Vicki's, and took a sip through the grainy salt on its rim.

'Do you like it?' she asked. 'The drink?'

'It's a little like lemonade.'

'It's strong, though. It has tequila and Triple Sec.'

He nodded as if he knew that.

'Well,' she said, 'shall we see what they've got?'

They studied their menus. The prices stunned Melvin. He had never eaten at a restaurant this nice, and never imagined that the food could cost so much. The price of the top sirloin was almost ten times the amount he spent for one at the grocery.

She can afford it, he told himself. She owns the whole clinic now. Thanks to me.

Still, the prices made him feel uneasy.

Maybe I'll pay for us, he thought. That'd make it all right. She said this was her treat, though. It might be rude if I try to pay.

'Their steaks are very good here,' Vicki said.

'Is that what you're having?'

'I think I'll have the prawns.'

The prawns, he saw, were less expensive. 'Go on ahead and have a steak,' he said, keeping the menu in front of his face so she couldn't see him blush. 'It's on me.'

'Melvin, no. I'm paying. I insist.'

'Hey, I got money I don't know what to do with.'

Her fingertips suddenly curled over the top of his menu and eased it down. She looked him in the eyes. His embarrassment fled as he felt a soft warm glow spread through him. 'My treat,' she whispered.

'But if you want a steak . . .'

'I don't even want to look at one.' She drew her arm back slowly. In the dim light, it was dusky and sleek. 'I want prawns. You may have whatever you wish. Have steak and lobster, if you like. Don't think about the cost.'

'Okay. I just wanted to . . .'

She touched a finger to her lips. 'You've given me so much already.'

'You made me take the car back.'

'That's not what I mean,' she said, 'and you know it.'

The waiter stepped up to the table. 'Are you ready to order, now?'

'I think so,' Vicki said. She glanced at Melvin. 'Have you decided?'

He nodded. He hadn't decided. He raced his eyes down the menu while Vicki talked to the waiter, didn't know what half the dishes were, didn't know if he should go ahead and order steak.

'And you, sir?' the waiter asked.

'I'll have the same as her,' he said, and felt a wonderful sense of relief when the waiter took his menu.

'And bring us a bottle of the Buena Vista Sauvignon Blanc,' Vicki added.

'Very good.' The waiter left.

'We having wine?' Melvin asked.

'Don't you like it?'

'Sure.' Grinning, he rubbed a hand across his mouth and felt crumbs of salt off his lips. 'We ain't careful, we're gonna get snockered.'

'We're celebrating,' she said.

She trying to get me drunk? he wondered. Or trying to get herself drunk?

She was already near the end of her second margarita, and her face had a rosy hue that wasn't there earlier.

She's just nervous, he thought. He remembered the way her hand had trembled when they clinked glasses. It's our first date, she has a right to be nervous. I'm pretty shaky, myself. But if she keeps putting down the booze . . .

She won't be in any shape to drive home.

I'll get her into my car.

Melvin's heart was suddenly pounding so hard he wondered if she might hear it.

'What're we celebrating?' he asked.

She finished her margarita, sighed, set down the glass, and licked the salt from her lips. 'What're we celebrating?' she asked, as if questioning herself. She leaned back. She stretched her arms across the top of the booth's cushion. The movement made her blouse pull slightly against the undersides of her breasts. 'Us,' she said. Her voice was soft, solemn. 'We're celebrating us.'

'That's . . . real nice.'

'A friend like you is very rare. I know you're too modest to admit you took care of Pollock. But that's all right. The thing is, I appreciate it. He was terrible to me, and you made him pay for it. It isn't just that I'm grateful. I *am* grateful. But it's more than that. It's that you cared so much. You actually risked your life for me. He might've *killed* you, or the cops might've got you . . .' She pressed her lips together. She looked as if she might begin to weep. 'I've never known anyone so gallant.'

Melvin swallowed, fighting the lump in his throat. 'I . . . I'd do anything for you.'

Leaning forward, Vicki reached her hand across the table. Melvin covered it with his hand, felt its gentle squeeze. He saw her look away. She drew her hand back moments before the waiter arrived with salads and a basket of bread.

Damn it! Why'd the bastard have to show up and ruin things?

When he was gone, Vicki stared into Melvin's eyes for a moment. Then, she began to eat.

Melvin picked at his salad. The white, lumpy dressing had a sour taste. He didn't like it, but the way he felt, he doubted that he could eat anything right now. His thumping heart made him light-headed. He felt hollow inside, and aching. Pushing the salad aside, he took a drink.

'You don't like the salad?' Vicki asked.

'The stuff that's on it.'

'Blue cheese dressing. It's my favourite.'

He sipped his margarita and watched her eat. After a few bites of salad, she took a roll from the basket and ate half of it before returning to her salad. She barely spared him a glance as she worked on the food. And she ate so slowly.

Melvin wanted her to rush and get done and talk to him.

She was almost finished when the waiter arrived again. This

time, he had the bottle of wine. He showed the label to Vicki, and she nodded. Then he uncorked the bottle. He poured a dab into her glass. She tasted it, said, 'Very nice,' and he filled both glasses. He set the bottle on the table.

Then, he was gone.

Vicki ate a big chunk of the blue cheese. She set her fork down on her salad plate, wiped her mouth with a napkin, and lifted her gaze to Melvin. 'I'm sorry you didn't care for the salad.'

'That's okay.'

'You should try a roll.'

He shrugged.

'Are you all right?'

'Yeah. Sure.'

'I didn't upset you, did I? What I said about . . . my feelings for you.'

'No. Yeah. I guess. I don't know.'

'You're not angry, are you?'

'Gosh, no.'

She drank the last of her margarita. 'I hope you're not worried that I might tell. I mean, it's our secret. I wouldn't breathe a word about it to anyone, not even to Ace.' Smiling, she shook her head. 'No one would believe me, anyway. They're all certain the nurse did it. Patricia something?'

'Maybe she *did* do it. That's what the cops say.'

'You don't have to play games with me, Melvin.'

Maybe you're the one playing games, he thought. But he couldn't bring himself to say it. He didn't want to believe it. This was all too good to be real, but why *can't* it be real? Resurrecting Patricia had been too good to be real. It had happened, though. This could be happening, too. Vicki might honestly like him – even love him – for what he'd done to Pollock.

'I'm curious about something,' she said. 'You don't have to tell me, but . . . it was fascinating the other night when you explained about digging up Darlene and setting up your science project. So how on earth did you manage to make it *look* like Patricia . . . took care of that creep?'

'Can't we talk about something else?'

'Sure. I'm sorry.' She took a sip of wine and looked around as if searching for the waiter.

'Somebody could hear us.'

'I shouldn't have asked. Forget it. I mean, I'm interested, that's all. But I can understand how you might be afraid of saying anything . . . too specific. It's okay. Don't worry about it. Ah, here comes the food.'

This time, Melvin felt grateful for the waiter's interruption. It saved him from getting in deeper. He didn't know what to do. Vicki was pushing to find out *everything*. Maybe she needed to be convinced that he really had done the job on Pollock. Maybe she was starting to doubt it. What if she should decide he *wasn't* involved, after all?

The waiter left, and Vicki began to eat.

Melvin looked down at his plate. Steam was rising off the asparagus and white rice. The prawns were smothered in a brownish sauce that smelled strongly of garlic. He forked one and tried it.

'Good?' Vicki asked.

'Yeah.' He supposed it was very good, but he had no appetite. He went ahead and ate, anyway. He ate, and drank wine, and watched Vicki. Though she sometimes glanced up at him, she didn't speak.

I should've told her, Melvin thought. I'm gonna lose her.

Then he reminded himself that she had eaten her salad with the same concentration. It's just the way she eats. Doesn't mean nothing.

What if I do tell her? he wondered.

That would mean explaining about Patricia. Would Vicki even believe him? She'd believe, all right, if he showed her Patricia.

Can't do that.

He could just imagine the scene. Patricia would fly into a jealous rage and Vicki, herself, might freak out when she realized what he'd been up to. Killing, resurrecting, *living* with a zombie. Even if she could accept all that, she was bound to figure out what he and Patricia had been doing together. That'd be bad enough, even if Patricia was just a regular person. But doing it with a zombie?

Can't ever let her find out, he decided.

She isn't gonna find out, long as I keep my mouth shut. I'll get rid of Patricia before Vicki ever steps foot in my house. She'll never know.

When she finished eating, she picked up the wine bottle and inspected it. Melvin saw that there wasn't much left. They had both been refilling their glasses during the meal. She poured more wine into Melvin's glass, then emptied the bottle into hers. 'Would you like some coffee or dessert?' she asked.

'I don't know.'

They'd have more time in the restaurant if they lingered over coffee and dessert. He wanted more time with her. But it would be even better if they were alone.

Maybe we can go someplace.

She has her own car. Ace's.

But she's had a lot to drink.

'You wanta have another margarita or something?' he asked.

Smiling, she shook her head. 'Oh, I don't think that'd be such a good idea. I know my limits. I wouldn't be in any condition to drive.'

'I'll drive you. You can leave the car here.'

The waiter showed up. 'Would you care for coffee?'

'No, I think we're all done.'

'Very good. Did you enjoy your meal?'

'Everything was delicious,' Vicki said.

He left.

Vicki lifted her purse off the seat beside her and set it on her lap. Melvin felt a pressure growing inside. As soon as she paid the bill, they would be leaving.

What'll happen then?

'I oughta drive you,' he said. 'You've had a lot to drink.'

'Don't be silly, Melvin.'

'We can take Ace's car. I can come back and get mine.'

'What would you do, walk all the way over here?'

'Sure. It ain't far.'

'I appreciate the offer,' she said. 'I really do. But that'd be so much trouble for you.'

The waiter returned. He had the bill on a small plastic tray. He set the tray on the table. Vicki quickly picked up the bill. She studied it for a few moments, then took cash from her purse. She placed three twenties on the tray, covered them with the bill, and smiled at Melvin. 'All ready?'

'Don't you gotta wait for your change?'

Shaking her head, she scooted to the end of the booth and stood up. Melvin saw that her blouse hung loose past her waist, draping the top of a white, pleated skirt. The skirt covered her almost to the knees.

She waited for Melvin to rise, then took hold of his hand. Her warmth seemed to flow up his arm. He felt as if his heart were swelling.

This is so great, he thought. This is so great – it *can't* end. We'll go somewhere, now.

It'll be *her* idea. Just wait and see. We'll get into the parking lot and she'll say, 'Why don't you follow me in your car? We can go to my place. Ace isn't home. We can sit around and have a drink and talk some more. I'd like that, wouldn't you?'

It'll *happen*. That's just what she'll say. She just paid for my dinner, for Christsake. And she still wants to know how I wiped out Pollock.

He opened the door for Vicki, and they stepped into the night.

'Will you walk me to my car?' she asked, still holding his hand.

'Sure.'

They started across the parking lot.

'Did you enjoy your dinner?' she asked.

'Being with you.'

She gave his hand a gentle squeeze. 'We'll do it again soon, all right?'

'Yeah.' Melvin felt himself sinking. She was getting ready to tell him goodnight. She wasn't going to say they should go somewhere now. Her suggestion that they soon have dinner again didn't help dispel his gloom. He wanted to be with her now – tonight. 'Next time, I'm gonna pay.'

'Next time,' Vicki said, 'maybe you'll trust me enough to be honest about things.'

Her words, though softly spoken, struck him like a punch.

'I *trust* you.' He sounded whiny to himself.

Vicki stopped beside Ace's Mustang, released his hand, and took the keys out of her purse. She faced him. 'I wish you did, Melvin. I don't know what kind of relationship we can have, if you feel you need to keep things from me. Frankly, I'm a little disappointed. If you can't be open with me . . .'

'I'll be open. It was just . . . we was in a restaurant.'

'We're not in the restaurant, now. Nobody's anywhere around.'

'Can't we go someplace? Can't we go someplace and talk? Like maybe your house?'

'Ace is there.'

'Well, how about we just drive? We can park someplace and . . .'

'I have to get home. I can't be away from a telephone. One of my patients is about due . . .'

'Huh?'

'I might have to deliver a baby tonight. In fact, we're lucky we made it through dinner. I can't go anywhere but home, Melvin. I'll give you a call in a few days.'

'A few days?'

'I need some time to think. I'm not at all sure about things any more.'

'Just 'cause I didn't tell you about Patricia?'

'I don't care about that. I'm interested, but . . . it's the fact that you're keeping me closed out. You're afraid to *reveal* yourself to me. That's what hurts.'

His mouth was dry, his heart slamming. 'What if I tell you I sent Patricia to waste him?'

'Did you?'

'Maybe.'

'See? You still won't open up. What do you think, I'm going to tell the police? Do you think I've got a tape recorder here, or something?' She suddenly pulled open her purse and thrust it toward his face. 'Look. You see a recorder in there?'

The lights of the parking lot were bright enough for him to see a billfold, a compact, a tube of lipstick and a small pack of tissues inside the purse. Nothing that resembled a tape recorder.

'Satisfied?' Vicki asked. She snapped the purse shut, whirled around, fumbled with the keys, got one into the door lock and opened the door. She tossed her purse onto the car seat. Then, she turned and face Melvin. She shook her head. 'I . . . I don't know what's wrong with me. I'm sorry. Will you forgive me?'

'Well, yeah. Sure. It's all right.'

Leaning forward, she brushed her lips lightly against his mouth. 'I'll call you,' she whispered.

He stood there speechless, amazed and thrilled, and watched her climb into the car. The door thumped shut. The engine stuttered to life. The headlights came on. The driver's window slid down.

Lurching forward, he reached through the window and clutched Vicki's shoulder. 'It was Patricia,' he blurted. 'She did it, but I made her do it. Hypnosis, that's how. Okay? Okay?'

She reached across her body and pressed Melvin's hand down on her shoulder. 'I'll see you tomorrow night,' she said. 'I'll call. Ace is going away, so we'll have the house to ourselves.'

She released his hand. She slowly backed up the car, and he felt her shoulder slide away.

Chapter Twenty-seven

She pressed herself against Jack. He embraced her. The muscles of his chest and arms were big and hard. Wrapped by him, Vicki felt small, protected, safe. She kissed him. She opened her mouth and tasted Jack's lips and tongue.

It was like standing in the first rays of sunlight after a night of awful darkness and numbing cold.

Too soon, he eased away from her and shut the door. 'That was well worth the wait,' he said. He reached out and lightly stroked her cheek. 'You look wonderful. And a little rattled.'

'It wasn't much fun.'

'Can I get you something to drink?'

'Coffee?'

He nodded. He took her hand, and led her across the foyer. They entered a living-room that seemed huge and plush compared to Ace's. The thick carpet felt soft under her shoes. 'This is very nice,' she said.

544

'Did you have any trouble finding your way?'

'Not much,' she said. In fact, she had been so distracted and dazed by the encounter with Melvin that she'd driven past the street and didn't even notice her mistake until she found herself a block from Ace's house.

She bashed her forearm against a dining-room chair.

'Ouch!' Jack said. 'You all right?'

Grimacing, she let go of his hand and rubbed her arm. 'Like you said, I'm rattled. And a little . . . tipsy. I had a drink before he got there. I don't think I could've faced him sober. Then, I wanted to loosen him up so we both kept drinking.'

'And who was this mystery date?'

'Melvin Dobbs.'

'You're kidding.' He led her into the kitchen, past a breakfast table, and pulled out one of the stools at the serving counter. While he held her steady, she climbed onto the stool. She leaned over the counter and braced herself on her elbows. 'Crazy Melvin?' he asked. 'That's who you had dinner with? The guy who's smitten with you? The guy who's missing a screw?'

'That's him.'

Jack frowned at her from the other side of the counter. 'Why?'

'I wanted him to admit killing Pollock.'

'And did he?'

'He did.'

Jack's eyes widened.

'That missing nurse? Patricia? He said he hypnotized her and made her do it.'

'Good God.'

'Yeah.'

'Do you believe him?'

Vicki nodded.

'Well.' Jack rubbed his jaw. He turned away and walked over to the coffee maker at the far end of the kitchen. 'No wonder you wouldn't tell me what you were up to.'

'I just didn't want you to worry. Or try to talk me out of it.'

'I would've done both,' he said. He scooped ground coffee into the filter and looked around at her. 'I knew you had guts, lady, but . . .'

'But you didn't realize I'm crazy?'

'I wouldn't go so far as to say you're crazy. Hey, you might slug me again. But why did you do it?'

'He has to be put away.'

Jack slid the filter into place, poured water into the top of the machine, flicked a switch that turned on a red light, and came back to her. He stood at the other side of the counter. 'Why do you suppose Dobbs made this confession to you?'

'He wants me to . . . approve of him. I let him believe he was doing me a big favour by killing Pollock. I mean, Pollock had insulted me in front of him. I as much as told him I thought it was great that he'd . . . stood up for my honour. By nailing the guy.'

'So he told you what he knew you wanted to hear. Whether or not he actually did the deed.'

She stared up at Jack. 'Hey, whose side are you on, here?'

'Who do you think?'

'You're making it sound like the whole things was a waste of time. God, I damn near *seduced* him.'

'Under which circumstances, any reasonable man – not to mention social outcast with questionable emotional stability who has been fantasizing about having you as his lover – would've admitted almost anything.'

'Come on, don't say that. It was awful. He . . . he *loves* me, Jack. And I encouraged it. I felt like the biggest liar of all time. I felt like such a shit, and you're telling me it means nothing that he confessed?'

'No, I'm not telling you that. His confession would be admissible in court.'

'So it's real evidence?'

'It is. But very weak. Any decent attorney would have no trouble at all convincing a jury that it was given under a form of coercion. You were dangling yourself in front of him like bait. Confess, and I'm all yours.'

Vicki felt herself blushing. 'I didn't say that.'

'From what you've told me, the implication must've been pretty clear to him.'

'So is it evidence, or isn't it?'

'It's enough to set an investigation into motion. It's probable cause for a search warrant.'

'Even to Raines?'

'He'd be a fool not to act on it.' Jack smiled. 'Of course, he *is* a fool. But Bob Dennison isn't.'

'Who's he?'

'The District Attorney. And also my fishing buddy.'

Vicki felt a grin stretch her face. 'Well, it sure pays to be well connected.'

'That it does. One way or another, I'm sure we can arrange it so that Dobbs will be visited by the authorities first thing in the morning.'

'Then what?'

'We hope they find something tangible.'

She nodded. 'Like Patricia.'

'Or her body. In fact, with what they apparently have on that woman, any physical evidence of her presence in the house should be sufficient grounds for hauling Dobbs in. And you never know what they might find. Pollock's service revolver. His badge. Even some of his blood might've gotten into the house. If Dobbs was involved, there's a very good chance they'll find something to tie him in.'

'Suppose they don't?'

'Then you're in trouble. Dobbs will know you're the one who fingered him, and he might not love you any more.'

'There's a mixed blessing.'

'You've gone this far. I don't suppose you'd let a little matter like that stop you.'

'I don't suppose I would.'

'We'll see to it that he doesn't get a chance to . . . visit his displeasure on you.'

'Thanks.'

Jack looked over his shoulder. 'Coffee's ready. Do you take cream or sugar?'

Melvin wished he could read the fucker's lips.

He had a very good view of Vicki's back. She had been sitting on the stool since he found the kitchen window. For a while, he hadn't seen anyone else. Then the man had come up to the other side of the counter and started talking to her. The angle was good, so Melvin could see him beyond Vicki's shoulder.

547

A big guy. He looked like a goddamn football player. He wore a white knit shirt that showed off his muscles.

Melvin didn't know who he was. He for sure wasn't the pregnant lady, though.

Keeping a safe distance back, Melvin had followed Vicki when she left the restaurant's parking lot. He wished she would drive faster. He ached for her to reach Ace's house. Though he couldn't be *with* her, at least he could watch her – find a window and spy on her. That'd be something. He was sure she'd change clothes as soon as she got there. He might get to see her slip out of that shiny blouse, step out of that long white skirt, maybe even take off the rest.

If she didn't take off her clothes, it would still be great to watch her. He knew he could look at her for hours, and every moment would be exciting.

But Vicki didn't drive to Ace's house, the way she'd said she would.

She lied to me, Melvin thought.

Did she lie about *everything*?

His mind reeled with confusion and loss.

Then, her car stopped at a curb. Melvin slowed down. He drove by just in time to see her reach the front door of a big two-storey house.

I know! he told himself.

He felt like a fool for doubting her.

It was nothing. Instead of going straight to Ace's house, Vicki had decided to pay a visit to the pregnant gal. Just look in on her, check on her progress.

She'll be there for a few minutes, then she'll head on home.

It's all right, after all.

Melvin parked near the end of the block. He thought he might wait in his car, but he quickly grew restless.

What if I'm wrong? he wondered. What if she's in there with a guy?

No, not Vicki. She wouldn't. No.

But Melvin couldn't get the idea out of his head. He wanted to believe in her, to trust her. But he had to know.

He walked back to the house.

Most of the windows had curtains that were shut, but not the kitchen. The curtains there were wide open.

First, he saw only Vicki. Then the guy stepped up to the counter.

Melvin tried to convince himself that the guy was the *husband* of Vicki's patient. She could be asking about the wife's condition. Any contractions yet?

Bullshit.

Who *is* he? What're they talking about?

It was like watching a drive-in movie without any sound. He could see Vicki and the guy perfectly. But the window was shut and an air-conditioning unit hummed loudly nearby, so he couldn't hear a damn thing.

If only he could read the fucker's lips.

Vicki turned sideways and slid off the stool. She stepped around the end of the counter. The guy was saying something. And watching her.

Melvin couldn't read his lips.

But he could read his eyes.

'How long have you lived here?' Vicki asked.

'What?' Jack called. 'You've got to speak up.'

'Wise guy.'

Jack smiled at her from the couch. It looked soft and comfortable, but Vicki had settled into an easy chair a short distance from the corner where he was sitting. 'What'd I do wrong, this time?' he asked.

'You bought a white couch and you gave me black coffee. I don't think the two would go well together.' She raised the cup to her lips. Steam drifted up, hot against her face. She took a sip of the coffee, and sighed.

'Take a chance,' Jack said.

'I'm fine here.'

'But out of reach.'

'We can admire each other from afar.'

'Should I confess to something?' he asked. 'Would that get you over here?'

The words made her stomach tighten. 'Don't rub it in, okay? I don't like what I did. It was a rotten trick.'

'Not nearly as rotten as committing murder. If your manoeuvres end up getting Dobbs put away, you've done society a considerable service. You'll have taken a killer off the streets. That counts for a lot.'

'I suppose.'

'No supposing about it. It's certainly possible that Pollock wasn't his first victim. And might not be his last, if he isn't stopped.'

'Possible, I guess.'

'That nurse, for instance. He told you that he hypnotized her?'

Vicki nodded, and took another drink of coffee.

'Pretty far out. But we're going on the assumption that he was telling the truth, right? So, if he put her into some kind of trance instead of just asking her politely to knock the guy off, that means she wasn't acting on her own volition. She was compelled to kill Pollock. So what happens to her afterward? Is Dobbs going to let her go on her merry way?'

'He could get her to forget everything that happened while she was under hypnosis,' Vicki said. She frowned into her coffee. A thought, a new idea, a realization heavy with portent was stirring somewhere deep in her mind. She concentrated, trying to force it to the surface. But Jack spoke again, distracting her.

'The nurse might forget it, but the cops know she was involved and they're looking for her. If they got their hands on her, they might make her remember.'

'If they hypnotized her again,' Vicki said, 'they might be able to get the truth.' What *was* that thought? Where'd it go?

'And if Dobbs knows enough on the subject to persuade someone to commit murder – I imagine that takes quite an expert – then he'd have to realize she's a threat to him. As long as she's alive.'

'Yeah.' Vicki searched her mind. It was like swimming under murky water, hunting a message hidden deep in the weeds along the bottom.

And having to come up for air when Jack spoke.

'It's my guess,' he said, 'that Dobbs has already killed the nurse. Eliminated the only person – except for you – who can tie him in.'

Vicki held up her hand.

'What?'

She shook her head and gazed into the coffee. She submerged herself again, thought of herself as taking a deep breath and plunging into the darkness. Going deeper. Her mind was a river and the lost thought was down there someplace. *Come on, where are you?*

Suddenly, Charlie Gaines was on her back, clinging to her, groping her, driving her down. The horrors of last night rushed in. She could feel him, feel the ache in her lungs . . .

'What's wrong?' Jack asked.

His words wrenched her to the surface. The coffee was shivering, the cup tinkling against the saucer. She rose carefully out of the chair, placed the cup and saucer on the table, then stepped around the table and sat down on the couch close to Jack.

He slipped an arm around her. She leaned against his side.

'I didn't mean to scare you, Vicki. But the fact remains that you've put yourself at considerable risk by . . .'

'It isn't that,' she said. 'I had . . . I flashed back to last night. Charlie. In the river.'

His hand gently covered her wounded shoulder. 'I'm sorry. You know, with all this Dobbs business, I'd almost forgotten about Charlie. That must've been so awful for you.'

Looking up at Jack, she managed a smile. 'Hey, it wasn't all bad. Afterward was pretty nice.'

'Till you conked out on me.'

'I hope you minded your manners.'

'It wasn't easy, but . . .'

The lost thought burst to the surface of her mind, full and clear. As if it had waited for her to stop searching, then popped up to surprise her. 'My God,' she muttered, stunned by what she suddenly knew. *Knew.*

'Honest, I was a perfect gentleman.'

'Hypnosis. That's how . . .' She squeezed Jack's leg. 'Melvin killed Charlie.'

'What?'

'Oh, Jesus. Melvin . . . he was doing me another favour, the scum. First, he gave me the car. Then, he "defended my honour" by making Patricia kill Pollock. And then . . . then he got hold of Charlie. He knew I owed money to Charlie. He knew I wasn't a partner at the clinic. So he got hold of Charlie and *helped* me.'

'That would explain a lot,' Jack said, staring at her, understanding. 'If Charlie was under Dobbs's influence when he called me in Monday morning . . .'

'I *knew* something was wrong.'

'I remember. You were concerned about his health, thought he might be dying.'

'Melvin made him do it. Hypnotized him, just like Patricia, and told him to make me a partner, make me *inherit* the whole clinic . . . Oh, damn it. The dirty . . . it wasn't any accident last night. Charlie's crash . . . Melvin must've staged it. He was *giving* me the clinic.'

'It makes sense,' Jack said. 'It's all supposition, but it sure fits neatly into the pattern. If he really did hypnotize Patricia and compel her to murder Pollock, which he's admitted, then the rest of it follows.'

She stared into Jack's eyes.

He believed her. He knew. She didn't have to convince him.

Something seemed to tear inside her.

She turned and hunched herself down against Jack's chest. He put his arms around her.

'I killed Charlie,' she whispered.

'No.'

'I did. I killed him.'

Jack held her gently. She could hear the quick beating of his heart.

My damn mouth, she thought. I murdered him when I told Melvin I wasn't a partner. When I told him about the loan.

'And Pollock,' she murmured. 'And Patricia, if she's dead. I killed them all.'

'Shhh.' Jack stroked her hair, caressed her back. 'You didn't do any of that.'

I stopped at Melvin's station. Bought gas from him. Thought the Arco might be closed. Couldn't wait for morning to fill the tank. That's how I started it.

No, I started it back in high school. Didn't tease him. Didn't torment him. I was nice to him.

I was nice to him, and two people are dead. Maybe three. Three lives.

Because of me.

Melvin, face pressed to the window screen, watched through a gap in the curtains. A tiny gap. No more than half an inch, but enough.

He saw Vicki when she twisted around on the couch, saw when she huddled against the big man's chest, saw when he put his arms around her.

The filthy, lying cunt!

Chapter Twenty-eight

'You might be wrong about all of this, you know.'

'I'm not wrong.' She rubbed her face against the soft knit fabric of Jack's shirt, feeling his sturdy chest beneath it, feeling his warmth. 'It was his way of . . . courting me. They'd all be alive.'

'You can't take the blame on yourself.'

'None of it would've happened.'

Jack's hands moved slowly up and down her back. In a gentle, soothing voice, he said, 'I was a prosecutor in Detroit for a short time. Before I moved here. I moved here because I couldn't stand it. The brutalities, the viciousness I saw every day. My last case, the one that finished me . . . two guys walked into a liquor store with shotguns. The owner, a fellow named John Baxter, didn't give them any trouble. He handed over all the money in the cash register. It was a lot of money. And the robbers had it in their hands. Then they proceeded to blast everyone in the store. They killed Baxter in front of his wife. She was bagging a six-pack of Pepsi for two teenaged girls who'd stopped by on their way home from the junior high down the road. They killed the wife and both girls. They killed a mother whose three kids were waiting in their car while she ran in for a carton of cigarettes. They killed a guy over at the paperback rack. And a stock boy who showed up when he heard the shots.'

'Horrible,' Vicki muttered.

'About as horrible as it can get,' Jack said. His caressing hands stopped in the middle of her back. In a low voice, he said, 'We got a murder-one conviction against the money in the cash register.'

Vicki raised her face and looked him in the eyes. 'Is that some kind of a bad joke?'

'A lesson,' he said. 'A lesson in blame. That pair of mutants went into the liquor store because they wanted the money in the cash register. In spite of that, you apparently think it's absurd to blame the money for the slaughter of those seven people. Isn't that right?'

'Of course.'

'Then how can you blame yourself for what Dobbs may have done because he wanted you?'

'How can I not?' she asked.

When she said that, she saw tears come into his eyes. He turned his head away quickly. Vicki raised a hand to his cheek. She eased his face around, stretched upward and pressed her lips to his mouth.

She sank into a warm, quiet place where there was only the feel of him. The moist softness of his lips and tongue. The gentle pressure of his hands. The firm muscles of his chest. The smooth skin she caressed through the shoulder and side of his shirt.

But she had to twist to hold him this way.

'I'm breaking,' she finally whispered against his lips.

'Can't have that happen,' he said. 'You're too precious to break.'

She brushed her lips against his, then climbed off the couch. She looked down at him. He was slumped against the cushion, big arms hanging at his sides, knees spread. His white shirt was askew, his hair mussed. His mouth, open just a bit, had a reddish hue around the lips from pressure and rub of the kissing. He gazed up at her with eyes that seemed, somehow, both calm and eager. She watched them lower slowly down her body, and up again, and linger on her face.

Her heart pounded. Her mouth suddenly felt parched.

Jack raised an eyebrow. He glanced at the length of the couch. 'Shall we stretch out, or . . . ?'

'What's upstairs?' Vicki asked.

'The bedrooms.'

'Show me?'

He pursed his lips and blew softly, not making a sound.

'Just a thought.'

'And a fine one, at that.'

Vicki stepped out of the way, and Jack got to his feet. They crossed the living-room, walking side by side, almost touching. At the bottom of the stairway, Vicki reached across his back and rested her hand on his hip. He moved in against her. She felt him caress her shoulderblade, sliding the slick fabric against her skin. Together, they climbed the stairs.

As they walked along the second-floor hallway, she looked at him. He faced her and smiled. She bumped him with her hip. His smiled widened.

They entered a room, and he flicked a light switch. A lamp came on beside the king-sized bed. The bed was made, the rest of the room tidy.

Vicki halted just inside the doorway.

Suddenly doubting.

He was a man who lived alone. His bedroom shouldn't necessarily be a mess, but . . .

He'd cleaned it up. Gathered the dirty clothes, hidden the clutter, put on fresh sheets.

Knowing I'd be here.

Knowing.

In the back seat of his car, Melvin stripped naked. He struggled into his greasy coveralls and pulled the zipper up. Then, he pushed his bare feet into the old leather shoes he liked to wear at the station.

Outside, he opened the trunk. He took out his tyre tool. It had a lug wrench at one end, a prying wedge at the other. It felt good and heavy in his hand. He lowered the trunk lid. Holding it down, he turned his back to it, hopped up, and drove it down with his rump. The latch made a quiet click.

He swung the bar, slapping it into his left hand as he walked toward the house.

I'll fix the bitch, he thought. The dirty, lying whore.

He couldn't stop *seeing* her. The way she turned on the couch and pressed herself against that bastard's chest. The way she kissed him. And how the guy's hands moved on her back as if he *owned* her.

The images sickened him. He felt as if cold hands were wringing his guts.

She'll be sorry. She'll be so sorry.

Melvin hurried alongside the house to its rear. The windows back here were dark. The patio, dim in the moonlight, was a concrete slab with a couple of lounge chairs and a barbeque.

The screen door wasn't latched. It squeaked as he eased it open. Holding it away with his back, he tried the knob of the inner wooden door. Locked.

He rammed the wedge of the tyre tool into the crack between the door and the jamb just where he figured the lock tongue should be. He threw his weight against the bar. The wood made crunching sounds. It bulged out, cracking. He drove the bar in deeper, working it back and forth, thrusting it, feeling the give of the lock's steel tongue.

The door swung inward.

He stepped into the house, drawing the screen door slowly shut. The kitchen was dark except for a glow of light spilling in from the entryway.

He listened. He heard only the pounding rush of his own heartbeat.

When he took a step, the sole of his shoe made a scuffing sound. He squatted down and loosened his laces. He stepped out of the shoes. The linoleum floor felt cool and slick under his sweaty feet.

He took a deep breath. He felt so tight and cold and shaky inside. If only he could calm down.

Calm down and enjoy what he was about to do.

He wished he could feel some excitement.

The kind of thrill he got when he nailed all the others.

But he couldn't. He hurt too much.

She had hurt him too much.

Now you're gonna pay for it. You don't fuck with Melvin Dobbs.

Silently, he made his way toward the light.

'Something wrong?' Jack asked, stepping up behind her. She felt the light pressure of him against her back. He put his hands on her sides. His warm breath stirred her hair, made her scalp tingle.

'It's . . . going awfully fast.'

'It doesn't have to.'

'I know I'm the one who suggested . . .'

'In the heat of the moment.'

'Yeah. I was a little carried away.'

His hands slipped around to her front. They made small circles, sliding the blouse against her belly. Vicki felt as if warm oil was being spread on her skin. She caressed the backs of his hands, his wrists and forearms.

'Shall we go downstairs?' he asked.

'I don't know,' she whispered.

She remembered her regret that she hadn't made love with Paul that morning so long ago on the diving raft. It had been their last chance, and she had missed it. There had been other men . . . a few . . . but she'd loved none of them.

Do I love Jack? she wondered. It comes down to that, doesn't it?

She knew that she cared for him, that she desired him. But love?

The feelings that she'd had for Paul certainly weren't there – the intimacy, the mystery, the ache of longing when they were apart. But maybe you only get that once. Maybe that's all they hand out, and Paul was it.

She had refused to settle for anything less than what she'd known with him. She'd looked back on their times together as the way it *should* be. Nothing afterward had even come close.

Jack comes close, she told herself.

I can't go through the rest of my life crippled by the memories of how it was with Paul. It was a brief, wonderful time, but it's gone. Forever.

And Jack's here.

And who knows about tomorrow. This could be it, our one and only chance, and if I don't take it maybe years from now I'll look back and wish . . .

'You're trembling,' Jack said.

'I know.'

'Let's go on down to the living-room.'

She guided his hands down the front of her blouse and up beneath it to her belly. As they drifted over her skin, she unfastened the buttons. She sank against him, reaching back and holding the sides of his legs. His hands moved slowly, lightly roaming as if he were a blind man who could only know her by touch, whose hands were his eyes and he wanted to see the texture of her skin and memorize every curve and hollow. Their slow exploration brushed her blouse open. Soon, they curled over her brassiere. Her nipples, already hard, ached against the lacy cups. She didn't want the fabric in the way, shielding her from the feel of his skin.

She wanted to reach up and open the catch at the front of her bra. She didn't do it. She rubbed his legs, and let Jack go on in his own way.

Come on, she thought. The bra.

A corner of her mind was amused by her impatience. Wasn't she the one who'd thought they should wait, see each other many times, slowly growing more intimate, slowly moving closer to a distant night when they would finally complete their long journey?

Then, she felt him unhook the clasp. Lowering her head, she watched his hands slip beneath the black lace cups. She moaned at the feel of him. His mouth pressed the back of her head. He roamed her breasts, his touch so soft it was like a warm wind. His fingertips drew circles on her nipples. Too lightly. Tormenting her. Making her squirm.

She reached behind him and squeezed his buttocks. As if this were a signal, he squeezed her breasts, kneaded them. Breathless, she brought her hands up, pressed his hands hard against her, then peeled them away and turned around and embraced him and found his mouth.

Melvin stopped in the hallway near the open door and leaned against the wall. Moaning, gasping sounds came from inside the room. The creak and squawk of bed-springs.

He knew what they were doing.

They wouldn't be doing it for long.

He wiped his lips with the back of a hand.

They're making it easy for me, he thought. I'll be on top of them before they know I'm there.

'No. Wait.' She sounded winded. 'Not yet.'

'What's wrong?' A man's voice.

'It's rubber time.' Melvin could almost see her smiling as she said it. Smiling and panting, her breasts rising and falling as she gasped for air, her naked body shiny with sweat.

'A rubber? Are you kidding?'

'I just don't want to take any chances.'

'Aren't you on the pill or something?'

'I'm not worried about birth control.'

'You think I've got diseases?'

'Would you rather argue, or . . .'

He moaned. A moan of pleasure. Melvin wondered what she was doing to him. He could guess.

In a low voice, the guy said, 'Hang on, I'll get one.' The bed creaked. There were quiet footfalls on the carpet.

Melvin raised the tyre tool, though he didn't think the guy would leave the room.

'I hate these things.'

'I know. It's like wearing a glove.' She sounded amused. 'Come here and give it to me.'

'That's not how they work.'

She laughed.

There were more footsteps. The bed squeaked again. Melvin heard the tearing of the condom's foil wrapper. He lowered the tyre tool and rested it across his leg.

'Think it'll fit?' the guy asked.

'Braggart.'

Then the guy went, 'Uhhhh. Yeahhh.'

Melvin could picture her unrolling the thing down him. He could almost feel the tightness of the cool moist tube, feel her fingers through its thin latex.

He'd gone to whores a few times over in Blayton. They'd made him wear one. But they'd made *him* put it on.

'There,' she said. 'All set.'

Melvin ran his tongue around inside his dry mouth. He took a deep breath. His heart was drumming. He was hard, and saw that the front of his coveralls jutted out like a tent.

The bed groaned.

'Oh, yeahhhh.' Him.

'It . . . doesn't feel like a glove to me.' Her.

'What does it . . . feel like?'

'A telephone pole.'

'Yeahhhh.'

Time to party, Melvin thought.

He pictured blood flying, spraying his coveralls.

Can't have that.

He rubbed his mouth. Crouching, he set his tyre tool on the hallway runner. He stood and slowly lowered the zipper of his coveralls. He shrugged the garment off his shoulders. It dropped around his feet, and he stepped out of it. Then he picked up the steel bar.

Panting, he leaned against the wall. It was cool against his back and rump. He listened.

'Oh . . . oh.' She sounded as if she was being beaten to death.

Any minute, Melvin thought.

'Oh! . . . Yes . . . Oh yes.'

Melvin stepped into the doorway.

A lamp beside the bed cast bright light onto their thrashing bodies. The guy was stretched out on top of her, half kneeling, his white rump flexing as he ran himself into her. Her hands were clenching his buttocks. Her legs were spread wide, knees high, heels digging into the mattress, pushing herself up to meet his thrusts.

Melvin walked silently toward the end of the bed.

He couldn't see their faces, so they couldn't see him.

She kept bucking herself up against the guy, gasping and murmuring. 'Oh . . . Oh, God . . . Yes . . . In, in.'

Melvin pictured himself ramming the iron right up lover boy's ass. That'd be a kick, but it wouldn't do the job.

He leaped onto the bed and dropped his knees onto the guy's rump, onto her hands.

Driving him down. The guy grunted.

She squealed.

'How's that for *in*,' Melvin gasped. Felt his knees sliding away. Threw himself forward and clutched the wet nape of the guy's neck, stopping the slide, and swung the bar.

The impact made pain blast through his bitten hand and streak up his arm to the shoulder.

But it sure did a number on lover boy. Knocked his head sideways. Sent a spray of blood slapping the wall.

'No!'

She had blood flecking her face. Her eyes looked ready to pop out of their sockets.

'Yes,' Melvin said, and smashed the lug-wrench end of the tool once more against the man's crushed temple. This time, the blood flew up spattering Melvin's face and shoulders. The limp body suddenly rocked beneath him. His knees slipped down the backs of the legs. He flopped, and before he could scurry up, something trapped under him – one of her hands – twisted and clawed his thigh and shoved between his legs. He flung himself backward just as it found his genitals. The hand clamped shut. The fingers bumped him. They didn't catch hold, though. Missed their chance to squeeze and crush, missed their chance to disable him. But the bump was enough to send a shock-wave of nauseating pain through his body.

He hunched over and grabbed the back of the dead man's leg to hold himself steady. He needed a second. Just a second to recover.

But the bitch didn't give it to him.

She lurched and twisted, throwing the body sideways, tumbling Melvin off the bed. His back slammed the floor. The guy landed on top of him. And she was on top of the body. Melvin could feel her up there, jostling the body, her weight shoving the bastard's butt against his face as if she were trying to smother him with it.

She wasn't up there long. Just long enough to untangle herself. Then she either rolled or fell off the pile. She hit the floor beside Melvin. He heard her hit, couldn't see her. Not until he flung himself over, toppling the body away.

She was scuttering toward the door on her hands and knees, whimpering, looking back over her shoulder. Melvin crawled over the body, got to his feet, and went after her. She pushed herself up. She stumbled into the hall. Melvin lurched through the doorway. She was already a few strides ahead of him. He cocked back his arm, ready to hurl the bar at her head. But what if he missed? Then he'd be without his only weapon and *she* might pick it up – use it on him. He kept the bar in his hands and raced after her.

But she was faster.

She's gonna get away!

He lost sight of her when she darted into the kitchen.

She's gonna get out the door and start screaming!

Melvin's shoulder hit the doorframe. He bounced off, grunting, and stumbled into the dark kitchen. And spotted her. She wasn't going for the door. Her pale figure was at the counter, reaching out, her back to Melvin.

He slapped the wall, raced his hand down it, and found the switch plate. He flipped the switch. As light filled the kitchen, she whirled around.

A butcher knife in her hand.

She stood there, gazing at him, blinking sweat out of her eyes, gulping air. Ropes of wet hair hung over her eyes. Her face was dripping, sweat mixing with the guy's blood and running down, dripping off her jaw. Her chest was heaving, her breasts shaking. Her wet skin gleamed as if slicked with oil.

She looked beautiful. Like some kind of warrior goddess.

Melvin stared. He *wanted* her. He'd only wanted to kill her, but now he ached for the feel of her savage body under him, writhing and slippery.

Beneath the desire, he felt a chilly stirring of fear.

'All right,' she gasped. 'End . . . of the line . . . fucker.' She took a step toward him.

Melvin fought an urge to back away. He bent over a little and raised the tyre iron. 'Come 'n' get it.'

She suddenly rushed him, snarling, feet slapping the floor, knife slashing.

Melvin's heart seemed to freeze.

She's gonna kill me!

He swung at her face. The iron bar knocked her jaw crooked. He saw her eyes roll upward as her head was whipped aside. At the same instant, he felt a streak of warmth across his belly. Not pain. Just a long line of heat.

But the blow from the tool had done its job.

He watched her spin away, head tipped back, arms flying out, knife sailing from her hand. She crashed against the floor, slid sideways on her belly, then lay motionless.

Melvin looked down at himself.

She got me!

He felt sick as he stared at the wound. It was five or six inches long, straight across the belly, just below his navel. A curtain of blood flowed down from it, sheathing his groin and thighs. His penis was shrinking, getting smaller and smaller as if it wanted to hide.

He fingered a raw edge of the cut. Peeled it back like a lip. Not very deep. But now it was beginning to hurt. To *really* hurt.

'You bitch!' he shrieked. 'Look what you done!'

She moved a little.

He hurled the bar. She flinched and gasped, 'Uh!' as it gouged the skin of her shoulderblade. It didn't stick, though. It bounced off and skittered across the linoleum.

Melvin, forearm to his slashed belly, hurried to pick up the bar. It had come to a stop beside the knife.

He picked up the knife, instead. When he straightened up, he saw that his legs were red all the way down to his feet.

He stepped over to the sink, being careful not to slip and fall on his own blood. There, he found a moist dishrag. Knife clamped between his teeth, he folded the rag and pressed it against his cut.

'You hurt me bad, you bitch.'

She just lay sprawled there. She bled where the bar had torn her skin.

Melvin remembered that she'd flinched and made a sound. So she wasn't out cold. Dazed, maybe, but not unconscious.

Still able to feel pain.

He straddled her and sat on her back. With the tip of the knife, he prodded her wound. She made a quick, high bleat and her muscles fluttered under him.

Melvin peeled the rag off his cut. He squeezed it into a tight ball, blood spilling out between his fingers. Then lay the knife between her shoulderblades, grabbed her hair, lifted her head off the floor, and stuffed the rag into her mouth.

If she was dazed, she came out of it when Melvin drew the blade across her brow. She gave a spastic jerk as if jolted by a charge of electricity. She shrieked into the rag. She rammed her hands and knees against the floor, started to push herself up. Melvin cut with one hand. With the other, he yanked her hair. With a wet, tearing sound, her scalp peeled back. He kept his grip on it and rode the crazed, screaming woman like a horse for a moment before she threw him.

He hit the floor, rolling, and got to his knees.

And held up the thatch of hair. It swayed, the flesh from the top of her head sprinkling a circle of blood.

'Scalped ya,' he said, grinning as he panted for air.

She wiped blood out of her eyes. Looked around. Scurried toward the tyre tool.

'No y'don't!'

Melvin sprang up. His feet flew out from under him. His rump pounded the floor.

Slipping and sliding on the blood, he crawled toward her.

She got a hand on the tyre tool.

He pounded the knife down into her back.

She flopped. She made a wet smacking sound when she hit the floor.

Melvin pulled the knife out, raised it high, and stabbed Ace again.

Chapter Twenty-nine

Vicki squeezed him as hard as she could, crushing him against her, then let her arms flop onto the bed. She slid her feet down the backs of his legs, and lay spread-eagled beneath his weight. He was still deep inside her. She was filled with him, peaceful and tired.

Jack pushed himself up enough so his face was above her. His chest no longer tight against hers, air came in, cool against her hot, damp skin. He stared into her eyes, searching them. He looked very solemn. After a long while, he said, 'I think I love you, Vicki Chandler.'

She felt as if her heart were swelling. She reached up and held his sides. 'I think maybe I love you, too.'

564

He eased down and gently kissed her mouth. When he pushed himself up again, he smiled. 'And it's not just your body.'

'Oh, sure thing.'

'I can take it or leave it.'

'Right.' She flexed muscles, tightening them around the hardness inside her, and watched Jack's eyes widen.

'On second thoughts . . .' he whispered.

She reached up and pushed her fingers into his damp hair. She drew his head down. She kissed him. She felt him start to move a little, squirm a little, tentatively pressing this way and that as if exploring the soft walls that held him.

'And one for the road?' she asked.

The exploration stopped. Jack raised his head. 'You're not going to leave, are you?'

'Indeed I am.'

'Why?'

She didn't want to leave. More than that, she didn't want to cast a shadow over their time together by ending it with an argument. 'Deep, dark reasons,' she said, and tried to look mysterious.

'Stay. Please.'

'I didn't bring my toothbrush.'

'I have a spare.'

'Oh yeah?' She smiled. 'Whose is it? Anybody I know?'

'It's new.' He had such sadness in his eyes. 'It's . . .'

'It's not about a toothbrush, honey.'

'What *is* it about?'

'You and me.'

'But I thought . . .'

'I'd love to stay. And sleep with you. And wake up in the morning in bed with you beside me. And have breakfast together. It would be wonderful. But I won't. That's something . . . I'd rather save.'

Jack nodded. 'I guess I understand. Something special. To save for another time. Like, for the honeymoon.'

She felt heat rush to her face. Her throat went tight. 'Yeah, like for . . . that.'

She stared into his eyes.

'I can feel your heart,' he said.

565

'I should think so.'

'Don't worry, I'm not going to drop the big question on you. You're not the only one around here who can save things for later.'

She felt neither disappointment nor relief, only the sense of wonder and excitement at knowing that he wanted her. He'd said that he loved her, but some people spoke those words easily. Now, he had gone so much further. He had let her know that he needed her in the midst of his life, part of him.

'Oh, Jack,' she whispered. She wrapped her arms around his broad back and kissed him. Gently at first, feeling tender and comfortable and glad, but soon with urgency as he began to move on top of her, began sliding himself within her hugging depths. His tongue entered her mouth and she sucked its thickness as he thrust, pounding her into the bed.

After bandaging himself in the bathroom, Melvin returned to the kitchen. He pulled the knife out of Ace's back. Then he turned her over.

'Not so tough now, huh?' he asked.

She looked like a *wreck*. A bald wreck. She still had lots of hair on the sides, but the top was a raw, skinned dome. It made her look a little freakish, like Lon Chaney in *Phantom of the Opera*. And all that red on her face and shoulders reminded him of Sissy Spacek in *Carrie* after they dumped the bucket of blood on her head at the prom. Her crooked, hanging jaw made her look like . . . Melvin couldn't think of a movie character. That part of her just looked like Ace after a run-in with a tyre tool.

The rest of her looked like that sexy babe in the second *Howling* movie. The one who kept howling and showing off her big knockers.

For a moment, staring down at her, Melvin regretted messing her up so badly. If he hadn't ruined her looks, he might've taken her home and brought her back to life.

But that had never been the plan, anyway.

The plan was just to kill her ass.

Vicki's best friend.

See how she likes it.

Lying cunt.

He dropped the knife onto Ace's belly. Then he picked her

scalp off the floor and gave it a toss. It dropped with a soft splat onto one of her breasts. He laughed at the look of it there. Then he moved it down to where the knife was. He grabbed her wrists and began dragging her.

A heavy thing.

His sore muscles ached, and he remembered that he'd been bent over just the same way, towing a body, last night in the river.

Killed Pollock for her. Killed old Gaines for her. She owns the fucking clinic because of me, even if she doesn't know it.

Told me I'm special.

Got rid of me and went straight to that big fucking asshole and started making out with him.

Gonna be real sorry, though.

Winded, dripping sweat onto Ace's face, he wanted to just let go and leave her in the hallway.

But his idea was neat. It was worth some work.

So he kept on dragging her. She was leaving faint maroon ribbons on the hallway carpet.

Somebody's gonna have a real job, he thought, cleaning up all this.

He dragged Ace past his coveralls lying in a heap beside her doorway. And kept on dragging her. Finally, he got her into the bedroom at the end of the hall.

This had to be Vicki's room.

Leaving her on the floor, he sat on a corner of the bed to catch his breath. His bandage had come unstuck during the long haul. It hung by one end. Blood was all over his belly and groin and legs. He pressed the bandage into place again, but the tape wouldn't cling. So he just held the bandage there until he could breathe again.

Then he let it dangle. He dragged Ace to the bed, jammed his arms underneath her body, gritted his teeth, and lifted.

Like picking up a damn horse.

But he got her onto the bed. He tugged and shoved until she was lying in the middle. Then he jammed a pillow under her head to prop it up. He arranged her arms so they stretched straight out away from her sides. He spread her legs wide. He admired the display for a few moments, wondered what to do with the scalp, then draped it over the toes of her right foot.

Nice.

He could just see the look on Vicki's face when he showed her.

Melvin found the knife on the floor beside the bed, where it had fallen when he lifted Ace. He took it with him, and went down the hallway to Ace's room. The dead guy was face-down, the broken side of his head against the carpet. The carpet looked as if it had soaked up gallons of blood. Melvin bet that if he stepped on it, over there, the blood would squish up between his toes.

Clothes were scattered over the floor near the foot of the bed. Jockey shorts, shoes and socks, a blue shirt and slacks.

A uniform?

He picked up the shirt. It had a colourful sleeve patch that read, 'Ellsworth Police Department.' A badge swung on its chest. A plastic name plate over the other breast pocket identified its owner as 'Milbourne.'

'Holy shit,' Melvin muttered. ' 'Nother cop.'

Cops carry guns.

A bright yellow jersey of some kind lay in a heap, partially covering the guy's pants. Melvin picked it up. A nightshirt with Minnie Mouse on the front. Once the shirt was out of the way, he spotted Milbourne's gunbelt and revolver.

Grinning, he waved it at the corpse. 'Thanks, buddy. Left mine home.'

The gun would come in handy when Vicki showed up. Without it, he might've been forced to mess her up. Now, he wouldn't need to get rough.

Just stick it in her face, she'll do what I say.

Step this way, sweetheart. Got something to show you.

My Ace in the hole, he thought, and chuckled.

He took the revolver and knife into the bathroom. He set them on the edge of the sink. Then he tossed his bandage into the wastebasket. The bandage on his right hand was loose so he shucked it off and tossed it. Most of his other bandages, he noticed, were hanging and about to fall off. A couple of them were gone, must've ended up on the floor someplace.

Well, none of the bites were all that fresh any more. The only wound that really mattered was the slice across his belly.

He wondered if he had time to take a shower.

Nice to be all squeaky clean for Vicki.

Bad news, though, if she walked into the house while he was under the spray. He wouldn't even hear her.

Just make it quick, he decided.

He stepped into the tub, skidded the plastic curtain shut, and turned on the water. When it felt hot enough spilling over his hand, he turned the shower knob. Spray spattered down on his back. He straightened up so it hit his chest. Head down, he watched the blood run down his skin. It turned the water pink in front of his feet.

The knife wound kept bleeding. Not much, though.

It reminded him of the Mouth of Ram-Chotep.

No stitches, though. No teeth.

He wondered if it needed stitches. Patricia could do that. She'd done a nice job sewing up the Mouth on Charlie.

Take Vicki home with him, he wouldn't trust Patricia with a needle.

She'd stick it in my eye.

Just have to get rid of her, Melvin told himself.

He pressed a washcloth against his wound, and turned his back to the spray.

Should've got rid of Patricia before, he thought. But he'd had no idea that everything would happen so quickly. It made problems.

He felt worn out.

He'd gone through so much, tonight.

And there was so much more to do. If only he could wish Patricia away. If only he could take Vicki home and not have to worry about dealing with that one.

Maybe keep Vicki in the trunk of his car. Go in the house without her, that'd make it easier.

If Patricia's as hard to rekill as Charlie . . .

He didn't want to think about it.

So much to do.

Made his mind feel soggy.

With a sigh full of weariness, he turned around and shut the water off. He held the washcloth to his wound, slid the curtain aside, and climbed out of the tub. Dripping, he stepped to the bathroom door and opened it. Cool air came in from the hallway. He listened. The house was silent.

Satisfied that Vicki hadn't arrived yet, he left the doorway and dried himself. He clamped the towel against his belly to stop the bleeding while he removed the adhesive tape and gauze from the medicine cabinet.

He used the entire roll of gauze, running the netted fabric back and forth several times across the length of his wound. It soaked up the leaking blood. The tape didn't stick well because his skin was slick. He kept wiping himself dry and adding more tape. Finally, the bandage seemed fairly secure.

He picked up the revolver and stepped into the hallway.

Though he liked the idea of being naked when Vicki showed up, he realized he would have to go outside, lead her to his car, drive her to his house. If he did that and somebody saw him not wearing a stitch . . .

He walked toward his coveralls.

Maybe wait till after she's here, he thought.

Might be awkward, though, trying to keep the gun on her while he dressed.

He put the revolver down, and climbed into his coveralls. They felt hot, confining. The fabric stuck to his damp skin. He left the front open, picked up the gun, and wandered up the hallway to Vicki's room.

He stepped inside.

His heart slammed.

He stared at the bed, at the stained coverlet and pillow.

Ace was gone.

Vicki, curled on her side, head resting on Jack's outstretched arm, lay motionless and stared at him. Only moments ago, she had been caressing his chest and he had mumbled a few words too low and slurred for her to understand.

His eyes were shut. His mouth hung open a bit. He was breathing slowly. She wondered if he was asleep.

She hoped so.

Asleep, he wouldn't give her any trouble about leaving.

She didn't want to leave. She felt lazy and comfortable and safe. She felt as if she were home. This was where she belonged, and Ace's house seemed like a long, empty distance from here.

If she didn't go, she knew she would regret it. She did want there to be something held back, something saved for another time. Not saved for him alone, but also for herself. A special gift hidden away, anticipated.

They had given their bodies and their hearts. All that remained to give was freedom from the ache of parting. It was what they both wanted. It was what she intended to save.

For the honeymoon?

She would *make* it wait for then, no matter how badly she wanted to stay.

Slowly, she lifted her hand off Jack's chest and rolled away from him. The bed made barely a sound as she stood up. Turning, she looked down at Jack. Except for the slow rise and fall of his chest, he didn't move.

Vicki felt the soft breath of the breeze against her skin. It was comfortable, now, but it wouldn't remain quite so warm as the night went on. The bed's top sheet lay rumpled on the floor. She crouched and picked it up, and floated it down over Jack's sleeping form.

He didn't wake up.

Vicki shook her head. Disappointed in herself. Knowing her only concern hadn't been for Jack's comfort. A corner of her mind had hoped the touch of the sheet would disturb his sleep and he would try to stop her from leaving.

She found herself wanting to kiss him goodnight.

Right. Why don't you just shake him awake and be done with it? Or climb back in bed and go to sleep?

Leave or don't. Stop playing games.

Resolved . . . resigned . . . Vicki gathered up her clothes. She carried them into the hallway.

She considered turning off the bedroom light and shutting the door. But the room going dark might awaken him. The door might squeak.

So she left the room as it was, moved silently through the hallway and down the stairs. At the bottom of the stairs, she put on her clothes. She carried her shoes into the living-room. There, she spotted her purse on the easy chair.

I ought to leave him a note, she thought.

Right, and maybe he'll wake up while you're writing it . . .

This isn't just another ploy to postpone leaving, she told

herself. He's going to wake up alone. He'll miss me, and he'll be hurt that I snuck away. I *have* to leave him a note.

Vicki sat on the chair, opened her purse, and took out a notepad and pen.

Melvin's mind reeled as he searched.

Ace was dead, damn it! The dead don't get up and run away!

No?

Where is she?

The bedroom window was open, but its screen was still in place.

He dropped to his knees and peered under the bed.

He rushed to the closet and yanked its door open.

He ran into the hallway.

He felt sick and dizzy. This *couldn't* be happening. It was like a rotten dream. Running down the hall, he wondered if maybe it *was* a dream. Maybe he'd fallen asleep in the shower and he would wake up in a minute choking on water – and Ace would still be lying in the bed where she belonged. Still dead.

I'm not dreaming, he told himself.

Ace isn't dead.

Or Vicki or *someone* showed up while he was in the shower and took her away.

He raced into the living-room. The carpet looked clean. If she'd come this way, there had to be blood. Unless someone was carrying her. Then, maybe . . .

The front door had a guard chain on it. She must've put the chain on so Vicki couldn't come in and surprise her with the cop.

She hadn't gone out that way.

Melvin rushed into the kitchen. His hip bumped a chair, crashing the chair against the edge of the table. He flinched, more from the sudden noise than the slight pain. Sidestepping, he swivelled his head.

The floor was smeared and splashed with blood over where he'd nailed Ace. There were even foot tracks.

But no Ace.

The screen door was shut. The inner wooden door with its splintered edge stood open.

He had left it open, himself, so . . .

He suddenly felt as if he'd been kneed in the stomach. He bent over, gasping, and stared.

At red smudges on the linoleum leading to the doorway.

His gaze followed them backward to the messy area.

He groaned.

He could *see* Ace. See her staggering in from the hallway entrance, slipping and sliding through the blood, coming out of it on this side, tracking it to the door.

To confirm what he already knew, he stepped up close to the screen door and touched its handle.

Sticky. His fingertip came away stained.

'NO! NO NO *NO* . . .!' He slapped a hand across his mouth to block the shouts.

Gotta calm down, he thought.

She's alive. She's outside. She got away. She's gonna fuck up everything.

No.

He pushed open the door and leaped onto the patio. He scanned the darkness of the back yard.

I'll find you. I'll find you, you bitch!

There was some kind of room at the rear of the lawn. A laundry room or something.

Melvin ran to it, flung open the door and turned on the light. No blood on the floor. But he checked a small enclosure beside the door. Nothing in there but a toilet. He hurried past a washing machine, a basin, a drier. He jerked open a pair of cupboard doors at the end of the room. Then he rushed back outside.

What if she got over to a neighbour's house?

Cops might be on their way.

I bet she can't talk. Not the way I fixed her jaw.

They'd still call the cops.

He ran. He ran for the corner of the house. The grass was wet and springy under his bare feet.

He'd left his shoes in the kitchen.

No time to worry about them.

He dashed alongside the house.

All that mattered was getting to his car. Getting to his car before the cops showed up. And driving. Driving to the other house. And blowing that fucker's brains out. And getting his hands on Vicki.

Take her home.

What about Patricia?

That's a good one. The whole fucking world was falling on his head. Patricia was just one little piece of it. The least of his worries.

Just worry about getting out of here and getting Vicki.

When he reached the front yard, he stopped running. He stuck the revolver inside his coveralls and clamped it against his side. He scanned the lawn, hoping to find Ace sprawled on the grass. But she wasn't there. On the sidewalk, he looked both ways. No sign of her there, either.

He wished he'd parked closer. His car was at the end of the block. He wanted to run, but forced himself to walk.

He watched the neighbour's house as he strode by. Lights shone from its windows. He saw no one peering out at him.

Ace might've gone to the house on the other side, he told himself.

Might've gone *anywhere*.

He kept looking back, half expecting to find someone rushing up behind him, yelling – maybe someone with a gun.

At last, he reached his car. He climbed inside. With a trembling hand, he fumbled the key into the ignition. His heart gave a sickening lurch as headlights appeared on the road ahead.

Cops?

He threw himself across the seat and lay there gasping, listening. The sound of the car came closer, closer. Passed him and faded.

Staying down, he twisted the key. The engine caught.

He pushed himself up, glimpsed the red taillights in the side mirror, then put the car into gear and turned the corner.

A car was parked in Ace's driveway.

She hadn't said anything about having company tonight. Maybe assumed I'd be staying at Jack's, Vicki thought, so she didn't bother to warn me.

She swung the Mustang to the curb across the street from the house.

Now what? she wondered. I don't want to blunder into something. She wondered who the man was.

Maybe it's not a man.

Of course it is.

Ace had broken up with Jerry a couple of weeks ago, and hadn't mentioned seeing anyone else. She'd had no dates since Vicki moved in.

Maybe she made up with Jerry.

Could be just about anyone, though.

Vicki sighed. She'd been so reluctant to leave Jack. It had taken all her willpower to resist the urge to stay with him. Now this. If she'd known Ace had company, she probably wouldn't have left.

Maybe I should turn around, she thought, and go back. No. I made my decision. It was the right decision. And I'm here.

Vicki climbed out of the car. She crossed the street and went up the walkway to the front door. She rang the bell. Waited. Rang it again.

That's plenty of warning, she decided.

She unlocked the door and opened it – three inches before the guard chain snapped taut.

Great, she thought. Hope they're not asleep.

She pressed the doorbell a few more times and heard the chimes ring through the house.

'Come on, gang,' she muttered.

Leaning forward, she eased her face into the gap and called, 'Ace? Ace, it's me. You want to let me in?'

Nobody answered.

Okay. They must be in Ace's room with the door shut. Either asleep or at a bad place to stop, too busy to be interrupted.

Vicki pulled the door shut. She dropped the keys into her handbag, and walked around to the back of the house. Light spilled out through the screen door. The wooden door was open.

If the screen's locked . . .

She tried its handle. The door swung open and she stepped into the kitchen.

And went numb.

Blood. Bloody smudges of footprints. And over there . . . over near the centre of the kitchen . . .

God, what happened here!

Gazing at the blood, she took a step forward and kicked

something. She looked down. A man's leather shoe. One of a pair just in front of the door. Crouching, she picked it up and turned it over. The sole was stained with black as if someone had walked through spots of grease in it.

Melvin? Melvin was here?

Maybe *still* here.

His car in the driveway?

God, Ace, no!

'ACE!'

A sudden noise like a chair scuffing the floor made Vicki flinch and jerk her head to the right. She dropped the shoe.

Curled under the kitchen table, staring at Vicki through the bars of chair legs, was a naked woman.

'Ace?' Vicki whispered.

Didn't look like Ace. Not with that bloody, distorted face. Not with that raw dome of skull. But the body . . .

'What did he do *to you!'* Even as Vicki heard herself blurt the question, she was lunging at the table. She looped the straps of her handbag over her head so the bag hung against her chest, then flung the nearest chair out of the way. She hurled the table up, overturning it. The vase of flowers flew off and hit the wall. The edge of the table crashed against the floor. She dropped onto her knees in front of Ace. Hunching over, she saw blood spilling from two gashes on her back. It came out in slow trickles.

Knife wounds? How deep? How much damage had the knife done, penetrating her?

No way to tell.

But if all the blood on the kitchen floor was from Ace, she'd bled a lot. And she undoubtedly had internal haemorrhaging.

She might be dying.

Vicki rolled her over.

Ace stared up at her, blinking.

'It's all right,' Vicki whispered.

Though her front was smeared with blood, there were no more wounds that Vicki could see.

Ace raised an arm. Clutched in her hand was a mop of hair. She reached up as if offering it to Vicki.

'Hang onto it, hon. I'm gonna get you to a hospital.'

She lifted Ace's other hand. The pulse was weak.

She looked across the kitchen at the wall phone.

What if Melvin's still in the house?

He's not. He'd be on me by now.

But calling for an ambulance . . . the volunteer ambulance. The alert would sound through town like last night. The ambulance drivers would leave their homes, drive to the fire station . . . It might take ten minutes to get here. Or longer.

We could be halfway to Blayton Memorial by then.

'Come on,' Vicki said.

She straddled Ace, grabbed her sticky arms and pulled. Ace came up into a sitting position. 'You've gotta help,' Vicki muttered. 'Can you help?'

Scurrying around behind Ace, she squatted and hugged her beneath the breasts and lifted. Ace shoved her feet at the floor. Vicki staggered backward a step as the weight moved up against her. Then, Ace was on her feet – balanced, at least for the moment. Vicki rushed in front of her. 'Grab on.'

She felt Ace fall against her. But she was braced. She stayed up. As Ace's arms went around her shoulders, Vicki bent slightly and reached back. She clutched Ace's rump, thrust it upward and bounced.

With Ace on her back, she hooked her hands under her big thighs and lurched to the screen door. She used Ace's knee to punch the handle, releasing the catch. She rammed the door open and lumbered outside.

And ran.

She didn't think she *could* run, but she did.

Ace like a giant child riding piggy-back. Her weight pounding down with every stride Vicki took.

But Vicki stayed up. She kept on running. Alongside the house, across the front yard, her lungs burning, her legs leaden.

If only it were *her* car in the driveway.

Whose was it?

Who cares?

She only cared about getting to the Mustang. Far ahead. On the other side of the street.

She blinked sweat out of her eyes. She wheezed for air. Ace started to slide down. She tugged her thighs and boosted her higher and kept running. Over the sidewalk and across the street.

At the Mustang, she whirled around. Ace bumped the side of the car. Vicki released her legs. Ace let go. Bracing her up with a hand against her chest, Vicki jerked open the door. She flung the driver's seatback forward. Ace, turning, bumped against her. Vicki caught her, guided her, shoved her into the car.

Ace fell across the back seat. Face down, she squirmed over the cushion.

Vicki raced to the trunk. She slipped the handbag straps off her head, dug out the keys, and opened the trunk. In the faint glow of the streetlights, she spotted Ace's blanket.

Ever since Ace had started driving cars, she'd kept a blanket in the trunk. *Never know when you'll wanta flop in the woods.*

Vicki snatched out the blanket, slammed the trunk, and rushed to the open door. Ace was on her side, curled up. Vicki leaned into the car and spread the blanket over her.

'Don't want the ER doctors drooling over your naked body,' she said.

The blanket was for warmth, not modesty. Standard treatment for shock.

Vicki slapped her haunch through the soft cover, then scurried out, threw the seatback forward and got behind the wheel. She started the engine, pulled the door shut, shifted and shot the car forward.

'Too bad you're in no condition to appreciate this, hon,' she called out. 'This is gonna be the quickest trip to Blayton in the history of man.'

Chapter Thirty

As a professional courtesy, she supposed, Vicki was led to the deserted office of the chief of surgery instead of a waiting-room. She was told to make herself comfortable. Then, she was left alone.

With tissues from a box on the desk, she wiped as much blood as she could from her hands and clothes. She wanted to sit down, but she knew that the back of her blouse must be bloody and she didn't want to make a mess on leather upholstery. Her skirt was clean in front. She twisted it around, then sat on the soft chair and leaned forward, elbows on her legs.

She flinched at the sound of the door opening.

I'm sorry, Dr Chandler, but we weren't able to . . .

The nurse who came in had a cup of coffee on a serving tray with a packet of sugar and a small plastic container of cream. 'Can I get you anything else? The kitchen is closed, but we have a vending machine in the lounge.'

Vicki shook her head. 'Thanks, I don't . . .'

The nurse set the tray on the desk in front of her. 'We've notified the police, Dr Chandler. They should be here shortly. They'll want to speak with you.'

She nodded.

'I'm sure your friend will be fine.'

'Thank you,' she muttered.

The nurse could be sure of no such thing, but Vicki appreciated the kind words.

When she was alone, she picked up the cup. She brought it toward her mouth. Coffee slopped out, splashing hot on her thigh.

She remembered joking with Jack about spilling coffee. Black coffee, white couch. That seemed like days ago. She wondered, vaguely, if he'd awakened yet and found out she was gone.

It took both hands to hold the cup steady. She drank, and set the cup down.

Jack. Thank God I didn't stay. Ace would've died for sure.

She might die, anyway.

Vicki wished she were with Ace in the operating-room. She'd asked to join the surgical team, but the doctor had taken a quick look at her and shaken his head. 'I'm sorry,' he'd said. 'No way. You're in shock, yourself.' Then he'd instructed the nurse to show Vicki to the office and 'look after her'.

Vicki supposed the doctor was right about keeping her out of the OR. In her condition, she certainly couldn't have done Ace any good and her presence might've been a distraction for the others.

But she hated just sitting here, not knowing.

Ace could be dead right now.

She'd been unconscious by the time they reached the hospital.

She'll be all right, Vicki told herself. She'll be fine.

We'll pop open a bottle of champagne for her homecoming, and get royally soused, and laugh about dumb things . . .

Vicki lowered her face into her hands and wept.

The nurse came in, followed by two men in slacks and sports shirts. Vicki stood up and faced them. Both men had thick moustaches. The older one, grey at his temples, wore a leather rig that held an enormous handgun upside down beneath his armpit. The other, with black curly hair, had a small revolver in a holster clipped to his belt.

Vicki tried to read the nurse's face. It looked solemn. 'Have you heard anything about Ace?'

'She's still in surgery. These men are Detectives Gorman and Randisi from the police.'

Vicki wiped her eyes. She looked at the two men.

Randisi, the curly-haired one, said, 'We'd like to ask you a few questions about . . .'

'It was Melvin Dobbs. He did it.'

'Dobbs?' Gorman asked '*The* Melvin Dobbs? The psycho? The guy they put away after he pulled the jumper-cable stunt on that dead cheerleader? What was it, ten, fifteen years ago?'

'That's him,' Vicki said.

Randisi glanced at the nurse. With a nod, she turned away and left the room.

'You were there at the time of the assault?' he asked.

'No. Melvin was gone when I got there. I *think* he was gone. I didn't look around. I just got Ace – Alice – out of there as fast as I could.'

'What makes you think it was this Dobbs psycho?' Gorman asked.

'It couldn't have been anyone else. He went to the house . . . because of me. I don't know why, maybe just to see me and talk, and maybe Ace tried to keep him out. See, he thought I was there. He was with me earlier, and I told him I was going home. Maybe he wanted to kill me or . . . abduct me or something. I don't know.'

'Had you quarrelled with him?' Randisi asked.

'I'd taken him out to dinner. I . . . baited him. I got him to admit he killed Dexter Pollock.'

The two policemen glanced at each other.

'I know,' Vicki said. 'Everyone thinks the nurse did it. Patricia Gordon. But Melvin *got* her to do it.'

'How did he manage that?'

Vicki almost told about the hypnosis. And how she suspected he'd also used hypnosis to persuade Charlie Gaines to make her a partner, then staged Charlie's crash. But she stopped herself. It would sound too much like hocus-pocus. These men might not buy it. Her credibility might start falling apart. 'I don't know how he did it,' she answered. 'He wouldn't tell me. But he *did* confess to making her kill Pollock. That was just before I left him. He must've got nervous, afraid I'd report him, so he went over to the house, thinking I'd be there.'

'Where were you?' Randisi asked.

'With a friend. Jack Randolph. At his house.'

'So,' Randisi said, 'you went to dinner with Dobbs, got him to confess killing Pollock, then you told him goodnight and went straight over to this Randolph fellow's place. Why Randolph? Why didn't you take your information to the police?'

'That's a good one,' she muttered.

'In what way?'

'I'd already told the Ellsworth police my suspicions about Dobbs killing Pollock. They acted like I was some kind of a flake.' She looked Randisi in the eyes. 'Which I'm not.'

'You don't seem much like a flake to me,' Gorman said.

'Who'd you tell in Ellsworth?' Randisi asked.

'Joey Milbourne. And he passed the word to Raines. I guess they had themselves quite a laugh.'

Gorman mumbled something. It sounded like 'dickheads', but Vicki couldn't be sure.

'So you figured,' Randisi said, 'there was no point in taking your information to Raines. He wouldn't act on it, anyway.'

'That's right. The man I went to, Jack, is an attorney. We discussed the situation. He was going to wait for morning, then go to Raines himself. If Raines wouldn't listen to him, he planned to see a friend of his in the District Attorney's office. One way or another, we figured we'd get someone to pay attention.'

'They'll pay attention now,' Gorman said. 'Where does this Dobbs fellow live?'

'In Ellsworth. His house in on . . . Elm Street, I think.'

Gorman got a sour look on his face. 'That's in the city limits,' he said to Randisi.

'Where did the attack take place?'

'Ace's house is on Third.'

'Damn.' Gorman shook his head.

'What's wrong?' Vicki asked him.

'We're Blayton PD. We've got no jurisdiction in Ellsworth.'

'So it's Raines's ballgame,' Randisi said.

'We'll contact him right now. If he gives us any . . . trouble, we'll . . .'

'There's something else,' Vicki said. 'If he needs convincing. Dobbs left his shoes on the kitchen floor. I know they're his. I've seen him wear the same kind at the gas station he owns. And they have grease stains on the soles.'

'We'll see that Raines picks him up,' Randisi said.

'He gives us any crap, we'll do it ourselves.'

Vicki looked at the two men. 'I'm really . . . Thanks. You're terrific. I was starting to think *all* cops were dickheads.'

Gorman blushed. Just a little.

Melvin was down in his basement laboratory when Patricia called from the top of the stairs. 'They're coming. They just got out of their car.'

'How many?' he asked.

'Two of them.'

Melvin climbed the stairs, looking up at Patricia. She wore one of his bright blue Hawaiian shirts, and nothing else. The tails draping her thighs were parted slightly, letting him see a hint of her blonde curls. Above the single button fastened at her belly, the shirt gaped wide enough to show the sides of her breasts.

She looked just right.

Melvin had dressed her for the occasion.

As he reached the top of the stairs, the doorbell rang.

'You ready?' he asked.

Patricia nodded. She had fear in her eyes.

He kissed her gently on the mouth. 'Hey, don't worry.'

'I don't want to lose you, Melvin.'

'Ain't gonna happen. Just do like I said.'

The bell sounded again. Patricia turned around. Melvin followed her, watching the loose, glossy shirt shimmer on the moving mounds of her rump.

'Sure hope these cops ain't a couple of fairies,' he said.

Patricia glanced back at him and smiled.

The bell rang again.

Melvin stationed himself against the wall beside the front door. The door would conceal him when it swung open. Patricia slipped the guard chain free and looked at him.

Melvin nodded.

She pulled the door open just a few inches. She peered out through the gap. 'Yes?' she asked.

'I'm sorry to disturb you at this hour, but . . . This *is* the home of Melvin Dobbs?'

'Yes?'

'I'm Chief Raines of the Ellsworth Police Department. This is Sergeant Woodman.'

The chief himself, Melvin thought. And sounding pretty nervous. Probably hadn't seen this much of a pretty young babe in a long time. Probably trying for a look inside the shirt.

Did the chief realize he was in the presence of Patricia Gordon, RN, who'd nailed Pollock?

'Is Mr Dobbs home?' Raines asked.

'Yes, he's upstairs. Won't you come in?' Patricia gave the knob a pull and backed away. The door swung closer to Melvin. It blocked his view of the men, but he saw Patricia beyond its edge.

She kept walking backward toward the stairs. The shirt trembled over her breasts. The gap below the single button seemed wider than before. Her hair gleamed in the lamplight. Her thighs flashed white.

Melvin grinned.

He heard the men step forward. A shoulder and left arm came into view.

'I'll just call him,' Patricia said, stopping at the foot of the stairs.

'Thank you.'

She spun around. The shirt tail swished, giving a glimpse of her buttocks.

Melvin heard a soft breathy sound, almost a whistle.

'Melvin!' she called up the stairway. 'There are gentlemen here to see you.' She waited a moment. 'Melvin?' she called again. Facing the men, she shook her head and rolled her eyes upward. 'He must be asleep. Should I go up and wake him?'

'I'll go with you,' Raines said. 'Woodman, you wait . . .'

Patricia whirled and raced up the stairs, taking them two at a time, her shirt tail flapping.

Both cops bolted after her.

'Melvin!' she shouted toward the top. 'Cops! Run!'

Melvin stepped away from the door.

'Hold it!' Raines snapped, drawing his revolver, aiming it at her.

Patricia stopped. She turned around. She had popped open the button on her way upstairs. The front of the shirt was wide open. She raised her arms.

Both cops, guns drawn, stood at the foot of the stairway and gazed up at her.

Melvin aimed at their backs. He fired both his revolvers at once. He kept firing, pulling the triggers as fast as he could. Through the roaring blasts, he heard one of the men yell, 'OW! OUCH!' as the bullets knocked him down. The other was silent.

When both guns were empty, one cop lay face-down on the stairs and looked as if he'd been trying to hug them. The other, who'd succeeded in turning around after the first shot caught him in the shoulder, was sitting on the floor, leaning back against the stairs, his legs stretched out. That one stared at the ceiling and twitched as blood foamed out of his mouth.

Grinning up at Patricia, Melvin twirled the guns and jammed them into his pockets.

'Reckon its Boot Hill for *them* hombres,' he drawled.

Patricia rushed down the stairs. She leaped over the bodies and threw her arms around Melvin. She was shaking. She squeezed herself hard against him.

* * *

Vicki sat, leaning forward, elbows on her knees, waiting. The two policemen, Gorman and Randisi, had gone away a long time ago to phone Chief Raines. Later, Gorman had returned alone to tell her how it went.

'Raines said he'd look into it,' he had told her.

'Look into it? Is that all?'

'He's not a great fan of yours.'

'I've noticed.'

'But he couldn't just ignore the attack on Miss Mason. Ace? Even a narrow-minded, stubborn cop like Raines has to do something about it if one of his citizens gets carved up like that. But he didn't want to believe that Dobbs was the perpetrator. Not on the basis of your suspicions. He said you've got a "burr up your ass" about Dobbs.' Gorman's face reddened when he said that. 'Sorry, but those were his words. He said you've been trying to get Dobbs put away so he'll stop . . . putting moves on you.'

'I guess we gave Milbourne that idea Sunday morning,' Vicki said. 'Joey Milbourne, one of his men. Dobbs had threatened Pollock's life right in front of us, and we told Milbourne that. But he wanted to know why we were out with Dobbs, and Ace had to go and tell him the creep has the hots for me. So Milbourne went and convinced Raines we were trouble-makers. So they didn't do anything about that bastard.'

Gorman shook his head. 'No accounting for fools,' he said. 'Any cop worth a damn would've pulled in Dobbs for questioning at that point.'

'So now Raines is willing to look into it? On the word of a flake with a . . . grudge?'

'I made it pretty clear he'd better.'

Vicki almost smiled. 'I bet you did.'

'I'm glad you told us about the shoes, though. That's what did the trick, finally made him decide there was sufficient reason to drop by the house and have a "chat" with Dobbs.'

'Tonight?'

Gorman nodded. 'He said he'd get right on it.'

Now, sitting alone in the office, Vicki looked at her wristwatch. Almost 3 a.m. Gorman had left her just after two.

Which meant that Raines had probably already had his 'chat' with Melvin.

Right now, Melvin might be in custody.

Or maybe he talked his way out of it, convinced Raines of his innocence.

That won't last long, she told herself. The minute Ace regains consciousness and names Melvin . . . she won't be naming anyone with her jaw in that shape.

Give her a pen and paper.

If she regains consciousness.

She will, Vicki told herself. She'll be all right.

She *can't* die.

My fault. It's all my fault.

Jesus, Ace, please.

Vicki lurched to her feet as the office door swung open. The nurse came in.

'How is she?'

'I haven't been told anything about her condition.'

Vicki nodded. 'Well, at least no news is good news.'

'I didn't say I had no news. Something came up. I thought you should know about it. We just got word to call in Dr Goldstein. He's our staff cosmetic surgeon.'

Vicki stared at the nurse.

A cosmetic surgeon!

For Ace's scalp?

They wouldn't bother, if . . .

'Oh, thank God,' she murmured.

'He's on his way right now.'

Vicki slumped into the chair.

'I don't know how long they'll be in there, but it's safe to assume that your friend's in a stable condition. Wouldn't you like to go home and clean up and get some rest? You've been through such an ordeal. You must be done in. And it'll be hours before you're able to visit with her. Why don't you call in around nine or ten, we can let you know when you'll be able to see her. Really. Waiting around here all that time . . . You'd feel so much better if you went home and slept for a few hours.'

Vicki nodded. 'Yeah,' she murmured.

Ace . . . she's going to live.

The awful tightness inside Vicki seemed to be melting, ice

going soft, warmth flowing through her body, soothing, making her weak.

Ace.

You made it, Ace. You made it.

Vicki drove. She drove through the warm night toward Ellsworth, though she wasn't quite sure where she would go when she arrived.

She knew where she wanted to go.

Jack's house.

But she didn't like the idea of walking in this way, all covered with dried blood. Maybe she should go to Ace's house first, clean up, put on fresh clothes.

I can't, she realized. I can't walk through that kitchen.

Besides, it would be stupid to enter Ace's house alone. For all she knew, Melvin hadn't been caught. He was probably in jail right now, but what if he wasn't? What if she walked into the house and there he was, waiting for her . . . with a knife?

She considered turning the car around and driving to her parents' house. They had kept her room ready for overnight visits, and some of her clothes were there. She could shower, catch some sleep, then return to the hospital, which wasn't much more than five minutes from their house.

But she would have to do a lot of talking – explain everything. She didn't feel up to that. And why upset them with all that had been going on? They'll be sick when they find out. Might as well spare them the agony for as long as possible. Once it's all over . . . really over, Ace recovering for sure, Melvin behind bars for sure . . . that would be the time to let them in on it.

Pay them a visit tomorrow . . . today, she reminded herself. It's been Wednesday for hours. See them this afternoon or tonight. That's soon enough. Spare them till then.

She parked in front of Jack's house. Leaning away from the seatback to climb out, she felt her blouse peel away from the upholstery.

You're in for a shock, Jack old pal.

When she stood up, her legs trembled. She held onto the open door to steady herself. The lack of sleep, the tension, carrying

Ace on her back, the relief she'd felt during the past half-hour or so – they had taken their toll. The nurse had been right. She was 'done in'. Not only sore in the arms and back and rump and legs, but deep-down weary.

She took a full breath. Even her *lungs* felt heavy and tired.

It's almost over, she told herself.

She swung the door shut, shuffled around the front of the car, moaned when she stepped onto the curb, and pointed herself toward Jack's lighted porch.

It would feel so good to hold him, sink against his strong warm body.

First a shower.

She wondered if she would be able to stay on her feet long enough for a shower.

Maybe Jack'll go into the tub with me, hold me up.

The thought of that sent a stir through Vicki that pushed away some of the weariness.

She tried the door. It was locked. Of course. She'd made sure it was locked when she left. She pressed the doorbell and waited, hoping the sound was loud enough to wake him.

Before she could press it again, the door swung open.

Chapter Thirty-one

Staring at her, Jack stepped away from the door and let Vicki enter. She pushed the door shut.

'What happened to you?' he asked.

He was frowning. He looked pale, and Vicki wondered if he had been up for a long time, worrying.

'I came from the hospital,' she said. 'I took Ace there. Melvin attacked her tonight.'

'My God,' he muttered. He reached out and pulled Vicki against him.

'I'm a mess,' she warned.

'Who cares.' He stroked her back.

She put her arms around him. His terry robe was soft under her hands.

'Was Ace hurt badly?' he asked.

'He . . . really wrecked her. But she's going to make it. I'm sure she's going to make it. The cops went to pick up Melvin. I'm such a mess. I'm so tired.'

'It's all right.' He gently stroked her back.

'I'm getting blood all over you.'

'Doesn't matter.'

'Can I use your shower? I . . . I'd like to get clean. And sleep. Is it okay if I sleep here?'

'Of course.'

Easing away from his embrace, she shook her head when she saw the hint of rust colour her blouse and skirt had left on the front of his light blue robe. 'Sorry,' she muttered.

'It'll wash.'

'We can throw it in the laundry like your shorts.'

'Not wearing any,' he said.

'I didn't suppose you were.' Her heart quickened and she felt a warm spreading glow.

She smiled up at Jack as she remembered his embarrassment when his skimpy briefs had fluttered to the floor of Ace's kitchen. That seemed like weeks ago. It was only last night. Tonight, the place on the floor where they'd dropped was smeared with Ace's blood.

Vicki's smile died.

'Come on,' Jack said. He took her hand and led her to the stairway.

She saw her note taped to the top of the newel post. Brushing it with a fingertip, she said, 'Didn't you read it?'

His face looked blank. 'I was asleep till you rang the doorbell. I hurried right down.'

'Don't you want to read it now?'

'It can wait. You're here. That's all that matters.'

Vicki felt a small pull of disappointment. Didn't he *care* what she'd written to him? Though the note was brief, it told of her love for him, her regret for sneaking out while he slept, her hopes that soon there would be no need for her to leave. She glanced back at it as she climbed the stairs. The note looked abandoned.

He's right, she told herself. What's the big deal? I'm here. We're together. That's what counts.

At the top of the stairs, he released her hand. 'You go ahead and take your shower. I'll phone the police and make sure they've arrested Melvin.'

'All right.' She didn't want to be left alone. But it would be good to know, for sure, that Melvin was in custody. 'When you're done, why don't you come in . . . and wash my back?'

Jack grinned in a way that made something go tight inside her. There was nothing of tenderness or love in that grin. It looked wolfish, leering. She supposed it was meant to be amusing, but it seemed awfully inappropriate.

'Very funny,' she muttered.

Walking through the hallway, she glanced back at him. He hadn't moved. He was watching her, hands thrust into the pockets of his robe. For a moment, she was reminded of the way Pollock used to look on those mornings when he waited for her in the apartment corridor to lecture her, to ogle her.

She entered the master bedroom. Staring at the bed, she was filled with a rush of memories: the feel of him inside her, his gentleness, their soft words, his hinting of marriage, the way she had ached with love when she covered his sleeping body with a sheet before leaving.

None of that fit in with the harsh, lusting way he'd looked at her in the hall.

What had changed?

Maybe nothing.

He's tired, she told herself. I'm tired. It was nothing. He was trying to be funny and I'm just not in the mood for it. Too much has happened.

She stepped into the adjoining bathroom, snapped the light on, and shut the door. Her hand curled around the knob. Her thumb jabbed its lock button down.

That's ridiculous, she thought. What's the matter with me? *What's the matter with him?*

You invited him in, and now you're locking the door?

He gave me that look.

Big deal. Forget it.

Shaking her head, she turned the knob. The lock button popped out with a quiet ping.

She moved in front of the mirror, and curled her lip when she saw herself. So much like last night. But instead of black, greasy smudges from Charlie's body, it was stains of blood from Ace. Even her chin, though she'd wiped it with a tissue at the hospital, had a reddish smear.

Quickly, she turned her back to the mirror. She slipped her blouse off, reached back and draped it over the edge of the sink. Then, she removed her bra.

The blood had soaked through to her skin. Her chest, her breasts, her belly – all were marred by faint spots and blotches as if she'd been sunburned through a torn garment gaping with holes.

She turned toward the sound of the door swinging open.

Jack stood there in his robe.

The nasty leer was gone, but his eyes lingered on her. She had an urge to cover her breasts . . . but that'd be absurd. 'Did you make the call?' she asked.

He nodded. 'They arrested Melvin. They've got him in jail.'

'That's great,' she said. But she felt no relief, only uneasiness about the change in Jack. 'Is something wrong?' she asked.

'No. Everything's fine. And you look . . . terrific.'

'I wish you wouldn't stare at me like that.'

He came toward her. Vicki took a step backward, then stopped herself.

This is Jack, for godsake. Jack.

He took her by the shoulders, drew her forward, and kissed her. His mouth felt quick and eager. More urgent than before, but so familiar. It opened. It sucked her lips, slid down and licked her chin. Where the bloodstain was.

'Don't,' she murmured.

Then moaned as a hand moved to her breast. His other hand tore the bandage from her shoulder. She flinched as the tape pulled her skin.

'Jack.'

He said nothing. He squeezed her breast. He squeezed her

bitten shoulder. The surging pleasure and pain made her squirm.

'You're . . . hurting.'

His mouth went away from her chin. He sucked the side of her neck. Her mouth fell open and she writhed, gasping. She dug her fingers into his buttocks through the thickness of the robe, and pressed him hard against her.

He no longer squeezed her shoulder. The hand roamed down her side, rucked up her skirt, hooked her panties down around her thighs.

His wet mouth slipped over her skin. He kissed her shoulder. Licked the wounds left by Charlie's teeth last night.

'Don't do that,' she murmured. 'Hey, come on.'

He bit.

Fire bolted through her body. She jerked rigid and cried out. His teeth sank deeper. She shuddered in spasms of pain as she felt them grinding her.

When she tried to twist away, he clutched her buttocks with both hands, lifted her, turned her, slammed her against the bathroom wall. The impact snapped her head back. It struck the wall. Her vision exploded with brilliant lights, then dimmed.

She told herself to move, to struggle. But her body wouldn't respond to the commands of her dulled mind.

She was aware of Jack sucking blood from her shoulder. She heard wet smacking sounds, slurping sounds. She felt no pain. Just pulling sensations.

Then she felt herself being impaled.

He sucked and thrust, pounding her limp body against the bathroom wall.

It went on and on. Vicki tried to lift her arms, wanting to make it stop. But they flopped uselessly at her sides, bumping the wall each time he rammed.

Later, she realized the wall was no longer against her back. Instead, there was the cool tile of the bathroom floor. She gazed at the ceiling. It took her a moment to become aware that Jack wasn't on top of her. She tried to lift her head, couldn't.

She heard thumping, splattering sounds. Familiar sounds. Water bashing down, filling the bathtub beside her.

The noise shut off.

Jack loomed over her. He straddled her hips, staring down.

His robe hung open. Across his belly, just above the navel, was a white strip of bandage. It looked like a mouth, the mouth of a strange design carved on his abdomen, drawn in lines that were threads of dried blood, leaking in places, droplets trickling down his skin . . . an upside-down pyramid inside a circle . . . ovals like eyes at the corners . . . the bandage its mouth.

A face. An evil face.

Something from . . . black magic? That changed Jack, made him evil.

And her mind pulled a memory out of its dense fog – Charlie sitting behind his desk at the clinic, specks of blood appearing on his shirt.

She gazed up at Jack's face. His mouth and chin glimmered with blood. Her blood. She searched his eyes. They looked down at her, wide, frantic, somehow both gleeful and frightened. She saw no hint of the Jack she had known, had loved.

'Melvin,' she muttered. 'Wha . . . wha'd he do . . . to you?'

The wild glee vanished from his eyes. His face twisted with fear and rage. 'You filthy rotten slut!' he squealed. 'You made me do it.' He swept down, bending at the waist, and his open hand smacked her cheek, rocked her head sideways. 'I wasn't supposed to touch you, damn it! You *made* me! He won't like it. He won't like it one bit! It's all your fault!'

Squatting beside her, Jack rammed his arms under her back and legs. He picked her up, lurched forward, and dropped her.

Into the bathtub. The cold water clenched her, covered her, but cushioned her fall. Softly, she bumped the bottom of the tub. She curled upward and caught a breath before Jack's hand clutched her face and pushed it down. The hand went away. She thrust herself up, gasping, and saw Jack climb into the tub.

He reached down for her feet. She jerked her legs back, knees rising out of the water, but he crouched and grabbed her ankles and pulled them toward him. Her back slid. Her face went under.

Forcing her eyes to stay open, Vicki watched him through inches of water that swirled pink from the blood of her shoulder. He stood, holding her legs up, yelling words that sounded faint and mushy.

Her heart felt like a bludgeoning club. Her lungs burned. *What did Melvin do to him?*

He's gonna drown me.

She squirmed and kicked, but he didn't loose his hold. She shoved her hands against the sides and bottom of the tub, trying to push herself up. And she *did* get closer to the surface, but Jack raised her legs higher. Her head pressed the bottom. Through the blurry pink, she saw her legs nearly straight up, saw her pubic hair and belly out of the water, felt her rump against Jack's legs, felt ripples on the undersides of her breasts. He almost had her standing on her head.

I'm gonna die, she thought. *Jesus, this is it.*

Then he shoved downward. She felt her back slide, her body unbend and enter the cold water, her head rise as it ran up the slope at the rear of the tub. Her face broke the surface and she gulped air.

Jack, crouching, still held her ankles. He glared at her. 'You won't tell him a thing!'

Vicki jerked her head from side to side.

'I didn't bite you, I didn't fuck you! Right?'

'*Right*,' she choked out.

'You came back and you were bloody so I let you take a shower. I wanted you clean for him.'

'Yes! Yes!'

'You're not going to tell on me.'

'No!'

'Promise?'

'Yes!' With a palsied hand, she splashed water as she drew an X on her submerged chest. 'Cross my heart. I promise. Please.'

Jack released her ankles. He stood and climbed out of the tub. Vicki sat up. 'Get out of there and dry off. You can wear this,' he said, and pulled the robe off. He tossed it to the floor, turned away from her, and reached for a towel.

He kept his back to Vicki and rubbed himself with the towel while she clambered over the wall of the tub. She flopped onto the floor, panting.

'Don't just lay there.'

The ceiling seemed to be spinning slowly, tipping.

'Move it!'

'My shoulder,' she muttered.

A dry washcloth fluttered above her, dropped onto her right

breast. Still on her back, she folded the cloth and pressed it gently against the torn flesh of her shoulder.

Moaning, she sat up.

Jack opened the bathroom door. 'I'll be right back,' he said. 'Don't try anything.' He stepped into the master bedroom.

Throwing herself forward, Vicki scurried on hands and knees toward the door. She was almost there when Jack spun around. He lunged for the door. She smashed it shut with a swing of her fist. The door slammed. She rose on her knees. Reached for the knob. For the lock button.

The door flew at her, knocked her hand aside, crashed into her forehead.

She came awake in darkness, her head throbbing and spinning. She didn't know where she was, but her wet hair forced the memory of looking up at Jack through the bathtub water. She remembered what he'd done before throwing her into the tub. She tried to think forward, to getting out of the tub, but the memories stopped with her still underwater and thinking she would drown.

She knew she was no longer in the tub. She was on a cushion. She was wearing something dry and warm on top, sodden and chilly lower where it clung to her rump and legs. Jack's robe? She remembered him wearing it when he squatted in the tub and grabbed her ankles.

Was she on the bed in Jack's master bedroom?

She tried to push herself up. The dizziness flipped her stomach. She grabbed the edge of the cushion and dragged herself sideways and vomited onto the floor.

When she finished, she rolled away from the edge. Lying curled on her side, she saw a seatback in front of her. There was dim light above it. And a head. A head that turned. A face that was a pale oval, dark smudges for its eyes and mouth. Jack.

The face turned away, and Jack kept on driving.

She knew where he was taking her.

To Melvin.

She tried to make herself as small as she felt, snuggling her back against the rise of the seat cushion, drawing up her knees, hugging her breasts through the heavy softness of the terry cloth robe.

595

Taking me to Melvin, she thought.

Following orders.

'Jack?' Her voice sounded small and far away. 'What did he do to you, Jack?'

'Remember what I said about telling,' he warned.

'I remember. I won't say anything. What did he do to you? How did he make you . . . we *loved* each other.'

'That so?'

'Oh, God,' she moaned.

'You're Melvin's,' he said. 'That's all I know. I wasn't supposed to touch you, just pretend I was your boyfriend and bring you back to him. That's all. But you had to flaunt yourself and tempt me, you damn whore, and I lost my cool.'

'It's that . . . *thing* . . . on your stomach. That face or whatever it is.'

'I wouldn't know.'

'Do you know who I am?'

'Vicki.'

Her heart seemed to jump, pumping blood into her head, making it throb. Squinting against the pain, she sat up. She scooted across the seat, away from the vomit, and swung her feet to the floor.

Jack twisted the rearview mirror so he could keep an eye on her. 'Don't even think about trying something. Last time, I almost broke your head open.'

She settled down against the cushion and stared at the back of his head. 'What's my last name?' she asked.

'I wouldn't know.'

'What do you know?'

'He drove me to the house and told me to wait for Vicki and take her to him. And not to mess with her. Remember that.'

'Jack. You didn't. You didn't mess with her. I'm not *Vicki*.'

'Bullshit.' He turned the car onto Elm Street. With a glance out of the window, she saw that they were only a block from Melvin's house.

'You'll find out when we get there,' she said. 'Melvin's really going to be mad.'

She felt the car slow.

'I know Vicki,' she said. 'She was supposed to show up at your house? Why? I don't get it.'

'Melvin knew you'd come back.'

'Not me. Vicki. Was she there tonight? After I left? I don't . . . Has she been . . . has she been *going* with you? Behind my back?'

Jack stopped the car. He twisted around and stared at her. 'What're you trying to pull?'

'That rotten bitch! Melvin wants her? He can have her! I'll take you to her. I know right where she is. Turn the car around.'

Jack shook his head. 'He said the gal who comes to the house would be Vicki. You're the one who came to the house.'

'But I'm not Vicki. I'm Jennifer Morley.'

'Wait. No. That's crazy.'

'I can prove it. My purse.' She paused. Her head felt as if it were splitting down the middle. 'You can see my ID. Where's my purse?'

'Back at the house.'

'Well, didn't you look in it? Why didn't you *make sure* before you . . . God, you're stupid. Melvin's gonna cream you when you walk in there with me. Jesus!'

'You're Vicki.' He didn't sound sure. 'You're just trying to trick me.'

'That note I left on the banister. If you'd read it, you'd know who I am. I signed it. I signed, "Love, Jennifer." Take me back to the house and I'll prove it. You've got the wrong person!'

'Melvin'll know.' He faced forward. The car began to move.

'I can be *yours*,' Vicki blurted. 'If you take me to Melvin, I'll be *his*. He didn't send you out to get me. He sent you for Vicki. So you won't be disobeying if you keep me for yourself. I can be yours, and I'll help you get Vicki. You can take her to Melvin, and keep me. I love you, Jack. I want to be with you, not with Melvin. Please.'

'I don't know,' he muttered.

'Jack. You want me, don't you?' Leaning forward, she reached over the seatback and placed her hands gently on Jack's shoulders. They hunched for a moment as if he expected an attack. She caressed him through his knit shirt.

He stopped the car. In front of Melvin's house.

'Keep going,' Vicki whispered, brushing her lips against his ear.

'No,' he said. 'You're going in.'

Her hands tightened on his shoulders. She saw herself grabbing his face, going for his eyes, gouging into them with her fingernails. The pain should incapacitate him, giving her a chance to flee. Blinded, he wouldn't have a chance of overtaking her. She'd get away.

But this was Jack, *her* Jack. As brutal as he'd been to her, it wasn't his fault. Melvin had him controlled. Somehow. And maybe it wasn't permanent. But if she blinded him . . .

As he pulled the key from the ignition, Vicki rammed him forward. He slammed against the steering wheel. The car horn blared.

She threw herself against the door, levered its handle and stumbled out. She had a stranger's legs, weak and trembling. But she kept them under her, staggering toward the rear of the car, looking back when she heard the driver's door squeak. Jack lurched into the street. She ran.

She sprinted, chin tucked down, arms pumping, legs flying out, bare feet pounding the blacktop. Though pain crashed through her head with every heartbeat, her legs began to feel right. Her own legs, her own body, running – just as she had run every morning, but this time with an urgency she'd never known before.

She heard Jack behind her. His slapping shoes. His huffing breath.

He'll never catch me!

She dashed up the centre of the road. She felt the breeze in her wet hair, on her face, on her chest and belly and legs. The robe, hanging loose, flapped behind her like a cape.

I can run like this all night, she thought. I can run right into the police station.

(Lot of good *that* would do.)

An intersection. Glaring brightness from the left.

She snapped her head that way.

A car rushed toward her, bore down roaring, then shrieking. Shrieking, though she thought she was safe from it, strides beyond its path.

She twisted around in time to see it hit Jack.

Even over the noise of the brakes, she heard the thuds of the impact. The bumper struck the side of his leg. It kicked both his legs high. His body shot over the hood. His head crashed through the windshield.

The car came to a stop just beyond the intersection.

The driver's door swung open. As a man climbed out, Vicki pulled her robe shut and tightened its cloth belt.

She wondered whether to run or stay.

There's no more reason to run, she realized. Melvin's house, far back from the road and alone on the block, was more than a hundred yards from the intersection. She could keep an eye on it. She could get away in the man's car at the first sign of Melvin's approach.

And Jack was no longer a threat.

'He ran right in front of me!' the man called to her. He sounded scared. 'You saw it, didn't you? Was he chasing you or something? What's going on?'

She walked toward him. 'He was after me,' she said.

'Wow. Oh, wow.' He stood beside his car, turning, looking at Vicki, then at the body sprawled motionless across his hood, then at Vicki again.

In the glow of the streetlights, he looked vaguely familiar. A short man, black hair in a crew-cut, eyes small and too close to his broad nose. 'Hey,' he said. 'You're someone. Vicki?'

She nodded.

'Wes,' he said. 'Wes Wallace. You remember me?'

'Sure.' From school. He used to pal around with Manny Stubbins. 'How're you doing?'

'Jesus. Not bad till a minute ago. Jesus H. Christ on a rubber crutch.' He walked closer to the body. Vicki stayed beside him. 'Who was it?'

'Jack Randolph,' she said, and felt a sudden aching tightness in her chest.

'You say this guy was chasing you?'

'He . . . he'd attacked me. I got away. He was trying to get me again.'

'Hey, so I'm some kind of hero, huh?' He leaned over the side of the car, and stared. 'Sure busted my windshield. Maybe I better try 'n' get him out, you know?' He clutched the back of Jack's belt and pulled. The body didn't move. 'Shit. Hung up.' Reaching through the hole in the windshield, he grabbed Jack by the hair and lifted. Then, he dragged the body backward and let the head down on the hood. He gave it a close look, and groaned. 'God, last time I saw something this bad was when Kraft and Darlene . . .' He turned away, holding his mouth and gagging.

Vicki saw Jack's head. Its crown was caved in. One eye had popped out, and dangled by the optic nerve against the side of his nose.

'Oh, Jack,' she whispered. He was no longer a monster, he was Jack again, the man she had held in her arms only hours ago, who had been in her and part of her. Bending over, she lay her arms across his back, pressed her cheek against him.

And felt a slow rise and fall as he breathed.

Vicki whirled around. 'Wes! He's alive.'

Wes was hunched over, vomiting.

'Hurry! Come here and help.' Not waiting for him, Vicki turned again to Jack. She pulled his limp arms down against his sides and shoved his spraddled legs together. She clutched him by the shoulder and hip, pulled, tried to roll him over.

Then Wes was beside her. 'Alive? Can't be.'

'Help me turn him over.'

Together, they tumbled Jack onto his back.

'Oh, wow,' Wes muttered. 'Look at that.'

Vicki looked.

A triangular shard of windshield glass was embedded in Jack's throat. Its point had entered his oesophagus, but the jugular and carotid hadn't been severed. Wes peered at it, his face inches above the glass.

A hand grasped Vicki's wrist.

She looked down.

Not Wes's hand. Jack's.

It seized her like a manacle. Gooseflesh like a swarm of spiders scurried up her back.

She looked at Jack. His one eye opened slightly, slid toward Wes.

'I'll be damned,' Wes said. 'I guess . . .'

'Look out!' Vicki cried when Jack's other hand darted up. Wes started to rise away. Vicki flung herself against the side of the car and leaned and reached for Jack's hand as it tugged the glass shard from his throat. But he was too quick. For either of them. Vicki reached and missed and Wes was unbending and Jack slashed.

Blood spouted from Wes's neck. It splashed Jack's face. Wes lurched upright, grabbed his throat and walked backward stiffly, blood shooting between his fingers.

'No!' Vicki shrieked. She twisted away from the car, trying to tug her wrist from Jack's grip, and saw Wes fall. His legs just gave out and his rump hit the blacktop and he sat there, spraying the front of his jeans.

She threw herself sideways, all her weight against the hand squeezing her wrist. Her muscles strained. She felt as if her arm might pop from its socket. But Jack didn't loosen his grip. As he slid off the hood, she reached with her other hand and snatched his thumb. She struggled to pry it away from her wrist. Jack dropped to the street, landing on his knees, staggering to his feet. She stumbled away as he came at her.

With a gristly ripping sound and a pop, his thumb broke.

Vicki jerked her hand free.

Before she could spin away, his other hand grabbed a lapel of the robe. He yanked her up against him. She faced his wide frantic eye, his empty socket, his hanging, swaying eye.

The blow came fast. His knee? It blasted Vicki's breath out and lifted her off her feet.

Chapter Thirty-two

Patricia, bent over the body of Chief Raines, prodded the green ooze back inside the gash with the fingers of one hand while she stitched the wound with the other. She was tugging her needle gently, pulling the thread, when the doorbell rang. She flinched. The needle jerked. The stitch pulled out with a silent tearing of skin.

She looked at Melvin, her eyes wide.

'I'll take care of it,' Melvin said.

'More cops?' Patricia asked.

'Maybe, maybe not.'

'Shouldn't I go up just in case? I can do my thing again.'

'Stay here and finish up with Raines.' Melvin backed away from the lab table. He crouched over the heap of clothing they'd removed from the cops. He had dropped the handguns on top of the pile. All four of them. Three were cop guns – .38 caliber Smith & Wessons, blue steel with four-inch barrels. One was his own Colt .44.

He'd emptied his .44 and Milbourne's .38 into Raines and Woodman.

The doorbell rang again.

'Melvin!'

'I'll take care of it.' He grabbed two .38s and charged up the stairs.

By the time he reached the top, he was labouring for breath. *These fucking better not be more cops*, he thought.

As he hurried through the hallway, he pointed both guns at his eyes. The blunt tips of bullets showed in the cylinder holes of just one.

'Shit,' he muttered.

He dropped the empty revolver to the floor.

At the front door, he flicked on the porch light and squinted through the peephole.

Felt a tight squeeze of shock and joy.

He released the locks, swung the door open, and stepped backwards as Jack entered the foyer.

He gaped at them.

At Vicki, at Jack.

Vicki hung limp in Jack's arms, her arms and legs dangling, her head drooping, her eyes gazing into space. Her hair looked damp and stringy, but otherwise . . . ah, so beautiful. She wore a powder blue robe that had fallen open. Melvin stared at her pale breast, its dark nipple, the sleek curves of her ribcage and belly and hip, the smooth side of her buttock, her long tapering leg.

Her beauty seemed all the more perfect compared to the ruin that was Jack.

The top of Jack's head was broken flat. His face was sheathed with dripping blood. And that *eye*. It dangled against his cheek like a bloody, peeled egg.

'What'd, you have some trouble?' Melvin asked.

Jack shrugged and grunted. Melvin saw the raw slot in his throat, and realized why he wasn't talking.

'Anyone after you?'

Jack turned, swinging Vicki, and rocked her back and forth as if gesturing out the doorway with her knees.

Melvin stepped past him. From the stoop, he saw his car parked at the curb and another car far down at the end of the block standing crooked just the other side of the intersection. Its headlights were on.

He wanted to ask what it was doing there, but Jack was in no shape to explain anything.

'Take her down to the basement,' he ordered. Then he shut the door and hurried towards the distant car. The grass in front of the house was wet and slick under his feet. Already, he could feel sweat making his silk robe cling to his back. He didn't *want* to be all hot and sweaty for Vicki.

Pain in the ass, he thought. The last thing he needed was to go running around like this. Now, when he finally had Vicki, he had to go chasing off. He should be inside with her.

Always some kind of fuck-up.

He felt cheated. As if the party had started without him. He wanted to *be* there. Instead, he was missing out. And getting himself breathless and sweaty.

His frustration changed to worry when he realized he wouldn't be there when Patricia saw Vicki.

Shouldn't have told Jack to take her down.

Shit!

He'd planned to get rid of Patricia before Vicki came along.

Should've taken care of her soon as the cops was dead, he told himself.

But he hadn't even thought of it. Too busy.

As soon as the cops were killed, he'd left Patricia alone and driven Jack home. When he returned, he found her trying to drag one of the bodies down the basement stairs. And *still* didn't think of wiping her out, even though Jack was all set and waiting and might show up pretty soon with Vicki.

After helping to move the bodies into the basement, Melvin had allowed her to do most of the work involved in resurrecting them. And never gave it a thought that time was getting short.

Stupid!

Now, she was down there and so was Vicki.

Shit!

She better not try nothing!

Huffing, Melvin rushed past the rear of the car. And saw a body lying in the street.

What the hell happened here?

Jack must've run into trouble, all right. But it looked as if he'd taken care of it.

Good fella, Jack.

Melvin approached the body. Standing above it, he recognized the bloody face. Wes.

Manny's gonna be pissed, he thought. The two guys were best buddies, and Wes was always hanging around the station when Manny was on the job.

Wes was a jerk.

The jerk's throat had been slashed open.

Melvin was suddenly quite pleased with himself. It had been a smart move, using Jack to bring Vicki in.

Good thing he didn't blow the fucker's head off and leave him dead in the house, the way he'd planned while he drove there from Ace's place. He'd almost done it the minute Jack opened the door. And came even *closer* when he found out Vicki was gone. It had suddenly occurred to him, though, that Jack might be useful. So he'd forced the man, at gunpoint, to drive him home. Got him inside and down to the basement, then whacked him with the barrel. It had been a cinch, wrapping his head in cellophane while he was out cold. Dead, and not a mark to show for it. With Patricia's help, they lifted him onto the table and got to work. They were down there, still at him, when the cops showed up. Once those two bastards were cancelled, Melvin had returned Jack to his own house. To wait for Vicki.

'Did a great job, old pal,' he muttered. 'Got Vicki for me *and* you wasted shit-for-brains.'

Bending down, Melvin set his revolver on the pavement. He grabbed Wes by the ankles and dragged him to the car. The socks, at least, weren't bloody. With keys from the ignition, he opened the trunk. He frowned at the body, wondering how to get it in without messing his good silk robe.

He looked around. The streets were deserted. The few nearby houses were dark at the windows.

Nobody's watching, he told himself.

They'd be out here by now, rubber-necking, if they'd seen the car or body.

So he took off his robe. He rolled it carefully and set it on the roof of the car. Strange, being naked in the street. He felt the breeze on his hot, sweaty skin. He was getting hard. He thought about the way Vicki had looked, her robe hanging open.

Vicki. Patricia!

Shit.

As fast as he could, he rolled Wes over, grabbed him under the armpits, hoisted him up, and dumped him head first into the trunk. He moved the legs out of the way. Then he lowered the lid, turned around, and bounced his rump on it until he heard the latch click.

He opened the driver's door. The overhead light came on. Glass from the windshield littered the seat, but most of it was towards the middle. So was most of the blood. From Jack's head? Had his head smashed the windshield? Was that how it got flattened?

Melvin brushed off the seat, climbed into the car, and drove it to the curb. He shut off the engine, killed the headlights, and opened the door. The ceiling light came on again. He looked down at himself. A small smear of blood on his chest. But both hands were red, and he'd used a hand to brush glass off the seat, so he probably had blood on his *rump*, too.

He didn't want blood on his beautiful robe.

Maybe Wes kept a towel for wiping the windshield.

Again, Melvin thought of Patricia in the basement with Vicki. She won't try nothing, he told himself. Wouldn't dare.

But he leaped from the car, threw its door shut, snatched his robe off the roof, and rushed to pick up his revolver.

* * *

605

'*Damn* him,' Vicki heard. It was a woman's voice. It seemed to come from a great distance. 'I'm not good enough for him? He prom . . . Put her down.'

Vaguely, she was aware of her legs being lowered. She felt a cool cement floor under her feet. Her knees buckled, but she didn't fall. Someone behind her (Jack?) had an arm tight across her chest, pinning her against his body.

She saw the arm below her breasts, saw her bent legs and the grey floor. The floor was spotted and smeared with bright, fresh blood.

She tried to lift her head, but it seemed like too much trouble.

Bare feet and legs came into her view. Then a shirt. A glossy blue Hawaiian shirt, hanging open. The person in the shirt was a woman. She stopped in front of Vicki, less than an arm's length away.

Vicki raised her head enough to see the slash across the woman's belly, just above the navel. It was cross-hatched with stitches. From the look of the healing, the wound was a few days old. This is what Jack must have under his bandage, Vicki thought. Though the shirt covered the sides of the design, she could see parts of the circle and pyramid and eye-like ovals, the same as Jack had, but faint. Faded pink lines on the woman's white skin. Almost gone.

A hand, slick with green fluid, reached out and grabbed Vicki's chin and lifted her head.

The woman had blue eyes, short blonde hair hanging in bangs across her forehead, a sprinkling of freckles over her nose and cheeks.

The nurse? Vicki wondered. The one who killed Pollock? 'Patricia?' she asked. Her voice came out weak, little more than a whisper.

'Yeah. And you must be Vicki.' She let go of Vicki's chin. 'You're not so hot. What's he want you for? Huh? He's got me, why's he want you?' She looked upwards. 'Where's Melvin?'

Jack grunted.

'MELVIN!' she yelled. No answer came. She called his name again. A grin spread across her face. 'He's gone? Well, now. Jack, go upstairs and keep him out. Don't let him down here.'

He made another grunt, this one rising like a question.

'Do it! *I* brought you back, I can make you dead again.'

Jack's arm went away. Vicki sank to her knees and slumped forward. Her face pushed against Patricia, eyes against the stitched wound. She heard the quick footsteps of Jack climbing the stairs.

Her hair was yanked, her head jerked backwards. Patricia gazed down at her.

'By the time *we're* done, Melvin won't want you any more. He'll toss his lunch just looking at you.' A hand flashed down at her, fingers hooked to rake her cheek.

She twisted her head and felt a quick scrape of fingernails as the hand swept by, nearly missing. The hand swung back at her. Pounded her nose. Then she was falling. Her back hit the floor. Blood was spilling from her nostrils. She licked at it as she pushed at the floor, trying to rise. Then she was sitting up, braced with straight arms.

Patricia sneered down at her. Legs spread. Hands on hips.

'You know Raines and Woodman?' she asked.

For the first time, Vicki noticed the men.

Two of them. Standing on either side of Patricia and slightly behind her.

Dead men. Dead like Jack. *I brought you back, I can make you dead again.* Dead like Patricia.

Dead, but not down.

Vicki's mind seemed to freeze.

The two cops (one was the chief, all right) both stared at her with frenzied eagerness in their eyes. Their faces were doughy white. Their bodies, from the neck down, were sheeted with blood.

The taller cop had dime-size entry wounds in the chest and belly, a bigger wound to the shoulder. He was leering at Vicki, rubbing his hands together.

Raines must've been shot in the back. His torso was pocked with big pulpy exit wounds, red globs and strings hanging out here and there.

Along with the rest of the wounds, each man had a horizontal slash above the naval, green fluid oozing from the stitched lips.

She saw Patricia's mouth move, heard a voice that sounded as if it came from far down a tunnel. 'Let's go to it, fellas. Have a go at her.'

Patricia sat on Vicki's legs.

The cops rushed forward. They dropped to their knees, Raines on her left, Woodman on her right. She swung at their reaching hands, trying to knock them away as she lurched and writhed under Patricia. Then, her wrists were pinned to the floor.

She felt hands – sliding, rubbing, squeezing, digging, twisting and pinching her.

She saw Patricia, beyond the moving arms, lean down and bite the back of a hand that was tight on her breast. The fingers trembled open. The hand let go. Patricia dropped lower, mouth wide. She felt the woman's tongue on her breast, felt the edges of her teeth.

Then Raines's face blocked her view. His mouth covered hers. His tongue thrust in.

She screamed into his mouth and heard a gunshot.

When Melvin saw Jack blocking the closed door to the basement, he groaned.

He wasn't sure what he'd expected. Patricia throwing a fit, maybe. Not posting a guard.

'What's going on down there!' he blurted.

Jack stood motionless.

'Get outa my way!'

Jack didn't move.

'Damn it! I'm your master! Move!'

Jack shook his head, his loose eye swinging.

Melvin raised his arm, aimed the revolver at Jack's good eye, and pulled the trigger. The gun blasted. The eye vanished. Jack's head crashed backwards against the door. It bounced off the wood, and Jack raised his arms. Melvin lurched away from the reaching hands.

The fucker's blind.

Just like Charlie, he remembered. And Charlie damn near killed me.

'Stop!' he yelled.

Jack grabbed Melvin's neck and started squeezing.

Melvin jammed the muzzle into the gash in the centre of Jack's throat. Half the barrel vanished inside the wound. He fired. The blast flung Jack against the door. The way his head drooped and rocked, Melvin guessed that the bullet had severed the spinal column, Just as he'd hoped. He watched Jack slump to his knees and topple forward.

He dragged the body out of the way.

He flung the door open.

Saw Patricia and Woodman and Raines on their knees on the basement floor. All three huddled over a sprawled body, their hands on it. All three looking up the stairway at Melvin.

'GET AWAY FROM HER!' he shouted.

As he rushed down the stairs, the two cops looked at Patricia. She nodded. They started getting up. Patricia stayed where she was, sitting on Vicki's thighs.

Melvin stopped at the foot of the stairs.

Vicki lay motionless except for the rise and fall of her chest as she gulped air. Her arms were still inside the sleeves of the robe, but the robe was wide open. Her skin was slick with blood. As the cops backed away, Melvin crouched and looked closely at her body. She had awful-looking bite marks on one shoulder. Except for that, her skin seemed to be unbroken.

'Get off her,' he told Patricia.

'It's not fair.' Her voice trembled. Tears filled her eyes. 'I love you. *She* doesn't love you.'

'She will. Same as you. Get off her. Now.'

Patricia sniffed. She wiped her tears away with the backs of her hands. And stared down at Vicki and peeled back her lips, baring her teeth. For a moment, Melvin thought she might lurch forward and try to bite Vicki's face, ruin her looks. But he had given her an order, and she seemed to know it was her duty to obey. Her chin shook. She rubbed her eyes again, then stood up and backed away.

Vicki hung limp in his arms as he lifted her and carried her to the table. He stretched her out on top of it. She lay there, gasping for breath, her gaze fixed on the ceiling.

Stepping back, Melvin glanced at Patricia. She stood beside the pile of clothes from the cops, head down, sobbing quietly. The cops had retreated to a corner of the basement. They stood side by side, staring at Vicki.

'Forget it,' Melvin warned. 'She's mine.'

He went to the basin, turned a faucet on, and dampened a

towel. Then, he returned to Vicki's side and began to mop the blood off her face and body.

She squeezed her eyes tight as if trying to shut out what was happening.

She looked beautiful and helpless. The rage Melvin had felt against her, earlier that night, was gone. He felt only tenderness and loss.

It wasn't supposed to turn out this way. He'd been so good to her. He'd given her the car, he'd killed Pollock for bothering her, he'd made Charlie give her the clinic. She was supposed to like him and be his girl.

But it was too late for that.

It had all fallen apart.

There would be more cops, soon. They'd come for him. The only way to have Vicki was to go away with her in the car. They'd live like fugitives.

But they'd be together.

Melvin tossed the towel aside. She was as clean as he could get her, for now. Except for the raw wound on her shoulder, she looked fine. Wonderful. He would bandage the shoulder later, and maybe there would be time for a shower before fleeing.

The thought of showering with Vicki brought a warm stir to his groin. He caressed her. Her skin felt damp and chilly from the moist towel. It had goosebumps. He felt her muscles quivering below the surface.

He looked over his shoulder at Patricia. She was staring at him, crying. 'Bring me the cellophane,' he said.

She nodded.

He bent down and kissed Vicki's mouth. Her lips were trembling. 'It's gonna be okay,' he whispered. 'It won't hurt much.'

He heard a metallic click behind him.

Whirled around.

Saw Patricia aiming a revolver at him.

Heard a roar and felt the bullet slam his chest.

Vicki, rigid and shaking, waiting for her moment to strike out at Melvin, bolted upright at the crash of the gunshot. Melvin hit the table. The back of his robe was embroidered.

THE AMAZING MELVIN.

610

Above the Z of AMAZING was a ragged hole.

He dropped out of sight.

Vicki flung herself off the table. She sidestepped, eyes on Patricia.

The woman was staring at Melvin's body.

But the cops were watching Vicki.

She dashed for the stairway.

They raced for her, silent except for their feet slapping the concrete.

She leaped, kicking high, her foot catching the third stair.

A tug at the shoulders stopped her.

The robe. One of the cops had grabbed the flapping end of the robe, had pulled.

She tried to shrug out of the garment.

But already she was hurtling backward down the stairs.

They were all over her. Tearing her flesh with their teeth.

She screamed and heard her scream and flinched and opened her eyes.

She was in the basement. Sitting on the cement floor, her back against the stairs, her arms high, wrists bound with rope and tied to the banister.

Though her head throbbed and all of her body felt sore, the robe was open and she could see that she hadn't been devoured. Nor had a design been carved on her abdomen – no pyramid inside a circle, no eyes, no stitched slot of a mouth. Her skin was red in places, scuffed and scratched, but uncut and unchewed except for the burning shoulder hidden beneath the robe.

She scanned the basement.

She was alone.

Even Melvin's body seemed to be gone.

She listened. There was the sound of her heartbeat, and nothing else.

Groaning as hot pain surged through her body, she pushed herself up to the next stair. With her teeth, she reached the clothesline connecting her bound wrists to the banister. She began to chew it.

She listened. Still nothing.

611

Had they actually left her?

It seemed too good to be true.

When the rope finally parted, she used her teeth on the knots at her wrists. They loosened. She slipped her hands free, grabbed the banister, and struggled to her feet. She turned around. The door at the top was open.

Slowly, she climbed the stairs.

Her heart jumped when she spotted the body beyond the doorway. Jack. But he was down.

She stepped around his body, watching it, careful not to get close. His head was turned away so she couldn't see his face. The back of his head was blown out. So was the nape of his neck. But she didn't trust him to be dead.

Standing near him, though out of reach, she stared at his back. Finally, she knelt and pressed a hand against his knit shirt. There was no warmth. She lifted one of his hands, and felt the stiffness of rigor.

At first, she was relieved.

Then she wept.

She knew she should hurry and get out of the house. The others might be nearby, just in another room, or upstairs, or maybe they had left the house and would be returning soon. But she stayed there on her knees, face buried in her hands, crying for Jack and for herself and wishing for a way to go back in time and do something different and make all of it not happen.

Finally, she forced herself to stand.

She limped to the front door and pulled it open. Brilliant sunlight stabbed her eyes.

Chapter Thirty-three

The scream that woke Vicki from a nightmare of being stalked by corpses wasn't her own. Pulse hammering, she climbed from bed and raced through the dark house to Ace's room. She flipped the light on.

Ace was sitting upright in bed, panting, her yellow Minnie Mouse nightshirt clinging to her body with sweat.

Vicki sat on the edge of the mattress and took hold of her hand.

'Melvin?'

'Who else? Shit. You'd think I'd be over it by now.'

'It may take a while,' Vicki said. 'Like years.'

'Here we are, our bods good as new – almost, and . . .'

'Better than new, in your case.'

'Yeah, right.' Smiling Ace patted her belly. She hadn't been noticeably overweight before the attack. Now, she was slim. By cutting back on her meals, she had managed to keep off most of the fifteen pounds she'd lost while her broken jaw was wired.

The only remaining mark of her encounter with Melvin was the thin faint line of a scar just below her hairline. The hair had started growing in white where her scalp had been reconnected, but she had used that as an excuse to visit Albert's New You Beauty Emporium in Blayton from which she emerged with her hair short, swept-up, spiky and purple. 'What are you going to do,' Vicki had asked. 'Join a rock band?' To which Ace replied, 'It's *me*, don't you think?'

'Better in some ways,' Ace said. 'But the damn nightmares. And half the time I feel like hiding in the nearest closet.'

'Me, too.'

'And crying for no reason. Really sucks, you know? How come our minds won't heal like our bodies?'

'Not as tough, I guess.'

'We're a couple of tough old broads.'

'You said it.'

'In the springtime of our spinsterhood.'

'Yeah, sure. This is the first night you've spent alone in a week.'

'Obviously, a bad mistake. Didn't have any crap-sucking nightmares when there was a guy in here with me. A mistake I've got no intention of repeating in the near future.'

'How long does Gorman have the night shift?'

'Jesus, I don't want to know. Maybe I'll have to change my schedule, stay up till he gets off.' Ace looked at the clock beside her bed. She groaned. 'Get out of here and let me get my beauty sleep.'

'Sure you're all right? I'll stay with you.'

'Get. I'm fine.' She waved a hand at Vicki.

Vicki squeezed her hand, then stood up. 'Guess I'll go out for some fesh air.'

She saw concern come into Ace's eyes. 'Do you have to?'

'I'll lock the door.'

'I'm not worried about me, hon.'

'Well, don't worry about me. I'm fleet of foot and tough as nails.'

'It's nothing to joke about.'

'I know. But I need to get out and run. I can't keep putting it off. I need to.'

'Shit. Be careful, huh?'

'Yeah. Sleep tight.' Vicki flicked the light off as she left the room.

She walked down the corridor. In her dark bedroom, she slipped her nightgown over her head. As she dressed for running, she thought about Ace's concern. Jack's body had been found where she left it in the house, but Melvin's body was missing. Patricia, Raines and Woodman had also vanished. Along with two cars.

Maybe Melvin had survived the gunshot. Maybe Patricia had taken him away and nursed him back to health.

But Vicki didn't believe it.

The bullet had killed him. And while Vicki was left bound at the foot of the basement stairs, unconscious, Patricia had cut on Melvin. Cut one of those weird designs and made him come back. Then, they'd driven off together. Two cars gone, so Raines and Woodman had probably taken off on their own.

Four of them out there. Zombies. Somewhere. Doing God knows what.

Thinking about it, Vicki felt a chill squirm up her back.

But for weeks she'd given up her morning runs, and she could feel the need for the calming exertion, the touch of the morning breeze on her quick body.

She looped the chain with its key and whistle around her neck, and walked to the front of the house. Before opening the door, she told herself it was perfectly safe.

They're gone.

The cops were still looking for them.

Some of those were very nervous cops – those who'd listened to Vicki and shaken their heads as if they thought she had slipped a gear or two, but who'd later looked at Melvin's collection of video tapes. They had pretended to think the tapes were faked. But she could see the change in their eyes.

Those cops believed.

She was sure they'd kept it to themselves.

Raines and Woodman were described in the press as missing persons, possible victims of Melvin Dobbs and Patricia Gordon. Dobbs and Gordon were wanted for the abduction of Vicki Chandler and for multiple homicides. They were considered armed and extremely dangerous.

But not zombies.

Vicki had told herself, countless times, that they would've been caught by now if they weren't far away.

She told herself that, again, as she stood at the door, wanting to go out and run, but afraid.

There's no need to worry.

She left the house. On the sidewalk, she looked up and down the block. She studied shadows cast by the streetlights. Satisfied that nobody lurked nearby, she stretched, twisted, touched her toes. Then she sat on the cool concrete, spread her legs and swivelled, reached to her toes, straining, finally limber enough to grab the soles of her shoes.

She got up and began to run. Twice, she circled the block, unwilling to venture farther from the house. But she felt a longing to break away. Ignoring the small pull of fear in her stomach, she headed for downtown.

Except for a few delivery trucks, the main street was deserted. She dashed past the Riverfront, past Ace Sportswear and the lighted doughnut shop with its delicious aromas, felt her legs begin to weaken as she sprinted past Handiboy, and slowed down in front of the clinic. By the time she reached the park at the north end of town, she was huffing and her legs felt like warm lead.

She slowed to an easy jog. And stopped at the top of the hill. Staring down, she saw the pale strip of beach. The dim shapes of the playground equipment. The slide and swing set.

Empty.

No Jack.

Her eyes grew warm. Her throat tightened.

She walked down the slick dewy grass of the slope, remembering how she'd fallen on her butt the morning she first met him. He had been a stranger, then, watching her from atop the slide.

For just a while, he had filled the empty place in her heart.

Now, he was gone.

Vicki walked on the sand. She climbed the metal rungs of the ladder and sat on top of the slide. The platform was damp. The wetness soaked through the seat of her shorts, but she didn't mind. She was sitting where Jack had sat, and she felt close to him.

From here, she could see the dark slope. She wondered if he'd been amused by her klutzy fall. After the fall, she had gone down to the shore. He must've watched her. She'd been itchy from lying on the grass. She'd stepped into the river and picked up a stick and used it to scratch her back. She'd been thinking about Paul, aching with the memory of the early morning she'd been with him on the diving raft.

The raft, now, was out of sight, hidden beneath a thick fog.

There had been fog that last morning when she was with Paul. A heavy mat of it that covered them as they embraced. Nobody could have seen if they'd made love. But they hadn't, and she remembered standing in the water, full of longing and regret, wishing she could go back to that time.

All the while, Jack had been watching. From here.

She'd been daydreaming about the only man she had ever

loved, and the man she was about to love had been sitting here on the slide, watching and wondering about her.

She closed her eyes and imagined the feel of Jack's big body against her, his mouth . . .

Sucking her shoulder, biting as he thrust, ramming her against the bathroom wall.

Her stomach clenched and she whimpered. Snapping her eyes open, she flung herself forward and shot down the wet ramp of the slide. She flew off its end, stumbled through the sand.

Ran, the memory pursuing her.

Paused only long enough to pull off her shoes and socks, then splashed into the river and dove. The chill of the water shocked her mind clear.

She thought, this is crazy. What am I doing?

I have a right to be crazy.

She arched to the surface and swam, swam towards the diving raft. She couldn't see it through the fog, but she knew right where it was.

It was home, that diving raft. It was where she had been happy and innocent and in love before the bad times came, before the loneliness, before the horror.

Treading water for a moment, Vicki heard it. Soft, familiar slurping sounds of the river's surface lapping the oil drums that buoyed it up. She swam towards the sound, and the weathered old wood appeared through the gauze of fog.

She climbed the ladder. She stepped onto the platform. It tipped and rolled gently beneath her.

Turning around, she looked towards shore.

There was no shore, only fog, pale in the moonlight.

She was surrounded by fog, alone on her raft, safe.

But shivering. The air, which had seemed so still and warm before she plunged into the river, now felt like an icy breath blowing through her sopping clothes, against her dripping skin.

She sat in the centre of the platform. She drew her legs up tight to her body and hugged them.

She sat there, shaking.

The sun will come up in an hour or so, she thought. It'll burn off the fog. It'll dry me and warm me.

617

She could swim ashore now and return to the house and take a long hot bath.

But it was good here.

She didn't want to leave. She wanted to wait for the sun.

After a while, the chill seemed to fade and her shivering stopped. She lay flat on the raft, her face on her folded arms. The planks grew warm beneath her.

Her eyes drifted shut, but she opened them quickly. With sleep, dreams would come.

The platform moved gently beneath her. The water lapped at the drums. Sometimes, birds cawed and squealed. Far away, a motor sputtered to life and Vicki imagined a man setting out in his boat to begin fishing.

Her eyes slid shut.

She was alone in a canoe. It seemed that Jack should be with her, but she didn't know where he was. Had he gone in for a swim? The night was clear, moonlight casting a silver path on the water. She turned the boat slowly, scanning the river for him.

And saw, off in the distance, the faint shape of a swimmer.

She called, but no answer came.

The swimmer came closer.

What if it's not Jack?

Fear made a cold, hard place in her stomach.

Splashing sounds came from the other side. She jerked her head in that direction, spotted another swimmer.

More splashing from behind. She twisted around. Still another pale shape was moving towards her through the water.

A fourth appeared beyond the prow of the canoe.

Another off the starboard side.

Oh, Jesus! I've gotta get out of here!

She dug her paddle into the water. It lurched and was jerked from her grip. It flew high and hit the water far away.

Hands clutched the gunnel. The canoe tipped. A head bobbed up.

She stared at the broad face, the slicked-down hair, the bulging eyes and thick, grinning lips.

'Did you save yourself for us?' Melvin asked.

'No!' she gasped. 'Get away!'

The canoe tilted the other way as black hands grabbed the

gunnels. The head that burst from the surface was charred and eyeless.

'He wants you, too,' Melvin said. 'Charlie's always wanted you.'

They both began climbing into the canoe. Patricia, naked except for a nurse's cap, was suddenly perched on the prow.

Vicki backed away. Hands clamped her knees, halting her. The hands of Raines and Woodman, both in the water, leering up at her from the sides of the canoe.

And someone was still swimming towards her. A vague, pale shaped in the water's blackness.

Jack?

It must be Jack. He'll save me.

'Jack!' she shouted. 'Help! Quick! They've got me!'

And Jack's voice came from the swimmer. 'Save some for me, folks.'

Melvin laughed.

All of them came at her. They threw her down. They piled on top of her, clawing, biting, ripping. She twisted beneath them. She writhed. She felt her belly split open. Someone bit her thigh. Her left breast was torn off and she saw it bulging from Patricia's mouth. Then Jack's face loomed above her. It came down, loose eye swinging. She felt the slimy eye slide against her cheek, felt his mouth cover hers, his tongue thrust in. She twisted and bucked, trying to push him off. The canoe capsized.

Cold water clutched Vicki, filled her mouth and throat.

Wide awake, she struggled to the surface. She grabbed the ladder of the diving raft, coughing and gasping, shaking from the terror of her nightmare.

When she could breathe again, she climbed the ladder. She staggered onto the platform and rested there on her hands and knees. Something was hanging from her. She lowered her head more. Her T-shirt was ripped down the front. Its dripping edges swayed. Her left breast was bare, the shoulder strap of her bra dangling from the cup bunched beneath it.

Vicki pushed herself up. Resting on her haunches, she studied herself in the faint light seeping through the fog. And pressed her lips tight as she gazed at the tangle of scratch marks on the pale skin of her breast and chest and belly.

She could hardly believe that she had done this to herself.

But she remembered tearing her nightgown once, soon after her arrival in Ellsworth. So she must've done this.

She had not only torn her clothes and skin, she had put up such a struggle against the demons of her nightmare that she had pitched herself into the river.

The body heals, why not the mind?

Could the mind get worse instead of better? She'd had horrid nightmares before, but nothing that caused her to do anything like this.

With trembling fingertips, she explored the scratches. Only those on her belly were deep. The skin there had been plowed up in furrows.

She pulled at the rumpled fabric of her bra and lifted it over her breast. She tucked the strap down inside.

And heard distant splashing sounds.

Her back jerked rigid. She listened.

The sounds, which seemed to come from behind her, were those of someone swimming.

She felt as if her wind had been punched out.

This can't be happening. I'm awake.

Am I?

Vicki sprang to her feet and whirled around. The platform dipped. She grabbed the ladder's uprights and held herself steady and gazed into the fog.

The swimming sounds came closer.

She saw a yard or two of black water beyond the raft before the whiteness closed off her view.

She heard only one swimmer.

Who is it? Melvin? Charlie? Jack? One of the others?

Maybe all of them were coming for her, the rest of them approaching from below the surface. They don't need air, she thought. They're dead.

How do they know I'm here?

My shoes, she thought. I left my shoes and socks on the beach.

Oh, Jesus!

'LEAVE ME ALONE!' she cried out.

The sounds of the splashing stopped.

'VICKI?'

A man's voice. Almost familiar.

'I'm sorry,' it called through the fog. 'I didn't mean to scare you.'

'Who are you?'

'Paul. Paul Harrison. We used to . . .'

'PAUL?'

He swam out of the fog and reached out with both hands and took hold of the ladder and looked up at Vicki. She stared down at him.

'Permission to board?' he asked.

Vicki nodded and backed away. Her heart slammed. She struggled to breathe.

He climbed the ladder and stood in front of her, slim and dusky in the vague light, bare except for clinging white undershorts.

A body she had seen countless times in cut-offs and swimsuits, a body she had held tight and caressed. So long ago.

So damn long ago.

Vicki shook her head. 'This . . . is impossible.'

'I heard about your problems,' he said. His voice was almost the same as she remembered it. A little deeper, more confident. 'I was in Guam until yesterday. I got into San Diego and ran into an old buddy. He told me about it. He didn't know it was you, but he remembered I used to talk about a girl in Ellsworth, and . . .' His voice went husky. 'Oh God, are you all right?'

Vicki didn't answer. She rushed to him and threw her arms around him.

He held her. He stroked her hair, her back.

His skin was wet and cold, then warm where it pressed her. There was muscle where he used to feel bony. But his body fit against her the way it used to, as no other body ever had, as if it had been made especially to join with Vicki's body and complete her.

'You're really back?' she murmured against his neck.

Paul nodded.

'I can't believe it.'

'Believe it,' he whispered.

'How did you find me?'

'It wasn't easy. I figured Ace would know. I called her about half an hour ago. She said you'd gone for a run. I remembered you and the river, so I tried the beach.'

'Saw my shoes and socks.'

'I *hoped* they were yours.'

'You could've called out, you know.'

'I wanted to surprise you.'

'You scared the hell out of me. I thought *they* were coming for me.'

'You don't have to worry about them any more. I'm here. Nobody's ever going to hurt you again.' His hands tightened on Vicki's back, pressing her hard against him. 'God, I've missed you.'

'I've missed you, too,' she murmured. 'God, so much. I thought I'd never see you again.'

'I always wanted to come back and look you up. I just didn't have the guts. I'm a leatherneck with one enormous yellow streak. I figured you'd met someone else, probably got married, had kids. I didn't want to know. I figured I'd missed out.'

'You didn't miss out.'

'Ace told me you're . . . single.'

'I been saving myself for you, hon.'

He laughed softly, and Vicki tipped back her head and watched his face come slowly down and waited for the feel of his mouth.

One Year Later

Chapter Thirty-four

'Nobody move or yer dead meat!'

Meg Daniels jerked with alarm at the rough shout, and dropped her loaf of bread on the floor. She stared at the two men standing in the 7-Eleven's doorway. A tall man with a revolver in one hand, a nylon satchel in the other. A shorter, stocky man with a sawn-off shotgun. Though the Bakersfield night was balmy, both men wore long coats. And ski masks.

Side by side, they strode towards the counter.

Meg wanted to back way, but she didn't dare.

The tall man dropped his satchel onto the counter. 'Fill it up,' he told the clerk.

The stocky man turned to Meg. He studied her through the holes of his mask. She trembled as she watched his bloodshot eyes roam down her body.

With the muzzle of the shotgun, he nudged her left breast through the thin fabric of her tank top. 'Nice,' he muttered. 'Real nice.'

'Don't . . . hurt me. Please.'

'Aw, I wouldn't *hurt* . . .'

The blast of a gunshot roared in Meg's ears. Whipping her head sideways, she saw the back of the tall man's coat puff out. Blood sprayed from a hole below his shoulders. But he didn't fall. Instead, he shoved his revolver towards the clerk and fired. His bullet slammed into the clerk's chest. The clerk staggered backwards, dropping his gun. He was still on his feet when the stocky man swung the shotgun and fired. The clerk's face from the mouth up flew apart in an explosion of red. Then he flopped out of sight behind the counter.

The tall man leaned forward, reached into the open drawer of the cash register, and started taking out money. He scooped up bills, tossed them into his satchel, and reached for more.

Meg, dazed, stared at the back of his coat.

The hole there was the size of a half-dollar. Blood was spilling out of it.

But he kept stuffing the bag with money.

'Yer coming with us, honey.'

The words seemed to come from a great distance. Meg thought, is he talking to me? Must be. Nobody else in the store.

'Hey, you!'

She turned her head. The stocky man was looking into her eyes.

'You got a problem with that?'

She shook her head.

The tall one closed his satchel and lifted it off the counter. He turned towards Meg. He had a leaking hole in the middle of his chest.

Why isn't he dead? she wondered.

'We're taking this one with us,' said the stocky man.

'Fine by me, chief. She's a knockout.'

Grabbing the front of her tank top, the stocky man yanked Meg forward.

And out of the store.

Towards a waiting black van.

'Would you like another drink?' Graham asked, seeing that she had nothing left in her glass but ice and a red swizzle stick.

She shook her head. Her hair swayed, shimmering golden in the soft lights of the cocktail lounge. 'Not here,' she said. 'But if you'd like to come up to my room . . . ?'

'You're staying here at the hotel?'

Instead of answering, she opened her clutch purse and took out a room key.

'Well, now,' Graham said.

'This is your lucky night.'

'I'll say.'

He could hardly believe his luck. He'd been striking out so many times since JoLynn left him and he moved to Tucson. Even when he did score, it was with women who were as desperate as he was: they were older, or plain, or fat, and all had personalities that were either bland or grating on the nerves. On a scale of one to ten, they ranged from about three to five.

This gal, Patricia, was at least an eight.

Lovely, golden hair. Warm blue eyes. A sprinkle of freckles across her nose. A quick, sly wit that tended towards the sarcastic but stayed short of mean. And a slim, lithe body that her dress did little to conceal.

More like a negligee than a dress. Low-cut and glossy white, with spaghetti straps and a slit that showed her left leg all the way to her hip. The smooth way it flowed down her body, Graham *knew* she wore nothing underneath.

She had only two minor flaws, or she would've been a ten for sure.

A face that was slightly too long. Not long enough to make her seem horsey, just enough so she couldn't be considered gorgeous.

And she was pregnant. Not grossly pregnant, but enough so her belly pushed out the front of her gown.

Graham was keenly aware of what was pushing out the front of his slacks as he climbed off the barstool. He buttoned his sports coat, hoping to cover it.

Patricia took hold of his hand.

'Burrr,' Graham said, smiling.

She smiled. 'Cold hands, warm heart.'

As they walked through the cocktail lounge, he thought about how her chilly hand would feel on his hot flesh.

They walked through the hotel lobby and entered one of the elevators. It was empty. Patricia pressed a button for the second floor. She looked at him and licked her lips. 'I'm going to devour you,' she said.

He said, 'Jesus.'

The elevator doors slid open. She led him through the corridor, and unlocked the door of 218. Graham entered first. No lights were on. When she shut the door, the room was dark except for a pale glow coming in through the glass doors on the far side.

She moved into his arms. He felt the firm mounds of her breasts and belly pressing against him. He kissed the side of her long, cool neck. He caressed her bare back. He ran a hand down to the slitted side of her gown, stroked the skin of her thigh and hip, inserted his hand beneath the fabric and found the silken smoothness of her rump.

She eased away from him, and for a moment he wondered if something was wrong. But only for a moment. Then she was undressing him: taking his coat off, opening his shirt and casting it aside, tugging at his belt, unbuttoning his waistband, skidding his zipper down, crouching as she drew his slacks and underwear down to his ankles.

He squirmed at the touch of her lips, her tongue.

'Delicious,' she whispered.

Then she stood up.

'Go in the bathroom,' she said.

'Sure. What for?'

'I like to do it in the shower.' She nodded towards the darkness of an open doorway. 'I'll be along in a minute. I'll make us drinks and bring them in.'

Incredible, he thought.

He took off his shoes and socks, kicked his feet free of the pants, and went into the bathroom.

He turned on the light. The brightness made him squint for a moment. Then, he saw himself in the mirror.

One nervous-looking guy.

Ain't nerves, buddy.

Jesus!

Shaking his head, he grinned at himself. His mouth was parched, so he stepped to the sink and turned on the faucet. He used a hand to cup cold water to his mouth.

He straightened up and turned off the water. He wiped his wet hand on his belly. He looked at himself again in the mirror, and again shook his head.

This can't be happening.

But it sure is.

Trembling, he stepped to the tub. He ran the water until it felt good and hot, then turned a handle and watched the spray shoot out of the shower nozzle. It felt cold for a moment, then hot. He climbed into the tub. He slid the frosted door shut, and waited beneath the beating spray.

She likes to do it in the shower.

Oh man oh man.

First, we'll wash each other.

He could *feel* it, feel her soapy hands sliding all over him, feel her breasts slick under his lathered touch.

Graham moaned as he saw her vague form through the shower door. He couldn't see much, just the pink tint of her skin.

The door slid open.

He saw the hammer in her upraised hand.

Saw the face behind her shoulder, bulgy eyes gazing at him, thick lips grinning.

The hammer crashed against his forehead. He fell. The back of his head slammed the bottom of the tub.

A shadow of consciousness clung to him.

'Turn off the water,' he heard through the ringing in his ears. Patricia's voice.

The spray stopped.

The two seemed rimmed with electric blue light as they climbed into the tub. They were naked.

'Shut the drain, honey,' Patricia said. 'We don't want to lose his blood.'

She crawled over him.

They both crawled over him.

He felt their teeth.

'Okay,' Vicki said. 'We're here.' She rested her paddle across the gunnels. Paul did the same. The canoe glided silently over the moon-sprinkled surface of the river.

Paul looked over his shoulder at her. 'We're where?' he asked.

'The special place.'

'We're in the middle of the river.'

'So we are.'

She crawled towards him, the canoe rocking gently as she moved. Paul turned around.

On her knees, she spread the blanket. She lay down on it, feet towards Paul. Lifting her head, she watched him come to her.

'What's the idea?' he asked.

'Gee, I don't know.'

Vicki turned onto her side. Paul stretched out next to her.

'Hope we don't get run over by a powerboat,' he whispered.

They moved closer together until their bodies touched.

'I've always wanted to do this,' Vicki said.

'The Huckleberry Finn in you.'

'Finn never had it so good.'

She hooked an arm over Paul's back, slid her other arm beneath his head, drew herself more firmly against him. She could feel his heartbeat and the soft warm touch of his breath on her face. The river gently lifted the canoe, turned it, lowered it, rocked it.

Something thumped the hull.

Vicki flinched.

'Just a piece of driftwood, or something,' Paul said.

Rigid against him, she listened.

'Hey, what's wrong?'

'What was it?' she whispered.

'I'll check.' He stirred, but Vicki clenched him hard against her body. 'I can't check if you're going to hang onto me like that.'

'Stay down.'

'Vicki.'

'Please.'

'Okay. God, you're shaking.'

'Just hold me. Hold me tight.'

'I'll do better than that.' He rolled, climbed onto her, covered her with his body.

'No! Get down here!'

'Oh,' he muttered. 'Aw, Vicki.'

She fought to hold onto him, but he pushed himself up and leaned out over the river. She heard a swish of water. Then he brought up a club of tree branch. He held it above her for a moment. Chilly water streamed off it, splashing her face and running down her cheeks. Then Paul flung the branch away. It plopped into the river.

Straddling her, he took off his shirt. He gently dried her face with it. 'Just driftwood,' he said in a low voice. 'It wasn't Charlie Gaines coming up to get you.'

'I'm sorry.'

'Don't be.'

'I've been looking forward so much . . . I thought it'd be so *neat*.'

He rolled his shirt and tucked it beneath Vicki's head. 'You just lie there, I'll take us back to shore. The bed may not be as romantic, but it'll be a lot more comfortable.'

Reaching up, she caressed his chest. 'I don't want to go.'

'Maybe next year.'

'Next year, I'll still wonder if he's down there. And the year after that. He's never going to be found.' She slipped her hands around Paul's sides and drew him down onto her. 'If Charlie's after me, let him come.'

'Maybe we'd better go home.'

'I don't think so.' Vicki pressed her open hands against Paul's ears and shouted into the night, 'HEY, CHARLIE! CHARLIE GAINES! IT'S ME, VICKI! NOW OR NEVER, OLD FRIEND! COME AND GET ME, OR FOREVER HOLD YOUR PEACE!'

For a long time afterwards, they lay motionless in the bottom of the canoe – listening.